RUMER GODDEN

IN THIS HOUSE
OF BREDE

UNABRIDGED

PAN BOOKS LTD : LONDON

First published 1969 by Macmillan and Co Ltd.
This edition published 1970 by Pan Books Ltd,
33 Tothill Street, London, S.W.1

ISBN 0 330 02641 0

2nd Printing 1971

For J. L. H-D.
who has endured us
for five years

Printed in Great Britain by
Richard Clay (The Chaucer Press) Ltd, Bungay, Suffolk

IN THIS HOUSE
OF BREDE

'Contains not one but perhaps a dozen stories, and impressively full of realistic detail . . . How vividly and individually some of these identically-clad women emerge! One remembers Abbess Catherine Ismay in her struggles to obtain wisdom and leadership; Agnes Kerr, the noble yet jealous scholar; Maura Fitzgerald, the devoted choir mistress whose love of beauty precipitates her passion for the gifted novice Cecily; the pitiable and repellent Veronica Fanshawe, with her small talent and her large vanity . . .'   *New York Times Book Review*

'It is impossible for Rumer Godden – that excellent storyteller – to write a dull book . . . the insidious magic of centuries-old tradition enfolds us, the idea of an enclosed House being not only a powerhouse of prayer but a place of intense activity . . . the story is told through several nuns and it is with their separate spiritual crises that we find ourselves actively concerned, actively caring.'   *The Daily Telegraph*

'Surpassingly good . . .'   *Saturday Review Syndicate*

'An important work of fiction about religious life . . . remarkably readable.'   *The Times*

By the same author in Pan Books

KINGFISHERS CATCH FIRE

All the characters in this book are imaginary, but many of the episodes are based on fact; some are taken from the life and sayings of Dame Laurentia McLachlan and Sister Mary Ann McArdle of Stanbrook Abbey. To many monasteries of Benedictine nuns I owe most grateful thanks; especially do I offer them to our English Abbeys of Stanbrook, Talacre and Ryde; also to Mr M. Kunihiro of The Information Centre, Embassy of Japan, for constant help given, and to James Kirkup, poet, for permission to quote from his book: *Return to Japan*.   R.G.

Ground Floor Plan

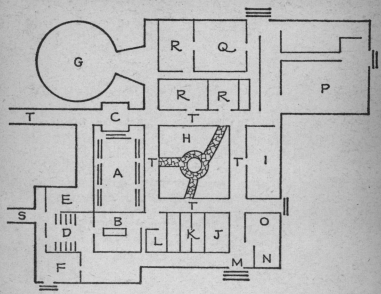

A Choir
B Sanctuary
C Bell Tower
D Extern Chapel
E Side Chapel
F Entrance Hall
G Chapter House
H Garth
I Refectory
J Large Parlour

K Parlours
L Sacristy
M Main Entrance Hall
N Guests' Dining Room
O Portress' Cell and Turn
P Kitchen
Q Recreation Room
R Libraries
S Cloister to Presbytery
T Cloisters

First Floor Plan

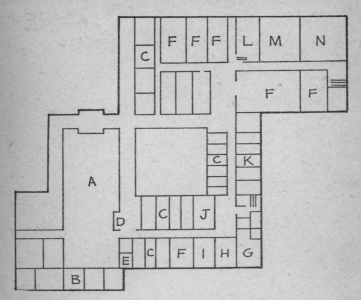

A Church
B Cells for Guests
C Cells
D Sick Tribune
E Parlours
F Sewing Rooms
G Abbess' Rooms
H Telephone Room
I Cellarer's Office
J Prioress' Cell
K Infirmary Wing
L Scriptorium
M Studio
N Bindery

The motto was 'Pax' but the word was set in a circle of thorns. Pax: Peace, but what a strange peace, made of unremitting toil and effort – seldom with a seen result: subject to constant interruptions, unexpected demands, short sleep at nights, little comfort, sometimes scant food: beset with disappointments and usually misunderstood, yet peace all the same, undeviating, filled with joy and gratitude and love. 'It is My own peace I give unto you.' Not, notice, the world's peace.

Penelope Stevens never forgot that morning. It was New Year's Day, 'which made it all the more heart-breaking,' she told her young husband, Donald, afterwards.

'Heart-breaking?' Penny could imagine the amused lilt in Mrs Talbot's voice if she had heard that. 'Isn't the first day of the year a good time to begin?'

To Penny it had not felt a good time to do anything; she and Donald had been up till four o'clock dancing the New Year in at one of Donald's 'important' parties, 'which was why, perhaps, I was so dim,' said Penny.

'Mrs Stevens, I have spoken to you twice! You are here to work, you know.'

'Sorry, Miss Bowman.'

Joyce Bowman was personal assistant to 'the mighty woman' as Donald called Mrs Talbot and was important to those who wished to 'get on' as Donald was always urging, and for a while Penny's fingers went so fast on the typewriter keys that she slurred letters together and had to start again with fresh sheets of paper. 'Three sheets!' she could imagine Miss

Bowman scolding, and 'You would never have been given this post,' the Typing Pool Superintendent told Penny. 'Never, if Mrs Talbot hadn't taken one of her fancies to you.'

'Taken a fancy to *me*?' Penny had been astonished. 'Why, she's as cold as . . . a flick knife,' said Penny.

'Flick knife was a good simile,' Mrs Talbot said when, long afterwards, Penny told her this story. 'I used to flick people. I still do. I must learn not to.'

Penny had known something was going on. Mr Marshall, from Overseas Press Division, had had a desk in Mrs Talbot's room all the week. There had been talks – 'but there often are' – there had been private meetings. If Penny had put into words what she sensed about that week it would have been a confirmation of what was rumoured through the whole Department: one of the four Controller posts in the office was vacant and Mrs Talbot was to be made that fourth, 'and how many women Controllers are there in the whole Service?' asked Penny. That morning the meticulously punctual Mrs Talbot had been late, very late. When she did arrive, a string of people had come in to see her, one after the other, and the telephone had hardly ceased; the inner office had hummed, but the outer office was the same as on any day; telephones ringing, Mrs Talbot's buzzer going, messengers coming in and out with files, the three typewriters – Joyce Bowman's, Cynthia, the senior typist's, and Penny's, all clicking and Penny's desk getting its usual muddle of copy paper, carbons, lists. 'Mrs Stevens, *why* can't you work tidily?'

Penny's eyes too, kept straying to the window; the window of the outer office looked northeast over London and, sitting at her desk, Penny could see far over the roofs to the thin green skyline of Hampstead and Highgate. A new office block hid the turrets and towers of Westminster but the campanile of the Cathedral could be seen overtopped by one of the new office buildings. Something happened to people's minds when man learned to build offices higher than spires, thought Penny, then blushed as she realized that the thought was not her own but Mrs Talbot's. 'Why do you have to blush when you talk about your Talbot?' Donald had once asked her, amused. Penny knew why but she was not telling Donald. Donald had the innate antagonism that a husband feels towards someone to whom his wife gives allegiance. 'You can be loyal without being enslaved,' he said resentfully.

'I'm not enslaved,' but Penny had not said it; with a wisdom older than her years she did not talk now about Mrs Talbot. At first, in the excitement of being promoted to Mrs Talbot's office she had – babbled, thought Penny now, and boasted, 'Mrs Talbot isn't only a director, she's...' Penny could not exactly express what she sensed Mrs Talbot was, and, 'she's special,' she said lamely.

'In what way?' Donald had raised his eyebrows.

'Well, she's the only woman director in the office. She has men as well as women working under her.'

'That must be difficult for the men,' said Donald.

'It isn't difficult,' Penny had said. 'It's easy.'

'She must be marvellous,' said Donald so drily that Penny should have been warned but, to her, Mrs Talbot was precisely that – marvellous.

Not that Donald was not marvellous too. 'Why he married me I don't know,' Penny told Miss Bowman. 'He's brilliant and so good looking. Isn't he good looking?' demanded Penny. Miss Bowman had to concede that Donald was exceedingly good looking, though she had only seen him when once – just once – he had come to collect Penny from the office. 'And he's so popular,' said Penny. 'He's such a brilliant conversationalist, and talented; he writes,' Penny said it reverently. 'One day he will be published.' She obviously had not a doubt of it. 'And I can only cook and sew and things like that,' she said.

'And wash and iron and clean and shop.' Miss Bowman was looking at Penny's hands. 'And go out to work and earn quite a good salary.'

'Donald earns far more.' Penny was earnest. 'He'll go far. They all say so. I only do it to help.' She had no ambitions for herself, least of all when she was with Donald. Penny was nineteen, a married woman, Mrs Donald Stevens, but she was still, as Donald often told her, hopelessly naïve. 'Perhaps it's lucky for Donald that you are,' said Miss Bowman which

11

Penny did not at all understand. 'And you should remember,' Miss Bowman added, 'remember that Mrs Talbot picked you out.' Penny still did not know why but it was true that on the rare times she went into Mrs Talbot's room she became a different Penny, someone in her own right, Penelope Stevens. Mrs Talbot expected you to be yourself – and more than yourself; she teaches me things, thought Penny, but it was more than that; it was as if Mrs Talbot stretched her, made her stand upright. One day I might even be – 'groomed' seemed asking a little too much – be tidy, thought Penny. Already there was a difference in the way she put on her clothes, held herself, talked or did not talk – even Donald had noticed it.

What did Penelope know about Mrs Talbot? Very little. Her name was Philippa but her peers in the office never called her Phil, always Philippa. She did not, like Penny and the other girls and women in the office, only hold a post; she had a career that had brought her a long way. She worked and consorted with men – 'High-up men,' said Penny – on equal terms. Often she was the only woman on a board or at a meeting – with the Foreign Office for instance.

Penny, as the most humble member of the outer office, had little to do with Mrs Talbot. 'Just as well,' said the Pool Superintendent, but Penny came under the 'Talbot image' as Donald called it. One mistake in a letter and it was sent back; no rubbings out were allowed; it was of no use, either, thinking of leaving at five o'clock every day. 'If there's work to do, we stay,' Mrs Talbot had said when she had interviewed Penny. It was that 'we' that explained Mrs Talbot's hold on her staff; if they worked hard, she worked harder. 'Doesn't your paragon have any private life at all?' asked Donald.

'She has a flat in Highgate, a housekeeper called Maggie and a cat, a Siamese, called Griffon. She told me that,' said Penny with pride. 'She doesn't take books out of a library, she buys them. I have sometimes ordered them for her; all kinds of books, sometimes in French,' said Penny, 'and, yes, Latin. Do you know, she has been studying Latin again – at her age.'

'How old is she?'

'She's forty-two. She gives dinner parties,' said Penny

dreamily. 'Sometimes in my lunch hour I buy things for her. She tells me to take a taxi.'

'What sort of things?'

'Oh, a special kind of crystallized ginger: smoked trout and pâté, profiterolles.' Penny had been fired with the idea of getting a jar of pâté de foie gras for Donald's birthday. 'In one of those dear little pots, but enough for two, just two, costs forty-five shillings!'

'Is Mrs Talbot good looking?' That was another of Donald's questions.

'N-no,' said Penny. 'She ... hasn't much colour but...' How could she convey the, to Penny, exquisiteness of Mrs Talbot? The ... the finish, thought Penny. 'She's groomed,' she said.

'That's money,' said Donald but Penny had a belief that had Mrs Talbot been poor, she would still have looked elegant. 'Yet her clothes are very plain,' said Penny. 'In the office she wears suits, plain suits, low heels, silk stockings, not nylons.'

'Mannish,' said Donald immediately.

'No, not at all,' said Penny. 'Her hair is long; it gleams. She has a little finger ring, not a signet ring but one huge pearl. It's real – and you should see her office...'

The inner office was like no other room in the building; it had ivy-green walls and white paint. 'I wonder how she got the Ministry of Works to consent to that!' Donald said when Penny described it. 'Perhaps she didn't,' said Penny. Mrs Talbot had a way of doing things she wished and taking the consequences. 'She has a picture,' said Penny. 'A Sisley.'

'An original?'

'Of course.'

'Well, she must be getting four thousand a year and probably has money of her own. Who is her husband?' asked Donald.

'I don't know,' said Penny. 'She isn't married now.'

'A widow or divorced?'

'I think she's a widow.'

'Does she have lovers? Most of these high-up women do.'

'If she does, they are her own business.' Penny spoke

13

sharply; she oddly resented Donald's asking that. 'She makes you feel she is her own business. There's hardly any office talk about her.'

'That must be uncommon.'

'She is uncommon. You should see her clock.'

Penny liked the clock even better than the Sisley. A clock like a large watch, a gold repeater that lay in its case on the desk. It was heavy. Penny had once lifted it when Miss Bowman told her to dust the desk after a storm had blown smuts in through the window. The clock's face was rimmed in a border of blue enamel and gold with a design of minuscule leaves; its hands were chased gold and it had a chime, rich and sweet, that would, Miss Bowman told Penny, repeat to the nearest quarter of an hour.

Once when Penny had taken some papers in – Miss Bowman was away and Cynthia had gone to get a cup of tea – Penny had dared to linger until Mrs Talbot glanced up. 'Can I do anything for you?' It was meant to be sarcastic and Penny's blush came up but she had to say it, childish though it seemed: 'It's almost a quarter past,' she said. 'I was hoping your clock would chime . . .' and Mrs Talbot had actually picked up the clock, pressed the knob and the chimes had rung, three – for three o'clock – then a stave of notes for the quarter.

'Thank you!' Penny had stammered. 'Thank you!'

'I rather like it myself,' said Mrs Talbot. 'Now . . . get.'

At half past eleven that New Year's morning there was a directors' meeting. Mr Marshall went, Mrs Talbot did not, but Cynthia was sent with Mr Marshall to take the minutes. At a quarter past twelve the buzzer sounded and Miss Bowman was told to go into Mrs Talbot. Penny heard Mrs Talbot's voice; it sounded curt. It was some time before Miss Bowman came out and when she did her eyes were red. Penny had raised her head but hastily ducked it again. What can she have done? thought Penny and made as much noise as she could with her typewriter to hide the other's sniffs. Mrs Talbot must have flayed her, thought Penny.

Presently Miss Bowman was quiet, but she did not work again. She put her papers into her drawer, confidential papers that no one else in the outer office was allowed to see, locked the drawer and stood up. 'Mrs Talbot is lunching with the Permanent Secretary,' she said. 'Will you wait and listen for the buzzer?'

'Yes, Miss Bowman,' Penny tried to put into her voice the sympathy she felt, but the older woman took no notice. 'Yes, I was dim,' Penny told Donald afterwards. On Miss Bowman's little finger was a ring with a large pearl. 'Why! You have a ring exactly like Mrs Talbot's.'

Miss Bowman made a noise like a hiccough and ran out of the room. Feeling mystified and important, Penny returned to the letter in front of her but she could hardly type. Something is happening, she thought. It was something that did not fit with Mrs Talbot's being made a Controller, something different. Her ear cocked to the inner office, Penny tried to concentrate on her letter but ... something is happening, she thought again.

At a quarter to one, Penny heard the private door from Mrs Talbot's room to the corridor unlocked, then closed and locked again. She is going to the wash-room, thought Penny. Mrs Talbot came back through the outer office. Penny stole a look from under her lashes; Mrs Talbot was wearing a hat and was freshly made up. Penny typed diligently but Mrs Talbot did not pass her; she stopped by the table. 'I want you for a moment, Penny.'

Penny! Not Mrs Stevens! An odd excited quiver ran through Penny, a premonition that, at the same time as the excitement, made her feel cold. Had she, like Miss Bowman, done something terrible? But then why 'Penny'? As she followed Mrs Talbot into the inner room, the back of Penny's neck and her hands were damp.

Mrs Talbot's gloves, long and mole-coloured – and clean as new, thought Penny – lay on the desk with her bag and the Sisley painting taken down from the wall. Why was it taken down? 'I'm just going,' said Mrs Talbot.

'Yes, Mrs Talbot.'

15

'I wanted to say "goodbye".'

Goodbye before going out to lunch? Again that quiver came as Penny raised puzzled eyes to Mrs Talbot's face. 'Goodbye?'

'Yes, Penny. I'm not just going out to lunch. I'm leaving.'

'Leaving?' The floor seemed to give a lurch and Penny clutched the back of a chair. '*Leaving?* But ... when?'

'Now. I'm not coming back.'

'But ... Mrs Talbot!' and, 'No!' cried Penny sharply. 'No!'

'Not "no", yes,' said Mrs Talbot, 'and I wanted to give you this. I believe you always liked it.' She picked up the clock and put it into Penny's hands. 'Don't drop it.'

'But, Mrs Talbot!' Penny was incoherent. 'Mrs Talbot. I ... you ...' and in a rush, 'I don't understand. Don't you want it?'

'I shall have no further use for it,' Mrs Talbot's voice sounded amused. 'It will probably surprise you, Penny, when I tell you I'm leaving to become a nun.'

'A *nun*!' Now Penny nearly did drop the clock and Mrs Talbot had to put out a quick hand. 'If I were you,' she said, 'I should put that in your bag to take home.'

'But ... a nun!' Penny – Pennywise, as Donald often said – blurted out the first thing in her mind. 'At your age!' then blushed even more hotly than usual. 'I'm sorry ... I mean ... but don't nuns usually go in at eighteen or very young?' Then, 'I'm sorry,' said Penny again, 'that was rude,' but Mrs Talbot was not angry.

'You are perfectly right,' she said. 'I should have thought of it long ago.'

'But a *nun*.' Penny felt stunned. 'And the clock! Are you sure?'

'Sure I'm going to be a nun or sure I don't want the clock?' Then the amusement went out of Mrs Talbot's voice. 'I am sure, Penny. Nuns don't need clocks. We have bells – or large silver watches. And I'm sure I'm going to be a nun, a Benedictine of Brede Abbey in Sussex.'

'But you ... oh, Mrs Talbot, no! Please no.'

16

'Please yes.'

Penny looked up and saw that Mrs Talbot was laughing at her, gently laughing. 'Do you think it will be the end of me?' Penny emphatically did but, 'I hope it will be the beginning,' said Mrs Talbot. She did not sound dismayed, only happy, thought Penny incredulously. Then Mrs Talbot was serious again and said something incomprehensible to Penny. 'I have a long way to go. Will you think of me sometimes, Penny? I shall be very much alone.'

The buzzer went and Mrs Talbot bent and listened to a man's voice. 'I'm coming, Richard.' Richard was Sir Richard Taft, the Permanent Secretary. Mrs Talbot picked up her bag and gloves and put the Sisley under her arm. She's going to give it to him, thought Penny and an intuition ran through her, a sudden awareness of something she, Penny, had once seen and not taken in – with my usual dimness, thought Penny. Once, long ago, when again she had been alone in the outer office, Mrs Talbot, with Sir Richard, had been wrestling with some knotty office problem in the inner room; the buzzer had sounded and Penny had answered it. As she had listened to Mrs Talbot's orders, Penny had been acutely conscious of Sir Richard standing by the window. She had felt him looking and for a moment had let her attention slip from Mrs Talbot; he was indeed looking but not at Penny – for him, the Pennys of the office scarcely existed – he was looking at Mrs Talbot and his guard was down. It was a look of infinite tenderness. Penny had been surprised that she, ignorant Penny, had been able to find those grave words: 'infinite tenderness' and, if only Donald looked at me like that, she had thought with a pang. Now suddenly she knew what it meant. Sir Richard and Mrs Talbot! thought Penny. Mrs Talbot and the Secretary! Of course! and Penny felt she had been entrusted with an immense secret.

'But . . . I'll never see you again!' It was a cry.

'Why not? You can come and see me.'

'I . . . could? Could I?'

'Yes. You will have to come. I can't come to you. I shall be enclosed.'

'Enclosed?' The unfamiliar word seemed to ring in Penny's ears. 'You mean – shut up?'

'Not shut up. The walls are not to keep us in but to keep you out.'

'But why?'

'An enclosed order is like a kind of power house,' said Mrs Talbot. 'A power house of prayer; you protect a power house, not to enclose the power, but to stop unauthorized people getting in to hinder its working.'

'Then, how would they let me come?'

'You wouldn't come into the enclosure. There are parlours to which people can come – lots of people.' Mrs Talbot turned to the door. 'I mustn't talk to you now or I shall be late for Sir Richard. I'll write to you. Goodbye, Penny. Try to be a little tidier for Mr Marshall.'

When she had gone, the clock in Penny's hand gave out a single deep rich chime that filled the empty office. Penny began to cry.

Only moments of that day broke through to Philippa, 'until the evening in the little train,' she said. Small things stood out sharply: Penny's face, her bluntness when she had said, 'At your age.' Why did Penny make more impression than devoted Joyce Bowman? Then, when at lunch Richard Taft had suddenly said, 'What about the food?' The head waiter was cooking their steak Diane in front of them. 'The food. Have you thought of that?'

Everyone outside the monastery, Philippa was to find, was concerned about the food. When Dame Catherine Ismay who had been Mavis Ismay entered Brede, her old Nanny had concealed a jar of malt and cod-liver oil in her trunk – 'You don't know what they'll give you to eat in that place, or what they won't give you.' Sister Cecily Scallon's cousins were to tease her unmercifully. 'You'll have lentils and fish. Ugh!'

'Bread and water on Fridays.'

'No. On Fridays you'll fast. And what about Lent?'

Dame Ursula Crompton, Brede's novice mistress, knew all about these postulant fears. 'Have you ever seen a nun who didn't look perfectly well fed?' When Sister Cecily came to think of it, she had not.

'I expect the food will be ordinary,' Philippa had said in the restaurant. 'I'm told the tea is terrible. I shall mind that. It will be one of the difficult things.'

'And this?' Richard had touched her glass. He had ordered a Chambolle Musigny – 'liquid rubies' Philippa had said as she tasted it – and she answered, 'I believe we have a glass of home-made wine' – Richard made a face – 'on the day of the miracle of Cana, and I have heard that once, on a great occasion, the monastery was given, fittingly, a bottle of Benedictine and everyone in the community had a sip.'

'You're joking.'

'As a matter of fact I'm not. Well,' she shrugged. 'I have been wonderfully good to myself all these years.'

'I give you six months,' said Richard.

Philippa laughed. 'I thought you were going to say six weeks. No, Richard, I shall stay – somehow.'

She had meant to spend the journey remembering, going through it all again in her mind, gathering up that long long thread into a ball – and keep it hidden in my hand, thought Philippa, for ever; she lit a cigarette and settled down but, as the train clanked slowly over the bridge across the Thames and the towers of Westminster sank away – I may hear Big Ben again, I shall never see it – when the brief stop at Waterloo was over and the train settled to its speed through the suburbs, weariness overcame Philippa. It had been a long morning, full of pangs and tearings and tears, beginning with the agonizing half hour when she had taken Maggie and her last suitcase, with Griffon protesting in a basket, to their new home, the flat Maggie was to share with her sister. 'It will be yours for always, Maggie.' 'To make a home for Griffon,' Maggie had said obstinately.

Griffon! 'We nearly all of us had had animals,' Philippa said long afterwards – all except Sister Julian who seemed to know from the beginning that animals were not for her. Cecily had had her spaniel: Hilary, the hunter her father had given

19

her – the only time anyone saw tears in those plain grey-green eyes was when Sister Hilary spoke of her hunter. It was better, Philippa found in the train, not to let herself think about Griffon. It was possible to shut Griffon out, not to think of Griffon – she had succeeded in doing that – but she could not always do it with Keith.

He came like a ruffle, a ruffle of wind on leaves or water, a cool little breeze. Well, Keith means a wind. Even as a baby he used always to be disappearing:

> Keith, where are you? . . . going round the garden without being seen.

The treble voice came back from unexpected places: under the arch of the steps; from the barn roof – 'You naughty little boy' – behind the hydrangeas. Philippa remembered the time he had climbed the great elm tree at Roughters, her mother's house, and fallen, plummeting down until a branch had caught him, hooked by the straps of his dungarees, and there he had dangled, quite trustfully, as she stood below talking, while her mother and Morton, the gardener, ran to fetch a blanket into which he had fallen, laughing. He was only four then, but he had climbed that lofty tree. Laughing . . . think of him like that, not:

> Don't cry Keith   breathe   breathe   I'm here
> quite close   Mother's here   breathe   and, 'picking
> up gold and silver . . . picking up gold and silver . . .'

With shaking fingers Philippa lit another cigarette and hastily returned to the day.

There had been all the office partings – she smiled again as she thought of Penny; for Joyce Bowman it was, Philippa knew, the breaking up of a whole life. Then came lunch with Richard, but that amputation had been made long ago. Then back to Highgate for the last time, to wash and brush up – she had wiped all the make-up from her face so that she looked ghostly pale – a ghost of the old Philippa.

Except for a small suitcase of night things, her luggage had gone in advance; there had been two cases of books for Brede Abbey library; everything else had gone into one small trunk. 'Good,' Dame Ursula was to say approvingly. 'Some postulants bring two or three.' In the trunk were the two long-sleeved high-necked black dresses she would wear as a postulant: black stockings and 'silent' shoes: plain under-clothes: two black shawls – those had been difficult to get in London and Maggie had crocheted them: blanket and sheets – 'not too luxurious,' Dame Ursula had warned her. A small workbox – Philippa had not owned such a thing since she was at school – a fountain pen, a plain silver watch on a pin – 'We don't wear watches on our wrists,' and a gold watch would have been considered 'unmonastic', a word Philippa was speedily to learn; she had given her gold watch to Cynthia: a Bible, a missal and a few chosen books. Philippa had only to pick up her suitcase, briefcase and go. Maggie would come in later and clean the Highgate flat; already it looked bare, the furniture stiff, the rooms deserted. It had been sublet for eighteen months. 'I hope you haven't burnt all your boats,' Richard had said.

'My heart tells me to, but my head says not,' answered Philippa.

She had locked the flat door behind her and given the key to the porter George as he held the taxi door open. George was the last of her 'people'; then she was alone. At Charing Cross, she went straight to the familiar four o'clock train; she had been down to Brede often in the last eighteen months, taking this same four o'clock train on Fridays to spend the weekend at the Abbey, though not taken it like this, thought Philippa; but as soon as it started, the throbbing pulse in her temples quietened, and, as the small houses and gardens, playing fields and factories slipped past the window she fell asleep.

She woke with a jerk. It was Ashford, the market town where she had to change and take a smaller train across the marshes. Always before, unless she had driven all the way from London, she had hired a taxi from Ashford to Brede but, during these last few weeks, she had been steadily divesting herself of all luxury and her car had been sold. 'At least let me drive you down,' Richard had entreated.

McTurk, a Controller himself and her immediate chief in the office, had offered too. It was odd that Daniel McTurk, hitherto a withdrawn, almost unknown little man – in the office he was called by his surname as if his given name were too intimate – should be the only one among Philippa's colleagues who understood what she was doing – and approved. 'You couldn't not,' he had said, 'not now,' but – and Philippa had learned it with the utmost surprise, and only when they reached these confidential terms – McTurk was inclined towards Buddhism and, thought Philippa, Buddhists understand contemplatives far better than most Christians . . . but, 'I should rather go by myself,' Philippa had said, and as she stood on the Ashford platform waiting for the small train to come in, she seemed already separated from the people around her. Tomorrow I shall not be among you any more; not 'of you' but mysteriously still with you, thought Philippa. As Lady Abbess of Brede had said, 'People think we renounce the world. We don't. We renounce its ways but we are still very much in it and it is very much in us.'

Now Philippa felt a strange love, strange because she would not normally have noticed any of the crowd, except as a conglomeration, as people in a frieze. Now the fat girl in the too bright, too tight, badly fitting coat and skirt looked wistful as if – and as often with over-fat people – another girl were prisoned inside, looking out of her eyes. The porter trundling a truck had dirty hands, stubble on his chin, but there was something brave and independent about him; the tired, petulant young mother with a still more tired and petulant small girl, an overdressed, whining little girl, had a pathos, Philippa felt – yet she had no affinity with young mothers and did not like whining small girls – who could? I'm looking past their faces, Philippa thought, looking into them. Perhaps it was the pulling up of her stakes, or claims, to her private loves, renouncing them, that had made room for these people in a kind of universal love, without any claims. 'I shall run the way of thy commandments when thou hast opened wide my heart,' the psalmist had sung. Was that, Philippa wondered, what was happening to her? This was not only love but compassion, being with another, sharing his suffering in fellow feeling, and Philippa's ironical smile touched her lips; how paradoxical to have fellow feelings when you are just about to leave your fellows!

The small train drew in and, still in this new dimension, thought Philippa, she found a compartment and put her shabby small case up on the rack. She had changed cases with Maggie. 'What! me take your beautiful little air case and give you that cheap thing!' 'It's what I need,' Philippa had said and, 'I shall not be going anywhere again.' Yes, this is almost the last step, she thought, as the train began to move and all at once she wanted to cry, 'Those inexorable steps!'

'My life was so beautifully arranged,' she was to say that over and over again: her flat in London overlooking a garden square, its rooms so finished and exquisite, with Persian rugs, furniture, pictures; Maggie, Griffon; her work, outstanding in her Department – 'I was becoming a personality' – her devoted personal staff, from Joyce Bowman to Penny: her colleagues, McTurk and the others; her galaxy of friends – and Richard; and then this came like dynamite, thought Philippa, and blew it all to bits.

'Why suddenly?' Richard had asked bewildered.

'It wasn't sudden, it was slow,' Philippa had said. 'Unforgiveably slow,' though she knew now that she had been seeking – freethinker and renegade as she was – seeking, until ten years ago, a whole decade, thought Philippa, she had gone one lunchtime into Westminster Cathedral, with its mysterious depths, the bleakness of its unclothed heights, the glimmer of its mosaics, the theatrical yellow arch behind the high altar, the scattered points of glowing gold from the candle-stands. She had thought the cathedral dark, vast and ugly compared to the patina and beauty of Westminster Abbey; then she had sensed the atmosphere of prayer; there was a coming and going, many people come to pray, not looking for history or beauty but prayer. 'I didn't know what I was doing there,' Philippa told Dame Beatrice Sheridan, sacristan at Brede, to whom in her early days she often talked. 'I was ignorant of the meaning of anything. I knew though that in churches one knelt down, so I went to a line of chairs and knelt.

'Being the lunch hour, the cathedral was busy and there was a queue of people, standing in line, I didn't know for what. I suppose I must have been looking towards them, perhaps looking lost or troubled, because suddenly an old man beckoned to me. He was a tramp.'

'Was he a tramp?' Unlike most nuns, who were more wary, Dame Beatrice often, quite calmly, found supernatural explanations for things.

'God knows,' said Philippa in the words of St Paul. 'He looked a very thorough and solid tramp.' She saw him now, dirty, unshaven, unlovely, in a drooping old overcoat, his trousers tied with string. 'Surely if there is a miracle, that is the miracle? That someone quite ordinary, by some not extraordinary action, can work providence?' To find a tramp in the cathedral was most likely. 'One of the good things about a Catholic church is that it isn't respectable,' she had told Richard. 'You can find anyone in it, from duchesses to whores, from tramps to kings.'

'I expect I looked towards the line,' Philippa told Dame Beatrice, 'wondering what they were doing because the old man beckoned me and gave me his place.'

'And disappeared?'

'I don't know,' said Philippa, which was true. 'I only know that somehow I seemed unable to move out of that line and the next thing I knew was that I was in the confessional.'

'And did you confess?' asked Richard – she had told him this story when she had broken her news to him. 'Did you?'

'Of course not. I couldn't. I didn't know how, but I asked the priest if I could come and see him.'

'And that was the beginning?'

'Of the practical things. Of course I didn't begin to realize then what I was in for.'

'And when you did realize?'

24

'I dodged,' said Philippa. 'Oh, I had plenty of excuse,' she told Dame Beatrice. 'It couldn't have come at a worse time. There was one thing I had been playing for – in those days for me it was *the* one thing, and I must own I was playing prettily; the next step up in my Department was a big step for a woman, but I think if I had waited a little longer I should have got it.'

Richard confirmed that. 'Indeed you would have got it.'

'For another thing,' Philippa went on to Dame Beatrice, 'I didn't want to be bothered. I thought I was very well as I was; a human balanced person with a reasonable record; with the luck of having money, friends, love – only suddenly it wasn't enough – not nearly enough.' Dame Beatrice nodded; this was what she understood. 'Everything seemed – not hollow, but – as if suddenly I could see beyond them, into an emptiness, and all the while there was this strange pull; no one can describe it to someone who hasn't felt it, and doubly strange for me because until then, such a thing had never crossed my mind.'

'That's what happens,' said Dame Beatrice.

'But *how* does it happen?' That was to be Mrs Scallon's wail for her Elspeth who was to become Sister Cecily, as it had been the wail of countless parents all down the centuries. 'No one in our family is a Catholic,' said Mrs Scallon, 'let alone a nun. *How* does it happen?'

'It happens in all sorts of ways,' said Dame Ursula Crompton, to whom, as Cecily's future novice mistress, it fell to see much of Mrs Scallon. 'Vocations can come to the most unlikely people in the most unlikely circumstances and there's no resisting. It's as if God put out a finger and said, "You."'

'I suppose it is the greatest love story in the world,' Philippa had said.

'Of course.' McTurk had been his usual matter-of-fact self. 'Like the merchant in the Bible who found the pearl of great price and gave all that he had to buy it.'

'But I should have thought I was the last person,' said Philippa.

'Why? You are a woman with plenty of acumen.'

'But can I do it?' In these last weeks Philippa had been more and more doubtful.

'A vocation is a gift,' said Dame Ursula. 'If it has been truly given to you, you will find the strength.'

In the train, Philippa began to feel she had no strength at all. The little train bumped and jolted its way slowly across the marshes, stopping at small lit stations with homelike names: 'Ham Street', 'Appledore': then wandering on through the flat marsh country where there seemed more sky than land – a fitting place for an Abbey, thought Philippa. The lights from the train showed sheep grazing on the flats where the dykes separated the hedgeless fields; now and again water glinted pale in the darkness that seemed to deepen as they neared the coast.

'I couldn't wait to get to Brede,' Cecily was to tell her.

'I just came when it was time,' said Hilary, and added, 'What else?'

'I grew more and more afraid,' said Philippa.

It was almost six o'clock when Philippa came out of the station into the town.

The wind was blowing fresh from the sea; its salt tang was revivifying after the stuffy train and she decided to walk up to the Abbey. She had only her light suitcase and briefcase to carry and the old town was so huddled together on its bluff, jutting out into the marsh, that it took only ten minutes to walk from wall to wall, up or across it.

The streets were steep and as Philippa climbed the heights the wind grew more than fresh; it buffeted round corners as only the Brede wind could; the narrow streets made air funnels and she shivered. The panic had come back; she felt cold, sick with apprehension.

Light fell from the house windows on to the cobbles; the pavements were so narrow that only one person could walk on them; a second would have had to step off to let the other by. The lamplight made each house look inviting, homelike; Philippa could see firelight, hear voices, children laughing. She caught a glimpse of a table spread for high tea; often the canned voice of radio; ordinary quiet people leading regular ordered lives and, again under her fear, that odd love came up – but now it ached. Then across this everyday life, came the sound of a deep-toned bell: three and a pause: three and a pause: again three and, after the pause, continuous changes for five minutes. It was the great bell of the Abbey, Mary Major, ringing the Angelus. Philippa stopped. She was visibly shivering and, making up her mind – or unmaking it – she turned into the Rose and Crown, Brede's oldest inn; habit taking over, she thought, and went into the saloon bar and ordered a double whisky. 'I had three in half an hour,' she told the Abbess afterwards. 'I don't know what the barman thought.'

The bar was comfortable with its warmth and light, its glasses reflecting the heaped-up fire; its cheer might be fictitious but it seemed a snug human place and Philippa sat on, spinning out that third drink. She seemed rooted to her stool; she sipped and smoked, stubbing out one cigarette after another. The barman looked several times at the tall figure sitting so silently with bent head but did not speak to her. Then the clock struck the three-quarters; in fifteen minutes the parlours of the Abbey would be closed. 'Are you going to stay here for ever?' asked Philippa of Philippa. Coward. Coward.

She stood up, fastened her coat, paid the man and turned to go. 'Not turned to go,' she said afterwards, 'turned to come.'

'You have left your cigarettes,' said the barman.

'I don't want them.'

'Giving up smoking?'

'Yes,' said Philippa and went out into the night.

'What do you ask?'
'To try my vocation as a Benedictine in this
house of Brede.'

BENEDICTINES OF BREDE
(when Philippa Talbot entered)

Abbess:
Dame Hester Cunningham Proctor

Choir Nuns:

Councillors
Dame Emily Lovell	prioress
Dame Veronica Fanshawe	cellarer*
Dame Agnes Kerr	mistress of ceremonies
Dame Maura Fitzgerald	precentrix (in charge of the choir)
Dame Beatrice Sheridan	sacristan
Dame Catherine Ismay	pharmacist
Dame Perpetua Jones	subprioress
Dame Colette Aubadon	mistress of church work
Dame Edith	printer
Dame Ursula Crompton	novice mistress
Dame Clare	zelatrix (assistant novice mistress)
Dame Joan Howard	infirmarian
Dame Domitilla	portress
Dame Camilla	chief librarian
Dame Mildred	in charge of gardens
Dame Bridget	first depositarian
Dame Teresa	bell-ringer
Dame Thecla	archivist
(an Ethiopian)	
Dame Gertrude	artist
Dame Winifred	assistant cellarer

* Cellarer: not, as it sounds, the keeper of the Abbey's wine cellars (there are none), but in charge of all material things, including finance.

Dame Monica	second chantress
Dame Margaret	assistant infirmarian
Dame Anselma Riordan	assistant mistress of church work
Dame Frances Anne	
Dame Simone	
Dame Paula	

Claustral Sisters:

Sister Priscilla Pawsey	kitchener
Sister Jane	in charge of the novitiate
Sister Ellen	in charge of the Abbess's rooms
Sister Stephanie	in charge of domestic work
Sister Justine	vestiarian
Sister Gabrielle	poultry keeper
Sister Hannah	bee-keeper
Sister Marianne	in charge of vegetable garden and orchard
Sister Xaviera	in charge of laundry

Novitiate:

Sister Julian Colquhoun	(Barbara Colquhoun)
Sister Constance	later Dame
Sister Benita	later Dame
Sister Nichola	later Dame
Sister Sophie	later Dame
Sister Louise	

Extern Sisters:

Sister Elizabeth	extern sacristan
Sister Renata	
Sister Susanna	

and fifty-four others, choir, claustral, extern and novices

In 1957, to the novitiate:

Sister Hilary Dalrymple	(The Hon Fiona Dalrymple)
Sister Cecily Scallon	(Elspeth Scallon)

I

The tower of Brede Abbey was a landmark for miles through the countryside and out to sea; high above the town of Brede, its gilded weathercock caught the light and could flash in bright sun.

The weathercock bore the date 1753 and had been put there by the Hartshorn family to whom the Abbey – in those days the Priory of the Canons of St Augustine – had been given after the Reformation; it had then been the Hartshorns' private house for more than two hundred and fifty years. When the nuns came they had thought it prudent not to take the weathercock down – 'Brede wouldn't have tolerated a Catholic nunnery here in 1837,' Dame Ursula Crompton told the novices. 'We had to disguise ourselves.' The cross was below, a stone cross interlaced with thorns – and it had known thorns; it had been thrown down, erected again and stood now high over the entrance to the church; it was said to be nearly a thousand years old; certainly its stone was weathered but, though the wind from the marshes blew fiercely against it and rain beat in the winter gales that struck the heights of Brede so violently, the cross stayed unmoved, sturdily aloft, while the weathercock whirled and thrummed as the wind took it. Dame Ursula had pleasure in underlining the moral, but then Dame Ursula always underlined.

The townspeople were used to the nuns now. The extern sisters, who acted as liaisons between the enclosure and the outside world, were a familiar sight in their black and white, carrying their baskets as they did the Abbey's frugal shopping. Brede Abbey had accounts at the butcher and grocer as any family had; the local garage serviced the Abbey car which Sister Renata drove; workmen from Brede had been inside the enclosure, and anyone was free to come through the drive gates, ring the front door bell which had a true monastic clang, and ask for an interview with one of the nuns; few of the townspeople came, though the Mayor made a formal call once a year; the Abbey's visitors, and there were many, usually came from farther afield, from London or elsewhere in Britain, from the continent or far overseas, some of them famous people. The guest house, over the old gatehouse, was nearly always full.

From the air, it would seem that it was the Abbey that had space, the old town below that was enclosed; steep and narrow streets ran between the ancient battlements and its houses were huddled, roof below roof, windows and eaves jutting so that they almost touched; garden yards were overlooked by other garden yards while the Abbey stood in a demesne of park, orchard, farm and garden. Its walls had been heightened since the nuns came, trees planted that had grown tall; now it was only from the tower that one could look into the town, though at night a glow came up from the lights seeming, from inside the enclosure, to give the Abbey walls a nimbus.

The traffic made a continual hum too, heard in the house but not in the park that stretched away inland towards the open fields; it was a quiet hum because the town was quiet and old-fashioned; besides, no car or lorry could be driven quickly through its narrow cobbled streets. The sparrow voices of children, when they were let out of school, were heard too, but the only sound that came from the Abbey was dropped into the town by bells measuring, not the hours of time as did the parish church clock, but the liturgical hours from Lauds to Compline; the bells rang the Angelus, the call to Chapter and the Abbey news of entrances and exits; sometimes of death. There was a small bell, St John, almost tinkling by contrast; it hung in the long cloister and summoned the nuns to the refectory. The bells of the Abbey, the chimes of the parish church clock, coming across each other, each underlining the other, gave a curious sense of time outside time, of peace, and the only quarrel the town had with the Abbey now was that the nuns insisted on feeding tramps.

A winding stone stair led up to the tower, going through the belfry above the bell tribune where the hanging bell ropes had different coloured tags. Though the bells were numbered, they had names. 'Dame Ursula says they are *baptized*,' said Sister Cecily. Dame Clare, the zelatrix, Dame Ursula's assistant, was more exact. 'There is a ceremony in the pontifical which is called baptizing the bells; it is, rather, a consecration,' but to Cecily they seemed personalities. Well, they are the Abbey's voice, but she did not say it aloud – already she suspected that this Dame Clare, so cool and collected, thought her, the new postulant Sister Cecily, whimsical; but the bells were the Abbey's voice and its daughters knew the meaning of every change and tone, from the high D of Felicity to the deep tone of the six hundred pounds weight of Mary Major; when this was rung, it made the whole tower vibrate.

The stair came out on a flat roof that had a parapet on which tall Philippa could rest her arms and look far out, over the marshes and the river winding through them, to the faint far line of silver that was the sea. I shall never see the sea again. That thought always came to her up here on the tower : 'I shall never see the sea.' She whispered it aloud. The silence the nuns kept most of the day for concentration and quiet sometimes made Philippa long to use her tongue, even to herself. But then I'm still new, as religious life goes, not quite four years old, new but with the dragging disadvantage of old habits. 'I shall never see the sea,' but Philippa said it with content. Four years had gone since she had made her solitary journey across the marshes, four years except for two months and a few days. If all went well she, Sister Philippa, would make her Solemn Profession next summer, take her vows for life in this house of Brede.

Philippa had discovered the tower in her second week at Brede, when Burnell, the Abbey's handyman, had pulled a muscle in his leg, leaving it stiff, and Dame Ursula had called on her strong young novices and juniors to do some of his

35

tasks: chopping wood and carrying it in for the common-room's great fire: carrying kitchen swill for the pigs: cleaning out the deep litter of the hen houses for old Sister Gabrielle, the poultry keeper. Philippa, neither young nor strong, had volunteered to go up and sweep the leaves out of the church tower gutter. 'Very well, if you have a head for heights,' said Dame Ursula. Philippa had, and, as a reward, had discovered the high platform, 'where I can get away,' she would have said – after only two weeks, she had wanted to get away. 'I can imagine you living with ninety men,' Richard had told her, 'but not with ninety women.' Yes, it's somewhere I can breathe, Philippa had thought of the tower and, in spite of Richard, breathe before going on.

From where she stood now, she could look down on her Abbey – it had become 'her' Abbey – look over its precincts, over the buildings, the outer and inner gardens and park to the farm outside the walls. The Hartshorns had pulled down most of the old priory, though they had left the L made by the refectory and library wings above the cloister that had been paced by those Augustinian Canons of long ago. The cloister, called the long cloister, was of stone, beautifully arched, its grey weathered, while the new cloisters that ran round the other side of the garth, as the inner court was called, were of red brick, with glazed windows – Lady Abbess shuddered every time she saw them. Another grief to her were the Vic-torian additions to the church in the sanctuary and extern chapel – 'Abominations of mottled marble,' she said. The choir itself was exquisite, part of the Augustinians' old church, with pointed stone arches and delicate tracery that matched the chapter house; the Hartshorns had kept that intact but used it for breeding pigeons. 'Pigeons in a chapter house!' said Dame Ursula. 'I rescued it from worse than pigeons,' the Abbess had said, 'from what our nuns did there when they got some money! they lined it with pitch pine and put in a plaster ceiling!' It was Abbess Hester who had restored it, uncovering the delicate arches that met at the apex of the roof. 'All that beautiful stone,' said Abbess Hester, glorying.

The buildings held spaciousness in refectory, libraries, workshops, though the cells in their long rows on the first and second floors were narrow. Across the outer garden a glimpse of the Dower House, used as the novitiate now, showed among its trees and, dominating the whole, the church with its tower on which Philippa stood.

The Abbey was hushed this afternoon in a hush deeper even than its normal quiet; though the nuns went about their work and the bells were rung at the appointed time, and the chant of voices came, as always, from the church, the hush was there, a hush of waiting. The parlours were closed. 'No visiting today,' said Sister Renata when she answered the front door. She and the other extern sisters went softly in and out, but they did not go into the town, where the news had spread. 'The Abbess is dying: Lady Abbess of Brede.'

This was the community recreation hour but, looking down, Philippa could see only two figures instead of the many, habited in black and white and as alike as penguins, that would usually at this time have been gathered in the park, or on the paths or pacing together in the cloisters. The prioress and senior nuns were keeping vigil in the Abbess's rooms, the others had withdrawn, some to their cells, most to their stalls in choir, to pray while they waited – Philippa, still renegade, seemed to pray best up here – but the life of the monastery had to go on and Dame Ursula had as usual sent her novitiate to the tasks they undertook in the afternoons for the community; gardening, helping the printers in the packing room, sewing or taking messages to relieve Dame Domitilla whose office as portress was arduous. The two small figures below were silently mulching the rose beds.

By their short black dresses and short veils Philippa knew they were Sister Hilary, a postulant of two months' standing, and the new postulant, Sister Cecily Scallon, who had arrived only yesterday afternoon.

'It is strange,' Dame Beatrice Sheridan had said when with Mother Prioress and the other councillors she had waited for Cecily at the enclosure door, 'strange how often an entrance coincides with a death in the house. One comes, in faith and

37

hope, to make her vows, as the other reaches their culmination – or should have reached it,' she could have said.

Lady Abbess Hester, old and mortally ill, was lingering – unaccountably; the inexplicable waiting had gone on now for thirty hours, all yesterday from the morning, through the night, all this morning and into this windless but chill October afternoon, a day and a half, and still it seemed she could not die. 'Why can't she?' The question was spreading and dismay growing through the grief, the stupor they all felt. 'What is troubling Mother? Why can't she die?'

Abbesses of Brede Abbey were elected for life and Abbess Hester Cunningham Proctor had ruled Brede for thirty-two years; she was now eighty-five but, up to yesterday, had still been active and filled with power – sometimes too much power, her councillors felt; headstrong was the right word, but they dared not use it. The community knew that their Abbess could be as wilful as she was clever and charming – and lately there had been favourites, that threat to community life – but still their trust in her was infinite, and her small black eyes, so filled with humour and understanding, had still seen 'every-thing,' said the nuns, and she seemed to know by instinct what she did not see. She had grown heavy for her height and she limped from a hip broken ten years before and that had never properly set. 'It was never given time,' the nuns said, but, 'no more oil in my bones,' said the Abbess. Her hands, too, shook; of that she had taken not the slightest notice.

As Dame Hester she had made her mark as a sculptor; it had been such a mark that, when she was elected Abbess, her friend Sir Basil Egerton, art critic and a keeper at the British Museum, had written: 'This is absurd. What time will you have now for your own work?' 'I have no "own" work,' she had written back. 'I do God's work.' It would seem that God had also endowed her with a genius for friendship, warm and lasting. All her adult life, she had worked and prayed only in the Abbey – 'I entered at nineteen' – and yet, from its strict enclosure her influence had spread far.

'Her life is a beacon,' Dame Ursula told her novices, 'that sends its rays all over the world and to unexpected places, unexpected people.' The Abbess's friends came from every walk of life from dukes to chimney-sweeps. The cliché happened to be true though the nuns had no inkling that the Duke of Gainsborough often came to see the Abbess, nor that she had a good friend, a woman chimney-sweep, 'who has often given me the most sane advice'. Happenings in the parlours, letters and telephone calls were, for every nun, strictly private. Some of Abbess Hester's friendships had ripened through decades – as with Sir Basil – from conversations in the parlour, where a unique mixture of wit, learning and humour had come through the grille, from thought 'and praying' the Abbess would have said – and from letters. 'Her letters ought to be published,' said Sir Basil.

'I suppose,' said Dame Maura Fitzgerald, the precentrix, 'we had taken it for granted she would live for ever.'

'No one lives for ever,' Dame Ursula made her usual truism.

At first it was difficult for the nuns to understand what had happened; they only knew that yesterday morning young Sister Julian Colquhoun had gone to the Abbess's room and had, of course, been admitted. 'Sister Julian who can do no wrong,' as Dame Veronica Fanshawe, the cellarer, said bitterly, Dame Veronica of the wistful harebell-blue eyes whose chin trembled at the Abbess's slightest reproof. Dame Anastasia, the nun telephonist who was at the switchboard next door, had heard Lady Abbess's, 'Deo Gratias,' giving permission for the Sister to come in, and then Sister Julian's blithe, 'Benedicite, Mother,' as she shut the door. Half an hour later Sister Julian had come out and had – she said – gone straight to the church where she had said the Te Deum. 'I was so happy,' said Sister Julian. A few minutes later Abbess Hester had had a stroke.

'But she can't be dying,' Sister Cecily had said yesterday when she was met with the news: 'I had a letter from her this morning.'

'We would have put you off,' Dame Emily Lovell, the prioress, told her, 'but you have had such a long struggle to get here that we felt we shouldn't.'

Cecily had had constant shivers ever since – shock, thought

Philippa; as a senior in the novitiate, Philippa had been asked to take the new postulant under her wing. Before she came to Brede, Philippa had not been close to young girls – Joyce Bowman had dealt with them – except perhaps Penny Stevens. Penny, Philippa thought, must be the same age now as this Sister Cecily, twenty-three, young girls, still at the beginning; they had not had time to be spotted and stained, chipped and scarred, thought Philippa with a pang of envy. There was an innocence about Cecily that reminded her of Penny; they had the same humility, probably because they had both been bullied – Dame Clare had told Philippa a little about Cecily's mother – but Cecily Scallon was beautiful as Penny certainly was not. Cecily was tall, not slim but giving the impression of slimness, because she carried herself so well. Her hair was ash-blonde, so flaxen fair that it was only when sun or lamplight caught it that it gleamed pale gold. 'People bleach their hair that colour,' said Dame Veronica, but Cecily's hair was natural and naturally curly. 'But it won't grow,' said Cecily who detested it; it showed under her postulant's veil in short feathery rings like a child's. Her habit of veiling her eyes by exceptionally long lashes gave her the look of a child too, a shy child. The eyes when she lifted them were dark, not black but dark brown. 'Striking with that hair,' said Dame Veronica, 'and that wonderful skin,' while Dame Maura, the precentrix, said, 'She looks like a seraph.' That was misleading: Cecily was too tall and too feminine to be a seraph – or a child.

There had been nothing misleading in Penny; she was stubby, grey-eyed with dark hair that always looked tousled, but Penny was firm – 'All of a piece, all through,' as Joyce Bowman used to say – and her eyes were as openly trustful as a dog's, while Cecily veiled hers from any direct gaze. Two girls, but utterly different and not only in looks and character; fulfilment, for Penny, lay in loving Donald, however he might treat her, Donald and, one day, Donald's children; while for Sister Cecily ... up on the tower Philippa said a prayer, not for the dying Abbess but for the new postulant.

The novitiate of any convent or monastery is, in a way, a

restless place with its entrances and sudden exits. 'They comes and they goes,' Sister Priscilla Pawsey, Brede's old kitchener said, 'but mostly they goes.' In Philippa's four years there, she had tried to keep her eyes down, her thoughts on her own purpose, as Dame Ursula directed, but she had not been able to help casting a professional look over her fellow novices and juniors. 'Haven't I sat on selection boards for years?' Even in her first days, – Sister Matilda won't stay, she could have said. Sister Matilda had kept the Rule with scrupulous fidelity – scrupulous exaggeration, thought Philippa. No bows had been as exact as hers, no books marked as correctly, no one else obeyed with such alacrity. By reason of nine months' seniority, she had been kind to the new postulants, always setting them right, ignoring the fact that Julian had a lifetime's knowledge of Brede and its ways. 'And I should let Sister Philippa manage her own Latin,' said Dame Ursula. 'My poor girl!' Julian had told Matilda afterwards. 'Sister Philippa took a "first" in languages at Oxford.' Everyone had been glad when Sister Matilda was sent away; Sister Angela too: '*She* sits about, waiting for someone to put a halo on her,' Julian had said. 'She certainly doesn't make much effort,' Philippa had to say. 'Only in trances,' said Julian, scornfully and, 'We don't put much faith in ecstasies here,' Dame Ursula had told them. 'The nun you see rapt away in church isn't likely to be the holiest. The holiest one is probably the one you would never notice because she is simply doing her duty.' Sister Angela had left after four months, but there were many who persevered in the life: Sister, now Dame, Benita, once a teacher of art: Sister, again now Dame, Nichola, daughter of a chemist – 'He lets us have drugs at cost price.' Sister Sophie, just senior to Philippa: Sister Constance, tiny and quick as a bird, who had come in Philippa's third year, as had Sister Louise whose father and brothers were miners.

From the beginning Julian had seemed to be set apart as a leader. In the novitiate it was Julian who calmed troubled waters and never seemed to have any troubles of her own; who somehow made a cross person less cross and who encouraged the others when a tedious task flagged. 'Let's all get at it,' she would say; her energy was infectious. 'She wants to put the world to rights,' but Dame Ursula had said it in affectionate amusement, and, 'How much better it is to curb than to prod,' said Dame Clare, who as zelatrix was Dame Ursula's right hand.

When the Abbess paid one of her frequent visits to the novitiate, it was Julian who had sat next to her, sometimes at her feet and the Abbess had allowed it. She would put her hand down and let it rest against Julian's cheek as she talked. If they were in the garden or park, Lady Abbess would lean on Julian, 'I need a strong young arm.' The others walked around or ahead of them, but it was Sister Julian who was close, whose laugh rang out; she seemed to give the old woman new life, but Philippa, by habit and long training, was cool; she made her own judgements and every now and again she had found herself wondering why Sister Julian had chosen to be a contemplative nun. Could it have been propinquity? thought Philippa.

Julian had first come to Brede when she was four years old; the same Julian, stocky and strong, with the same dark curly hair and bright brown eyes. She was the daughter of James Colquhoun, one of the Colquhoun Brothers of the building firm, who had built the new cloisters. Often, when he had come to inspect the work, Mr Colquhoun had brought his small Barbara, the future Julian, with him. Even at that age she had wanted to stay. 'But nuns have to work,' said her father.

'I can work,' said four-year-old Julian.

'What can you do?' the Abbess had teased her; even then, the community said, Julian had been Lady Abbess's pet.

'I can laugh and I can sing.' The Abbess had been delighted. 'A perfect Benedictine!' she had told Mr Colquhoun, and fifteen years later Barbara became Sister Julian. It had not stopped at Julian; her brother John, the only son, was a monk. 'Two out of three are a lot to give,' the Abbess told the Colquhouns.

'If God wants them, who am I to say "no"?' Mr Colquhoun

had said and, 'We still have Lucy – perhaps she will give us some grandchildren. I should dearly have liked a son to come into the firm – maybe it will be a grandson.'

Julian Colquhoun should have made her Solemn Profession in February of the coming year. 'February the 19th, to be exact,' said Dame Domitilla. 'Sister Philippa is due next, on the 1st of July.' Dame Domitilla, as portress on the 'turn', knew all the comings and goings of the Abbey, took in the post and sent it out and, with the years, had become like a reliable clock, telling the exact time or date of any event in Brede Abbey. Her memory was phenomenal and the nuns vowed she could recite the register: 'June 19th, 1953. Entered, Barbara Colquhoun as choir postulant, in religion Sister Julian, elder daughter of James Colquhoun and his wife Helen Baird. Born August 24th, 1934.

'January 1st, 1954. Entered, Philippa Talbot (widow *née* Sweeney) as choir postulant, in religion Sister Philippa, only daughter of the late Giles Sweeney and his wife Isabelle Cayzer, deceased. Born June 30th, 1911.'

'And no two entrances could have been more different,' said Dame Domitilla.

When Julian came, the Abbess had taken her, as it were, from her father's hands. Father, mother, brother – the young monk John – and the little sister Lucy had all come with Julian, spending two days at the Guest House, and though there had been tears and embraces before she knocked at the great enclosure door, it was with pride that they saw her go through. Mr Colquhoun had made handsome financial arrangements for her; it was all sure and firm. Philippa, that uncertain prospect, came alone; she had given her briefcase to Sister Renata, the extern portress, to send through the 'turn' to the Abbess. It contained transfer notes for shares worth round about five thousand pounds, 'to go on with,' Philippa told the Abbess and the cellarer, Dame Veronica. 'There may be a gratuity to follow in lieu of my pension. There would have been a gratuity if I had married ordinarily – but will this qualify as a marriage? I don't know. My friends are looking into it for me. It's a tricky point.' She had added, 'I thought I should make the investments for you. I didn't know how good your man was.' Dame Veronica had given a little gasp, but Philippa did not realize that she had been presumptuous and the Abbess only said gravely that the money seemed well invested.

Abbess Hester had sent for Philippa yesterday – 'Only yesterday,' whispered Philippa now on the tower – and told her it had been decided to bring her into the community for the last six months of her Simple Vows. 'It's absurd to keep you in the novitiate any longer.' She had put her hand on Philippa's shoulder. 'You have fought a manful battle, as I knew you would.' She had said that yesterday morning; indeed, it had been as Philippa was leaving the Abbess's room that Julian had come so blithely towards it.

Julian's brother John had spent the weekend before at Brede – 'Providentially,' said gentle Dame Beatrice to whom most things were providential. 'If he had not come, Sister Julian might have made a terrible mistake.' Brother John Colquhoun had changed his Benedictine Order for a missionary one in India, the Brown Brothers, and at the end of his year as a novice there, had been sent back to England to take a year's course in hydrostatics.

'What on earth's that?' asked Hilary.

'Water engineering,' said Julian and she had said, 'You shall all see him,' as one granting a rare privilege. 'Mother says he will talk to the whole community this Saturday in the large parlour about his province in Bengal – the work and problems there. You can't imagine what it is like,' said Julian, with shining eyes.

'I can. I once lived there,' said Philippa. Now and again Sister Philippa lifted the curtain over these – to the others – tantalizing glimpses of her past. 'I believe Sister Philippa has been *everywhere*,' declared Sister Constance, but if Philippa had, she did not say a word about it to Brother John and he had breezily taken it for granted that there was no one in his audience who had been out of Britain except Dame Thecla, the Ethiopian who, to the least observant eye, was not English,

44

and he had explained things, 'not exactly in one-syllable words, but very nearly,' as Dame Agnes said.

'Wasn't it *deeply* interesting?' said little Sister Constance.

'Not deeply,' said Philippa.

'Oh, Sister!'

'It couldn't be; he is not a deep young man' – any more than Sister Julian is a deep young woman, Philippa had wanted to add, but refrained. Not yet ordained, Brother John was only twenty-four and exactly like Julian – or as Philippa had sensed that Julian was. He looked like her, thick set, cleanly, with the same bright brown eyes, the same enthusiasm. His hair was crew-cut, his cassock short. 'John's a worker,' said Sister Julian proudly.

'And he thinks we are not.'

That had been evident, evident too that Lady Abbess had not been entirely immune from the missionary fever that was spreading. 'Brother John thinks you would be interested,' she told her senior nuns on the Sunday following the talk, 'to meet him for an informal discussion in the parlour, perhaps five or six of you at a time. He asks me to say there will be no gloves on. That's good because we have a great deal to learn.'

'Hasn't he?' they had wanted to ask, but were silent.

'Shall we say after None in number three parlour?'

There was another silence, then, 'Yes, Mother, if you are interested.' The Abbess had felt the silence and over-rode it. 'I am interested and you should be too – unless you prefer to shut your minds.'

'Why do we have to waste our time with this young whipper-snapper?' Dame Agnes Kerr, the tart old scholar, had asked when the Abbess had gone. 'Why?'

'He is Sister Julian's brother.' That was Dame Veronica. She and Dame Agnes were seldom in sympathy but over this, for different reasons, they were at one.

'Mother is building too much on that girl,' said wise Dame Agnes. 'Far too much,' and wondered why Dame Veronica's harebell-blue eyes had looked at her, with such fear? thought Dame Agnes uneasily.

To Dame Agnes, Sister Julian and her brother with their

new-fangled ideas were like woodpeckers busily making holes until the life of the tree was destroyed. 'They don't care a rap for history or tradition, and are completely ignorant of them. They won't even listen.' It was the beginning of the restlessness, the growing power of the young.

'I don't like to see these,' Brother John had said, tapping the grille of the parlour. 'I look forward to the day when the bars will come down and you can mingle freely with your guests – perhaps even wear lay clothes as they do.'

'Just as we did a hundred years ago,' said the young councillor Dame Catherine Ismay.

That took him aback.

'Didn't you know?' asked Dame Beatrice, sweetly. 'When we first came to Brede that was how we had to live. We could not wear our habits, and were not allowed enclosure until 1880. We had to fight to get our grilles.'

'One who informs, ought to be himself informed, not?' Dame Colette, who was French, asked of the air.

'But then you could open a hospital, run a school,' he argued.

Dame Maura, the precentrix, rose with a swish of skirts. 'I have an organ practice,' she announced and left the parlour. Dame Maura was privileged – and did not believe in wasting time.

'We kept a school in those days. Now, thank God, we don't have to,' said Dame Agnes.

' 'Why thank God?' he had bristled.

'Because it took us away from our proper work.'

'Which supports the likes of you.' Dame Perpetua, Brede's stout, steady, subprioress, was always forthright.

It was the old argument. 'Our Lord taught and healed . . .' said Brother John.

'And prayed; withdrew into the mountain or the wilderness to pray,' said the nuns.

'Do you not believe in prayer?' asked Dame Colette.

'Of course – but if you are shut away it must be limited.'

'Or concentrated,' said Dame Catherine Ismay.

'Brother John, you want to be a missionary,' said Dame

Agnes. 'Then you might reflect, Brother, that the greatest missionary of modern times was, and is, little St Thérèse of Lisieux who never, even for five minutes, left her cloister.'

John Colquhoun, though, had become likeable when he talked about his work, 'his, not ours,' said Dame Agnes. The Brown Brothers were called 'Brown' – 'not because we have Indian priests, though I'm glad to say we have many, but from the coarse brown clothes we wear'. They were Indian clothes, a kameeze, loose tunic shirt, and loose trousers coming in to the ankle, 'much more practical for manual work than a tunic and scapular.' The mission was a new venture in India's 'moffusil' or countryside and was formed, not to open schools or hospitals, but for agriculture and irrigation. 'Farms and wells,' said Brother John.

'What could be needed more?' asked Lady Abbess.

The Order lived as the peasants did; their centres were village huts; the brothers slept on charpoys, Indian string beds; ate Indian food. 'And we need sisters'; his eyes had swept over the ranks behind the grille. 'Sisters for the women, to teach them hygiene, how to look after their children and feed them better; how to make the most of what they have: plant vegetable gardens and rear chickens and bring back the village handicrafts. Every minute counts.' His face had burned with zeal and there had been an answering fire in the eyes of many of the nuns, especially the young ones. 'Wonderful, wonderful work,' said Sister Constance as they had all talked of it in the novitiate during recreation. 'If one could do it, but it must be terribly hard.'

'Is it harder than ours?' asked Philippa.

'Of course it is,' said Julian but Philippa had shaken her head. 'Is it easier to "be" than to "do"?'

'I don't know what you are talking about.' The blood had risen in Julian's cheeks. 'Those poor poor people. Look at our clothes, our habits,' she had cried. 'They ought to be made of the cheapest serge.'

'Why?' asked Philippa. 'We weave our own, and handwoven cloth wears better than serge, especially cheap serge.'

'Yes, I have had this winter habit for thirteen years,' Dame Ursula had put in.

'But our white linen. Our shoes.' Julian had been up in arms. 'We should be barefoot like the Poor Clares.'

'The Poor Clares do more manual work, less study,' said Dame Ursula. 'With our long hours of stillness, bare feet would not be practical.'

'They would be exaggerated,' said Dame Clare.

'I still feel ashamed.'

'Did Mary feel ashamed for not helping Martha?'

Philippa still had not learned to let an argument go, or temper it; she still used the quick riposte, 'and we haven't a chance against her,' muttered Julian but, 'The Church needs many, many Marthas,' Dame Clare had said gently, laying her hand on Julian's.

'Yes!' cried Julian. 'Look at the state of the world.'

'Which is why she needs a few Marys too.' Philippa had undoubtedly been right but she had had a rebuke from the zelatrix.

Brother John Colquhoun had left Brede on the Monday after that memorable weekend; he had telephoned Julian that evening and later that night she had gone to Abbess Hester and asked permission to telephone her father and mother. On Tuesday morning she went to the Abbess again.

Kneeling by her chair, Julian had told her she would not now be taking her vows at Brede. 'I see where my real vocation is.' She would be joining the Brown Sisters, 'as soon as John can arrange it.' Her father and mother approved and they would write to Lady Abbess. 'It will be work, real work, and with John. I shall have to start all over again.' Julian had had a new humility but her face was radiant; this undoubtedly was the path for Julian. She thanked the dear Abbess and dear Dame Ursula and Dame Clare for all their love and care. 'For all you have taught me, and I know, dearest Mother, you will give me your blessing.'

The Abbess had succeeded in blessing and kissing her – until then she had not said a word – and Julian had danced away. Twenty minutes later Sister Ellen, who looked after the Abbess's rooms, had found Abbess Hester slumped and unconscious in her chair.

But, no matter what the affection or the hopes, thought the nuns, a great Abbess does not die because a junior nun leaves, even one as dear as Sister Julian. 'It doesn't *happen*,' they would have said, but it was happening now. 'Yes, she's defeated this time,' Doctor Avery had said. He had been the Abbey's doctor for a score of years and had come at once. The Abbess was paralysed, except for the smallest movement of her head and fingers, and unable to swallow; Dame Joan, the infirmarian, had stood by the bed, hour after hour, constantly moistening the strangely swollen lips. Abbess Hester was plainly dying – 'A matter of hours, perhaps even an hour,' Doctor Avery had said.

The whole community, the choir nuns in their cowls, had lined the long cloisters, each carrying a lighted candle, and knelt as the enclosure door opened; escorted by the sacristan, Dame Beatrice, softly ringing her little silver bell, and by Dame Agnes who, as mistress of ceremonies, bore a lighted candle before him, Dom Gervase, Brede's young chaplain, had carried the holy oils and the Blessed Sacrament to the Abbess's cell. The nuns followed after, singing the 'Miserere' and knelt, as many as could, in the Abbess's rooms, the rest on the bare floor of the corridor. Dom Gervase put down the ciborium on the table, ready with its white cloth, candles and crucifix and came to the bedside, but Abbess Hester had motioned him away by the restless movement of her head, while her fingers plucked feebly in distress, at the sheet. Her lips formed the word 'No', though only a distorted sound came through; then the prioress, bending over her, thought she heard the word 'want' welling up from the mind below that thickened speech, 'Wa-ant.'

'I am here, dear Mother,' said the prioress as she had said day in, day out, all these years.

'Wa-ant.' It went on after Dom Gervase had gone away. 'I shall be waiting, every minute,' he had said, 'but I think we should send for Abbot Bernard.' Abbott Bernard Rossetti was

Abbot of Udimore Abbey, twenty miles away, companion monastery to Brede; for years, he had been Abbess Hester's trusted counsellor and friend; he had come at once but she had given him no flicker of recognition.

'Wa-ant.'

'Want some*thing* or some*one*?' The prioress, Dame Emily, bent low. 'Is it Dame Veronica?' she had asked, selfless, as always.

Mother Prioress looked as white and strained as if it were she, not the Abbess, who was dying, and – how thin she has grown, thought the nuns, almost emaciated.

As subprioress, Dame Perpetua was below, holding the reins, the guiding strings as, since she took office, she had held them a hundred times when Abbess and prioress were locked away in the Council or other business. 'But not business like this!' said Dame Perpetua. Dame Perpetua was as simple as she was downright and she had not tried to stop the tears running down her cheeks as she went about her work; the work was carried out as usual from her room or in the refectory or choir, and, 'She's the only one of us who can sing through tears,' said the nuns. 'We don't usually lament over a death,' they would have said, 'but this is worrying.'

Next to prioress and subprioress in importance was the cellarer, Dame Veronica of the harebell-blue eyes that were 'always brimming', as Dame Agnes said in irritation. Dame Veronica was the most baffling of all Abbess Hester's appointments; the Rule of St Benedict lays down that a cellarer should be 'wise, of mature character, not a great eater, not haughty, not excitable, not offensive . . . not wasteful'. 'Well, Dame Veronica is not a great eater,' said Dame Agnes.

The cellarer before had been the younger Dame Catherine Ismay, who had held that office for six years and who seemed to have all the qualities needed; Dame Catherine was capable, unhurried, noted for her evenness, and sturdy, perhaps too sturdy for the Abbess. Three years ago when the day for Distribution of Offices had come round, contrary to all expectations Dame Veronica Fanshawe, pliant Dame Veronica, had been appointed in Dame Catherine's place, though it had not been done without arguments from the Council, arguments produced with reverence and politeness, unshakeable, but of no avail. In those days, Dame Perpetua, in whose eyes Abbess Hester was the pattern of wisdom, had been on the Council; she and, as always, Dame Emily as prioress, and Dame Beatrice, who saw only the best in everyone and would not go against the Abbess, voted with her for the appointment. None of the arguments had been repeated to the community but, in the way of communities, the nuns seemed to know about them without being told and, when Dame Perpetua became sub-prioress, leaving a vacancy on the Council, the community had elected Dame Catherine Ismay.

The Abbess had been quick to catch the unspoken criticism and it did not make her like Dame Catherine any better, though Dame Catherine had had no choice but to accept what had happened to her: to be displaced as cellarer, when, because she held that office she had automatically been a councillor, and then to be elected councillor again. Now she was the youngest on the Council as she had been the youngest cellarer ever appointed at Brede but she took it with her accustomed quietness. 'Quietness or aloofness?' asked Dame Agnes. It was hard to tell.

As Dame Catherine knelt now, she was bigger, taller than the rest, except for the immensely tall precentrix, Dame Maura. Dame Maura was slim and with her height gave the effect of a mast in a ship scudding before the wind, perhaps because she always moved too fast. Dame Catherine, proportioned like a Brunnhilde, seemed more the figurehead of the ship, first to breast calm or storm; now her face was shut in prayer and an almost visible strength flowed to the tormented figure on the bed.

Dame Beatrice Sheridan knelt closer; though as sacristan her work was exacting, she had been appointed a councillor by the Abbess, whose right it was to appoint three out of the requisite six, the community electing the others. The Abbess had chosen wisely because Dame Beatrice was much loved; no one had ever heard her say an unkind word of anyone. 'She's not of this world at all,' said Dame Veronica.

'Which will make her of singularly little use on the Council'; that was Dame Agnes.

'Perhaps we need her to keep the peace,' was Dame Maura's retort.

Dame Maura Fitzgerald and Dame Agnes Kerr were the two most prominent nuns in the community, prominent because they were outstanding. 'I think of them as twin towers,' Philippa said once, 'which is odd because Dame Agnes isn't tall.'

Dame Agnes Kerr was little and bony, even her shoulders looked sharp. She had a red lump on her forehead that the younger nuns said was a third eye, seeing even farther than the other two that, with their red rims and sandy lashes, were so shrewd they stripped away all humbug and pretence. Brede was proud of Dame Agnes. 'She is our acid test,' said Dame Maura. When Dame Agnes was working, she was like a terrier down a foxhole. 'And she will always get her fox,' the Abbess had said.

Dame Agnes was not only a classical scholar but also a mathematician; she had been Eighth Wrangler at Cambridge and, since coming to Brede, had specialized in Anglo-Saxon; she was writing a book on the history, in art, literature and devotion, of the Holy Cross, 'been writing it for fifteen years,' said Dame Veronica who, herself, wrote poems.

Dame Maura Fitzgerald, precentrix in charge of all music and Brede's first organist, was equally noted. 'People come from all over Britain to hear our chant,' Dame Ursula told her novices.

Dame Ursula was not kneeling in the Abbess's room; as mistress of novices her first duty was to the novitiate; Dame Ursula was called Ursa, the Great Bear, or Teddy according to her moods, 'though we're not supposed to nickname,' Hilary warned Cecily. With the councillors knelt French Dame Colette Aubadon, mistress of church work: Dame Camilla, the learned old head librarian: Dame Edith of the printing room, Dame Mildred, gardener, while Dame Joan Howard, the infirmarian, stood on the other side of the bed from Mother Prioress.

52

'W-ant.'

'Is it Dame Veronica?' but Dame Veronica seemed as if she too had had a stroke and was semi-paralysed. 'She hasn't once been in the proc's room since Mother fell ill,' said Dame Perpetua wrathfully. The proc's room was the procurator's or cellarer's office where Dame Veronica's 'second', young Dame Winifred, was trying to fill her place. At her name, Dame Veronica looked up, white and cowed as if she were terrified, and the nuns had to push her forward, but when she knelt by the bed and quavered, 'Mother,' the Abbess's restlessness increased, the fingers plucked in torment. 'W-ant.'

'Want Sister Julian?' When the prioress asked that there was a sudden stillness in the old body and, 'Send for Sister Julian,' said the prioress.

Sister Julian did not want to come. 'She'll try and make me change my mind.'

'Don't be silly, child,' said Dame Perpetua who had gone in person to fetch her. 'Mother cannot even speak.'

When Sister Julian was defiant, her underlip stuck out and, with her tear-stained face, she looked like a cross child, but when she came to the bed, all her inherent kindliness warmed her into pity, deep sadness and regret for this ruin of her dear and august friend. 'Oh, I didn't mean to do this. I didn't mean to,' she whispered, shrinking against the prioress and, kneeling by the bed, 'Dear Mother. Dear, dear Mother,' she said, over and over again, but the head still moved, the fingers twitched and, 'Want,' came again. Then it was not Sister Julian.

Dom Gervase tried once more, his dark young face tense with the anguish of his grief. Lady Abbess had been his lifeline but, for all the upholding power of his office, he could not reach past the trouble that tormented her, nor could Abbot Bernard; even he could not soothe her, but towards that evening another word had come welling up, forced out by great effort. The prioress thought it was 'tell'. 'Want. Tell.'

'You want to tell us something, Mother?' but the Abbess could only say 'tell'. 'Why?' asked the nuns. 'What could she have to tell?' 'Why should she be so troubled? She cannot be afraid.' No true nun is afraid of death. 'I wish I knew when I was going to die,' ninety-six-year-old Dame Frances Anne often said, 'I wish I knew.'

'Why, Dame?'

'Then I should know what to read next.'

In the early hours of the morning, those hours of low ebb when so many souls slip quietly away as if all resistance were gone, the 'want' gave way to 'sor-ry'. 'Sorry.' The prioress knew the Abbess's every shade and tone – she would have believed she knew her every thought – and her quick ear had fathomed that this 'sorry' was not only regret; there was con-trition, deep contrition. 'Then it is not only Sister Julian; it is something Mother has done, for which she cannot forgive her-self.'

Mother Prioress had not said that aloud but the infirmarian had caught the 'sorry' too; Dame Emily and Dame Joan looked at one another and, as if it were a contagion, deeper qualms spread through the monastery: 'something Mother, our Mother has done.'

There had been, they all knew, no suggestion of impro-priety, even in thought, with Sister Julian. In the last years there had been favourites but never inordinate love. 'Lady Abbess has loved more people than most of us could begin to know.' Dame Ursula often said that and, 'we have only one love to give,' Abbess Hester had told the community at one of the conferences she gave twice a week. 'We don't give bits of our hearts but love everyone with the love we give to God. That keeps it safe.' That was how she had loved Sister Julian; though often she had not been exactly wise over her, the nuns knew and trusted that. Now it was as if the Abbey trembled. Something – and Sister Julian's defection may have been the spark that lit it – something had been brought home. 'Sorry.' The word was clearer now though it still seemed to come from a depth they could not reach; tears slid down from the Abbess's closed eyes and soaked the pillow. Abbot Bernard came to the bed again. 'Dear, dear friend. Dear child . . .' but again the head moved in refusal and again the effort welled up from the Abbess, 'sorry.' As the second afternoon waned, it

54

seemed to the waiting nuns that the weary word would never end.

It was Dame Catherine who stood up. She was always strong and, though now she was as white and worn as any of them, resolution shone in her hazel eyes, such resolution that Dame Joan made way for her. Dame Catherine stilled the Abbess's fingers by taking the shaking hands in her own firm grasp; her voice was strong as she spoke. 'No matter what it is,' she said. 'You have said sorry. We have all heard. No matter what it is, we shall deal with it. Dear Mother, there is no more you can do now. Lay it down.'

She knelt and kissed the Abbess's hand and went back to her place with such swiftness that when the Abbess's black eyes opened it was only the prioress, Dame Emily, she saw.

She looked at her, a look of gratitude, affection and respect; then the Abbess gave a sigh, closed her eyes, and head and fingers were still.

Back in her corner, Dame Catherine felt her face burning; she thanked heaven for the wimple that hid the nervous patches on her throat and the veil that shadowed her face. 'What made me do that?' she asked herself. She, the most contained of creatures? And a voice in her, the same voice that had impelled her forward, answered, 'Someone had to,' and to do anything else would have been a betrayal of what she had clearly seen as duty. 'They may think it was Dame Emily,' she comforted herself. 'Mother herself thought it was,' and, 'as long as it was done, what does it matter who did it?'

Up on the tower, Philippa, lost in her prayer, felt a vibrating under her feet as soft-toned Michael began to ring; it was the Passing Bell.

55

2

The great bell, Mary Major, took over from Michael; it tolled once every minute, the solemn death toll sounding through the Abbey, across the marshes and down into the town. 'She has gone, then,' said the townspeople, and those who were Catholics among them silently made the sign of the cross.

The Abbess had not been able to speak to make her last confession but Dom Gervase, hastily summoned, had given her absolution; nor could she swallow the Holy Viaticum, food for the unfathomable journey she was to make nor kiss the crucifix, but the prioress had held it to her lips.

The nuns, as they gathered, had knelt, some sobbing, some white and quiet, round the room and down the corridor as Dom Gervase administered Extreme Unction, touching eyes, ears, nostrils, lips, hands and feet with holy oil in the sign of the cross, sealing the five senses away from the world: '*By this holy anointing and of his most tender mercy, may the Lord forgive you whatever sins you have committed through your sight*' or '*hearing*' or '*sense of smell*' or '*speech*' or '*touch*'. Dom Gervase's voice had faltered as he began but it had grown firm and clear as he prayed. Then the nuns had heard the words: '*Go forth O soul, out of this world in the name of the Father Almighty, who created you . . .*' and a moment after, '*We commend to Thee, O Lord, the soul of Thy servant Hester.*' Dom Gervase read the words in the silent room. '*Dead to this world, may she live to Thee, and the sins she has committed in this life, through human frailty, do Thou in mercy forgive . . .*'

56

Philippa, kneeling almost at the end of the long line of nuns in the corridor, heard a small gasp and looked up to see Cecily Scallon opposite her; among the habits, the postulant's dress looked thin and skimpy; the short veil had slipped back from the soft hair. She looked too shocked to cry but Philippa saw that she was still shivering – and violently. Dame Ursula was with the senior nuns, in the Abbess's room, and four or five juniors separated Cecily from the zelatrix, Dame Clare; without a sound Philippa rose, stepped across, knelt down again by Cecily and took the girl's hand in her own.

The last toll ended. Then, as the nuns rose stiffly from their knees, the voice of the great bell sounded again, beginning the first of the three tolls for Vespers. Silently the nuns filed down to fetch their cowls and go to their station in the cloisters, then, two by two, paced in procession into choir where the Abbess's crook lay across her empty chair which was already draped in black. When Cecily saw that, she gave another gasp; coming into church she had walked as was prescribed – Cecily had been studying monastic observances for years and had kept her eyes down, her hands together, but now, in her place she looked up and saw the black drapings, the laid-down crook that seemed so eloquent and her distress was audible all through the choir. Dame Clare laid a restraining hand on her shoulder; it was not too early for the newest postulant to learn that nothing, not even the death of a most holy Abbess, could be allowed to disturb the Divine Office.

There were absences. Dame Joan and her 'second', Dame Margaret, were upstairs in the Abbess's cell, ready to wash and prepare the body for its lying in state. 'But where is Dame Veronica?' whispered Dame Joan.

Dame Veronica should have been there; it was the cellarer's duty to take charge of the body until it was brought down to the church where it was given into the care of the mistress of ceremonies. The cellarer was needed for the laying out; it was she who had to say the accompanying prayers. In fact Dame Veronica should not have left the Abbess's cell but, 'I think she's in the proc's room,' Dame Margaret whispered and Dame Joan, tired out and grieved to her depths, failed to keep back a small but impatient click of her tongue as she went to look.

The proc's room was a busy place, with its two desks, two typewriters, telephone, filing cabinets, shelves of stationery. It had a silver cupboard, small stores cupboards, a locked drugs cupboard. The storeroom proper opened out of it but the proc's room was always full; there was the basket for shoes that needed mending: the shelf for electrical repairs: a table heaped with objects that had been lost, now found, but not claimed. Anything and everything went to the proc's room: presents that had not yet received the Abbess's approval: things to be changed: things so old they really needed to be replaced – 'past mending,' a nun would say regretfully. Dame Veronica used often to put up pleading notices: '*Please* add a note to say where this comes from': 'What needs to be *done* with this?': 'Where *is* this?' and, frantically: 'Please bring things on Monday mornings, *not* on Sunday afternoons.' 'Things! Things!' Dame Veronica often wanted to cry, 'After all, I wasn't brought up to this.'

'Not at Orford Hall,' Dame Agnes said it deliberately and afterwards to the prioress, 'I'm sorry, Mother, but what do Orford Halls matter here?'

At first the importance of being cellarer had buoyed Dame Veronica up and carried her through the work and, in those first days, she had not been too proud to seek help from Mother Prioress, but the prioress perhaps understood too well what Dame Veronica's limitations were, and more and more, Dame Veronica's pride had taken over; but with the pride came a secret weariness and her difficulties with the work increased. 'I am, after all, a poet,' she wanted to cry, but not for worlds would she have complained to the Abbess. Most of the consequences of her shortcomings fell on young Dame Winifred, but Dame Winifred was loyal and did not blink an eyelid when Dame Veronica said picturesquely, 'For me to be cellarer is a heavy cross.' That had ceased to be picturesque this last year and had become a fact.

On the back wall of the proc's room, and too large for it, hung a crucifix; it was so large that the foot of the cross came

58

down almost to the skirting. It had been sent to Dame Veronica by a Yorkshire business man who, unlikely as it seemed, had read and been touched by her poems, when they were published on the Abbey's own press, the Brede Press. It was a small plain edition though, as with all Dame Edith's printing work, the paper, print and binding were outstanding, 'More outstanding than the poems,' Dame Agnes had said, and justly. Dame Veronica's poems were uneven in calibre. 'She can be charming,' said Dame Beatrice. 'Charm isn't a quality of good poetry,' snapped Dame Agnes, 'and some of these are "kitsch",' but the book had found a way into some surprising minds. It was, of course, anonymous, 'by a Benedictine of Brede', and the crucifix had been sent 'for the poet'.

The Yorkshireman had evidently thought 'the bigger the better', and the Abbess had flinched when she first saw the glossy plaster, the bright brown curly hair, the red paint-splashed blood. 'Ugh!' the Abbess would have said, except that no one could say that about a crucifix, but Dame Veronica's taste was more naïve. 'She's really a little bourgeoise,' Dame Colette had once said, exasperated, and had gone straight to her cell and forced herself to bend down and kiss the floor for her lack of charity. With the crucifix Dame Veronica had seen only the suffering and its message. 'Mother, it speaks! I don't think I have seen another where our Lord has broken knees, though of course He must have had with three falls.' She had also been immensely touched by the gift, 'It was sent for *me*. Fancy!' and at once, 'Where will you put it, Mother? In the music library?'

'N-no,' the Abbess had said.

'I just thought – the one there is so small. Would you like it in your room? Your own one is small too. It would go beautifully.'

The Abbess had visibly recoiled; the crucifix in her room was of olive wood, two hundred years old.

'Then where, dear Mother?'

'In the proc's room, of course.' The Abbess had been grateful for the inspiration. 'It was sent for you and you shall have it.'

'But . . . it will be hidden.'

'It won't be – if it speaks for you.'

'When I look at it, I can do *anything*!' Dame Veronica had declared but now Dame Joan found her kneeling beside it, her eyes closed, her face as livid as its paint.

'Dame, we're waiting for the laying out.'

'I – know.'

'Then will you come?'

'I'm coming,' said Dame Veronica but did not move.

'Come, Dame.' The infirmarian tried to help. 'You have seen death before,' though as a matter of fact, since Dame Veronica's appointment only one nun had died.

'This is – Mother.'

'All the more reason why everything should be done properly. Please get up,' but Dame Veronica would not move. When Vespers was over, Dame Joan went to fetch the prioress but she was speaking on the telephone and Dame Joan came back with the subprioress, Dame Perpetua. The little cellarer had moved but only to kneel closer, pressing her cheek against the pierced feet. 'Pierced like me,' she had whispered with Dame Veronica's usual drama.

'It's the same for all of us,' Dame Perpetua argued but Dame Veronica shook her head. 'For me, it's different. I wish it were not.'

'All the same, Dame, you must come.'

'I'm coming.'

'Then come.' There was no movement. Stout bustling Dame Perpetua was sensible and perspicacious. 'Do you want the community to know that Dame Winifred had to do your work?' she asked. It was the right question. Dame Veronica's eyes flew open and, though they were wet, as were her white cheeks, she got to her feet.

'You must remember,' said the prioress when Dame Perpetua went to her in indignation, 'remember it is difficult for Dame Veronica to steel herself to things.'

'But for one of us seniors to behave like that . . .' Dame Perpetua's plump face was creased with worry. 'Mother Prioress, is something really very wrong?'

'Let us hope,' said the prioress after a moment, 'that this is just Dame Veronica.'

Lady Abbess Hester lay on her bed, dressed exactly as on the day of her Solemn Profession in her habit and cowl. Her hands were clasped over the wooden crucifix; her face, with the eyes closed, slept quietly at peace. One by one, the nuns came in to kneel beside the bed, perhaps to put a flower or a posy among the many others – though posy flowers were difficult to find in October – to say a prayer, reverently kiss the hem or the sleeve of her habit, then quietly make way for the next-comer. All through the night the nuns watched, two by two in turn, though others came in and out; in the early morning the plain coffin, made by Burnell in his workshop, was brought, and the Abbess was lifted into it. The prioress drew the veil down over her face for the last time, and Dame Veronica, calm now the others were watching, fastened the lid; then eight of the strongest nuns carried the coffin downstairs where it lay, covered with a velvet pall, on its wheeled bier, in the middle of the choir. Six tall candles, in silver candlesticks, guarded it and at its foot was a vase of lilies sent by Sir Basil Egerton.

None but her daughters' hands had touched the Abbess; everything was simplicity and should have been serene. 'In the midst of life we are in death,' said the medieval Responsory 'Media Vita', but when the nuns came into choir to sing the Office and the steady cadences rose, as they did every day, all through the day, it was the opposite: 'in the midst of death we are in life'. The Church does not weep for death and, in the Abbey, there was none of the funeral pomp of undertakers; there should have been no gloom, yet gloom there was, worse, almost a sense of doom and, oddly, of disorder. It was perhaps because this death was different from any the nuns had known – as if Lady Abbess Hester, in some way, did not belong to them; it was oddly public; the outside world intruded, like those lilies, thought Philippa. They sent their fragrance into the choir – almost overwhelmingly; indeed their scent made Dame Veronica sick again. 'Perpetually sick.' Dame Joan was

61

irritated. At a time like this, she felt Dame Veronica should have kept her sickness to herself. Mother Prioress was dropping on her feet; she had been up for most of three nights, first with the dying Abbess, then keeping watch; there were letters and telegrams to be sent: endless telephone calls in and out.

'It's the Bishop, Mother.' '*The Times*.' 'It's Sir Basil.' Dame Domitilla, the portress, even with extra aids to help her, had hardly had a moment's rest, taking in telegrams and flowers; the Abbey began to fill with flowers – 'far, far too many', said the prioress – it seemed almost unseemly: extravagant.

The guest list, too, grew longer every hour and extra hands were needed in the kitchen for the guests' luncheon and the kitchener, Sister Priscilla grew distracted. Dame Maura gathered the chantresses for the dirge that was sung on the afternoon of the second day. 'A noble Abbess deserves a noble dirge,' Dame Maura said, and their faces shone. It was a noble dirge but when after the 'Subvenite', that asked the angels to come and lead the newly freed soul into heaven, the precentrix and her three chantresses intoned '*All things are alive, in the sight of their King*,' their supple voices rising and falling, Dame Perpetua of all people could not go on; she was overcome with weeping. 'And I condemned Dame Veronica,' she said. 'I am ashamed, but Mother's death *shouldn't* be like this,' said Dame Perpetua.

Philippa was deputed to try and spare the prioress, to take messages, run errands, fetch wanted people. 'It's a shame to turn you into an errand boy,' said the prioress.

'Mother, I would do anything.' Philippa wanted to go on, but emotion and presumption would not help; Mother Prioress had the tremendous Requiem to get through, thought Philippa, and all those people to see and, of course, the life of the monastery to keep flowing.

The Requiem was on the third day, a Solemn Pontifical Mass, in the presence of the Bishop of the Diocese, sung by the Abbot President, assisted by Abbot Bernard of Udimore

and Dom Gervase. Other Bishops and Abbots knelt at prie-
dieux in the sanctuary, which was lined with monks and
priests. The monks of Udimore sang alternately with the
Brede choir for the Kyrie and Dies Irae, and joined with the
choir for the rest, singing with the full and clear virility
Abbess Hester had loved; no one broke down, Dame Perpetua's voice kept its full beauty, yet the nuns' hearts were
heavy.

The Abbess's friends and relatives filled the extern chapel,
overflowing into the porch and the garden beyond. Sir Basil
was there; Canon Giles Drinkwater, the Anglican theologian:
Mrs Abel the chimney-sweep, countless others. Four of Abbess
Hester's great-nephews carried the coffin to the Abbey grave-
yard where, after all the pomp, Abbess Hester Cunningham
Proctor would lie under a small wooden cross identical with its
sisters; row upon row in this quiet place, guarded by tall yew
hedges; even in death the nuns kept their enclosure. Two
bowls of flowers were put on the grave; one of violets, one of
wild orchids from an Afrikaans friend, flown from South
Africa. Dame Beatrice, as sacristan, put torches at the head
and foot of the grave where they burned all night. The rest of
the flowers, except one or two bunches sent by the prioress to
the infirmary, were heaped at the foot of the statue in the ante-
chapel, our Lady of Peace.

It was over. The ritual, each ceremony, carried out with
beauty, dignity and love. It was over, 'and the empty time has
begun,' said Cecily.

It was a strange emptiness. A few of the oldest nuns had
experienced it before; in her seventy-eight years of religious
life Dame Frances Anne, for instance, had known the election
of four abbesses, but Abbess Hester Cunningham Proctor had
ruled for so long that, for most of the community, the experience was new.

At first it did not seem so empty; Lady Abbess: Mother
Prioress: it was so natural for the second to step into the place
of the first, as the nuns always and instantaneously filled in for
one another, that for a short while there did not seem any
question but that Dame Emily would be elected Abbess as

unanimously as, once upon a time, Dame Hester had been chosen. 'But is it fair,' said Philippa, 'to ask it of someone so worn and tired?'

The juniors, not having a vote, felt they could discuss the coming election. 'But they shouldn't,' Dame Agnes, that stickler, told Dame Ursula, 'it's nothing to do with them.'

'It is to do with them.' Dame Ursula was warm. 'It is to do with the least and newest postulant. After all, they will spend their lives under the new Abbess.'

'You hope,' said Dame Agnes tartly. 'The Scallon postulant looks very shaky to me.'

Cecily was shaken. 'I had *counted* on finding Mother here.' Philippa had heard Cecily sobbing in the night, almost all night – she herself had been wakeful, as were nearly all the nuns. Philippa would have gone in to Cecily, but cells were sacrosanct – only Dame Ursula or Dame Clare could have done that and Philippa guessed that Cecily would far rather they did not know. In the morning Cecily had looked so desperate that Philippa had tried to hearten her by saying, 'It's not irrevocable, you know. No one will think any the worse of you if you find the Abbey too hard without Lady Abbess.' Cecily had turned what Philippa thought was a startled glance on her; then she said in a low voice like a shamed child, 'It's just that ... I had wanted, I needed – to tell her about the lunch party.'

'A lunch party?'

'Yes. The day I entered, my mother gave a farewell luncheon for me. It was dreadful. No ... I was dreadful,' said Cecily.

She could hear her mother's voice now: 'I won't have people saying we bundled you off. They might think there was something wrong, a family rift or you had had an unhappy love affair.'

'Couldn't they think it was choice?' but Cecily had bitten that back; instead, 'It – it will all be so complicated,' she had stumbled over the words. 'I – I wanted it simple, quiet and – kind of usual.' She had picked up her spaniel Rory and held him tightly to give herself courage, while Mrs Scallon tapped with a pencil on the blotter. 'Mummy, can't you understand?'

'No,' said Mrs Scallon.

'I thought – if I could leave, just simply, as if it were every-day . . .'

'You *can not* pretend,' Mrs Scallon had said, 'that this kind of thing is everyday.'

'If only I could have belonged to a family like Sister Hilary's,' Cecily said longingly to Philippa, 'like the families in Ireland or America where it is part of family life, and a privilege, for a daughter or sister or cousin to be a nun. In ours, you would think no one had ever joined an Order before.'

Cecily had waited seven years. 'Wasted seven years,' she had said rebelliously. 'You are not twenty-one; you cannot enter without your parents' consent.' Everywhere she tried, that had been said to her, and, 'I shall never consent, never,' Mrs Scallon had declared.

It had begun when Cecily was sixteen – which was, she had to admit herself, quite out of the question. Then seventeen: 'Far too young to know your own mind,' and, 'Eighteen! Ridiculous!' Cecily had advanced the case of St Thérèse of Lisieux, as girls, wanting to marry young, have always advanced Juliet, but, 'St Thérèse? Never heard of her,' Mrs Scallon had said and, when Cecily had explained, 'That's different. She was French.'

'It's just a phase.' Cecily's Aunt Elaine, wise in the ways of the world, had comforted Mrs Scallon. 'Girls go through phases like that. It's probably anaemia.'

'Anaemia?' Mrs Scallon had been indignant. 'Elspeth isn't in the least anaemic.' Elspeth was Cecily's baptismal name. 'Look at her lovely skin,' and, 'Aunt Elaine has always been jealous of you,' Mrs Scallon said to Cecily. 'She would have liked Larry Bannerman to fall in love with Jean.'

'Oh, Mummy!' Cecily had protested.

'Perhaps *that* would bring you to your senses,' Mrs Scallon had said bitterly, but, 'It has been my experience,' Dame Ursula, equally wise in spiritual matters, could have told her, 'my experience that once a young girl has fallen truly in love with our Lord she will never look at anyone or anything else in that way; you must remember,' she cautioned, 'that love and falling in love are two different things; we nuns love people – and love greatly – but,' and she quoted the Abbess, 'with the same love we give to God. That keeps it safe.'

'Nineteen – far too young,' Mrs Scallon had still said to Cecily, 'Twenty, too young.'

'*You* never had to struggle,' Cecily said enviously to Hilary.

'Only with myself,' said Hilary.

'Yourself?'

'I was like the little girl in the story who was asked what she would say if she were told she would be a martyr. "I should say 'What?'" she answered. I went on saying "What?" for a long time,' said Hilary. 'My father had given me my first real hunter. I nearly didn't come,' said Hilary.

'Somehow, in spite of everything, I knew that I should come,' said Cecily. 'Though I still couldn't see how.' Then she had visited Brede purely by chance. 'My music brought me; it was to hear the plainchant – and then I knew,' said Cecily. 'I knew quite certainly. I only had to have the courage.' That was the rub. 'I could have entered at twenty-one but I still dallied – two years more. Lady Abbess didn't hurry me.'

'Let's hope they come round,' Abbess Hester had said. 'It will be happier for everyone. Prayers *are* answered,' she had heartened Cecily and, at last, 'If at the end of the year you still want it . . .' Mrs Scallon had said ungraciously.

'I shall still want it,' and now, almost miraculously it seemed to Cecily, her name was in the register under Hilary's.

'October 4th, 1957. Entered, the Honourable Fiona Dalrymple, as claustral postulant, in religion Sister Hilary, second daughter of Viscount Seaton and Clare Gore Rokesby, his wife. Born October 4th, 1938.'

'It was my birthday present,' said Hilary.

'October 23rd, 1957. Entered, Elspeth Scallon, as choir postulant, in religion Sister Cecily, younger daughter of Major Austin Scallon and Eleanor St George, his wife. Born April 12th, 1934.'

'It *is* miraculous because I have always given in,' said

Cecily. She had given in about the lunch party. 'Not a large one,' Mrs Scallon had said. 'Just the family and a few intimate friends.'

'But they are the worst.'

'Elspeth!'

'They *are*!'

But, 'Aunt Elaine,' Mrs Scallon had been inexorable, 'and Uncle Arthur and the cousins; yes, Moira and Jean. Major Fitzgerald, of course, and the Baldocks; Mrs Bannerman and Larry,' and, 'I didn't behave very well,' Cecily told Philippa now in a low, shamed voice. 'I wanted – I needed – to tell Lady Abbess.'

What no postulant was prepared for or had ever visualized was the welcome each found on the other side of the enclosure door. 'What do you ask?' The ritual question was always put and the postulant, kneeling, answered, 'To try my vocation as a Benedictine in this house of Brede.' That was what the novice mistress schooled them to say but it was reported that when Mother Prioress, acting for Abbess Hester, had put the question to Cecily Scallon, Cecily had simply gasped, 'To come in.'

The first steps the postulant took inside the enclosure were down the long cloister as she walked with the Abbess and the councillors straight to the church. The nuns sang: '*In exitu Israel de Ægypto, domus Jacob de populo barbaro: Facta est Judaea sanctificatio eius Israel potestas eius,*' the song that the children of Israel sang as they left Egypt; 'Her entrance is the postulant's Passover,' explained Dame Ursula, 'her entrance into the Promised Land. Egypt symbolizes the worldly world she has left.' The age-old words were sung to the Tonus Peregrinus with its fitting wandering air and, I have been wandering a long time, Philippa, those four long years ago, had thought.

The singing had filled the arched stone cloister that, she had thought too, must have a patina of praise and song; for how many postulants had these words been sung while the high note of the entrance bell told all the community that another aspirant had come? Voices: singing: bells: joy: they had been the balm to Cecily's sore heart.

In the church the postulant knelt with the Abbess on the step facing the sanctuary, as the Abbess presented the new-comer to her Lord, and on each girl, as on Philippa, a stillness always fell as if from a quietening hand; stillness, the scent of flowers and, above all, the lamp burning, showing by its live small flame that the Presence was there, unseen but on the altar; it was the first time any of them had seen it through the grille, yet it looked nearer.

With a deep genuflexion they left the church for the chapter house where the community waited. Here the postulant was given her new name: 'You will be Julian for beloved Julian of Norwich.' 'You will remain Philippa.' Did they keep my own name because they thought I wouldn't stay? Philippa had wondered. It had seemed hardly likely she could stay, and she had remembered how Penny in the office had blurted out, 'at your age!' At Brede, Dame Agnes Kerr, formidable on the Council, had made the same objection. 'Her ways will be fastened on her. This Mrs Talbot has held a high position.'

'Doesn't that prove her worth?' Dame Beatrice Sheridan had asked.

'Not necessarily,' said Dame Agnes.

'Think, Dame. That position was in the Ministry of Trade and Information.' It had been plain that the Abbess was championing Philippa, 'and a government ministry is not made up of fools.'

'No, Mother, but such success in the world will be difficult to discard, if not impossible.'

'It's a case of the parable of the rich man and the needle's eye,' said Dame Veronica.

'I agree,' the Abbess had said, 'but think how that parable ended,' and when she named Philippa as Philippa, Abbess Hester had said, 'You shall have a brave name, from a man's, Philip; Philip was one of the twelve, and there was St Philip Neri.' Hilary, when her turn came, would have liked to be plain Jane, 'but there is a Jane already,' the Abbess told her. Indeed there was: Sister Jane who looked after the domestic side of the novitiate and taught the budding claustral sisters. Generations of novices had passed through her hands.

Unlike Julian, Philippa and Cecily, Hilary had entered as a claustral sister. 'But her father is Lord Seaton!' Cecily, brought up in Mrs Scallon's shibboleths, was bewildered. 'She had a title. She was an *Honourable*, the Honourable Fiona Dalrymple.'

'I want to be lay,' Hilary had said that from the beginning. 'Call it claustral if you must. I like plain words better. I'll work in the kitchen or laundry or garden or look after the pigs, but I can't do all that Latin; and as for singing solo or reading aloud . . .'

'But, what did your family say?' asked Cecily.

'I have a vocation,' said Hilary as if that settled it.

It was Dame Emily, the prioress, who had given Cecily her name. 'You will be Cecily, from St Cecilia because you have brought us music.' They did not know then what music.

In the chapter house the novice mistress took charge of the postulant, presenting her to the nuns in turn, to be given the Pax, the Kiss of Peace. '*Kiss* the community!' Philippa had shrunk in dismay when Dame Ursula had told her about the Pax. 'Kiss them all! But, Mother, I smell of whisky.'

'Postulants smell of all kinds of things,' said Dame Ursula placidly. 'Living as we do, in such pure air and almost without smoke or fumes, our sense of smell is keen. They smell to us of railway carriages, of cars, oil and petrol: of face powder and scent. Whisky is a good strong smell but cheap scent, for instance, is very disagreeable. You won't smell of that.'

In this first moment of meeting, to every postulant the community was a sea of faces, of black veils and habits, white fillets and wimples.

'All these Dames and Dames and Sisters,' Hilary had said. 'I'm lost.'

'Well, there are ninety-six of us,' said Dame Ursula. 'Sixty-two "dames" or fully professed choir nuns, and twenty-one claustral sisters. You will meet the juniors and novices afterwards; the extern sisters you already know.'

Some of the nuns had passed their golden jubilee, fifty years of religious life; the youngest might only that month have taken her Solemn Vows but there was no difference in their dress; each wore her long tunic and scapular, her wimple, fillet and veil: her girdle and ring and, for the choir nuns, the cowl, long and loosely fitting, with wide sleeves, worn in choir and in chapter on all occasions of importance. Yet it was amazing how the same habit could look so different; on the French nun, Dame Colette Aubadon, it was chic, while dear Dame Perpetua always looked bundled and untidy. They were each different in shape, walk, ways of speaking, traits, affinities – 'And problems and opinions!' the Abbess had often said. 'You will never get to the end of the surprises in your community,' she told the new postulants. Each nun gave the Pax with a smile of encouragement, often a hug, a whispered, 'I am so glad,' perhaps even tears of gladness. For Sister Julian there had been many such whispers, for Sister Hilary the same; there had been an especial warmth for Sister Cecily because of the shock of not finding the Abbess and because she looked so forlorn, but, for Philippa, a certain restraint – and it isn't only the whisky, she had thought – a restraint . . . even timidity . . . as if she were still Mrs Talbot – but unmistakable admiration. Even if I don't succeed they honour me for trying, for coming, and words had come into Philippa's mind: 'Not what thou art, nor what thou hast been, beholdeth God with His merciful eyes, but what thou wouldst be.' It was McTurk who had quoted that; McTurk who alone had understood. 'What thou wouldst be.' Philippa's eyes had been suddenly blinded.

The nuns had seen too many postulants come and go to be excited, yet it was always a serious moment; if the postulant proved faithful – 'and fruitful for us' – she would be sister to them all, 'And sisters are born, not made,' the nuns could have said. This ceremony in the chapter house was, for most of them, the first time they had seen the stranger now admitted to their enclosure. Even those who had seen her in the parlours seldom knew what she was really like. 'We don't see our visitors walking, or in full daylight.' There were four scriptural tests, 'And it's odd how often they are right,' said the nuns; gait: apparel: laughter: teeth: and, though the community's eyes had been taught that they must be guarded against being too penetrating – curiosity was unmonastic – the postulant was summed up, especially her apparel. Almost all the nuns were acutely observant of clothes and, perhaps because of their own perpetual black and white, they revelled in colours; they had, for instance, been disappointed in Hilary's tweeds. 'Those dreadful thick stockings,' said Dame Veronica.

'Thick stockings are de rigueur with tweeds,' said Dame Colette.

Dame Veronica flushed. She did not like it to be thought she did not know what was de rigueur, 'I was, after all, brought up at Orford Hall,' she said.

'I never cared what I looked like, anyway,' said Hilary.

Sister Julian Colquhoun's tartan skirt, black jersey and coat had been approved – but then everything in Sister Julian had been approved by almost everyone; the new Sister Cecily's dress and matching coat were delightful. 'That love-in-the-mist blue,' said Dame Beatrice. 'It was bought for Larry Bannerman,' but Cecily did not tell them that, nor, 'Mummy insisted, though Dad needed a new overcoat.' The nuns had liked Philippa's quiet grooming. 'That suit was Chanel,' Dame Colette pronounced. They liked the way she walked; the Scallon postulant held herself well and she had such pretty teeth, really like pearls. Julian was the only one who had laughed but then Julian obviously had felt at home and now the nuns were remembering what old Sister Priscilla had said after Julian's reception, 'too much at home', and had immediately been talked down: 'Sister Julian belongs here.' 'This is "at home" for her,' but it was the old claustral sisters who always knew. They were of the old school, simple, largely uneducated, serving the monastery, 'as our Lady must have served in Nazareth', Abbess Hester had often said. They were as holy as they were humble, but with the deadly knowledge of old family servants and, 'That one won't stay,' they said, or, 'She's likely.' Now and again, 'She'll do.' After meeting Julian, Sister Priscilla had stumped away. 'Too much at home.' The nuns remembered that now.

Every day, after None, Dame Clare, as zelatrix, gathered the postulants and novices together to teach them how to mark the places in their choir books and how to read the Ordo Divini Officii, 'for tomorrow,' said Cecily on the afternoon of the funeral, and she burst out, 'We go on as if nothing had happened.'

'No, we don't,' said Dame Clare. 'We just go on.' Her long white fingers deftly turned the pages of Cecily's book, putting in the markers, helping her to keep up with the others, until the quivering grief grew quiet; then, 'This is what Mother would have wished, would have done herself,' said Dame Clare. 'We are Benedictines, and St Benedict himself laid down that "nothing should be preferred to the work of God", which is the Office, Sister, our Opus Dei. Now try and use your markers and see if you can follow the order.'

At Brede the Divine Office was sung in its full solemnity and it was intricate work, not only to follow but to be part of each Office, to find one's way among antiphons, psalms and canticles, the chapters and responses, collects and hymns, and particularly the nocturns and lessons of Matins. '*May our voices, our tongues and our minds, our every faculty sing Thy praise,*' the nuns sang in the opening hymn at Terce. 'Yes, the whole of you must go into it,' said Dame Clare, 'and unless you are aware, tuned, you will make a mistake – and make it for everyone.'

'Don't,' said Cecily and quailed in horror.

'I'm not expected to sing,' Hilary said firmly; the claustral sisters, unless they wanted to, and had a suitable voice like Sister Louise's clear treble, did not act as chantresses. 'I needn't,' said Hilary.

'No, but you need to follow,' said Dame Clare, 'and you should be doing that by now.'

'But all these first-class feasts and seconds and third class and memorias,' groaned Hilary. 'And all those propers and seasons!'

'Proper *of* the Seasons, Proper and Common *of* the Saints,' corrected Dame Clare and, to help Hilary's bewilderment,

'Don't you see, it's like a pageant. Our Cardinal has said the liturgy entertains as well as feeds us.'

'*Entertains?*' Hilary was so flatly dubious that all the others laughed.

'Yes, we're not angels but humans,' said Dame Clare, 'and human nature is made so that it needs variety. The Church is like a wise mother and has given us this great cycle of the liturgical year with its different words and colours. You'll see how you will learn to welcome the feast days and the saints' days as they come round, each with a different story and, as it were, a different aspect; they grow very dear, though still exacting.'

To Philippa the chant was the nearest thing to birdsong she had ever heard, now solo, now in chorus, rising, blending, each nun knowing exactly when she had to do her part. On feast days, it took four chantresses to sing the Gradual in the Mass, four more for the Alleluias, rising up and up, until it seemed no human voice could sustain it. 'I don't know how you do it,' Philippa had said to Dame Maura.

'Oh, the cherubim come down from that painted reredos behind the altar and help us,' said Dame Maura.

For Brede, as in most monastic houses, the Conventual Mass was the most important act of the day. 'Not that everyone can go to it,' Dame Ursula told the novitiate. 'There are those who have to keep the wheels turning and they have to make do with an early Mass; and there are the sick, who have to make illness their prayer.' The Office centred round the Mass, giving the day one theme, making of it one continuous prayer. 'Everything we do, outside choir,' said Dame Clare, 'our work, our reading, our private prayer, even our meals in the refectory are simply pauses, meant to prepare ourselves for our real work, the Opus Dei – and that needs discipline.'

Discipline. At the sound of the bell, a speaker must stop – 'Well, not in mid-sentence,' said Dame Clare, 'but stop.' A writer must stop too even in the middle of a paragraph, the artist must lay down her brush, the cleaner her broom or dust-pan.

Lauds, Prime, Terce, Sext, None, Vespers, Compline;

seven times a day – and the long office of Matins, not, as its name suggested, a morning prayer but which, with its nocturns and lessons, its twelve psalms, is the great night vigil of the Church. 'Yes, one suffers for the Office,' Dame Clare said. 'The getting up, and staying up: the continual interruption to ordinary work, singing no matter how one feels, day after day. Nuns have no holidays.'

That had been what Philippa had been most afraid of, the intensity of the work.

'You afraid of work!' Richard Taft had said.

'Richard, have you ever tried to pray for fifteen minutes, even five, without letting your attention wander? The Office at Brede takes six hours and we have private prayer as well.'

'But what *use* is it?' Richard had been exasperated. This had been in the days when Philippa had first told him of her intention, and been involved in endless and fruitless arguments; how strange that two people, both speaking English, should yet be using different languages. 'What use?'

'Man, you always want everything to be immediate and apparent.' McTurk, who had often come in on these arguments, had tried to help, his r's rolling as they always did when he was moved. 'There are things visible and invisible,' said McTurk and the nuns endorsed that.

'Nowadays there's a tendency to make everything utilitarian – even the things of the spirit,' said Dame Clare. 'Beware of this,' and 'That wasn't the way of the saints,' said Dame Ursula. 'They didn't set out to be of use.'

'Nor they did,' said Hilary in surprise.

'And you needn't worry about being useful,' said Dame Ursula. 'When you have become God's in the measure He wants, He, Himself, will know how to bestow you on others.' She was quoting St Basil. Then her face grew wistful, ' "Unless He prefer, for thy greater advantage, to keep thee all to himself." That does happen to a few people. Yet, paradoxically, they have the greatest influence.'

'Like Dame Beatrice,' said Sister Constance.

'Or a lay sister quietly saying her rosary.' That, surprisingly, was learned Dame Clare.

'Yes, because what is really apostolic, what really speeds God's glory,' said Dame Ursula, 'is not the time given to work but the holiness of the worker.'

'Us holy!' said Hilary.

'Isn't that what you come for? To try at any rate?'

'Cripes! I never thought of that.'

'Prayer has power.' Philippa had said that to Richard, as she had said it to Penny. 'It's the only thing that holds when everything else fails. As individuals I expect that nuns, like everyone else, are poor and faulty creatures – unfortunately we bring ourselves with us when we enter – but as a community Brede has done astonishing things.'

Philippa never forgot her first sight of the notice board at Brede; it was put up in the ante-chapel close by our Lady of Peace; the votive light kept burning there seemed an emblem of hope. Any nun could put a notice up on the board; there were lines from letters, cards, messages, each a cry for help, some touching, some comic: on a half sheet of cheap lined paper, 'I want prayers especially that I may get married to a man I'm interested in, but he's not so interested in me. Please, dear Mother, ask the sisters to pray that he may go ahead; I'm worried as I'm over thirty.' Prayers were asked for a young priest going on a lonely mission: for an expectant mother facing a hazardous confinement: from a husband whose young wife was dying – 'She's only twenty-two and we have a year-old baby. She can't bear to leave us.' Dame Beatrice wrote to that girl every day. Prayers were asked for the sick, the dying, for sinners, for men and women in prison; for hopes and joys, anxieties, searing sorrow, and each met with a brimming response. 'We have you tucked in our sleeves,' Dame Perpetua had written to the expectant mother, 'In our sleeves,' and it was true. Every nun had her personal post and a continual stream of letters went out, 'lifelines', many people called them; each anchored in the strength of prayer. 'And we pray for our brothers and sisters in the active Orders, who have little time to pray for themselves,' Philippa had told Richard. 'And we pray in reparation, to make up for all those who won't or can't pray for themselves – especially anyone in grave sin.

75

That's why communities say the longest and most arduous Office at night – the time when most sin is committed in the world.'

'You mean a little Carmelite might sit up and pray for a murderer?'

'She has, with results,' said Philippa.

'Mother Prioress is wonderful.' That was an accepted fact in the monastery but now, 'Is Dame Emily very old?' asked Hilary. 'She is twenty-five years younger than Abbess Hester was,' said Philippa, but to Hilary's nineteen there was little difference between sixty and eighty-five and, 'She's old,' said Hilary.

'Not old, worn out,' said Philippa.

Dame Emily had always been self-effacing in the shadow of the Abbess, a presence more than a person; now she stood revealed and the whole community woke to the fact of how thin and tired she was. 'It's remarkable,' Philippa had once said, 'how much one notices a nun's eyes.' Wimple, fillet and veil made a frame that set them off so that they were enhanced. Philippa thought of Dame Veronica's beautiful eyes, of Dame Beatrice's, a paler blue but that had a shine that made them almost luminous. Dame Ursula's were like pebbles behind her spectacles; Dame Clare's were grey and set straight, her eyebrows fine – almost like circumflexes; Dame Maura's were piercing, her eyebrows thick; Dame Catherine's hazel eyes had a direct gaze. 'It was Lady Abbess who taught me to look directly at people,' she said; 'before that I was always hiding.' The Abbess herself had had quick black eyes, lively and snapping, but one doesn't notice Mother Prioress's eyes at all, thought Philippa; they are too sunken and the puffed flesh round them looks as if it were bruised – with patience and suffering? wondered Philippa and she asked Dame Perpetua, 'Is Mother Prioress ill?'

'I hope not,' Dame Perpetua said, startled. 'She never seems to be,' and then uncertainly, 'I don't know.'

'One wouldn't know,' said Philippa. 'The habit somehow blots her out – or holds her together,' she added.

As steadily as ever the prioress went about her own and her Abbess's duties, but more and more she seemed to Philippa like a shell. While Abbess Hester had been alive and needed her there had been fire – a sacrificial fire, thought Philippa – but now there was nothing to feed it with and it was as if it had gone out. Uneasiness began to spread through the community, opinion was shaken. 'We don't want any more declining years,' Dame Agnes, as usual, dared to voice the feeling of many of the nuns.

The feeling was not to be tested; the Saturday after Abbess Hester's death was the eve of the feast of the Kingship of Christ that fell on the last Sunday of October. As always the Vespers of the Eve anticipated the feast, and Mother Prioress, solo in Lady Abbess's stead, began the antiphon: *'Dabit illi Dominus Deus, sedem David patris ejus. The Lord will give him the throne of David, his father.'*

Mother Prioress loved this feast. 'We must not think only of Christ on the cross,' she had said in the conference she had given that very afternoon. 'We must think of him crowned and of His glory.' Now she was lost in the beauty of the words the choir was singing, words that shone out in their richness: *'He shall be king over the house of Jacob for ever, and of his kingdom there shall be no end.'* Suddenly her voice faltered and seemed to die on the air. She gestured helplessly to Dame Perpetua who, after a moment's plunging silence, valiantly took up the antiphon; chantresses and choir joined in as the nuns saw Dame Emily groping her way out, with Dame Joan who had darted to her side; before they had gone a few steps, the prioress swayed and would have fallen but strong Dame Catherine was there; she and the infirmarian carried the prioress into the open air of the long cloister; she was as light as a child.

'So you have betrayed yourself at last,' said Doctor Avery and was rewarded by a wan smile. 'I have been expecting this,' he told Dame Joan.

'What are you going to do with me?' The prioress's words

jerked and seemed to die from want of air as they had in the choir.

'Put you into hospital again, but for observation and complete rest.' He was as brisk as he always was when he had made up his mind – irrevocably.

'Doctor, I can't.'

Doctor Avery had met this before; he understood something, but not all, of the purgatory it meant for an enclosed nun to go into a big up-to-date hospital, especially for one who, besides being ill, was tired – and wounded in body and mind, as he sensed Dame Emily was. With their vow of poverty the nuns had to go into the public ward; he could not save them from that though it meant lying in what, to them, was an exposure. Used to hard pallets, they could not, they told him, rest on the spring beds; the fluorescent lighting was a glare that hurt eyes after the dimness of Brede where modern lighting was only installed in the workshops; they stifled in the central heating after the Abbey coolness where the heating system was kept at its lowest and often did not work at all, but worst of all torments, he knew, was the noise after the silence; the chatter and clatter and bustle – but he guessed it was not any of this that made Dame Emily beg, 'Oh no, Doctor! You can't. I can't.'

'Why?'

'I can't leave Brede just now.'

'Why not?'

'You don't know, they don't know what – I think they will have to face.'

'They will face it,' said the doctor with certainty.

'Lady Abbess . . .'

'You can't cover up for her for ever.'

'I can't leave them unprepared – unprotected.'

'I knew you were obstinate,' said Doctor Avery. 'I never knew you were conceited.'

The prioress gave him another of her rare smiles. 'Please.'

'Let's be sensible,' said Doctor Avery. 'You can have one interview with someone. Some*one*,' he said with emphasis.

'But which one?' asked Mother Prioress. 'Which?'

3

Which?

That was the question in everybody's mind now that the prioress was 'sequestered' as she had put it to Dame Joan.

'Is Mother Prioress severely over-tired?' Dame Perpetua had asked Doctor Avery. As subprioress she was now acting head of the monastery and it was she who saw the doctor. 'Is it just over-tiredness, or ...' – she hardly dared to say it – 'something serious?' It was in distress that Dame Perpetua reported his answer to the councillors.

'You know that four years ago Dame Emily had an operation.'

'I remember,' said Dame Maura, 'but she recovered.'

'We were not told what it was for,' said Dame Agnes.

'She did not want it told. It was for cancer of the breast. They removed one and all was well for a while. Last year she developed secondaries, tumours in the bone.'

They were aghast. 'They must have been agonizingly painful!'

'She was often in great pain,' Dame Perpetua went on, as tears began to run down Dame Veronica's face. 'Doctor Avery said he would have given her amidone, but she wouldn't take it; she said it made her sleepy.'

'Sleepy!' Doctor Avery had said, in wrath.

'Did Mother Prioress know what this meant?' Dame Agnes asked now.

'Yes. She didn't want anybody else to know, but Doctor had told Lady Abbess of course.' Dame Perpetua did not retail what he had said of their Mother. 'I told her,' Doctor Avery had said, 'but in her manifold activities and enthusiasms, Lady Abbess was apt to forget. I reminded her when I could. Dame Emily would never remind her.'

'You make us ashamed,' Dame Perpetua had said.

'I don't blame you. I blame that charming and utterly head-strong late Abbess of yours. No, I do blame you,' and his usually mild and wise eyes were angry. 'You behaved like sheep,' but he had said it was not the cancer that had made Dame Emily collapse; her heart was affected. 'She has had two attacks of paroxysmal tachycardia. This was another, more severe.'

'Didn't Dame Joan know?' asked Dame Perpetua.

'In part. Dame Joan is an excellent nurse but she is not trained,' said Doctor Avery. In the traditional Brede way, Dame Joan had been bellringer, portress and zelatrix before becoming infirmarian.

'Can Mother Prioress get better?'

'Of course not, but she can end her days in peace.'

'Here? At home?'

'I will let her come back when you have a new Abbess who can put her under obedience.' Doctor Avery knew their ways. 'Talk about the divine right of kings . . .'

'What will happen now?' asked Dom Gervase.

As soon as Abbot Bernard heard about Dame Emily, he had driven over from Udimore Abbey, to see if there were any help he could give Dame Perpetua. Never in its history had Brede lost Abbess and prioress together. 'I don't know of any house that has,' said Abbot Bernard.

'I suppose Dame Perpetua will manage with the Council's help until Father President can come,' Dom Gervase's voice was curiously flat and heavy, without life. 'Then there will be a new Abbess – but it can never be the same.' Dom Gervase said that with a sudden passion and bowed his head on his hands.

They were in the presbytery where Mrs Burnell had brought them a tray of tea. 'How many different houses of nuns have identical traycloths edged with crochet?' said

Abbot Bernard, to cover up the other's emotion. 'I would recognize this old-fashioned look anywhere.' No answer.

The older monk looked at the close-cropped dark head; in spite of the cropping, the hair still crinkled like a young ram's. Yes, a ram's, thought Abbot Bernard. The boy is quite a fine specimen – to him, Dom Gervase's thirty-eight years still made him a boy. He *should* have been all right, thought Abbot Bernard.

Dom Gervase's study looked out on a small private lawn; it was in this room, with its heavy furniture, or in his small bedroom, that he spent his solitary days – except for Burnell and visiting priests, the only male among ninety-six women – a strange existence for a young man.

'If a young priest is appointed chaplain to a monastery of nuns, there is a reason behind it,' Dame Agnes had said, nodding her head.

'Perhaps he needs a sabbatical period for study, or perhaps he is writing a book,' suggested Dame Beatrice.

'He may have been ill,' said sympathetic Dame Veronica. 'I know what it is to be highly strung.'

'Or else something has gone wrong,' said Dame Agnes. Something had gone wrong with Dom Gervase: he had been trained for teaching, 'and a notable failure,' he would have said. He had never been able to keep order, let alone discipline his boys, but his superiors had assigned him to sixth forms where his brilliance was invaluable. Then at thirty-six, and ten years ordained a priest, he had been sent to Kildown, a secondary school in the slums of Salford and, 'I couldn't take it,' he had confessed in shame to Lady Abbess.

'Well, you don't use diamonds to cut stones,' the Abbess had said to the prioress afterwards.

Dom Gervase had always been delicate, so highly strung he seemed to live on wires; he had been appalled at the squalor and misery round the school; everything he had to teach seemed to him useless and he had been afraid – 'Yes, afraid,' said Dom Gervase – 'of the boys.' He had never met boys like them. 'They are usual, ordinary boys,' Dom Thomas, the headmaster, had told him. None of the other monks had had any difficulty. They had a joviality and balance that knew how to take the toughness, when to joke and when to clamp down; but to Dom Gervase the boys had seemed monsters that grew to one many-headed monster. 'They soon took the measure of me,' he said and one evening in his fifth term, when he had been alone, correcting or trying to correct, in a pile of dirty exercise books, the ill-written, smudged and, what seemed to him, infantile responses to the essay he had set, a gang of boys had burst into the classroom. What happened, Dom Gervase never told, but he was found unconscious on the floor, smeared with soot and covered in chalk and ink, with blood from a broken nose, his habit half-torn off; one shoe was in the waste-paper basket, one filled with urine, his classroom was a waste of upturned desks, torn-up books, ink thrown to the ceiling, walls and windows daubed with obscenities. 'But these are boys,' Dom Thomas had said again. 'Ordinary usual boys!'

'Not with me.' Dom Gervase had blamed no one but himself; he could not live with that blame and when he became fully conscious he had had a nervous breakdown.

'It doesn't sound promising,' Dame Agnes had said when, four months later and convalescent, he was posted to Brede and the Council was told a little of his history. 'What use will he be to us?' But from the first the nuns liked his gentleness, the beauty with which he said Mass, his scholarly Latin – and his humility. In the confessional, they said, he was inspirational. He, in his turn, liked the nuns but with Abbess Hester it had been more than liking and, 'I believe they sent me here because of her,' he said now.

'She was a great lady,' said Abbot Bernard. 'It is true, sometimes I was worried . . .' but Dom Gervase had not heard that afterthought. 'A great lady.' Even as he talked of Lady Abbess his face was transformed. 'And she did great things,' said Dom Gervase reverently. 'Do you know, Father, I think the best of them was that she taught me to laugh, not least at myself, but I can't laugh now,' said Dom Gervase.

'You will,' said Abbot Bernard but Dom Gervase shook his head and sat staring out at the small lawn where the dark laurel bushes were shaken by the cold wind. Beyond, at the front of the house, Sister Elizabeth, the extern sacristan, had lit one of her autumn bonfires, and blue smoke curled up from the burning beech leaves; Dom Gervase seemed to smell their acridness. 'There will be a new Abbess,' he said. 'A new Abbess!'

He turned to meet the old man's quizzical gaze, and his lips tightened. 'Don't worry, Father. I shall do my duty.'

'If it's no more than that, won't it be most unhelpfully bleak for her?' asked Abbot Bernard.

One of the tasks that faced Dame Perpetua as acting head of the Abbey was to see Sister Julian's parents, the Colquhouns.

They had come to the funeral – Lady Abbess Hester had been their revered friend – and they took Julian away next day, but, tactfully, had not come then to talk over the necessary arrangements for the return of her dowry. 'That can wait until you are over the first shock,' Mr Colquhoun had written. Now he came with his wife and, 'You must see them with me,' Dame Perpetua told Dame Veronica. 'You know far more about it than I.'

'Yes,' but Dame Veronica's voice was faint.

'As cellarer, money is your concern, Dame.'

Dame Veronica did not answer but her hands were gripped together under her scapular and her chin quivered. All the nuns knew that quivering. Dame Veronica had always hated dealing with money and this was a question of a considerable amount, ten thousand pounds that, under Canon Law, had to be repaid to Julian, but looking at Dame Veronica's distressed face the subprioress asked, 'The money is there, I suppose, Dame?'

'Of course it is there.'

'Where?' Dame Perpetua was an innocent over the Abbey's financial affairs. 'Where?'

'In the bank, on deposit, where else? Surely you know a dowry must not be touched, not even invested until after Solemn Profession.' Dame Veronica's voice was unnecessarily sharp, thought Dame Perpetua.

The Colquhouns gave Brede a thousand pounds. 'Well, you

have kept Sister Julian – Barbara – for four and a half years.'

'That is most generous,' said Dame Perpetua, 'isn't it, Dame?' she asked, turning to Dame Veronica, but Dame Veronica only twisted her hands in silence. 'We shall return you nine thousand then,' said Dame Perpetua. 'That is right, Dame?'

'Yes,' whispered Dame Veronica, but in such a way that Mr Colquhoun said, 'I wish we could leave it all with you but it is Barbara's portion.'

'And the Brown Sisters need it,' said Dame Perpetua warmly, but afterwards, 'How could you,' she said to Dame Veronica. 'You made the poor man thoroughly uncomfortable. He was only asking for what is his own. He has his son, the little girl Lucy and his wife to provide for. Mother would have been most upset; they are such dear friends and she loved Sister Julian.'

'Sister Julian!' cried Dame Veronica passionately. 'If only we had never heard of Sister Julian,' and she burst into tears.

It was a time of tears; every day the emptiness seemed worse; every day there was more confusion and nerves and tempers were growing frayed. Dame Perpetua, for all her worth, was no leader; she could not control Dame Agnes, nor Dame Maura. Already they were in command of the choir – 'Perhaps the one place where I could have coped,' said Dame Perpetua – and it only took a few days to bring them into collision.

'If only Father President would come and we could hold the election,' sighed Dame Perpetua.

'Yes, we're like a hive without a queen,' said Philippa. She had said something of the kind to Sister Cecily that morning. In the refectory Philippa was reader for the week and Cecily was taking her first steps in learning to serve from the pantry, so that both were at second table; after it, they walked through the cloister together. It was recreation hour, they could talk, and Philippa had said, 'I wonder which one of us has been fed on royal jelly?'

'I know one,' said Cecily.

'Who?'

84

'You.'

'I?' It was the first time Cecily had seen Philippa flush; it was a flush of anger. 'Don't be *ridiculous*.' It was the Talbot voice but Cecily was steady.

'If you were a choir nun of ten years' standing, there would be no question.'

'You don't know what you are talking about!' Self-contained Philippa for once was incoherent. 'I haven't even begun to catch up. You don't understand,' said Philippa more quietly. 'All my grown life, it seems to me now I have been – acting in authority ... yes, acting,' said Philippa, 'because I wasn't a full person. I was so busy,' said Philippa, 'that I had no time for myself. Now, at last, at Brede I have a chance to be no one. That's what I need because I must begin again; in all those years I hadn't advanced one jot.'

'Not advanced! *Look* who you were,' Cecily interrupted.

'Who I wasn't,' said Philippa. 'Don't be silly, child. Think,' but Cecily lifted an obstinate face.

'I don't need to think. I know.'

Brede believed in friendship. 'There is nothing more wonderful than spiritual friendship,' and, 'Have as many particular friends as you can,' Abbess Hester had often said, 'but many, not one.'

Nothing and no one must be clung to. Philippa could still feel the way Cecily had clung to her hand as they knelt in the corridor as the Abbess died. Philippa had found it touching but, 'It's as well for Sister Cecily that you are going into the community,' said Dame Clare. Cecily, though, was woebegone. 'Now there will be no one,' she said. 'No one.'

'As you get to know the others, there will be plenty,' said Philippa, but she guessed that though Sister Cecily seemed so docile she was not to be easily won; she was not at all forthcoming with Dame Ursula and was oddly silent with Dame Clare but, where Cecily loved, thought Philippa, she would give her whole trust.

In the community Philippa gratefully breathed the larger air; much as she liked and honoured Dame Ursula, and had a true friend in Dame Clare, it was good to be free of constant scrutiny and care. Now she was least among sixty-two choir nuns, free, in the Benedictine way, to make her own path, making it what she could, though until she was professed, she was in the nominal charge of Dame Perpetua. 'What a wonderful thing is obedience,' said Dame Perpetua. 'Do you know, if I hadn't been put in charge of you, I should never have dared to speak to you – and think what I should have missed.'

'And I,' said Philippa sincerely.

Dame Perpetua's simple imagination, though, could not visualize what her new charge had been. 'I'm told, Sister, that you were a trained secretary.'

'Once,' Philippa had to look back to her long-ago starting days.

'And you speak French, dear child?'

'Yes,' said Philippa.

'And Italian?'

'Only a little. You see, I specialized in Oriental languages.'

Dame Perpetua blinked. 'Oriental? Don't say you speak Chinese.'

'No, only Japanese.'

'Well! Well! Well!' Then Dame Perpetua recovered. 'I doubt if we get any call for that. We do get Japanese letters of course, just as we get letters from India and Africa. It was always one of Mother's dreams to make a foundation from Brede, overseas. We had hopes from Dame Thecla, but no more Ethiopians have come yet – still perhaps one day . . . but I don't think any of the letters were written in Japanese. However, French will be most useful.'

A temporary desk was put for Philippa in the small alcove outside the Abbess's empty rooms, close by the telephonist's cell and, 'Could you,' asked Dame Perpetua, 'clear some of these letters? Especially the foreign ones? I can't read a word of them,' said Dame Perpetua.

There was, everyone knew, as Dame Perpetua knew herself, no question of her being elected Abbess. 'Imagine it!' she said to Philippa with her usual frankness. 'If it had not been for my voice,' Dame Perpetua had a strong rich contralto – 'I shouldn't have been a choir nun at all.' Lady Abbess Perpetua

Jones. She grew hot as she thought of it. 'Me giving confer-ences, sitting in the abbatial chair!' All the same, Dame Per-petua had her dignity. 'You had better let me or Dame Catherine take over the letters,' said Dame Agnes.

'No thank you,' said Dame Perpetua. 'I can manage with Sister Philippa. She can answer letters much better than me.'

'Than I,' Dame Agnes could not help correcting.

'You see how I need her,' said Dame Perpetua unperturbed.

'She has no authority . . .' Dame Agnes began.

'She has the grammar, I have the authority,' Dame Per-petua drew herself up to her full plumpness. 'Mother made me subprioress, Dame, and subprioress I shall remain until our new Abbess relieves me of that office. Thank you, Dame Agnes.'

Everyone loved Dame Perpetua as, for quite different reasons, they loved Dame Beatrice Sheridan, but loving was not the decisive thing in the election of an Abbess. 'I can't imagine their electing dear Dame Beatrice, though I should like to,' said sharp little Sister Constance. 'We should all turn into angels.'

'Or devils,' said Philippa.

'Do you have parties and canvassing?' McTurk wrote teas-ingly to Philippa and, 'You forget, we keep silence,' Philippa wrote back. There was partisanship, of course, but it was characterized by extreme quietness. Each nun had to decide for herself and make no declaration, indeed give no inkling of what she was deciding, but the new Abbess must be over forty, probably one of the councillors and in these days it was as if every senior, each member of the Council, was held in a bril-liant light. Even Cecily, who as the latest comer was 'on the doors', responsible for opening and shutting them for the com-munity as they went in and out of choir and refectory, would stand and wonder, 'which'? 'Will it be you?' 'It won't be you.' 'It might be you.'

Dame Maura Fitzgerald and Dame Agnes Kerr were the obvious ones. Dame Maura with her commanding height would make a noble Abbess but there would be a great loss because she would have to give up the choir; Dame Monica, second organist and chantress, was gifted but she was not a Dame Maura. Dame Agnes had renown and absolute integrity, 'And she's a disciplinarian,' said Hilary; in the novitiate they knew that very well. Dame Agnes taught them Latin three times a week. 'She would make a good Abbess,' said Hilary.

'Would she?' Philippa had come over to see the novitiate during recreation. 'I don't think the Rule is meant to clamp down on one's life. It has to fit everyone, to be able to bend, not break. That is its gift. It's not meant to be rigid.'

Both Dame Agnes and Dame Maura were adept at keeping their faces; in public they greeted one another with the utmost courtesy but they knew, and the whole community knew, of an old old hostility between them.

It had come to a head long ago in the music library. Dame Agnes had gone to Dame Camilla to ask for the plays of the tenth-century nun, Hroswitha.

'Dame Maura has it. She is working with it in the music library. I'll keep the book for you when she returns it,' the librarian promised, but Dame Agnes had not been mollified.

'How long has she had it?'

'I think about a month. She shouldn't be much longer.'

'She shouldn't be as long. I'll go and find her.'

The music library where Dame Agnes had found the precentrix was one of the most pleasant rooms in the house, with long windows that opened on the garden. Its walls, instead of the usual monastery white, were washed pink; 'They deepen at sunset,' Dame Camilla was wont to say. Its floor, as were all the monastery floors, was bare but pale under the wax; its tables were covered in grey formica, the gift of Dame Benita's brother. 'It's a modern room,' she said happily, but that July afternoon its sunniness and peace had been broken by the swish of Dame Agnes's skirts. Dame Maura had recognized the swish and braced herself. 'I believe you have the Hroswitha plays.' Dame Agnes had planted herself in front of the table.

'Yes, Dame. I'm working on "Abraham", trying to fit music to it; quite a work but I thought it would be good for the novitiate to do for Mother's feast day. Little Sister Nichola

88

has written a counterpart, "What Isaac thought." A play by a nun of the tenth century and another of the twentieth; it should be interesting.'

'Most interesting, but unfortunately I must have the Hroswitha. You know we are making a new translation – the last was 1923 – and this morning I had an urgent call to finish, from the publishers. It seems someone else is putting a new edition on the market. As it happens, I have only Abraham to do; it shouldn't take me more than a few days.'

'A few days! Mother's feast is on the fourteenth and we must have time to rehearse.'

'I have to send in my manuscript.'

'Surely there's not such a deadline? Publishers always try and rush you,' Dame Maura had pleaded. 'I will be as quick as I can.'

'Then you won't give it up?'

'I can't.'

The two nuns had faced one another. Dame Maura was sitting down but even so she was as tall as Dame Agnes; she seemed to dominate but no one dominated Dame Agnes Kerr or frustrated her.

'You can't? Then I shall go to Mother.'

'You won't tell her! That will ruin everything.'

'You give me no option. One is a permanent work,' said Dame Agnes. 'The other a passing entertainment.'

'Dame, it's a question of waiting such a little while. I will try to get it finished today or tomorrow. Surely two days can't imperil your book? The novitiate are so looking forward to this and nothing would please Mother more ...' but Dame Agnes had not been moved.

'You have had that book a month and no one has the right to do that in a community library. I too shall only keep it two or three days, but I need it now. *Now*.' She had not said 'or else', she did not need to; Dame Maura had handed over the book.

They had not accused themselves afterwards of being uncharitable as Dame Colette had done over Dame Veronica, because each was convinced of the total unreasonableness of the other. It was never alluded to again, but the community sensed there was a rift. Now, if either Dame Agnes or Dame Maura were elected, what would happen to the other? And what would be the lot of those who consciously, or unconsciously, were followers of them? 'We don't want any more favourites,' the nuns could have said.

It was significant that no one considered Dame Veronica Fanshawe; in these days the nuns found the cellarer disturbing; she looked so stricken, white and ill. 'She says she has palpitations,' Dame Perpetua said, worried, to Dame Joan.

'She has emotions, if you ask me,' said Dame Joan. 'Since Mother Prioress had her heart attack, Dame Veronica is sure she has a bad heart.'

'You sound most unsympathetic, Dame.'

'I am,' said Dame Joan. 'I had Doctor Avery examine her from top to toe. There is nothing organically wrong.'

Dame Ursula Crompton, as novice mistress, was used to guiding and directing; at least a quarter of the present community had been her novices but, though affection and loyalty prevented them from saying it, the thought was in them all; must we listen to Teddy's platitudes for ever? 'She is so good and careful and kind,' said Cecily. 'And so flat,' she might have added. 'It's not her fault,' said Cecily suddenly. 'She hasn't the mind.'

'Well, there are all sorts of minds in a community,' said Hilary, a little nettled. 'Most are valuable.'

'Not in an Abbess,' said this strangely unswerving Cecily.

Dame Colette Aubadon? She was mistress of church work, in charge of the vestment-making and silk-weaving rooms.

Besides weaving much of the black cloth for their own habits and making thick grey winter stockings on the stocking machine, three of the nuns, Dame Colette as chief, and her aids, Dame Anselma and Dame Sophie, were skilful in weaving silks and brocades for vestments, and several nuns could weave orphreys, the narrow bands that decorated chasubles and copes. The vestment room was a treasure house of stuffs and colours. 'If you are starved for colour, go and look in there,' was often said, but the riches were not for the Abbey. Church work earned quite an income for Brede, Dame Gertrude and Dame Benita making the designs, but always guided by Dame Colette's unerring taste. 'Elegant' was the word used most to describe Dame Colette, elegant and quick, probably too quick with her judgements, her temper and her wit. She would make a graceful Abbess, but not a comfortable one, thought Philippa, and, 'It would be odd to have a Frenchwoman as Abbess of a house of the English Congregation,' said insular Hilary.

There was still, of the councillors, Dame Catherine Ismay. She had presence, no one could deny that; she was heavy yet moved with unmistakable grace, and in her way had beauty – 'She's like the Flemish Madonna Sir Basil gave to Mother' – the only valuable painting in the house. Nuns who had been at Dame Catherine's Clothing ceremony remembered the length and colour of the chestnut hair that had been cut off; her health and vigour showed in the glow of her skin, her confidence in the direct look in her eyes. She doesn't keep them lidded, Philippa thought. Dame Catherine would have said, 'Not now.' As a young nun she had had to battle with shyness. 'It's being such a big girl,' she had said, hopelessly, to Abbess Hester.

'All the more of you to fight,' said the indomitable Abbess.

To Dame Catherine it had been a silent bewildered grief when Abbess Hester had turned against her. 'Dame Veronica was made cellarer in the Distribution of Offices in January '55,' Dame Domitilla ticked it up accurately. 'Dame Catherine was made a councillor the following year.' That had brought the estrangement, and Dame Catherine's shyness, back; she had a reputation for dealing with difficult cases in the parlour but with her sisters in the community she was over silent. Dame Agnes called her 'a cloister within a cloister', and, 'We don't know her,' almost all the nuns could have said, but, 'I know her,' said Philippa.

Dame Catherine came to the novitiate to teach Church History but it was not of these classes that Philippa was thinking. She knew Dame Catherine as the others did not.

Before Philippa came to Brede – and when she had come – over and over again it had been impressed upon her that she would find the life hard. 'I need it hard,' she had said. 'I need to be purged and cleansed,' and at first, she had been impatient when it was tempered for her. Dame Ursula had told her to stay in bed every morning of her first week and rest until Dame Clare came to call her after Lauds and Prime, 'but I'm not ill,' and how chagrined she had been, in the six weeks of her first Lent, when the edict came: 'Sister Philippa is not to fast. She is to have meat.'

'But, Mother Mistress . . .'

'You won't need extra penances. We know what an effort this must be for you.' Dame Ursula had laid her hand on Philippa's arm and the green eyes behind the spectacles shone. The spectacles were of the cheapest kind but they could not hide the joy and admiration that transfigured the plain face, and Philippa was moved again as she had been with the Pax. It was only a moment, then duty said, in the uncompromising voice used by an old-fashioned novice mistress to her charges, the 'Great Bear' voice, 'It is Lady Abbess's order and it's far more salutary than fasting for you do what you are told.'

'But will you be able to be obedient, a stiff-necked creature like you?' McTurk had asked; obedience was the stumbling block for almost everyone, but Philippa found it restful. 'Thank God I shall never have to give orders again,' she wrote to him. None of the things she had anticipated as being hard, were hard; not the cold, nor the long hours of prayer. It was the little things that were Philippa's danger; things so little they made her ashamed; Dame Agnes, though Philippa did not know what Dame Agnes had said, had been right: the habits of success were fast in Philippa; indulgences that had become habits. Other postulants and novices were not old enough to have them as embedded but for Philippa, in those first months at Brede, they were like hooks being torn out of her flesh. 'I didn't know you had been a compulsive smoker,' said Dame Ursula.

'Nor did I,' said Philippa but, 'A cigarette. If only I could have a cigarette.' It had become an obsession; 'and a bath: if only I could have a hot bath.' At home she had relaxed every evening, in her bath, steaming hot and scented, soaking away the tensions of the day before dinner; she had had her own particular powder, oils and soap; the monastery made its own soap. 'I never understood the word "lye" before,' said Philippa: ' "to clean harshly, as washing soda." It scours you clean.' The ancient building had only two bathrooms; one in the infirmary, the other for the Abbess; a third was being planned for the novitiate. 'We don't want our modern postulants to have too much of a shock,' said the nuns; it was typical of them to give to the young first, but bathrooms or not, the nuns were scrupulously clean: every night they had to take their jugs to the hot tap, one on each corridor, then, standing on a sugar sack for a bathmat, strip in the unheated cell. 'You will wash from head to foot,' Dame Ursula told the postulants on their first day.

'S-St M-Melania never washed more than her f-fingertips,' Julian had rebelled one icy January day.

'That may be, but you will. We are supposed to live like the poor,' said Dame Ursula, 'and this is what the poor have to do. Half the families in Britain have no bathrooms.'

'They b-bath in f-front of the k-kitchen fire,' said Julian.

The food at Brede was ordinary, largely tasteless but healthy because most of it the nuns grew themselves – Sister Marianne ran the vegetable garden and orchard – then why had it given Philippa such indigestion? Had it been nervous tension or was it perhaps the tea? 'I'm told the tea is terrible,' she had said to Richard's inquiry but, at Brede, her first winter, Philippa learned the reason for the English addiction to tea; the cup of hot strong tea at breakfast, after an hour and a half of singing in the choir, was badly needed; it not only warmed but stimulated; the cup after None put heart into her before Vespers, but the indigestion had grown so bad that Dame Ursula noticed and questioned her.

'You could have asked for hot water to weaken your tea,' she had said.

'And be singular?'

'Better to be singular than ill,' said Dame Ursula, but

Philippa was almost morbidly aware of drawing attention to herself. 'I was so afraid they would send me away,' she said afterwards and, 'It's just that I have been spoiled with China tea,' she had hastily told Dame Ursula.

'Sister Philippa has lost her looks,' Dame Maura had said at community recreation.

'She looks ravaged.' Dame Colette's 'r's still showed that she was French. 'Perhaps she should not persist.'

'She isn't sleeping,' said the Abbess. 'I know that. Dame Ursula expected her to ask for sleeping pills. She never has.'

'I should have thought our long days of work and mental effort and plenty of exercise would make anybody sleep,' said Dame Veronica. 'I am delicate, and a difficult sleeper yet I sleep.'

'You didn't enter at forty-two.'

The Office dictated the hours of sleep. Half an hour after Matins came Curfew when all lights were put out. 'At the time I often started to read or work,' said Philippa. 'I seldom went to bed before one; Maggie did not wake me, with my breakfast tray, until eight.' Philippa lay in the dark, trying not to toss or turn because it made her bed creak. All round her, in the novitiate, the others had slept peacefully – or snuffled. Dame Ursula's snores came through the ceiling. There had been nothing to do but lie and try to relax and, yes, suffer, thought Philippa, because it was in those hours that the thought of Keith came back, not the ruffle of clear wind, free, but Keith down – down in the trickling dark. 'Where are you, Keith?' No answer. Only the muffled crying, muffled by rock? suffocation? distance? they did not know.

> Keith don't cry   try not to cry   breathe   listen
> I'll count   one-two one-two one-two   Mother's
> here   don't cry   we're coming.   Her cracked voice
> singing: 'picking up gold and silver ... roll out the barrel
> ... there was a little man and he had a little gun ...'   If
> I was you, Ma'am, I would let them take you away now

Philippa would find herself bathed in sweat.

She tried to think of Christ's last night in the Praetorium.

What did our Lady do in those hours? She must have been waiting, watching; three days for her too, thought Philippa, but though she had tried to fortify herself with such thoughts, doubts would come up again. What am I doing here? I was mad. Richard's 'criminal waste' rang in her ears; familiar doubts but tormenting, and bitterly she had reproached herself for them; it was a shock when she discovered later that many of the nuns had these 'two o'clock devils', as Dame Clare called them.

Towards three or four, Philippa, exhausted, would fall asleep too heavily, so that it seemed only a moment until the caller of the week opened the door, put her head in and switched on the light – that blinding overhead light that was another discomfort – and called loudly, 'Benedicite.' It was five o'clock, half past four on feast days, time to rise for Lauds. When Philippa, blear-eyed, heavy-lidded, gave the required answer, 'Deo gratias,' she felt, every morning, the 'thank God' was a lie.

The sleeplessness had gone on, night after night. Am I going to be ill? thought Philippa. She could easily have been ill and the thought used to come: Let me be ill, that will let me out. Then she would round on herself and, If you are ill, she told her body fiercely, I shall take not the slightest notice. She had not fallen ill but the nagging thought had persisted – if only I could have a cigarette.

The silly longing showed signs of becoming a running sore and Philippa had realized that she had never gone an hour a day without lighting a cigarette, 'which meant, for me, relaxing,' she told Dame Clare. 'When I had to think, having it to fidget with, the very smell, helped me to think, concentrate.' She had developed a trick of rubbing her thumb against her fingers which Dame Ursula, perhaps persuaded by Dame Clare, had not corrected, though Philippa had sometimes done it deliberately; yet she had often been infuriated by the others: Dame Ursula's perpetual little sniff: Julian's way of humming under her breath as she worked: Sister Sophie's habit of tapping a pencil on her teeth. 'Will you stop that *maddening* little noise!' and Sister Sophie had looked at

95

Philippa in alarm, while Sister Nichola said, 'It offends Her Majesty.'

From the first the novices and juniors had found Philippa difficult. 'She spoils things,' said Sister Benita. 'She makes us know how silly we are.' Even Julian had shied away from talking to Sister Philippa. 'She can't help being superior, but she is.' Philippa had known she should not let them see how worrying she found their daylong company. 'Try, my dear. Try,' Dame Ursula had encouraged her. 'It's just a mortification.' 'A typical Teddyism!' Philippa said to Dame Clare, who was not amused. 'We don't use nicknames, Sister, and especially not for Mother Mistress who should be revered,' and she had said, with scant sympathy, 'The other novices try to keep things pleasant – and try their best. At least you could be polite.'

'Thank God we have silence most of the time,' Philippa had written to McTurk. 'Recreation seems the longest hour of the day. Serves me right; I'm so used to being on a pinnacle.' The pinnacle had tumbled now. 'Your age is against you.' If Dame Ursula had said that once, she said it a hundred times, and it was unmercifully true: while Philippa had toiled, the young ones, notably Julian, finished their housework, gobbled up the unfamiliar words and phrases of the liturgy, found their mark-ings, learned to chant, compelled their bodies into discipline, while she had felt hopelessness creeping into her very bones. 'It's like trying to be a ballet dancer; you can never achieve that if you start too late.' Only a dogged obstinacy had held her, but . . . if I could have a cigarette.

The worst time was twilight. As the days grew longer and lighter and dusk came later, melancholy would descend, long-ings, a sinking and an infinite loneliness as if she were es-tranged, not only from all she had left, but from everyone in the Abbey – except perhaps the Abbess – and I cannot go bothering her with my dolours.

Dame Ursula and Dame Clare had seen the melancholy and had learned – odd though it seemed to Dame Ursula's way of thinking – that Sister Philippa was better if left to fight it out alone. 'Go down to the bottom of the garden,' said Dame

Ursula, 'and turn and see the lights and think of the warmth of interest and companionship we have here – and everything we need. Then think of those who have nothing, the truly lonely, the sick, the refugees. That will make you feel better.'

'Go down to the bottom of the garden,' said Dame Clare, 'and look back and see our buildings against the sky, particularly if there is a gale and the weathercock is spinning. You will see the Abbey riding with the church cross at its prow – the light from the west wing just strikes it. The Abbey is like a ship under its flag and makes you proud to be in it,' but Philippa standing far out in the dark, had felt nothing at all. 'They don't understand because they can't. No one can, not even Mother.'

She had not known then of the discussions, the watchful eyes. 'Will Sister Philippa hold out?' 'Be able to go on?' 'Sometimes I wish I could give her a stiff brandy and soda,' said Abbess Hester.

That was what Philippa needed in those twilight times. It was as simple as that. She could despise herself thoroughly but the truth remained. 'I suppose it is the habit of years, but it would lift me, make me more charitable.' Once she had even put on her black postulant coat – after all I'm only trying, not yet dressed as a nun – and gone down to the park wall where a buttress of brick made it easy to climb. Why not climb over and slip down to the Rose and Crown? That was when she had found a ten-shilling note in her pocket. Ten shillings of temptation. This is absurd, she told herself. We have a door. I have only to tell Mother I am going. That night she had walked up and down the path that ran along the wall, her nails pressed into her palms.

'But smoking and drinking for a nun.' Dame Beatrice had been distressed.

'St Benedict himself allowed a little daily wine,' Dame Veronica had pointed out.

'That was in Italy,' said Dame Ursula who had come to the Council with her report – her tone said clearly that anything might happen in Italy – 'They go in for such things, we don't.'

'Properly used, there is nothing against smoking and alcohol,' said the Abbess, 'except our wish for poverty. They are extravagances, not sins.'

'And a very silly habit,' Dame Agnes had been totally unsympathetic.

'Think of Manley Hopkins's sonnet,' said Dame Catherine, 'his "cliffs of fall ... Hold them cheap ... who ne'er hung there."'

There had come a night when, unable to speak, Philippa had taken a cloak from a peg by the novitiate door – Dame Clare's cloak? a junior's? she had not cared – and had gone out, leaving the sheltered garth and garden for the open park to feel the cold and wind on her face and to walk – violently, thought Philippa – away from the house, up along the avenue that spanned the width of the park, an avenue of copper beeches, their top branches bending and straining in the wind.

It had not been quite dark, clouds were chasing across a half moon; every now and then a twig snapped and whirled down through the air. It had been too cold and windy even for her desperate mood and she turned into the 'pleached alley' that bordered the lawns, pleached because of the thickened interlacing of the old espaliered peach trees, planted, so history said, in the reign of Queen Elizabeth the first. The branches broke into timid blossom in spring, but the park was too cold for them and the peaches were hard and green. The alley made a sheltered walk for the nuns who often paced there and that night Philippa had caught the white shine of a wimple and underveil; someone from the community was out too, making, Philippa guessed, her evening prayer; the nuns often came out for that half hour, morning and evening, to sit or stand in some specially loved spot, or to pace as they prayed, but not in the wind and cold, thought Philippa. It must be someone who, too, wanted to be alone, to get away.

Philippa had shortened her long strides and slowed to quietness so that she could pass, in monastic fashion, without interrupting the other, but the moon came out and showed her face which must have looked wild and distraught because the nun had stopped. The postulant dress and short veil were unmistakable and, 'Sister Philippa!' said the nun. It was Dame Catherine Ismay. She had put out a hand to find Philippa's that was clutching the cloak.

'You're cold' – Dame Catherine's hand had been warm, surprisingly firm and strong; Philippa could feel it still – 'cold and distressed,' said Dame Catherine. The compassion in her voice had seemed to plumb Philippa and, as if it had made a crack in the wall of her reserve, that surface composure under which she had hidden all these weeks, Philippa had felt tears beginning to well; they had seemed to have come not from her eyes but deep in her, welling up with such force that she shook with the effort of holding them back. It had been no use and in a moment she, dry-eyed stoical Philippa who had not wept even when Keith died or when she and Richard had made their decision, was weeping in a storm of tears, perhaps the tears of a lifetime, that had shaken her as helplessly as the beech trees in the wind. Dame Catherine had stood by, concerned but letting them flow, releasing Philippa's hand so that she could find her handkerchief, and saying nothing until Philippa had managed to gasp, 'I'm . . . so . . . sorry.'

'Don't be. We have all done this when we were new. We call it "having monsoon".'

'I . . . never . . . have before.'

'Perhaps that's why,' Dame Catherine had said, and presently, when Philippa had quietened, 'Come and walk.' She had slipped her arm under Philippa's and together they had walked up and down the pleached alley for half an hour talking of trivial things.

That night Philippa had slept.

Dame Agnes, Dame Maura, Dames Ursula, Beatrice, Colette, Catherine: each in turn seemed focused in a strong light that, while it showed their virtues, showed each blemish too, 'as if none of them will do,' said Hilary.

'One must,' said Philippa. 'It will resolve itself.'

Dame Ursula endorsed that. 'You may be – no, I know you are – wondering who will be elected Abbess,' she told the novitiate – 'Dear Teddy! as if we weren't all deep in it,' muttered Hilary – 'You don't really know the community,' went on Dame Ursula, 'so that none of you can possibly judge between those who stand out as possible choices.'

Sister Constance blushed but, 'Isn't it our duty to be concerned?' asked sensible Hilary. 'It's for life – and so it is grave.'

'It's not your duty, you have no vote,' said Dame Ursula, 'but it is very grave; so much so that it seems as if there's no one who can fill Lady Abbess's place, but remember God never asks us to do something without giving us the strength. Becoming Abbess will call out qualities in the one chosen, that we, and she, do not think she possesses.'

'It will need to,' said Philippa, when Cecily repeated what Dame Ursula had said. 'It will be very hard coming after Lady Abbess Hester Cunningham Proctor.'

On the morning of the thirteenth of November, feast of All Saints of the Benedictine Order – 'Who ought to guide us,' said Dame Perpetua – all the solemnly professed choir nuns assembled in the choir after Mass. The Abbot President, head of the English Benedictine Congregation, came from the sacristy with his two monk scrutators. Dame Agnes as mistress of ceremonies locked all the doors leading to the choir : the main door from the long cloister, the door on the first floor that led from the sick tribune where nuns who were ill could be wheeled to hear Mass, and the door from the bell tribune leading to the bell tower; then she unlocked the wicket in the grille. The Abbot President took a roll call, each nun as her name was called rising in her stall and answering, 'Adsum.' The Abbot put on his purple stole and, as the community knelt, said the confiteor and gave them absolution. Then, with his hand on the Gospels, he took the oath to conduct the election with complete fairness. The two scrutators put their hands between his, promising absolute secrecy.

On a table in the choir lay a crucifix and, as there was no prioress present, Dame Perpetua took the oath in the name of all the community, swearing that she would vote before God for the one she considered most worthy of the office : that she had made no compact with another, nor anyone with her: and that she would vote for the new Abbess in accordance with her conscience. Each nun followed in order of rank confirming Dame Perpetua's oath with the words, 'Item testor et juro' – 'I likewise testify and swear.'

Printed lists of all the choir nuns in solemn vows and over the age of forty were distributed; each nun finding her own name cut out. With her scissors she too cut out a name and, again in order, going to the grille, dropped the name into the box of one scrutator and, folding up her list so that none should see where it had been cut, stuffed it into the other. Dame Perpetua voted by proxy for the prioress.

There was a tense expectant silence of hopes, fears, silent prayers, silence filled only with a faint rustle as the two monks in their plain black habits sorted and counted the slips of paper at a side table. In tense stillness the older monk wrote – 'names', thought the nuns, following his hand on the paper: names, not yet a name – with Abbess Hester there had been only one voting, almost unanimous. A new abbess needed two-thirds of the votes, plus one, or a two-thirds majority and the Abbot President rose. 'There is no election,' he announced. 'I will read out the names and the votes given': and he read out:

Dame Maura Fitzgerald	18
Dame Agnes Kerr	16
Dame Catherine Ismay	13
Dame Beatrice Sheridan	10
Dame Colette Aubadon	4
Dame Ursula Crompton	1

There was a sigh as he said, 'Please distribute fresh papers.'

It took longer; the nuns needed time to think and it seemed even longer before the Abbot President announced again, 'There is no election.' It had, though, coagulated:

Dame Maura Fitzgerald	25
Dame Catherine Ismay	22
Dame Agnes Kerr	15

There was a stir. Dame Maura had gained seven of the votes, Dame Catherine had made a surprising bound upwards, Dame Agnes had lost one and the thoughts were almost audible. Dame Agnes would be eliminated.

'If it's not irreverent to say so, it must be rather like a race,' wrote McTurk. 'The odds must shorten, the favourite comes up or an outsider.'

'There is no election.'

Dame Catherine Ismay	37
Dame Maura Fitzgerald	25

On this third voting Dame Catherine had gained the whole of Dame Agnes's vote, but it still was not enough. Papers were distributed again.

Dame Maura's dark face flushed darker as she sat as erect as a soldier, her eyes looking straight ahead. Dame Catherine seemed stunned; it was only afterwards, when she had to move, that she found her feet and hands were so cold they seemed turned to lead, while sweat broke out on her neck and on her forehead; her fillet was soaked. There was a gathering dread in her heart. No! Please no! The minutes seemed to go on and on with the steady rustling of the papers.

At last the Abbot President rose; the community rose too, and he announced, 'Reverendissima Domna Catherina Ismay Abbatissa electa est.'

Enough had 'gone over' as the nuns said. It was suspected there was still a core of faithfulness to Dame Maura, but the Abbess was Dame Catherine Ismay.

4

She was Brede's thirteenth Abbess. 'Perhaps there *is* something in numbers,' said Dame Domitilla. 'The election was on the thirteenth; you started with thirteen votes.'

'Yes, it's an augury,' said Dame Perpetua, her face beaming; Dame Catherine knew, without being told, that Dame Perpetua's vote had been hers from the start. Thirteen abbesses – a long line, stretching from Dame Elizabeth Paget, first Abbess of the house of our Lady of Peace, little England, at Beauvais in France, to Abbess Hester Cunningham Proctor, and now thirteenth, and least, thought Dame Catherine, 'I'.

The nuns of Brede traced their origins back to an ancient and proud tradition. 'There were Benedictine nuns in England in the seventh century,' said Dame Agnes; houses at Folkestone, Whitby, Minster, Ely, and Barking. When these were sequestered at the Reformation the nuns were scattered, but their traditions were handed down in the old Catholic families, from aunts to nieces, old cousins to young cousins, godmothers to god-daughters in the faithful, persistent way of women until, in the seventeenth century, a little band of them emerged, driven to new boldness. Nine resolute young women escaped from England, 'at the risk of their lives,' Dame Ursula would impress on each succeeding novitiate, 'and led by a Lady Elizabeth Paget, opened a house at Beauvais in Northern France'. She turned to Hilary. 'Am I right in thinking your family are offshoots of those Northumberland Pagets?'

'Yes, the Dalrymples,' said Hilary. 'Perhaps I am a great, great – I don't know how many greats – a very distant cousin of that Elizabeth.' Those nine young nuns had called their house 'Our Lady of Peace', a touchingly confident name for those perilous times.

For the next hundred and seventy years other adventurous young women, travelling in secret, had found their way from England and Scotland to Beauvais. They often brought their maids and dependants with them from whom an equally sturdy lay-sistership grew up. 'But choir and lay have always worked together,' said Dame Ursula, 'as they do now. Everyone has always shared the burden of the work of house and garden.' Indeed the choir nuns provided the – as it were – unskilled labour because they went to help where necessary, often working under a lay sister expert in charge of kitchen, laundry, poultry or garden. 'And you don't know,' Dame Ursula said, 'what a profound effect it has on people, to see a young noblewoman working in the kitchen, a scholar labouring and doing exactly what she is told in the vegetable garden. In those days, gentlewomen didn't do such things. We were revolutionary.'

Though Beauvais was in France, the house was firmly English; only English and Latin were spoken. The 'little England' of Beauvais lived up to its name; it gained a reputation for beauty and peace, a place of quiet and culture in the troubled times, but, 'in human life, peace is transient', this was Dame Catherine, who taught Church History in the novitiate. 'We may enjoy a little pocket of peace, vouchsafed for a while, but no one should count on it.' The French Revolution was at its height in 1793 when the Beauvais house, like most religious houses, was seized and its nuns imprisoned.

'You may wonder,' said Dame Ursula, 'why our Abbess, for her pectoral cross, wears that humble little wooden one on a cord. You would expect it to be a gold cross, inlaid or set with amethysts and once upon a time our Abbess wore a cross like that, but it was seized in those troubles. Mother's cross, rough and humble as it is, was made by a princess; the Princess Marie Hortense of Savoy, who was in that prison with our nuns. She carved this little wooden cross with her penknife from pieces of a broken chair and, on the morning that the tumbril came to fetch her for the guillotine, she gave it to our then Abbess, Lady Abbess Flavia Vaux, and said, "I give you the most valuable thing I possess." She could not say more because of the guards, but think of it,' said Dame Catherine. 'For a princess the most valuable thing she possessed was a rough little cross. Mademoiselle, as they called her, was guillotined the same day, so you can see why that cross is so eloquent, and more precious to us than gold. Our Abbesses have worn it ever since.'

The Beauvais nuns would have gone to the guillotine too if Robespierre had not died; the fanaticism waned and they were released on condition they left France. They decided to come to England in spite of the danger – 'There was nowhere else for us to go – and, half starved, ragged and penniless, twenty-seven of us landed at Dover.' Only twenty-seven out of thirty-eight; eleven had died of malnutrition and prison fever; one, an old nun, Dame Benedicta Laidlaw, had died of a heart attack when the Beauvais house was invaded; one nun, trundled off the boat on a handcart, was paralysed. 'It was a terrible time,' Dame Ursula said when, at recreation, the novitiate talked over Dame Catherine's lesson. 'Nobody wanted us, most people were afraid of us, but the spirit was wonderful, and it was here in this district of downs and marshes on the borders of Sussex and Kent, that – after several tries – we found a home.' 'You know the portrait that hangs in the refectory,' Dame Catherine had said. 'It is Elinor Hartshorn's. She allowed us, not to buy Brede Abbey – many people then would not sell to nuns – but gave it to us. We had to keep it a secret though; Dom Aidan Pattinson, who came to see her for us over arrangements, had to come disguised as a country squire, and it was still years before we could bring back our customs, and wear the habit. When that was possible we had not even a pattern and had to write to Arras; the Arras nuns, bless them, sent a complete habit and cowl for the Abbess. More years went by before we could put up the "grates", as they called our grilles, and have true enclosure, enclosure for life in this house.'

Dame Ursula's first lesson to any postulant was on the meaning of that enclosure. She gave these lesson-talks three times weekly to the novitiate; 'They go on for ever,' Hilary warned Cecily. 'Dame Clare's are far more pithy.'

'You have to know all these things,' said Dame Ursula, 'because you, in your turn, will have to pass them on.' It was like a torch that went from hand to hand – and there was much to learn.

'It will be some time before you take any vows,' Dame Ursula always said. 'Maybe a long time, but you must understand them.' 'Understand what we are in for,' muttered Hilary.

'We Benedictines do not take the same vows as other Orders: poverty, chastity and obedience. For us, our first vow is of stability, stability to our chosen house. St Benedict laid down,' said Dame Ursula, 'that a monastery should be as self-contained as possible, with its own farm and orchard, its vegetable garden, poultry and, in the old days, its watermill; its own bakery, its weaving, bookmaking – handwritten then, now it is printing – so that "its members should have no need to go abroad",' she quoted, ' "which in no way can be good for them".'

The second vow was the famous Benedictine 'conversion of manners.' 'I'm glad you teach them manners,' Mrs Scallon had said. 'Young people's manners are deplorable these days.' 'Which of course isn't true,' said Dame Ursula. 'Many of you have excellent manners.'

Conversion of manners though meant far more than that; it was an entirely different way of thinking from the world's, 'and turns your ideas topsy-turvy,' said Hilary: self-effacement instead of self-aggrandizement: listening instead of talking: not having instead of having: voluntary poverty. 'They are dear, good girls,' Dame Ursula often said of the novitiate – it did not matter which novitiate – 'If only they wouldn't be so ardent. They want to sleep on planks, go barefoot, which isn't necessary, but they won't use up a reel of thread, or make a pencil last, or darn or patch which is necessary,' and, 'what is the use,' she said to Philippa, 'of taking a vow of poverty if you look to the house to provide you lavishly with everything you need?' Philippa had to smile at the thought of Brede being lavish. 'And our poverty,' Dame Ursula taught, 'doesn't simply mean doing without – a great many poor people are niggardly hoarders; it means being willing to empty yourself, be denuded, giving and giving up.'

'Think of all you gave up to come here,' Cecily said to Philippa; her brown eyes were again bright with admiration.

'Yes, a cat and a clock and some dear little sins.'

'The newspapers said far more than that,' Cecily was indignant.

'Did they now? Do you believe all you read in the papers?'

'Don't tease. You wouldn't joke if you knew how they helped me,' said Cecily. 'My mother was impressed. You gave up all that.'

'And what did you give?' Philippa was serious again. 'You and Sister Hilary and Sister Constance and Sister Louise? I was like an orchard where the fruit is ripe, but some has fallen in windfalls, some been spoiled by wasps, some sold,' Philippa's voice was low, 'or given away or wasted. The owner comes and gathers what is left and gives it to God. That's what anyone does who gives up in the fullness of her life, leaves it for Him; but the one who comes at nineteen or twenty or even twenty-three,' she said, looking at Cecily, 'gives the whole orchard, blossom and fruit and all.'

There were grounds for Philippa's regrets. Dame Agnes, too, was worried. 'She is extremely mature in the worldly world,' said Dame Agnes, 'but a beginner in ours. Ideally the two should mature together; if they don't, there is this unevenness, so difficult to redress. Can anyone ever really start again?'

'Sister Philippa is making a valiant try,' Dame Clare defended her.

'I grant you that, but for her it is far more difficult than for anyone less gifted; just because she is so unusually capable and with so many resources there must always be this instinct to decide, to settle matters for herself, be reserved. A religious must reserve nothing,' said Dame Agnes.

There was always this emphasis on giving – being fit to

give. 'A monastery or convent is not a refuge for misfits or a dumping ground for the unintelligent,' Abbess Hester had often said, 'nor for a rebound from an unhappy love affair – though a broken heart can often find healing in one of the active Orders, it will not do for us – nor are we for the timid wanting security or the ambitious wanting a career,' and, 'Anyone who comes here with the idea of getting something is bound to fail,' Dame Ursula warned all her postulants.

'But every human motive is, in some sense to get, to find,' Philippa would have argued, 'if only satisfaction.' Yet the paradox remained: only by giving completely was there any hope of finding.

'Have you told me everything?' Abbess Hester had asked Philippa in her days of candidature.

'No, Mother.'

The Abbess had not questioned further. She had only said, 'You will.'

The third vow was Obedience, 'and you don't know what you are in for when you take that,' said the nuns. Obedience was the rub for them all – all through their religious lives. It must, too, be prompt and whole-hearted, 'which means what it says,' said Dame Clare, 'doing what is asked of you with your whole heart, even if you don't like it, even if you can't agree. It's not blind obedience,' she said. 'You cannot be asked to do anything you know is wrong, such as telling a lie, or hurting someone. It is submitting your will, even when it goes against the grain; giving up your judgement and accepting your superiors' – even such a weak superior as I,' said Dame Clare. 'Our Abbess, we believe, is the representative of Christ – God – it is in her name "Abbess" from "Abba", Father. That is why we hold her in such reverence; kneel to her, make the deep bow when we pass or meet her.'

'And she will be Abbess for life,' said Cecily. 'It must be terrifying.'

'Domna Catherina Ismay Abbatissa electa est.' Dame Catherine had had to step out of her stall as Dame Agnes bowed before her; step out of it for ever, though that realization had not come to her then, and go to the wicket where she had knelt, thankful to kneel, while the Abbot President confirmed her as Abbess in the name of the Holy See, giving her the pectoral cross, the ring, the seal and the keys of the monastery. The bellringer had slipped up to the bell tribune to set the bells ringing; the doors were unlocked and the claustral sisters and novitiate trooped in.

Dame Agnes led the new Abbess to the abbatial chair, its mourning gone now, as the President intoned the Te Deum and the nuns took it up. Can they feel thankfulness and praise for this? Dame Catherine had wondered, but the voices had been strong and clear as if shaken into vigour after the days of hesitancy. The very newness of the idea of Abbess Catherine Ismay had shaken them. Then, one by one, Dame Perpetua first, the nuns had come, each kneeling and putting her hands between Abbess Catherine's to show fealty, homage, obedience and to be given the kiss of peace. Peace and love to each; she had tried to show it, but what must Dame Maura be feeling as she knelt to her? Or Dame Agnes, those great nuns? She had been heartened by Dame Perpetua's open approval, the gladness in Dame Beatrice's eyes, the delight in Philippa's. Then Dame Perpetua, acting for the prioress, had led Abbess Catherine up to the Abbess's rooms, the whole community following. As they reached the top of the stairs, they had heard the sound of castors; Sister Ellen and Sister Stephanie were wheeling away Abbess Hester's small bed, bringing in a larger one. The homely sound had seemed suddenly to crystallize the morning's happenings, make them positive. Then I'm not dreaming, thought Abbess Catherine.

The rooms themselves were ready, the larger study swept and polished as only Sister Ellen could polish; a fire was burning, fresh flowers had been put in the bracket vase on the wall, clean paper in the blotter. 'But these are all Mother's,' Abbess Catherine had wanted to cry. 'How can they be for me?' and her own voice had answered, 'Not for you. For the Abbess of Brede.' The prie-dieu was in an alcove that made a small oratory – I should feel Mother's spirit there. It was not the utilitarian prie-dieu they all had in their cells with its shelf for books, a top that opened like a desk, a cupboard with shelves below; even the kneeling board lifted to show a space where each nun kept her cleaning things: a tin of polish, scouring powder, shoe blacking. An Abbess would have no need of such things – she had not time for them – and this prie-dieu was handsome, of oak with a kneeling cushion – Mother needed that; her knees were old; for me it should be taken away. Dame Catherine's few books were already on the shelves, her one picture hung on the wall, though Sir Basil's Madonna was still over the fireplace. 'Then my things have been moved already,' she had said, dazed. 'Of course,' said Dame Perpetua, 'we look after you now. I'll leave you,' she said, 'until it's time for Sext. I expect you would like to be alone for a little,' and she had given the deep bow before she went respectfully away. The bow had been like a blow. Abbess Catherine had shivered and fled to the small chapel of the Crown of Thorns that opened out of the choir.

The nuns saw her go and Dame Beatrice guarded the door as Abbess Catherine fell on her knees close to the chapel grille. 'I can't. I can't,' she had cried it silently, her face hot though her knees and feet and hands were cold. 'I can't.'

Dame Catherine had a brother who, like Sister Julian's, was a monk, but ordained priest when he was still very young, and a bishop now. When they were children, Mark and Catherine had taken a vow together. 'Whatever you do, I will do too. Whatever you are, I will be too.' Mark had been ten, Catherine six, and she could remember how, sitting up in one bed, they had pricked their wrists with Mark's penknife and held the two together so that their blood could mingle. 'It's a blood vow,' Mark had said solemnly. He was a Benedictine novice while she was still at school; then, for her, there had been Paris, further study in Rome, and when at last she had come home, she had still dallied, just staying at home, playing tennis, picnicking, going to every party and dance she could. Had her father and mother, Dame Catherine often wondered afterwards, been trying to tempt her away from religious life – she was their only daughter – or had they been testing her vocation? Had she herself been trying to stifle the call that matched Mark's? It was odd, she thought, that she who was so shy had, in those last months in the outer world, been almost feverishly gay.

One night, it was in June, she had gone to a dance at the big house of the village, she, the doctor's daughter. She had always loved dancing; like many large people she was light on her feet – and had danced herself giddy that night and had come home at three in the morning. She could still see every detail of her coming in: the colour of her dress, dark gold satin – an odd choice for a girl – but it set off her white skin and the chestnut of her hair; the necklace she had borrowed from her mother rose and fell with her excited breathing. She had almost got engaged that night. The hall was dim, the moonlight fell through the open window, warm moonlight, and then Catherine had seen a line of light under the surgery door. It was not her father, she knew; it was Mark, home for a few days, but still working. Mark! She had not spoken but, as if he had answered her, the door opened and he had come out, holding his book. His face, so young, looked tired but – exalted, the young Catherine had thought – and as satisfied as if he had been drinking at some refreshing spring! 'He shall be as a tree planted by running water,' she had found herself thinking; she had looked at his black tunic and cincture, and her own dress had suddenly seemed tawdry.

Her eyes had begun to burn, her heart to pound. Mark had been unaware. He was smiling at the sight of her. He thought I looked radiant, remembered Abbess Catherine. He should have seen his own radiance! 'Was it wonderful?' he had asked and Catherine had answered, 'Yes,' and then said what she knew had been beating in her brain all evening, all night – and all the months before, months she had spent running round and round and round – 'It was wonderful, but no place for me.'

'What you do, I shall do too: whatever you are, I will be too.' That childish vow was fulfilled. 'You a bishop, I an Abbess,' she had whispered it aloud in the chapel of the Crown of Thorns and, at that, realization overwhelmed her. Everything she cherished at Brede would, for her, be gone: the

111

anonymity that was such balm to her: her manual work –
there would be no time for the fine weaving that was so restful
– 'Dame Catherine's orphreys' – nor for translating – she was
in the midst of a new book on the Qumran Caves by Father
Pierre Benoit of the Order of Preachers – that would have to
be left, nor would there be the lessons in Church History she
gave to the novitiate and found so interesting. She must not
have special friends, must give up the joy she had taken in her
talks with Dame Emily, once her own novice mistress, the
recreation quips with Dame Colette and her companionship in
the vestment room and, latterly, the growing friendship with
Sister Philippa; the Abbess must be for everyone, nothing is as
lonely as a throne, and she, Catherine, would not possess
Abbess Hester's warm genius for getting beyond it. The
silence Dame Catherine had found so fruitful must be continually broken in upon; worst of all she, to whom it was still
an ordeal to take a solo part in choir, or to act as reader in the
refectory, meet strangers in the parlour – though she had successfully hidden all this, too successfully she could have said –
must now be always solo, leader in everything, unmercifully
prominent. An Abbess cannot lift a little finger but it is seen
and marked by her nuns; she must lead, inspire, and every
hour of the twenty-four hours of each day until she died, bear
that awesome responsibility of souls and, in her own monastery, consent to be the representative of Christ.

'I can't,' Dame Catherine had cried in the chapel and at
once felt the need to be where all the nuns went for strength
and comfort, reassurance and love; as if drawn, she had got up
from her knees and gone into the choir itself, to kneel on the
step behind the grille, the step facing the sanctuary where,
long ago, she had knelt as a postulant in her first hour in the
enclosure. Once again it was as if a quietening hand was laid
on her panic; with her eyes on the small flame that had never
gone out since the community came to Brede, she whispered,
'I can't,' but it was acceptance now. 'I can't,' whispered Dame
Catherine, 'so You must.'

The bell began to ring for Sext. She rose to her feet and
walked towards the abbatial chair.

112

It was not until after dinner – in the strange seat at the high table – giving the knock, the rap with the small wooden mallet that was the Abbess's signal, walking behind the procession to sing the dinner grace in choir, that Abbess Catherine had been able to go to her rooms. 'Go and rest,' Dame Perpetua had urged her. 'I will take recreation today.'

The Abbess had gone into her new cell; it was smaller than the study and as humble, she was glad to see, as any nun's, with its bare floor, narrow bed and chest of drawers below the crucifix, her own crucifix. Only the prie-dieu was missing, there was an armchair instead – cushioned, thought Abbess Catherine, with distaste – missing, too, were the customary basin and jug, and she remembered that the Abbess had a bathroom, a bathroom to herself, while the others washed in basins on the floor of their cells. That had brought the unwelcome thought: there could be no more of those informal and friendly meetings in the interval between Vespers and supper when the nuns hurried to draw off their cans of washing water while the water was really hot.

Her bed was made up and ready. Abbess Catherine took a step nearer and caught her breath; the pillow and white counterpane were strewn with small picture cards and nose-gays such as the extern sisters were often asked to place in the guest house to welcome some especially loved guest. No names were attached, no words written on them; they were not needed – the nuns who sent them could guess what that welcome would mean to their new Abbess – but there was one exception: a few of Dame Mildred's carefully grown white violets were gathered into a bunch with a card on which Abbess Catherine recognized Dame Maura's writing: 'For my Abbess and dearest Mother with love, loyalty and prayers of her devoted daughter, Maura.'

Sister Ellen, coming in with the small pile of Dame Catherine's underclothes, found her new Abbess on her knees by the bed, sobbing as if her heart would break. The door had been open, the Sister had thought the Abbess had gone to recreation – 'or I shouldn't have come in.'

Sister Ellen was ninety-two, 'Long past her work,' said

Dame Veronica, but she was still scrupulously clean and tidy and, 'I can polish with the best of them,' she would say indignantly. Abbess Hester had refused to have anyone else. The old Sister was tired with the changing of the cells, the emotion of putting her beloved Abbess Hester's few things away; she was shaken out of herself, or, 'I would never have done as I did,' she told Abbess Catherine afterwards. She put the linen down and Philippa, who had come up from recreation to catch up with her pile of letters, never forgot what she saw then. 'It gave me a glimpse of what it means to be elected Abbess.' Letters in her hand, she had followed Sister Ellen through the open door of the Abbess's room, and for a moment stood transfixed by what she saw in the cell beyond.

Abbess Catherine was far taller than Sister Ellen but the Sister would never have dreamed of sitting down on her Abbess's bed; instead she had knelt beside her, reached up and put her arms round the big strong body, cruelly shaken now – for the moment Sister Ellen's thin old arms were the stronger. 'Don't cry, my Lady,' she was saying and Philippa saw she was rocking Abbess Catherine as if she were a child – to Sister Ellen, of course, Abbess Catherine was still young. 'Don't cry. It will be all right. You will see. It will be all right.'

Philippa silently went away.

5

The life of the great monastery flowed as steadily as a river, no matter what rocks and cross currents there were; Philippa often thought of the river Rother that wound through the marshes of Kent and Sussex, oldest Christendom in England, watering the meadows whose grass fed the famous marsh sheep, then winding below the town to the estuary that flowed to the sea. Brede Abbey was like that, thought Philippa, coming from far sources to flow through days, weeks, years, towards eternity.

In religion a different year revolves within the natural one, the seasons making a background for it. Philippa was now seeing the cycle for the fifth time; it began as autumn reddened the Abbey's wild cherries and sent the yellow birch leaves spinning in the park, while the beeches in the avenue stood deep in fallen leaves; the hedges were bright with rose hips and briony berries and Dame Beatrice's vases for the sanctuary were filled with michaelmas daisies or sent the pungent smell of chrysanthemums into the choir. There was a crisis of apple picking; even choir practice had to be missed and Sister Hannah, who had been a farmer's daughter, took the honey off her bees, working all night with two volunteers to help her; one, this autumn, was Sister Hilary, turning the handle of the extractor and letting the trickles of liquid gold drain through the tap into the jars.

Every year Sister Hannah wrote to the famous Brother Benedict at Holne Abbey in Devon to tell of her harvest. 'It's small compared to his, but then we don't sell much of it.' Pots of honey did appear in the extern sisters' shop, with baskets of apples and nuts from the nut-plantation, but most of the produce was for the Abbey. Like squirrels, the nuns were gathering their winter store.

The grey squirrels were everywhere in the park. Starlings made most of the bird noise now; their moulting time was over, they chattered with joy, sounding like bird castanets. The robins still sang from dawn to dusk and there was a caricature of a blackbird's song, titmice calls, a woodpecker's laugh and, every late afternoon if the sun appeared, thrushes poured out their song. 'Which is more beautiful?' Dame Beatrice asked. 'A spring blackbird's song or a winter thrush's?'

At this afternoon time in autumn, the nuns loved to be out in the garden, garth or park, to walk along the beech avenue or up and down the pleached alley, bare now, or on the narrow brick path that ran below the boundary wall, all paths where generations of Brede nuns had paced up and down, measuring the half-hours of their silent prayer. The November gales and storms drove them into the cloisters; only the hardiest in the community put on their cloaks, drawing the hoods up over their veils and keeping their heads down against the wind. The wind helped the rooks to pull their nests to pieces, and the grass was strewn with twigs, while the lawns were dotted with seagulls driven in from the sea; their early crying round the tower broke into the singing at Lauds and Prime. Dame Bridget, the Abbey's dedicated ornithologist, reported a flock of redwing from the North, 'come for our hollyberries,' and she predicted, 'We shall soon have colder weather.'

Dame Bridget was usually right; in most years, it was not long before the Abbess ordered the central heating to be put on 'in spite of the cost'. 'What did we do once upon a time?' asked Dame Agnes who did not like the innovation. 'We had plenty of novices and juniors to saw wood and stoke the fires,' was the answer. The young ones still carried in logs and brought up coal for the Abbess's room and the infirmary, but there were fewer young and when the common room fire was lit, as it was on special occasions, it held only huge logs,

116

trundled in on a make-shift trolley which had once been the undercarriage of a perambulator.

After Christmas there was usually snow, giving a new beauty, an even quieter hush to the monastery grounds, 'and there's nothing to spoil it,' Philippa had said her first winter. 'No traffic, no footsteps' – except when the paths were swept by the novitiate. The pond was frozen over, the moorhens ran across it with their absurd long-legged run and Dame Bridget's bird table was besieged. 'I wish some benefactor would send us coconuts and seed,' she lamented. Sister Priscilla gave all she could spare, but it was difficult to feed birds in a frugal monastery where even the crumbs were eaten in the refectory. Each nun, at the end of each meal, was bound to sweep her crumbs up into a little pile at her place and swallow them. 'And the birds are not the only beggars,' said Sister Priscilla. There were always tramps ringing the extern bell; they were never refused a meal, even if it were only doorstep-thick slices of bread and cheese, a mug of cocoa. 'We give what we have,' said Sister Priscilla. 'Last Boxing Day we fed fifty-one men,' said Dame Domitilla, but the nuns could not give what the monastery did not possess and there was one especial hen blackbird that haunted Dame Bridget with its soft 'took' of hunger. 'One of the hardest things about being a nun is that you have nothing to give,' she said.

The first sign of spring was the reddening of the willow boughs above the pond; the snow and ice melted and the brick paths that had been too slippery to walk on were wet; if anyone stepped on the grass, it was so soft and water-sogged that mud squelched up. 'I do nothing but brush the skirt of my habit,' Hilary complained. 'That's because you forget to turn it up,' said Dame Clare. The nuns often turned up the skirts of their habits and pinned them round their waists above their strong blue petticoats. Spring seemed all mud, cold and spring colds, the sore throats and influenza that so agitated Dame Maura. 'How shall we ever have a full choir for Easter?' she used to worry, but presently it grew warmer, the garth was a sheet of crocus, there were snowdrops and violets in the dingle and, in Dame Teresa's bog garden round the pond, the first dark purple clumps of dwarf iris appeared. 'There's blackthorn out,' several of the nuns said as if they had made a discovery but, 'It's been out since Christmas,' said Dame Maura. 'Didn't you notice I put a big bowl of it in front of our Lady in the music library? I had kept it a week in the warmth and it came out in full blossom.'

Up on the tower Philippa could hear the bleating of the lambs, the sound carried inland from the marshes. In the orchard and along the avenue, daffodils came up in the grass and there were nests everywhere. Brede was a natural bird sanctuary; even the cats left the birds in peace but then, 'monastery cats are not like other cats,' Sister Renata, Philippa's friend among the extern sisters assured her. Sister Renata had an affinity with cats and when Philippa said, 'I have – had – a Siamese called Griffon . . . I had to leave him,' Sister Renata had put out a quick hand and squeezed Philippa's.

The monastery had its cats; there was Grock with his one green eye; the other had been lost in a fight when he was a whole tom and he was called Grock because of his swollen and misshapen face. Grock had attached himself only to Abbess Hester; he had no use for any other nun, not even for Sister Priscilla who fed him. There was the little she-cat, Wimple, a Benedictine in her black and white, the white running under her chin, which explained her name. There was also the extern Bonnie, short for Boniface, who never grew much bigger than a kitten and who, Sister Renata swore, would catch butterflies but with a mouth so soft that when he brought them to her he would open his mouth to let them go and they would fly away. 'He wouldn't chase birds. None of our cats would,' said Sister Renata. 'Too well fed,' said Sister Priscilla. She had once given Grock a herring for his dinner, 'the same as we were having'. He looked at it, 'and his tail went swish-swish,' Sister Priscilla told afterwards. Then he had fixed her with his one eye, baleful now, picked up the herring and stalked off with it. Sister Priscilla had followed to see what he would do. Grock had walked majestically upstairs to the Abbess's door where he scratched to be let in, giving his peculiar miaow, which was hoarse, unmistakably Grock's, and Abbess Hester, as she always did, had let him in. He laid the herring at her feet and his tail went 'swish-swish again,' said Sister Priscilla.

Wimple too had the nuns on a string, as Sister Priscilla would say. There was a custom in the community for the nuns, on their way to breakfast after Prime, to stop at the statue of our Lady with the Holy Child in the long cloister, to say three Hail Mary's there. Wimple was impatient for her breakfast and she would walk among the kneeling figures, giving them small pushings with her head; one hand after another would come out, not to push her away but to stroke her. Wimple was perverse; she would come into the refectory through the ever-opening service door and walk through the room to the other, demanding to be let out. Unlike Grock's, Wimple's miaow was piercing and could, at dinner and supper, interrupt the reader so that Sister Xaviera who doted on Wimple would get up and let her out. In a moment or two, the little cat would walk in at the service door again.

Almost all the nuns loved animals and birds, especially young ones. 'Well, I suppose we're starved for them,' said Dame Perpetua. Sister Gabrielle, the poultry keeper, had coops out every spring for hens and their chicks; young moorhens hatched out in the nests on the pond, ridiculous dabs of black; while swallows had built under the eaves of the Chapter House for centuries. 'There's a pair of goldcrests nesting in the larches,' Dame Bridget was breathless with excitement. Goldcrests, so tiny that they made their wren relations look large, were rare in Kent and Sussex. 'They're like olive-green elves,' said Dame Bridget, showing them to a chosen few. 'Look, you can see the cock's orange crest.' The monastery sow farrowed in the spring. 'I have just seen a piglet born,' Dame Teresa came running in. 'It was pink and folded, looking as if it were wrapped in cellophane; the sow ripped that off, gave the piglet a swipe with her snout and it stood up, shook out its ears and tail, then ran round her and started to suck. It was like a miracle!'

In the garden the hedges were no longer clipped as tidily as they had once been – 'Yew, not box,' Cecily Scallon said

119

regretfully when she came; she had always thought her visionary convent or monastery would have box hedges – nor were the lawns mown and rolled to their old perfection. 'If ninety-six women can't keep a garden, they ought to be able to,' Abbess Hester had said, but the ninety-six women now had too many other things to do; pressures and demands, even in the Abbey, had increased and more of the big garden was being allowed to go back to woodland but, 'We are so fortunate,' Dame Ursula said often. 'Think of the Newgate nuns in London, shut in between those city streets with their roaring traffic. That's real renunciation for you – no garden at all.' Dame Mildred, the gardener, managed a procession of flowers, from the pinks and yellows of spring to what she called 'the purple time', lilacs, iris and the deep purple of pansies. As summer advanced, she had roses and lilies, mixed borders with the blue of delphiniums, anchusas and flax, pink of lupins, and poppies, phlox and sweet peas.

In a hot summer even the lightweight habits were too warm – close-fitting wimples and fillets were apt to get crumpled and limp – and the younger nuns wilted. 'We don't take any notice of little things like heat,' said Dame Clare who looked as cool and as immaculate as always; then the garden colours deepened: yellows and bronzes and reds came up: scarlet of berries and, in the dingle, crocuses again, but the pale autumn crocus that a once-upon-a-time chaplain had brought the nuns from Switzerland. Sister Elizabeth made her bonfires in the front of the house and they burned too in the enclosure, along the avenue; there was a smell of woodsmoke in the air, the dew lay late, sometimes all day on the grass; soon the November mists and gales would come; the year had slipped away again.

Abbess Catherine thought it fitting that she was made Abbess at the year's ebb; she who was so obscure after the renown of Abbess Hester. 'To intrigue to be Abbess' was the most grave of the faults in the List of Grave Faults, 'and anyone who intrigues for the office deserves to get it,' Abbess Hester used to say. As this, to Abbess Catherine, strange

November passed, the days seemed to slow more and more, and the weather was grey, with chill and mist. 'It's all dismal and dying, full of howling winds and holy souls,' Hilary had burst out on All Souls Day but, 'Advent is coming,' said Dame Ursula. 'Wait.'

Now that an Abbess had been elected a feeling of confidence and settlement was in the Abbey, even among those who had not voted for her. On the second day Abbess Catherine had given her first address to the community in Chapter and, 'By the grace of God,' she would have said, managed to speak simply but with a dignity that won approval. 'I must say she is clear and direct,' said Dame Agnes.

'And humble,' said Dame Maura.

'Edifyingly humble,' Dame Beatrice used the word which was a favourite one among the nuns in the sense of 'building up'; a good action by anyone strengthened the whole community, a bad one 'dis-edified', or pulled it down. 'Yes, I believe we were guided.' Dame Beatrice was sure of it.

'We need to be guided!' Abbess Catherine would have said. 'You will soon learn the ropes,' Abbot Bernard had comforted her, but she was finding these ropes, these guiding lines, intricately knotted and some, she suspected, inexplicably tangled.

'Benedicite, Mother. I . . .'

'Mother, I . . .'

'I . . .'

I! 'Did you ever notice,' Abbess Catherine asked Dame Perpetua, 'how often even we nuns used that word?' and there were so many 'I's ranging from old Dame Frances Anne and bedridden Dame Simone – I must go in to her this evening; Dame Joan says she is not so well – to the youngest, little Sister Cecily Scallon.

Here the Abbess caught herself back; Sister Cecily was not the youngest; Sister Hilary, Sister Louise, Sister Scholastica were all younger and, 'Why do I think of Sister Cecily as little?' the Abbess asked Philippa, who had brought in a sheaf of letters to be signed – Philippa was still working as an unofficial secretary, 'Just to help through these first weeks,' said Dame Perpetua – 'Sister Cecily isn't little,' said the Abbess.

'No one could be little and sing like that,' said Philippa.

Because she herself had serious difficulty with the chant, Philippa still went to the novitiate choir singing lessons and so was present when Dame Maura first heard Cecily sing. Cecily had come with the rest of them into the chapter house where the lessons were given; Dame Maura seemed immensely tall in the round room, dark and intimidating, but Cecily, usually so nervous, had looked at her with confidence. 'We will take the sequence "Lauda Sion" from the Mass of Corpus Christi,' announced Dame Maura. 'It was written by St Thomas Aquinas and is set to the melody of a sequence of Adam of St Victor so it is not very old, only thirteenth century.' These introductions were just names to Hilary, though of course she knew of Thomas Aquinas, but Cecily drank in every word. 'Stand properly,' Dame Maura had told the girls in their half circle. 'You can't sing if you slouch. Keep your hips behind your shoulders. Eyes should be down,' she said to Cecily, 'so that you can follow what you are reading,' and, to everyone, 'pronounce the "e"s as in "met" and bring the "d"s well forward.' Cecily's eyes followed every movement, every word but, 'Just listen for the first few minutes,' Dame Maura had told her, 'until you are a little accustomed.' Cecily's lips moved but she had said nothing.

The juniors and novices began, but at the verse: '*Dogma datur christianis quod in carnem transit panis...*' Dame Maura had stopped them wearily.

Three times a week Dame Maura laboured at these singing lessons and had little reward. 'It's always the way,' she said. 'The unmusical want to sing, and the musical want to listen!' She spent her days coaxing shy voices out or trying to make poor ones – 'respectable,' said Hilary. 'Possible,' said Philippa.

In Philippa's early days the precentrix had taken her apart after every lesson and made her hum to the piano. 'Just hum on "F" or "F" sharp,' then made her descend on a scale of five notes; go up again by semitones, over and over. At first it had been to such little avail that when the question arose as to Philippa's Clothing, Dame Agnes had advanced that it was impossible to accept her as a choir nun. 'A choir nun is one

122

who sings in choir. Sister Philippa cannot sing. Therefore she shouldn't be clothed.'

Abbess Hester and the Council all knew Dame Agnes had an implacable distrust of Philippa. In the Council she was quite open about it. 'I was against her coming in the first place. I am against her still.'

'Why, Dame?' but Dame Agnes took refuge behind this indisputable difficulty. 'The reason I have advanced does away with any other. Sister Philippa cannot sing. Ask Dame Maura.'

'It is certainly her Apollyon,' admitted Dame Maura. 'I don't understand it,' she had told Philippa. 'You have a good speaking voice, even a rich one, and surely you cannot be shy.'

'I used to give lectures,' said Philippa, 'to large audiences,' and she said, 'It's not only my voice, it's myself.' This had been in the time of her sleeplessness, her loss of weight, her struggles. Dame Maura had been unfailingly understanding and championed Philippa in the Council, as did the Abbess, but Dame Agnes had been, 'preposterous,' as the Abbess and Mother Prioress, Dame Emily, had said afterwards.

'If Sister Philippa really has the courage and humility you all vaunt,' Dame Agnes had said, 'let her be clothed as a claustral sister.'

'That would be absurd.'

'Not as absurd as a choir nun who cannot sing.'

Abbess Hester had finally settled it. Sister Philippa should be received for Clothing. 'After all,' said Abbess Hester, 'you have put up with my voice all these years.'

'Dearest Mother, that's entirely different.'

'It seems to me exactly the same. I can't sing, I never have been able to, but I can intone quite respectably; so will she. Dame Maura will see to that.'

Dame Maura had seen to it, labouring patiently, as she was preparing to labour now with the small half circle facing her.

' "Dogma datur christianis",' she had said, marking the 'd's. ' "Quod in *car*nem," roll your "r"s in "carnem"; you make it sound like "canem". The bread was transformed into *flesh* – not into a dog!' Hilary and the novices giggled but Cecily was serious, only waiting for the moment when she could start.

Philippa had heard a minute hiss from her when Sister Scholastica went flat.

'Again,' commanded Dame Maura and had given one of her rapid strings of instructions that Philippa found so difficult to comprehend. 'Take no notice of the quarter bar, but snatch a breath at the half bar, and lay the cadence down gently. Gently!' said Dame Maura darting a fierce look at Hilary. 'You can allow a distinct pause at the double bar, then resume a tempo. Now altogether, and you,' her dark gaze had come to Cecily, 'try to join in.' They began and Cecily had not tried to join in, she sang; her voice, clear as a cuckoo call, yet unmistakably full of power, rose with the others. For a moment they saw the surprise, the interest in Dame Maura's face, then not by one iota had the precentrix betrayed the excitement she must have felt; her arms lifting in her long sleeves, she conducted with her hands, drawing them on until they had finished. Then, 'Again,' she said. 'Sister Constance, watch the marks. Sister Philippa, try a little more power.'

'I shall croak if I do,' said Philippa.

'Then lift your voice. Begin by lifting your chin and *breathe*,' but as the Lauda Sion Salvatorem burst forth – Sister Cecily seemed to have galvanized them all into new life – it was too much for Dame Maura. 'Go on,' she had said to Cecily, signing to the others to stop, and Cecily sang alone.

Dame Maura had had to wait until after Vespers for the moment when she could fly to Abbess Catherine's room. 'Mother! That blessed child! In all these years of waiting – she says she waited six years – she was getting ready, studying for us! At the Academy schools she took organ and singing...'

'Organ?' The Abbey needed organists. 'Does she play well?'

'I haven't heard her yet.' Here Dame Maura did not know whether to be annoyed or to laugh. 'What did you think of the organist last night?' she had asked Cecily when she had kept her for a short talk after the practice, and those brown eyes, candid and innocent, were lifted to hers. 'I thought she was very promising,' said Cecily.

'Promising?' Dame Maura was nonplussed.

'She must learn how to pedal,' Cecily had said with all the

severity of the young. The organist had been Dame Maura.

'But I taught myself,' Dame Maura said. 'This girl is almost a professional. While she was working in London she joined the Bach Society where she often sang solo; at weekends when she went home she used to go to the cathedral and have lessons with Doctor Shepherd, *the* Doctor Shepherd. Mother, it's a voice like a flute, with such range and power! For years,' said Dame Maura almost in a vision, 'we haven't been able for instance to sing "Gaude, Gaude, Gaude, Maria Virgo" from the Sarum Antiphonal. It's too difficult for anyone here. Now we can. Think what it will be like to hear it again – and so many other things. Oh, Mother!'

Philippa could have told the Council part of the reason why Dame Agnes was so opposed to her. 'It was my fault,' she could have said. When Dame Agnes gave a Latin lesson she gave no quarter, overlooked no slip. Philippa, when she came, expected no quarter, made no slip, but still Dame Agnes had singled her out – as if for combat? Philippa had wondered.

'I hear, Sister Philippa, you are quite a Latin scholar.'

'I was more for modern languages,' Philippa said carefully. 'My Latin is very rusty now, and I'm afraid my knowledge of liturgical Latin is almost nil.'

'Remarkable, when you are intelligent and have been a convert for – is it six years?' but Philippa had known, as soon as she had spoken, that the sort of false diplomacy she had used so easily in the outside world would not deceive Dame Agnes. Then was Dame Agnes jealous? She couldn't be, thought Philippa – in those days she still had illusions about nuns. Dame Agnes, in fact, was like a robin instinctively defending its territory – she would have been shocked if she had realized it was jealousy. She envied the clarity of the younger woman's mind and Philippa was so much quicker than Dame Agnes who felt herself beginning to be slow; she even envied Sister Philippa's slim height, her carriage and the grey eyes that were so beautifully set: they would be more noticeable still when they were framed by the wimple and fillet.

'If you have been small, plain and sore-eyed all your life,

distinction gives you a pang, even if you are a nun,' Dame Agnes could have said, and unconsciously too she felt that her position at Brede was threatened. 'Sister Philippa took a first in languages at Oxford,' Dame Beatrice in her sweetness had remarked happily to Dame Agnes, 'that should be a bond between you.' To Dame Beatrice, innocent of all ambition, it would have been a bond. To Dame Agnes it was like a barb.

The novitiate learned Latin, not only for the chant but, too, for reading books and to help in the work of transcribing and translating what would otherwise be lost – 'So few people in this day and age can really read Latin,' said Dame Agnes. In Philippa's first lesson Dame Agnes had taken her class, at Dame Clare's request, through the hymn and psalms of Lauds of the next day. When she read the Divine Office, Dame Agnes's face lost its sharpness and settled into the peace of someone totally absorbed by what she was doing. 'This is our craft,' she said, using the word in its highest sense. 'The craft of a contemplative religious, and as a good workman, an artist, loves his craft, we must delight in ours.'

Dame Agnes had read the hymn and passed the book to Sister Benita whose words had sounded blurred and stumbling after hers, and brought curt rebukes. Sister Sophie came next. She, Nichola and Benita were all in the novitiate then and Sister Sophie was sharply corrected as was Sister Nichola. Julian had read only two verses, guided and helped by Dame Agnes; last of all she had passed the book to the newcomer, Sister Philippa, and, What shall I do? Philippa had asked herself. Dissemble or just read? She had raised her eyes for a moment to the small ones studying her under the black veil and Philippa knew afresh that with Dame Agnes only truth would do – but truth kept modest, she thought – and without making an especial effort she had read the hymn through, with one or two mistakes, genuine ones – 'I am rusty,' she had said with truth at the end. Dame Agnes had made no comment but Dame Clare, who was at the lesson to help the postulants, said afterwards, 'You read Latin well, accent and phrasing and voice.'

There came a day when Dame Agnes arrived in high good humour. 'I met Dame Agnes in the Via Crucis cloister – I had just made the Stations of the Cross—' Sister Sophie had warned, running in before her. 'She was positively twinkling, so look out!' Dame Agnes, they were sure, would set them a trap.

'There's nothing like a puzzle to keep young people on tiptoe,' she often said, and she had had a good catch for her group that morning.

The class had risen to greet her with a chorus of 'Benedicite' and, when she had made the sign of the cross, said the collect 'Actiones', she went to the blackboard and chalked up: 'Videns regem splendide vestitum arma praeclara elephanta loricatum loricis regis exercitus miratus est.' Then, with that twinkle Sister Sophie had seen, asked, 'Sister Benita, will you translate?' With a puzzled face the Sister had looked at the board and after a few moments began: 'Seeing the king splendidly apparelled . . . but does "praeclara" go with "elephanta"?' she asked doubtfully. 'The king couldn't be "loricatum loricis" – harnessed with harness.'

Sister Nichola in her turn could only add the last words, 'that the army was lost in wonderment or admired whatever it is that comes before.' Even Sister Sophie had been lost.

'Try again,' said Dame Agnes. 'Remember that in Latin you can leave out the conjunction "et",' but Sister Sophie still stumbled.

'I am sure our scholar, Sister Philippa, can do it,' Dame Agnes had said in acid tones.

Dame Agnes was used to make juniors blush and quake before her but Philippa kept a calm face; the gaze of her eyes was level and, 'It's not easy to prick that one,' murmured Dame Agnes.

Here she was wrong; that morning Philippa had been extraordinarily vulnerable, weary to her bones after a sleepless night and, just before the Latin lesson, had had a long struggle with the chant when even Dame Maura grew impatient. Philippa was discouraged and tired, more tired still of curbing herself to be tactful. 'Our scholar can do it.' Her temper could flash as well as Dame Agnes's and, 'Yes, Dame,' she had said with dangerous quietness. 'Elephanta is a Greek accusative. The catch is in the Latin author's use of a Greek form, isn't it? It simply means . . .' and she read off 'At sight of the king splendidly apparelled, the shining weapons and the elephants equipped with harness, the army was lost in amazement.' The class had been silent except Sister Benita who had said under her breath, 'Clever Dick!'

Dame Agnes had gone red to the tip of her nose. 'Sister Philippa,' she had said. 'I don't think you need any lessons in Latin from me.'

'And she wouldn't give me any more – though it was true I was rusty – and she won't forgive me,' Philippa said, but it was not for the Latin nor the unconscious jealousy that, to give Dame Agnes her due, she had opposed Philippa's Clothing; though Dame Agnes was sharp and prejudiced, she was fair. 'She may *sound* uncharitable but uncharitable she is not,' Abbess Hester used to say. Dame Agnes sensed something in Sister Philippa Talbot, 'That disturbs me – I say this for the Sister's own sake,' she said. 'Something is not right.'

She had brought this up again when, just before Abbess Hester's death, there had been the first discussion in Council about Sister Philippa's Solemn Profession. 'What is not right? Be explicit, Dame,' but Dame Agnes could not name what she felt; each objection she made she could, in reality, have answered for herself, and yet . . . 'Sister Philippa is cold,' she said.

'She is not,' Abbess Hester had been firm. In one of those long-ago preliminary interviews in the parlour she had asked Philippa, 'Were you happy with your husband?'

'No, Mother.'

'Whose fault was that?'

'Both of ours. It's nearly always both.'

'I'm glad you said that, without excuses,' said the Abbess and, her eyes looking deep into Philippa, asked, 'You were even in those days a career woman?'

'Yes, but not only,' Philippa had taken the point. 'After I came back to London I could have married again.' The Abbess said nothing and Philippa went on. 'He was married and had children, so we stopped.'

'You were able to stop?'

'Thank God,' said Philippa. 'I didn't want to have that on my conscience.'

'How long ago was this?'

'Nine years.'

'Then it has nothing to do with your wanting to enter religious life?'

'Nothing.'

'H'm.' The Abbess had considered then asked, 'Have you seen him since?'

'I see him almost every weekday. He's the Permanent Secretary, head of my Department.'

'H'm. Did his wife know?'

At that Philippa had hesitated. 'If she had been ... alive to him, she couldn't have helped knowing, but she wasn't. Richard is very lonely. That was what made it so hard for both of us, but I'm glad now – for myself. For me it was ...' – Philippa could have used Dame Beatrice's favourite 'it was providential' – instead, 'if we had been able to marry, for me it would have turned out "second best".'

The Abbess had smiled. 'I'm glad you are loving. A cold heart is no good for a religious.'

'Sister Philippa is opinionated,' Dame Agnes had gone on in the Council.

'Well, at her time of life, one would expect her to have opinions,' said Abbess Hester, 'and I have found nothing wrong with them.'

'She is deceitful.'

'Not deceitful, reserved.' Dame Catherine as she was then had a fellow feeling with Philippa as she spoke, but Abbess Hester had said thoughtfully, 'Many people have sensed that.'

In the novitiate it had been noted that Sister Philippa never talked about her family and background. 'She's cagey,' said Sister Benita, 'when she could be so interesting. Dame Ursula says she has worked in Tokyo and Washington, been in India, all over the world. Think of that.'

'Well, do we want to know about her wonderful past?' asked Sister Nichola, whom Philippa always nettled. 'I'm sure I don't. Isn't there a proverb,' she had asked, 'that says, "Keep at three paces distant any man who doesn't like music, or bread, or the laugh of a child"? Well, Sister Philippa hates music.'

'Does she?' asked Sister Julian.

'She isn't very good at it, is she? And she never eats bread if she can help it – I suppose to keep that elegant figure – and she takes not the slightest interest in children; she didn't even glance at the snap of my cousin's little boy.'

When Cecily came, she too wondered about Philippa and children. In gratitude for Philippa's kindness in those first difficult days, Cecily had asked Dame Ursula if she could give Sister Philippa her own small statue of the Infant Child of Prague, the sturdy small boy with the crown and orb. 'She hasn't a statue, Mother. I know because I asked her.' Dame Ursula gave permission but Philippa had refused so definitely and firmly that Cecily, young as she was, had sensed something withheld. 'Reserved. Hah!' Dame Agnes had pounced. 'Now we're getting closer. Of course she is adept at keeping her face, but yes, there is a reserve. I think it is something dark.'

'You sound like a clairvoyant,' said Dame Maura, but the Council had not dismissed what Dame Agnes had said.

After living long years on what is a supernatural plane – 'because that is how we try to live' – many of the nuns had a sensitivity to trouble as unerring as if it had a shape, or colour or smell, and several of the councillors had to admit that there were things they could not fathom in Sister Philippa.

'Do you mean something Sister Philippa has done?' Dame Veronica was roused to ask.

'No – no,' said Dame Agnes. 'I think she would have told that – at any rate to Mother.'

'Perhaps it was something done to her,' suggested Dame Catherine and Dame Agnes had lifted her head and nodded.

'That she is holding to.'

'I wonder what it is?' said Dame Veronica with a touch of her old curiosity.

In the Christmas after Abbess Catherine's election Dame Veronica was sadly changed; 'A wraith of herself,' said the nuns. Last year she had been its life and soul, revelled in it, in spite of the extra work which always fell heavily on the cellarer; 'We are such an immense family.' To begin with, almost every nun had a family of her own; fathers, mothers, brothers, sisters, aunts, cousins, friends were mysteriously brought into fellowship with the community and, though Mrs Scallon could not believe it, the families felt this too; they were enlarged through the one who had left them, because now they too had a bond with Brede Abbey. 'I have met people I never dreamed of meeting,' said Dame Nichola's mother.

The community knew the Ismays as they knew the whole tribe of Joneses, Lord and Lady Seaton as they knew Sister Louise's miner father, and many were the cross-family letters and Christmas cards sent out; the nuns wrote most of their Christmas letters and small home-printed cards before Advent began, relying on the extern sisters to post them on suitable dates – while letters and cards and parcels poured in to accumulate for Christmas day. There were very few for Philippa; Maggie faithfully every year sent a snapshot of Griffon 'to show you he is alive and well', and a Christmas cake she had iced herself. Philippa had never had the heart to tell her the Abbey was inundated with cakes and sweets while it was fruit and provender they needed; McTurk though sent three whole cheeses; 'It's expensive having such a large family of friends,' Abbess Catherine wrote to him in thanks and, 'I never thought I should taste Stilton again.' From Joyce Bowman there was a book token, 'which we can always thankfully use,' wrote Philippa, and every year brought a card from Penny; Philippa could imagine her anxious studying of holy pictures, lighted candles or stained-glass windows, suitable for that unknown creature, a nun, but though Philippa always wrote in return for the card, Penny had never come to see her.

Philippa's post was the least but there was another nun who seemed to have no family – or dealings with her family. Dame Veronica had many cards and presents but none, the Abbess noted, from any Fanshawe. 'Has Dame Veronica no relations?' Abbess Catherine, who was worried about Dame Veronica, asked the portress in confidence. 'She has a brother,' said Dame Domitilla. 'He came to see her last August after eleven years. I remember exactly. It was August the 8th. He has made three visits since.' His visits, though, had not seemed to make Dame Veronica exactly happy but Sister Renata, who usually let him in, could have told that he was a queer sort of brother for Dame Veronica. Sister Renata would not criticize or she might have said, 'He looked so shabby and ... "furtive" ' was the word she would have used.

'Perhaps he's a professor,' Sister Susanna, an extern too, had suggested. 'They don't care about their clothes. Or he might be a painter. You know how artistic Dame Veronica is.'

'She has felt Mother's death terribly,' the nuns said now, and yet, 'Why so much more than any of us? We all loved Mother with our whole hearts,' but Dame Veronica looked increasingly haggard and ill.

Checking the outgoing post-bag the Abbess had come across an envelope addressed, 'Paul Fanshawe Esq, Orford Hall, Orford, Lincolnshire'; not an open envelope for a card but a letter. All through Christmas and Epiphany-tide Dame Veronica went to the turn every day to tell Dame Domitilla exactly where she would be – if visitors came unexpectedly it was often difficult to find the nun they wanted to see; there was the sad tale of Dame Teresa's brother on a literally flying visit from New York, arriving without notice, 'for only two hours', and having to go away again without seeing his sister. 'I was up in the bell tower trying to clean out the bells.' No one had thought of looking for Dame Teresa there. 'I shall be in the proc's room,' instructed Dame Veronica, or, 'I am going to the library,' 'I shall be with Lady Abbess,' but, though Dame Domitilla noted it down, nobody came.

In this, Abbess Catherine's first Christmas as Abbess, she

learnt the strength of her twin towers, Dame Agnes and Dame Maura, 'and their generosity,' she said. As mistress of ceremonies and precentrix they 'upheld me,' she told them; Dame Agnes was vigilant to prompt and help through all the complicated ritual, Dame Maura at the organ sustained the Abbess's voice, 'and fitted in with my every breath,' said Abbess Catherine. With Christmas and Epiphany-tide coming so soon after her election, she had made no change in the office holders; 'I will ask the obedientiaries,' she had said in chapter, 'to continue in office until the new appointments.' She could not, for instance, change Dame Beatrice now. 'It wouldn't be fair to plunge a new sacristan straight into the Christmas feasts,' but she herself was faced with this plunge and into the leading role – it is the Abbess who acts as hebdomadarian, taking the lead in choir in all the great feasts of the Church. On the morning of Christmas Eve, in the dim dawn light, the community went in procession to the chapter house to hear her sing the Christmas Martyrology; it was the custom at Brede for the Abbess to sing it, where in other monasteries it was sung by the precentrix, 'and Dame Maura would have done it so beautifully,' mourned Abbess Catherine.

Standing under an arch of holly, evergreens and mistletoe lit by scores of candles, Abbess Catherine began the long chant; not long in words but in its intricacies of melody; it was the chant of Christmas, its mystery and history, from the creation and beginnings of the world, through the Old Testament, the patriarchs, the foundations of Rome, to the opening of the New Testament, 'all woven together into a marvellous whole,' said Cecily. Though, out of respect for Abbess Hester, not one of the community would have uttered it aloud, there was a tonic effect for them all in Abbess Catherine's strong well-rounded voice, her clear enunciation. Abbess Hester's old voice, especially in these last years, had wavered, sometimes quavered and been hoarse and, when she had failed to find a voice at all, as had happened two or three times at Christmas, the prioress, Dame Emily, who had supplied for her, had a tone that, though true, was thin. The Christmas Martyrology, thought the nuns, hasn't come through to us like this for years.

'It was splendid,' said Dame Perpetua in the Abbess's room. 'You made it splendid.'

'It wasn't I,' said Abbess Catherine. '*It* is splendid. That is the blessing of the liturgy, it wipes out self.' She had resolved to put all thought away for these few days, all the difficulties, worries and fears, but some still broke through to her: the stony look on Dom Gervase's face, lit by the candle flames above his white vestments, 'Will he ever take to me?' Dame Veronica white, tight-lipped; it was reported that she had wept all through the midnight Mass, 'and we ran out of candles,' said Dame Perpetua, 'which is her charge.' Even Dame Beatrice was roused to say, 'I put a reminder note in the proc's room three times!'

It was the novitiate's privilege to decorate the choir – 'Well, we clean it every morning,' said Sister Louise – and every year they thought of something different. 'Not just wreaths and evergreens,' said Sister Constance. Sometimes the decorations outstripped themselves. 'Do you remember the year it was all oranges and green paper ribands?' asked Dame Maura. 'It looked like a fair and the oranges fell down on our heads.'

'I remember the year of the apples,' said Dame Veronica. 'They took all our precious Cox's.'

'But when they were polished and put on wreaths they were exceedingly pretty,' said Dame Beatrice.

'Mother's throne looked like a greengrocer's shop,' said Dame Agnes.

On the night of Christmas Eve the Abbey was so still it might have been thought to be empty, or the nuns asleep, but when the bell sounded at ten o'clock, from all corners, especially from the church, silent figures made their way to their station in the long cloister, and Abbess Catherine led them into choir for Christmas Matins. The first nocturn from the book of Isaiah was sung by the four chief chantresses: '*Comfort, comfort my people says your God. Speak tenderly to Jerusalem and cry to her that her warfare is ended, that her iniquity is pardoned. A voice says "Cry!" and I said, "What shall I cry?" All flesh is grass, and all its beauty is like the flower of the field...*' Voice succeeded voice through two hours until the priests, vested in white and gold, with their servers came in procession from the sacristy for the tenderness and triumph of the midnight Mass. Lauds of Christmas followed straight after and at two o'clock the community went to the refectory for hot soup, always called 'cock soup' because it was the first taste of meat or chicken they had had since Advent began; the soup was served with rice – 'beautifully filling,' said Hilary in content – and after it came two biscuits and four squares of chocolate. 'Chocolate!' 'We need to keep our strength up,' said Dame Ursula.

In the twenty-four hours of Christmas they would spend ten hours in choir, singing the Hours at their accustomed times, and the second 'dawn' or 'aurora' Mass of the shepherds as well as the third Mass of Christmas which came after Terce. The wonder was that the nuns had time to eat their Christmas dinner, most of it contributed by friends, 'and at least half given away,' mourned Dame Veronica. Nor was there time to open the letters and parcels. 'Some won't be opened until the new year,' Dame Clare told Cecily. All gifts had to be taken to the Abbess; some were welcome in the proc's room as presents for priests or children, most were shared in the community; some were given back to the nuns for whom they were sent, a few judged unsuitable. 'I'm sorry, Sister Louise, but we can't allow a transistor.' 'This enormous box of chocolates must be kept for the children's party.' 'That scent must go to the parish bazaar.' Talk was allowed all day but there was little time for talk; for one thing, the notice board was weighed down with pleas for prayers, 'but I loved it, loved every moment,' said Cecily. How was it, then, that standing in the empty novitiate common room on Christmas afternoon, she found herself so desolate?

Dinner, and the long grace sung in choir after it, was over and most of the nuns had gone to their cells to rest; even Hilary had flung herself on her bed and fallen asleep, but Cecily was wide awake. The novitiate seemed deserted, the fireless room felt chill and in the grey afternoon light, already turning to shadows, it looked bleak. Cecily was still not used to Brede's absolute plainness; there was nothing in any of its

135

rooms that was not essential for its purpose. In this there was simply a row of lockers, two bookshelves, a long table and upright wooden chairs; the only cushioned chairs were in the infirmary; even the old nuns sat upright, even those in wheel chairs, until they could sit no longer. Walls were white-washed, 'which is at least better than most convents' brown and cream,' Dame Benita used to say, but she longed to make them pink or primrose; the floors were of plain waxed wood, or stone – the refectory was flagged; curtains, when there were any, were plain white. The Abbey's only colour was in the church, in the richness of its stained glass, in altar vestments, red, purple, green, rose, white and gold or black as the days demanded. There was colour in bookbindings, and in the crafts the nuns worked at, their painting, illuminating, weaving, embroidery; it was in flowers and the deep red of votive lamps burning at the foot of the statue of our Lady of Peace in the ante-chapel and, most important of all, before the altar. There were paler colours in the different framings made by the windows, of sky, trees, the garth, the garden or the park beyond.

To Hilary, straight from her Northumbrian castle, the stone corridors and high rooms seemed natural, but the Scallon home, though shabby, had been one of warmth and the cosy prettiness of chintz and white paint. If only there were a fire, thought Cecily. She gazed out where the garden looked sodden, and as desolate as she felt, in the fading light.

'My worst time is twilight,' Philippa had told Cecily.

'Mine is teatime.'

'I never had tea.'

'Tea!' said Hilary. 'Coming in from hunting, stiff and cold and aching, to thaw by a big fire with strong tea, toast, plum cake.'

Cecily had never hunted but, she thought, when people are badly off, as Mrs Scallon never ceased to say the Scallons were, tea was the time for entertaining – except that luncheon party, thought Cecily, wincing – and on Christmas afternoon Mrs Scallon always gathered the relations for tea. All of them, except Cecily, would be there this year; Daphne and her husband home on leave from Hong Kong, the children, the cousins, Jean and Moira, Aunt Elaine, Uncle Timothy. Cecily could hear the chatter, the cousins giggling – they and she had always giggled together. She saw firelight on white walls, the laden tea table with the Christmas cake everybody had stirred – the Scallon family stirred Christmas cake, not pudding. Cecily could smell chrysanthemums and the scent of the violets she had always given her mother for Christmas – I left the money with Dad this year for that. Suddenly she seemed to catch a whiff of the soda mints her father took for his indigestion and, if I stay here I shall cry, thought Cecily. She fled from the novitiate, over the grey garden to the garth. 'You should have your shawl,' Dame Ursula or Dame Clare would have cried, but Dame Ursula and Dame Clare were not there to see. No one was there and Cecily ran on into the empty choir that still smelled of incense. 'I don't suppose I am allowed here at this hour; I should be in the novitiate, but I don't care.' Cecily was not often rebellious but now she was defiant.

She had no place of her own yet in choir – nuns were not allowed a stall until they made their Solemn Profession – and postulants, novices and juniors knelt or sat on either side of the nave, nearest the grille and farthest from the abbatial seat, in pews called the 'nobodies'. Cecily did not go there now but crept up to the organ loft where the big organ was built into its niche, placed so that the organist could see the sanctuary in a mirror, and from which she could follow the Abbess or hebdomadarian.

Cecily ran her hand longingly over the three manuals, the Choir organ, the Great organ for diapason tone mixture and reed and the soft Swell organ enclosed in its box; she dared to switch on the current, draw out a stop. If only I could play something, thought Cecily, I should feel better, but she did not dare. Imagine it, shattering the quiet! Very gently she pressed down a key but even that seemed to strike the walls and vibrate up to the arches so that she hastily took her hand away. She must not even play. Tears began to spatter on the ivory; the more she tried to stop them, the more they came and she let herself down on the floor and, putting her head sideways, clinging to the organ, her tears had their way.

In all those years of futile argument, Mrs Scallon had not once elicited tears, though she had known just where to argue. 'Your father is twelve years older than I. When he goes, I shall be left alone. If I get ill . . .'

'You have Daphne.'

'Daphne is married.'

'You would have let me get married.'

'That's different. Quite different. I should never have been selfish enough to stand in your way for that. You know I hoped and prayed . . .'

Cecily knew very well what her mother had hoped and prayed for and she had said hurriedly, 'Mummy dear, why should you get ill? You're perfectly strong.'

'You're heartless. Utterly heartless.'

Cecily had only wanted to get to Brede – That's why I ran away, thought Cecily, but now – almost – she wanted to run back. If Abbess Hester had been here : if Sister Philippa were still in the novitiate : if there were anyone, someone, and the tears came faster now. The nuns could have told her that no postulant or novice worthwhile, gets through her six months or year without tears, but there was no one to comfort or tell, and Cecily wept until, overcome by the smell of incense, her tiredness and the unaccustomed crying, she sank lower on the floor, her head pillowed against the organ bench, and went to sleep.

Dame Maura, coming up to the loft before None to arrange music for Vespers and Benediction, found her there. All she saw at first was the gleam of a white collar, the pale outline of Cecily's cheek and, where the postulant's veil had slipped back, her hair, a tumble of curls, and Dame Maura was reminded of what she had seen long ago in Assisi, the curls St Francis had cut off from St Clare, the night she ran away to him; through more than seven centuries they had kept their faint gold. Dame Maura switched on the light but it did not wake Cecily and the precentrix saw her lashes were still wet; very tenderly she touched the girl's cheek with her finger but Cecily did not stir, and after a moment Dame Maura slid into the organist's long seat and began to play; she, confident and in charge, had no hesitation in playing on Christmas Day.

Cecily woke to a tide of music coming from over her head; she seemed to be drowning in music and for a moment she was bewildered. Then the wooden walls of the loft, the groined arching above it, the geometrical pattern of the painted front pipes came into focus: beside her were Dame Maura's black skirts, her moving busy feet and Cecily saw where she was, and with whom. Slowly she knelt up, her hand on the bench as she watched Dame Maura's hands and let the peace of the music, the lift it always brought her, flow through her. Dame Maura was playing Bach's 'Jesu, joy of man's desiring', its graceful flowing triplets played on string stops and flutes against the melody, tender as Dame Maura played it: then the chorale was emphasized on a small beautifully voiced reed. The chorale ceased; the triplets grew softer, softer, more caressing, intimate and loving until they came to rest on a chord that was scarcely audible. 'O-oh!' breathed Cecily.

'I think,' said Dame Maura, lifting her hands, 'that Thomas Aquinas and John Sebastian Bach must occupy thrones side by side in heaven.'

'Handel?' Cecily advanced timidly.

'Much lower down, with St Bernard perhaps,' said Dame Maura decidedly. 'St Augustine will be among the cherubim with King David, and whoever it was who composed the Easter Mass.'

'And the plainsong "Christus factus est",' Cecily said it in comradeship and Dame Maura nodded. 'But this was – exquisite,' Cecily touched the music.

Dame Maura got up and, putting out a strong hand, pulled Cecily to her feet. 'You play it.'

'May I?' Dame Maura noticed that Cecily showed no hesitation or fear though she had not touched the big organ before. The precentrix stood behind Cecily listening to every note as the music swelled out, tracing again the pattern of sound she herself had just made, following her, yet making the whole subtly different, lifting it and, Dame Maura thought, giving it an added dimension, a sureness she recognized. This child is going to be a master. Dr Shepherd did his work well.

Cecily finished; she too drawing out that final chord until the last vibration died. Then, 'I needed that,' she said. 'Oh, I needed that!' There was a deep satisfaction in the voice and, Dame Maura thought, relief. 'Would you like,' she asked Cecily, 'to play Lady Abbess into Vespers with that tonight?'

'I? With the Bach?' Again Dame Maura had expected hesitancy, a pleased blush perhaps, but Cecily's face was alight with joy. 'Oh! would you let me?'

'If Dame Ursula makes no objection.'

'She won't. I'm sure she won't. Oh, Dame!' and Cecily got up, came round the organ bench, knelt and, holding Dame Maura's hand in both her own, kissed it.

Dame Maura looked down on the kneeling girl. Then, 'My dear child, I'm not Lady Abbess,' she said and disengaged her hand. She let it rest for a moment on Cecily's hair, straightened the crooked veil, then, 'Dame Ursula will be looking for you,' she said. 'I'll come and speak to her later..You had better run back to the novitiate now.'

On the twenty-ninth of December, the feast of St Thomas of Canterbury, the Archbishop came to Brede to give Abbess Catherine the abbatial blessing and formally enthrone her in the presence of the whole community, of the Abbot President, Abbot Bernard and his monks, and of her own family. To her great joy, Bishop Mark Ismay was at a special prie-dieu in the sanctuary.

'I clung to St Thomas,' Abbess Catherine told Mark afterwards, 'and tried not to think of myself.' St Thomas of Canterbury, martyr in the ranks of the martyrs that have had fresh recruits in every age since the death of Christ. St Thomas, a Catholic murdered by Catholics, died for the Church's liberty and, a bishop may not flee, like the hireling shepherd, thought Abbess Catherine, nor may he hold his peace; he is bound to preach, 'in season and out of season', no matter how unpopular he becomes – unpopular even to death. '*I am the Good Shepherd.*' The words of the Gospel as the deacon read them, '*I am the Good Shepherd. I know my sheep and my sheep know me,*' became a living actuality for her.

140

That was the meaning of the crook. Abbess Hester's family had had a crook made for her, a stem of rosewood with a crook of silver, embossed with the roses of the Cunningham family – 'roses with thorns,' said Abbess Hester – and tipped with ivory. To Abbess Catherine's delight Bishop Mark brought her a plain crook from the Sussex downs. 'Beautiful as Mother's was, I like this far, far better,' said Abbess Catherine. Abbess Hester had had her coat of arms above the abbatial chair, but Abbess Catherine was a country doctor's daughter and had a simple crest. Even so she preferred to use the Abbey's. 'Let me keep to simplicity,' she said. Only that, she felt, and humility could balance this terrifying power.

6

When the archbishop had given Abbess Catherine the crook he
had said, 'Receive full and free power to rule this monastery
and community of Brede and everything that is known to per-
tain to the same, within and without, in spirituals and temporals.' Today it was temporals.

Two days after Epiphany, the eighth of January, Abbess
Catherine had declared a 'cell' day, a day on which domestic
work was cut to a minimum and the nuns need not attend their
workshops; apart from choir and refectory, they were free to
do as they liked. In summer many of them would have gar-
dened – they loved to give Dame Mildred an extra hand and
many of them had some small patch in the gardens for which
they were responsible; Dame Teresa's bog garden round the
pond had been made entirely by herself as had Dame
Camilla's herb patch. 'My fingers itch to get at some earth,'
she said, but it was too cold for gardening, though Dame
Mildred could be seen intrepidly raking up leaves for her
cherished compost heap. Dame Benita went to help her 'as a
change from the studio,' she said, but most went to their cells
or the warmer common room to catch up with letters – all
those Christmas 'thank you's'. 'I am going to spend the day on
my bed with a book,' announced Dame Agnes, while Dame
Maura, who had been sent a tape of Mozart's four Horn Con-
certos played by Dennis Brain, said she would be holding a
music session if anyone cared to hear it in the music library.

'Mother Mistress,' said Cecily, 'Dame Maura says she has
permission for me – for us – to go to the music library and
hear Dennis Brain playing Mozart if you say "yes".'

'I'm sorry I can't say "yes",' said Dame Ursula. The novitiate were making a shadow mime of The Fleury Play of Herod for Abbess Catherine's feast on April 30th; that was a long time off, but the puppets and stage had to be made, the score rehearsed and, 'We have so little spare time, so this is a golden opportunity to start,' said Dame Clare. Cecily was singing the Angel and, 'That's the opening solo, the Angel's address to the shepherds; they can't do without you,' said Dame Ursula. 'Run along.'

'Yes, Mother.' There was not a murmur or the plea, 'Mother, couldn't we *possibly* rehearse this afternoon?' as Sister Constance would have said – not even a trace of disappointment, and Dame Ursula sighed.

The novice mistress was old and experienced. She had been able to deal without a ruffle with ebullient Julian, as she dealt now with Sister Louise's hasty judgements and her jealousies, with Sister Constance's faint slyness, with forthright Hilary. Only that morning Hilary had bounced in on Dame Ursula in her cell, where the novice mistress was writing a letter. 'Mother, have I a vocation?'

Dame Ursula had looked up mildly, 'Only you can answer that.' Then quietly she added, 'I think you have a very strong vocation.'

'Damn,' said Hilary but Dame Ursula had heard her telling the others proudly, 'Teddy thinks I have a strong vocation.' That was natural, lovable, as were Hilary's faults; she was always in trouble with Sister Jane. 'Sister Hilary, have you *never* cleaned a saucepan before?'

'No,' said Hilary.

'Thorough, you must be thorough,' was Sister Jane's maxim. 'I could never canonize a saint who wasn't thorough.' She was in charge of the cells and often saved the girls from trouble. 'Sister Constance, you have left your window off the latch *again*. One day it will blow into the garden. I did it for you *this* time,' and she would do it again, but she was appalled at Hilary's untidiness. 'Anyone would think you had had a nanny to pick up after you.'

'I had,' said Hilary.

Sister Cecily was of different calibre; what calibre, Dame Ursula, experienced as she was, found difficult to say. When Sister Cecily was pleased or touched, she was 'transfigured,' Dame Ursula said; happiness shone through her, 'as if she only had one skin.' Dame Ursula was not given to flights of fancy but, by her refusal just now, she felt as if she had snuffed out a light – which was of course exaggerated. Was Sister Cecily herself exaggerated? 'If there is any instability, religious life will make it worse.' That was a precept every Abbess and novice mistress had to keep in mind but Sister Cecily was not unstable. Dame Ursula knew, as the Abbess and Council knew, of the long steady battle Cecily had fought for her vocation; how tenaciously she had held to her purpose; and how sensibly she had prepared herself, 'though Mummy never guessed what lay behind the music. Poor Mummy!'

For that Christmas Day Vespers, Sister Cecily had played with the greatest aplomb; and yet aplomb was not a word that seemed to belong to Sister Cecily. 'Is this your girl who was so timid and shaky?' Dame Agnes had asked.

'Her music, such a gift, is of course the greatest help,' said Dame Ursula and, 'Work is a great splint,' said Dame Clare.

'To hold a weak limb?' asked Dame Agnes.

'But is Sister Cecily weak?' That had come up when Dame Ursula had been making her monthly report on the novitiate to the Abbess and Council and, over Sister Cecily Scallon, had called in her zelatrix.

'Is Sister Cecily weak?'

'I don't know,' Dame Clare had said. 'I cannot, as it were, see her.'

'In what way, Dame?'

'There's her timidity, her quietness – the way she takes refuge under someone's wing.' 'Abbess Hester's,' Dame Clare and Dame Ursula could both have said that; Sister Philippa's and – as they knew perfectly well – now it was Dame Maura's – 'Yet paradoxically there's a steadiness,' said Dame Ursula, 'and a serenity.'

'And great sweetness,' said Dame Maura.

'I find myself baffled,' said Dame Clare. 'No, I don't see

her,' and she had said slowly, 'of course, being a postulant is tricky.'

'Yes, one is a sort of hybrid,' said Dame Maura. 'It's far better when one is clothed.'

'Then you see what they are really like,' said Dame Ursula. 'But . . .'

'But, Dame?'

'We don't want to hold out false hopes.'

'Being a postulant is tricky,' Dame Clare had repeated that as if she had hold of the tail of some idea and wanted to catch it before it vanished. 'Sister Cecily doesn't seem to find it tricky.'

'She was woefully homesick on Christmas Day,' said Dame Maura.

'I'm glad to hear it,' said Dame Ursula. 'Someone without feelings and faults to conquer . . .'

'That's it!' broke in Dame Clare. 'She hasn't any faults, and that makes her . . . like a person without a shadow.'

'Perhaps there are no shadows for her,' suggested Dame Beatrice, but Dame Ursula had shaken her head. 'There must be,' and on this cell day, 'How did Sister Cecily sing the Angel?' she asked Dame Clare.

'Truly almost perfectly,' said Dame Clare and Dame Ursula sighed.

Dame Perpetua went to Dame Maura's session – music was a deep love – and, 'If Dame Anastasia came too,' she asked Philippa, 'could you manage the telephone and answer Mother's bell?'

'Of course,' said Philippa. Abbess Catherine seldom rang her bell; she still instinctively got up to go in search of anyone she needed, besides, 'I like to go about among you,' she said when Dame Perpetua tried to save her but today she was too busy to come out of her room; once again she was engrossed by the Abbey accounts.

It had been the duty of the two depositarians, those inde-fatigable book-keepers to prepare the 'status' of the Abbey and present it to the new Abbess; for the last few days Abbess

Catherine had been going through it and, as if the nuns sensed she had a heavy task, they forbore to knock at her door, that incessant knocking, all the minutiae of requests and permissions. 'May I lend this book to Dom Placid O'Hara?' 'Mrs Forrester is coming to the parlour at half past four. She has suggested that Professor Forrester gives a lecture to us on the twenty-fifth or twenty-sixth. What shall I say to her?' 'May I write to the *Tablet* about...?' 'Mother, I feel so tired, I don't know what to do with myself. May I have a morning's rest?'

'Almost everything you ask, in reason, will be allowed,' Dame Ursula had told her novitiate, 'but remember, the best nuns are those who try not to ask.' Yet, even for these, there were many occasions when they had to go to the Abbess's room. It's an iniquitous system, Philippa had thought at first, but was it? She, Philippa, or another nun secretary, sitting just outside in the alcove, could have taken half a dozen messages and requests and brought them in at one time, but that would have meant coming between the Abbess and her flock.

Like many things at Brede, it was wiser than at first appeared; the Abbess was taxed in time and patience, but in this way she knew and could keep a finger on everything that happened in the Abbey; it gave her a closeness to her nuns that nothing else could have done. An Abbess has to know even what she would far rather not know, and Philippa soon learned to keep her eyes on her work and away from the continual comings and goings – though how Mother gets anything done, I don't know, thought Philippa.

'It's why I can't get to grips with these books,' Abbess Catherine could have told her.

The heavy account books, made and bound in the Abbey,. were minutely kept and had to be totalled every month and brought to the Abbess to approve and sign, but had Abbess Hester gone, not just through them, but into them? wondered Abbess Catherine. The account books were, of course, familiar to her; as cellarer she had spent ten years with them and there were much the same entries; the same names: grocer, butcher, fishmonger, hardware shops; there were items for travel: Dame Edith to London to see an eye specialist; an especial specialist – Dame Edith's eyes were valuable to the community: fare, expenses, specialist's fee, were all carefully noted down: there were payments for clothing – though we make most of our own: shoe repairs :\ once we did our own, perhaps we shall have to again: stationery, a heavy expense as was postage and money spent on books; these were unchanged – except the figures. 'Expenses have risen,' she had said to Dame Veronica after the first cursory look.

'I knew you would say that.' There had been something less than respect in Dame Veronica's tone. 'Costs have risen too.'

'As much as this?'

'Yes.' It was unadorned and Abbess Catherine had felt the latent hostility, but she knew that for Dame Veronica there could have been no more dislikeable choice for Abbess than herself – an Abbess who had been cellarer – and who knew the work through and through. Dame Veronica had added, almost with defiance, 'Mother approved.'

The Abbey's money came in four ways: in rents from its farm, its outlying cottages and the grazing rights on the marshes it owned: from its earnings which were meagre – Benedictines were bound to charge modest, often less than commercial, prices for their wares: from old-age pensions and a few widows' pensions, though these were outbalanced by stamp payments for the younger nuns: by gifts, and donations including dowries which at Solemn Profession could be invested. The books and files for these last were kept locked, only the Abbess, prioress and cellarer were allowed to see them; it was these that were on Abbess Catherine's desk now and, as she turned the pages, more and more they dismayed her: the cottages where the Abbey's old pensioners lived – a former shepherd, 'from the days when we had sheep': a retired handyman: Burnell's old and indigent parents – were mortgaged, as was a good deal of the land; mortgages and second mortgages, noted Abbess Catherine, turning the pages; shares too had been sold and the Abbey's resources had dwindled – to danger point. On the margins were pencilled figures as if Abbess Hester had tried to make the accounts add up differently but they were of course correct. Yet Dame

147

Bridget, that careful depositarian and her aid, must have wondered – and worried. Then why didn't they speak? wondered the Abbess. Why didn't Dame Veronica? Why had they not warned Abbess Hester and the Council? They had simply accepted: it was blind obedience and into Abbess Catherine's mind came the words that Dame Perpetua had since told her Doctor Avery had said: 'I do blame you. You were like sheep,' and, 'Talk about the divine right of kings.' With a sinking heart Abbess Catherine wondered what the Abbot President would say, and wondered too how much of this he' knew. The accounts had to be presented to him every three years and were due to be shown in the course of the present one; she scalded at the thought.

There was no blunting the fact that things had become lax; well, business and accounts are not Dame Veronica's strong point, she thought, but Mother ... Abbess Catherine wanted to shy away from the thought of criticizing Abbess Hester, yet when she looked at the accounts for building, she was as astounded as she was dismayed. What Lady Abbess had done! When one added it up, what she had spent! And how cunningly, thought Abbess Catherine. Her right hand must hardly have known what her left hand did, and she had thoroughly hoodwinked her Council. First a window restored here, an arch uncovered there; steps put back to their original stone, but not essential steps, and echoes of Dame Edith's perpetual request to the Council came now to Abbess Catherine. 'Can't we have proper steps in the print room?'

As the printing work expanded – and it had done wonders under Dame Edith's clever hand – it had been necessary to take in a third room and a door had been cut to the old dairy from the second printing room; unfortunately the dairy was on a different level and until steps could be built up to it, Dame Edith had contrived temporary steps with boxes, not exactly safe for anyone carrying heavy plates or rolls of paper; 'It's just while we wait,' Dame Edith said.

'You'll wait,' predicted Dame Agnes.

The steps were still that flight of boxes but the building work had not been all for appearance; it was Abbess Hester who had put in the central heating, 'But she encouraged us to economize on that,' the Council had to admit, and it was always breaking down. 'Mother isn't interested in central heating,' said Dame Agnes. 'It's old stone.' 'Stone disease, if you ask me,' said Dame Agnes.

'Dame, that isn't fair,' said Dame Veronica. 'Mother thought of the sluice in the infirmary and the lift; think what a boon that, especially, has been.' It was a boon; nuns who were crippled or had bad hearts could get down to the choir, the garden, the parlours; it had changed their lives but, 'we never had these things before,' said Dame Agnes.

'Poor people don't,' said Dame Perpetua. 'They take the rough with the smooth.'

'And we must live like the poor.'

'If we have such monies,' and Dame Agnes sounded doubtful, 'they should be used, not for ourselves, but for apostolic purposes. Perhaps towards a foundation . . .' It was still a grief that Brede had never made one. Pixham Abbey had made a thriving foundation in Brazil, 'and *look* what Dom Benet Owen is doing in Bangalore.' The younger nuns said that wistfully.

'You can hardly make two dreams come true.' Dame Agnes's third eye saw that most clearly. 'Mother's dream just now is stones and mortar.'

There had been endless warnings among the senior nuns on the Council, endless . . . preventions, thought Abbess Catherine now, but still a bathroom had been added to the infirmary, another was building in the novitiate; Abbess Hester had wanted six for the community, 'and that's not enough.'

'But Mother, we should have to go on the mains. Our pump could never give so much water. We should have to pay water rates. Think of the cost.'

'Cost! Cost! Cost! That's all you ever think about.'

'We have to think of the cost.' The bathrooms had been voted down in chapter. The new cloisters had been built because they were the gift of a novice's father, 'but a limited gift,' Mother Prioress, Dame Emily, had warned Abbess Hester. As it had been a large expenditure the whole chapter had

149

had to be consulted; stone to match the old long cloister would have been prohibitive in cost and the nuns had voted for the comparative cheapness of plain red brick, the floor to be of tiles, easily cleaned, with windows that could be opened in summer and, 'closed in winter,' said the older nuns gratefully. 'Brick!' Abbess Hester had moaned in despair. 'They have no eyes.'

'You can't expect them to have,' Dame Veronica, that ardent confidante had said. '*They* are not artists.'

In Abbess Hester's last two years Dame Veronica had been much to the fore, important and self-important.

'Our cellarer is a magician,' Abbess Hester told architects and builders. 'She'll find the money,' and Dame Veronica had blossomed on the admiration but, '*How* is it found, Dame?' asked Dame Agnes.

'Oh, economizing, whittling down on something else.'

'Are you quite sure it is not the Abbey's reserves that are being whittled down?' asked Dame Agnes.

It was Dame Veronica who, two years ago, had suggested – 'As if anything needed suggesting' – that the long cloister should be restored. 'It's of historical interest,' she had said in Council, 'and the work needn't be very expensive. In fact, we needn't put it to the chapter – and it would please Mother so much.' To the Council's surprise, Mother Prioress, Dame Emily, had voted for it, with the Abbess, Dame Veronica and unpractical Dame Beatrice. Why? Mother Prioress was usually sensible and restraining. Why? And Dame Agnes, Dame Maura and Dame Catherine, silenced and worried, had unwillingly guessed the answer: Dame Emily had reasoned it could not cost a great deal – and will keep Mother quiet and happy. Had it come to this? they asked themselves; had this become a mania? The word had hung in the room; they would not even whisper it. Had Lady Abbess Hester really got Dame Agnes's stone disease?

Unfortunately the long cloister took more money and time than they had dreamed. In the high arch at the southern end that led into the ante-chapel and choir the architect had seen a small patch of loose stonework; he had climbed up a ladder to investigate and pulled some of the stones out by hand; tell-tale white strands were revealed that, when the top of the wall was opened, spread in a dense white cobweb up the vaulted ceiling. Dry rot. The dreadful words sounded through the Abbey. In conscience, he said, he must examine farther. 'Into the roof of the choir where the timbers are equally old; it may have spread.' The fungus had indeed spread, but the other way; the lead covering on the choir roof had deteriorated, 'and seriously,' he said, 'letting the rain in,' and the rot had spread to the cloister roof from the underside of the gutter which ran the whole length of the choir wall; the seating of the queen post trusses supporting the roof were affected too. 'In fact, if we had *not* restored the cloister, the choir roof might one day have come crashing down on our heads,' Abbess Hester had said.

'Yes, it was providential,' said Dame Beatrice, but the bill had been over four thousand pounds. That was when the Abbot President had allowed the mortgages; had had to allow them. 'And how shall we repay them?' Dame Agnes had asked.

'Somehow,' Dame Veronica had said it so blithely that Dame Agnes lost her temper.

'*How*, Dame?' 'But all that happens, if you ask a direct question,' said Dame Agnes afterwards, 'is that Dame Veronica looks pathetic, her chin starts to quiver and Mother tells you to leave her alone.'

'Her task is quite difficult enough without this continual criticism,' Abbess Hester had said severely.

The second time Abbess Catherine had made an assault on the books Dame Veronica had not been available. Dame Joan had put her to bed for three days' complete rest. 'Why she seems so ill when she isn't at all, I don't know,' the infirmarian told the Abbess. 'Doctor Avery says he can find nothing wrong; of course she herself is convinced that she has a weak heart and half a dozen other things – an ulcer among them. Can't you talk to her, Mother?'

Abbess Catherine wanted to say, 'I can't,' but instead, 'I will try. Meanwhile rest would be wise.' Meanwhile, too, she herself had to try and plumb these swollen figures.

'What is this item that keeps recurring?' she had asked Dame Bridget, the first depositarian. 'S.F. What does that mean?'

'It stands for Sinking Fund,' said Dame Bridget.

'Why only initials?'

'Because I wasn't sure it was that. To begin with it was, but afterwards ... we didn't know what to put. Mother ... Lady Abbess ... started it as a fund to help pay off a small loan we had from the bank when we installed the lift.'

'I remember,' said Dame Catherine. 'But that was repaid.'

'Yes, but Mother kept this one, a savings bank to help pay for some extra building; any sum over from different expenditure was put into it; small change given back from expenses: little donations ...'

Dame Winifred, the second cellarer, had confirmed this and, 'Mother sold a few things,' she added.

'Sold them?' Abbess Catherine was startled. 'Without telling us?'

'Oh, nothing valuable. Dame Veronica knew, and,' Dame Winifred hastened to explain, 'they were small superfluous things, some of them had been unused for years. I remember some Victorian candlesticks. They went to a little church in Wales, very reasonably.'

'I thought they were a gift.'

'No, Mother. And there was some lace. We don't use that any more.' Dame Winifred hesitated. 'The lace was valuable. I think Dame Beatrice thought it had gone to be repaired. It is all entered,' said Dame Winifred.

'There must be quite a sum in the fund by now,' said Dame Bridget and, when Dame Winifred had gone, 'I think that Mother was saving up for one of her pet schemes, repairing the old fountain in the garth. She always wanted to be rescuing something, as you know.'

Stone disease. Abbess Catherine tried not to think that.

'Is this a separate account?' she had asked Dame Bridget. 'There is nothing in the bank statements.'

'It wasn't in the bank,' said Dame Bridget. 'I didn't like it, but Mother kept it in an old money box. I entered it as "Sink-

152

ing Fund", because I couldn't very well write "money box" for the monks and Father Abbot to see. It seemed a little like keeping cash in a teapot but Mother relished little schemes like that. It wasn't so little though,' said Dame Bridget. 'There should be something near a hundred pounds in there now. I have entered ninety-three pounds, eleven shillings and three-pence, but Mother often slipped in little extras without telling me. There may be even more than a hundred pounds.'

'Sister, have you seen a money box?'

'Where Mother kept her pennies?' asked Sister Ellen. 'Dear! how could I have forgotten to give that to you. See, here in the little cupboard in the panelling.'

'I didn't know there was a cupboard.'

Sister Ellen had chuckled. 'Mother would have liked you to say that! She always said she should be allowed one secret,' and the Sister had shown Abbess Catherine a hinged panel over the fireplace. 'I'm so bent over I have to stand on a chair to reach it and so had Mother, but you are tall enough. I hope it isn't sooty. It usually is,' said Ellen. 'Wait, my Lady, I'll fetch a duster,' she scuttled out, while the Abbess looked at the box in its niche.

It was a child's money box, a miniature cash or deed box with a handle and slit in the lid, brought by some long-ago postulant perhaps to hold her humble savings – if they could, claustral sisters brought the sum of twenty pounds with them.

Sister Ellen had done that. When she was young, in her hamlet parish in Ireland, the priest had given her a pamphlet in which there was an article by Lady Abbess Scholastica Bruce Grey of Brede, Abbess before Abbess Gertrude, who was before Abbess Dorothy, who was before Abbess Hester. Sister Ellen loved to tell how she had read the article and then and there made up her mind, 'That's the lady for me.' She had asked the priest to write the necessary letters for her and, saving literally penny by penny until she had the twenty pounds, she had found her way to Brede. 'I walked right in and never walked out,' said Sister Ellen.

Abbess Catherine had touched the little money box gently;

it had held, she was sure, months and years of purpose, devotion and toil, and, 'Mother relished little schemes like that,' Dame Bridget had said. With the understanding of love, Abbess Catherine had almost heard Abbess Hester's own chuckle at this private small device for getting around the Council and contriving her own way. It was not exactly monastic procedure but there was no real harm in it, and the chuckles would have been gleeful, Abbess Catherine had thought with tenderness – rather like a child's – or Sister Ellen's. Perhaps we could restore the fountain in the garth with this money as a tribute, thought Abbess Catherine. Mother hated to see it broken.

Sister Ellen brought the duster and Abbess Catherine had reached up and carefully wiped the box; 'It's clean,' said Sister Ellen in surprise. 'I must have dusted it and forgotten. Usually it makes the duster black!' Sister Ellen pattered away and Abbess Catherine lifted the money box down; it chinked but, it's not very heavy, she had thought.

She had carried it to her desk and searching among the keys in the drawer, had found one that fitted, turned it in the lock, and lifted the lid; inside were three shillings in coppers.

When Dame Veronica was back in the community, Abbess Catherine had asked her about the money box. 'Can you throw any light on this, Dame?'

There was no answer. A curious stillness had come over Dame Veronica. She is going to faint, the Abbess had thought and half rose in alarm, but Dame Veronica had answered. 'I suppose . . . Mother spent it.'

'A hundred pounds, without telling us?'

'It wasn't all that. It couldn't have been.'

'Dame Bridget says it was.'

'This perpetual totting up, totting up!' Dame Veronica burst out. 'This niggling, niggling.'

'This was a sinking fund, Dame, Abbey money. It has to be accounted for.'

'Suppose I tell you it was not a sinking fund, not latterly.'

'What was it then?'

'A private charity.'

The way Dame Veronica had said those words had given Abbess Catherine a strange apprehension as if a warning bell had sounded; the next words did nothing to lighten it. 'I'm telling you the truth.'

'Why shouldn't you?' but even as the Abbess said that she had known that nuns do not have private charities, not even an Abbess and she had to ask, 'What charity?'

'It was private.'

'Dame Veronica, I know you had Mother's confidence, but Mother is dead. A hundred pounds, or ninety-six or whatever it was, is a large sum of money – for us. If you know where it went – and I presume you do – you will have to tell us.'

For a moment she had thought Dame Veronica would tell; her hands twisted, the chin quivered and she half turned towards the Abbess, as if she were on the brink of – something, thought the Abbess, who kept still and found herself inwardly praying. Then Dame Veronica lifted her eyes. 'Mother, will you give me a little time?'

Dame Veronica had not called Abbess Catherine 'Mother' before; her voice was soft and, moved, the Abbess had looked at her, but there was no softness in the eyes, and Abbess Catherine had known with certainty that Dame Veronica was acting. Acting! But why? In bewilderment, Abbess Catherine had let her go.

The almost empty money box had given Abbess Catherine a shock, shocked her into reality, she admitted afterwards. To hoard money in a secret place was a little thing – indulgently she had thought that before she opened it – a little thing, but was it? 'Allow one small fault and you will get another.' How often had her novice mistress, Dame Emily, wise Mother Prioress, said that? Dame Ursula was probably saying it now in the novitiate – and in an Abbess a fault is magnified. 'To whom more is committed, more is required,' said the Rule. On this cell day, Abbess Catherine's heart was heavy and she felt the humble light wooden pectoral cross as heavy too, almost unbearably heavy, on her breast. It was not the money that worried her most, or not chiefly the money; with scrupulous care and economy and a new firm cellarer – I must hold the Change of Offices very soon – resources could be built up again. It was what was taking place in Dame Veronica that was the searing worry, and what had taken place in – 'Mother,' whispered Abbess Catherine. The figures in the long columns were beginning to dance in front of her eyes and she got up and went to the window; spears of rain were falling, darkening the garth and the roof of the new cloister where she could see one or two of the nuns, wrapped in their cloaks, pacing in spite of the strong westerly wind that often blew through Brede. My daughters, thought Abbess Catherine, many older than myself. 'It will be hard for you, coming after Abbess Hester,' the Archbishop had said, when he had talked to her alone in the parlour on the day of her blessing; he had meant, coming after the fame and veneration, the friendship and the wit. This was another kind of inheritance. 'If I only knew what it was, what is wrong, I could face it,' whispered Abbess Catherine. 'If I could only know.'

Philippa would have liked, this cell day, to do what Dame Agnes was doing, lie on her bed with a book, but she had been watchful; since that moment, never betrayed, when she had seen Abbess Catherine broken down for those few minutes in Sister Ellen's arms, she had felt bound to her Abbess in an especial way. Meeting her later that day Philippa had gone down on her knee in the corridor and kissed Abbess Catherine's hand, murmuring, 'I am so glad.' The pressure of her fingers had been returned with a whispered, 'Pray for me.' No other sign had passed between them; Philippa had come in and out with letters, taken orders – sometimes Abbess Catherine did not even lift her head from her writing – but Philippa knew, without telling, that her presence, working quietly outside the door, gave some support and, more than ever that morning, she felt she would rather not leave the Abbess.

'You make me feel guilty,' Dame Perpetua had said.

'Dear Dame! You have worked day and night. Go and enjoy the music. You know it would be wasted on me. I have nothing else to do and there's a pile of letters not even opened yet.'

Now Philippa was clearing her desk, not as quickly as in the old days but even more carefully. A quality she had long seen and appreciated in the monastery letters and writings was their clarity; even the nuns' handwriting seemed to become as unmistakable and clear as their thoughts. 'Well, they are un-cluttered,' said Philippa. The typewriter she was using was antique but polished to cleanliness and she had to smile when she thought of what her old office, Penny Stevens in particular, would have said if they could have seen their Mrs Talbot now, answering the telephone but referring all important calls to Dame Perpetua or Lady Abbess, as Penny herself had done to Miss Bowman, taking them letters, written or typed, to sign – Penny had not been allowed to do that for her.

Most of the letters were condolences: from friends or other houses and Orders. 'I see by the obituary notices that your dear and venerated Lady Abbess has gone home to God . . .'

'I was sad to read that Lady Abbess Hester Cunningham Proctor . . .'

'Our prayers and love are with you.'

'No one was like her . . .'

'Your hearts must ache . . .'

To each went a letter and a copy of the memorial written by Dame Agnes and duplicated by Dame Edith in hundreds on her machine. 'You may not have heard that Dame Emily Lovell, our prioress, was taken ill . . .' Philippa finished her sheet, slid out her paper and addressed the envelope, put it on the pile for Dame Perpetua to sign and reached for the next letter.

It came from Paris and was written in a bold, careless hand, using black ink; the paper was thick, its envelope addressed simply to 'Brede Abbey, Brede, East Sussex.' As Philippa slit it open, a photograph fell out, a postcard-size photograph of a bas-relief in stone, a tall Saint Benedict holding a crook and the book of the Holy Rule. She looked at its few lines, it's not finished, thought Philippa, but already austere, expressive, strong and beautiful. A feeling stirred that she knew whose work it was.

The letter began: 'Mesdames,' which was unusual; it was

written in French. As she began to read it Philippa thought it another letter of condolence:

'It was with sincere regret that, coming back to Paris, I learned of the death of Lady Abbess Cunningham Proctor. The day Sir Basil brought me to Brede, I was deeply impressed by our meeting; to meet her again was each time a pleasure but her letters I shall keep all my life and it made me happy to work for her.'

Work for her? wondered Philippa.

'I do not know to whom I should write but if it is to a newly appointed Abbess, may I salute you. As you will see from the photographs the St Benedict is almost finished; I think it has come out well. Indeed we are all highly pleased here and hope you will be too. St Scholastica you have seen, so that the two side panels are ready to complete. The stone has been cut for the rest; the altar block is ready and the crucifix finished. I am ready to carve on site.

We shall therefore prepare for the dismantling at Brede straight after Epiphany as we had planned and I have arranged with Messrs Berthoud and Sons to start on this work on the 12th January.'

In four days' time! thought Philippa, startled.

'As soon as they have finished – they estimate about a fortnight – I shall arrive. I shall bring three men and two lorries so you will be invaded. Indeed I would postpone as you have had this so recent death, but am anxious to get to Chicago where a work is waiting for me. Also you, Madame Abbess, would like the new apse and altar in place for Easter. We shall be quick and careful.'

It had a footnote: 'I enclose the account for the stonework,' and was signed 'Stefan Duranski'.

Duranski! I thought I recognized him, recognized his work,

thought Philippa. No wonder the St Benedict was beautiful. Duranski has not done anything better, she thought, studying the photograph. 'Then you know his work?' Dame Perpetua was to ask and Philippa had to refrain from saying, 'Everybody knows it.' If this was only one panel, what would the whole be? And, thinking of the yellow and dark plum-colour mottled marble of the present altar, the barley sugar twisting of the pillars upholding the ornate canopy, the simpering cherubs of the painted reredos, Philippa rejoiced, but the letter was not hers and should be seen at once. She got up and knocked at the Abbess's door.

'Benedicite, Mother. I was told to read all letters that came in French but this is for you, and in view of the time-factor it's important.'

Abbess Catherine looked up, dazed with figures. 'Who is it from?'

'Stefan Duranski, the sculptor.'

'A condolence?'

'No, Mother. It's to say the altar and panels for the church are ready.'

'The altar?' The dazed look went, as if the Abbess had been given an electric shock. Philippa laid the photograph and letter in front of her. Abbess Catherine read it through once, twice, then asked, as if still more shocked, 'Where is the account?'

'I think it's under the letter.'

'Did you look at it?'

'No, Mother.'

The Abbess looked and looked again. Then, 'Please find Dame Veronica,' she said.

For the first time since Abbess Hester's death, Dame Veronica was happy – or had found a short respite from unhappiness. No letter had come for her, no visitor – but as the new year came in without a message or a visit and Epiphany passed, Dame Veronica knew there would be none, and knew the storm must break. Two or three times she had gone to the Abbess's door, once even lifted her hand to knock and could not. 'Not to her,' whispered Dame Veronica and each time had gone away to her stall in choir, meaning to wrestle this out with herself – those stalls had seen many battles – but none like this, thought Dame Veronica, none, and she tingled with shame and dread. It was the shame she could not face. She tried to pray but could not. 'Nemesis must overtake me. Till then I'm not fit to pray.'

She was better in the proc's room, surrounded by mundane things, duties to be discharged, endless small worries, requests that kept her mercifully busy, and the broken knees of the figure on the crucifix comforted her; He had known what it was to fall. He knew agony and He would understand. Dame Veronica was frightened now of God, but not of Him, Christ, God made man, was human. Human! He can understand, and now, suddenly, on the morning of this cell day He had sent her a small unexpected balm; Dame Veronica was finishing a poem.

She had begun it in Advent in the dreary days after Abbess Catherine's election, been 'vouchsafed' part of it – Dame Veronica always said her poems were 'vouchsafed' – but only part, and in her worry and stress she had not been able to finish it. Now Dame Winifred, in an effort to cheer her superior, had brought in some winter jasmine and put it in the vase on Dame Veronica's desk. Dame Winifred could not have known the poem was about winter jasmine. Against the centre arch of the long cloister Dame Mildred had planted a cutting and it had grown into an enormous bush, its dark green sprays starred with yellow were effective against the grey stone.

Dame Veronica often rearranged more artistically flowers that other nuns had done, 'Then wonders they are annoyed,' Abbess Hester had said. Dame Veronica rearranged Dame Winifred's and had started the poem again:

> Each year a pang; first shiver of the birth
> of our December spring.
> The earth
> Trembles into yellow. These Advent flowers bring
> promise . . .

It was coming and, to add to the balm, Dame Edith had

come up from the printing room to tell Dame Veronica they planned to reprint her book of poems. 'We are sold right out and it is still in demand.'

'Does Dame Agnes know?' but Dame Veronica stifled that question as unworthy. She could never quite vanquish her chagrin that in the community it was Dame Agnes who was regarded as Brede's first author, 'Though she has only edited collections of letters, written treatises, done translations of Hroswitha and of Aelfric's Sermons and is still on her big book.'

'Only,' said Dame Edith.

'It's not creative,' argued Dame Veronica.

Dame Agnes was the first to acknowledge that. 'I'm only a grubber,' she would have said but it was remarkable grubbing; there was her book; for fifteen years – 'Fifteen years!' said Dame Veronica – Dame Agnes had been researching on the Holy Cross as found in English literature, art and devotion. 'Not that there's any difficulty in discovering material,' she said. On the contrary, she often thought she was drowning in it. Many people had heard of the great poem, 'The Dream of the Rood', but there was a mine of other treasure in medieval English writings, in romance, and lyrics and carols, and the literature often merged into devotion. Aelfric's sermons had started her off and she had just finished translating the Portiforium or personal prayer book of St Wulstan of Worcester. '1059,' said Dame Agnes and her face filled with reverence as she described it to the nuns at recreation. 'It contains what is almost a "little office", a complete litany on the Holy Cross. It's beautifully copied in Latin and West Saxon by a scribe who evidently wrote both alphabets.'

'But when is it to be published?' asked Dame Veronica as she always asked.

'When it is finished.' The answer was always the same. Meanwhile Dame Veronica's book had come out and she was collecting poems for another. 'Then why should Dame Agnes . . .' but today her mind was too filled with the jasmine poem for such nagging questions:

See. The wands are tipped
spear sharp with sorrow.
but that will be tomorrow...
The first stone spatters the Child...

When Philippa knocked and came in, Dame Veronica was jerked back into the unwelcome present. 'One moment, please,' she said, before Philippa could speak. She left the poem; her hands fluttered over the table, moving objects; she wrote a swift note, took up some papers, put them down again, tried to put a bill on a spiked holder but did not succeed so that the bill fell on the floor. Philippa picked it up and put it on the spike but Dame Veronica did not notice. She got up and went to a cupboard to put some electric light bulbs away, then altered their shelf. She scarcely knows what she is doing, thought Philippa. When at last the message could be delivered, Dame Veronica did not at first move or speak. Then, 'Very well,' she said. Her voice had become a whisper. She kept her face turned to the cupboard and put her hands under her scapular but Philippa had seen that they were trembling.

'Benedicite, Mother.' It was stiff – Dame Veronica's eyes had taken in the account books still spread on the desk and, 'You want me about the accounts again?' Abbess Catherine noted that she did not wait for her Abbess to speak first. Abbess Hester must have allowed her to take liberties.

'We will go through the accounts later. Sit down, Dame.'

Dame Veronica sat on the edge of her chair, her hands still under her scapular, her eyes looking at the floor, a smile at the corners of her mouth. Philippa, experienced, would have seen the nerves in that smile, guessed that the hands were pressed tightly against the elbows, noted fear and dismay in every rigid line, but Abbess Catherine could not see past the hostility. 'I sent for you, Dame, to ask you about this.' She held out the letter from Stefan Duranski.

'It has come.' Dame Veronica seemed unable to speak above a whisper. She had grown very pale and her eyes, now that she looked at Abbess Catherine, seemed enormous. 'It has come.'

162

'You knew about it?'

'I – can hardly bear to talk about it.' Dame Veronica's eyes filled. 'I know how it will be misunderstood.'

'Misunderstood?'

'It was to have been the big surprise for Easter.'

'For Easter?'

'That was Mother's plan. I was the only one who knew.' Even now there was pride in Dame Veronica's voice. 'Mother commissioned the altar and the panels for remodelling the apse eight months ago.'

'But . . .' Once again Abbess Catherine seemed dazed. 'The Council refused even to consider it.'

At the beginning of the year before, Abbess Hester had called an extraordinary Council meeting and, without the usual preliminary circulating, had laid the Stefan Duranski drawings and plans before her councillors. The Abbey church, like the choir, was arched in stone, beautifully proportioned and still had its old painted vaulted ceiling, but it was ruined by the heavy marble apse below the rose window which could hardly be seen for the altar's ornate overhanging canopy, its pillars and reredos. Some of the nuns – notably Dame Beatrice – loved the cherubs, wreathed with rosy clouds, but Abbess Hester had shuddered from them as much as did the artists, Dame Gertrude and Dame Benita. 'Wait till Dame Gertrude and Dame Benita see these plans,' Abbess Hester had said with a chuckle of delight.

Sir Basil had brought the great Hungarian sculptor to Brede two years ago, 'and he's after my own heart,' Abbess Hester told the community when photographs of Duranski's sculpture had been handed round at recreation: a Mary Magdalen for a cathedral in France: a Pieta for a new church in Milan: an Adam half-finished in Chicago. 'That is a bronze,' the Abbess had said. 'But Stefan Duranski says he works best in stone. He carves directly into the stone without making a model. A true sculptor,' and, 'we might have guessed,' said Dame Maura.

At the extraordinary meeting they had reached the point of consternation. 'He will reveal the old stone of the apse,' Abbess Hester had told them. 'We shall see the rose window at last; he will make a pilaster at each east end corner of the sanctuary, and there will be a low centre panel linking them; the altar, of plain polished stone, will be brought forward to the centre of the sanctuary, the middle of the floor.'

'The *middle*?' asked Dame Beatrice.

'That is the new trend in France. Think of the Matisse chapel in Vence. I hope that here too our priests will soon be saying Mass facing the community.'

'Never!' cried Dame Beatrice in horror.

'The cubic altar on its steps will be the centre of interest, architecturally and literally,' Abbess Hester had rushed on, 'with the pilasters emphasizing the corners of the sanctuary; they will be carved as you see, with bas-reliefs in stone – St Benedict and St Scholastica – with these two slit windows cut to give them a sharp side light. At the back, the horizontal panel, again of stone, will be carved with symbols of corn, wine and oil. The altar will, as I say, be plain, carved on the frontal with one word "Pax" in a circle of thorns with rays. The new crucifix which Stefan Duranski will carve of oak will be on the grille facing the altar so that we shall, as it were, look out with it.'

'But ... this will cost a fortune,' Dame Catherine had said.

'Six or seven thousand pounds.'

'*Six or seven thousand pounds for some pieces of stone!*' Dame Beatrice could not believe it.

'Stone carved by Stefan Duranski,' Dame Veronica flashed. Her eyes had shown that she, too, was seeing visions. 'People would come to see it as now they go to Vence for the Matisse Chapel. We should have that treasure here. *Here!* Think of it ...!'

'But I like the altar we have now,' said Dame Beatrice. 'Our dear cherubim. Mother, you wouldn't do away with those?'

'They can be hung as a painting somewhere,' said the Abbess; she had not needed to add 'out of my sight.' 'The main design ...' but the prioress had broken in. 'Mother this sounds as if you were seriously considering ...'

'As we are,' said the Abbess.

'I must remind you, Mother, that when we discussed with

Mr Dutton' – Mr Dutton was the bank manager – 'about the expense of the long cloister, he said we were reaching the utmost limit . . .'

'And think of Father President,' said Dame Beatrice. 'Last year he cautioned us.'

'Think of the General Chapter,' said Dame Agnes. Besides the Abbot President's inspection a summary of accounts went every four years for auditing to the President and General Chapter of the English Benedictine Congregation. 'We should be given an even worse character for extravagance than we have now.'

'We don't go to the General Chapter for another three years,' said Dame Veronica. 'And by that time the altar will be installed. They can't take it away.'

'Thank you, Dame Veronica,' Abbess Hester had said and then had turned to the others. 'There is a lack of vision, a lack of courage, about this Council that I don't like to see. Nothing is ever done,' she said, with her voice rising so that it rang in their ears, 'nothing can be done by doubt and quibbling and picking holes. You have not even looked at the sketches.' That was true; they had been too appalled to look. Her voice had become calm as she said, 'I should scarcely embark on a project without knowing how it could be paid for, would I?'

There had been a silence. In conscience they could not agree with that and, darting a look at them, Abbess Hester had gone on. 'Though I am not at liberty to tell you the circumstances yet, I know where to get the money. In fact, I shall have it in less than a year, next March. Dame Veronica knows as well – if this reassures you. I am sure, too, I can get the community to agree.'

'And I expect she could have,' Dame Agnes had said afterwards. 'She makes it sound so plausible.'

'Dame Veronica,' Abbess Hester had said finally, 'will you tell the Council that I am right and we can pay for this.'

Abbess Hester had commanded but it had not escaped the councillors how Dame Veronica's tell-tale chin had shaken, nor that she gave a wild look round as if wishing she could escape. 'Why, oh why, did Mother appoint her?' Dame Maura said afterwards, and this time Dame Agnes did not hold back her instant thought, 'So that she could be cellarer herself.'

'Can we, or can we not, pay for it?'

'We can get the money, Mother, but . . .' they had all marked the 'but'.

'Wouldn't it be better, dear Mother, to wait until the money does come and then discuss this again?' That had been tactful Mother Prioress.

'Even then,' Dame Beatrice had said, 'should a monastery spend so much money?'

'I suggest it should not,' said Dame Maura.

'I'm afraid I feel the same way,' said Dame Catherine.

'And I. Even with the possibility of some windfall,' said Dame Agnes. 'It's an impossible project, dear Mother.'

The interest, the hope, that had set Abbess Hester's face alight, went out, a fire quenched. They had not liked to see it go, any more than one likes to see the quenching of an eager child. As everyone in religion knows, they knew it was only the childlike who accomplish impossible things; only they are single minded enough but, 'we had to refuse it,' Dame Catherine had said, and now, as Abbess, said it again to Dame Veronica, 'You knew we had to.'

'I trusted Mother,' said Dame Veronica, 'though none of you did.'

'That is not fair,' Abbess Catherine kept her voice level – she would not allow herself to be drawn into battle with Dame Veronica. 'We all trusted and revered her, but on this one point of building and restoration she needed restraining.'

'Restraining!' cried Dame Veronica. 'Stone disease! Dame Agnes said that. Actually said it. You all thought Mother was unbalanced, didn't you? Even Mother Prioress. Well, I didn't. She was not. She was visionary, in a way you couldn't, or wouldn't, see. Always trying to tie her down . . .'

'To realities. Dame, you had better look at this?' Abbess Catherine held out Stefan Duranski's account.

Dame Veronica stopped short, her eyes turned to the floor.

'Look at it, Dame.' Abbess Catherine's voice was peremptory, but Dame Veronica hid her face in her hands.

'I can't.'

'We shall all have to look at it,' Abbess Catherine waited until the hands came down. Then, 'Mother told us she would have the money this March . . .'

'Yes.' It was a whisper again.

'Where was it to come from, Dame?'

'From – Sister Julian.'

'Sister Julian!'

'Barbara Colquhoun, that's her proper name. She should never have been called Sister Julian,' said Dame Veronica. 'I told Mother not to count on her. She wouldn't listen,' and Dame Veronica said, almost in a gabble, the words came so fast: 'You – as cellarer then – must remember that when Barbara Colquhoun entered, her father arranged for her dowry to be in two parts; one half to be for Brede in the ordinary way, the other half for his precious Barbara to allot as she chose when she made her Solemn Profession. She was only five months from that, the day she told Mother she was going. Mother was certain she could influence her to make a donation for the new altar. Oh, if I had had that much money! It always seems given to the wrong people – a builder's daughter! Mother thought she had Sister Julian in the palm of her hand – and Sister let her think so almost up to the last – and Mother died in torment. Dame Agnes said she built too much on that girl. She didn't know how true that was.' Dame. Veronica's voice was shrill, her body was trembling; the Abbess noticed how dry her skin looked, how pale her lips. What a state she is in, thought the Abbess. There has been too much strain, and, 'Quietly, my dear,' she said, 'quietly.'

'How can I be quiet? Barbara Colquhoun killed her.'

'No, Dame.' Abbess Catherine spoke firmly. We must keep reality in this, she thought, and aloud, 'Sister Julian had to do as she did, but you . . .'

'Yes, blame me. I must be blamed.'

'You are cellarer.' They both knew that was the indictment. 'When Sister Julian left, you knew what must happen.'

'Knew! Do you think it hasn't been with me every minute of the day and night? Hammered into me, like nails.'

'Then why didn't you tell us? We would have shared it, and helped,' but Dame Veronica had shrunk into herself.

After the Council meeting at which the Duranski plans had been shown, she had made an effort to conciliate Dame Agnes. 'Must we cross one another?' she had asked in her most winning way – and Dame Veronica could be most winning. 'We both know Mother works with her whole heart and mind for Brede. Then shouldn't we try and help her? Not impede?'

It had been that moment after Vespers when the seniors hurried upstairs to fill their jugs – old-fashioned hot-water cans – while the water was really hot before it was drawn off for washing up in the pantry after supper. A jug, wrapped in a towel, stayed hot. The tap – the only one in that corridor – was just outside the lavatories and as the seniors often dallied for a word or two, a short discussion, Dame Agnes had named it the Privy Council.

'Dame?' Dame Veronica's eyes had been brimming with the effort of her earnestness – and from fright, thought Dame Maura, who was standing by. 'Why not?'

Dame Agnes had put down her water can and stood upright. 'Because I dread it.' Her voice shook with feeling in a way Dame Veronica had never heard.

'D-dread it?'

'Yes. Dread what is going to happen – to her and to us, if this goes on – if it isn't stopped.'

'Surely it's our duty to help and support her.'

'Not by being blind,' said Dame Maura who had come up behind Dame Agnes.

'By keeping things balanced,' said Dame Agnes.

'You are a councillor. That means responsibility,' said Dame Maura.

'It *is* our responsibility,' said Dame Agnes.

Dame Veronica had looked at the two towers and fled.

'Why didn't you come to us?' Abbess Catherine asked now.

'I ... couldn't,' and Dame Veronica said with great tiredness, 'Perhaps I hoped Mother would send a miracle. Or that Stefan Duranski would go away to America – or it was all a bad dream. I was silly, wasn't I?' and she began to laugh.

Philippa, outside the door, heard that hysterical laughter. It ceased so abruptly that she wondered if the Abbess had slapped her cellarer, but Dame Veronica had gained control of herself and stopped with a queer little hiccough and once again sat rigid looking at the floor.

'You have been through a time of extraordinary difficulty and strain,' Abbess Catherine tried to put understanding and sympathy into the words. 'Quite apart from your work which is a heavy responsibility, as I well know. I have been cellarer . . .'

'Yes.' A small polite word, but not as Dame Veronica said it.

'If anyone should be able to understand, I should.'

'Yes.'

Abbess Catherine decided it was of no use to go on. 'The councillors must be told,' she said. 'I shall call them after None this afternoon. It's short notice, but we can't keep this to ourselves a moment longer than is necessary.'

'We must do as you say.' Again, nothing in that but the emphasis on 'we' and 'you'. I must try again, thought the Abbess. I can't let her go like this. But Dame Veronica had already risen.

'And you must tell them about the money box.'

What made Abbess Catherine add that now? In the shock over the altar, she had almost forgotten the money box. Dame Veronica grew more rigid, then she swayed. Once more Abbess Catherine thought she was going to faint; her hands were gripping her skirts, her face was not pale but leaden, and, she minds more about that hundred or so pounds than about the Duranski thousands, thought the Abbess. Why? and, 'Dame, tell me,' she said.

It was meant as a plea, but as soon as she had said it, Abbess Catherine knew it was wrong. 'Won't you tell me? Can't you?' might have been better, spoken with compassion and love. Above all, an Abbess must love; now dismay seemed to have chased out love.

Dame Veronica stiffened again. Then words seemed to be wrung from her, not venomous but in despair. 'If only you were Mother!' She made a travesty of a bow and left the room.

After midday dinner, Abbess Catherine gave the knock of dismissal and rose: '*Tu autem Domine, miserere nobis,*' intoned the reader. '*Thanks be to God*' the nuns responded, '*Let all Thy works praise Thee, O Lord. We give Thee thanks for all Thy blessings,*' and the community went in procession to the choir for the formal grace, singing as they went. 'We must always, everywhere, give thanks,' Dame Clare told Cecily. 'We must learn, as St Paul says, to be grateful.'

Cecily did not need reminding. She was profoundly grateful, 'every minute of the day,' she would have said. She fell blissfully asleep at night. After the shocks of the first few weeks, 'without Lady Abbess Hester, without Sister Philippa,' she had taken to monastery life with the ease of a bird released into the air.

In the church, for grace, the hebdomadarian, choir leader of the week, gave out the Pater Noster and sang the versicles: '*He has distributed freely. He has given to the poor,*' and the response swelled: '*His righteousness endureth for ever. I will bless the Lord at all times, His praise shall always be on my lips.*' Cecily chanted it with mind, heart and soul but when Dame Clare looked at her, the zelatrix saw only exaggeration, a girl too starry-eyed, and sighed; when Cecily sensed that Dame Clare was looking at her, her chant ceased.

Today at the end of grace, the Abbess did not leave the church but waited in the long cloister until Dame Veronica came out when she beckoned her. 'Dame, I want you in my room.'

'If only you were Mother.' Abbess Catherine had not ceased to hear that – reproach, as she thought it. I have failed. Failed badly. Looking down from the high table at dinner, she had seen that Dame Veronica ate nothing, could eat nothing, thought the Abbess. 'I tried, truly I tried,' but Abbess Catherine had no one to whom she could say that. I must not trouble Mother Prioress with my failures. She had telephoned Doctor Avery for permission to tell Dame Emily what had come to

170

light. 'She knows that something distressed – no, tormented – Lady Abbess's last hours. If Dame Emily knew what had been worrying her she, herself, might rest.' Doctor Avery had agreed but said, 'Only stay ten minutes.'

'I guessed,' said the old weary voice. 'Guessed it was something to do with Sister Julian's money but I had not dreamed of this.' Dame Emily had taken Abbess Catherine's hand. 'My poor child.'

Abbess Catherine would have liked to kneel down by the bed and burst into tears as she had in her cell that first day. 'I feel so new, Mother, so lost,' but she had only pressed the thin hand and laid it down saying, as she had said to Abbess Hester, 'We will deal with this.' Dame Emily though, could see the trouble in her eyes and, 'Treat her with the utmost sympathy,' she advised. 'Remember, dear child, Dame Veronica is very proud.'

Now in the ante-chapel Dame Veronica's eyes flickered away from the Abbess in such misery that Abbess Catherine's heart ached for her. 'Come, my dear. I think we need to talk.'

At once there was a hardening. 'Please, I don't feel well.'

'Then come and we'll sit down.'

'I have such palpitations.'

'We'll call Dame Joan.'

'Please no. She'll make a fuss.' Dame Joan was the last to do that but Abbess Catherine let it pass. 'If I could lie down a little . . .'

Abbess Catherine hesitated. She had a strong feeling that Dame Veronica should not be left alone. If you are in the outside world, thought Abbess Catherine, a misdemeanour or fault can go almost unnoticed; conscience is not as tender, as cleansed and polished with many rubbings as with us – examinations of conscience every day, every week a Chapter of Faults, and instant acknowledgements. Yes, thought Abbess Catherine, it is the difference between a rough and pitted surface and one so planed down and polished that the least mark shows. Dame Veronica was obviously excoriated, in torture, but – what is the use of pressing, thought the Abbess, when she so dislikes me? Yet . . .

At that moment Dame Veronica looked her straight in the eye. 'You are worrying about the Council meeting. You needn't. I shall be there.'

Back in the proc's room, Dame Veronica knew she could not be there. 'Not like this,' she whispered aloud. She felt too ill; she had hardly been able to get up the stairs and now her heart was leaping and she was breathless and dizzy. I shall have to go to Dame Joan, but she shrank from that. Go and be laughed at! 'This is just fear,' she told herself. 'Panic.' That was true. Her face and neck were clammy; it was fear that made her knees weak. 'You have disgraced your office.' No one would say it but it would be true; there was not one of them but would think it. Dame Veronica would have given worlds now to have taken back some of her self-importance, her pride. 'Mother, why did you let me? Why didn't you curb me? You encouraged me,' she wanted to cry, but she could not, in justice, fasten it all on Abbess Hester. Abbess Hester had had nothing to do with ... Paul. Even his name seemed to blister Dame Veronica. They will have to know everything. *Every* thing! she thought. There is nowhere to hide.

She would have knelt on the floor, holding her arms wide like the figure on the cross, sharing the suffering, but a spasm of pain made her double up. How can Doctor Avery say there is nothing wrong with my heart? 'It's wind, that's all' he says. I should see a proper cardiologist. I'm ill. Ill! thought Dame Veronica.

The clock struck two as she sat, bowed at her desk where the poem, with its disjointed lines, still lay on the blotter. Two o'clock. One hour to None, and then she must face the Council – be stripped and nailed, thought Dame Veronica dramatizing. Let them hammer in the nails. Well, I deserve it.

> Earth trembles at this blossom for, see
> the dark green wands are tipped
> spear-sharp to pierce with sorrow ...

For a moment the stillness that mysteriously she had put into the lines stilled her. I must go and lie down, perhaps rest ... and painfully, pressing her hands down on the table, she got to her feet but the room seemed to swim around her and, I must take something, thought Dame Veronica. There was brandy kept for emergency in the drugs cupboard. She would take a little brandy. If Dame Joan has shut me off from her, I will treat myself, thought Dame Veronica. A dose of brandy, then go and lie down.

All drugs were in the cellarer's charge, the infirmarian taking what was needed for the day or night, and Dame Veronica got out her keys. As the cupboard door swung open, her eyes fell on a small squat bottle, the pills Doctor Avery had given Mother Prioress, Dame Emily, for her heart, quinidine.

'I hope I haven't caused too much inconvenience.' Abbess Catherine rose to greet the councillors who had gathered outside her door and come in all together. 'I had to call you suddenly because . . .' she broke off. 'Where is Dame Veronica?'

The Abbess had not been at None; Sister Dorothy had scalded herself badly in the kitchen and Abbess Catherine stayed with her until Doctor Avery came. Now, 'Dame Veronica wasn't at None either,' said Dame Maura.

'Would you ask Sister Philippa to go and call her? She will probably be in her cell. She went to lie down and may have fallen asleep. While we are waiting, as Dame Veronica knows it all, I will explain,' and she began the opening prayer.

They were all making the sign of the cross at the end when there was a sharp knock at the door, and without waiting for the 'Deo Gratias', Philippa opened it. 'Forgive me, Mother, but please come to Dame Veronica at once.' It was the old decisive Mrs Talbot. 'I will get Dame Joan,' but the Abbess had already passed her. 'Dame Veronica seems to be in a coma,' Philippa told the councillors. 'Will someone telephone for Doctor Avery and get Father Gervase?' Dame Agnes went quickly to the telephone, as Philippa sped on to the infirmary and Dame Beatrice rose. 'I will prepare,' she said, and went down to the sacristy.

In Dame Veronica's cell, the narrow room was neatly set in

order, the window shut. Dame Veronica was lying on the bed in her habit, but without her veil; the blanket was thrown back; one hand was outflung, the other at her throat as if she had tried to tear off her wimple – struggling for breath, thought Philippa. Dame Joan gave a choked little cry, 'She's dead,' but Abbess Catherine had gone down on her knees by the bed, one hand under the folds of the habit. 'She is breathing – just.'

'Dame Agnes is telephoning for Doctor Avery.'

'He has just left us,' lamented Dame Joan.

'What happened, Sister?' the Abbess asked Philippa.

'I saw the token on the door,' – a white handkerchief was hung on the doorknob if a nun did not want to be disturbed – 'so that I knew Dame Veronica was in her cell. I knocked and knocked again and called. Then I put my head round the door and went in. I knew Dame Veronica wasn't well.'

'How could you know that?' Dame Joan had not much respect for a junior nun's knowledge.

'I haven't been able to help noticing Dame Veronica.' When Dame Veronica had come out of the Abbess's room that morning, she had leant against the door she had just closed, her eyes, shut, her throat working as if she could not breathe and Philippa had stayed quietly at her table, bent over her letters until Dame Veronica was able to walk away. At Sext Philippa had seen her, not singing but looking straight ahead; her eyes seemed huge in her face and, 'I have seen her bend almost double, as if she were in pain,' said Philippa.

'She said she had palpitations,' said the Abbess. 'It must have been a heart attack,' but, 'Dame Veronica's heart is perfectly sound.' As she spoke, Dame Joan was working, loosening Dame Veronica's clothing. 'Doctor Avery examined her just before Christmas. She has nervous indigestion which gives her spasms, but this . . .'

'Look,' said Philippa. She had glimpsed a little bottle, hidden behind the books on the prie-dieu beside a medicine glass. Dame Joan pounced on it. 'Mother Prioress's quinidine. I gave it back to the drugs cupboard only last week. If she has taken that . . .'

'How many were in it?' asked Abbess Catherine. 'Can you remember?'

'Doctor Avery prescribed thirty.' Dame Joan spoke slowly, carefully. 'Mother Prioress took it for that one day – here and in the ambulance. That would have been . . .'

'Count them, Dame.' The Abbess did not mean to be curt but the same dark thought was in them all, and, looking at Abbess Catherine's anguished face, Dame Joan said firmly, 'Dame Veronica was convinced she had a bad heart, Mother. This is heart medicine. She took it for that.'

'Yes,' said Abbess Catherine. 'Yes.'

'She must have taken five or six,' said Dame Joan, and to Philippa, 'Sister, has word been sent for Father Gervase?'

Philippa nodded. 'Dame Beatrice is preparing.'

'Ask her to hurry,' said the Abbess. 'Then wait at the enclosure door and bring Doctor Avery here when he comes.'

A notice was put on the board asking for prayers 'For Dame Veronica who has had a heart attack.'

'I suppose we can call it that?' said Dame Joan.

'Indeed you can,' said Doctor Avery who had been caught on his way home.

The Abbess was not at Vespers, nor in the refectory for supper nor at Compline. Dame Perpetua, taking her place, was grave and the community guessed something of the struggle that was going on in the infirmary's treatment-room where Dame Veronica had been carried. Abbess, prioress, cellarer, struck down one after the other! but the nuns knew that the best help they could give was in trying not to let the dismay spread. If there was curiosity – and there must be curiosity, thought Philippa who had dreaded questions – little of it showed. She was not asked questions, not even by Dame Agnes. After Vespers most of the community stayed in their stalls to pray for Dame Veronica or went to their cells to do the same; those who had work to do, did it. Dame Edith and her aids had an urgent set of leaflets to get out; Dame Colette was working against time on a set of vestments. The younger nuns took example from the older and it was only one or two 'inveterates' as Dame Agnes called them who whispered and speculated together. 'What is happening?' 'What *is* this that has fallen on Brede? Three! One after the other!'

'Not three,' the Abbess could have told them. 'This is all one. It stems from Abbess Hester.' One fault allowed – no, encouraged – can grow in a community like the mustard seed into a monstrous tree. 'No one lives to herself.' Over and over again, the Abbess thought that in the long watches of the night. That was what I was doing, when I was no longer cellarer. Living to myself, aloof – almost; there had been only the one small episode with Sister Philippa in the pleached alley to redeem that. If I had not shut myself in for so long, thought Abbess Catherine, I might have been able to find the right compassion, share, suffer with Dame Veronica. 'You couldn't have been expected to,' Dame Perpetua's sense would have said, '*Look* how she behaved!' but, 'I am expected to,' was the answer for an abbess. *There must be no limits.*

Philippa, coming in with letters, saw that scrawled in Abbess Catherine's big writing on a pad on the desk and Philippa looked at the words for a long time.

Abbess Catherine learned that night what it was to be a mother. At first it seemed in the infirmary that they must lose. 'The heart has almost stopped,' said Doctor Avery. He had given a first injection in Dame Veronica's cell – 'coramine', he told Dame Joan – now he gave adrenalin as well. 'She must not die. She must not die like this,' Abbess Catherine cried silently; as she and Dame Joan rubbed feet and legs, her lips moved ceaselessly. Dom Gervase was praying in the ante-room.

Then slowly there was a pulse, almost imperceptible at first, but the heart, under Doctor Avery's hand, had quickened, though it was an uncertain beat at first. Dame Veronica opened her eyes, her hands fluttered out in bewilderment, then, as slowly she took in the doctor and priest – Dom Gervase, had come when Dame Joan called out – bewilderment gave way to consternation. 'The meeting,' she gasped. 'The meeting.'

'No meeting for you.' Dame Joan spoke out of common

sense. She had no idea what Dame Veronica was talking of. 'You lie still.'

'Lie still,' said Abbess Catherine and took the weak hands.

Dame Veronica began to vomit. 'Good,' said Doctor Avery. 'With any luck she will get it all out of her stomach which will save us washing it out.' To Abbess Catherine, holding her, supporting her, 'with such tenderness as I cannot tell you,' Dame Joan said afterwards, it was as if Dame Veronica brought the whole past up, dredges of bitterness and jealousy, fear, prevarication, 'and worse,' gasped Dame Veronica. 'Worse. You don't know . . . about . . . Paul,' and when she lay back exhausted and Dame Joan was sponging the sweat from her face, she still clung to Abbess Catherine's hand. Presently she fell into a deep sleep.

Daylight was coming into the cell when Dame Veronica spoke again. 'She will do now,' Doctor Avery had said; an hour after she fell asleep, he had risen and stretched up exhausted. 'Keep her warm and absolutely still. She will be all right,' but Abbess Catherine had not left her that night.

'Mother,' it was a whisper, 'I took Mother Prioress's medicine.'

'I know.'

'Q-quinidine.' Dame Veronica shut her eyes but tears found their way under her lids, tears of weakness and contrition, real contrition, thought the Abbess, and pityingly she asked, 'Were you so afraid to face us?'

'It was so that I could face you.' That was surprisingly firm and Abbess Catherine's heart lifted. 'I felt so ill,' Dame Veronica was whispering, 'my heart was jumping so. I'm sure Doctor Avery is wrong.' It was the old complaint but her voice tailed off. 'One shouldn't take other people's medicines but this helped Mother Prioress. I thought if I took a shock dose and lay down . . .'

The Abbess laid a hand on her. 'You could face the meeting?'

'Yes.'

'Thank God,' said Abbess Catherine silently. 'Thank, thank God,' but the weak voice went on, 'I only took five.' Five white pills to do all this, but 'Five!' said Dame Joan, when the Abbess told her. 'I couldn't be sure but on an empty stomach five would be enough to stop the heart completely. She's lucky to be here.'

'Didn't you know how dangerous it was?' Yesterday Dame Veronica would have dodged that question, though vivid in her mind was Dame Joan's bringing the bottle back to the drugs cupboard. 'I don't want to keep this in the infirmary.' Now, in this new found purgation, Dame Veronica told the truth. 'I knew there was a risk.'

And she had had a warning – or given herself a warning. When she had turned to go out of the proc's room, as always she had looked at the big crucifix. 'I think always when I come in, my eyes go straight to Him. When I go out, I take leave of Him,' she could have said and, 'I knew if I did this I might ... I was on the brink of something dreadful then and I seemed to cast myself in front of Him though I was standing still.' She remembered she had whispered, perhaps whispered aloud – because I was beside myself, thought Dame Veronica; that was the right description: she had seemed outside her body, looking at herself as at a pitiful stranger with that deadly little bottle in her hand; she had whispered, 'If it happens I'm not afraid to face You. You understand.'

'But I had gone away from Him,' Dame Veronica said now, though the Abbess could not follow. 'Other things crept in.' Her voice was getting weaker; it came in jerks and the Abbess had to bend over her to hear. 'I was ... in love with myself,' said Dame Veronica. 'I think I always have been – I loved to be important ... singled out ... that's why I lent myself to the altar and the money ... to have Mother's confidence. In love with myself, which is ... pride,' and in a rush, 'Mother, I haven't told you about Paul.'

Dame Joan had come in and was standing by the bed. She took Dame Veronica's pulse. 'She shouldn't talk,' and she said in a loud, sensible voice, 'What you need is a cup of tea, and you too, Mother.' Gently but firmly she loosed Dame Veronica's hand and helped Abbess Catherine to her feet.

*   *   *

'Mother did this? *Mother?* But she couldn't have done,' said Dame Beatrice.

'Unfortunately she did.'

It was a depleted Council that met again in the Abbess's room, three councillors instead of six, and the gaps 'ached' as the Abbess said, ached all the more for the shock she had just given. 'Unfortunately she did. The altar, pillars and panel are ready to be installed.'

'How much is the account?' Dame Agnes, as if she had been stunned, had said not a word until now.

'For the work up to date, four thousand three hundred and fifty pounds. Two hundred for the crucifix.'

'Four thou...' Dame Beatrice could not finish the terrible words. She said, as she had said before, 'for pieces of stone!'

Stone carved by Stefan Duranski. They could hear Dame Veronica's voice saying that.

'It seems incredible,' said Dame Maura, 'but I should guess it is cheap for Stefan Duranski. Isn't he getting ten thousand pounds for his Adam? The work of a great artist has a high market value, especially these days. Duranski's value will increase.'

'Then in a way Mother was visionary.'

It eased the shock to let them talk but Abbess Catherine had to continue and as she told the story of Lady Abbess Hester's reliance on Sister Julian Colquhoun – her anticipation of the dowry – their faces changed; Dame Beatrice's grew white with distress: Dame Maura's eyes glittered as if they had met a challenge, while Dame Agnes's wrath and concern sent patches of red to her nose and her cheeks and seemed to inflame the red lump on her forehead. 'But this *is* incredible,' said Dame Agnes at the end. Incredible! A word they were to use again and again. 'Where was Mother Prioress?'

'Shut out,' Abbess Catherine wanted to say, but instead, 'Mother Prioress did not know.'

'Dame Veronica?' Dame Maura asked that.

'Dame Veronica knew.'

They were aghast. 'Knew, and is cellarer.'

179

'Neither spoke nor warned us!'

'Connived.'

'Dame Veronica was always a weak link,' said Dame Agnes.

'Don't say that,' Dame Beatrice still had pity. 'We can only be as strong as we are. She must have suffered terribly to bring on such a heart attack. You know how sensitive she is.'

'By which you mean always brimming.'

'Only because she is so responsive. Tears are a part of that. Remember how she throws herself heart and soul into any project.'

'As she did about the altar,' Dame Agnes was dry.

'The altar and what else?' groaned Dame Maura.

'Do I have to tell? Am I bound to?' Abbess Catherine had asked Abbot Bernard.

It was Dom Gervase who gave her the idea of asking the Abbot to come. 'I have heard Dame Veronica's confession – as she tells me you have,' said Dom Gervase, 'but I'm afraid my sympathy may outrun my judgement. I know what it is to be disgraced...!'

'Not in this way. It was not your fault.'

'Weakness is a fault,' but Dom Gervase was not as grave over himself as he used to be; he was grave, though, over Dame Veronica. 'She needs better help than mine,' but when Abbess Catherine asked the Abbot to come, it was for herself, not Dame Veronica. New found antennae of wisdom seemed to have grown; Dame Veronica was still Dame Veronica: and it seemed safer not to give her any fresh importance; their own house chaplain's humility and unswerving realism were, Abbess Catherine felt strongly, the sanest help Dame Veronica could have now.

'My name is not Fanshawe,' Dame Veronica had said. 'I was born Maisie Shaw, not Margaret Fanshawe as I am listed in the register,' and with a shudder, 'Maisie is a horrible name. It's true we lived at Orford Hall because my mother was the housekeeper. I knew it better than any Orford because I used to pretend the Hall belonged to us. My mother had been a housemaid there as a girl; she came back when she was widowed – or perhaps she wasn't widowed. We never knew our father.'

Dame Veronica had taken her hand out of the Abbess's as if she must tell this tale alone. 'And you never told Lady Abbess Hester?' Abbess Catherine felt she hardly dared speak for fear of arresting this painful cleansing but she had to make it complete.

'Never. I had been Fanshawe so long before I came here – called myself Fanshawe,' Dame Veronica corrected herself – 'that it seemed to me true. Yes, I had come to believe it myself. Dame Veronica Fanshawe. It felt true and yet, suddenly, it would all seem to be hollow. If only,' said Dame Veronica, 'I had told Mother. If only I had come here as Maisie Shaw ... but you don't know what it was like,' said Dame Veronica. 'If we had been brought up by ourselves in some little house, but it was Orford. I have always told people I lived with the Orfords and it was true, but I didn't say how we lived with them.

'We used to play with Damaris Orford but when it was time to go in, she went indoors by the front, we had to go round by the back.' Dame Veronica's voice was full of bitterness. 'She had her tea in the drawing-room or her own sitting-room; we in the kitchen. I was allowed to exercise her pony in term time when she was away at boarding school. Once I entered it in a gymkhana though I had no proper riding clothes. I won a cup as the best child rider. Lady Orford wasn't pleased; Damaris had never won a cup, and there was no more riding for me. Oh, Lady Orford was kind – in her sphere, to me in mine. She gave me Damaris's clothes – when Damaris was finished with them. I not only wore them, I copied everything Damaris did; talked like her, behaved like her, as much as I could. She went to boarding school, then Paris, and I had to go to work. Why should one girl be born like a princess and another, just as good and far prettier, have to slave? I remember,' said Dame Veronica, 'my mother's suggesting I train as a children's nurse, or a cook. Lady Orford had offered to pay, and to my mother those were high class posts, but I stared at her and said, "I? Be a *servant*?" She said ...' Here the iron went out

181

of Dame Veronica's voice and her chin quivered. 'She said, "I am a servant." I can still see her face when she said that, the dignity. When we were very small – before she got the Orford post – she used to get up at four and clean offices before she started her regular work, to get more money for us; we were always neat and clean and well fed, but I was cruel. It was then I decided,' said Dame Veronica, 'I should be a nun as soon as I could. Nuns have no class.'

'Should have no class,' said Abbess Catherine.

'I brought that with me,' Dame Veronica admitted. 'I could say it governed my life. Lady Orford didn't pay for any training because I went out as a governess – a mother's help at first. I detested children but I can act. I never deceived the children though – children always know – but I deceived the parents and I worked hard. Soon I was desirable; Margaret Fanshawe, brought up at Orford Hall. You don't know, Mother, how adept I grew and I was quite safe. Lady Orford had died – she had been a widow for years; Damaris married in America – a rich man of course – the Hall is far away in Lincolnshire and it was sold and mother moved to the Lodge as a kind of caretaker. I had four years in France, governess at the Château Lefèvre near Tours, which is why my accent is so good – I learned far more French than the children learned English. Then I came back to England. I had had enough of children and became companion to old Mrs Lake. Governesses and companions are anonymous and that was where I met Father Dugdale who was the link with Brede. Margaret Fanshawe seemed eminently suitable to be a choir postulant though I think Sister Priscilla and Sister Jane had their suspicions, but what could they say? Mother and the Council were, in their way, innocents; they didn't know guile when they saw it.'

'Guile?' asked the Abbess. 'Surely by your own efforts you had worked and planned to come here?'

'To be a Brede nun, part of a noted Abbey. To be called Dame. That's why I came but it wasn't why I stayed – miraculously. I came for all the wrong reasons but it overtook me and I found I had a vocation. That was true,' said Dame Veronica, 'the one thing that was true.

182

'I suppose there were signs before,' she said. 'I could have married – or not married – several times. There was always that other and easier way. I was exceedingly pretty and Madame Lefèvre in France and Mrs Lake both tried to sponsor a marriage. They were fond of me; yes, my credentials go back a long way. I had made my story proof – for everyone but myself. Over and over again I wanted to tell but could never face the shame,' and Dame Veronica whispered, 'I even forbade my mother to come here.'

'Your mother is alive?' The Abbess was startled.

'Yes. God pity her,' said Dame Veronica, 'because we didn't. I used to write to her sometimes, but I always told her not to come.'

'But . . . she must have been wonderful and devoted.' Abbess Catherine was shocked.

'She says – not "naow" for "now", and "cike" for "cake", but very nearly; sometimes she drops her aitches.'

'Oh, my dear child!'

'I know! I know it was contemptible but . . . you don't know – no one can!' said Dame Veronica passionately. 'It served me right when Paul came instead.'

'Paul. Your brother?'

'Yes, my brother. My little brother.' Dame Veronica spoke with a mixture of tenderness and sadness. 'Paul was different. We put all our efforts into him, Mother and I. That's why I went out to work so young. Well!' Dame Veronica gave a shrug. 'He went to prison for the first time when he was twenty. I don't know,' said Dame Veronica, 'how he found out where I was. My mother would never have told him, never, but he may have found a letter or a card and then . . .' Dame Veronica sat upright in bed, her eyes fixed on the opposite wall. 'He came here to see me last August, first of all. He called himself Fanshawe too. I gave him that idea. He had helped me fake my birth certificate – he was a clever faker. Paul Fanshawe. I don't know what the extern sisters thought, he was so shabby; just out after ten years, his fourth sentence, down at heel, and down and out. He said he would tell Lady Abbess if I didn't . . .'

'Didn't what?'

'Give him money.' Dame Veronica's face was drained of all colour, her lips seemed blue. 'You must lie down,' said Abbess Catherine. 'Don't talk any more,' but, 'Let me finish,' said Dame Veronica. 'Now I have begun, let me tell it all. All. I gave him money...'

'But ... you hadn't any.'

'No. I found out what it means when nuns have nothing to give of their own, so I took what wasn't mine.' She turned to the Abbess. 'Can't you understand? He is my little brother, even if he is a criminal. To see him like that: shabby, hopeless, beaten, only he wasn't beaten. I should have known that. And I started it,' cried Dame Veronica. 'He didn't ask me that first time but I gave him ten shillings. I thought I could tell Mother that I had done wrong and given money to a tramp and she would forgive me, but as soon as he knew I had access...' Dame Veronica clenched her fists, her head bowed, then slowly lifted. 'He never stopped writing. He came twice more though I begged him not to. He wanted a pound; then five pounds: then another five. It wasn't difficult with all the building and the work going on. In her last years Mother was not too exact, and Paul got facsimile bills that I made out. It was only little sums until...'

'Until...'

'The last time he came was in November and said if I gave him a lump sum he knew a way of doubling it; he swore he would bring it back. It would give him a chance, he said, and he would go straight, not trouble me again, nor trouble our own mother. He had been bleeding her too – said he had to bleed her though he hated to do it. He begged her for her sake. It was a long long interview and I believed him. Lady Abbess Hester had died. There was the upset of the election and no one would have time to think or, come to that, knew exactly about the money box. I opened it and gave him the whole – it was a hundred and four pounds, eighteen shillings. I left the coppers. Then the days went on and on all over Christmas-tide without a sign or word from him, and I knew he had cheated again – and it must be found out.'

'And you still didn't tell.'

'I couldn't tell. A nun ought to be impeccable.'

'My dear child!' said the Abbess again. 'None of us is that.'

'I should have been so ashamed.'

'There isn't one person here who wouldn't have opened her whole heart to you.'

'In pity,' said Dame Veronica, her lips tight.

'We are sisters, Dame, which means your brother is ours.'

'Yes. You brought a bishop into the family,' Dame Veronica spoke with something of her old spite. 'I brought a thief.' Then she changed, the pride crumbled. 'I am a thief myself. I have to remember that.'

'Must I tell the Council?' Abbess Catherine asked Abbot Bernard.

'You are reluctant to?'

'Father Abbot, I should hate to. It's not only Dame Veronica. It exposes Mother, Lady Abbess Hester, still more. If she had not been so avid about the building . . . so occupied.'

'I see.' Abbot Bernard had been Abbot of Udimore for fifteen years and he was wise. He was watching Abbess Catherine through the grille, noticing a new thinness and tautness and her tired and troubled face. 'What about you?' he asked.

'Me?'

'Dame Veronica has made you suffer acutely.' Abbess Catherine made an impatient little gesture but he went on. 'Not only Dame Veronica. Lady Abbess Hester as well.'

'And?'

'You might justifiably feel ill-used. They have left you a pretty pickle. It will take a long time to put it right. In fact, I don't know how you can put it right, but there will have to be stringent measures and you may seem a pinch-penny Abbess, too severe. If you told the community something of this, it would excuse you.'

She did not immediately protest her selflessness and that pleased Abbot Bernard. She weighed what he had said, then slowly shook her head. 'I should rather go without that – if it's possible. Father, what would you do?'

185

'Tell the community in chapter about the altar; it is anyway inevitable they must know; tell them the amount of the debt. Let them make their own conclusions about Lady Abbess Hester, but don't indict her by telling about her plan for Sister Julian. Dame Veronica will merely be blamed for conniving.'

'And then?'

'Well, you are Abbess. If you wish to donate the sinking fund – isn't that what they called it? – shall we say to the Prisoners' Welfare Society, that is your business. Your depositarians may think you unduly magnanimous but they can't gainsay you, the amount's not big enough, and we can explain to Abbot President.'

'Thank you, Father.' Abbess Catherine looked suddenly younger, her cheeks flushed, her shoulders straightened with relief. 'And Dame Veronica herself?'

'I should let it lie. I'm sorry,' said Abbot Bernard. 'I didn't mean to be so apt. Dear Catherine, remember that people need only be told as much of the truth as they are entitled to know, and nuns are people. As I see it – the only person entitled to know about Dame Veronica's background is you, her Abbess, and she has told you. She is a senior nun, and in many ways lovable; it would do no good to upset that, causing more distress, more dismay. No, I see no point,' said Abbot Bernard, 'after all these years, in forcing Dame Veronica Fanshawe to be Dame Veronica Shaw.'

Now, in the Council, Abbess Catherine was thankful she could listen and not have, in conscience, to add fuel to the fire; but perhaps she was too silent, because the councillors' talk stopped. They were looking at her. 'Mother, this is, above all, terrible for you,' was the feeling of them all and, 'Instead of lamenting,' said Dame Agnes, 'let's see what we can do.'

'There are a few ideas,' said Abbess Catherine. 'I am examining the possibility of raising another overdraft with Mr Dutton, but of course we must consult Father President. Then we might try and sell the altar and panels though that will be difficult as they are designed to fit our apse – and we should have to ask Mr Duranski.'

'They belong to us, not to him,' said Dame Agnes.

'Not until they are paid for,' Dame Maura pointed out.

'And it won't help Brede to antagonize a famous artist,' said the Abbess, 'nor . . .' but she did not go on; it was in all their minds, 'nor discredit a famous Abbess.' 'As it is,' said Abbess Catherine, 'this will have to be told in chapter. It concerns the whole community.'

After a moment Dame Maura asked, 'There are funds on deposit, Mother?'

'Yes. Quite an amount.'

'Yet we can't pay Mr Duranski from those?'

'No. While that money is there,' said Abbess Catherine, 'the future of every nun here is safe – even if she brought no money with her. We never know what we might have to draw from it; one of us might be too incurably ill to be nursed here.'

'Or go insane and have to leave.' Dame Beatrice's tone seemed to show that nothing that happened at Brede could surprise her now, but the others were not listening; they were waiting for the Abbess to go on, but Abbess Catherine was silent.

Presently Dame Beatrice spoke again, and quite differently. 'This is all very painful – especially for you, dear Mother – but while concerning ourselves, and we have to concern ourselves, should we distress ourselves so much? Lady Abbess Hester said – I remember it vividly – that we had neither faith nor vision. Perhaps she is right and this is the way it is meant to happen. Brede is not a house of business. It is a house of prayer.'

'Prayer must be founded on common sense,' said Dame Agnes.

'Not necessarily so.' Dame Beatrice was quite unruffled. 'It often seems against sense. I shall pray. We must all pray.'

'Like a child asking the bank manager for a bag of money to take home to Daddy?' In her worry, Dame Agnes's sarcasm was biting but, 'Exactly. Exactly like that,' said Dame Beatrice.

7

'When you are in trouble,' Abbess Catherine told herself, 'think of a bird caught under a net; the more it struggles and makes a flutter, the more it gets enmeshed; if it is still and looks about for a hole, keeping its strength, it has a chance of escape.' She tried to work methodically, causing the least possible ripples of alarm and no one, seeing her going about the Abbey, taking her place in choir, chapter or refectory or at recreation, could have guessed the sick hollowness she felt. Nor did they know that, unable to sleep, she often came down into the choir at night and spent long hours in prayer, kneeling where Abbess Hester had often knelt, among the 'nobodies'. Many of the nuns, though, noted as Abbot Bernard had noted, that a few weeks of being Abbess had made her thinner, pale and tired. 'Well, she has had a fierce baptism of trouble,' said Dame Maura.

'An incoming Abbess almost always has someone near her who knows administration,' Abbot Bernard said to Dom Gervase. 'She has a prioress or, as would have happened had Dame Emily been able to be elected, has been prioress herself, but Abbess Catherine is alone.'

'Terribly alone,' said Dom Gervase.

Every evening at Vespers in these days Abbess Catherine, as if echoing the Abbot's words, thought, as the antiphon to the Magnificat was sung, of the Visitation when the Virgin Mary, with the angel's announcement beating in her heart, had gone 'in haste' as St Luke says to visit her far older cousin. Why, wondered Abbess Catherine, did theologians always teach – and we take it for granted – that Mary went simply to succour Elizabeth? Probably she did do that, but could it not also have been that she needed the wisdom and strength of an older woman? How wonderfully reassuring Elizabeth's salutation must have been: 'Whence is this that the mother of my Lord should come to me?' A recognition without being told, and Mary, as if heartened, touched into bloom by the warmth and honour of that recognition, had flowered into the Magnificat. If there were only someone I could talk to, but Dame Emily was still in hospital, Abbot Bernard had the heavy burden of his own Abbey and even to her councillors an Abbess must not lay her feelings bare. Abbess Catherine, passing Philippa at her desk in the alcove, would think, I wish I could put you on the other side of the grille and talk to you as Mrs Talbot, but Sister Philippa was still, officially, a junior nun, and the Abbess passed on into her solitary room.

The first steps had been taken: 'All the steps that I can see,' said Abbess Catherine. There were three new councillors: Dame Colette and Dame Ursula, elected by the community; and lively young Irish Dame Anselma Riordan, appointed by the Abbess. 'Mother, isn't she very young?' objected Dame Agnes; it had become settled in the nuns' minds that the Council should be composed of what could be called 'elders'. 'She is a senior,' said the Abbess, 'and we need freshness of mind.' Three were necessary; there could be no question of Dame Emily Lovell's being able to serve on the Council again, or keep her office as prioress, and it was decided to make her, on her return, a Dean, as it were, of the Abbey, holding no office but much honoured with an especial seat in chapter and at the high table, and still to be called 'Mother'. 'One can't imagine her back in the ranks,' said Dame Maura, though Dame Emily would have retired there quite content.

Dame Veronica – 'thankfully,' said the Council – was more than at the end of her five year term as councillor; she had remained because the cellarer automatically was on the Council. Now her illness made it natural that she be deposed. 'She must never hold a responsible office again,' Abbot Bernard had said.

Abbess Catherine was still haunted by the memory of that initial scene with Dame Veronica. 'Act prudently,' the wise voice of St Benedict came down fifteen hundred years, 'prudently, lest, in seeking too eagerly to scrape off the rust, the vessel break. Remember that the bruised reed must not be broken.' And I nearly broke it, thought Abbess Catherine. If she had died! 'I didn't understand how far Dame Veronica had gone,' she told Dame Joan. 'Lady Abbess Hester, with her marvellous intuition, would have known, but I could only go by right and wrong.'

'If we all did that, none of this would have happened,' said Dame Joan. 'I am just plain shocked,' she said, but all the same she put a posy of winter flowers, a christmas rose and jasmine, on Dame Veronica's tea-tray and herself cut the bread and butter extra thin. 'You are too good to me,' said Dame Veronica and, still weak, relapsed into tears at the sight of the jasmine. She wept again when officially she had to give up her cellarer's keys – but that was from relief, she told the Abbess.

Abbess Catherine held the Chapter for the Deposition of Offices in the second week of January when, beginning with the least important or newest of the offices, she deposed their holders one by one.

For three days she sat alone at the high table, the nuns having returned to their old places in order of seniority at the main tables, and all during those days she spent hours closeted with her councillors, debating the appointments, new and old.

Then the bell rang out for Abbess Catherine's first Chapter for the Distribution of Offices and the nuns gathered to know their fate for the coming year – or perhaps years; they expected that some would be reappointed in their old positions, some faced with what was quite new, but now it was a major reshuffle. 'It's like pulling a stone out of a carefully balanced stone wall,' Abbess Catherine had said to her councillors. 'Much of the wall comes tumbling down.'

Some nuns, for the good of the Abbey, could not be changed: Dame Maura as precentrix: Dame Edith as printer: Dame Colette as mistress of church work: Dame

190

Mildred and Sister Marianne as gardeners. They were experts, 'But we must all give more time to the training of the younger ones,' Abbess Catherine said in her address, 'train them not to work with you, but to take your place.' It seemed almost like heresy to suggest that anyone could take the place of any of these nuns, but their aids were reappointed with this more than direct recommendation. 'I sniff the wind of change,' said Dame Agnes. She was right.

Dame Beatrice had been sacristan for sixteen years, steeped, immersed in holiness and in quiet, and to give this up for day in, day out Abbey affairs was a shattering loss to Dame Beatrice, but, 'Dame Beatrice, we appoint you prioress,' said Abbess Catherine and Dame Beatrice bent her head so that her veil hid what might possibly have been a telltale face.

She had guessed of course; when the office of sacristan had been discussed, she had naturally retired, but she had also not been present at the discussion for prioress. 'Will she have the necessary firmness?' Dame Agnes had asked.

'I think she will, in time,' said the Abbess, 'and we need her. The whole community loves her. I am going to be unpopular and they will need someone to love.'

Dame Agnes had guessed, with an equally sinking heart, that she would be cellarer.

'Dame Winifred?' the Council had suggested.

'She is too young to have the authority'; said the Abbess, 'though she has done very well in lieu of Dame Veronica, that has only been for a few days. This cellarer will have to be stringent in economy. Dame Winifred has worked three arduous years, but under Dame Veronica. We need a change of policy.'

'But Mother,' said Dame Beatrice, 'Dame Agnes's book.'

'She has finished her book,' said the Abbess quietly. 'She is only tinkering,' but she did not like to say that; instead, 'There comes a time when the amending and re-amending must stop and the book must go out. Dame Agnes, I believe, has reached it.'

Dame Winifred was appointed sacristan. 'She has had these years of temporal things. This will be a reward for her, and we know she is capable and faithful,' said Abbess Catherine. No one in the Abbey was happier that night than Dame Winifred.

Dame Ursula – and in the Chapter Abbess Catherine gave her a long and grateful commendation – was to take Dame Agnes's place as mistress of ceremonies.

'But Dame Ursula has been novice mistress for so long.'

'Yes,' said Abbess Catherine. She did not add, 'that is why,' but said, 'she has worked devotedly but she is getting older and must be very tired.'

'Then ... as novice mistress?'

'I should like to try Dame Clare.'

'But Mother, she is so young.'

'Young, but quite experienced and very gifted; she has a knack of managing people without saying much. I believe, too, we need someone young, more up to date, à la page if you like, for our nowadays girls.'

Once upon a time there had been no great hiatus for a girl between life at home and life in the monastery.

In the middle ages a family, unless it were rich, had the same, mainly vegetarian diet, a girl wore the same linen or woollen for her clothes. She had the habit of working by daylight 'instead of turning night into day, as they do now,' said the disapproving Dame Ursula.

At home there was little more heating – 'Heating is a comparatively modern invention,' said Dame Agnes with distaste; she was one of those who had opposed the central heating, 'though they keep it so low it hardly exists,' said Cecily feelingly.

If a girl were of gentle birth, her day was usually sedentary and confined; every family had its set time of prayer, and above all, she was content to play a passive part, to submit to other people's judgement, be ruled, whereas now ... 'If anyone had told me I would give up my will to another, I should have said I should rather be shot,' said Hilary, and, 'People think we don't know how the world is changing,' said Dame Maura. 'Even if we couldn't read or listen, we should know it with each postulant who comes.'

Dame Clare was appointed novice mistress – 'We shall do

nothing but read,' Hilary pretended to groan – and, 'The young are very much to the fore,' said Dame Agnes.

'We think of them as young but they are grown women and mature,' said Abbess Catherine. 'Many of them more mature than some of us older ones,' she could have added with a sigh.

'Mother, what are you going to do with me?' After the Distribution of Offices, Dame Veronica, still thin and pale, had come and knocked at the Abbess's door.

'I was coming to see you in the infirmary,' said the Abbess.

'I am nearly well now. I should work, try to pay back. Mother, you should punish me. Punish hard,' Dame Veronica's hands were pressed together under her scapular; tears were brimming.

'I think you have been punished enough,' said Abbess Catherine. 'Sit down, dear child,' and as Dame Veronica sat, 'I have had a letter.'

'It – hurts when you are so good to me,' Dame Veronica interrupted.

'Let's think about the letter.' The Abbess held up her hand and Dame Veronica had to be silent. 'As soon as you are quite strong, you will help Dame Camilla in the library. I know you will do it tactfully; she is getting very old and her eyes are bad. Meanwhile there is something I have kept for you : a Mr Digby of Mortimer and Digby, the publishers, has written saying they want an especial book and think it might come from Brede; it is to be a kind of birthday book for children, not of birthdays but name days, feasts, each with its special saint, as many as you can get in a year, one for boys and one for girls perhaps, in short poems. I believe you could write them.'

'Write poems *now*?'

'You could do it well.'

'But I *love* writing poems.' The tears spilled over. 'I need to do what I hate as – as an atonement. Mother, give me the hardest, dirtiest work in Brede. Let me clean out the hen houses, dig in the vegetable garden.'

'You are supposed to have had a heart attack,' said the Abbess. 'We must be consistent.'

'Send me to the kitchen then. I'll peel potatoes ... scrub and scour.'

'I think that would annoy Sister Priscilla.'

'Let me look after Dame Simone.' Dame Simone, though five years younger than Dame Frances Anne, was senile, bed-ridden and incontinent.

'Sister Mary does that very well and Dame Simone would miss her. Dame Joan and Dame Margaret help her too, and you are not strong enough to lift her.'

'But I *ought* to be humiliated.'

'There is nothing humiliating in doing a claustral sister's work.' A little of Abbess Catherine's patience was wearing thin. 'We all scrub and peel potatoes and look after ill people when the need arises. Wouldn't the best penance,' asked Abbess Catherine more gently, 'be in doing what you are asked? What you can do.' She smiled and said, 'Talking of atonement, the advance they offer against royalties is a hundred guineas, one hundred and five pounds.'

The Abbey had seldom had such an upheaval – but Mother has moved them round with admirable diplomacy, thought Philippa – 'and there will be more to come,' the Abbess could have said. Just as Dame Maura had been saying, 'my choir,' for years, so Dame Mildred talked of 'my garden'. 'I'm not going to have Dame Sophie ruining my garden,' she complained to the Abbess. 'Our garden. Dame Sophie's as well as yours,' the Abbess had corrected her. For Sister Priscilla it was 'my kitchen'. It would have to be changed; the Abbess knew that, and much else changed too – The cats! thought Abbess Catherine. All those kittens! and none of us must be attached – 'But change it slowly,' she told herself, 'even imperceptibly' – and first she had to find this vast sum of money. Money! Money! Money! she thought, and pressed her hands each side of her aching head.

'As your penance you will say the "Miserere".' The winter morning light came through the long windows of the chapter house, accentuating the black and white of the rows of nuns.

At each Chapter of Faults, the Abbess called on six nuns to make full and clear confession of any wrong they had done; now the last of these rose from her knees, bowed and went back to her place. 'Are there any acknowledgements?' the Abbess asked as she always asked, and a miserable figure in a black postulant dress and veil stood up.

'It's dreadful, being a possie,' Hilary had said in sympathy to Cecily. 'You are marked out even by the shape of your veil.'

'Yes, even by your shadow,' said Cecily and, 'What shall I say?' Cecily had asked Dame Ursula in panic. Now, 'My Lady, I . . .' she began.

Just after Christmas the bathroom in the novitiate had been finished. It was a bare small bathroom by worldly standards, holding a narrow bath and a basin, and with linoleum on the floor, but the novitiate had painted its walls primrose, the woodwork white; it gleamed attractively and the water was 'hot!' said Sister Constance. 'What luxury.'

'Yes. We must be deeply grateful and remember that the nuns in the Abbey haven't this,' said Dame Ursula, and the young sisters had looked suitably moved, but a few nights later – Dame Ursula's last night with them – an icy January night just before Curfew, the Great Silence had been broken by a frantic knocking on her cell door. 'Mother! Mother! Oh come! Please come.'

Dame Ursula, in her warm night tunic and night veil, was just getting into bed but, throwing her shawl round her, she flung open the door, to find Sister Cecily, her face ashen, her body shivering. 'Mother! Come and see what I have done.'

'Is it a fire? Is someone hurt? Speak, child,' but, 'It was an accident,' moaned Cecily, 'an accident,' and she had seized Dame Ursula's arm and propelled her down the passage like the wind – 'And I'm seventy-five, remember,' Dame Ursula told the Abbess – down the passage and the stairs into the new bathroom. 'There,' panted Cecily, 'there!'

All that month Cecily had been sleepless from the cold – there was no heating in the cells and the straw mattresses were thin – but there were no hot water bottles in the novitiate and

Dame Ursula did not suggest that Sister Cecily might ask her mother, Mrs Scallon, for one; 'I should rather be cold,' Cecily would have said and Dame Ursula knew the look of stone that would come on the girl's face. 'Mummy would say, "I told you so. I knew you wouldn't stand it,"' and the novice mistress had contrived a hot-water bottle for Cecily. The Abbey bought its ink in bulk and Dame Ursula had purloined one of the big empty bottles of heavy brown earthenware with a narrow neck; she cleaned it out, made sure its cork was secure and gave it to Cecily. 'Put that in your bed, child. The earthenware will hold heat for a long time.' It had become Cecily's greatest comfort.

That night, after Matins, she had gone to the bathroom to fill it; carefully she stood it in the basin and ran the tap until the water was hot. It was her turn to stoke the boiler and she left the bottle to fill from a slow dribble of the tap while she shovelled the coke. She washed her hands, turned off the tap, corked the bottle and lifted it out, 'but I forgot that it was wet'. It had slipped through her hands, landed with a crash in the basin and gone through it. Now, in the new basin was a large round hole, the exact size of the big ink bottle which lay unscathed on the floor below. 'Look!'

Dame Ursula looked and, though her heart ached for Cecily's stricken face, she had sat down on the edge of the bath and laughed.

It was no laughing matter to Cecily. 'It never is,' said Hilary. Hilary could sympathize because she was in constant trouble; she left taps running, tops off bottles, polishing rags not put away; she scorched and tore. 'Didn't *anyone* ever teach you anything?' asked Sister Jane in despair. In her first month, helping too enthusiastically with the cleaning of the choir, Hilary had knocked over the heavy lectern, sending it crashing to the floor and buckling its brass. 'We didn't let you in to smash up the Abbey,' Abbess Hester had said when Hilary was sent to her, but not even Hilary had broken anything as badly as this.

'I have,' said Philippa. That had been on Sunday when, as always on Sundays and important feast days, the novitiate had joined the community for recreation and Cecily had come straight to Philippa. '*You* have?'

'When I was a novice I broke a wing off one of the stone angels in the choir.' Philippa had been using a step-ladder to stand on while she dusted the high window sills and, lifting it to put it away, had caught one of the angels below the organ loft, breaking a wing. 'I remember I had to acknowledge it before the whole community and make satisfaction by kneeling, holding the wing, in the middle of the refectory until Mother gave the knock.'

'I can't very well do that with the basin,' said Cecily in relief.

Abbess Hester had been given to minutiae but when Abbess Catherine took her first Chapter of Faults, she had said, 'Let's have no laundry lists but real self-accusations, and not more than three. If you have ten faults, choose the three most damaging to the common life.' Each nun knelt. 'My Lady, I . . .' Abbess and community listened and the Abbess gave a penance. 'You will say the twenty-second psalm.' 'Read Chapter seventy of the Rule.' 'Say the Miserere.' Now and again she gave a short harangue but seldom to the one concerned, usually to all.

When the last of the six had stood up and bowed, the Abbess asked her question. 'Are there any acknowledgements?' When Philippa had said, 'My Lady, I have broken an angel,' an irrepressible ripple of mirth had run round the community.

The Chapter of Faults had the effect of welding the nuns together and making them like one another. 'You can't be afraid of someone, even as sharp and clever as Dame Agnes,' said Cecily, 'when you have seen her kneel down before us all, even us young ones she teaches, and say, "Three times yesterday I said things that cut," or "I lost my temper." '

'Especially when you know you will probably lose yours tomorrow,' said Hilary.

Strange things came out in the Chapter of Faults and, sometimes, endearing things. 'I accuse myself of 'aving done a h'act of charity in such a h'ugly manner as I'll never be h'asked to do another,' said one of the old claustral sisters, and from a nun, stickler to the letter of the Rule about possessions, 'My Lady, I have broken our false teeth.'

Abbess Catherine gave the knock for Sister Cecily to rise almost as soon as Cecily had knelt in the refectory. 'I couldn't bear to think,' Abbess Catherine said afterwards to Dame Beatrice, 'that here was this child, sick with contrition about a cheap basin' – she had seen that when Cecily went to her place at the novitiate table she had scarcely eaten anything – 'sick over this when her mentor and leader, our Mother, has plunged the Abbey into debt for thousands of pounds!'

'A basin isn't cheap if it is bought with frugalities,' said Dame Beatrice.

'No,' said the Abbess. 'It's all one and the same – but that basin can be replaced.'

'So can the thousands of pounds.'

'I wish I knew how.'

She had seen the bank manager, Mr Dutton, but against the already large overdraft she had no more security she could offer. 'The deposit money?' suggested Mr Dutton.

'Those are, as it were, in Trust.'

'The Abbey itself?'

'We could do that, but . . .'

'But?' Mr Dutton was sympathetic.

'I feel I can't. The cottages are already mortgaged; the farm land let.'

She would, as soon as means were found, have to consult the Abbot President; she could have consulted Abbot Bernard now, 'but I feel we should, rather, try and keep this in the house.'

'How?' asked Mr Dutton.

'I don't know how.'

When Abbess Catherine left the parlour where she had seen Mr Dutton, she walked thoughtfully up to her room; the one or two nuns she passed, seeing her abstraction, made their bows without speaking, but as she went through the alcove, Philippa stood up. 'Mother, may I speak?' and, without waiting, in her earnestness went on, 'I know an Abbess doesn't go to a junior nun for advice, but I can't help knowing or guessing your worry, Mother, and . . .'

'And?'

'Problems used to be my daily lot,' said Philippa.

The silence in the chapter house could be felt as Abbess Catherine, standing, laid the position before the community. 'We are committed to the altar and the new apse. The – the means' – for an instant her voice had hesitated – 'means Lady Abbess Hester had counted on are not forthcoming, so that we have to face this debt. Our cottages are mortgaged and the holders may foreclose which would mean that our pensioners will lose their homes. The farmland is let on a long lease we cannot break, so that it would be difficult to find a buyer for that. We have no assets that are free except . . .' and she looked over their heads through the windows to where the beeches along the avenue stood sentinel and white with rime against the sky.

'There is a way,' Philippa had said.

When Abbess Catherine had taken Philippa into her room, Philippa had listened – 'doesn't comment but listens with her whole attention,' Abbess Catherine told Dame Beatrice, 'really listens'. 'Yes, that was one of her assets,' McTurk could have told them. 'She listens, then, while the rest of us are mulling over the problem and wondering, she has seen a way to a solution.' With Abbess Catherine, Philippa had not been as quick as that; she had asked several questions, studied the bank statements and the status of the Abbey, then gone away to ponder. A few hours later she had knocked at the door. 'There is a way – I think – but it is so hateful that I dread to tell it.'

'Is it the only way?' asked Abbess Catherine.

'The only way that I can see, but it would be a terrible deprivation for us all.'

'Much better to be for all,' said Dame Beatrice. 'Then each can feel she helps.'

'What is it we must do?' Abbess Catherine had asked.

'Get planning permission,' said Philippa.

'Our park is fifteen acres,' Abbess Catherine said now in the chapter house. 'Brede is an expanding town, land is short and the most desirable part of it is up here on the hill. We have applied for planning permission to build houses on seven of our fifteen acres.'

Abbess Catherine kept her eyes away from Dame Agnes sitting two seats from her.

Dame Agnes had come to her room after the Council's second 'extraordinary' meeting. 'Mother, may I ask you something?'

'Of course.'

'I am your cellarer now and concerned with temporal things,' said Dame Agnes, 'so I must speak. Mother, about this solution; did you send for Sister Philippa or did she bring it to you?'

'She brought it to me.'

'And managed you into it.'

Abbess Catherine's colour seldom rose : it rose now. 'I don't understand.' She had spoken with a new haughtiness.

'Please forgive me, Mother, but this is what I have been dreading all along.'

'It would be better to be more explicit.' Now it was really distant. 'Can you be more explicit?'

'Yes,' said Dame Agnes. 'Mother, don't you see that what I said in Council long ago is true? That was Mrs Talbot speaking, not the Sister Philippa we are hoping and trying to adapt to our ways. Our way is faith and hope and dependence on God, as Dame Beatrice said; I see now she was right. The Mrs Talbots of this world are clever, adroit, but they cannot refrain from interfering, setting the world to rights, or what they think are rights. This is the immediate solution.'

'It happens to be the only one.' Abbess Catherine's voice had been cold.

Dame Agnes shook her head. 'It's the worldly one,' and she had said, 'Mother, I must say this in chapter.'

'Of course,' and Abbess Catherine dismissed Dame Agnes with that.

Seven acres! Almost half the park! A sound like a faint hiss filled the chapter house: it was not a hiss but a catching of breath all round the room.

'I am assured permission will be granted. This does not mean the land will be built on – yet. No one can build until we sell but planning permission means the price will rise to perhaps nine hundred pounds an acre, nine times its present value, and, on that security, the bank will lend us the money we need.' Another sound, but of relief, filled the room.

'But banks don't like long-term loans,' said Abbess Catherine, 'and this will only be for a year – if Father President approves. We have, of course, to get his permission. A loan for a year. We shall hope and pray that in that time something will intervene.' It would be a miracle, she almost said.

'And if it doesn't intervene?' The unspoken question was on everybody's tongue but Dame Thecla asked it.

'If it doesn't intervene, we shall have to give up our seven acres.'

Dame Anselma passed round copies of a map of the Abbey and park and the new plan. 'As you see,' said Abbess Catherine, 'the wall would be moved nearer and built higher. It would have to be built higher because houses would be on the other side. We shall hope it is a private buyer who will want to build with space, but if the Town Council takes it for development, we should have to accept that they may perhaps build terrace houses, ten to an acre.'

'Ten to an acre! That's iniquitous,' Dame Agnes had exploded in Council.

'That is all the space those people have. We should try to think of it like that,' said the Abbess.

'But they have all the world to go out into; we only have our park, and think of the *noise*!' Dame Agnes had seemed to look at Abbess Catherine with that third red eye. It was then that she had asked, 'Do I detect that our business-minded Mrs Talbot had something to do with this?'

We should lose our woodland, the nuns thought now, as they looked at the plans. Lose the long walk, the pleached alley, the dingle, the avenue. 'We should still have the gardens, the orchards, the vegetable garden and garth, and we should plant new trees,' said the Abbess.

'In fact, have plenty of space,' said Dame Beatrice and she said, as Dame Ursula had said to the novices, 'We should think of the Newgate nuns.'

Dame Beatrice spoke with a vitality the community had not heard before as she went on, 'The money realized would free Brede of debt, redeem the mortgages on the cottages and make them safe for our old people – and it will pay for the new altar and apse.'

To trade an altar and stone panels, however beautiful, for the freedom to walk, for woods whose wildness made another world for the nuns where wild flowers, birds, small animals abounded. They would all be driven away, thought the nuns. To lose the dingle where the moorhens had their pond and where the Canons used to fish, and the bog garden – my water lilies, thought Dame Teresa – lose the avenue with its broad walk and double row of noble trees – they would all be felled, thought the nuns – and the little pleached alley. To trade these living things for stone, life for ambition! 'I shall never be able to look at that altar without choking,' Dame Anselma had said in Council. That was the feeling of them all.

Dame Bridget stood up. 'And if the land is not used for building? If we sold it as woods and farmland?'

'It is worth perhaps a hundred and twenty pounds an acre.'

'Which would not be enough,' Dame Bridget said sadly and sat down.

Dame Winifred asked the question Abbess Catherine herself had asked. 'This is probably superfluous,' said Dame Winifred, 'but, Mother, is this the only way?'

'The only way we can see, unless we go to Father President and confess we cannot meet our debts and ask if he and the General Chapter can arrange a loan elsewhere to save our house.' There was again that ripple of distaste among the nuns, but Dame Agnes stood up, a lone figure, and began to speak.

'The suggestion of getting planning permission is brilliant, a clever solution, but . . .' The 'but' rang in the room, then Dame

Agnes went on, 'with Lady Abbess's permission I should like to put it to you again. She has said it is the only way except to go to the General Chapter for help. Well, why not? Wouldn't it be better to do that? We religious should not be proud; does it matter if we are humbled for the sake of God? We are all ready to be noble and abnegate ourselves, but what are we really doing? If the park is curtailed we think we should be robbing ourselves. No! We should be robbing God. This is His House; that is why people come here, to find Him; we are only the custodians and we have no right to give away what is His. It would be quite wrong,' said Dame Agnes firmly, 'to reduce our already not large enclosure; to do our work satisfactorily we must have elbow room, breathing space; Mother Prioress has instanced the Newgate community, but she did not mention that they have a country house to which they can go in turn for refreshment. We cannot get away, even for holidays. We are not so strong and steady that we can take risks, and we must not unfit ourselves. Let us apply to Father President and the monks for help.' There was silence as Dame Agnes sat down, then a fidgeting stir.

The Abbess rose. 'I shall ask you to vote,' she said. 'Do we raise the loan on our own land, knowing that it may bring us this ... deprivation?' She did not have to embroider that – each nun knew what it would mean. 'The white balls are for "yes", the black for "no".' When the boxes came back to Dame Beatrice as prioress, she had no need to count them; there was one black ball ... she knew it was Dame Agnes's.

The contractors came to take down the altar and dismantle the apse. A temporary choir was arranged, facing the chapel of the Crown of Thorns where Dom Gervase now said Mass. The main sanctuary was full of canvas sheeting, scaffolding, dust and noise. The workmen were puzzled at having to break off for the Office, when extern Sisters Elizabeth and Susanna served them with quantities of tea, and puzzled too by, in the mornings, having to wait to come in until the Conventual Mass was ended. 'Can't you start your prayers earlier?' the foreman asked Sister Elizabeth.

'As it is, we start at half past five.'

'Half past five. Cor! That's two hours.'

'And begin again at nine for an hour and a quarter, but while this work is going on, we do that in the large parlour.'

'Cor! What do you find to say?'

When they had finished, the empty sanctuary looked big, its walls rough where the ornamental marble had been prised away. The cherubim mourned by Dame Beatrice – and many of the other nuns – had been moved into the ante-chapel, 'so you can still look at them,' the Abbess told them. With the ornate canopy removed, the ceiling showed its ancient colours, the rose window its jewels; Abbess Catherine had taken the opportunity of having them carefully washed and cleaned. 'We never knew they were so beautiful,' and the community had to acknowledge that Lady Abbess Hester had undoubtedly been right; 'except the price, the heavy price!'

To Abbess Catherine's surprise and Philippa's dismay McTurk took the same view of the planning permission as Dame Agnes. He had descended, as he did every now and then, to see Philippa, always bringing a present for the Abbey. 'A sensible present,' said Sister Priscilla, 'that we can use, perhaps cook'; a side of gammon: cheese: a crate of apples: boxes and boxes of biscuits. With Abbess Catherine's permission Philippa had consulted McTurk. 'What a busybody you are,' he said to Philippa.

'You mean I shouldn't have advised it? But it was obvious.'

'It wasn't obvious to the nuns,' said McTurk. 'I am sure no one here at Brede knew the value of the land. Religious don't think along those lines and I believe monastic possessions are not sold for profit; perhaps they are deliberately undersold. It's only you, with your tradesman's workaday knowledge, my dear, who are sophisticated enough . . .' McTurk was upset. 'I'm sure it's not wise. It offers an immediate solution, but space is the health of your bodies and souls.'

McTurk's eyes, so like a monkey's, Philippa had often thought, brilliant in his wizened face, expressive, oddly sad, holding prescience of things far beyond himself, looked at her through the grille and must have seen her distress. Philippa's usually pale face had a spot of colour on either cheek, her eyes, usually so level, were looking down, her fingers, usually quiet under her scapular were drumming on the sill. McTurk put his hand through the grille and stilled them.

'Shall I never learn?' Philippa spoke in misery. 'Of course I see it now – too late. It will be difficult, no, impossible, to stop it. I may have done Brede irreparable damage.'

'It may never happen,' said McTurk.

'I wish I had the faith to think so. You're right, I am a busybody. I suppose it's second nature. I *will* learn,' said Philippa. 'I shall hold my tongue, keep myself back, efface my meddlesome self – this me.'

'You can't,' said McTurk.

'Why not?'

'For the simple reason that they will never let you. To deny your gifts would be cheating. We can overcome our second natures, my dear, but not our first, and you were born to take responsibility, to lead.' He spoke seriously but Philippa only laughed.

'I can't do that here. There is always Dame Agnes to take me down.' Then she spoke seriously too. 'These walls are my shield; here, thank God, I am a nobody, almost anonymous, a very young-in-religion, unimportant Benedictine nun.'

8

It was by chance that Abbess Catherine saw Stefan Duranski arrive.

Dame Emily was to come home. 'Home!' she had said when she was told in hospital, only the one word but her joy seemed to shine through her thin face. The Abbess had gone herself to fetch her and, as the car driven by Sister Renata came up the drive to the enclosure gate, the way in was blocked by a lorry; beyond was another lorry with a crane; both were loaded with sheeted shapes. As the lorries ground round the loop of the drive to the church and the Abbess's car went on, the three nuns saw an estate car parked by the front door; two men were in it, and a third was standing on the drive, a bulky man with huge shoulders made bigger by a massive sweater and with a head of dark curly hair. 'Mr Duranski,' said Abbess Catherine as their car went through the enclosure gate.

'Then the new altar has come,' said Sister Renata.

It had come, and with it the panels and a curve of plain stone to fit the apse below the rose window; this piece would be carved in position. 'It's a question of light,' Stefan Duranski had written. One by one, the pieces were lifted by the crane on to the rollers – wheeled trolleys; fortunately the old stone flags of the porch leading to the extern sanctuary were on ground level, the pieces were easily rolled in and a phase began in the Abbey of which its daughters had not dreamed.

Stefan Duranski, with his curly hair, brown eyes, snub nose and plumpness looked far younger than he was, 'like an infant John the Baptist,' said Dame Maura. He was as enthusiastic as a child too – 'I couldn't tell him how dismayed we were,' said Abbess Catherine – and as direct: 'I can't get used to you,' he told her. 'You are too young to be an abbess,' and she answered as she would never have answered before to a stranger, 'That's what I think,' but added, 'I should be old enough. I'm almost fifty.'

'And I too am fifty – but my eyes,' he said, meaning 'except my eyes'. 'They are five years old and five hundred,' he said gravely.

Abbess Catherine felt those eyes looking at her as they talked; they looked in a way she had not felt for a long time. Abbot Bernard, wise and penetrating as he was, saw the habit, the pectoral cross – and the soul, thought Abbess Catherine, as Bishop Mark now did, though for him there was always the accompaniment of the young sister he had known and loved. Stefan Duranski saw the woman. And we are women, thought Abbess Catherine. How many people forget that? How we forget it ourselves!

She guessed that he was not concerned with uniforms or offices, not even as symbols, but looked through them to people: not only flesh and bones, but hearts, thought Abbess Catherine, because he knows they are intrinsic. She had heard he had an unswerving eye for beauty. 'I am not beautiful,' she would have said and yet knew he found her beautiful; there was pleasure in his eyes as well as respect, and she was warmed as she had not been warmed – since I became a senior nun, she thought, and somehow stopped loving. There was a tremulous flutter in her like a young girl's – and I didn't laugh at it, she thought afterwards, it was too badly needed.

He and she had talked only about the necessary arrangements; Dame Agnes was called and Sister Elizabeth, the extern sacristan, and the work was planned: a plinth to be placed in the middle of the sanctuary, the altar itself to be set on it; then Stefan Duranski would carve the front, 'in place,' he said, 'which is ideal, and as Lady Abbess Cunningham Proctor promised me.' The two tall panels would be erected, the sidelights cut and the finishing carving done on them: the curved panel that joined them would be put in below the window; the crucifix hung on the grille facing the sanctuary; the nuns would see of it only the shape of the cross and a glimpse of the thorn-crowned head, but they were to find that even more moving than the front view. 'This will all take me and my men till Easter,' said Stefan Duranski, 'when you must have your full church again.' After Easter he would come back and carve the centre panel – 'in place again. She promised me,' – he seemed half afraid they would stop him doing that. 'It is the light,' he repeated. 'In so many places they do not understand the importance of light, the way the light falls. If I carve in place, I shall be able to make it . . .' and he spread his hands in, not hope, but confidence. Perhaps, though, he had felt a certain blankness of response; the confidence gave way to an uncertainty, as if there were something he could not plumb. 'You do wish me to do it?' he asked, and, 'We shall have to get over our feeling about the altar,' Abbess Catherine told the Council. 'Yes,' said Dame Beatrice, 'after all, though the park is nice to have, the centre of our life is our church.'

One of the first things Stefan Duranski had asked was, 'The sanctuary is, of course, temporarily empty?' Abbess Catherine knew what he meant: and had answered, 'The tabernacle is in our chapel of the Crown of Thorns which we shall use meanwhile.'

'Good,' said Stefan Duranski. 'Then I can smoke and play my guitar,' which had startled Dame Beatrice. 'I play very softly but it loosens me – and you won't sweep up round me, will you?' he asked Sister Elizabeth. 'I need my dust.'

'But cigarette butts,' pleaded Sister Elizabeth, remembering the dismantling men.

'Give me a bucket. We can empty that.'

'A bucket in the sanctuary!' said Dame Beatrice, but there were many buckets, of sand and cement, of stone chips, as well as the cigarette bucket which Sister Elizabeth sensibly filled with sand.

Stefan Duranski did not have to be told about the time of the Conventual Mass, or the singing of the Offices, but acquainted himself with them and, as soon as the nuns came in behind the canvas screens that were stretched across the grille, he would signal his men to stop work. Sometimes they stayed, though usually they went out. He himself would sit and listen. 'I like it,' he said. 'It helps me to look.'

He had to work through the other Masses but, Dame Winifred said, he always stayed the work at the consecration bells. 'And that from a man who says he is a pagan!' said Dame Beatrice.

Between him and Dame Beatrice – though he was the cause of uprooting her cherubim – an instant liking had sprung up; also with Dame Agnes whom he teased. Dame Maura he admired – sometimes she came to the organ and played for him – but he was a puzzle to Dame Perpetua. Why that stone should cost so much she could not see, 'and he doesn't look like someone who needs money. He seems so at home here with us.'

Dame Ursula was not only puzzled, she was horrified. To her Stefan Duranski was a complete mystery. 'He can't be poor, but look at his clothes!' Internationally famous, he earned these, to them, enormous sums of money, yet he wore a pair of dusty jeans and the massive loose jersey that they knew was torn at the shoulder – they had seen it when he took off his smock. 'No, thank you,' he said when Sister Elizabeth offered to mend it, 'it frees my arm.' He wore ski socks that fell over the espadrilles in which he padded about among the dust and chips of stone. 'He isn't even clean,' said Dame Ursula.

'Stone dust won't brush off like wood dust,' said Dame Gertrude. 'I remember Mother telling us that stone dust clings.'

'But what will visitors think?' said Dame Ursula.

Visitors were not allowed in the sanctuary while the work was going on, but they could meet him on the drive or going in and out of the extern cloister. 'What will they think?'

'That we are privileged,' said Abbess Catherine.

Soon the altar and panels were placed; the men – all but the foreman Ralph who acted as fetcher and carrier – left, and Stefan Duranski started to carve. 'He must be happy,'

Philippa said in recreation. 'He always says it's his ideal, to carve where the work is placed, although he works a great deal in what he calls his "stone shed" in Paris.' She went on, 'It really is a shed, small and shabby and covered in his loved dust. It's the same shed he had while he was poor when he was just starting. He says he has never had time to move.'

'Says? Then you *knew* Stefan Duranski?' Dame Veronica had reared up her head and Philippa, wishing she had kept quiet, had to say, 'Yes. Anna Fouldes, the artist, was a friend of mine and she took me to see him sometimes.'

'Anna Fouldes!' Dame Gertrude and Dame Benita heard that across the room and, this being recreation, Philippa was plied with questions and she was grateful that Abbess Catherine refrained from asking if she would like to meet Stefan Duranski again.

'We will let him get on with his work in quiet,' said the Abbess, but, 'Mother,' said Dame Perpetua, 'couldn't you ask him if he could do something about our Lady's hand?'

Philippa had broken the angel in the choir, but that was not unprecedented: long, long ago Dame Perpetua, as a novice, had knocked off a hand from the statue of our Lady of Peace in the ante-chapel. 'Dame Perpetua says she was as clumsy as I am,' said Hilary comforted but Dame Perpetua had not ceased to reproach herself, and this seemed a golden opportunity. 'Couldn't you ask him, Mother?' she said wistfully.

'But, Dame, she is in plaster.'

'He could model a hand or carve it in wood and stick it on,' said Dame Perpetua in blithe ignorance. 'Then we could paint it pale pink. Please, Mother?'

Abbess Catherine knew he would shudder but to please Dame Perpetua she asked him. 'I will look,' said Stefan Duranski; Sister Elizabeth brought him to the enclosure door where Dame Agnes and Dame Perpetua met him to escort him down the long cloister to the church.

'In the enclosure?' Dame Beatrice had been doubtful. Besides priests and doctors only three classes of persons were allowed in an enclosure: reigning members of a royal family: cardinals: and plumbers – which meant all workmen.

'He is a workman,' said Abbess Catherine, 'and a strangely humble one,' she added.

'I broke that hand off thirty-three years ago,' Dame Perpetua told Stefan Duranski. 'Every day I pass it several times and it is such a reminder. Can you make another, Mr Duranski? Can you?' Stefan Duranski saw the distress in her face, the reproach as fresh now as when the damage was done. 'Can you? Without it costing too much?' pleaded Dame Perpetua.

'I will . . . think of something,' he said gently.

'Lady Abbess, can I have your drinking bowl?'

'My what?' asked Abbess Catherine.

'I think it is a drinking bowl, but long – like that,' Stefan Duranski measured the full extent of his arms. 'They did eat and drink from it – animals, I mean, perhaps pigs. Now they have aluminium, the kind they push up and rattle, you can hear them from the presbytery.' Stefan Duranski was staying with Dom Gervase who found him a great change from visiting priests. 'Now they have aluminium,' Stefan Duranski repeated. 'The old is stone.'

'You mean a trough. Is there one?'

'Lying among the nettles. I have been poking, you see. It must have lain there for centuries. I had my men turn it over. It is a lovely bit of stone.'

'But . . . what will you do with it?'

'Carve it,' said Stefan Duranski. 'It is seldom one finds stone weathered like that – and I think that, no, you should not contrive with that abominable figure of plaster out there.'

'Our Lady of Peace? Many of the nuns love it.'

'I do not think,' said Stefan Duranski – for all his years in America and England his th's still sounded like Z – 'I do not think Lady Abbess Hester loved it.'

'N-no,' said the Abbess.

'I shall carve you a Lady of Peace. I shall split this piece of stone, using the part that is at present plinth. You will see, it will carve itself.'

'But Mr Duranski, we can't pay you.'

'You have paid me already,' he said, 'just to come here;
211

besides, it is your trough. If your nuns grieve for the other –
well, ask Dame Perpetua to break it some more.'

The trough was carried up from the farm – a special gang of
men had to be recruited – split and rough shaped outside, then
set up in the sanctuary. 'Is he to carve that here too?' asked
Dame Ursula.

'I think we must show him that courtesy. He says the light
is much the same as in the ante-chapel though he will finish it
off there.'

'But a statue from a trough!'

'And a pig trough at that.' The Council did not know
whether to be shocked or amused. 'If he is doing it for nothing,
he is making us a most valuable present, judging by his other
prices,' said Dame Agnes. 'But . . .'

'After all,' said Dame Beatrice, 'our Lord used the most
homely and earthy of things : he mixed clay and spittle.'

'But *can* Mr Duranski carve from a *trough*?'

'Wait and see,' said Abbess Catherine, but even she had no
inkling of what they would see.

What appealed particularly to their monasticism was the
simplicity with which he worked. Some sculptors, he admitted, used power-driven chisels; that needed a different tech-
nique, as he explained to Abbess Catherine. 'The thought goes
from your head, along your arm to your fingers, to the cutting
edge all in one go; there is no time to decide a new "where".
For me, the less apparatus the better. I like mallet and chisel.'
Twelve years ago, he told her, he had bought seven chisels, a
mallet 'and a sheet of sandpaper. Cost to me, three pounds,
and I have used them ever since.' He carried his tools in a big
duster and laid them out on it on the floor until Sister Elizabeth brought him a table. 'This is luxury,' he said, reproving
her. Nor would he use a riffler on his surfaces, nor oil. 'Only a
very little sandpaper now and then. And never never will you
wash this stone,' he told the extern sisters. 'Water will ruin the
surfaces at once.'

'Then how . . .' began Sister Susanna, but he stopped her. 'I
will buy you a feather duster.'

From the worry and upset that had surrounded the apse and

212

altar another feeling had emerged, one of hope and cheer. Though nothing had changed, another dimensión was in the monastery. 'I suppose it's having a "creating" in our midst,' said Abbess Catherine.

'This deserves the name creation,' said Dame Gertrude. 'I thought when I entered Brede, I should never see great sculpture or painting again except in photographs. That was a real grief to me but if I had stayed in the world, I should never have seen anything like this.'

'Nor I,' said Dame Benita.

More and more, in their scant free time that February and March, the nuns would steal into the choir that looked so strange with rows of hired chairs facing the chapel of the Crown of Thorns. They would lift a corner of the canvas that screened the sanctuary and watch through the grille. Once Dame Clare brought her novitiate. 'Do they disturb you?' asked Abbess Catherine.

'Who?' asked Stefan Duranski, and when she told him, 'I didn't know they were there. Your nuns,' he said, 'have a great advantage over other women. They are silent.' It was the silence of Brede that pleased him. 'I can hear life,' he said.

To the nuns it seemed that life was growing under his hand. The sanctuary looked as strange as the choir with its ladders, buckets and shapes of stone; the upright – block was too solid a word for it – the upright shape the trough-plinth had made, seemed itself to be the rough shape of a woman but veiled from head to foot. On the floor a debris of stone accumulated, hunks to begin with, then chips, then dust which got into and overlaid everything. The skull cap Stefan Duranski wore was not an affectation but a necessity: without it he would never have got the stone dust out of his hair. The centre panel was still empty, waiting for its relief of corn sheaves for bread, grapes for wine, olives for oil, the corn and wine for the substances offered in the mysteries, oil for the priesthood that could transform them. The crucifix lay sheeted on the ground.

After five o'clock, when his man, Ralph, had gone, Duranski worked alone on the figure; the sound of his chisel and mallet was the only noise until he put them down to stretch his arms

– their span was enormous – then he would pick up his guitar and softly strum as he walked round and round the statue. 'Mother, are you going to let him?' asked Dame Ursula.

'Yes,' said Abbess Catherine. 'He plays it well,' and, 'think of the Jongleur de Notre Dame,' said Dame Maura.

He liked it when she or her 'second', Dame Monica or, sometimes, Cecily, practised the organ. 'Music makes the work grow,' he said.

The statue seemed to emerge almost naturally from the stone though again, statue seemed the wrong word, it was so alive. 'He's uncovering it,' said Dame Gertrude marvelling.

After the novitiate had watched him, Sister Constance had said, 'It's like us. We come as a rough piece of stone and have to be carved and shaped to have meaning.'

'But he can only shape,' said Cecily. 'He can't put anything there that wasn't there before.'

'Still more like us,' said Philippa who had come, as she sometimes did, to see them at recreation; she came for Cecily; instinctively she knew that Dame Clare and the Council were doubtful about this girl.

It was told in the Abbey that Dame Emily Lovell, when she was novice mistress, had never clothed a novice who had not stayed. Dame Ursula, who succeeded her, had had several disappointments, notably Sister Julian. 'But she wasn't a disappointment to me,' said Sister Priscilla. 'I thought what I thought, and seeing her in the habit showed me I was right. It didn't fit her.' Julian's habit had fitted perfectly well in the actual sense, but the nuns knew what the old kitchener meant; the black dress, long scapular, white wimple, fillet and veil, which covered from top to toe was, by paradox, extraordinarily revealing. 'I knew too,' said Sister Jane, 'and I told Mother Mistress, but she wouldn't listen.'

Dame Clare was being careful – over-careful, thought Philippa, looking at Cecily's innocent face.

For Holy Week and the week after, the octave of Easter, Stefan Duranski would leave Brede. 'For one fortnight, no more,' he said.

'But your letter said you were going to Chicago.'

'I have changed my mind.' For the first time Abbess Catherine found him peremptory. 'I shall let you drive me away for that little while but I am coming back: to do the panel, to finish our Lady – and to see you,' he shot at her.

'And Chicago? Your urgent business in Chicago?'

'Chicago must wait.'

The fortnight would give time for the Clothing which could be held during the octave. Both postulants were due – 'Sister Hilary overdue,' said Dame Domitilla, of Hilary's reception there was not a doubt, 'in spite of her faults and untidiness,' said Dame Clare, though when Sister Jane was asked for her opinion of Sister Hilary and Sister Cecily, she had drawn herself up and said, 'I am extremely edified by the behaviour of the *choir* postulant.'

'Poor Sister Hilary,' said the Abbess and laughed, but even with Sister Jane's tribute, Dame Clare asked for more time for Sister Cecily. 'I still find her baffling,' said Dame Clare.

'Can you still not say why?'

'She's good.' Dame Clare said it so helplessly that they had to laugh. 'I mean, she is too good to be true, yet it is true.'

'Yes,' said Dame Maura.

'If only – she would be a little bit silly.'

'Perhaps she isn't silly. Perhaps she just is good,' said Dame Beatrice.

'Yes, but most of us when we come have a struggle to adapt ourselves, to conform; we have difficulties. Sister Cecily seems to have none at all. She seems not to have to make the slightest effort. She lives up among the stars,' said Dame Clare.

'Bring her down to earth,' said Dame Agnes.

'I try, but she immediately folds.'

'Not with me,' said Dame Maura.

'No, but even with her singing . . . she sings as if she were trying to please; she has one eye on you most of the time.'

'She won't stand alone?' asked the Abbess.

'Yes. No,' said Dame Clare almost in a breath.

'One cannot alternate in religious life,' said Dame Agnes.

215

'And there must be a modicum of spunk.' The blunt word coming from Dame Beatrice was so unexpected that they all looked at her, but Dame Ursula took that up, her spectacles glittering. She had always been indignant when one of her fledgelings – 'goslings', the old Abbess used to tease her – was criticized, and she was still not used to Sister Cecily being Dame Clare's postulant. 'Didn't it take spunk to revolt against that overbearing mother?'

'Was it revolt or escape?' asked Abbess Catherine.

'She could have married.'

'We don't know that. It is what the mother said.'

'Yes, poor child!'

'Poor child.' Abbess Catherine was more thoughtful still. 'It is significant that all of us, except perhaps Dame Maura, seem to think of Sister Cecily as a child. She is twenty-three, a strong grown woman.'

'Yet that's just what she isn't,' said Dame Clare.

'Musically she is more,' said Dame Maura.

'Yet, with us, she is more like eighteen – or less.'

'Perhaps Mrs Scallon touched her with frost,' said Abbess Catherine.

She, as Dame Catherine, had been present with Lady Abbess Hester at the first interview any of them had had with Mrs Scallon – 'and Major Scallon,' Dame Catherine had said, as they recounted it afterwards. 'Though it's difficult to remember about him. He was so overshadowed.' Mrs Scallon had been – 'pitiful', Abbess Catherine could say that now, though at the time it seemed like virulence. Mrs Scallon had sat on the edge of her chair, her rings and bangles making glittering bands on her fingers and wrists, too many rings, too many bangles, Dame Catherine had thought; they jangled as she moved, and she moved often and jerkily with nervous tension.

'Naturally,' said Abbess Hester afterwards. It was the first time Mrs Scallon had come any length on Cecily's road, had faced an actuality, 'and she is giving up a most beautiful daughter,' said the Abbess. Not only that; they could guess, in spite of the show of rings, that money was scant, and much thought about in the Scallon household – Cecily had told them

Major Scallon only had his pension and, 'My daughter would have made a good marriage,' Mrs Scallon told them, 'if it hadn't been for this nonsense.'

'Can you call it nonsense?' Abbess Hester had asked mildly. 'All down the ages, thousands of intelligent women have made it their chosen way of life.'

'Because they had nothing better to do.'

'On the contrary; because they knew there was nothing better they could do.'

'Pshaw!' said Mrs Scallon, or a sound very like it and, 'Carlotta!' Major Scallon had expostulated helplessly.

Mrs Scallon, Abbess Catherine remembered, had an extraordinarily pale face, and her eyelids were hooded over eyes that were – saurian? Dame Catherine had thought. Yes, like a python – a pythoness. She seemed to have crushed all life out of her husband; Major Scallon looked ill and shabby; his suit, carefully pressed, was old-fashioned and shone at the elbows: he smelled of soda mints. Dame Catherine had seen him take one out of his pocket and quietly put it into his mouth – nervous indigestion, thought Dame Catherine – but it was from him that Cecily got those dark eyes and, when he smiled or his humour was touched as Lady Abbess Hester knew how to touch it, his face too was transformed; but in the parlour he had been too much disturbed to do more than cluck his ineffectual 'Carlotta' as he tried to check his wife and, remembering that interview it was no wonder, thought Abbess Catherine, that Sister Cecily was this baffling mixture of timidity and ease.

On the morning after the interview at Brede, Cecily had found a letter by her bed. 'It was from Mummy,' she had told Abbess Hester. 'It said if I did this, came to Brede, I should have nothing from her – she's the one who had a little capital – no money, nor my share of the house, or of her jewels – she sets great store by her jewels – they should all go to my sister Daphne.'

'Did you mind?' asked Abbess Hester and Cecily had laughed; then she was sober. 'I only mind that, if you take me, I must come almost empty handed. I can't save much;

working in London and paying for my music, I have only a hundred and fifty pounds.'

'Did your father have a say in this?'

Cecily shook her head. 'Dad ... can't,' was all she would say but the Abbess had understood. All the same, at the interview when Mrs Scallon had almost run out – the three nuns, Abbess Hester, Dame Catherine and Dame Ursula had simply let her speak – Abbess Hester had turned to Major Scallon and asked, 'And Major, what do you say?'

He had cleared his throat, braced himself and said, 'I think Kitten should try—' his eyes went unhappily to the grille. 'She will never be satisfied with anything less.'

'Less!' Mrs Scallon had snorted.

Dame Catherine had noted that 'Kitten', and her voice had been gentle as she had said, 'You will get used to the grille. After a time you will find it makes no difference.'

'Perhaps,' said Major Scallon. It was then that she had seen his smile.

'You see, they are all ganged up against me,' Mrs Scallon was saying. 'I'm defeated, as I always am.' Her glance had swept round the parlour, back to Abbess Hester. 'I suppose this is as good as anywhere else. I hope you understand when I say at least it isn't common.'

Abbess Hester had bowed her head in acknowledgement but, 'I thought the time had come,' she told Dame Catherine afterwards, 'to turn the tables – just a little.'

'I gather you think we might be suitable for your daughter, Mrs Scallon, but we must not go too fast. We have also to think "Is she suitable for us?"'

'Don't you *want* her?'

'It's not a question of wanting; all candidates ...'

'*Candidates?*' Mrs Scallon had bristled. 'You ought to be down on your knees thanking God there are girls who want to join you.'

'We are,' said the Abbess. 'We pray for vocations, of course, but we must be as sure as we can be that they are the right ones. Your daughter seems an exceptionally sweet and gifted girl but ...'

'But what?'

'We haven't known her very long. We have to find out more about her – which is why I am so glad you have both come today. We need to know about her health, her history, heredity.'

'Heredity. The Scallon side is middle class,' said Mrs Scallon, 'but mine, the St Georges, are *good* family.'

'Good for religious life? That's something different. Most of us here are quite ordinary people, but has your daughter inherited, for instance, some of your – shall we call it "emotionalism"?'

'My . . .' Mrs Scallon had stared, but the Abbess went smoothly on. 'On the other hand, you may have taught her a great deal of control. Perhaps too much; she seems almost unnaturally quiet and silent for a young girl, but one must say she has been steady and brave all this time.'

'When I was fighting for her.'

'When you were fighting with her.'

'Insufferable woman!' Dame Catherine had heard Mrs Scallon say that as she left the parlour and it was true Abbess Hester had been formidable, yet Dame Catherine remembered her cautioning Sister Cecily: 'Try not to call me Mother in the parlour if your own mother is there. It would wound her.'

'Touched with frost,' said Dame Clare in the Council now. 'That's what I'm afraid of.'

Dame Clare fitted her name; she had clear eyes and she knew one of the great difficulties with her young girls was that they would have to mature without most of the incentives that, in the outside world, made a man or a woman adult. 'Take poverty,' she had said when talking of this to Philippa. 'A man who is poor in the world has to work hard, drive, to make up his deficiencies, but a religious, though poorer, is secure; he has food, clothing, a roof; he can depend on that for life. Take chastity: a young nun has to realize what it is she has renounced; love, human love and marriage, must be shown to her as tender and desirable, as is the gift of children. She must learn there are *not* compensations,' Dame Clare's eyes flashed

219

as she thought of 'all the twaddle people talk'. 'The lack of these things will gnaw at her all her life, leave holes in her, yet she must be just as warm, as self-denying and hard working as any wife or mother, and just as loving, without anyone to hold to. Somehow most of us do it. Lady Abbess Hester used to say, there may be lazy Benedictines and comfortable Poor Clares, but she had never met them. Somehow we do it, but can Sister Cecily?'

'We don't want a perpetual sweet pea,' said Dame Colette and, 'Take away her music,' said Dame Agnes suddenly. Dame Maura made a movement which she instantly quelled, but Dame Agnes had seen. 'It is for the girl's good,' she said with unaccustomed gentleness.

'She has an outstanding gift for music,' said Dame Beatrice slowly.

'A gift can be a refuge and a disguise,' said Dame Clare. 'Yet I don't like stifling...'

The Council was as divided as she.

'I feel to be given the habit will help,' Dame Maura spoke directly to the Abbess. 'It is a declaration that Sister Cecily needs.'

'A deprivation would be wiser, to challenge her,' said Dame Agnes.

It was put to the vote. Dame Maura, Dame Ursula and, after consideration, Dame Anselma, voted for Cecily's Clothing. Dame Beatrice, Dame Agnes, Dame Colette against it. Finally, 'I think we must test it a little further,' said Abbess Catherine who had the casting vote, and it was announced that Sister Hilary Dalrymple would be received for Clothing the Tuesday after Easter; Sister Cecily Scallon must wait.

'How did she take it?' asked Abbess Catherine.

'She said, "When you think I am ready, I shall be,"' Dame Clare sounded thoroughly exasperated.

As Holy Week opened Stefan Duranski's unfinished statue was carefully wheeled to the back of the extern chapel and sheeted; his tools were gathered up into the old duster; they and the guitar went with him. 'But we shall *never* get rid of the dust,' said houseproud Sister Susanna. The sanctuary seemed unnaturally quiet without him, yet as if it were waiting, with the curved back panel still blank between the two tall ones. These were now unveiled, lit with their slits of daylight or, at night, by softly diffused lighting. The crucifix was in its place; the new altar would be used for the Easter ceremonies and the nuns would have the, to them, extraordinary experience of Mass facing the community. 'I don't know if I dread it or look forward to it,' said Dame Veronica.

'I dread it,' said Dame Agnes. 'It will be as if the priest were giving a performance, not leading us to God as he does when he faces the altar,' but many, especially the younger ones, thought it would make the Mass even more intimate, 'as if we were gathered round the table.'

'It's not a table; it's an *altar*,' said Dame Agnes.

The Archbishop was coming to consecrate it in July when he would also receive Sister Philippa's Solemn Profession – and perhaps give Sister Cecily the habit. 'We'll see,' said Dame Clare.

'I'm glad for Sister Hilary,' Cecily said it obstinately to hide her pain and disappointment.

On the day of Hilary's Clothing the Abbey guest rooms were crammed with visitors; it had never known such a galaxy of earls and countesses, lords and ladies, bishops, two monsignori; Hilary's mother, father and sisters came, her grandmother, uncles, aunts, cousins, 'the whole clan,' she said, as well as her august godfather and godmothers. It outshone Lady Abbess Hester's funeral. Seldom had there been such splendour and rejoicing.

'And the same day she'll go back to the novitiate and to her work helping Sister Priscilla in the kitchen,' said Cecily marvelling.

'Well, Sister Priscilla's the dead spit of my Aunt Victoria,' said Hilary.

'Of the *Marchioness*?'

'Yes, only much more particular.'

A luncheon was served in the guest dining room for the visiting clergy and family and once again it was reported that

Dame Domitilla had not had time for a mouthful of dinner, she was so busy passing dishes through the turn, while the extern sisters were run off their feet. Even the day smiled for Hilary; it was perfect April weather, clear and sunny, the garth and park filled with daffodils.

Philippa had been deputed to help Dame Domitilla at the turn and when the rush was over, she stepped out for a moment into the garth to feel the sun and air; there she met Cecily, sent over from the novitiate with a message. Cecily, Philippa could guess, was feeling like Cinderella; it was recreation time, they were free to talk, and Philippa called her; together they started to pace for a few moments round the garth. As they came to the long cloister where the sun fell through the high arches, they stopped together in front of the cloister statue of our Lady with the smiling Child; laid on the plinth at her feet was a bouquet, white narcissi with sprigs of white heather: Hilary's.

Hilary was a nun now, her hair cut, her habit put on, her girdle buckled round her, the scapular over it, her white veil on her head; the time of aspiration was over, she was embarked on the real road.

Philippa's own Clothing had been simple; as a widow she had only had a 'monastic family' ceremony behind the grille, not wearing white but simply changing her postulant dress for the habit. Nothing had impeded her; as if Dame Catherine had exorcised her that night in the pleached alley, her torments had stopped as suddenly as if she had gone out of their reach. 'What did you do?' she asked Dame Catherine.

'I? Nothing. You had already done it.'

'But I was in such distress and you ...'

'I was there, that's all. That is what a community means,' Dame Catherine had said. 'We are all there for one another. It's as simple as that. We may quarrel, we may find ourselves going down another staircase to avoid meeting some particular nun, but in times of stress...' Philippa remembered that strong arm under hers as they had paced and Dame Catherine had talked, not of anything in particular, but of calm usual things; of her father who was a country doctor: of the spring:

and the moon: yet all the time below it, flowing strongly, steadily, was that current of help.

Philippa's Simple Profession had been different. Then she had known panic. 'After None you will stay behind in Choir until I come to fetch you,' Dame Ursula had said, and Philippa had known that the moment had come.

'Simple Profession seems quieter, less dramatic than the Clothing, but it is far more thorough,' Dame Ursula had said and Philippa had known that, all the week, every nun in the community had had to go to the Abbess and give her opinion – of me, thought Philippa, wincing; it began with the Council, the councillors like all the others going in singly, and ended with Philippa's fellow novices and, as she had knelt in the empty choir, she knew what was happening in the chapter house: Lady Abbess would tell the nuns her own opinion, the opinion of the Council, and the ballot box would be taken round; the nuns' hands were hidden by their sleeves; no one could see which ball, black or white, a nun put in. If there were more than a third of black balls, the novice would not be allowed to stay.

For the one left behind, the time seemed endless; Philippa had felt as if she were suspended, hung between the Abbey and the world outside. She could hear the seagulls round the tower; they sounded like voices wailing, seeking or mourning her and, odd, she had thought, I never seriously visualized coming out of Brede again; it had not occurred to her, but in those minutes it occurred painfully. She could have blushed to think how once she had taken it for granted that, if she made enough effort – steeled herself – it would be settled. 'I know,' Dame Clare said afterwards. 'I was as confident. Once upon a time I even thought God had taste, choosing me!'

Dame Perpetua had been more blunt. 'Weren't you surprised that God should have chosen you?' a young woman reporter, writing a piece on vocations, had asked her. 'Yes,' Dame Perpetua had answered, 'but not nearly as surprised as that He should have chosen some of the others – but then God's not as fastidious as we are,' said Dame Perpetua.

Philippa had known that afternoon what 'hung in the

ance' meant. If those black balls came down too heavily she must leave. She thought of all she had done in the past year – and not done; there were endless little faults of observance, frictions, impatiences, lukewarmness, gaps. She had not been liked in the novitiate – except, at the end, by Cecily. Dame Agnes, she felt, would certainly come down against her and Dame Agnes had her following. Dame Maura? Philippa had striven mightily to please her, but the precentrix's standards were high; and there might be other nuns, whom Philippa did not even know, who all this time had been taking silent cognizance and might genuinely think Sister Philippa too old, too habit-ridden, not strong enough – that loss of weight and the lines in her face – too opinionated and strong-willed. 'But I can't come out now,' Philippa had whispered. 'Go back to the old life, the mill and the race, start it all again. What was I doing in those days? Really doing?' She had bent her head until her forehead touched the cold wood of the book rest. 'I must if I must, but please . . . please.'

If a place has been filled with prayer, though it is empty something remains; a quiet, a steadiness, Philippa had thought of a mosque she had seen in Bengal, a mosque of seven domes, eleventh century, and, as with all unspoiled Moslem mosques, empty, not a lamp or a vase or a chair; only walls glimmering with their pale marble. She remembered how, her shoes off, she had stood there, not looking but feeling. 'No one is there,' 'God is there'; and here, in Brede Abbey, the quiet was stronger – and close. The light flickering by the tabernacle was warm, alive, and as if they were still there she heard what the nuns had sung last night at Benediction: *'Christus vincit, Christus regnat. Christus imperat'* with its three soft repeated cadences. *'Christus vincit'* and, 'Thank you,' Philippa had whispered, 'thank you for bringing me where I am,' and, 'even if You send me away, I shall be here for ever.'

'My dear child.' Abbess Hester had her arms wide to embrace Philippa who had been fetched by Dame Ursula. Keeping to tradition, the novice mistress had made her face grave so that no inkling of her news had shown and, when Philippa had followed Dame Ursula upstairs to the Abbess's room, her heart had been jumping so violently that she was breathless.

The councillors were all on their feet and Philippa had looked at the circle of their faces: Dame Beatrice's so loving: Dame Maura's filled with encouragement: Mother Prioress, happiness in her eyes: Dame Agnes's expressionless: Dame Veronica's, her eyes wet with emotion – 'It's always *such* a moment' – Dame Catherine's lit. 'My dear child. We have received you to Simple Profession,' but the Abbess's hug never reached Philippa. A sudden buzzing had come in her ears, a coldness on the back of her neck and hands; the room and the nuns had seemed to lift before her eyes as her knees buckled; to her surprise – and disgrace, thought Philippa – she had fainted.

I felt it as much as that, thought Philippa in the long cloister this April day, and yet she had an instinctive feeling that she did not, and could not, feel as deeply as the silent girl beside her, looking down at the bouquet: Sister Cecily, left behind, still at the crossroads, the outsider, the only one in the monastery now in the short black dress and postulant's veil.

Philippa wondered if Cecily would cry and almost put her arm around her, but an instinct told her it was better to leave her alone. Cecily stood silent; hurt, sorrow and a very human envy in her face; then, as Philippa watched, it was suddenly illumined; Cecily knelt and touched the flowers with a finger, lifted her face to the statue as if she said a hasty prayer, then got up and turned back along the cloister. 'Sister, where are you going?'

'To Lady Abbess.' Cecily still found it difficult to call Abbess Catherine 'Mother'. 'To Lady Abbess, to tell her.'

'You can't.' Even renegade Philippa was appalled.

'Why not?'

'It's out of the question.'

'It's not. Saint Thérèse of Lisieux went to the Pope,' said Cecily and was gone.

'Didn't that take spunk?' Dame Maura could not forbear asking Dame Beatrice when the Council was told.

It happened that Abbess Catherine had gone from the busy parlours to her room for a few minutes' respite – she had seen visitor after visitor, relative after relative, all the bishops, and, 'My voice is giving out,' she told Dame Beatrice. She had also to open the day's letters and had called the new prioress to help her. Then the knock had come and both nuns lifted their heads. For once Dame Beatrice had put the white token on the door, 'Not to be disturbed.'

'It must be something urgent,' and the Abbess called, 'Deo Gratias.'

The door opened to reveal Sister Cecily. 'Benedicite, Mother.'

Abbess Catherine looked hopelessly at the prioress, who asked, 'Sister, is this urgent?' Dame Beatrice said it with a mixture of sternness and reproof, but Cecily had already come in, shut the door and knelt down by the desk. 'Is this urgent?'

'It is urgent,' said Cecily.

'Then what is it, child?' asked the Abbess.

'Mother,' said Cecily, 'I have come to ask you to change your mind.'

'Change my . . .'

'Because you have made a mistake,' said Cecily. Dame Beatrice caught her breath with angry astonishment, but Cecily's voice was as gentle as it was grave and firm, and she was looking up at Abbess Catherine with absolute trust. 'Mother, you should let me be clothed *now*.'

Dame Beatrice had recovered. 'Sister! Are *you* telling Lady Abbess what she should or should not do?'

Cecily's eyes went to her for a moment. 'No one else can tell her,' she said, and came back to the Abbess.

'To dispute with your Abbess is a very grave fault.' Sweet Dame Beatrice sounded as sharp as Dame Agnes.

'I am not disputing,' said Cecily. 'I am asking. If Mother says "no" . . .' Suddenly Cecily could say 'Mother'.

'Of course she will say "no". Postulants can't run the Abbey.'

'Abbesses run the Abbey,' said Cecily. 'That's why I have

come.' She put her hands on Abbess Catherine's knee. 'Mother if you say "yes", they will *have* to let you.'

'You could be sent away for this,' but Cecily did not even hear Dame Beatrice's voice. She did not take those confident eyes off Abbess Catherine.

'I have never been more taken aback,' Abbess Catherine told the Council afterwards.

'Yes. Quelle impertinence!' said Dame Colette. Even unconventional Dame Anselma was shocked.

'It was not impertinence,' Abbess Catherine spoke slowly. 'Indeed I believe it was far from it.'

She had not, to Dame Beatrice's further astonishment, ordered Sister Cecily from the room. She had, though, said 'all the usual things', as she told the Council now: 'that if a purpose is firm, a little opposition only strengthens it. That patience is as much part of a vocation as fervour.' 'To subdue your will . . .' she had said, but Cecily had made a movement there. 'Did you want to say something, Sister?'

'Mother, it's not only *my* will.'

'Whose then, Sister?'

'God's.'

'Are you sure?'

'Quite sure. If it isn't – if it's just mine, not God's, I don't want it.' Cecily had looked round the Abbess's room. 'Wild horses wouldn't have made me come, interrupting you, Mother. This has.'

The Abbess had gone on talking, 'sensibly,' she said, but even to herself the words had sounded dim and hollow – old words that did not apply in this case. 'I think the girl must be out of her mind,' Dame Beatrice had said when Cecily had gone and the phrase that had come into Abbess Catherine's own mind was, *'We are fools for Christ's sake,'* and, 'I have never felt a stronger compulsion to give in,' she told the Council, 'but it wouldn't have been good for the girl . . . most girls,' she added now.

She had sent Cecily away. 'You can tell Dame Clare you have been with me,' but at the door Cecily had come back and knelt again, 'You're not angry with me, Mother?'

'Never that.'

Abbess Catherine had looked after Sister Cecily for a long time when the girl had shut the door and gone. She had stayed silent and the letters were left unopened.

That evening a telephone call had come from Stefan Duranski. He would be delayed: 'Asian flu which I don't think risking to give all of you.'

'No indeed,' said Dame Maura. 'The havoc that would wreak in the choir!'

He would be delayed, he said, for at least a fortnight. There was a Council meeting next morning and Abbess Catherine asked her councillors to reconsider the case of Sister Cecily.

Cecily was clothed in the second week of May, six months and ten days from her entrance. The weather did not smile for her as it had for Hilary; the sun and balmy warmth had gone: it was grey and cold, with a sky full of rain. 'My mother will say it is weeping,' said Cecily.

'I only hope you don't perish of cold,' said Dame Clare, but nothing could have made Cecily feel chill that day, she was so lit with happiness, and as the procession came through the church door into the sanctuary, there was something more than the usual stir at the sight of the figure in white and a cloud of lace, walking between her matrons of honour, in front of the bishop and behind the monks and priests.

'She looked exceedingly pretty,' said Dame Veronica.

'Pretty! Don't you know beauty when you see it?' said Dame Agnes. To Abbess Catherine's surprise, Dame Agnes had supported Sister Cecily. 'That was genuine,' she had said, but all the same she had added, 'In my young days a postulant would no more have dared to argue with a senior nun, let alone her superior, than a child would have dared to argue with its teacher in school.'

'Children are taught to argue now in school,' Abbess Catherine had said calmly.

Cecily would have liked to be clothed by Dom Gervase in a simple ceremony at the grille, but it was decided that the Abbess's brother, Bishop Ismay, whom they all called Bishop

228

Mark, would come. 'The only one who could at such short notice,' said the Abbess and, 'I thought a bishop would make it easier for your mother,' she told Cecily.

'A wedding without a bridegroom,' Mrs Scallon saw only the empty place. 'It's a mockery.'

'There is a bridegroom,' said Cecily.

'Pah!'

'Oh, Mummy, don't.' Cecily spoke as that helpless girl Elspeth, and Mrs Scallon fell into the old lament. 'You could have married anyone, *anyone*,' which meant, as Cecily wearily knew, Larry Bannerman. On Elspeth's twenty-first birthday, old Mrs Bannerman had sent her the set of her own emeralds: necklace, ear-rings, brooch; in the face of Mrs Scallon's anger, Elspeth had sent them back. Mrs Bannerman had been bitterly angry too. 'Don't kiss me. You have hurt me. Now you'll hurt Larry.'

'If I were marrying a prince or a king...' Cecily began now, but it was hopeless.

'You are marrying an idea.'

'People often do marry ideas,' Cecily said defensively.

'But a day comes,' said Mrs Scallon, 'when they find, or should find, the idea is a person. That's when the marriage holds or breaks.'

'Mine won't break,' said Cecily with a lift of her chin.

'We'll see,' said Mrs Scallon.

She had refused to get the customary wedding dress for Cecily. 'It doesn't matter about the dress,' said Cecily. 'I'll borrow Sister Hilary's.'

'You're a different shape,' said the Abbess.

'Couldn't I wear my postulant's dress and be clothed at the grille like Sister Philippa?' Cecily had coaxed again but, 'You are not a widow,' said Abbess Catherine. In the end Cecily wore her sister Daphne's.

The nuns had seen many Clothings but few like Sister Cecily's. 'I have never seen anyone as radiant,' said the Abbess, 'unless it was Dame Maura as she played.' '*Jesu corona virginum,*' sang the choir, and indeed Cecily looked a virgin crowned. 'Golden hair, golden voice,' said Dame

Maura. When Cecily sang her responses and the flute voice rose, pure and clear, Bishop and monks exchanged glances. 'You won't see or hear the like of that again in your life,' Bishop Mark said to Abbess Catherine afterwards. 'A voice and a face like that. It isn't fair.'

'Is she so beautiful?' The Abbess sounded as if she were pleading. 'Has Lady Abbess been won over by the beauty?' She had felt that question in the air. 'Well, Mother, we can only hope you are right.' That had been the politely censorious remark of Dames Beatrice, Colette and Clare – all experienced nuns. 'Is she so beautiful, Mark?'

'Undeniably.'

Sister Cecily's that day was beauty no one could deny, like the wand of a lily, or a tree in white blossom, thought Philippa; in the sheath of white satin she seemed slim and tall, her veil of fine lace making her look taller. Old Sister Priscilla became biblical and called her a pillar of cloud. In the end Mrs Scallon had contributed the family wedding veil. 'Let them see we at least have lace,' and, 'If I had known Lady Seaton was coming, of course I should have given you a dress.' The novitiate had spent hours taking Daphne's in, but Mrs Scallon did not know that – 'And you had her wreath of pearls.'

Cecily was quite unconscious of her effect. She looked young, dignified as she walked and the scent of the white freesias she carried – given her by her father – came into the choir to the nuns.

Cecily knelt before the Bishop, facing the ranks of priests and monks. 'What do you ask?'

'The mercy of God and the grace of the holy habit.'

'Do you ask it with your whole heart?'

Her whole being seemed to breathe as she answered, 'Yes, my Lord, I do.'

'God grant you perseverance, my daughter.'

She stepped to the prie-dieu set ready with its white cushion.

'*Veni Creator Spiritus*,' sang the choir, the hymn to the Holy Spirit; prayers were said, psalms chanted, then Cecily's

230

two matrons brought her forward – 'Very young matrons,' Abbess Catherine said.

'And both Hons,' Mrs Scallon told with relish afterwards. 'The Honourable Sybil and Honourable Monica Dalrymple.' Sister Hilary had telephoned home asking if her twin sisters could come and act as matrons for Cecily, as they had acted for her, and Lady Seaton had not only said 'yes,' but had brought them. She was in the front pew of the extern chapel with Major and Mrs Scallon. 'I cannot imagine anyone who could help us more than your mother,' Cecily had told Hilary gratefully. It certainly soothed Mrs Scallon's grief to have luncheon afterwards with a viscountess and a bishop. 'If I had known I should have brought Aunt Elaine,' she told Cecily and in church, with Lady Seaton beside her, Mrs Scallon mercifully kept her sobs quiet.

Bishop Mark was praying: *'O God, who hast called us from the vanity of this world to follow our vocation ... keep Thy handmaid, our sister, always modest, sincere and peaceful, ever mindful ...'*

Again the sweep of song came as the voices rose and fell: *'Tu es Domine'* the antiphon rang out and then the psalm: *'The lines have fallen to me in pleasant places ... and my inheritance pleases me exceedingly,'* as Cecily, with the young twin matrons, came to kneel in front of the Bishop in his carved chair. Philippa caught a glimpse of her face, serious, withdrawn under the softness of the veil – and so adamant, thought Philippa. She could hear Mrs Scallon weeping; she doubted if Cecily heard. *'Bless the Lord, that he hath given me understanding ... Thou wilt show me the path of life, the fulness of joys ... delights at my right hand for ever ...'*

The two girls took off the coronal of pearls and lifted the veil away, took too the necklace Cecily was wearing, then Cecily bowed her head, but there was little hair to cut, it was so short already; Bishop Mark, with the scissors Dom Gervase handed him, cut off a curl. *'She shall receive a blessing from the Lord and mercy from God the Saviour.'* To the singing, Cecily left the sanctuary to go into the little room where Sister Elizabeth and Sister Susanna were waiting to help her off with the bridal clothes and put on the black shoes and thick stockings, the plain undershift. With a towel round her shoulders, Cecily sat on a stool while Sister Elizabeth cut the rest of her hair short, running the clippers up the back of her neck. Cecily looked like a boy, 'but it still curls,' said Sister Elizabeth. Then, 'and at long last,' whispered Cecily, the black habit went on, the cap and wimple like a helmet, 'It fits like a glove, in *every* way,' said little Sister Renata.

As clergy, guests and community waited, Dame Maura played, while on the empty prie-dieu the heap of white flowers was eloquent of all that Cecily had now left; as she came back, Dame Maura, thinking of that memory, known only to herself, of the sleeping face pillowed on the organ bench, wet lashes, wet cheeks, tumbled curls, went into the Bach, 'Jesu, joy of man's desiring,' and Cecily looked up at the organ loft with a quick smile.

The first sight of the habited figure always brought, as the nuns knew, a stir among the relatives and friends. Mrs Scallon gave a low cry as she saw this stranger girl, unfamiliar in the long dress that made her look so tall, the helmet-shaped white framing her face so that the brown eyes looked enormous, but Lady Seaton's hand came into Mrs Scallon's and held it.

Cecily had another swift smile for her father, then was grave again as she went with her matrons to the altar steps where Bishop Mark gave her the girdle: '*May the Lord gird thee with justice and purity*'; they buckled it on: the scapular: '*Receive the yoke of the Lord and bear His burden which is sweet and light.*' They put it over her head, arranging it back and front; the white veil, mark of novices, which the two girls unfolded and put on, pinning it to the cap. Then Bishop Mark gave Cecily a lighted candle: '*Receive this light in thy hand,*' and they saw the glow of light on her face, illuminating it again in the folds of the white veil. 'What an exquisite girl your daughter is,' whispered Lady Seaton. The Bishop prayed, '*Grant her grace to persevere ... so that with Thy protection and help she may accomplish the desire Thou hast given her ...*'

Then he spoke directly to Cecily who knelt at the prie-dieu, her candle set on a tall silver candlestick beside her; he warned her of the life she must expect, its abnegation, the renunciation of almost all pleasures of the senses; of the hard work, the obedience, the silence, the loneliness, 'from now until death if all goes well.' When he had finished, Cecily came and knelt and kissed his hand and the singing broke into the Te Deum, echoing up to the church roof, the organ weaving in with the paean of praise as the procession left the sanctuary, the new novice and her small matrons walking before the Bishop, priests and monks; Dom Gervase carried the cross, Major and Mrs Scallon, with Lady Seaton and the extern sisters came behind. The procession wound through the Abbey grounds into the forecourt through the big outer front door and the high hall to the enclosure doors where Cecily knocked.

'Open to me the gates of justice,' the full clear voice rang out.

The nuns answered from inside. 'This is the gate of the Lord ... the just shall enter,' and the door opened, showing Abbess Catherine with her crook, the whole community behind her.

On the threshold Cecily knelt and sang, 'This is my resting place for ever ...'

Bishop Mark said the last prayer and signalled to Cecily to rise. She went to her mother; for a second they stood face to face, then Cecily leant forward and gently kissed her. She was kissed by Lady Seaton, then, going to her father, threw her arms round him in a whirlwind hug, muffling her face against him. 'Goodbye, Kitten.' It was a whisper and Cecily hugged him again. Then Bishop Mark gently took her from her father to Abbess Catherine. 'We thereby entrust to you our sister and pray that, under the guidance of the Holy Rule and through obedience she may deserve to obtain perfect union with God. May the peace of the Lord be always with you ...'

He blessed Cecily who went through, and the doors were shut.

9

For a time the sun seemed to have disappeared in continual
rain and the Abbey was dark and chill. Dame Agnes had
turned the central heating off long ago – 'Central heating in
summer! Absurd!' she pronounced. 'It's only early summer,'
said the Abbess – and everyone was cold; the black crocheted
shoulder shawls the nuns wore in winter came out again and
Dame Ursula had chilblains, 'chilblains in May!' 'If we're not
careful we shall start on an epidemic of colds,' warned Dame
Joan. 'There are far too many sneezing visitors in the parlours,' but 'Be brisk. Move about,' was all Dame Agnes said,
though her own nose was red at the tip.

Stefan Duranski was back to carve his panel and finish the
statue. He at least was not cold; he was too busy and generated
warmth and activity; the sound of his mallet and chisel and of
his guitar were heard in the choir and Abbess Catherine dared
not acknowledge even to herself how glad she was to see him.
'What have you all been doing to yourselves?' he asked. 'You
look pinched.'

'I think we are all a little tired,' she said, 'after the fasts of
Lent. In Holy Week and at Easter the choir work is heavy, we
have had two Clothings' – and Dame Agnes has been practising her economy, she could have said.

Dame Agnes was paring expenses so rigorously that the
community was growing restless; almost every evening a thick
anonymous soup appeared in the refectory for supper, soup
that Sister Priscilla concocted from left-overs – it was being
rumoured that she scraped the plates: impudent Sister Louise
declared that in hers she had found the identical piece of

gristle she had not been able to eat last Sunday and had left on her plate. The soup was served with dry bread.

The best of the garden produce went now to the shops in the town; the extern sisters had told Dame Agnes of a stall in the market that every Thursday sold flower bunches and Dame Mildred was made 'to part with everything,' she declared to the Abbess in dudgeon. The altar and the shrines suffered. Only the cracked and sub-standard eggs were kept; the new-laid dozens that were the pride of Sister Gabrielle's heart were sent to market. Dame Agnes had stopped buying coffee – or sugar for the table, 'sugarless tea except for the very old'. Even soap was rationed and tooth powder took the place of paste. 'A tin should last you six months,' said Dame Agnes to each recipient.

'And the diets!' she said to Abbess Catherine. 'Did you know there are thirty nuns on thirty different diets? It's enough to drive anybody mad. Do I really have to sanction extra eggs and extra meat for young Sister Louise?'

'Sister Louise has diabetes, Dame. She must have protein because her carbohydrates are so limited.'

'And meat twice a day for Dame Nichola, liver three times a week. It's such a price.'

'It's what Doctor Avery ordered. Dame Nichola is anaemic.'

'And all this fruit for Dame Maura; tomatoes are so expensive just now.'

'Dame Maura is being treated for arthritis in her wrists – a vegetarian diet is part of the cure. Dame Maura's wrists are exceedingly valuable to us,' and at Dame Agnes's disbelieving face, Abbess Catherine said, 'You must steel yourself to it, Dame. Sometimes we have to spend to get.'

Abbess Catherine herself had made economies in the workrooms and libraries – 'though I hate to curtail books.' Dame Agnes followed her : the Brede printed writing paper was to be kept only for the most important letters; the rest to be written on cheap paper bought by the gross in blocks. 'But the ink runs,' said the nuns.

'It wouldn't, if you didn't use so much.'

Letters received were to be carefully slit open and the

velopes used again with economy labels. 'It isn't dignified,' protested the nuns; each was to think carefully before she used a stamp. 'Our postage bills!' said Dame Agnes in horror.

Stringency, severity, were her watchwords and each new ruling brought, Dame Veronica felt, a reflection on herself so that she was in a perpetual bath of tears. 'Well, you wanted humiliations.' Abbess Catherine found in herself a tendency to snap at everyone. 'Don't go too far,' she told Dame Agnes.

'We need to go far.'

'Dame, you are savings pennies and shillings when we need thousands of pounds.'

'I am aware of that but shillings will help – besides it brings home that buildings have to be paid for.' Dame Agnes was snappy herself. 'Are we getting any further?' she demanded.

'Not really,' Abbess Catherine sighed. The months were going by without any lightening of the overdraft; it was a dark cloud coming nearer. 'Before we know it, we shall be in January again,' said Dame Agnes.

'Oh, Dame! Not as bad as that.'

'It is,' said Dame Agnes obdurately.

Now Stefan Duranski's kind eyes searched Abbess Catherine's. 'You are low down, down,' he said, and suddenly, 'Give them all a bank holiday.'

A bank holiday. Abbess Catherine ordered the nearest monastic equivalent, a cell day, and sent for Dame Agnes and the caterer. 'Give us a really good meal, something filling.'

'Such as?'

'Roast lamb and pancakes,' said Abbess Catherine without thinking.

Dame Agnes sanctioned Irish stew and hasty pudding and got her first reprimand from her new Abbess. 'It's not your business to penance the community! Mortification should never begin in the kitchen.'

Though the weather changed, Abbess Catherine could not lose her despondency. There were gleams that she clung to; the steady effort of the nuns: Dame Emily's recovery; it was slow; she would be very frail, Doctor Avery said, but she was

236

better and at peace. She seemed utterly content to leave everything in Abbess Catherine's hands. 'She doesn't know how
they tremble.'

Dame Veronica, writing her poems, seemed engrossed by
them and was tactful and helpful with Dame Camilla. The
apse and the statue were growing under Stefan Duranski's skill
– 'It's heartening to see something that *is* progressing,' said
Abbess Catherine. The sheaves of corn with the Host, the
grapes with the chalice, the branches of olive with the priestly
hands, were carved and the statue was shaping, though Duranski had turned its back to the grille so that the nuns could not
see the face.

Now and again he came to one of the parlours in the evening
to talk to Abbess Catherine – when she had time. They talked
of external things : his work on other churches : the exhibition
planned for him next year in Paris : of other artists : but it was
more than words; Abbess Catherine had never, she realized,
had a man for a friend; Abbot Bernard was, rather, counsellor
and guide. 'I had young men in love with me when I was a girl
but they were not friends.' Perhaps because she and Mark had
been all in all to one another, they had shut out friends, 'and
since I left home I never had occasion or opportunity.' The
community had never known of the celebrity, the calibre and
unusualness of many of Abbess Hester's visitors; now Abbess
Catherine was experiencing a little of that richness. 'Mind on
mind kindles warmth,' she could have said, and these occa-
sional talks gave balance. 'They seem to let me out of myself,'
she told Abbot Bernard. 'They give me confidence, perhaps
because Stefan Duranski is so confident himself. It's not con-
ceit; it's a belief and interest in other people.'

'I can believe it,' said Abbot Bernard. 'He is doing a great
deal for Dom Gervase.'

The chaplain had been extremely averse to having Stefan
Duranski in the presbytery, but it was impossible to stay aloof
with him, not to thaw and the young monk had come to love
and trust him. 'And I like the way his foreman, Ralph, is one
with us; Mrs Burnell thought Ralph should eat in the kitchen,
but Duranski said, "Then let's all eat in the kitchen. When we

are at work we share and share alike." ' These masculine evenings were toughening Dom Gervase; he found himself talking as he had not been able to talk even to Abbess Hester. 'I believe soon I shall be able to teach again,' he told Abbess Catherine.

The dark face with its nervous lines looked more relaxed than Abbess Catherine had ever seen it. 'I have found a friend,' Dom Gervase could say that as well as she. 'Yes, I shall be able to teach boys,' and he laughed, 'any boys.'

'And I am learning perhaps to be a human Abbess,' said Abbess Catherine, 'and not a figurehead,' but a human is prey to doubts and fears, and Abbess Catherine's seemed to rise around her like demons. The money; always this money; how strange for a religious to be obsessed with money – and personalities: Dame Agnes, Dame Veronica, Dame Emily: and now she had added to them with Sister Cecily. 'But Mother, what made you change your mind about her?' That had been Dame Colette's puzzled question in the Council. 'What made you?'

Abbess Catherine could only answer, 'Sister Cecily herself.'

'I thought we were to wait for some kind of test,' said the prioress.

'Wasn't this a test?' but Dame Beatrice shook her head.

'She nerved herself to come. It was a crisis.'

'And a religious isn't built by fits and starts,' said Dame Ursula.

'I have only faith to go upon,' Abbess Catherine had said, 'That and a strong compulsion,' but she had known what the prioress was thinking, and many of the others: Lady Abbess Hester would never have allowed this.

Yes, I must seem variable to them, thought Abbess Catherine. How silly to risk one's reputation for a young girl, and it wouldn't have hurt Sister Cecily to wait another two or three months as Dame Clare had wanted. Yet Abbess Catherine felt it would have hurt; she could still feel the force that had driven Cecily to her. 'If you are in charge of a soul of extraordinary mettle, you must do extraordinary things,' but she could not say that – yet, thought the Abbess. The girl had to prove herself first and meanwhile it was no light thing to over-rule the novice mistress whom you yourself have appointed – and why add to the worries just now?

A bogey among the worries was her own lack of time. She had learned that, as Abbess, there was one thing she could count upon – never to have ten minutes of uninterrupted time. Dame Beatrice was still too new to the office of prioress to save her and give her the hour or half-hour Dame Emily had been able to charm, by some wiles of her own, each day for her Abbess. Abbess Catherine had been tempted to keep Philippa at her post in the alcove outside the door but, 'no favourites,' she told herself. 'No friends,' and Sister Philippa willy-nilly had had to know too much, be too concerned, 'which is not right or fair so close to her Solemn Profession,' said the Abbess. Philippa had been appointed as 'second' to Dame Winifred, the new sacristan.

Dame Winifred, though thorough, was slow and more used to handling tins and packets than precious crystal and gold; Sister Philippa was deft and would provide the necessary polish and speed. 'You seem always to be the oil poured on the wheels,' said Abbess Catherine, and now Philippa was gone she realized some of that oil – 'A little, very little,' Philippa would have said – had been poured on her own. The Abbess was trying in vain to write notes for a conference to be given next day in preparation for the feast of Saint Basil and had already been interrupted four times. 'Abbess Hester must have written hers in the middle of the night,' said Abbess Catherine, but resolutely began again:

'In his Rule, St Benedict twice expresses his deep admiration,' she wrote, 'for the manly and vigorous type of holiness ... He alludes, with especial reverence, to the outstanding master of the monastic life, St Basil the Great, who ...'

Knock!

'St Basil the Great, who ...'

Knock!

Last time it had been Dame Paula who wanted to write a letter of protest to *The Universe* – 'Don't you think, Dame, there have been too many protests already?' It had taken some time to talk Dame Paula out of it; before her Sister Xaviera had burst in with the news that Wimple had had more kittens... 'Well, *really*, Sister!' Abbess Catherine had been sorely tempted to say, 'I *am* trying to write a conference,' but, 'Two are black, Mother, one has a little white nose; there's a tabby, and the sweetest little tortoiseshell. That's a little "she".' The Sister had been so simply happy that Abbess Catherine had managed to curb herself, though she almost wrote: 'Great – with a little white nose...' but St Basil would have understood, she thought wearily.

This, though, was Dame Domitilla's unmistakable knock. Someone must have come to the parlour – or else it was a telegram. Abbess Catherine sighed and laid down her pen.

Dame Ursula had been fond of telling her novices the story of a theologian who was so busy working on his treatise of the Love of Christ that he did not answer a knocking at the door. The knocking was so insistent that at last he got up, flung open the door to berate the interrupter and found it was Christ himself. 'It's only a story,' Dame Ursula would say unnecessarily and, being Dame Ursula, would underline its parable. Abbess Catherine did not encourage legends or mythology but, 'Perhaps those interruptions came to me three times today,' Abbess Catherine was to say that evening. It was, she remembered afterwards, the thirteenth of June. 'Thirteen again!' said Dame Perpetua.

'Deo Gratias.' Abbess Catherine had called to Dame Domitilla to come in.

Cecily had not known that she was singing until the Abbess came round the corner.

Cecily had been sweeping the novitiate courtyard, sweeping up every twig and leaf and speck so that it would pass Sister Jane's eye and, all unconsciously, had started to hum, but her voice had lifted. As soon as she saw Abbess Catherine she stopped. 'I'm sorry, Mother. I was breaking silence.'

Abbess Catherine looked at her latest novice, broom in hand, blue aproned, her face blooming with exercise and health – and something else, thought the Abbess. 'Sister, are you happy?' she asked.

'Mother, I'm happy up to here,' Cecily put her hand on the crown of her head.

Abbess Catherine almost went away – it seemed cruel to interrupt. Tempted by the now golden weather and the dark thoughts in her room – also wanting time to think when she had left the parlour – Abbess Catherine had come herself to find Sister Cecily; she had crossed the garth and garden in the sunshine, coming through the hedges that smelled spicy in the warmth, to the novitiate and to its courtyard filled with sun and song. It's a shame, thought Abbess Catherine – but everyone is so doubtful of this child – and she said, 'Sister, I want you in my room. Go and tell Dame Clare where you will be, and come.'

'There is a visitor for you, Sister Cecily.'

'A visitor?' Cecily, as she knelt by the desk, had been remembering the last day she had knelt there, her heart beating so strangely in her throat, her hands cold with terror, yet under that strange compulsion – but 'a visitor'. That jerked her out of what she had wanted to say, which was: 'Mother, I still feel I have never thanked you properly. Thank you. Thank you. Thank you.' Cecily knew that, except for relatives or very near friends, visits in the novice-year were discouraged, and her eyes widened. 'Mother, is something wrong at home?'

'Not that I know of,' said Abbess Catherine.

Yet, why is she looking at me so intently, thought Cecily.

'I don't want to upset you, Sister, but I think you should see him.'

'Him? Dad? My father? Something *has* happened.'

'Not your father. This is a young man. Laurence Bannerman.'

'Larry!' Abbess Catherine had expected Cecily to go crimson, but the girl turned white. 'Mother, I can't see him.'

'That was my first reaction, then, as I thought about it seriously, I decided otherwise. Sister, I think you must.'

'*Please*, Mother.' The words were appalled.

Abbess Catherine took Cecily's hand. 'Sit down, Sister ... Now who is Laurence Bannerman?'

'They all thought I was going to marry him.' Cecily sat on the edge of the chair. 'My mother had set her heart on it. You see, we are so poor, struggling along on Dad's pension and my mother's few dividends. Mummy would struggle, keeping up appearances; it was just appearances, underneath it was bitter.' Cecily winced. 'They sold things to send us to the right schools. I didn't want to go to the right schools – at that cost.' It came in jerks. 'But perhaps she was wise – for what she wanted. Larry's mother wanted it too. Larry's a farmer – at least he has four farms' – the Abbess could hear Mrs Scallon speaking; 'He's rich and – Larry's a dear.' Cecily's hand trembled in the Abbess's. 'If I could have, I would have, Mother, but ... on my last day,' Cecily took her hand away, 'On my last day, Mummy gave a lunch party.'

Cecily, trying to be what Lady Abbess Hester had said she must be, generous and loving in those last days at home, had gone through the ritual, cleaning and dusting the drawing-room, putting out extra ashtrays, washing the glasses they had had to borrow, doing the flowers. Mrs Scallon, she remembered, had been even more fussy than usual about the flowers. 'What would you like? It's your party.' Mysteriously it had become Cecily's party. The pudding had been one of Mrs Scallon's favourites – mushrooms in grass: the mushrooms were meringue shells, lined with chocolate and turned upside down on fondant stems; they stood on a base of chocolate mousse with fronds of angelica grass. Cecily had made the mousse and meringues the day before, but had to decorate them – it took an hour. Her father had come and stood by her as she arranged them in the pantry, watching while she cut the angelica grass. 'Damned flummery!' he had said suddenly.

'Dad, I wanted to come out with you, walk to the top field,' Cecily had said.

'Better do as your mother wants,' said Major Scallon and walked away.

There was one thing Cecily had determined she would do –

give her spaniel, Rory, a last brush. As soon as the pudding was finished, the table set, the fire lit in the drawing-room, guest towels put in the bathroom, she had washed her hands and brushed her hair, and whistled for Rory. She had whistled and whistled; he would not come – as always he knew when something was happening to her. He growled when she had picked him up to carry him into the cloakroom, but he was shivering. It had been a mistake to go near Rory that morning; as Cecily brushed, tears had fallen on his head and run shining down his black coat, helpless tears.

'Elspeth.'

She had whipped round. It was Larry Bannerman, Larry come early. He was standing in the doorway of the cloakroom, looking at her with an expression on his face that had made her turn quickly back to Rory; even Rory was safer than that look on Larry's face.

'Why do you let them make you go?' His voice had been angry.

'No one's making me. I want to go.'

'Then why are you crying?'

'Don't you expect me to feel it?'

They had hurled these angry questions at one another. 'Do you think I'm made of stone?' cried Cecily.

'Yes,' said Larry tersely.

Stone. Marble. Hard as nails. 'Oh, I'm not, I'm not.' She had begun to cry again, and Larry had taken one step nearer.

'Elspeth! Elspeth! My little love.'

'Larry! *Please* go away.'

Instead he had come nearer. 'You don't want to go.'

'I do! I do!'

'It's an idea that's got hold of you.'

'No, Larry. No.' Cecily had said it breathlessly between the sobs that shook her. 'It's my life,' she might have said. 'Don't you see I'm fighting for my life.'

'Elspeth, I love you.' He had stood there, his eyes pleading, very much as Rory's eyes pleaded when they looked up at her, only Larry looked down. Cecily did not know what it was in

243

her that had made her able to harden her heart, even against these two; that gave her the strength to do it. 'Elspeth!'

She whispered, 'Larry, couldn't you love Jean?'

His eyes had blazed at that. 'You're not the only one who can set their heart on something,' and Cecily had burst into louder sobs. 'Oh, Larry! Go aw-a-ay.' He had turned on his heel and gone. Cecily had heard his steps ringing on the tiles of the back passage as she had stifled her sobs against Rory's coat. Now, in the Abbess's room she seemed to hear those steps again and, 'Why has he come?' she asked, white to the lips.

'I think to try and get you away,' said Abbess Catherine. 'It seems your mother has told him about your Clothing. He is a very determined young man and a fine one, Sister Cecily. He would make you a good husband.'

The dark eyes looked suddenly bright – with anger, thought the Abbess – as if they said, 'You too,' and Cecily flushed. 'Mother, you're not asking me to go?'

'Of course not. Unless you want to.'

'Never! Never! Never!' Cecily shook with her vehemence. 'I have told Larry again and again but, like them all, he won't believe me,' and she besought, 'You believe me, Mother?'

'I believe you, but I want you to realize the price.'

'The . . . price?'

'That we have to pay . . . which is why I want you to see him.'

'Mother, won't you tell him?'

'He won't take it from me,' said Abbess Catherine. 'He will only think we are keeping you from him. He loves you,' said the Abbess.

'I know,' Cecily lifted those dark eyes – Abbess Catherine had never seen such a velvety brown. 'I love him too. Once, when I was young . . .' – the Abbess's lips twitched, Sister Cecily looked so young now, sitting like a schoolgirl on the edge of her chair – 'I took it for granted I should marry him,' said Cecily, 'until I went to Paris and met Andrée – mother had arranged an exchange; we couldn't afford a finishing school for me – I met Andrée and – this. Andrée had a vocation; she's a Poor Clare now. I knew then I could never marry Larry – or anyone; but I do love him. You can't help loving Larry.' She looked at Abbess Catherine piteously.

'Does that take away from this?'

'Of course not,' said the Abbess.

'But why can't things arrange themselves better?' cried Cecily. 'My cousin Jean loves Larry. Why can't he love her?'

'We don't know what is better,' said Abbess Catherine. 'We only know things are a kind of crucible, especially love; and now, Sister, if you love Larry, you must see him, for his sake and for ours,' but Cecily still dodged.

'Mother, I can't.'

'Cecily,' Abbess Catherine's voice was very tender. 'I think that all your life you will have the faculty of making people love you, perhaps more than you want. Your mother's love is like that, possessive, and perhaps his.'

'But I don't *do* anything,' Cecily protested.

'You don't have to,' and, looking at her, Abbess Catherine thought, you were born with great beauty of body and, I begin to think, of soul. The two attract like a magnet.

'It isn't my fault,' said Cecily, as if she read the Abbess's thought.

'It's your responsibility,' and Abbess Catherine leaned forward and took Cecily by the shoulders. 'I felt like a doctor shaking a baby into life,' she told Dame Beatrice afterwards. 'Grow up!' she said. 'Grow up.'

For a moment the shield came down, that stony look; then Cecily looked up again, her eyes wide open. 'Mother, that day of the lunch party – I ran away.'

Elspeth had not been able to stand any more. She had shut Rory in the cloakroom, crept upstairs, put on her coat and gloves and scarf, snatched up her case and purse, stolen down the back stairs and run through the back gate and away down the road. 'Dad came after me and found me at the bus stop, but he did not make me go back. He drove me straight here. It was cruel to my mother, cowardly, but I couldn't face them. I wish now I had. I wish I hadn't run. I – panic, Mother.'

'I know,' said the Abbess.

'On Christmas Day too I nearly gave in – if it hadn't been for Dame Maura.' Cecily drew a sharp breath of fear. 'That frightened me. I began to wonder if my vocation was a kind of obstinacy, against my mother.' Abbess Catherine forbore to say that was what they had all been wondering. 'But it isn't,' said Cecily. 'It isn't. I knew it when I saw Sister Hilary's bouquet. That's what made me dare to come to you. I knew then that it was everything and I must not wait another minute. Everything,' said Cecily, 'which is why I can't see Larry.'

'Which is why you can see Larry,' The Abbess stood up. 'He is in number three parlour. You may have half an hour.'

As Cecily reached the door, Abbess Catherine called her back. 'Remember, even though he is expecting it, seeing you in the habit and behind the grille will be a shock to him. Be gentle.'

'Hullo, Larry.' The 'hullo' sounded strangely out of place.

'Elspeth.' Lady Abbess had been right. Larry was startled, more than startled. He stared, stared again, then, caught unawares, sank down on to the wooden chair as if he had been stunned. 'Elspeth!' and Cecily saw what she had never seen before – or dreamed she would see – a man weep. Larry put his head down on his arms on the wide shelf of the grille as if to shut out the sight of her and was shaken by sobs while Cecily stood helplessly behind the bars, looking down at his bowed head. It was worse to hurt Larry than her father, or mother, almost worse to face him than to have faced Lady Abbess over the Clothing. Why was it so much more alive? It was like a physical pain and when Cecily spoke it was too violently, too unkind. 'Oh, Larry! Why did you come? It's seven months . . .'

'Seven months, three weeks and two days. You see I know and care.' He thrust that at her.

'I care too,' said Cecily in misery.

'Then come *out*.' He stopped and looked round. 'I suppose someone is listening to us?'

'We're not that kind of monastery,' said Cecily in scorn.

'I don't care what kind of monastery it is. Your mother told me of that mock wedding,' said Larry in disgust.

'Mock!' Cecily thought of Hilary's bouquet lying at the feet of our Lady, of the scent of her own white flowers, the voices that had sounded – like angels, thought Cecily – of the solemn moments of renunciation and the putting on of her girdle and scapular and veil, and, 'Mock!' she said, almost with a little hiss, 'you don't know what you are talking about!'

'And soon you will be taking vows, signing your life away.'

'It's what I hope and pray for.'

'No, Elspeth.'

'Yes.'

'I shall pray too,' said Larry. 'And I'll out-pray you, because I'll never give up. Never.'

'Larry, don't.' She had sunk down on one of the parlour chairs and he had sat up so that their faces were almost on a level, the bars between. 'Larry.'

'Don't keep on saying my name as if you were rubbing it in.' He held the grille bars. 'Elspeth. Wake up. Stop all this nonsense.'

'I am awake and it isn't nonsense.' Nonsense could not hurt – so excruciatingly.

'It may not be nonsense for some. It is for you.'

'It isn't.'

They were squabbling almost as they had as children.

'This abbess of yours says you are free – quite free to go.'

'And to stay.'

Cecily spoke pityingly. Oddly enough, she did not think of running away from the argument and the pain, the sight of Larry's face, ravaged – by what I have done to him, thought Cecily; she felt as if she were bleeding herself. Were the nuns teaching her – not to feel, she felt too much already – but to consent to feel? Not run away and, for instance in this present moment – so dreadfully present she could have said – to think of Larry, not of herself? But no matter what she felt for him, she could only say, 'I shall stay, Larry.'

'No.' He brought his fist violently down on the shelf. 'No!

247

Come away with me now. Marry me and be real – a real woman, a wife, with children. You love children, Elspeth.'

'Perhaps more than ever now,' said Cecily.

'Then? Don't you want to be a woman?'

'I am a woman. Larry, look at me.'

'I can't see past all those trappings.'

'That's the trouble,' said Cecily sadly. 'So few people can – but please try.'

Reluctantly he looked straight at her face, a look that grew ardent, thought Cecily, her heart sinking. The old Elspeth would have dropped her lids under that gaze but Cecily made her eyes steady. 'Don't I look happy?'

'Damnably happy,' said Larry.

'If there were anyone in the world I could marry,' said Cecily, 'it would be you. It always has been you.'

'Well then?'

'I said, "in the world". You wouldn't want me if I were married to someone else, would you?' He did not answer. 'Would you?'

'This Christ!' said Larry, his teeth clenched. 'Jesus Christ who died two thousand years ago.'

At that a fierceness woke in Cecily, a zeal she had not felt before and that, oddly enough, let her speak quietly.

'He hasn't died – because He is God. Men and women, thousands of them still leave all that they have – and might have – to follow Him. I'm not the only one . . .'

'You are for me. I love you, Elspeth.'

Cecily shook her head. 'You're blind, Larry. I'm not Elspeth any more. I'm Sister Cecily.' She stood up and put her chair away, neatly in the monastic way. 'You'll have to learn to call me that.'

'I call you Elspeth.' He got up too, in Larry's old abrupt way and picked up his hat. He seemed immensely tall, broad and alive in the small dark parlour and, tall though she was, he looked down on her. She felt his warmth and strength, almost she could smell his tweeds and his freshness. 'So long,' said Larry and went out.

Larry's words were often old-fashioned, slang borrowed

248

from his mother but, 'So long.' The words seemed to fill the parlour. Cecily sank down again, her hands gripping the ledge, her forehead against the cold bars, that quivering tearing inside her. The happy cocoon that she had thought was Sister Cecily had been torn open, and a weak little moth was struggling for life inside.

The bell began to ring for Sext. Taking refuge in obedience Cecily put her chair in its neat place for the second time and went to choir.

Abbess Catherine's morning had been taken up with Larry Bannerman and Cecily; Sext came and dinner with its long grace; recreation needed to be spent with the community – 'And I had to get a breath of air,' said Abbess Catherine, but the best and longest time for work was between None at three o'clock – it finished at quarter past – and Vespers for which the first toll went at a quarter past five. Two hours, thought the Abbess. I must be undisturbed, and she did what was seldom, indeed, almost never, done – put a token on the door knob, that forbidding white, and began to write.

'In his Rule, St Benedict twice expresses his admiration for the manly and the vigorous type of holiness . . .' It seemed better to start again. 'He alludes with great reverence to . . .'

Knock.

She did not answer.

Knock.

She went on writing.

Knock.

With a smothered exclamation she gave in. 'Deo Gratias.'

Knock.

'Deo Gratias.' She called it loudly this time, but no one came in. Instead – Knock.

'Deo *Gratias*. Come *in*!'

Knock.

Abbess Catherine lost her temper. She got up from her chair so quickly that she sent it rocking, and in three strides was at the door which she flung open with such force that her hand caught in the cord of her cross. The cord broke – it must have

249

been rotten – the cross fell on the hard wooden floor and broke too, came apart, but Abbess Catherine was staring – at emptiness. No one was at the door and the alcove was empty.

'Well, really!' said Abbess Catherine. Swiftly she went through the alcove to the corridor but there was only Sister Ellen down on her hands and knees at her eternal polishing. 'Who dared to come to my room just now, knock and run away?' The Abbess was almost storming and Sister Ellen got to her knees bewildered. 'Who dared?'

'N-nobody, my Lady.'

'What do you mean, nobody?'

'Nobody has come down the corridor, my Lady. I didn't hear anybody knocking.'

'Then you must be deaf and blind,' stormed the Abbess.

The old nun had dignity. 'I have been here for the last quarter of an hour, my Lady, and I am quite in my wits.'

'I . . . beg your pardon,' said Abbess Catherine, 'but . . .'

'No one has come,' said Sister Ellen.

'Are you sure?'

'Quite sure, my Lady.'

'Then I'm sorry, dear Sister,' and Abbess Catherine went back to her room and found she was shaking. Someone must have heard the anger in her 'Deo Gratias' – 'Forgive me,' murmured the Abbess – her angry steps, and fled; or else, too late, seen the token and realized she should not have disturbed . . . Sister Ellen after all was over ninety and engrossed in her polishing – but to find no one outside the door had been a shock. No one, the alcove empty, thought Abbess Catherine; it seemed strangely impressed on her but, I must be overwrought, she thought, hearing knocks when there are none, and I should not lose my temper like that. Her hands were shaking too as she picked the pieces of the cross off the floor and carried them to her desk. For nearly two hundred years you have been honoured and revered; then in one little moment of anger I smash you to bits. She could have wept.

The crosspiece, come away, had splintered along one edge, the longer vertical had cracked, and she saw that in the hollow into which the crosspiece had been socketed, the wood was crumbled and soft. Well, after nearly two centuries the wood must be dry. Abbess Catherine tried to fit the crosspiece back into the socket but it would not fit; she felt with her finger and there was something in the socket – something hard that felt like – a bead? wondered Abbess Catherine, a bead embedded in the wood. Then she saw there was a corresponding hollow in the crosspiece – a hollow to fit over the bead? It felt like a bead, but why put a bead into a cross? and, as she felt it delicately with her little finger, Abbess Catherine found that the bead was oval, had – edges, she thought. Her heart began to beat quickly. It's not a bead! With her little finger she scraped away the wood dust and what seemed a film or coat of wax, like candle wax, she thought, and was rewarded by a glint of red. It's not a bead, it's a jewel, hidden! She picked up her paperknife and with its sharp tip gently prised the oval up. It came out on her hand – a small oval, the red showing through the dried grease. She scraped it again and, going to the window, moved her hand in the sun; the red was warm, with a deep jewel light. Could it be – a ruby? thought Abbess Catherine.

'What can Mother want with surgical spirit in the middle of the afternoon?' Dame Joan wondered. 'As far as I know there hasn't been an accident and all her cleaning is done for her.'
'And why a jeweller?' Dame Domitilla wondered too.
'Dame, what was the name of that jeweller who came to see Lady Abbess Hester when I was cellarer?' asked Abbess Catherine.
'There's the little jeweller in Brede,' said Sister Renata who happened to be at the 'turn', 'Mr Winter at the watch shop.'
'A Brede jeweller would be no good,' said the Abbess. 'This was from Hastings.'
'I remember,' said Dame Domitilla. 'It was Mr Rootham from Rootham and Bagnall, the big jeweller's shop. That was five years ago this July. Mother wanted to sell a monstrance; we thought it was set with opals and Mr Rootham came himself. They turned out to be moonstones, poor and scratched at that . . .' but Abbess Catherine was gone.

251

'Get me Mr Rootham of Rootham and Bagnall in Hastings,' she said to Dame Anastasia at the switchboard. 'Mr Rootham himself if you can.'

'Mother didn't even say "please",' Dame Anastasia said afterwards.

Once again Mr Rootham came himself, bringing his loupe and scales and looked at the stone through the loupe in the best light Brede parlours could provide, and in the sunlight.

'Is it – is it a ruby?' Abbess Catherine asked.

'Undoubtedly. Undoubtedly a ruby.' The little man seemed – excited? thought Abbess Catherine.

'But rubies are not very valuable, are they?' she asked, 'as precious stones go?'

Mr Rootham smiled. 'They are often more valuable than diamonds,' he said, and Dame Beatrice gasped. 'That is because they are so rare. It may surprise you, Lady Abbess, but I can tell you that, in all my years, I have never had one of any size in my shop – indeed, I haven't seen one like this. It will have to go under the magnifiers of course, but it is a Burma ruby about six carats and, I think, a fine one.'

'How fine?' they both wanted to ask, but Mr Rootham was still examining it; instead, 'I thought good rubies had to be dark – as pigeon's blood,' said Abbess Catherine.

'That's the way they are described,' Mr Rootham spoke almost absently as he turned the stone this way and that. 'They should be, rather, a warm red, this deep intense colour.' Abbess Catherine had taken the stone to her bathroom and with hot water melted off the wax – 'put there to hold it,' Mr Rootham had said – and then with Dame Joan's surgical spirit cleaned and polished it. 'To think, after all these years, it should shine like this.'

'That is its intrinsic shine – the marvel that makes a jewel,' Mr Rootham spoke almost lovingly. 'I'm glad you sent for me this afternoon,' and, '. . . a princess of Savoy,' said Mr Rootham. 'She must have prised it out of a ring or a brooch, probably a ring, perhaps even before she was taken to prison, and hidden it somewhere about her person. Then when she knew she was going to her death, hid it so ingeniously and gave it to your Abbess in the only way she could. What a story! What a story!' said Mr Rootham.

'I give you my most valuable possession.' Abbess Catherine's fillet was sticking to her forehead. 'We nuns had always taken it for granted she meant the cross. "My most valuable possession" – and she meant just that.'

'Yes. What a story! What a story!'

'Mr Rootham.' The Abbess's voice was hoarse. 'Can you give us any idea how valuable it is?'

'Even in the days of the princess, it would have been worth a good deal,' said Mr Rootham. 'It could have saved your penniless Abbess and her nuns some of their privations. Nowadays? Well, I can only tell you that prices go up and up as the stones become more rare.'

'But if it is as fine as you think?' Dame Beatrice could not restrain herself any longer. 'How much?'

'Say . . . a thousand pounds a carat.'

'And . . . it is . . . six carats.'

'Thereabouts – between six and seven. Bringing the scales over here may have upset the delicate balance. I cannot be quite accurate,' and then Mr Rootham became businesslike. If Lady Abbess would entrust the stone to him – 'I shall give you a receipt, of course' – he would take it up to London in the morning, to Garrards, the Court Jewellers. 'They are always interested in fine stones and know where they can place them, which I do not, and with this history . . .'

'We might get six or seven thousand pounds!' Dame Beatrice sounded breathless. Abbess Catherine could not speak at all.

In the hour between supper and Compline, Abbess Catherine tried to calm her turmoil of mind – turmoil, exaltation and wonder. 'That knocking!' said the prioress.

'Dame Beatrice,' Abbess Catherine spoke seriously and slowly. 'We both know that there is nothing that cannot be true, that is impossible, but you are to say to yourself what I said to myself: Sister Ellen is very old and you know what she becomes when she polishes – wrapt; someone light-footed

could have passed her without her knowing. The – unpardon-
ably – angry voice in which I said "Come in" could easily
have driven that someone away, or she may suddenly have seen
the token on the door, or perhaps I am imagining knocks. You
can't wonder.'

'That may all be,' said Dame Beatrice; 'I still think you
were privileged.'

'If I were, it would be almost sacrilege to mention it; doubts
and controversy would be cast, and doubts and controversies
are human. No, we shall keep to what is rational – except
between you and me. The community will be told the cord
broke, the cross fell, came apart and we discovered the ruby.
That is wonderful enough – and we shall wait to tell them
anything until we know what Garrards will offer, if they offer.'

'Mr Rootham is taking it up *himself*,' said Dame Beatrice in
complete faith.

'He may be mistaken' – yet Abbess Catherine knew he
would not be.

The receipt was locked in her desk drawer and the whole of
her echoed Dame Beatrice's, 'It's like a miracle. It *is* your
miracle,' but work must go on. 'Use every odd space, each ten
minutes.' Dame Emily had always taught her novices that;
'It's how all our tasks are done,' and Abbess Catherine made
herself set to work on her paper again. 'St Basil the Great
whose festival we are keeping tomorrow', she read it over. 'In
his humility St Benedict calls his own Rule "a little Rule for
beginners", and the Rule of St Basil "the perfection of wisdom" . . .' Half an hour passed – Dame Beatrice must be keeping watch – and her pen was really moving busily when –
'knock' sounded on the door. The Abbess looked up quickly,
half rose, but it was only Dame Domitilla. 'Mother, our Lady
of Peace is finished.'

Abbess Catherine looked up in bewilderment.

'Our Lady of Peace, Mother. The statue. Mr Duranski has
sent round to ask if you would come down into the choir and
see it.'

'Please tell Mr Duranski tomorrow . . .' It was on the tip of
Abbess Catherine's tongue, but she paused; the statue had

been carved here at Brede, for Brede and under Brede auspices; in a special way it was theirs because they had seen it grow. They could almost have been said to have worked with Stefan Duranski; there must have been a prayer for every stroke of his chisel; she could imagine the surge of triumph and impatience he was in – and he was her friend. The pen was laid down and she rose.

The choir was empty except for Sister Philippa who was arranging the book on the lectern, finding the places for Compline. Abbess Catherine beckoned her and gave her the key that opened the wicket to the grille. Philippa pulled aside the canvas curtain to show the lights full on in the disused sanctuary that was still littered with chips and stone dust. Stefan Duranski, his skull cap removed, was standing beside his statue which was turned round to face the choir. Abbess Catherine's hand tightened on Philippa's arm.

Our Lady of Peace stood on her pedestal, a suggestion of the round world on which there were faint markings of clouds and seas; the lights made shadows of her veil and robe so that she looked alive and her stone seemed not cold as most stone did, but to glow as if it had a life of its own. 'Well, it is very old stone,' Stefan Duranski was to say, 'weathered by centuries; old stone gets a patina like that.' The carving was primitive, some even left in the block as if it were still held primevally, and the heart behind the Baby was concave, holed as with a sword point; one hand held him, the other extended as if held over the world. The Baby looked out with eyes that saw far, while hers saw only Him. 'Where did you learn to do that with eyes?' whispered Abbess Catherine.

'From my mother,' said Stefan Duranski, but she saw he was close to tears.

Philippa did not speak, only looked. Then Abbess Catherine put her hand through the wicket. 'Thank you,' she said to Stefan Duranski. 'Thank you from us all and thank you for making her and for making her here.'

As always when he was moved he was brusque. 'Why don't you sell her?' he said.

'Sell her?'

'To help pay for the altar.' He did not say how he had fathomed their trouble. 'I could probably get you four thousand for her.'

As she had felt with the princess's ruby, for Abbess Catherine it was as if the sky had opened, but, 'She isn't ours,' she said.

'It was your trough,' said Stefan Duranski. 'As for the carving, that's my present. Of course she is yours.' He looked at the figure. 'One of my very best,' he said. 'It must have been the prayers.'

'Mother, I know it's late, but could I speak to Duranski in the parlour for ten minutes?' Abbess Catherine noticed that Philippa called him simply Duranski in the French way, and remembered that Philippa knew him. 'I had thought you would have asked to see him before now,' she said, but Philippa shook her head.

'I wanted to be quiet, but now I have something to say to him. May I? I shall only be ten minutes.'

'I will tell Dame Domitilla to send round for him,' but the ten minutes had not gone when Philippa knocked at the Abbess's door.

'Mother, that statue, our Lady of Peace, belongs to Brede.'

'She should – but if Mr Duranski says we can sell her, there is the debt . . .'

'I know.' Cool Philippa seemed as excited as a young girl. 'I am asking you to sell her. If you will accept, Mother, I have bought her for Brede.'

'*You* have?'

'Yes. Duranski has agreed. He's delighted.'

'But how?' asked Abbess Catherine. 'Get up, Sister.' Philippa was kneeling. 'Sit down,' but Philippa stood, so light with happiness that she seemed poised.

'In a little while, Mother, if things go well we shall have to talk about my property. Although I brought a dowry . . .'

'A generous dowry.'

'I didn't bring the whole. I had to buy an annuity and the lease of a flat for Maggie, my housekeeper, that took almost all

256

the residue, but McTurk – Mr McTurk,' she corrected herself – 'has been fighting to get some sort of gratuity for me in place of the one I should have had if I had left to get married in the ordinary way; it is a nice point. I had a letter from him this very Monday,' said Philippa, 'to say the Treasury had agreed to an ex-gratia payment. I hadn't really taken it in deeply – money seems so far away here.'

'It is for most of the community.'

'But it came home, while you were talking to Duranski. There should be quite four thousand pounds which he thinks a fair price for the statue. I was going to ask you to put the money towards the debt – in effect it is the same – though it is not enough,' said Philippa regretfully.

'But it may be enough. Sister, we may even be overflowing.' Abbess Catherine stood up, took Mr Rootham's receipt out of her drawer and laid it before Philippa. 'Read that.'

Philippa read aloud: 'Received from Lady Abbess Catherine Ismay; one Burma ruby, approximately 6–7 carats' – 'He brought his jewel scales,' put in Abbess Catherine – 'formerly the property of Princess Marie Hortense of Savoy and bestowed by her on Lady Abbess Flavia Vaux, August 1794.' 'You cannot imagine,' said Abbess Catherine, 'how staid Mr Rootham enjoyed writing that.'

'But ... over six carats,' Philippa said when she had heard the story, 'and from the French court. Mother, it may be worth ... anything.'

'Mr Rootham said it might be a thousand a carat,' and, 'Suppose it were six carats.' Abbess Catherine tried to keep her voice level; 'If it were six, with your four thousand ...'

'We should have more than enough!'

'And suddenly – out of the blue – all in one day.' Abbess Catherine was incoherent and Philippa put her arms round her and hugged her. 'If you can imagine two nuns in a mixture of a war whoop and a Te Deum,' Philippa wrote to McTurk, 'that's what we did.' Both of them were flushed; Abbess Catherine's eyes were wet. 'It's too late to tell everyone tonight – though I should have liked to – but tomorrow in chapter, instead of my conference ... Think of the jubilation, the relief . . .' and, 'I felt more cock-a-hoop than if I had pulled off the most complicated government multi-million deal,' wrote Philippa to McTurk.

It was merciful, she thought, that it was almost time for Compline, then holy time, Matins and the Great Silence, or they would have gone to bed too elated to sleep – and Abbess Catherine looked worn out.

As the roll for Compline began she picked up the receipt to put it away again. It was then, glancing at the letters on her desk, that she said, 'Sister, I think you knew a Mrs Farren.'

She saw a stillness fall on Sister Philippa, such tenseness that the Abbess was startled. Sister Philippa had gone white. 'A Mrs Farren, Sister?'

'I did once,' Philippa made her deep bow and was gone from the room.

IO

'How well providence works things out,' said Dame Beatrice. 'All the worrying tangle of ends and threads weaving together into a new and exciting pattern. Instead of being poorer we are richer, much richer in every way.'

'It is our dear Mother working for us,' said Sister Priscilla whose faith had never wavered. 'I knew when they made all that fuss and got so upset, she wouldn't leave us in the lurch. Yes,' said Sister Priscilla, nodding her head, 'make no mistake. Mother is working for us in heaven.'

'I don't think that's likely,' said Dame Agnes when she heard, 'Mother never gave a thought to money on earth.'

'Do you know, I think it is,' said Dame Beatrice. 'She will have realized ... and the breaking of the cross – just then – Mr Duranski's generosity, Sister Philippa's wonderful donation, all stem from her.'

Garrards had made an offer for the ruby. Mr Rootham had telephoned from their shop in London. 'I believe you couldn't do better,' and a letter had followed. It repeated what he had said in the parlour. The ruby was a fine stone, a Burma ruby, of excellent colour; its weight, seven carats ... Mr Rootham had underestimated these; the magnifiers had proved the stone almost flawless. Its interesting history gave it added lustre and Garrards were happy to offer six thousand pounds. 'A little below my estimate,' said Mr Rootham, 'but they have, of course, to set the stone and find a buyer.'

Six thousand pounds. 'Well!' said Dame Perpetua after the story was told in chapter. 'We were astonished at Duranski, so much money in those pieces of stone, but they at least are large. This! Thousands of pounds in something not as big as my fingernail! Well, we live and learn!'

'Do you know,' Dame Beatrice was reluctant to cast any shadows on the marvel but felt she had to speak. 'Now I have had time to think, I liked it better as it was.'

'Liked what, Dame?'

'The cross,' said Dame Beatrice. 'Princess Marie Hortense's cross as we have had it all these years. I don't want to be ungrateful, but that is what I feel. "I give you the most valuable thing I possess." '

'Well – and didn't she?' asked Dame Perpetua.

'It seems that we mistook her. To me,' said Dame Beatrice, 'it was more valuable to us without the ruby.'

Of Philippa's four thousand pounds the chapter was only told there had been a donation.

'Don't let *anyone* know,' she had begged, but, 'No more secrets from the Council,' Abbess Catherine had been decided about that. 'The Council must know.' When the councillors were told – and Dame Perpetua – they were dumbfounded until Dame Agnes said, 'Sister Philippa seems born to be thrust into extraordinary prominence.'

That was what Philippa felt – no matter how she tried to eschew it. On the seventh of July – four years, six months and six days from her entry – she made her Solemn Profession, taking vows for life in one of the most ancient ceremonies of the Church. The Archbishop professed her from the newly consecrated altar, though, as a widow, Philippa stayed behind the grille. Maggie was there and McTurk – not of course Richard – Joyce Bowman, no one else. Philippa's voice was strong now, 'though horridly untuneful,' she still had to say, and she was able to sing out the triple 'Suscipe', '*Accept me, Lord, as Thou hast promised, and I shall truly live*' that each time was repeated by the community.

She had lain prostrate while the Litany of the Saints was sung, the long scroll of honoured names – and who knows, thought Philippa, from what obscure convent or quiet cell would come some Professed like herself, though with merits a

Philippa did not possess, whose name would be added to them? Then, at the open wicket, she knelt while the Archbishop gave her the cowl, which her matrons put on her, the full black veil of a solemnly professed nun which they pinned on her cap, the ring by which her marriage, as a bride of Christ, would be made whole. As a widow she could not be given the mitra or crown, token of virginity. 'I have to forfeit that,' but she was given the book, the breviary, sign of her right to sing the Divine Office in choir. 'She will not go all the way,' Dame Agnes had predicted. But I am here, thought Philippa, here – miraculously.

'It has been a long hard road,' Abbess Catherine had said to her that morning. 'Especially at first, those small tormenting things.'

'They were only pin pricks,' Philippa could say that now.

'Martyrdom by pin pricks can be very painful,' said Abbess Catherine.

Philippa had never seen McTurk's face as little quizzical, as serious, as it was when she had glimpsed him through the grille in the moment of taking round her chart, the chart of her vows that she had just read out and signed and that must be shown to everyone in the choir, signed too by the Abbess and which would then be laid upon the altar.

McTurk surprised her. 'A Solemn Profession isn't touching in the way a Clothing is,' she said when she saw him three days later in the parlour. A choir nun of Brede keeps silence for three days after her Solemn Profession; nothing is allowed to intrude on her, and McTurk, surprisingly again, had waited in the town all that time. 'It isn't touching.'

'Certainly not,' said McTurk. 'It was awe-ful, full of awe. I know now,' he said, 'at least, have an inkling of what it means to love God with your whole heart and mind and strength.' *Having seen Him, I love and trust Him. He is the love of my choice,* Philippa had sung, *until death.* Awe-ful and full of joy – happiness was too light a word – a joy that was in the whole monastery that day. For this day, in the refectory Philippa sat on the Abbess's right hand at the high table, her place decorated with flowers; in her cell her bed was strewn with messages, cards and flowers. And I thought I wasn't liked, thought Philippa, misty-eyed. 'Dame Philippa,' said Dame Perpetua, giving her a hug and a kiss. 'Dame!' There was hardly a nun in the community who did not embrace her. Sister Priscilla waddled up from the kitchen and gave her a smacking kiss; even Sister Jane came who, in the novitiate, had found Sister Philippa nearly as useless as Sister Hilary. 'Dame!'

'And now what?' asked McTurk.

'As far as anyone in the world will know, nothing,' said Philippa. 'No one will hear any more of me; six hours a day in my stall in choir; two, perhaps of manual labour in the house or garden; some time for study; silence; singing; prayer; living; room to live. I shall disappear, be almost anonymous. Yes, I have learnt now. No more Philippa Talbot,' she said, glorying. 'Arranging, deciding, settling – that arrogant creature!'

'Then what will she do?' asked McTurk.

'Simply grow,' but McTurk's wise monkey eyes grew quizzical again. 'Difficult to grow without yourself,' said McTurk.

'Could I see Mrs Talbot?'

'Mrs Talbot?' For a moment Sister Renata had to think. 'Oh! Dame Philippa Talbot.'

'D-dame?'

'Yes. She is professed now,' and as Penny still looked puzzled, 'Benedictine choir nuns are called Dame,' and Sister Renata asked, 'Does she know you are coming?'

'No, but please find her. I must see her. It's not a visit. Tell her it's Penny – Penny Stevens from the office, her office, and . . .' Penny took a deep breath, 'it's a matter of life and death.'

Sister Renata looked at this unknown young woman whose hair was dark and rough and who wore, to Sister Renata's eyes, most outré clothes: an orange and black woven dress too warm for the day, no hat, lipstick that made a gash of her mouth, but whose face was white, its nostrils pinched and whose hands were clutching her handbag. 'I'm sure we can find her,' said Sister Renata and, Tea, strong tea, she thought to herself.

'Penny Stevens,' said Penny again, 'and it *is* a matter of life and death.'

In the chapter house the Abbess's weekly conference was coming to an end. 'We did not come here to find graces just for ourselves,' said Abbess Catherine; she preferred to speak standing, her nuns sitting in their double row of seats round the room. 'Not just for ourselves; the interior life engages our whole being – its discoveries, the growing intimacy with our Lord which is one of its fruits – fascinates us and this is the very temptation, because it tends to shut us in on ourselves.'

Philippa was not listening; she had emerged from her days of silence feeling as if she had been standing in strong sunlight, and ordinary life was still blurred and shadowy for her. Lady Abbess's words went on over her head while she watched a lark. 'I never had time to watch larks before. Odd, one has to leave the world to discover it,' she had said to Dame Perpetua who answered, 'We only leave the worldly world.'

Now through the tall arched window opposite, Philippa could see the sky in its summer blue; she could not hear the lark's song through the glass but could see it, the shape of a minuscule cross in the sky; it had been winging its way up and up, these twenty minutes. Did it hope one day it would not come down, but be taken up into some invisible heaven beyond that blue? As she thought that, it suddenly closed its wings and plummeted down, falling in a few seconds out of the window's range, back to its nest in a furrow of the field or park – or is it too late in the year for a nest? wondered Philippa – she must ask Dame Bridget – but back to earth in a matter of seconds after that long effort of trilling and upward beating of wings. H'm, thought Philippa, parables in front of your eyes, but . . .

She was given a sharp nudge by Dame Sophie, youngest of the professed choir nuns and next to Philippa in religion. 'Mother looked at you *twice*,' she told Philippa afterwards. 'I thought you had gone into a trance.'

Abbess Catherine was summing up; '. . . and when we need consolation, succour,' she was saying, 'we don't seek it from strangers; we go to someone who, we know, has in his or her soul a fund of strength, whom we can trust to help us without weakness. Today is the festival of our sister monastery of Pixham, dedicated as you know to our Lady of Consolation; this morning they called her "blessed in her strength". She is blessed in her gentleness and sweetness but the source of these attractive qualities is her strength of soul. Let us, of our Lady of Peace, take our pattern too from her. When we are fixed in our loyalty to God's slightest requirement, and are strong enough to answer it, then and only then are we capable of being a comfort to others, a consolation,' but the words made little impression on Philippa; she was still thinking of the lark.

It was one of the few times Dame Perpetua reprimanded her. 'Though you are professed, I am subprioress; you should have been listening. It was meant for you.'

'For me?' Philippa's eyebrows went up.

'For every one of us.' Dame Perpetua had caught Philippa as she was walking to the refectory after None to get a cup of tea, to which the nuns helped themselves from urns on a side table. Philippa usually avoided tea but it was a thirsty afternoon. In the long cloister Dame Perpetua planted herself in Philippa's way, then drew her apart. 'For every one of us,' she said again. 'Mother is right. We get too shut in on ourselves. We come from the masses and should be one with the masses – always,' said Dame Perpetua, and the old Talbot impatience flared up in Philippa.

'If you enter at nineteen or twenty, yes, you may need to be reminded, but I have had half a lifetime of other people's troubles, concerns and interest. You don't work in a Department of eighteen hundred men and women without meeting endless difficulties,' and, standing in the sunlight of the cloister, she said, 'I have done my stint.'

'Stint?' asked Dame Perpetua. 'That sounds like a measure.'

'It is a measure,' said Philippa, 'a fair share. Enough,' but, 'I don't think you'll find,' said Dame Perpetua, 'that God has measures.'

Philippa did not get to the refectory. Dame Domitilla was at her elbow. 'Dame Philippa, Mother says you may go to a Mrs Stevens in number four parlour.'

Much talking had gone on in the small parlour rooms at Brede.

'I once read,' said Dame Perpetua, 'a description, written by someone who ought to know better, of enclosed nuns as being like lilies growing in a sheltered greenhouse and fed daily with a mixture of pasteurised milk and snow! Well, there may be communities like that, but I wonder if there is anything these walls haven't heard.'

'You see,' Philippa told Penny, 'parlours get their name because they are "parloirs" – places for talking.'

Each was divided in half by the grille, the front half opening into the extern cloister, the back on the new cloisters and the enclosure. The floors still had their ancient oak boards; there were straight-backed chairs, a wide sill each side of the grating with a double-fronted drawer below it through which, when the Abbess granted the key, books and papers could be passed back and forth. Philippa, coming quietly in, saw a small hunched figure on a chair, a tray of tea untouched beside her. 'Penny?' The figure started. 'Is something wrong with Donald or is it you?'

Penny had stumbled to her feet – how small and untidy and woebegone she looked.

'You or Donald?'

'Neither. We're ... perfectly well,' Penny was staring.

She hasn't seen a grille before, Philippa reminded herself, nor me in a habit.

'You're ... thinner.' Penny spoke in a whisper. 'It makes your eyes look big ... but ... oh, Mrs Talbot!'

'Dame Philippa. You'll have to try and learn to say that now. Penny, you haven't had your tea.'

'No. I came from London ... but ... I don't want any.'

'You do.'

'Mrs Talbot ... Dame ... could I talk to you?'

'Of course, but tea first.' It was the old authoritative voice with a hint of amusement in it and it seemed to lay a calming hand on Penny, as Philippa had meant it to. 'Why, it's cold.' She had put a hand through the bars to feel the teapot. 'Wait a moment,' and Penny blinked as with a swish of skirts Philippa was gone. 'No,' Penny had started to say, 'I couldn't drink any tea,' but when in a few moments Sister Renata brought a fresh pot and Philippa had come back and begun a light office gossip – how Miss Bowman was now personal assistant to Sir Richard and Penny, promoted, had gone with her; how McTurk had been given the CMG in the Birthday Honours and, 'Have you still got the clock? Do you make it chime?' asked Philippa – Penny ate and drank and had to admit she felt better. The tea was warming, 'all down inside me. I don't know why I felt so cold on such a warm day,' while the brown bread and butter was good. 'We bake our own bread here,' said Philippa and, 'Now,' she said as Penny slid the tray aside. 'You didn't come to talk gossip. What is it?'

'It's – it's – I'm going to have a baby.'

Philippa was suddenly still; the same tense stillness Abbess Catherine had seen. For a moment she sat looking down at the sill, her hands pressed together under her scapular. Dame Perpetua, like the novitiate, had noticed that she did not share the nuns' love of and interest in children and babies.

Every Christmas the Abbey gave a party for the children of Brede town; it was run by the extern sisters in the large front hall, but all the nuns contributed by dressing dolls, wrapping parcels, making sweets for doing up in bags, decorating the big tree, and most of them listened at the enclosure door, listening to the fun, but Philippa found an excuse to be at the other end of the Abbey. Nor would she look at the Child in the Christmas crib – just as she avoided Him in statues or paintings. 'Dame, don't ask me,' Philippa had begged, and Dame Perpetua had pressed her shoulder and left her alone. That was all Philippa asked, to be left alone – so that I can keep Keith just as that ruffle of wind, laughing – but now she braced herself. 'Isn't that lovely and exciting?' she asked it as a question; she had taken in the trouble in Penny's grey eyes, the worried way she pushed her hair up, making it rougher – Why *won't* she brush it? thought Philippa. 'Isn't it?'

'It was, after our doctor, Doctor Murdoch, said "Yes, it was true." I felt so full of riches, I couldn't tell anybody. I hugged it to myself. I felt like – like a cocoon.'

Philippa nodded. 'One does.' It slipped out, but Penny was too absorbed to notice. She went on. 'Then...'

'Then?'

'I began to think ... and oh, Mrs Talbot, I daren't tell Donald.'

'But, Penny!'

'I know,' said Penny miserably.

'He's your husband.'

'That's why. He'll be angry and then ... I'll feel as if he had hit it. Oh, I can't explain.'

'Try.'

'You see,' Penny took a gulp, 'he doesn't want children, at least not yet. He thought when we had been married much longer, about ten years and he had got on ... he made me promise to be careful. I thought I was, but of course I wasn't. We tried the pill, of course, but I forgot to take them. Anyway, I'm frightened of the pill. Then I went to the clinic. It wasn't that I didn't know,' said Penny, 'or didn't try ... Donald always says I'm careless but perhaps subconsciously...' the broken jerked sentences came out. 'Yes, I did want a child,' said Penny, but, 'You see, Donald's clever. He will go a long way – if he's not bogged down.' Philippa could hear clearly when it was Donald speaking, and not Penny. 'I thought I could stop it, and I went back to Doctor Murdoch, but he wouldn't do anything.'

'Of course he wouldn't. Doctors don't like doing it, even when there are strong reasons. Here there's no reason.'

'But there is,' said Penny, with earnestness. 'Donald's going in for water ski-ing – it isn't only sport, it's the thing to do. He makes useful contacts. If I have to stop working, we couldn't afford it and – and we have just moved into a new flat. They won't allow babies.'

'These are not reasons, they are pretexts. Wake *up*, Penny.'

'But people do do it,' argued Penny.

'People do all kinds of hideous things but they don't know

what they are doing. You do,' said Philippa, 'or you wouldn't be here.'

Penny conceded that. 'But it will upset everything.'

'Babies do, because they are people from the very beginning.'

'That's what I feel. I feel it here,' Penny's hands went to her breast. 'It's mine,' she spoke fiercely; then her eyes clouded, 'but I'm sure Donald won't have it.'

'He will,' said Philippa, 'if he's the right kind of man.'

'Oh, he is, he is,' Penny was always loyal.

'Penny, listen to me.' Philippa had forgotten herself in her concern. 'You and Donald are both well and strong and young. You earn enough money to buy a house if that is necessary. There are no reasons, except selfish ones, why you shouldn't have this child. It's a privilege,' said Philippa, 'and even to think for one moment of doing anything else is evil – *evil*, Penny.'

'That's what I thought you would say,' said Penny in content.

'You knew very well what I would say.'

'Yes, but I wanted to hear you say it.' Then again there was that clouding. 'You say it as a nun. Would you have said it as Mrs Talbot?'

'I should certainly have said it as Mrs Talbot,' and Philippa leaned forward and through the grille put her hand on Penny's. 'Penny, think of him – or her – listening to your clock.'

'I want to see Dame Philippa Talbot.' The way the young man said it was so crisp, even hectoring – as if he would not put up with any nonsense – that Sister Susanna, who had answered the front door, felt her colour rising.

'I shall have to ask if she can see you.'

'She saw my wife.' There was a pause. 'Tell her my wife, Penelope Stevens, is ill.'

'Please tell her,' Sister Susanna silently corrected. 'I will find out.' She did not show him into a parlour but left him in the hall.

Abbess Catherine sent for Philippa. 'Do you know this young man?'

'Donald? Only through his wife. She was the junior clerk in my office.' Philippa felt a shiver of anxiety. 'She came to see me last week because she was having a baby,' said Philippa in a rush. 'I don't know what has happened – but something to bring him here. Penny went away happy and confident and brave.'

'Brave? Then there was an obstacle.'

'There shouldn't have been. I was sure . . .' Philippa broke off. Had she been so sure? No, I was anxious, thought Philippa. She had written to Penny, but her phrases had sounded stilted, too general. They wouldn't have reached her, thought Philippa. It needed a Dame Beatrice or a Dame Perpetua and now . . . but Abbess Catherine touched her lightly on the shoulder. 'Go and see this Donald.'

'It isn't as if it had been a hole-and-corner business,' said Donald. 'I do take care of her. It was a proper doctor and a nursing home and I took her there myself,' said Donald virtuously. 'They let her out next day.'

'Too soon,' said Philippa.

'Nowadays it's nothing.'

'Nothing,' said Philippa, looking at him. So this was Penny's Donald, tall, well dressed – much better dressed than Penny – taking the eye with his height, waving blond hair, cleft chin and handsome tan. Yes, extremely personable, even good looking, and Philippa thought with a pang of Penny's plainness. She could see how wonderful he must appear to Penny, but Philippa's experienced eye had noted that Donald was already a little too fleshy – and petulant – about the mouth, she thought, spoilt. 'Nothing,' she said again. 'Perhaps that is the trouble. Penny went from here full of hopes and plans. What did you say to her, Donald – I can't call you Mr Stevens – to make her change her mind?'

'We had a quarrel, as a matter of fact, when she told me. At least, she didn't have to tell me; it was at breakfast. She was sick.'

'How dreadful for you,' said Philippa, and he reddened.

'What man could have liked it?' Donald demanded. 'I see. I ought to have been sympathetic.'

'You could have been – under the circumstances.'

'Penny was – apologetic. That always exasperates me. I had *told* her to be careful, but Penny's so frightfully careless. Of course I mean to have a child one day, preferably a son, but not now. To have a baby now, when we had just taken our flat, spent money on it, when things are in the balance for me and ...'

'You are going in for water ski-ing?'

Donald's head came up. '*That* wouldn't have mattered. Penny's inclined to make a fetish of anything I do.' Philippa nodded. 'But she told me she had been to see you. That made me see red.'

'Yes. You never liked me, did you?' said Philippa. 'That doesn't matter. Go on. What happened when you had said all this – as I imagine you did?'

'Penny said, "If you don't want our baby, I don't either," and I said, "That's all right then." She said, "I'll make arrangements." I could tell by her voice she would rush off and do some fool thing, so I said, "You won't. It must be done properly. We'll ask Myra," Myra was a girl I knew – had known. She was a bit of a ...' Donald hesitated. 'Penny knew about her,' he said as if that salved it.

'And what did Penny say to that?'

'She went still, the way Penny does and said, "Very well." She whispered it again, "Very well." I thought it was a threat but no, she only said that I must do the asking as I knew Myra best. So I did – which wasn't pleasant for a man,' said Donald. 'I must say Myra was most helpful and kind. She arranged everything and tried to cheer Penny up.'

'And Penny wouldn't cheer.'

'She made no attempt,' said Donald, exasperated. 'Before it, she was like somebody sleepwalking – you don't know how silent Penny can be; then, when she came back from the Home, she just lay in bed, wouldn't get up, wouldn't eat, wouldn't speak, just *wouldn't*.' Donald exploded in wrath – and in fear, Philippa thought – and then he said, like a

frightened, helpless and far more likeable young man, 'She's
. . . she's bleeding. She says that's normal, but is it? As much
as that?'

'Have you had the doctor?'

'I wanted to get that doctor, the one who did it, but she got
into a fearful state, said she would lock the door.'

'You could have got your own doctor.'

'I couldn't very well. Doctor Murdoch – well, he's a bit of a
stick; he wouldn't have approved. Then this morning early she
was so white, so cold, yet she was sweating, clammy. I think she
was hysterical again. She kept calling for you and something
about chimes. She was asking you to forgive her and flinging
herself about. The only way I could get her quiet was by
promising to come here myself. I – didn't like the look of her,'
Donald confessed.

Philippa had risen. 'Donald, this is dangerous. You must go
straight back. How did you come? By car?'

'My car's laid up. I had to take that God-awful train.'

Under her scapular Philippa looked at her watch. 'Look, I'll
get them to telephone for a taxi. You can catch the fast four
o'clock from Ashford; that will get you to London in an hour.
Take Penny straight to hospital or get your own doctor at
once.'

Philippa disappeared, then came back. 'A taxi will be here
in ten minutes. Sit down,' but Donald was pacing. 'Is Penny
alone?' Philippa kept her voice calm.

'I got Susie, our old daily woman to stay with her.'

'Good.'

'I don't know,' said Donald. 'Susie's full of old wives' tales;
she might make Penny worse.' He paced restlessly. 'You don't
really think . . .'

'I hope not, but bleeding is always serious. The taxi will
soon be here.'

Donald walked to the wall, came back, sat down. Then he
demanded, 'Chimes. What chimes?'

'The chimes of a clock I gave her. We talked about your
baby listening to them,' and Philippa asked, 'Donald, didn't
you even think about the baby?'

'There wasn't a baby, only a germ.'

'Think straight.' The glint in Philippa's eyes made Donald sit up. 'There was a baby, a complete baby, your son or daughter.' How many sorry stories, thought Philippa, this parlour had heard. 'That's why Penny is grieving.'

'It's not only grieving,' said Donald, and he burst out, 'What is it that's killing her? We agreed.'

'Yes, poor Penny.'

'I told her we'll have another baby one day.'

'If you can,' said Philippa. 'A baby doesn't always come for the asking. *It* might choose to be expedient.' Then she said, 'I can guess Penny feels an ineffable sense of wrong.' The sadness in Philippa's voice made Donald look at her through the bars. 'Guilt – if you prefer it,' said Philippa.

'Did you put that into her head?'

'I didn't. It was in her head and her mind and her heart. That's why she came to see me. Now she can't forgive herself . . .'

'Excuse me,' it was Sister Susanna at the door, 'but there's a call for Mr Stevens from London.'

'From London.'

'Yes. A Doctor Murdoch, from the Samaritan hospital.'

Donald flung a wild look as if for help at Philippa; he seemed unable to move. 'Go and answer it,' Philippa had to say and Sister Susanna, who had summed up the situation, put a hand on his arm and said, 'Come, I will show you.' Philippa waited behind the grille; afterwards she found that one of her hands had been clenched so tightly on the grille bars that the knuckles were white.

When Donald came back he was dazed. 'Miss Bowman from the office came to see her.'

'Joyce! Thank God for that.'

'She called Doctor Murdoch at once. He took Penny to the hospital. She is haemorrhaging badly – still talking of you and that I had promised to see you. That's how they knew where to find me.'

'And?'

'They are operating now. They telephoned to ask my per-

272

mission.' He shuddered. 'They have given transfusions but Penny is unconscious. I must go at once. Doctor Murdoch said ... he said...' But Donald could not tell her what the doctor had said; he leant his head against the grille and shut his eyes. 'He didn't go for me, but he will. He should.'

'Donald,' said Philippa. 'We shall be praying for Penny – and for you. Prayer is a force and it's strong. May I tell Lady Abbess?' He nodded dumbly, and she put a slip of paper into his hand; like all the nuns she hoarded scraps of paper, backs of envelopes, margins, on which to write notes. 'That's our number. Telephone me this evening.'

'You can come to the telephone?'

'Of course. Nuns are not antiques, you know. We use type-writers and vacuum cleaners and washing machines, go in cars, and planes – drive them – cars, not planes.' The ordinary talk took some of the tenseness out of him. Then Sister Susanna came to the door; 'Your taxi,' and he got up to go.

'I shall be with you, all the way,' said Philippa.

'Ought I to have told you?' Philippa was in the Abbess's room.

'Certainly not,' said Abbess Catherine. 'What a nun hears in the parlour is as secret as what a priest hears in the confessional. The Church lays down that only if you need to consult an expert, a doctor or a priest, or a nun who has some special knowledge, may you tell one other person – and you must have the confidant's permission. But you could have put Penny Stevens's case – not her name but her case – up on the board for prayers.'

'I needed an expert,' said Philippa shakily. 'I'm still being independent, trying to go it alone,' Lady Abbess Hester had said that of her in Philippa's third year when Maggie had been critically ill with pneumonia and Philippa had not asked for prayers. 'I didn't like to bother people.' 'Sister,' Abbess Hester had said, 'how long have you been practising prayer – really practising it?'

'Since I came here – and a little before, perhaps five years.'

273

'And I for sixty-five years. Don't you think I should know more about it than you? You need the community.'

'She is alive.' Donald's voice on the telephone was husky, barely audible but Philippa caught the words. 'Very, very weak. They gave her five pints of blood.'

'You are staying in the hospital tonight?'

'She – your Miss Bowman – told me to keep away.'

Joyce! Joyce! thought Philippa and, into the telephone, 'She shouldn't have done that. Joyce is always fierce over someone she loves and we all love Penny – but it is you she needs.'

'I ... do you think so?' That was so hesitant, humble, it did not sound like Donald.

'Of course, you are the sun and the moon and the stars to Penny,' Philippa brought out the old cliché deliberately. 'Of course you must stay – and we shall be with you.'

'You?'

'Yes. Lady Abbess appealed to the community. She said she would give special leave to anyone who would give time for prayers during the night for a girl who was desperately ill. They will come.'

'But the nuns don't know her.' He sounded incredulous.

'They know her need. We won't let Penny go.'

Watching, keeping vigil, in the stretches of the night, Philippa found that Abbess Hester's old rebuke was as just now as it had been two years ago and that she, Dame Philippa, was still a novice in prayer. Abbess Catherine told her she might watch from the end of Matins at ten until midnight – again from two until four. 'Then go to bed until after Lauds. You must get some rest.'

For the first hour, three nuns knelt with her. Dame Beatrice, Dame Colette, young Dame Sophie. From eleven Philippa was alone and that hour seemed unending, yet she was grateful for the little experience she had – grateful that I am able to pray at all, she thought, remembering old times when crises had broken through the veneer of every day, as this had now for Donald and Penny. She remembered those hectic dis-

274

jointed prayers that could not find words, let alone thoughts; the blind appeals where now, at least, she turned naturally to the fount she was coming to know more and more. 'You can do nothing of yourself,' the old Abbess had said. 'But you can make yourself an instrument through which strength can flow.'

In the big church there was only the glimmering sanctuary lamp, carefully filled each day after Vespers by Sister Elizabeth, and the votive lamp she had left tonight in the chapel of the Crown of Thorns. 'If you want to read, switch on a reading light,' Dame Winifred had said, but Philippa did not want to read, but knelt in her stall. She had a stall of her own now. After her Solemn Profession, when the Clergy and guests had left, she had come back with the community to the choir, kneeling in the centre while the Collect of thanksgiving was sung. Then the Abbess, with the mistress of ceremonies, came and took her by the hand and led her to the stall assigned to her. The Abbess herself lowered the seat and put the new Dame into it; the stall was now Dame Philippa's, hers by canonical right as an official representative before God of the Church. 'In other words, you are now a professional,' Abbess Catherine had told her. The nuns prayed in their cells, in the garden or park, in any favoured spot, but for most of them there was no place where they were as happy or as at home as in their stalls.

Now Philippa knelt, trying to join herself steadily to that bed in London with the machinery of a big hospital round it, and to Penny lying still and flat under the sheet – it must be hot in London – the drips fastened to arms and legs. Donald in a chair perhaps by her, or worn out, asleep.

Sometimes Philippa found words: 'O God, at whose bidding the sands of our lives run fast or slow, accept the prayers of thy servants for her in her sickness. We implore thy pity. Save her from peril and change our fear to joy.' Fear to joy. Fear to joy. Fear to joy. The words hammered in Philippa's brain. 'Restore her in body and mind.' Sometimes it was without words: the healings in the Gospels grew vivid: Peter's wife's mother, ill of a fever: the nobleman's son: 'Come down

275

before it is too late,' the nobleman had entreated. The servant of the centurion, the blind and the lame and the possessed: the lepers: the woman who touched the hem of Jesus's garment – even to touch it was enough; power went out of him and she was healed. Philippa said the steady decades of the rosary she took from her pocket – our Lady's lifeline, Sister Priscilla called it; saying the beads, she declared, made a chain at whose end was a firm anchor; now each bead was for Penny, but the effort of holding her in unbroken thought made Philippa so tired that she would have swayed but for the wooden ledge against which she knelt, and the lamps seemed to swim in their own light. 'With the manifold help of thy compassion . . .' She had to gather herself again. 'Give me strength to comfort them . . .' and, how little, infinitesimal we are, she thought.

At midnight, when the clock sounded out its slow chimes and Philippa, obedient, stumbled to her feet, her knees were stiff, her mouth dry. But have I to leave Penny alone, she could have cried. The next moment, in the doorway she met Dame Agnes. 'Dame Agnes for me?' she said, marvelling, to the Abbess next morning – though nothing had been told, the nuns' sixth sense would probably, she guessed, have told them that the case was hers. 'For me?'

'Not for you. For a girl in peril; real peril to die with that on her soul,' said the Abbess. 'Dame Agnes has an extraordinary power and great faith. If anyone can storm heaven, she can – and she will do it gladly.'

In the dim choir Philippa, looking down into the older nun's face, saw only its outline under the veil but Dame Agnes was purposeful and wide awake. She had her books and her spectacles; she snapped on a light and moved straight to her stall. It was the Great Silence, when nobody must speak but, as Dame Agnes passed, she made the gesture of sleep, pillowing her cheek on her two hands, nodded encouragingly, and gave Philippa a little push to send her on her way.

Only one light was burning in the long cloister as Philippa came out; no sound came except the faintest echo of bells as the wind from the sea blew into the belfry. A leaf rustled as it was blown along the cloister floor, dried and fallen already, thought Philippa, though it's only July. In her wrought-up state, it seemed a bad omen but, as she went, she met another figure, Dame Maura. Those two antagonists, Dame Agnes and Dame Maura, would now kneel together, praying for the same end – and then, how big we are, thought Philippa.

She found a note in her cell 'Dame Anselma will call you at a quarter to three.' Philippa took off her shoes and veil, stretched herself fully dressed on her bed and feel asleep.

When she came back into the choir, Abbess Catherine was there, kneeling in the 'nobodies'. Dame Ursula, Dame Nichola, Dame Bridget, other figures stole in and out but, 'Mother stayed with me until dawn, and I have never felt such strength,' Philippa told Dame Perpetua afterwards. 'Think, at one time I didn't know her! Now – I couldn't live without her!' said Philippa.

Abbess Catherine that night was a bulwark against fear and Philippa was grateful. This is the time, in the small hours, she thought, when resistance is weakest. She seemed to see Penny's face, small, unconscious, upturned and white, her hands still. 'If Penny dies, having done this,' Philippa had said that in dread to Abbess Catherine. 'Most of us die in our sins,' the Abbess had answered, 'but no one knows what happens in those last few moments. God is infinitely merciful; besides, hasn't this child repented over and over again?' But Philippa found she was praying now as she had never prayed before; yet, with all the strength of her appeal, there was peace. 'Not my will but thine be done,' and, 'Into thy hands I commend . . .' She was not tired now, but seemed borne up and it was with surprise that she heard sounds, seagulls flying round the tower, while, dim out of darkness, a faint light was gathering in the church. The Abbess had gone and presently the clock struck four; Philippa must go but, as she rose to leave the choir, she heard a familiar sound of skirts and not so silent footsteps and a slight creaking of stays, and knew it was Dame Perpetua. Penny would have found Dame Perpetua reassuring, homely where she would have been scared into stupidity by Dame Agnes or the majestic Dame Maura, overcome with awe by the Abbess. 'I have your girl tucked in my sleeve,' Dame Perpetua would have said.

The garth was dim in the colourless light, the shadows grey. The wind had dropped but Philippa could see the seagulls, still inland and wheeling round the tower with their cries. She remembered how sailors say they are the souls of Liverpool seamen – Liverpool men because, legend says, they are the worst and so their souls are lost. The gulls cry their nickname, 'scouse'. Philippa shivered as if the dawn had touched her with a cold finger. 'It's because you're tired,' she told herself.

'Dame, you are wanted on the telephone.'

Philippa, in her blue apron, her eyes smarting with tiredness, her back aching, was cleaning out the cowl room, the cloakroom where the nuns hung their cowls and could wash their hands before going into choir. 'It's from the hospital,' said Dame Domitilla. Even crabbed Dame Domitilla had sympathy in her voice and smile. Nuns of Brede are not supposed to run; Philippa ran to the telephone.

'Donald?' she could hardly say it.

'She is awake and talking.' Donald's voice was so excited that he seemed to babble as he went on but, 'Thank God,' said Philippa.

'Yes, she has had a cup of tea. Do you know they have given her nine pints of blood?' Then he paused. 'Did you pray?'

'Yes,' said Philippa.

'Dame Philippa, I asked you about a Mrs Farren.'

'Yes, Mother.' Philippa tried to guard herself against the gaze of the hazel eyes looking at her so intently across the desk.

'I have to bring the subject up,' Abbess Catherine went on, 'because it's the case of a vocation.'

The guard fell. 'A *vocation*.'

'We have a letter from her daughter.'

'From *Katie*!' Philippa seemed not able to believe her ears...

'Yes – Kate, Kate Farren. She wants to be admitted here.'

'Here!'

*I'm on Tom Tiddler's ground   picking up gold and
silver   gold and silver   breathe   breathe   don't cry
Keith   don't cry   we're coming as fast as we can   gold
and silver*

Philippa's fingers found the rough serge of her skirt and
held it tightly.

'If it were not a vocation, Dame, I wouldn't trouble you,'
Abbess Catherine, Philippa knew, would never press. 'And it's
an interesting case. This girl comes of quite humble people but
would have to be admitted as a choir postulant on her own
qualifications. The father is a railway man; in the war he was
in the army and was promoted to be sergeant but seemed content to go back; he is a porter now at Huddersfield. The
mother died – ten years ago.'

'I didn't know.' Philippa managed to say it.

'There are smaller brothers and sisters; an aunt helped to
bring them up. This Kate is the eldest by seven or eight years.'

'She would be.'

'. . . and academically brilliant. Through grammar school
she got to university and is now a teacher – but she became
one, she says, only to earn money for her dowry here. It seems
the seed was sown when she read in the newspapers about your
entrance at Brede.'

'Those cursed papers,' – but Philippa did not say it.

'As a child, she says, she had an admiration for you, though
too shy to show it.'

'I only saw her once or twice.'

'Well, it seems it's there still.'

Philippa gave a sound like a small groan.

'She fixed her heart on following you as a Benedictine and
made a firm intention to enter Brede. She has been reading,
studying, and,' Abbess Catherine went on, 'I have an accompanying letter from her parish priest. I have seldom read a
warmer recommendation. He and the father and the girl are
coming to see us . . .'

'No!' but Philippa bit back the word.

'She says she is sure you will speak for her.'

Philippa swallowed, but made no sound.

'Well, Dame?' The Abbess waited, then: 'She says her mother worked for you.'

'Yes,' said Philippa.

'In what capacity?'

'She was nurse to my child.'

'Your *child*?'

'Yes.'

'But you are listed as having no children.'

'I haven't.'

'Then. . . ?'

'I had a little boy – who died,' and before the Abbess could speak, Philippa said, 'It's years ago. There is – no point in talking of him.'

'Wouldn't it help to tell me about him?'

'No, Mother – if you don't mind.' Philippa evaded the pity and affection. 'If you don't mind.'

'Very well – but I must ask you this, was it anything to do with Mrs Farren?'

> Let Darrell hold it like a good boy . . . No . . . Keith . . . I was only trying to make him behave like a little English gentleman . . . the small fist clenched against the big authoritative fingers prising . . . Don't pay any attention he always runs and hides when he's upset . . . he'll come out

'Dear Philippa,' said Abbess Catherine. 'I don't want to pry, but if you know anything against Kate Farren's mother you are bound to tell us.'

'She . . . only acted as children's nurses do.' The words came out as monosyllables. 'She couldn't have been expected to guess . . .' Then Philippa gathered herself together and the grey eyes looked levelly at the compassionate hazel ones. 'Mrs Farren did nothing, Mother, that should penalize this girl. I'm sure she is as good as they say – but please, Mother, need I see her?'

Kate Farren was admitted at eleven o'clock on a morning of that September and named Sister Polycarp. 'Well, I'm a queer fish, so that's right,' she said contentedly.

That was what the Council had felt. Brede had never had a candidate quite like this before – 'Not even me,' said Dame Perpetua – and there had been fierce argument.

'If ever any girl were in earnest,' said Abbess Catherine, 'it is Kate Farren.'

'Yes, Mother, but there have to be other things than earnestness and worth.'

'What other could there be?'

'For the choir, a degree of culture and breeding, certainly of manners.'

'I agree with Dame Agnes on that,' said Dame Maura. 'Mother, you interviewed the father?'

'He rather interviewed me,' and the Abbess smiled.

'How many old and ailing have you?' Will Farren had asked. 'I'm not going to have my girl, with her brain, turned into a sick nurse or a slavey.'

'She will have to take her turn at such tasks, as we all do,' the Abbess had said.

'Is it fair turns?' His Yorkshire was as rich as Sister Polycarp's could be.

'Your daughter will have to try and see.'

The aunt, Aunt Tib, who had brought Kate Farren up had come with a basket of her Bakewell tarts for the Abbey. 'They are "giving" people,' said the Abbess. 'I must remind you how this girl worked and saved for her dowry; how her father put down a part of his savings, a working man's savings, to make up what she couldn't save. We offered to remit it but she refused. "I'll come with the right amount." '

'Except that she said, "Ah'll coom wi t'reet amoont," ' said Dame Agnes.

'She puts it on for you,' said Abbess Catherine, but, 'She's certainly of the people,' said Dame Ursula uncertainly.

'We are all of the people,' Dame Anselma had been hot with indignation. 'Any other pretence is nonsensical.'

'Not to recognize differences is more nonsensical.' Dame Agnes was heated too. 'The standards of Brede must not go down.'

'I do not think,' said the Abbess, 'that the Farrens will put them down. It will have to be put to the vote, but it is my opinion that we cannot turn this strong, true, capable and loving soul away.' Abbess Catherine had seldom spoken so forcibly in Council, and the vote was won.

'Which one was Dame Philippa Talbot?' Sister Polycarp asked Dame Clare after the entrance ceremony had ended in the chapter house.

'Dame Philippa? Now I come to think of it, she wasn't there. She is second sacristan,' said Dame Clare, 'and, I expect, had work to do in the choir.'

Philippa had arranged that. 'I see by the list,' she had said to Dame Winifred, 'there is a Mass at eleven in the chapel of the Crown of Thorns. May I answer it?'

'Certainly, if you wish.'

'You cannot come between a girl and her vocation' – Philippa had endlessly told herself that – 'you cannot, but you need not go out of your way to meet her.' It was easy to avoid someone in the big Abbey; like Keith, Philippa had the art of disappearing. The girl would live in the novitiate – at any rate for five years – in choir and refectory her place was apart. 'I need hardly see her,' but Sister Polycarp was early and the high-toned entrance bell caught Philippa in the sacristy where she had been preparing for the Mass, and, carrying her book and small handbell, she met the procession of Abbess, councillors and the new postulant as they were leaving the choir. Philippa had a swift impression of what she would have called 'a gawk of a girl', in a cheap, turquoise coat and skirt; a girl with sandy hair like Mrs Farren but with a thin face, strangely intent. Philippa shrank back against the wall to hide herself; she shut her eyes but seemed impelled to open them again and found Abbess Catherine looking at her, a look that took in the book, the bell, the whole. Abbess Catherine comprehended perfectly.

An odd defiance woke in Philippa. 'This Mass must be answered, Mother.' She almost flung that at the Abbess in silent dialogue.

'Of course – but Dame Winifred should have been the one

to stay. You knew Kate Farren as a child. In charity you should be in the chapter house now to welcome her.'

'I have no charity. Kate Farren is nothing to do with me.'

'Perhaps not Kate Farren, but Sister Polycarp will be your sister.'

'I am doing nothing to impede her, and at least this will spare me from giving her the Pax.'

'Spare you?' The Abbess's look altered to one of such grave disappointment that it struck Philippa as if with a shaft, but it was too late. The priest in his vestments was entering the chapel of the Crown of Thorns. Keeping her eyes down, giving the bow, Philippa had to go past the procession to the chapel grille . . .

'In nomine Patris et Filii et Spiritus Sancti . . .'

'Introibo ad altare Dei.'

'Ad Deum qui laetificat juventutem meam.'

Philippa hardly knew she said the responses.

picking up gold and silver   we're coming we're coming as fast as we can   Keith   breathe   roll out the barrel   the animals came in two by two   picking up gold and silver

By a supreme effort Philippa rose to her feet for the Introit.

II

The papal flag flew at half mast from the tower; Pope Pius XII, venerable and holy, had died. All these last days the nuns had kept him in their minds and prayers; now, while he lay in state in the basilica of St Peter's, a catafalque was set up in the sanctuary at Brede with black velvet hangings and tall candles. On the day of the funeral, a Solemn Dirge was sung.

Then there were days of prayer that followed the fifty cardinals as they went to their conclave in the Sistine Chapel which Dame Clare described in the novitiate, showing pictures of the Michelangelo ceiling where the painted Adam just missed touching the finger of God – Dame Clare did not underline the parable. Instead she told how the cardinals would sleep in improvised cells, take improvised meals, the doors of the chapel sealed and locked, no one allowed out or in.

At Brede the community had a radio in the large parlour and, waiting, as the world waited, they heard how ten times smoke from the burning ballot papers went up, each time darkened by the wet straw burnt with them to give black smoke, showing that the ballot was inconclusive.

The younger nuns hoped for a progressive Pope, the older ones were silent, remembering Pope Pius. 'We shan't see his like again,' said Dame Perpetua. Then the excited voice proclaimed the eleventh smoke, a spiral of white, strawless, and they heard the cry that went up from the crowd, thousands strong, in St Peter's Square: 'We have a Pope! We have a Pope!' The voices were of acclamation but in Brede's large parlour, depression filled the room. 'Cardinal Roncalli?' asked the nuns disbelievingly. *'Roncalli?'*

'But who is he?' That was the question asked by many. 'They have chosen an old man,' said Dame Anselma in disgust. 'An interim Pope,' and, '*He* won't rock the boat,' said Dame Paula who was emerging as the Abbey's progressive nun.

'That may be what they think they have chosen,' said Dame Colette. 'I heard from Paris when he was made Papal Nuncio to France. Very few people know him, but we French do. Don't underrate this Pope, Dame. I think he will give us surprises.'

'And it's no wonder we don't know him,' Abbess Catherine said. 'He has been in Turkey, Greece, Bulgaria and was Patriarch of Venice; he must know the world.'

'But he's so fat,' said the new little Dame Constance with distaste when the first pictures of him were put on view. 'Fat and small and bald.' 'And so old,' said Dame Paula. 'Not my idea of the Holy Father at all,' said Dame Anselma, while Dame Beatrice, remembering the upright ascetical figure of Pope Pius, his fine-drawn aristocratic features, those calm deep eyes, where Cardinal Roncalli's were black and twinkling, could not help mourning. Then, 'John,' said the Abbess. 'A curious name to choose.'

'Yes, he has broken precedent,' said Dame Agnes. 'There hasn't been a John for five hundred years.'

'He has broken precedent!' Young Dame Paula approved of broken precedents.

Abbess Catherine liked his reasons, simple ordinary reasons: 'John was the name of his father: the first name of St Mark, patron of Cardinal Roncalli's loved Venice.'

'And of John the Baptist, the forerunner,' said Dame Paula.

'And of John the evangelist,' said Dame Agnes.

A change of feeling had come; there was hardly a nun who did not feel it – it was as if something new had started in the world.

'A foundation! You mean we, Brede, might make a foundation?'

'Well – we mustn't go as far as that yet.'

'Mustn't we?' Dame Paula said it wistfully. Nuns should not know jealousy, or if they did, certainly not show it, but Brede had not been able to help being envious when news from other houses reached them ... of Dom Benet Owen's growing activities in India; of Indian postulants at Freshwater in the Isle of Wight; of Pixham's flourishing community in Brazil, 'and now there is talk that they have a hope in Sweden' – while Brede ... 'It's only us,' said Dame Paula which was, of course, untrue; if a few communities were expanding, many houses were closing down. 'Think how lucky we are in our continuing vocations,' but now, no matter how Dame Agnes cautioned, a whisper was running through Brede: 'Japanese postulants'. 'Talk about new!' said Hilary, and even Dame Paula had to say, 'We never even thought of Japan.'

A Father Vincent Conway of the Order of the Holy Name had come to talk in the large parlour about his work in the province of Nagano, and with him had come a Japanese gentleman, a Mr Konishi. The nuns had been struck by the courtliness of his manners as he bowed to them, then made way for Father Vincent; he – Mr Konishi – had not spoken at all. They had been struck too by the extreme beauty of his clothes, the cashmere overcoat, deep prune colour, a glimpse of a heavy silk shirt, and the hand that held his cigarette case, though he did not take one out, had a little finger ring with what looked like a grey pearl. 'It was a smoked pearl. I asked him,' Dame Anselma told them afterwards. Since the discovery of the ruby, the community was keenly observant of jewellery. 'You see, we are getting worldly,' said Dame Beatrice.

Mr Konishi had seemed the epitome of worldliness; who could have guessed he might be the instrument of their old dreamed hope. 'Not the instrument – the king-pin,' said Dame Paula afterwards. It was obvious though that he was rich. It was not only his clothes or the pearl. There was a sleekness that spoke of care and grooming with a peculiar thicksetness that was well fed, solid and plump. Plump was a good word for him – 'like a ripe plum,' said Dame Benita – and the likeness to a fruit was enhanced by his rosiness, a rose suffused on Mongolian yellow. He was not young; the stiff black hair was blended with grey; he had a small lip moustache that had a look of softness like two paint brushes, thought Philippa, while his eyes, black too, were shrewd. All through the talk he had sat in his corner outside the grille, never taking his eyes off the nuns. 'I don't believe he heard one word,' said Dame Paula. 'He was studying us from top to toe.'

Afterwards the councillors had met him with Father Vincent in the large parlour. 'Mr Paul Konishi.' He presented each of them with his western-style card:

> Mr Yoshio Paul Konishi
> President
> Konishi Oil K. K.
> No 12 Mitsubishi Building
> Chiyoda-ku
> Tokyo

There were other addresses in Kuwait, Beirut and Paris. 'Worldly,' the councillors had thought until Father Vincent said, 'It is Mr Konishi's ambition to help found, one day, a contemplative monastery in Japan.'

'In Japan?'

'Indeed yes,' said Mr Konishi, and beamed.

'But,' said Dame Anselma, 'forgive me if I am very ignorant, but would not a Japanese monastery properly be Buddhist?'

'Properly? Properly?' Mr Konishi seemed to swell with indignation. 'Madame Nun, you do not know your history.'

'The Japanese martyrs,' whispered Dame Agnes.

'Yes indeed,' Mr Konishi had caught the whisper. 'We, though Japanese, are old, old Christians and – yes, martyrs. What of Nagasaki?' he demanded, 'Nagasaki in 1597? Again, 1614 and 1626 when one hundred and seven died for the faith? What of Thomas Tamaki who was only ten years old and died with smile and perfect courtesy? Of little Thomas Acofari who was buried alive? We were burnt, beheaded, crucified, Madam Nun!'

'I am sorry,' Dame Anselma was abashed. 'I apologize.'

'I accept,' said Mr Konishi and bowed. 'One day we shall bring back that splendidness – without the physical, of course. We need it, ladies. We need it, Mother Abbess.

'It is my dream,' Mr Konishi went on, 'and I hope not an idle air dream, to bring the contemplative ideal to Japan. Christian, of course,' he said, with a darting look at Dame Anselma, and now he, not Father Vincent, became the spokesman. 'My nation, as all nations, is becoming a land without peace, without thought, without mind, Madam Abbess. We are suffocating our spirits in commercial and material things. This is not envy,' said Mr Konishi earnestly. 'I am a rich man, with much business, so I have succeeded in all these things, but I know that they are empty. This is why we have made this plan, Father Vincent and his priests, the Bishop and I. You may think an impossible plan, but I feel it here,' and Mr Konishi tapped his breast where a perfectly folded silk handkerchief showed in his breast pocket. 'One day it will be possible.

'When that time comes, I shall buy a site, not too far from the city, but far enough, where there are hills and a lake – beauty; I am a business man but my heart aches for beauty.' Mr Konishi's eyes were visionary. 'The house which I hope to build will be Japanese style with modern plumbing of course, but completely Japanese with gardens, many gardens. There will be silence as here; no loudspeakers, no transistors which I *detest*!' He was suddenly passionate. 'You do not know, Mother Abbess, how loudspeakers, radio are ruining my land. Here will be none. All noise, all commerce, will be forbidden; not even Coca-Cola barrow or ice-cream bicycle will be permitted. People will not eat, they will think. A garden will be there for public meditation; there will be rooms for wise speaking like in this parlour, speaking softly of wisdom. There will be heard running water, insects, rustle of bamboos and, from its nuns, the only sound, bells – no, perhaps gong-beats – to mark the hours of prayer; that and the sounding of chanting. Japanese people like your plainchant – I have taken many records – we detest polyphony. Yes, one day, between us all, we shall create a house of peace and, from it, the influence will spread far ... far.'

The nuns felt that they were being enchanted. Father Vincent tried to 'catch us by our coat-tails – or the skirts of our habits – and bring us down to earth,' as Dame Maura said afterwards. 'Yes, Paul,' he said to Mr Konishi, 'but first steps first. Before anything can be thought of, we have to persuade Lady Abbess and her community to allow our candidates to enter Brede ...'

'Enter *Brede*?' cried Dame Ursula, but Mr Konishi broke in again.

'They are ready, five of them. There is my daughter, Mariko Mary – I give you their names in the western way, with given names first – Mariko she is twenty-five, and Sumi Tanaka, her maid, who has been brought up with her is the same. Sumi will be what you call "lay".'

'Claustral,' Dame Agnes had corrected.

'There is Yoko Matsudaira, an old friend of our Bishop; she is eldest, thirty-seven, very holy woman, calm – though she has led a problem life. There is Yuri Teresa Sugami; she was an orphan left in front of a Catholic orphanage; the nuns brought her up so she is very suitable; then a girl, Kazuko Miyazaki – of her I hesitate, but Father Vincent thinks much of her, and she has been in commerce and that is very useful. These will be the first ...' It took some time to calm him and let the Abbess ask her questions.

'Mr Konishi,' said Abbess Catherine, 'the first question must be – have they vocations?'

'They will get them,' said Mr Konishi, before Father Vincent could speak. 'They will get them here.'

'But ... vocations are not "got"; they must come, be inborn.'

'Nicodemus had second birth, and these ladies have the dispositions. We have carefully seen to that.'

'But do they *want* to come?'

'Certainly they want. One, as I say, is my own daughter, close to me. She wants what I want,' and, as the nuns did not look convinced. 'I do not think,' said Mr Konishi, 'you understand the Japanese mind; this is a project, Madam Abbess, and they will tunnel their thoughts into it. Naturally they will suffer a little – in diet for instance – but I will send you provisions and they will soon be accustomed.'

Father Vincent, intervening again, was reassuring, 'and practical,' said Dame Agnes. The five would-be postulants had been living together in Tokyo, studying, reading, keeping times of prayer. 'Not the Divine Office, of course,' said Father Vincent, 'the Little Office of our Lady. They are in earnest, I promise you.'

'You will keep them five years, ten, fifteen,' said Mr Konishi, 'no matter how long – naturally I shall pay for them – keep them until they are imbued. Others will follow them, I hope. Then perhaps one day they will come back and perhaps too you will give us nuns from Brede to guide them, nuns who will stay ten, twenty years with us. In this way we shall found a house of contemplation, get truth; meditation, prayer. You will vow them to it.'

'That is the right way,' even Dame Agnes had to admit it.

The Abbey was swept with Japanese fever, especially when the community heard Mr Konishi's full story. It seemed Father Vincent had not brought him to Brede : he had brought Father Vincent. 'But why Brede?' Abbess Catherine had asked him. 'How, Mr Konishi, did you happen to think of Brede?'

'I did not "happen to",' said Mr Konishi. 'I was *directed*. That is what I believe. Long years ago,' said Mr Konishi, 'when my wife was a girl, she came to Paris with her father. You must know that my wife's family was exalted, much, much more exalted than I; her father was of enlightened ideas and he placed her, his daughter, for a while in school in Paris, what you call a finishing school, and think! who should be there in that school but a Miss Alice Cunningham Proctor, own niece to your late reverend Abbess. More,' said Mr Konishi almost in triumph, 'what happens but that my wife is invited to make a visit in the vacation to the family Cunningham Proctor. Young Japanese girls in those days do not visit, but marvellously – though after careful examination – her father let her go. She came here to Brede. Imagine, she might have been in this very parlour; and she talked long, in French of course, with Madam Abbess Cunningham Proctor. It made a deep impression, so deep that . . .'

Mr Konishi stopped and drew from his breast pocket a thin oblong book, once maroon coloured, but now blackened and discoloured, tattered and soiled, but the nuns recognized it. 'Our manual for oblates,' Dame Agnes whispered.

'Yes,' said Mr Konishi: 'In the bombing of Tokyo,' and now his voice grew low, 'in the bombing my home took fire; most of it was burnt; also my wife, two sons.' He took no notice of their murmurs of sympathy, of Abbess Catherine, but looked over their heads. 'Please do not mention. I do not speak of it myself. Mariko, my daughter, who will come to you, was baby then in the country with her nurse. Among things that were saved was a box; it belonged to my wife – a small private treasure box, and in that box was this book. I have carried it ever since. An oblate, I think,' said Mr Konishi, 'is a man or woman in the world who is affiliated to a house, a kind of brother or sister . . .'

'A true sister,' said Abbess Catherine.

'My wife wanted that,' said Mr Konishi. 'I know it now. Madam Abbess, I was imprisoned during the war; I had much time to think. I came back to Tokyo a thoughtful man. It was then that I found this book – a message from my wife, I am convinced. You see why I say this is directed.'

Old Sister Priscilla Pawsey, when the news filtered down, was entirely of Mr Konishi's opinion. 'It is Mother again,' she said. 'Our Lady Abbess Hester. I won't say this Mrs Konish – or whatever her name is – hasn't something to do with it, but mark my words, it's our Mother, Lady Hester.'

Philippa knew little of the excitement. She was too immersed in her work in the sacristy. Of all the offices, to be infirmarian was hardest, sacristan next, and this extended to their seconds. The sacristans had to be up before the other nuns, were last of all to bed and were liable to work all day, yet no office was more dearly loved or more sought after. 'If I could be sacristan for one day!' Cecily said longingly. 'Think of it. It would be your own church in a way; you would be responsible for it; your mind drawn back to it all day! To be sacristan!'

'You, you'll end up as precentrix,' said Hilary.

On important feast days the sacristan and her seconds were scarcely out of sacristy or choir; there was the care of the linen and vestments, red, green, purple, black, white, with deep rose colour used for 'Laetare' or 'refreshment' Sunday, each set with its orphreys of gold or silver or flashing colours in weaving or embroidery. The sacristans put them out for the day, laying them in long double-fronted drawers, so that the extern sister sacristan could take them out on her side. There was the polishing of the gold and silver vessels and candlesticks. It was the sacristan who counted the number receiving communion – Sister Elizabeth, extern sacristan, counted the Abbey guests – and filled the ciboriums with the right number of wafers; it was she who opened the wicket in the grille for the nuns to go to communion and, when the last had gone back to her place, locked the wicket again and, through the rows of kneeling nuns, restored the key to the Abbess.

When Mass was over, the sacristan's first duty was to wash the chalice. When touching it, she must not speak. If visiting priests said a private Mass in the chapel of the Crown of Thorns, it was she or her aid who attended and made the responses and there might be as many as five or six Masses in a day. As Dame Beatrice had once been, Philippa was steeped, immersed in holiness; even to come out into the Abbey, itself permeated with prayer, was to step on to different ground. 'I feel at last I am advancing,' she wrote to McTurk and when she heard of the Japanese idea: 'Why not?' she said, unconcerned. 'I should think Japanese women would be "naturals" for contemplation. How interesting,' she had said, scarcely interested, and had gone back to her work, but no one, not even a nun who is sacristan, can stay in the choir all the time.

Looking out of the common room window at recreation

Philippa had seen three almond trees in flower in the garth, blossom pink against the grey. 'Wonderful in this cold,' said Dame Veronica, and, 'I have seen almonds and plums flowering in snow in Japan,' said Philippa.

'In Japan?' At once a knot of nuns came round. 'We must learn all we can, before the postulants come.' That was the mood of the moment. Everyone seemed positive that they were coming. Mariko Konishi: Sumi Tanaka: Yoko Matsudaira: Yuri Sugami: Kazuko Miyazaki: the strange sounding names were becoming almost familiar. Every book on Japan had been taken out of the library, customs and ideas had been discussed, but oddly no one had thought till now of Dame Philippa. 'Well, one can't guard every word,' she said afterwards to Abbess Catherine, and that afternoon she had been totally unguarded.

'Yes, almond blossom in snow, like a Japanese print,' and questions poured on Philippa. Then Dame Sophie asked, 'Do you know Suwa, Mr Konishi's home town, where he hopes, perhaps, to buy a suitable site?'

'Suwa,' said Philippa dreamily. 'Yes, we used to go there for our leaves now and then. It's only about a hundred and twenty miles from Tokyo. You go through mountains with birch trees, streams, brownish earth; the birches would be in bud now. Near Suwa the country gets flatter, pampas grass coming into flower – or should I say "into plume"? There are villages standing in rice fields, with low thatched houses. In autumn they hang corncobs in brilliant colours under the house eaves and what one thinks at first are flowers, but they are persimmons, coral red. Suwa town has old paved streets. There was a special inn ... I liked it best out of season when most of the houses were shut up. It was a little desolate there, but the lake was beautiful, empty and so still you could hear the bamboos rustle. A Japanese will tell you that is Japanese silence.'

'Go on,' breathed the nuns.

'There are specifically Japanese sounds,' Philippa was back a long way, 'a sort of whoam-whoam – that's the treadle for flailing when the rice is being harvested, and the clitter-clatter of wooden pattens on the path; just as the paper door screens make an unmistakable soft shirring when they are slid back. There are Japanese smells too. You know you are in France, for instance, by the smell of gitanes, coffee, chestnuts, bread a little sour, aniseed and garlic; in Kyoto, where I lived as a child, there were street smells mingled of bath-fumes and woodsmoke, of Peace and Ikoi cigarettes, hot soya sauce, dried fish, pickles, seaweed – and pomade, the scent of black Japanese hair heavily pomaded; but Japanese bodies have a clean fresh smell and their breaths smell of peppery rice crackers and hot saké. My nurse smelt like that. There are tin braziers along the pavements, with burning sushi and o-bento boxes . . .'

Philippa broke off, suddenly aware of the growing circle of listeners.

'You love Japan,' said Dame Veronica's soft voice.

'I suppose it's in my bones,' said Philippa. 'You may remember I was born in Kyoto, and lived there till I was twelve. Tokyo was my first and my last posting overseas,' and she quoted:

> 'Hito wa iza
> Kokoro mo shirazu.
> Furusato wa
> Hana zo mukashi no
> Ka ni nioikeru.

That means: . . .

> . . . the human heart
> Is unknowable.
> But in my birthplace
> The flowers still smell
> The same as always.'

and she repeated

> 'Hana zo mukashi no
> Ka ni nioikeru.'

'Of course, you speak Japanese!' Philippa looked up quickly and saw she had three councillors in her audience; Dame Ursula who had spoken, Dame Anselma and Dame Agnes who were exchanging nods.

The great difficulty over the coming of the Japanese postulants had been the language.

Mr Konishi's Mariko spoke French – 'As I myself speak French and Arabic better than English, my business contacts being there.' Sumi Tanaka spoke only Japanese as did Kazuko Miyazaki. Yoko Matsudaira had picked up English in the bar in Tokyo where she had once worked. 'But it is pidgin American and *disgraces* her,' Mr Konishi had said. Father Vincent assured the Abbess that they were all studying English now. 'But they must be fluent,' Abbess Catherine had insisted, 'fluent – or they will be lost.'

'Remember, they will be faced, not only with English but with Latin and the chant,' Dame Agnes had reminded them.

'Madam Nun, we have Latin and the chant; have had them for centuries,' said Mr Konishi.

'But all our ritual,' said Dame Beatrice. 'How shall we explain?'

'And you will not allow an interpreter?' asked Mr Konishi. 'Not even so that we shall lose no time? I myself would willingly come . . .'

The thought of Mr Konishi in the enclosure was too much for the councillors and there was a gale of laughter.

'I would rank as a workman,' he said with dignity.

'They will need someone to help them with every detail of the life,' Abbess Catherine had explained when she had recovered herself. 'To watch over them, explain, anticipate.'

'To guide,' and Mr Konishi had argued no further but had sat mournfully tapping his fingers on his knees. 'A year. At least a year. A year wasted!'

At the next meeting with Father Vincent and Mr Konishi, Mother Prioress, Dame Beatrice, showed 'a most unmonastic pride,' as Abbess Catherine teased her afterwards.

'There are not many houses, I think,' said Dame Beatrice,

295

'that can offer quite such resources in their communities as Brede,' – 'and she positively bridled,' said Abbess Catherine.

'Wouldn't it surprise you, Father Vincent,' the prioress went on, 'and you, Mr Konishi, if Lady Abbess were to tell you we have discovered we have a nun here in our Abbey who has lived in Japan for years and who speaks, reads and writes fluent Japanese?'

Philippa knelt by the Abbess's chair. 'Mother, may I take the discipline for an extra time each week?'

The nuns took the discipline every Friday, alone in their cells; how hard or how lightly they applied it was left to themselves, but the whistling sound of its regular swish swish filled the dormitories as the corridors outside the cells were called. On big feasts the whisper would go round: 'The string band won't play tonight.' The disciplines were made of nine light cords, but each one was knotted at the ends; they were made in the Abbey by old Dame Frances Anne who looked as if she were put together of fine pink and white china; her legs were useless but her hands were extraordinarily strong – 'Sometimes I think all my strength has gone into my hands,' said Dame Frances Anne. Only recently Philippa remembered, an afternoon concert of chamber music had been given to the community in the large parlour and she had watched Dame Frances Anne, in her wheelchair, sitting beside Abbess Catherine, her head nodding to the music, her eyes rapt while all the time her fingers tied and retied those wicked little knots. 'But it doesn't really hurt,' said Cecily, who had secretly tried it.

'I believe if you dip it in hot wax it's vastly improved,' said Hilary.

It could, though, sting and had the salutary effect of a blood-letting. 'Yes, it does seem to drive the old Eve out of one,' said Dame Beatrice.

'I don't think you know much about old Eve,' said Philippa.

'You would be surprised,' said Dame Beatrice. It was humiliating. 'You use it where one whacks small boys,' Dame Clare told the novices. 'And nowhere else,' she said firmly, 'and only as long as it takes you to say the Miserere, which may *not* be drawn out.'

She remembered the time when Mrs Scallon had read in a magazine about the taking of the discipline and had descended on Brede, demanding to see the novice mistress. 'Will you use this on Elspeth?'

'Certainly not,' said Dame Clare. 'Our declarations lay down that "Corporal punishment may never be administered by another's hand." The nuns use it on themselves.' 'But I don't think she came to find out if we were beating Sister Cecily,' Dame Clare had reported to Abbess Catherine. 'I had the feeling she was seeking to ferret out something ... unfresh,' said Dame Clare.

'You are training them up to be a set of perverts,' Mrs Scallon had said.

Dame Clare's reply had been even. 'Sexual perversion can manifest itself as masochism, of course.' She thought Mrs Scallon had not expected her to be as direct. 'And of course we must be vigilant, but perverts are the exception, don't you think so? Our rules are not drawn up for them but for normal people. Sister Cecily is quite normal.'

'Thank you,' said Mrs Scallon, but she had demanded to see a discipline. 'Will she use this?'

'She may, when she is farther on.'

'Farther on?' The head reared up.

'It's not suitable for everyone,' said Dame Clare. 'The ways used for penance do not matter very much, provided there is penance, but all the great religious traditions of the world have techniques to help control the flesh,' and Dame Clare went on, 'like fasting – even breathing exercises, yoga – but for us the attempt is illuminated by the passion of Christ.'

'I don't understand,' said Mrs Scallon.

'Our whole Christian life is a dying to selfishness – wasn't it Monsignor Knox who said the cross was "I" crossed out? The sufferings and grief sent us are usually enough to effect this – if we let them,' Dame Clare's eyes had been kind as she looked at Mrs Scallon, 'if we pick up our cross daily as He told us, but for most of us, weak and soft as we are, some voluntary token penance that hurts is a help in schooling us to accept what God sends. Many people in the outside world too find that the discipline helps them. I had a young aunt, beautiful and gay, in the full stream of a busy social life, who took it every week. It isn't only for peculiar people like nuns,' said Dame Clare.

'May I take the discipline?'

Now and again permission was given for an extra penance but only if a nun asked for it; often the request was refused and now Abbess Catherine considered Philippa carefully. She noticed that, as Philippa knelt, she did not look at her in Dame Philippa's usual way, but kept her head turned away; noticed too the tell-tale tenseness. 'Is it really necessary?' she asked.

'I can't subdue ... make myself behave,' said Philippa. No more was forthcoming though the Abbess waited. At last, 'If you must, you may,' said the Abbess, 'but only twice a week. Penance isn't meant to achieve a victory, Dame.'

'Then what?'

'A surrender.' The Abbess spoke with extreme gentleness. 'Philippa, won't you let me try to help you?' but Philippa had risen.

'No one can help me Mother. May I go?'

12

It was on a windy, cold day of Lent that the summons Philippa was expecting came for her. 'Dame Philippa, Mother wants you in her room.' For a moment Philippa lingered in the choir, putting a last touch to the markers in the book on the lectern, straightening the cushion on the abbatial chair. She would have liked to kneel down in her own stall for a moment, but a summons was a summons. On the way through the garth she caught a glimpse of the flowering almond trees, more than ever looking like a Japanese print. She averted her eyes and went on, pulling her shawl closer around her.

Abbess Catherine had Mother Prioress with her. 'You needn't kneel, Dame. Please sit.'

Philippa sat silently down and waited for it to come.

'Dame Philippa, you haven't been professed very long but you are experienced and have gifts we haven't; so, for the sake of these Japanese postulants who are coming from so far away, we are appointing you as zelatrix to the novitiate instead of Dame Paula who will take your place in the sacristy.'

Silence. Philippa's head was bowed as if the Abbess had dealt her a physical blow. Abbess Catherine and Dame Beatrice exchanged glances.

'You may say what you feel, Dame.'

'I . . . was expecting this . . . only because I speak Japanese, of course.'

'Exactly.'

'But – Mother, please no.'

'My dear, why not?'

'It . . . isn't . . . suitable.'

The word took the Abbess and Dame Beatrice by surprise. 'It seems eminently suitable,' and Dame Beatrice said with her luminous smile, 'You have been in Japan. You speak and write Japanese. You will understand these, to us, strangers.'

'*Please* no.'

'Why not?' and the Abbess repeated that. 'Why not?' and then, 'Tell us, why not?'

'Because – as zelatrix to the Japanese I should be zelatrix to Sister Polycarp.'

'Well?' Abbess Catherine's voice was cold.

'I can not be that,' said Philippa.

Sister Polycarp had been clothed, again not without argument. 'She doesn't know how to behave,' had been one of Dame Agnes's objections.

'She was only being practical,' Dame Clare defended her.

One of the farm calves, let in to graze in the Park, had broken into the garden when the novitiate was there at recreation. They had all tried to help Burnell corner and catch it. The calf had been too nimble for them until Sister Polly had picked up the skirts of her dress, girded them round her waist and had run, her long legs encased in black stockings and black knickers. The calf crashed through a hedge, Sister Polly cleared the nearby gate, turned the corner, caught the calf and led it back to Burnell. 'Well, I won the high jump and hurdling in the inter-school sports,' she had said to the clapping novices when she came back, panting, but, 'In your knickers! In front of Mr Burnell!' scolded Sister Jane.

'He must know that girls have legs.'

'Yes, but nuns . . .'

'That's what's false,' Sister Polycarp had declared. 'Nuns have legs and arms and heads and hearts and it's time the world knew it.'

'They have them without parading them,' said Dame Clare, 'that's the difference.'

It would take time for Sister Polycarp to see that. 'But she will teach herself restraint,' Dame Clare was certain of it.

'As Sister Polly has taught herself everything,' said Abbess

300

Catherine. She and Dame Clare both liked the big raw-boned girl more and more but, 'She has such aggressive elbows,' Dame Maura had said doubtfully.

'Well, she has had to fight,' said Abbess Catherine.

'And I should guess a tongue she cannot hold,' said Dame Agnes.

'She says you get used to belting out after six years teaching in a Huddersfield school,' said Abbess Catherine. 'I believe her,' and she said, 'I am firmly of the opinion that Sister Polycarp should be clothed.'

The Clothing had been 'Nice and plain,' said Sister Polycarp. 'No bishops or Monsignori for me. Just Father Tweedie from our parish and Dad and my Aunt Tibby and our Margery and Tom. Being on the railway, Dad gets the fares so he can afford the guest house fees. Aunt Tib has never had such a rest in all her days, bless her. The plainest part was me,' said Sister Polycarp. 'Aunt made my dress, God help us! I must have looked like a camel in a lace curtain.'

'Did you ask my dad about Dame Philippa?' she had asked Abbess Catherine afterwards.

'No,' said the Abbess. 'I thought it would seem like prying.'

'I didn't know her little boy died. I thought Mum just left.' Sister Polycarp was troubled and, 'Why didn't Mum tell me?' It burst out.

'I expect it was painful for her too. He was Dame Philippa's only child. There was an accident, I think. Dame Philippa doesn't talk about it.'

'No. She still won't speak to me. She avoids me.'

'It is understandable,' Abbess Catherine had said. 'Try and understand.'

'I understand,' said this new girl, but her face was more thoughtful still; a thin face, almost gaunt, thought the Abbess. Sister Polycarp had worked hard and long under poor conditions, but she had her father's deliberate eyes, his steady warmth. Nicknames had not been allowed in the Abbey before, but she had swiftly become Sister Polly. 'It is understandable,' said Sister Polly now, 'but someone as big as Dame Philippa should have been kind.'

'Should,' not 'could,' noted the Abbess.

'I can not be that.'

Abbess Catherine seemed to be studying her own hands on the desk; then she fingered her cross; the pectoral cross was a new one now of olive wood, strong and plain; the Savoy cross, its broken bits left broken, was kept reverently with Brede's other relics.

The story of the princess's cross was still told in the novitiate with the added drama of the hidden ruby. 'But I still liked it better as it was before.' Dame Beatrice was obstinate. 'It *was* more valuable.' A pectoral cross, though, in any form is a pectoral cross and now it seemed to gather Abbess Catherine's forces. 'Dame Philippa,' she said, 'your little son died, but many many other mothers have lost a child – perhaps, like you, their only child. It isn't a unique experience. They must, they have to, get over it.'

'Yes,' said Dame Beatrice, pityingly.

There was no movement from Philippa.

'Of course we don't know how he died . . .'

'No,' said Philippa. 'You don't know how he died.' She got up, went to the window, and against all monastic courtesy turned her back on the Abbess and prioress. 'I will tell you.'

I'm on Tom Tiddler's ground picking up gold and silver . . . Sing the doctor had said sing anything keep on singing talking singing let him hear your voice . . . picking up gold and silver A tactless song for poor Louis Freymus but the only song that came into my head at first . . . sing any song . . . Tom Tiddler's ground Lily Marlene I saw three ships a-sailing Roll out the barrel . . . sing talk He may not be able to hear you but try sing talk talk . . . don't cry Keith try not to cry it wastes breath breathe breathe breathe like a big boy I'll count one two one two one two we're coming as fast as we can I'm here quite near Keith Mother's here picking up gold and silver, gold and silver . . .

'The only people I have ever told,' said Philippa aloud,

302

'were my chief, Sir Richard Taft, and, for some reason just before I came here, McTurk.'

'Not even Lady Abbess Hester?' Abbess Catherine put the question.

'No, not even Mother.' There was a pause; then, 'It began with a nugget,' said Philippa.

'A – what?' asked Dame Beatrice.

'A nugget. A small nugget of gold'; as Philippa said it she saw Mrs Farren's authoritative fingers prising it out of the little clenched hand – trying to prise it. 'Keith would not give it up.

'In the second year of the war,' Philippa went on, 'I was posted to Washington. My – husband had gone into the army at the beginning; he died of wounds afterwards on the Burma railway. I took Keith with me to America. Women trained like myself were in short supply and I knew the work would be intense. Keith was only five and I wanted him to have an English nurse, so I took his nanny, Mrs Farren.' The sentences came out short, in jerks. 'I offered to take Katie too, but she had started school and was with her Aunt Tib up in Yorkshire; it seemed safe to leave her there.

'In Washington the work was intense – overwork and worry, too much responsibility. I wasn't very old then,' said Philippa. 'There was overcrowding too. I caught Spanish flu badly, and was sent away on sick leave. We went to California for the sun. I had friends in Beverly Hills, Louis Freymus the film director and his wife Belle. They had children – one was a boy, Darrell – and a dear coloured nurse, Sadie, so I took Keith and Mrs Farren. Louis owned a vineyard and one day we all drove out to see it and have lunch with his manager. It was to be a party. Keith was excited because, on the estate, there was a gold mine, no longer worked but now and again they found a few grains of gold. Louis promised the boys they should wash for gold. He told Keith he might find a nugget.'

What's a nugget? . . . A 'normous piece of gold (that was Darrell Freymus, two years older than Keith) . . . Big as a brick? . . . Course not you nut might be big as your fist . . .

To be called 'nut' by a boy as big as Darrell had seemed equality to Keith and a smile had spread over his face as he contemplated his doubled fist.

Hastily Philippa went on. 'The vineyard was spread over two hills with a river between, pebbles and pools more than a river because the water had been diverted; there was a subterranean river somewhere in the hills; we could hear it in the caves that lined the low cliffs on each side. It was the streams from that river, Louis said, that had brought the gold down in silt and gravel from the hills. The old mine was in the biggest cave, with a stream still on its floor. Above, it was a labyrinth of low tunnels and workings, some made by the miners, some by streams, but dried out now. We could see old timber stands and shorings. There was an echo. Louis shouted and the echo came back. It was hard to tell where anyone was . . .'

Keith! Keith! . . . and the echoes came from roof and tunnels Keith! Keith! . . . it had been like mocking . . . Keith where are you? . . . and Keith where are you? came back.

'Keith was fascinated.' Philippa stared out of the window on to the garth without seeing it. 'He had always been an odd little boy; he loved disappearing. He said, "We could go up there and hide," but Louis was stern about that. "It's dangerous. No one knows what hidden shafts are there. Old mines are supposed to be filled in but the river and rains break away silt, shift rock. No one is to go up there," he said, "no one. Do you understand? There are loose rocks and silt and gravel that could come down and those tunnels go back and back and get narrower; even grown men don't go there," and he said to the children and nurses again, "Anyone who comes down by the river doesn't go into the cave. Understand?"

'He and the children started washing in the gravel of the stream; the little boys were serious with their sieves, their jeans rolled up, arms bare and wet and brown in the sun. The nurses sat apart and knitted and talked. Talked.' There was an edge in Philippa's voice as she said that.

'Go on,' said the Abbess.

'Belle and I walked up the hill through the vines. I remember the blue,' said Philippa, 'and the smell of the vines; blue sky and the blue colour where they had been spraying copper sulphate on the leaves. The peace and sun. The war seemed very far away; we could hear the children splashing and laughing. It seemed a blessed spot...' Her voice trailed away.

'Go on,' said Abbess Catherine again.

'Keith gave a shout. He had found his nugget. Louis had taken it in his pocket to plant for him, but Keith never suspected. Five years old is easy to deceive. When Keith showed it, he was bursting with pride.'

I'm going to make it into a wedding ring for you... She's got a wedding ring you nut... She'll have another mine nut ... They could have gone on calling one another nut all day.

'Other guests came for lunch,' Philippa went on. 'We sat at trestle tables under the vines and Louis cooked on a barbecue. We drank the vineyard wines. The children and nurses – another nurse had come – had theirs on the house verandah. We could hear them laughing – laughing.'

It was the laughter that, ever since, Philippa had tried desperately to hear; not that muffled crying; laughing, sitting in the sun, the rough wood of the table warm under her elbows; sitting, eating, drinking the sun-warmed wine. 'It was the last time I ever sat like that,' but she did not say it aloud.

'The children finished,' she said, 'and Darrell Freymus came and said they were all going down to the river to paddle. Keith still had his nugget. He had shown it around.'

I found it. Will it be worth a whole dollar?... Nut! it's worth dozens of dollars

'The guests asked him, "Keith, what are you going to buy with all that gold?"'

305

A spitfire and a car a jersey for my teddy and nine trumpets ... Nine? ... For my friends I have nine friends and a lovely crane that picks things up and drops them down again ... I thought you were going to make a wedding ring for me Philippa had teased him ... Besides, Keith had said gravely ...

'The children went to the river. We sat on talking over our coffee, never dreaming. Three nurses were there. Three,' said Philippa. 'Then Darrell came back alone. He was dirty and hot and out of breath – and frightened. He came and stood by Louis and whispered, "Dad".

'"Darrell I'm talking ..." But "Dad" ... it was more urgent ...

'He said, "Dad, come. Please come. Keith's gone."

'"Gone? Gone where?"

'Darrell said, "I don't know. In the cave. I said, 'Come out, you nut,' and he didn't. I heard him crying."

'"Where?"

'"Down," said Darrell and started to cry himself.

'Louis jumped to his feet and said, "My God!"

'When we got to the river,' said Philippa, 'the nurses were still talking.'

I'm on Tom Tiddler's ground picking up gold and silver
sing   talk   count

'It was Sadie, the Freymus nanny who told us what had happened. They had been paddling just by the cave and Darrell and Keith had had a fight over the nugget. Darrell wanted to hold it. Keith wouldn't let him. He put it behind his back and said, "It's mine." '

Keith let Darrell hold it like a good boy. ... I'm not a good boy ... Keith!

'Mrs Farren tried to prise it out of his hand,' said Philippa. 'Afterwards she wept and said she was only trying to make him behave like a little English gentleman in front of the Americans. He didn't behave at all like a little gentleman. He said, "I hate you." '

Philippa could see the small angry face, the disdainful nostrils, but made herself go on. 'He said, "It's mine. I found it all by myself." She said, "That you didn't. Kind Mr Freymus put it in the stream for you to find."

'Sadie said Keith went pale, then red. Then he threw the nugget at Darrell and ran into the cave. Sadie said he must not do that but Mrs Farren said he wouldn't go far. "Don't pay any attention; he always runs and hides when he's upset. He'll soon come out," and they went on down the river gossiping.'

Philippa stopped. Abbess Catherine and the prioress were still.

'It was Darrell who went after Keith. He found him behind a rock, hiding. Darrell told him he could have the nugget.'

It's yours   yours   honest . . . I don't want it . . . C'mon it's yours . . . I don't want it

'Darrell came closer and Keith ran away, up beside the stream, into a dark tunnel. I know why,' said Philippa. 'He didn't want Darrell to see him crying. Darrell went after him, and Keith ran farther into a side tunnel. It was low, just high enough for a little boy but dark. Darrell had to grope. He could her Keith ahead of him. Then he said there was a cry; a slither and scrabbling – then silence; then crying. Darrell said, "Keith, where are you? Come out. Come out, you nut." There was no answer but he heard crying.'

Where Darrell? . . . Where? . . . Where? Louis   Belle Philippa frantically asked him but Darrell could only say Somewhere down

'It took us time to find the place,' said Philippa. 'The old mine was a labyrinth, tunnels winding, shafts, old workings and we only had two torches. We called and our voices came back, only our voices. There was a smell of earth, wet rock, gravel trickling. Darrell kept saying, "It's this one . . . that

307

one . . ." We stopped and listened: listened; listened. Then, suddenly, almost under our feet I heard crying – Keith crying.' Philippa's nails were biting into her palms as she tried to keep emotion out of her voice. 'The tunnel was rock, so low we were almost bent double, but the torches shone on a crack in the floor, a narrow jagged slit, like a rock crevasse. It was slimy. We could see on the edge where his hands had scrabbled. It was only inches wide – room for a child to slip through, no one else. It wasn't straight down. Our torches only shone a short way, then it was black. If it had been forty or fifty feet deep,' said Philippa, 'as some of the old shafts were, he would have been killed outright; this was only eighteen feet down, and Keith was alive. He was alive for three days.'

The prioress covered her face with her hands but Abbess Catherine, at her desk, said, 'Go on.'

'It took a day,' said Philippa, 'for the machinery to come, but the place was soon swarming with men; men from the vineyard, farmer neighbours, firemen, police, engineers – and crowds. I didn't know about the crowds until they brought me out. An ambulance came and a doctor. He stayed all the time. I was lying down,' said Philippa, 'my face to the crack, calling to Keith. When he heard my voice, he cried louder, so we knew he wasn't stunned. Louis said there must be some sort of space where he was, a pocket in the rock, or he would have been asphyxiated. They pumped oxygen down – and he cried again. I thought I heard words: "Mummy . . . come," ' said Philippa, 'and "hurt" . . . but I couldn't be sure. They brought arc lights but we still couldn't see down. We let down a torch, lit, hoping he could use it, and thought we saw reflected light.

'They tried pick-axes first . . . then there was so much machinery . . . I remember shapes. They tried every way to widen the crack, but each time the rock broke off and lumps went down. "Keith! move!" we shouted that down. Afterwards we knew he couldn't have moved,' said Philippa. 'His legs were broken. The whole shaft was narrow, slimed, so it was slippery. They made a winch to see if somebody could be let down. I was the thinnest and I tried first, tried – my clothes were stripped away but my shoulders stuck. I pushed and pushed, they were torn and scraped and my head felt bursting. It had to be head first,' said Philippa, 'a miner's lamp strapped to our heads, hands out like diving. A boy tried; he got farther but he fainted. People came off the road to try. Louis had offered ten thousand dollars, but it wasn't only that – anyone would have done anything. There was a dwarf; he was diminutive but thick; it was no use. There was no room for anyone but a child and we couldn't use a child.

'The second day,' said Philippa, 'there was no more crying. I thought I heard whimpers – perhaps I didn't. They drove drills each side of the shaft as near as they could to see if they could get through below, but they met rock and dared not use dynamite. Part of the tunnel came down and buried two men; they were dug out.

'We did silly things,' said Philippa to her silent audience. 'Once we had caught a word. The men thought it was "Daddy". It couldn't have been. Keith hadn't seen his father for two years. I thought perhaps it was "teddy". Louis sent all the way back to Beverly Hills for Keith's teddy bear. We let that down. Belle sent down milk and ice cream, and all the time I lay and talked and counted and sang – songs, rhymes, any rhymes. Sang, talked, told stories. They tried to make me go away. I went for a few minutes now and then for a drink and to the lavatory, but only if Belle took my place. The doctor stayed with me. He and Louis.'

Breathe Keith   I'm here   we're trying to come as fast as we can   picking up gold and silver

'I expect we went on long after Keith could hear. We went on but there was no sound.'

Dame Beatrice was sobbing now; the Abbess stayed still.

'On the third day,' said Philippa, 'Louis came to see me and said they were going to stop the oxygen. I went mad then; I tore at them and at the crack. I raged and fought and upbraided ... those men who had been working all those three days. I remember the doctor held my arms down and carried me out to the cave and forced me to be still. He said: "Keith's unconscious now, Mrs Talbot, probably already dead. If he isn't, don't revive him." '

Why? Why? Why? He's so close   so close it's only eighteen feet   Why? Why? Philippa could hear her own voice screaming and Louis's quiet Philippa   we cannot get him out   we cannot get him out.

'I remember it was dawn,' said Philippa. 'A glimmer of light in the cave so that the arc lights were pale. They had built a stockade to keep people out, but hundreds were there – even at that hour. They had stood all night.

'In the cave the men were standing round; most of them had been there the whole three days: farmers in jeans: police... They were stained with earth and water, grimed, glistening with sweat; some of them were bleeding, and I ... I must have looked ... The crowd was silent,' said Philippa, 'but an old fireman came up to me – he had been a miner. I had fallen on my knees – my legs wouldn't hold me up – and he put his hand on my shoulder. He said, "I should let them take you away now, Ma'am, if I was you. We're going to widen that shaft – and dig."

'Louis had been right,' said Philippa. 'There was a space at the bottom, a small box of rock. Keith had dragged himself against one side. Of course when they got him he was crushed by the falling rock and earth, but his eyes were open. They brought him up in the bucket they had been using to clear out the debris. The old fireman was right. I ought to have gone away.

'I remember Belle and the doctor washing me,' said Philippa. 'I wouldn't let the nannies near; washing earth and blood out of my hair, bandaging my hands – the nails were half gone – my shoulders were flayed. I remember an injection. When I woke,' said Philippa, 'the little boy Darrell came into my room. He came to my bed and said, "Mrs Talbot, here's Keith's nugget." We buried it with Keith.'

'It was eighteen years ago,' said Philippa. 'I only had Keith for five. We were all most sensible ... I went back to Washington and work, sent Mrs Farren back to England; then it was Tokyo, then London, more and more work. They said I was obsessed with it. I had a full, busy life. I fell in love and then came the wonderful privilege of my vocation. I can think of Keith calmly now; Keith as he was, my little boy, not what they brought up in the bucket out of that shaft.

'Sister Polycarp was thousands of miles away; she probably hasn't an inkling. It was in no way her fault but Dame Clare was my zelatrix,' said Philippa, 'and I know what constant thought and care and, yes, I believe love, she gave me; I would if I could, but, near Sister Polycarp – to look at she is so like Mrs Farren – near her I can't shut out the sight of those three nurses gossiping by the river ... I can't.'

'My dear. My dear.' Dame Beatrice's compassion could bear it no longer and she came to the still figure by the window to enfold her in sympathy and sweetness. 'My dear! Now she has heard, I am sure Mother will never ask you to. I'm sure,' but Philippa turned and in surprise saw that Abbess Catherine was still studying her own hands on the desk as if – Philippa had the sudden thought she were asking them to guide her.

What had I expected, thought Philippa – sympathy, fellow tears, an embrace?

'My dear! My dear!' Dame Beatrice could not say enough, her arms were round Philippa, but Philippa felt as if she were stifling. Then Abbess Catherine rose, over-topping the other two nuns, and took those loving arms away.

'You are exhausted,' she said to Philippa. 'You would like to be by yourself. Go and lie down quietly or go into your stall.' She put her own arm lightly on Philippa's shoulders, light but strong, thought Philippa and guided her to the door. 'Mother Prioress is right,' said Abbess Catherine. 'I shall never ask you.'

13

For every religious, Holy Week is the most moving time of the
year. At Brede the church was never empty; recreation was
suspended and each nun was quiet, withdrawn, except for the
part she must play in choir. 'In the liturgy of Tenebrae, of the
last three days of Holy Week,' taught Dame Clare, 'the
Church mourns over Jerusalem and celebrates the Passion of
our Lord in primitive chants drawn from the Jewish tradition
itself; they must often have been on the lips of Christ and the
apostles.' On Maundy Thursday Cecily was allotted the first
Lamentation and, as she prefaced each verse with the singing
of the Hebrew alphabet, Aleph, Beth ... she was doing what
any of the apostles might have done in the synagogues along
the Sea of Galilee. 'The psalm, In Exitu Israel,' explained
Dame Clare, 'is the exact counterpart of that of the Jewish
Passover night, and was probably sung by our Lord in the
Upper room.'

On that same day, the Abbess, following her Master's
example, became the servant of the whole community, serving
them at midday dinner. The sight of the refectory was inviting: each place was laid with a snow-white napkin, a glass of
wine, a bunch of grapes, a small wheaten loaf and a brown
earthenware bowl of vegetable soup. Apricot puffs and cheese
were laid along the side tables. When the nuns were seated, the
Abbess came in, wearing a white apron and white sleeves and
with her came the kitchener, Sister Priscilla, bearing a great
silver salver of fish. The Abbess went to every nun, serving her
and laying beside her plate a nosegay of small flowers: violets,

wood anemones, primulas, grape hyacinths, tiny ferns, pink heaths.

Later, in the chapter house, Abbess Catherine, girded with a towel, would kneel before twelve of her daughters, drawn by lot – 'I must cut my toenails,' Dame Nichola had said in panic – and reverently wash their feet just as Christ did to his apostles. 'I have set you an example,' He told them, 'to teach you what to do.' That night the Mass re-enacted the Last Supper, when Jesus took bread and broke it, took wine, and spoke the words that consecrated them and gave them to his disciples, the gift to the world for all time, of the Eucharist. Then, just as Christ had gone from the upper room to the Garden of Gethsemane and was seized in the midst of his disciples, so the Host was taken from the altar's tabernacle and borne in procession to a small side altar made welcoming with flowers and candles; the church was left stark, the high altar stripped of its linen, the empty tabernacle doors flung open. Bells were replaced by the dry sound of clappers.

For the long hours of the Good Friday vigil, a heavy wooden crucifix lay before the empty tabernacle as the nuns chanted and prayed the terrible saga through. The names mingled: Judas, Malchus, Annas, Caiaphas, Herod, Pontius Pilate, Barabbas, Simon of Cyrene: the women of Jerusalem, the two thieves and the centurion: the two Marys who stood with our Lady at the foot of the cross. 'The women didn't run away,' said the Abbess.

Christ died and, as if the Abbey had died too, came the long pause of Holy Saturday, 'Surely the longest day in the year,' said Dame Beatrice until, at night, hope came back to the Church as, long ago, hope had come to the apostles. The new fire was kindled in the church porch, the huge Paschal candle, inscribed with the date of the civil year, and painted with symbols of the Resurrection, was lit from that new fire and the priest took the first step inside the darkened empty church; he raised the candle and cried, 'Lumen Christi,' 'The light of Christ.' Three times the cry echoed as the new light was passed from candle to candle, the boy servers who came from the town lighting their candles from the great one and bringing them to the wicket where the Abbess met them with hers; she passed the fire to the rows of nuns, each holding her candle until the whole church was illuminated.

As the candles caught their light one from another, Cecily had a vision of the flame running in the same way from one church to another throughout Christendom, far around the world: new light, new joy, fresh hope. Thousands of candles, pure wax, wax of bees, made through the year by the wings and work of infinitesimal creatures like us, thought Cecily, made for this night. 'This is the night,' intoned the priest, 'the night on which heaven was wedded to earth. On this night Christ broke the bonds of death,' and, 'the night shall be as light as day, the night shall light up my joy.'

The priest blessed the new water and led the renewal of baptismal vows until, just before midnight, Mass began, the first Mass of Easter when linen, flowers and candlesticks were brought back to the altar as the celebrant began the opening of the Gloria, 'Gloria in excelsis Deo . . .' Every bell, every stop on the organ, every voice joined in the triumphant response: 'Glory to God on high,' and it was Easter Sunday.

Every Easter brought a card for Sister Cecily; every Christmas brought one too, but each was addressed to 'Miss Elspeth Scallon'. The Abbess, knowing Mrs Scallon's handwriting only too well, guessed they were from Larry Bannerman. On Cecily's fourth Easter, Abbess Catherine asked her how she answered them. 'I send them back,' Cecily's mouth was set and she tilted her chin. 'When he writes to me as Sister Cecily, I will answer him. Isn't that right?' and, as Abbess Catherine did not answer, 'Mother, I am Sister Cecily, so isn't it right?'

'It is right,' said the Abbess. 'It isn't kind.'

A flush of red stained Sister Cecily's neck and cheeks under her clear skin. That had gone home, thought Abbess Catherine, but, 'Mother,' said Cecily, 'this is Paschaltide, the – the most crucial time of our whole year, when our Lord came back to show He wasn't only the victim but the conqueror – for us all.' She was carried away, and her eyes were filled with ela-

tion. 'Mother Mistress is giving us the most wonderful conferences every day. You don't know how wonderful they are. I
can't let Larry disturb me now. He hurts with those cards and
he means to.'

'So you hurt back.'

'I ... need to concentrate,' pleaded Cecily. 'Mother, I can
feel my mind stretching, stretching!'

'And your heart?'

Cecily stopped as if she had fallen in midstream – and into
cold water, thought Abbess Catherine. 'You think I'm unkind?'

Abbess Catherine did not answer that; instead, 'What else
did our Lord show us, Sister?' she asked. 'In this Paschal
time? I expect, like you, after all the suffering, betrayal, de-
sertion, intolerable disappointment and being hurt, He would
have liked to have taken refuge with His Father, but He stayed
on earth and what did He do? He didn't try then to teach us,
bring us up – that was left to the Holy Spirit. He did simple
ordinary loving things: *loving* things, Sister, like consoling
Mary Magdalen, walking and talking with the disciples, breaking bread with them, cooking their breakfast. Didn't you,'
asked Abbess Catherine, 'come here to try and follow Him?'

Cecily's face was a study. 'But ... if I did write to Larry,
what could I say?'

'Those same simple ordinary things – about our Easter and
Lent. How you hate cocoa.' Cecily raised a surprised face;
how did the Abbess know that? Cecily always obediently
drank it. 'I hate it too,' said the Abbess and quoted:

> 'Cocoa is a cad and a coward
> Cocoa is a vulgar beast.

Chesterton wrote that. He was a right-thinking man, wasn't
he? Tell Larry about the idea of our Japanese postulants,
about the path you and Sister Hilary are making out of those
old bricks for the water garden, about our everyday life. After
all, nothing would convince him more clearly that you are
Sister Cecily.'

'It is right, but it isn't kind.' Wasn't that, thought the Abbess, an echo of Sister Polycarp's, 'It is understandable – but she should have been kind.'

This Easter brought no balm to Philippa. Mercifully, the sacristans were so busy she had little time to think; as on all great feasts the shelves of the 'turn' that revolved between the two sacristies glittered like a jeweller's shop with chalices, patens, ciboriums, cruets and candlesticks. There were vestments to put out – 'By the dozen,' as Dame Winifred said – but for all the work, the time seemed to drag for Philippa. Abbess Catherine had protected her – 'as far as I can,' she said. The simple announcement had been made, 'The Japanese postulants will not be coming for another year,' but the reaction was not simple; there was not only disappointment but a feeling that Brede Abbey had failed, done less than it could. No one put it into words, but many a nun was perplexed; there was too a feeling of blankness. 'Reaction from Japanese fever perhaps,' said Dame Maura.

'This wasn't Japanese fever. It was real.' If Dame Agnes said that, it was true and the Council was more deeply perturbed than ever.

Father Vincent had concealed his disappointment and quietly accepted the decision, but Mr Konishi was not as well schooled in the omnipotence of Lady Abbesses and he argued vehemently. 'But you can command,' he said. 'Then command this Dame Philippa.'

'To force someone, Mr Konishi, is never wise and there is a reason for this decision, Mr Konishi – a tragic reason.'

'Past or present?'

The question was so unexpected that Abbess Catherine was jerked into saying, 'Past.'

'Then she must forget – and forgive.' Mr Konishi was shrewd.

'She can't – yet.'

'She can. She is a *nun*.'

'Still quite a new nun,' said Abbess Catherine. 'Give her time.'

Mr Konishi was not sympathetic. 'I believe this Dame

Philippa was sent here to Brede for this very purpose. Why else,' asked Mr Konishi, 'should Father Vincent and I come? Why did my wife guide us to Brede, the only monastery in England, I am sure, that has a Japanese-speaking nun? It was meant,' said Mr Konishi, 'and to impede a meaning is not good.'

Dame Agnes felt that too. 'It isn't good for the house to backstep,' while Dame Maura, troubled, said, 'It won't make a welcome atmosphere if, when they do come, the postulants find out there is one of us who refused her help. We gather that, in a way, Dame Philippa did refuse.'

'She – made a plea,' said Dame Beatrice, 'and you do not know what lies behind that plea.' She gave a shudder.

'No; but Mother Prioress, the house is more important than the feelings of any nun.' That was the general opinion and Philippa felt, for the first time, what it meant to be at odds with her community; she felt, as she told Abbess Catherine afterwards, as if she were being shot by invisible arrows; arrows of surprise, unspoken questions. 'Held up by language difficulties when Dame Philippa speaks Japanese?' 'I felt like St Sebastian – without the saint,' Philippa told the Abbess afterwards and, unlike Sebastian, toughened her resistance, filled with a most unsaintly panic and obstinacy. She could feel herself drawing into herself, hunching her shoulders against them; and in the night, every night, she was lying on the rock floor again, her face to the dark ragged crack.

Breathe Keith   breathe   don't cry

'How ironic that, of all girls, Kate Farren should come to Brede,' McTurk had written. 'What irony!'

'Yes, if iron is cold, relentless,' Philippa wrote back, and, 'There is no way out; Sister Polycarp must not be penalized and I cannot leave. I am vowed to this house.'

'It is an impasse,' said the Abbess.

'They say spring is poetical,' said Dame Joan. 'They should just come to the infirmary; I have never heard such wheezings and coughs and colds. Dame Frances Anne has bronchitis; there's an outbreak of sore throats and I don't know how many people in bed.'

'I know,' Dame Maura said it feelingly. 'There were barely two dozen of us able to sing last Sunday.'

'Then, "This is the last straw!"' Dame Joan cried one rainy morning, coming in to report to the Abbess. 'Dame Clare has just sent Sister Polycarp over from the novitiate; she can't be kept there because of the others. She has spots.'

'Spots?'

Later in the day it was confirmed that Sister Polycarp had chicken-pox.

'Her father came to see her, and brought her two small brothers. It seems that one of them was already feverish. These families!' Dame Joan was wrathful. 'People think you can't catch things through a grille. Chicken-pox! Now what?'

'I expect most of us have had it.' Abbess Catherine was soothing. 'But put up a notice that anyone who hasn't must give in her name to you. We must be watchful.'

Cells were moved round to make an isolation ward on the attic floor and Sister Polycarp was incarcerated there. 'Poor girl, she will be lonely.' Dame Joan was divided between that concern and the hope that no one else would get it; the novitiate fortunately had all had it, and for Sister Polycarp there had, of course, been little or no contact with the community, 'and chicken-pox is contagious, more than infectious,' said Dame Joan, but Sister Polycarp had been working under Sister Justine in the "black room", 'and a scab *might* have fallen on a habit or a cowl.' Dame Joan tried to explain it afterwards.

'How could it – when she had no scabs?' Dame Beatrice held firmly to that and Dame Joan had to admit there had been no scabs then – not even spots. Thinking it was an ordinary cold, Dame Clare had kept Sister Polly in bed for two days before there was a vestige of a spot. 'It isn't possible that Sister Polycarp passed it on.'

'Not possible,' said Dame Beatrice, 'but she did.'

'Not chicken-pox! That's too childish,' Sister Polycarp had

318

exclaimed when it declared itself. Sister Polycarp was put out but to Philippa it came as a thunderbolt.

For two days she had felt as if her limbs were clogged; her head and her eyeballs ached – and the back of her neck. Influenza, she had thought, and on the evening of the second day knew for a certainty she had fever; but it was after Compline, the Great Silence had begun and – I shall be in bed anyway, she thought. Better to wait for the morning before bothering Dame Joan.

At dawn, Dame Sophie, as caller of the week, knocked at Philippa's cell, called 'Benedicite', put in her hand and turned on the light; Philippa, who had tossed and ached all night, hot with fever, filled with a strange pricking and pain, the back of her neck an intolerable ache now, sat up and reached for her shawl, meaning to tell Dame Sophie she was afraid she was ill, and ask her to call Dame Joan or one of the aids: as Philippa reached for her shawl she saw her arm covered with small darkish red blisters; she looked at the other arm, it was covered too, as was her chest when she opened her night tunic. There were no looking glasses in the cells and she had to call Dame Sophie. 'Dame, look at my face. Have I spots?'

'Spots?' Dame Sophie was backing away. 'You're *covered*!' Then, both together, they said, 'Sister Polly's chicken-pox!'

'I suppose it *is* chicken-pox,' said Dame Sophie. 'It looks like plague.'

'I wish it were,' said Philippa. Then she began to laugh, laughed so that Dame Sophie grew alarmed.

'Dame, do you feel *very* ill?'

'Yes,' said Philippa, laughing.

'Then – what are you laughing at?'

'At myself. My little puny self,' said Philippa.

For the first few days Philippa was too ill to know much about her incarceration. 'Her age is against her,' said Doctor Avery, but Dame Catherine guessed it was the weeks of strain before, the pent-up resistance and the old nightmare about Keith. 'She hasn't much weight to spare,' Doctor Avery said, worried, and the rash was virulent. 'The poison coming out,'

319

Philippa had gasped to Abbess Catherine in a lucid interval and, 'How many skins does one have to shed?' but she was often delirious and how much Sister Polycarp gathered or learned she never knew.

In her attic isolation cell Philippa was aware of a presence – sometimes it seemed no more than that – but who was always there, in the night as much as the day; someone who bathed wrists and head with heavenly cool water, brought cooling drinks, smoothed creased sheets and pillows, anointed spots that burned and itched. Sister Polycarp looked after Philippa unemotionally, firmly and thoroughly. 'No credit to me,' she said afterwards. 'I had it lightly, you very badly – besides what else had I to do, shut up in those two little rooms? And I had to help Dame Joan. She was run off her feet. There has been a real epidemic.' The epidemic, though, was influenza, not chicken-pox. Sister Polycarp and Dame Philippa were the only two to catch that. 'You see,' said Dame Beatrice, 'you see!'

Philippa and Sister Polycarp, willy-nilly, spent almost three weeks – 'nineteen days,' said Sister Polycarp – in one another's company and, 'Why was I making such a fuss?' asked Philippa.

Sister Polycarp did not talk much, nor smile, but she gave a grave attention, and had a look on her big-boned face as if she were drinking in every minute of the life of Brede. Now and again she would 'take off', as Philippa was to tell Dame Clare who nodded and said, 'Her ideas are often renegade.' Some of the nuns, and many of Brede's traditions, seemed to her antique, but she brought a scholarly mind to bear on them, unlike Julian in her time or Sister Louise in the present, 'and she has a better brain than Dame Paula, our avowed rebel.' In argument Sister Polly could often worst Philippa who was astonished at the grasp of the girl's mind. 'Its width if not its depth,' she told Dame Clare; but Sister Polycarp was deepening: perhaps these three weeks were fortunate for her too. For instance, she had dismissed Latin with scorn. 'It's dead.' Dame Agnes, as cellarer, had no time now to give Latin lessons and had been succeeded by Dame Ursula, 'Who drives me mad,' said Sister Polly. Philippa was able to persuade where Dame Ursula had prodded, to travel at speed where Dame Ursula had plodded and, on their last evening together in the attic cells, Sister Polly made a stiff, shy speech of gratitude. 'Latin isn't so bad now, thanks to you.'

Sister Polycarp asked Philippa no questions, but on that same last night, when they were standing at the attic's small west-facing window, watching the sun go down: 'I'm sorry,' said Sister Polly, 'sorry your little boy died.' Philippa was still. 'My mum must have been more than sorry,' said Sister Polly, 'I can guess that was why she never told me,' and Philippa had put her hand on the big-fingered one and pressed it.

Philippa spent the final days of her isolation alone. Sister Polycarp shed her last scab ten days before Philippa and departed, whistling, to the novitiate though she sent Philippa notes. Alone in the high cell, higher even than the trees, Philippa did much thinking.

On the twenty-first day of her isolation Philippa was pronounced clear. 'You can stop ringing your leper's bell,' said Doctor Avery. 'Have a good disinfectant bath, and wash your hair; put on clean clothes and you can go back to life.' Philippa had a deep bath – 'my first for more than six years,' she wrote to McTurk – and when her short hair was dry and she had on fresh linen, Dame Joan brought her a new habit, sent by Dame Agnes. 'You have had your old one ever since you came, and before that it was Dame Anne's, so you deserve it. I shall burn the old.' The new habit was hand woven, so soft and fine that Philippa felt as if she were dressed in silk. Feeling new from head to foot, she went to the Abbess's room and knocked.

'Well! Sister Polycarp won that round,' said Dame Agnes. 'What *do* you mean?' Abbess Catherine was almost sharp. 'Dame Philippa has just come to me and said that if a zelatrix is still needed for the Japanese – and the others – she is ready.'

'How kind of her.' Dame Agnes was dry.

'Dame, what *do* you mean?' Dame Beatrice was really pained. 'Dame Philippa has fought a painful and powerful battle with herself and won,' but Dame Agnes shook her head.

'Dame Philippa won't have won until she can do what she is asked, what is needed, without a battle,' she said.

14

On New Year's Day the Japanese postulants invited the community to a tea ceremony, a last celebration before they were Clothed.

They had arrived the May before, a little group shepherded by Father Vincent, proudly escorted by Mr Konishi. 'I have never been more moved than when I stood to see them go up to the enclosure door and knock,' he told Abbess Catherine afterwards. 'It was the moment,' he said, 'that perhaps I have worked for all my life – and now, think, six months have already gone! Now we are really on the way,' he said.

During December Abbess Catherine had sent for the Japanese postulants one by one.

'Mariko' or 'Sumi', 'Yoko', 'Yuri', 'Kazuko' – 'you want – desire – wish to be clothed, wear the habit?' Each had looked at her in surprise. 'But – that is the next thing we have to do,' said Yoko Matsudaira.

'Yes, but only if you want it, if you feel it with your whole heart.'

'What else would be in our hearts?' their faces seemed to say. 'We came to England to be made nuns.'

'But you must not stay if you are not happy.'

'I am happy,' but it was a sing-song as if it had been drilled on their lips. Only Yoko had said, 'I very much love,' but Yoko had settled from the beginning. She was older than the others, seen more of western ways, but even for her it had not been easy. 'The eyelids of a samurai know not moisture', said the old proverb; Yoko was daughter, grand-daughter, great-grand-daughter of many generations of Samurai, and she was brave,

323

not stoically brave as the other Japanese were, but brave enough not only to endure but to try and comprehend with body, heart, mind and soul.

She was a widow, married just before the war to a graduate of the military academy, a boy of brilliant promise but, 'killed,' Yoko told Philippa, 'within two months. All my expectations – smash!' She had lost her father and brother too, and was left with her mother and a small sister. 'Mother was very weak, sister young, I have to earn money.' Yoko had worked in a bar in Tokyo where, 'I learn much – horrible things,' was all she would say. 'It was suffering and degradation for a well-born girl,' Mr Konishi explained. She had become a Catholic – 'If not I go out of my mind,' – and when her mother died and her sister was safely married, she had gone into a convent where the nuns worked in the city among the flotsam of young girls in the bars and brothels. But Yoko longed, 'not for "active",' said Mr Konishi, 'but for "contemplative" life, a life of prayer for all those poor people she had met. Victims,' said Mr Konishi, 'of that sad tinsel life.'

Yoko was surely a case of those who entered a monastery from disgust of the world, 'and yet,' said Philippa, 'she is gay and steady, infinitely understanding.' Yoko had a strange tip-tilted face with beautifully arched eyebrows, a wry small mouth and a haoit of shrugging. 'Shrugging off everything,' said Philippa, but already, and long before she came to Brede, Yoko was steeped in prayer. 'A mystic from a low-life bar. That is paradox for you,' said Mr Konishi.

'Yes; Yoko, I'm sure, is a positive,' Dame Clare was able to say after the first few months.

'And, I believe, Mariko,' said Philippa.

At first Mariko Konishi and Sumi Tanaka had clung together like a pair of frightened kittens – 'If kittens can have black eyes,' said Philippa – 'but now they are separating, going about "waving their tails",' said Philippa. The Tanakas had, for generations, been the servants of Mariko's mother's family, and the two girls had been brought up together, a gentle cultured little mistress and a gentler little maid. 'But you must understand, Mr Konishi,' Abbess Catherine had said, 'that

324

though Mariko is a choir postulant and Sumi is claustral, she will no longer wait on Mariko. Here we are all servants. Remember . . .' – Abbess Catherine had discovered he loved texts – 'remember when our Lord washed the disciples' feet.'

Mariko was a beauty – a Japanese Cecily, thought Philippa -- but small, plump, beautifully formed, with a skin 'like a white-heart cherry' as Dame Gertrude, the artist, said. Mariko was graceful and deft, as feminine as a flower; at first Philippa had thought she might simply have been following the father she adored, but soon began to guess it was the other way round: Mr Konishi was following Mariko because, Philippa and Dame Clare had more than a suspicion, Mariko was one of the few, again like Cecily, for whom the call had been immediate and clear. Sumi too seemed certain, though she was timid, easily frightened, too anxious to please. Sumi had the almost white alabaster skin of some Japanese girls, big eyes, wide nostrils that gave her a look of alarm. 'But she is devoted,' said Philippa, 'capable of great devotion.'

Of Yuri she was not so sure: was she simply following the others? Yuri had been trained by her orphanage as a nurse and was far more decisive than the rest. Philippa could not help thinking she should be managing a household – husband and children; 'but I really don't know,' said Philippa. 'They are not easy to fathom.' Least of all did she know Kazuko, who remained obstinately sullen and withdrawn. It was a difficult situation, 'but better not probe any of them too much,' Philippa advised, 'or they will think they have failed and we could have a suicide.' She was not joking, but the advice, Abbess Catherine noticed, was tendered – not given decisively – tendered with humility and courtesy. Dame Philippa had changed. 'I scald when I think how discourteous most people are in the outside world,' she said. 'I was always laying down the law, interrupting, not letting other people speak!'

'You are a necessary part of our plan,' Mr Konishi had told her. 'I believe you were sent here for that.'

'Then perhaps Sister Polycarp was sent here for me,' said Philippa.

She had begun to see, as Cecily once had seen, that she had

been weaving herself into a private world of content and quiet. She had loved her work in the sacristy and the editing of St Hildegarde's Sermons – that amazing character whose writings can be compared with Dante's and Blake's. The Abbess had been working on them herself besides her work on the Qumran caves, but had had to put them aside when the election came, and had passed them on to Philippa. There had been quiet hours in the library, quieter in the choir and sanctuary, with the great outlet of the Office and Mass running through the days to bind them to a whole. Dame Clare had been right, it was a pageant – and there was enough manual work and time out of doors 'to keep me aired and walked', Philippa wrote to McTurk, 'and I can always go up the tower'. Once again, her life had been beautifully arranged and once again she was jerked out of it; yet she was glad Sister Polycarp and Mr Konishi had led her into this obedience – and he had been right, she was necessary. There had been so much to explain and smooth over – on both sides.

Some things were easier than for western postulants. The nuns marvelled at the Japanese control. 'Well, Japanese girls, brought up traditionally, have a strict training,' explained Philippa. They were used to kneeling, 'but kneeling down,' she said, 'folded down on their heels. It is rude to fidget, or move your feet or even shift your position.'

'I wish all my girls had been trained like that,' said Dame Clare. The deep bows to the Abbess, or in ceremonies, came naturally. 'There never were such bows,' said the nuns, though the Japanese bowed with the palms of their hands laid flat above the knee as they bent themselves double. There was the habit of quiet movement and, 'I have never seen such exquisite manners,' said the prioress.

'They are almost too perfect,' said Abbess Catherine. 'One never knows what these young women are thinking.'

Philippa could guess some of the thoughts; for instance, about the Abbey gardens and the vases of flowers: Brede garden, of which Dame Mildred was so proud, seemed to the Japanese an untidy wilderness, formless and without meaning. 'In Japan,' said Yoko when pressed, 'the whole has to make one scene, even the smallest garden. If there are only two stones and one tree, it has to make a composition.'

'Stones? You mean a rockery.'

'No, a design. We have some gardens only of stones, no flowers.'

'No flowers! How very odd. That can't be a garden.'

'Is,' said Yoko, smiling.

When the nuns arranged flowers, 'you put so much,' said Mariko. Dame Winifred had showed her some vases of daffodils for the ante-chapel.

'You have famous flower arranging in Japan, I know,' said Dame Winifred, 'show me and I will do it your way,' and was nonplussed when Mariko shook her head. 'You would have to study for years.'

'Years to arrange a few flowers!'

'I did,' said Mariko. 'It was part of my education and for Yoko too. In Japan it is an art.' Mariko did not mean it to sound derogatory but Dame Winifred was put out for the rest of the day.

Except for Yoko – and Kazuko who had been to commercial college – the postulants were country-bred, not conversant with the West, and there were many things they missed – and thought barbaric. 'The bathroom: a lavatory in the same room as the bath!' they recoiled.

They did their best to make no difficulties, even about food. 'I shall fly everything to London for them twice a week,' Mr Konishi had said.

'That would hardly be in keeping with our idea of poverty,' said the Abbess.

'What then?'

'They should eat what the poor people of Japan eat – as long as it is nourishing. We can get rice for them here, and vegetables, fruit and fish – if they will eat our fish.'

At first they had wanted to eat with the community, except Yoko who had sampled western cooking, but enthusiasm soon waned. 'It's so tasteless,' Yoko had to confess to Philippa. 'You don't use any spices.' The Japanese, Philippa knew, could not bear the smell of mutton and, 'Tongue – of a beef?'

327

said Kazuko, shuddering. 'Ham in slices, cold!' Sumi had said in astonishment and was hushed by Mariko. In the end, they took turns, two by two cooking in the novitiate kitchen and Mr Konishi provided a few stores: soya sauce, dried fish, wakame and yakinori – 'which is seaweed,' Philippa told Sister Jane – Japanese pickles and bean paste; but the Japanese postulants had breakfast with the rest in the refectory; the only time Philippa saw the politeness break down was when Kazuko, whose control was not as perfect as the others', tasted the monastery tea.

Now the nuns were to sip Japanese tea and watch the elaborate ritual. Yoko told them, 'You may be thinking this is the last time we shall make our tea ceremony, but no: it has been connected with monasteries for hundreds of years.' Buddhist monks, she told them, believe that tea makes the mind alert for meditation 'and with us, for prayer,' said Yoko.

'Yes, look what a difference that cup of tea Mother allows us now makes in the early mornings on feast days when the work is especially heavy. What a difference it makes to our singing,' said Dame Maura.

The effect of the tea was enhanced – 'made more thoughtful and wise,' said Yoko – by the ritual surrounding it.

'Dear me! We should never get started if we had to do all this,' said Sister Priscilla.

'Your way is more practical,' Yoko said with her disarming smile. 'Practical but meaningless,' Philippa guessed she might have added.

Mother Prioress, Dame Beatrice, had suggested that the ceremony be held in the common room but, 'It must be somewhere empty,' said Yoko.

'Empty?' Dame Beatrice was puzzled and Philippa had to explain the idea of relaxed simplicity that lay behind a tea house. 'Small huts or pavilions scattered about a garden, perhaps.'

'Yes, a tea house should be rustic,' said Yoko and sighed.

'Not in this icy weather,' said Dame Beatrice.

In the end the ceremony was in the solarium, cleared and cleaned and polished by the novitiate, when its floor was spread with Japanese matting, on which the nuns would sit. 'But we should have cushions,' said Mariko anxiously. There were chairs for the older nuns and, for Mother Abbess, as they insisted on calling her, an especial high cushion that Yuri and Sumi had made and stuffed. Behind her place they made the tokoma – or niche as Philippa had described it – and filled it with a text written in Japanese and a flat dish that held a single Christmas rose, a spray of berries, some stones and lichen. Dame Winifred averted her eyes from it.

Mr Konishi had sent the utensils: the iron trivet and round charcoal burner, the heavy iron kettle, a lacquer container for the fine powdered uji tea – long-handled spoons shaped like a pipe for measuring. Mariko, in her silks, made the tea as the one best versed in it. 'I am better at serving gin slings and whisky sours,' said Yoko. Sumi helped Mariko, both kneeling, folded down on their heels, as they measured, poured boiling water, and whisked the tea with a fine bamboo brush.

The little cups were handleless and of such fine china that, 'I'm afraid I'll crush them,' said Hilary, of the large hands. All the English nuns felt large and clumsy: Dame Colette and the handsome Ethiopian, Dame Thecla, were graceful, but even they felt heavy beside the Japanese who were all in full ceremonial dress, Mariko's kimono bearing five of her family's crests; five were for most important and formal occasions. The crests shed their lustre too on little Sumi, in her more humble kimono. 'My family also,' said Sumi, but Kazuko looked at them with jealous eyes.

Philippa had sad work with Kazuko that afternoon. To Philippa's eyes Kazuko's kimono was as attractive as the others, certainly a better one than Sumi's, but Kazuko always measured herself against Mariko and was miserable because she thought her kimono too plain. 'It's the colour of young grass,' said Philippa, trying to cheer her, and Mariko herself had given Kazuko an obi, stiff with gold over its orange, but Kazuko's face was still sullen and she would not leave the novitiate. 'Do it without me.' Mariko's five crests loomed large in Kazuko's mind, and, 'I too ugly,' she told Philippa despairingly.

'Now I am really ugly,' said Hilary, trying to help her, but, 'Sister Hilary is noble, nobly-born,' said Kazuko to Philippa in Japanese. 'Then for her it does not matter.'

Kazuko had a wide mouth, a strangely flat nose, high cheekbones – all ugliness in Japanese eyes – added to which her skin was dark. 'Not only dark,' groaned Philippa to Dame Clare, 'it's too thin.' Kazuko was perpetually feeling slighted, hurt and offended. In spite of Mariko's sweetness and Yoko's encouragement, she persisted in being sulky and withdrawn. 'Should we clothe her?' asked the Abbess. 'It's the only thing that will help her,' said Philippa and Dame Clare agreed. 'It's that or send her back.'

To the nuns it was as if a flight of birds of paradise had flown into their midst. In the raw January afternoon the colours, folds and shadings of the kimonos shimmered and swung, while the tinted linings, lime green, saffron yellow, coral, showed their deeper colours at hem and sleeves. The black heads were bent as the young women bowed in front of each guest with the small ceremonial fans held out. 'It's a feast of such colours that I shall see it all my life,' said Dame Gertrude and, 'Think how they will look at Candlemas,' said Dame Beatrice.

On the second of February, Candlemas Day, the feast of the Purification of our Lady, the Japanese postulants would wear these same kimonos for the last time. Mariko had wanted to wear a western white wedding dress for the Clothing. 'When my cousin was married she had five wedding dresses, two western and three Japanese.'

'Which did she wear?' asked Cecily.

'All five,' said Mariko.

'You mean . . .'

'She continually changed – that was to show the high position of the family. I could change at the Clothing,' but Philippa persuaded Mariko to be the same as all the others. 'And it would not be practical,' she said. 'Remember you have a bigger change to make than any other bride – from all this beauty to the habit.'

She had suggested a special habit designed on kimono lines;

330

Japanese dress became all the Japanese, but in their western black postulant dresses they – all but Yoko who was tall and slim – looked lumpish, short-legged, long-backed; the kimono gave them length, the wide obi with its padded and folded taiko broke the back line but, at the idea of a dark cotton kimono they were all, even Yoko, shocked and hurt. 'We want to be nuns.'

'With your habit.'

'Ben-e-dic-tine.' Mariko still spoke English in syllables.

'Please,' echoed Sumi.

For Kazuko, the thought of the Clothing was spoiled by the shame of her kimono and Philippa was thankful when it was all over and the five were dressed alike in the habit and white veil; it was remarkable too, how their difference of race and figure disappeared, remarkable and heartening and, yes, the habit seemed to fit them. 'Even Sister Kazuko,' said Dame Clare.

'Even Kazuko.'

'It's odd. When Lady Abbess Hester died it seemed as if everything were finished,' said the nuns. 'Instead we grow richer and richer. Who would have dreamed, two years ago, that we should have Japanese novices here?'

There were only four 'white veils' now: Yuri, two months after her Clothing, had given up and Mr Konishi had flown her back to Japan, 'where she will soon be betrothed,' said Mr Konishi. 'Well, to have a good, well-brought-up family is to serve God another way.'

'And for four out of five to persist is remarkable,' Abbess Catherine cheered him.

'Yes. This Dame Philippa, it seems, is an excellent influence.' Abbess Catherine agreed. Mrs Talbot, she could have guessed, would not have tolerated anyone slow, but Dame Philippa was patience itself with, for instance, Kazuko, 'Far more than I,' Dame Clare admitted. 'I find Kazuko exasperating.'

'But they treat me as a guru.' Philippa had the feeling of being caught in a net.

'That's how they look on you,' said the Abbess.

'I don't want to be anybody's guru. God forbid!' Philippa could have said. 'I have had enough of that,' but a zelatrix has to think of her novices, not herself and, 'Don't try to detach them yet,' Abbess Catherine was saying; 'they are not ready. They will need you for a long time.' Philippa tried to keep herself subservient in every way to Dame Clare, but it was plain that the Japanese knew who their real Mother Mistress was – 'and not only the Japanese,' said shrewd Dame Clare. Philippa would have been still more alarmed if she had known what the novice mistress said to the Abbess: 'Mother, it is Dame Philippa who should be over me, not I over her; anything else is ridiculous.'

'She doesn't try to usurp, I hope.' Dame Agnes's suspicions died hard.

'Indeed not, but it is evident,' said Dame Clare. 'Not for anything she does, but because she *is*.'

'Is who?' The little nun bristled.

'Is Dame Philippa.'

There were two new western postulants: an American, Sister Agatha, and Sister Michael, a northcountry girl, university friend of Sister Polycarp's. 'You see, as often happens,' said Dame Beatrice to Philippa, 'you started a chain.'

'And is *this* young woman to enter as a choir nun too?' asked Dame Agnes. 'She's another Polycarp.'

'She is, and I believe we need her. These Sister Polycarps will teach us things,' said Abbess Catherine. 'For one thing, they let in fresh air. Custom can stale.'

'The strength of a monastery is that it keeps its traditions.' Dame Agnes never lost sight of that. 'It must guard its treasure.'

'Yes, Dame, but what is its treasure? Its heart, and that must keep beating, not be moribund. The world is changing fast.'

'We're not in the world.'

'We are. The world is still here. You said, Dame, that in Lady Abbess Hester's day, Sister Polycarp – and Sister Michael too – must have been lay sisters; that was so, but this

332

is today. Perhaps tomorrow there will be no division among us, claustral or choir, when everyone of us, with our different degrees of gifts will be able to wear the cowl when, whatever our background, we shall truly be sisters. Perhaps Sister Polycarp is meant to teach us that.'

'There would be an immediate lowering of standards.' Dame Agnes was aghast. 'Fortunately it's impossible,' she said.

15

One Sunday that summer, McTurk brought two Buddhist monks to Brede. 'I must put up a *little* opposition,' he told Philippa. One was a Lama, the other his attendant young monk; they had come out from Tibet with the Panchen Lama and, anticipating the troubles to come, the double dealings, these two had refused to go on to Peking, but stayed in India to found a Buddhist monastery just over the border as a refuge when the Chinese came. The elder, Lobsong Rimpoche, gifted, smooth, cultured, with perfect English, had come to Britain and the continent to lecture, trying to raise funds; the younger, Tsarong, was learning printing, 'which is why I thought Brede would be particularly interesting for him,' wrote McTurk.

They spent the day and came to Vespers and Benediction, sitting in the sanctuary, the Lama on a golden cushion, young Tsarong on a scarlet. In their plum-coloured robes, the sleeves and vests of the saffron-coloured under-robe showing, they were so immobile and dignified that their faces seemed carved in the candlelight. 'This is the real thing,' Lobsong Rimpoche told Philippa in the parlour afterwards. 'I did not dream that such a life existed in England.'

After Vespers, young Tsarong and McTurk went to the large parlour to talk to Dame Edith and the Abbess about printing, while Philippa entertained Lobsong Rimpoche in a small parlour next door. She was called out for a few minutes and when she came back, the old man had taken a prayer-wheel, small, of copper and silver, from the pouch of his robe and was turning it as he sat. He did not put it down but continued to turn it as they talked, and Philippa remembered the prayer wheels that the Japanese peasants sometimes set in streams so that the prayers ran on as they worked; prayers that spun through the hours, days, months. 'Brede years are like that,' she told McTurk. 'The year of prayer, of liturgy, revolving within the natural year.'

On her seventh Christmas, she wrote: 'There is a story about Newman that I like very much. In his room he had a picture – I think his landlady had given it to him – of the Blessed in Paradise praising God, and every time he came in and out, he used to smile at it and say, "What! Still at it?" That about sums up life at Brede` from Christmas Eve to Epiphany – scarcely one hour free.'

The great feasts took their way: Christmas-tide with the Nativity: the next day, the 26th of December, St Stephen, the first martyr. On Holy Innocents Day the novitiate behaved like 'unholy innocents,' as Dame Agnes said, but she could not be annoyed because, by tradition, for this one day they were given the freedom of the house, rampaging into the work-rooms, climbing up into the loft to raid the store of apples; they played the organ, drove the tractor – the Japanese noviti-ate looked on in astonishment – and ended up in the Abbess's room where they roasted chestnuts on her fire, opened a box of chocolates left from Christmas and talked. 'Even Sister Cecily lost her halo today,' teased Hilary, 'she took off a gatepost with the tractor.'

Christmas-tide – forty days, not twelve as thought in the outside world – ended with Candlemas or the Purification of our Lady when, mysteriously, lilies always appeared in the sanctuary and ante-chapel. 'Lilies in January!' Only Dame Colette and the Abbess knew they were sent from Morocco by Yves Gilabert, the painter. 'I used to play with him when we were children in the Parc Monceau and he never forgets.' It was Dame Colette too who always went into the kitchen some days before Epiphany to bake the cake of the Three Kings for the community, a cake like a cartwheel, a custom she had brought from France; she had to be tactful with Sister Pris-cilla whose cakes were often sad in the middle and heavy. 'I wish Dame Colette could make the coffee too,' was the thought in many minds. On the rare occasions they had coffee it was gritty.

Ash Wednesday brought another forty days – of Lent. 'Forty, always forty,' said Sister Scholastica, 'Christmas, Lent, Paschaltide, forty days in the wilderness, it's a mystic number.'

'Like Ali Baba and the forty thieves,' suggested Hilary.

Lent was a time of cleansing; 'It's quite cheerful really,' Philippa told doubtful Sister Michael. 'It's a spring cleaning, that's all.' She did not say that, for herself, Lent usually began with a splitting headache – there was no early cup of tea on Ash Wednesday to help through the longer hours of choir; and the dinner of boiled cod and rice pudding, a supper of lentils and cocoa, all Lenten fare, lay heavy on her always chancy stomach.

Scales appeared in the refectory for weighing the stipulated amount of bread for supper and breakfast. 'If only we could have porridge,' sighed Sister Polycarp. 'Such good weight in your stomach. My Aunt Tib's porridge! That's grand stuff for filling you.'

'Sister Polycarp, never think about the refectory until you are in it.' That was a monastic maxim, 'but it haunts me,' said Sister Polycarp.

For Hilary, the penance of Lent was the reading – not even the claustral sisters escaped. 'In the days of Lent,' said the Rule, 'they [the religious] shall each receive a book from the library to be read straight through from the beginning, nothing missed.'

'And each means you too,' Dame Clare told Hilary.

Dame Veronica had worked for days under Dame Camilla laying suitable books out ready for Abbess Catherine to choose. 'We thought, Mother, that Dame Bridget would find this interesting...' or, 'Dame Sophie has not read any St Augustine.' 'But mine's in Latin,' wailed Sister Polycarp, 'it can't be for me,' but it was. 'When you have struggled to the end, you don't know how cock-a-hoop you will be. You will really have done something,' Philippa encouraged her.

On Ash Wednesday afternoon each nun had to give in her Poverty Bill, an exact account of everything she had in her cell and, if she had one, in her work-room. 'We don't want to collect things,' Dame Clare explained to her novitiate. No nun, from the least to the most important, escaped. Abbess Catherine was gentle, if inexorable – 'and very thorough,' said Dame Veronica feelingly. 'Do you really need all those books? Choose three.' 'One watch is all you can use,' or 'Dear child, you seem to have enough pens for an army.' 'Everyone should have the same,' was the hothead cry of some. 'If you pause to think, you could not say that,' said Mother Prioress in mildness. 'Dame Agnes, for instance, may need twenty books; Dame Perpetua needs one, as she would tell you herself, or perhaps none.'

The fourth Sunday in Lent came as a respite. Laetare or Refreshment Sunday. There were flowers in the sanctuary and shrine, the vestments were rose-coloured and, 'Silverside and dumplings for dinner,' Hilary, who still worked in the kitchen, whispered to Sister Polycarp. 'Sister Hilary, Sister Polycarp, you will *not* think or talk about the refectory until . . .'

'*Gaudate cum laetitia*': 'Rejoice and be glad', the community sang. It was a taste of joy, 'a breather,' as Hilary said, before going into Passiontide, the great drama of Christ's journey from Galilee to Jerusalem and his surrender into the hands of his enemies. On the eve of Passion Sunday, all the statues, crucifixes and paintings in the Abbey were veiled in purple and for Palm Sunday, palms, real ones, were blessed, the echo of those long ago Hosannas in Jerusalem. Then it was Holy Week and the glory and hope of Easter.

On sunny days that summer, a ray of light used to fall at None, slanting down to the place in choir where Cecily stood or knelt. It bothered Cecily but she did not ask to move, only marking her books with extra care because of the difficulty of seeing through the dazzle, but Dame Maura would often find that, in spite of herself, her eyes had strayed to look across at Cecily's face, tilted, as it were, in an aureole. Cecily was well on in her Simple Vows now, as was Hilary – 'almost old inhabitants,' as Hilary said – and often now Cecily, as she sang, would lose herself in the chant, be as unconscious of any gaze as a butterfly lifting and expanding its wings in the sun, and sending their colours shimmering into the world. Her voice is like that, thought Dame Maura, shimmering with colour and richness – and had to catch her gaze back, recollect herself with a shock. If Cecily caught her gaze, subtly the voice altered; there was a strain and that alloy of self-consciousness, wanting to please. 'Be careful of yourself,' Dame Maura told herself. Fortunately for her, the summer was wet and rainy, most of its days grey.

For the big feasts – Christmas, Easter, Pentecost – the guest house was always crowded, and guests overflowed into lodgings in the town. 'When most people go to the seaside, or fly to Paris, there are still very many who seem to want to come to us. If we go on like this we shall have to have a guest mistress,' said the Abbess.

Sister Renata and Sister Susanna in turns controlled the flow into the parlours. There were many visitors these days for Dame Philippa. The story of Penny had circulated and Philippa was beginning to find herself almost a welfare officer for her old Department; a zelatrix with the four Japanese especially in her charge, it was difficult to find time, 'but I feel I must.' Yet sometimes, 'Who are all these people? Why do they come?' she wanted to cry. Most of the nuns asked that question; 'parlouring' was exhausting work. 'Who sends all these people; what starts them off?' To Sister Jane or Sister Priscilla or Sister Ellen there was no question – 'The Holy Spirit, of course,' and Sister Jane would have added about this work what she said about cleaning saucepans, 'Be thorough.'

Pentecost was truly the feast of the Holy Spirit when it had come down on the lonely little group of apostles so full of fear in the upper room. 'But they should not have been so fearful,' said Mariko. 'They had with them our Most Honourable Lady.' The novitiate, a little group themselves, had been listening to Dame Clare talking of Christ's promise of 'the Paraclete, the Holy Ghost, whom the Father shall send in my Name, He will teach you all things and bring all things to your mind.' 'The Holy Spirit, who turned a fisherman – and such

338

an uncertain impetuous fisherman – into the first and greatest Pope,' said Dame Clare, 'just as He has made the son of a poor Italian farmer into our own Pope John. He showed a peasant girl how to defeat an army, and took an obscure little bourgeoise, so delicate that she only lived until she was twenty-three, and made her into the most powerful saint of modern times. Why,' said Dame Clare with a satirical little flick of her moth eyebrows, 'He might even make a saint of one of you.'

'Over Sister Jane's dead body,' said Hilary and Dame Clare was pleased to see that Yoko looked at Mariko, Mariko looked at Yoko.

Dame Veronica's mother, Mrs Shaw, came to Brede now every Whitsun but, 'You're sure that Maisie – Dame Veronica – doesn't mind, Madam?' The 'Maisie' and 'Madam' slipped out.

'It's going to be joy and comfort for her, wait and see,' said Abbess Catherine but, looking at the round back and shoulders bent with work, the hands that Mrs Shaw kept carefully hidden in her cotton gloves until she forgot as she talked, the same harebell-blue eyes as Dame Veronica's but faded with tiredness, sadness, disappointment and pain, Abbess Catherine found it difficult not to let indignation swell.

She was glad she had managed to say nothing because the second year Paul came too, a Paul in a decent suit and with work. 'Perhaps if you stop being ashamed of people you can do something for them,' Dame Veronica said afterwards, but the Abbess had taken the very earthy precaution of asking Abbot Bernard to see Paul as well, 'just to let him know we have strong males at hand' and, 'It has been made wonderfully easy for Dame Veronica to be magnanimous. She has had a great lift,' said Dame Beatrice who had become tempered with a little realism. It was a lift that lasted all summer – 'and may last many more,' wrote Mr Digby of Mortimer and Digby. 'Books for children endure and this may be a classic.'

The thistledown idea that had blown on to Abbess Catherine's desk that day from Mortimer and Digby and she had caught at as a means of helping Dame Veronica had held a seed that had burgeoned. 'Yes, like the mustard seed in the parable,' Dame Veronica told the woman reporter who came down to interview her. The children's calendar of saints – 'My Name Day', she had called it – had suddenly become a bestseller in every sense of the word. It had sold in thousands and been translated into nine languages – 'there will be more,' wrote Mr Digby. Magazines and Digests had printed some of the poems – 'and paid extraordinary sums, considering how little the poems are.' They had been made into a record, 'and paid the money box back over and over again,' Dame Veronica said with bliss. She had thought she could never be happy again; now she was so happy that the great feasts of that summer passed for her like a golden pageant: feast after feast: Trinity Sunday: Corpus Christi: the Assumption of our Lady.

'It was just a task,' Dame Veronica told the reporter. 'Lady Abbess allotted it to me.' The reporter liked that. 'And you still will be anonymous?'

'Of course, we all are.' It was spoken modestly but Dame Veronica was not anonymous in the community. 'How this has revived her,' the nuns said that thankfully at first. 'She is like her old self.'

'Yes, what a pity!' said far-seeing Dame Perpetua.

'When any nun in a contemplative house has a real gift,' – every novice mistress often had to say this to a postulant; it had had to be said, for instance, by Dame Ursula to gifted Dame Benita, – 'a real gift, though of course she uses it here, she makes in the house as little remark as possible.' Dame Ursula had been firm about that. 'Lady Abbess Hester used to be an outstanding sculptor – her work went all over the world, earned press reports, interviews, but we, in the community, knew little about it. We simply admired the statues.' Nor had Abbess Hester let it interfere with the long chain of offices she had held, or with her hours of prayer. Dame Gertrude was another such. Now Dame Benita herself was having an exhibition of her posters at a gallery in London; it disturbed the rhythm of the house not at all; no one who met Cecily would have guessed her rising reputation in music – she did not guess it herself. 'None of these are what we are here for,' they would have said, but now Dame Veronica was letting herself be more poet than nun, 'and on slender grounds,' was the opinion of the old book-learned Dame Camilla.

On the feast of Corpus Christi, one of the holiest days of the year when all minds and hearts were turned especially to the Blessed Sacrament – 'or should have been turned,' said Dame Perpetua – the choir at Vespers missed one of its four chantresses, Dame Veronica who had been appointed for that day. She was deeply contrite; 'I was carried away.'

'But *where* were you, Dame?' Dame Maura was as astonished as she was angry.

'Far out in the park, pacing, with a poem – yes, I was carried away.'

'From all those peals? That singing?'

'From everything,' said Dame Veronica.

Mr Digby came down to Brede anxious to commission another book. 'If you can think of an idea.'

Dame Veronica could think of several. She outlined some to the nuns at recreation. 'A clock of Love,' she said. 'Poems founded on twelve texts on love, each matching the number of words to the hour. One o'clock, the first, will have one word, "Love". Two o'clock, two.'

'Difficult to find, I think,' said Dame Colette.

'Three o'clock, "God is love," and so on, with, on the cover, a golden clock with angels guiding the hands.'

'Suitably sentimental,' said Dame Agnes.

Dame Veronica's colour rose, as did her voice. 'Remember it's for children.'

'Children have taste and sense.'

'Or the Life of the Little Flower,' Dame Veronica turned her back on Dame Agnes, 'told in nursery verse. I could call it Rose Petals or Flowerets.'

'A pretty idea?' Dame Ursula asked it uncertainly, sensing the silence of the others but, 'Bring me a basin,' said Dame Agnes.

It was then that Dame Veronica turned to Dame Agnes and said with dangerous sweetness, 'Of course *you* don't understand, Dame, but ideas have to be publishable.'

Dame Maura arose with a swirl of sleeves and said, 'Let's

ask Mother to re-read that last and extraordinarily interesting letter from Mr Duranski in Chicago.'

Everyone was glad to change the subject.

These were grievous days for Dame Agnes. Though she had tinkered, as Abbess Catherine had said, with her book for another two years, it had gone off at last, erudite and finished to the last footnote, only to meet with the news that the publishers who had sponsored it had been taken over – 'After all, it is years and years,' – by a less scholarly firm that found themselves unable to publish such a book. Nor could the literary agent to whom Dame Agnes had then sent it find any firm that would. 'It should be published because it is unique,' he had written, 'but I am afraid it is too specialized, the subject too remote.' The Cross too remote! To Dame Agnes that was part of the heartbreak.

'Can't we publish it ourselves?' Abbess Catherine asked Dame Edith.

'Mother, we can't. It's over five hundred pages long, not to mention the reproduction of manuscripts, paintings and sculpture. It's a major work and we haven't the facilities.'

The Brede Press produced fine books of poems, letters, translations, liturgical extracts, all of them hand printed, often illuminated, bound in the finest cloth, vellum or leather. 'If we printed this, supposing we could,' said Dame Edith, 'each copy would cost us about twenty pounds.'

'Which isn't feasible,' said Abbess Catherine.

It was grievous – 'and a reflection on our times,' said Dame Beatrice – no publisher for a treasure of learning, half a lifetime of knowledge and research, 'while for Dame Veronica's twaddle...!' Dame Maura was especially wrathful. The whole monastery was grieved but Dame Agnes took it well. 'Perhaps one day a publisher will come,' she said and gave the heavy manuscript into the Abbess's keeping, but the nuns noticed that Dame Agnes grew quieter, her sharpness lost its bite and, too, she began to look frail, while Dame Veronica went about the Abbey humming and rhyming, 'and falling into trances,' said Dame Perpetua.

342

On the feast of the Sacred Heart the Abbey prayers seemed to echo its timeless beating. 'I was turning out a box of books in the attic,' Philippa wrote to Penny, 'when I came across a thickish small book called "Ancient Devotions to the Sacred Heart". I was going to throw it away when my guardian angel made me open it. It was early thirteenth century, yet exactly what I need today – and you too, I can guess.'

Philippa wrote to Penny almost every day now. Penny was expecting another baby, longed-for, hoped-for, but the omnipotent Donald had been 'sacked', wrote Penny in indignation; it was the right description; Donald was like someone humiliated and looted. 'It was his too forward-looking policies,' wrote Penny, loyal as ever – his brashness, thought Philippa – meanwhile Penny had been promoted again, 'so I want to keep on working as long as I can.' Donald had found another post – 'of course,' wrote Penny – but he would have to start again at the bottom, and with less money. 'We shall have to give up this flat. He says "never mind, he'll sing in the streets for this baby", which is wonderful, but I can't help staying awake worrying – and being frightened.'

Philippa was able to help, not only with Penny's problems of work but with Donald's. Twice he had been down to see her. It seemed odd from behind the grille, to show someone how to write an appraisal of a marketing situation and how to set out statistics. Philippa also tried to help with the worry and fright. 'It's for you too, Penny,' she wrote of the old book on the Sacred Heart. 'Listen; ". . . whoever you are, whatever you are, there is room for you in Him . . . the hearts of mortals will forsake you but the most faithful heart of Jesus will never deceive, will never abandon you." Donald, and his new work and worries,' wrote Philippa, 'you with yours and new responsibilities, the baby and all your hopes for him, gather them all up and put them into that great heart, and *go to sleep*.'

The feast of the Assumption of our Lady fell in a week of blazing August weather when to come down in the earliest of early mornings was stepping into a paradise of stillness and freshness; then the year deepened to autumn.

In September the swallows flew, wheeling about the garth for days, filling the air with the sound of wings and cries, an excitement about them until one chosen day, instead of scattering, flock after flock keeping together, rose high above the Abbey, wheeled and disappeared towards the south. For Brede the cycle of the year went on. 'I always think of September as a time of warm colours,' said Dame Mildred. There was clear sunshine and in her flower beds was the rich gold of rudbeckia, deep purple and rose from Michaelmas daisies, flaring dahlias, and in the vegetable garden scarlet runner beans, tomatoes, dark-veined cabbages. 'Soon I shall have to ask for potato-pickers,' said Sister Marianne, 'and more for the apples.' The garth seemed to glow and the liturgy of these days added its especial truth and beauty to the whole.

Dom Gervase was away for the last Sunday of October, the feast of Christ the King. 'Father Gervase has gone as supply teacher for a fortnight to Bishop Palin's Grammar School for Boys.' Perhaps only Abbess Catherine and Abbot Bernard fathomed what lay behind that simple notice, they and Stefan Duranski. 'Pray for him,' Abbess Catherine wrote when she sent Stefan Duranski the news. 'It's an experiment – he knows it – and those boys are tough.'

His place for the fortnight was taken by Dame Thecla's brother. Brede had had its Ethiopian nun for eighteen years but it was the first time it had met an Ethiopian priest. Brother and sister had not seen one another all that time, 'But in our family we have three centuries of Catholics and we are used to separations and hardship,' Dame Thecla said. Their father was a chieftain and his children looked kingly; not tall – 'It's the way they carry themselves,' said the Abbess – slender and handsome with chiselled features but broad lips.

To celebrate the Mass of the feast, Abba Poemen wore his own vestments of gorgeous brocade, richly jewelled and flowing from his shoulders in heavy folds; the cope fell away from a narrow silk tunic with long sleeves so that when he lifted his arms in supplication or blessing and at the elevation, the effect was beautiful. His dark, long-fingered hands on chalice or paten seemed eloquent of the day. 'I thought of Balthazar of the Three Kings,' said Dame Emily Lovell. It was on this feast three years ago that she had tottered and fallen. 'We never thought I should see it again, yet here I am,' though often in the sick tribune overlooking the choir. Dame Emily was so frail her body seemed made of spun glass, but her mind was as clear as crystal.

All Saints was a day of joy, then the white vestments for the blessed were exchanged for black – mourning for All Souls.

'But don't think of Purgatory as all suffering,' Dame Clare told the novitiate in her morning address. 'Saint Catherine of Genoa called it blessed,' she said, and quoted : ' "Apart from the happiness of heaven, I think there is no joy to be compared with that of the souls in purgatory because they are at peace; true peace knowing their salvation is secure and welcoming this means of paying for their infidelity." It always brings a feeling of great satisfaction to pay one's debts,' said Dame Clare, 'but remember Karl Rahner says, "As to the detailed structure of the process, especially its connexion with any place, we have no information either from Scripture or from a definition of the teaching Church," so don't go thinking of Dante's leaden cloaks for liars or of the sulphur kingdom; just pray for them instead,' said Dame Clare.

Each nun brought her list of names, the names of her own dead; the lists would lie on the altar all November in remembrance as, slowly, the year ebbed. In the grey November days once more, it seemed as if it would never wake again, until . . . 'In that day . . .' the voices rang out the new promise. Advent – the wheel had turned round again. 'Advent to Advent, spun continuously,' Philippa wrote, 'but we nuns are the wheel.'

Their different avocations were twined with the seasons of prayer : for Sister Gabrielle it was the newly hatched chicks in their coops and runs set at Easter in the orchard : the putting down of eggs, when they were plentiful, in pails of isinglass against the winter : the culling of table birds and probably especial cockerels for the Abbey's Christmas dinner. 'We don't run to turkeys.' For Dame Mildred it was flowers; Dame

Mildred was often to be found, skirts turned up, gumboots on her feet, an old panama or felt hat perched on the top of her veil, gathering a collection of hornbeam twigs, sticky buds, or catkins or budding rowan to bring indoors. 'I have been making my prayer,' she would say. 'I don't know what the theorists would make of it and I don't care; just look at the pattern of that tree against the sky,' or she would be found kneeling on the earth, examining a minute wild flower through a magnifying glass. 'Only God could make a thing as perfect as that,' but she would also tell its colloquial and botanical name and where it would be found and how it would grow. Her borders were a mixture of wild and garden flowers: foxgloves and spirea grew with roses – and such roses. There was one white rose bush that flowered in June – 'That one's for me,' she said.

'Why for you, Dame?'

'I shall die in June.'

Dame Mildred did die that June and her coffin in the choir was heaped with those white roses.

With Dame Maura, of course, it was music; not only her own, and perpetual work in Brede choir but the advice, even lessons, she gave to musicians who came from far and wide; there was too the continual beginning again in the novitiate. The Japanese had been a problem. At Abbess Catherine's suggestion, Dame Maura had handed them over to Dame Monica who struggled with the two strongly marked vowels, the sibilants, the Japanese habit of singing through their noses instead of impolitely opening their mouths.

Dame Maura had not liked to delegate but she had enough to do with the others and, especially under her care, the steady blossoming of Sister Cecily. On All Saints Day, the singing had been especially remarkable and the precentrix had come to Abbess Catherine with a suggestion of making a gramophone record from Brede, 'like the Epiphany Jubilate of Solesmes. These are getting popular,' said Dame Maura. 'I think it would do well and I should like to do our Mass and Vespers of All Saints. Musically, it's one of the gems of the year's repertory,' she said.

346

'*Blessed are the peacemakers,*' she could hear Sister Cecily's voice as the joy rose up to the splendid – 'Yes, splendid,' said Dame Maura – flight of melody. '*Blessed are those who are persecuted for righteousness sake*' – a shout of triumph. 'Then it falls,' said Dame Maura, rapt herself, 'in steady rhythms,' – she was using her hands as if she were conducting – 'until it comes to rest, stilled little by little and ends in the chant of the glory of the Kingdom of Heaven. That is how I should describe it,' said Dame Maura. 'If we do it, we should of course have to school ourselves to perfection, beginning with the chantresses. Could I take time to practise them, Mother?'

'Of course.' Abbess Catherine was kindled by the enthusiasm.

'I should need Sister Cecily for solo singing and the organ. Would Dame Clare . . .'

Dame Colette's year was a round of vestment colours, and of different orphreys, orphreys with stylized peacocks, perhaps long-tailed, the eyes in the tails green on a red ground. 'Peacocks are a symbol of the resurrection,' said Dame Colette. Often there was a design of corn or wheat on a cream ground, red gold corn with blue green leaves; some of the orphreys were woven on small hand looms, some embroidered; then they were banded on to the silk or brocade.

One afternoon, the Japanese novice, Kazuko, was sent on a message from the black room where she was sewing to the vestment room. 'Will she be able to find her way there?' asked Sumi who had been stitching with her.

'It will do her good to try. She really must . . .' but Sister Justine broke off; it was not for her to bring up the novitiate.

Kazuko's Clothing had not solved her problems, and it seemed as if her novice year must be extended for a second one. 'There is some kind of . . . block,' Philippa had said.

'I think she really cannot be as intelligent as the others,' hazarded Dame Clare; she could not say it positively because none of them knew.

'She must be intelligent,' said Philippa. 'Mr Konishi knew her work in Tokyo. She had a responsible position.' Kazuko was certainly quick at the Japanese typewriter that so intrigued the nuns, not as fast as Yoko but adequately quick and, 'Father Vincent says she made great strides as a Catholic,' said the Abbess.

'She is not making great strides here,' said worried Dame Clare.

Kazuko was always acquiescent, impeccably polite, but her smile was never as complete as it could have been, her eyes were wary. She did not talk about her family as the rest continually did, showing endless snapshots – 'There probably isn't a household in Japan, except the peasants', that hasn't a camera,' said Philippa. Kazuko's father and mother were dead; she had no brothers or sisters. Her father had worked 'in textile', that was all Mr Konishi knew. In Latin and the chant, Kazuko made no progress at all, 'because she will not try in front of the others,' reported Dame Monica. 'She should make her Simple Profession next March,' said Dame Clare and she told Philippa, 'I'm sure you are gentle with her, Dame, but be even more gentle.'

'It's not me she is afraid of,' said Philippa, 'it's the other Japanese.'

'But why?'

'We don't know why.' Even Yoko, to whom everyone told everything, had not learned by one syllable what was wrong. 'We don't know why.'

'We should have sent Sister Kazuko back with Sister Yuri,' said Dame Clare. 'I'm afraid we shall have to send her now.'

'Which will finish her,' said Philippa.

Kazuko had not been to the vestment room before except when, on first arrival, the Japanese had been taken on a tour to every cranny of Brede, but then the vestment room had not been working. 'Besides, there was too much to take in,' said Philippa. This afternoon, Dame Colette was weaving silk for a set of vestments designed for a church of St Philip Neri, a set in deep rose, its orphreys woven with the mystical rose in shades of cream, black and red on a gold ground. Dame Colette seldom wove the silk for a set nowadays. 'I wish I could weave more,' she said regretfully, 'bought silk is never the same, but it takes too long and becomes too costly, so we usually buy silk or brocade, weaving only the orphreys,' but this was an especially valuable gift from a rich widow in memory of her husband. The chasuble hung in its rose folds from its hanger, the maniple and stole beside it, while Dame Colette had on the loom the long strip that would go to make the chalice veil, the burse and the tabernacle curtains. Dame Anselma and Dame Sophie who helped her had gone up to the refectory for a cup of tea and Dame Colette, who abhorred tea, was alone. Kazuko paused in the doorway, her small black eyes went directly to the silk on the loom; she bowed. 'Maa! Kirei na koto! Nante kirei na iro desho! Beautiful! What a beautiful colour!'

Dame Colette looked round, saw it was one of the Japanese, then recognized Kazuko and smiled. Kazuko, as though drawn, came a step nearer. Droppers-in were not welcome in the vestment room; the least dust or draught blowing in a smut could ruin a breadth of silk, 'also we have to concentrate,' but Dame Colette was now a councillor and all the councillors knew about Kazuko. Dame Colette nodded encouragingly. 'Would you like to see?'

'Yes . . . if you please,' but Kazuko still hesitated.

'Come in. Come in.'

'I . . . can . . . incoming?'

'Of course.' Kazuko came and with the small steps all of them used went up to the stand.

'You can look,' Dame Colette was going to add 'not touch', but Kazuko had already taken the silk of the chasuble in her hands. Dame Colette almost cried out peremptorily – none but those concerned dared to touch her work – but something in the way Kazuko ran one hand over the silk while the other held it beneath was not only careful but expert. 'S-silk, pure ssilk!' Kazuko spoke with strange satisfaction. She looked more closely at the weave, 'inspected it,' Dame Colette said afterwards, paused at a minute unevenness and clicked her tongue disapprovingly, but, running over the rest, approved it. 'Good . . . very good.' Then she came over to Dame Colette's loom.

'You want to see?' Dame Colette rose off the high bench and Kazuko slid into her place.

'It's called a loom. Loom.'

'Yess. In Japanese "hata",' Kazuko said it serenely. She also said something else Dame Colette did not catch; the next second to Dame Colette's fright and consternation, Kazuko began to work the loom. 'Sister!' but Dame Colette's cry was lost in the busy clacking. 'Sister! my silk . . .' but, 'Is good,' Kazuko almost shouted and, confident, wove on.

Dame Anselma, coming back from tea with Dame Sophie, stood transfixed in the doorway; not even they, expert as they were at the small orphrey looms, were allowed near Dame Colette when she was weaving on the large one; and trained as the two younger nuns were, their weaving was nowhere near being as fine as hers. Dame Colette's hot temper too was renowned but now she stood by, 'positively purring,' Dame Sophie told later, while the Japanese girl worked the loom – 'not only worked, it flew,' said Dame Sophie. Kazuko's hands were smaller than Dame Colette's; they were plump, the fingers short with oddly thickened nails, but the shuttle went back and forth smoothly and swiftly, faster than with Dame Colette herself.

When Kazuko stopped and got off the bench, the nuns clapped. 'Mais, c'est formidable,' Dame Colette when she was excited always went into French. 'Formidable!' Kazuko, her cheeks red with happiness and confidence, bowed and rebowed.

'Mr Konishi told me a little of Sister Kazuko's history but never told me she could weave,' said Abbess Catherine, but now, 'My father at last,' said Kazuko, meaning at the peak of his career, 'was one of silk weavers to Imperial palace. He teach me when I so small.' She showed the height of a small girl. 'Now most peoples, they want synthetic,' all these new words Kazuko seemed able to rattle off, 'is little pure silk now; too expense. Firms now have machine. I hate machine,' said Kazuko passionately. 'So all right! I say I do not weave.'

'We certainly don't want machines here,' said Dame Colette, and to the Abbess, 'To find an expert silk weaver, ready made!'

Already she was making plans. 'Mother, there is a request in

350

from Scotland, almost identical with the St Philip one, but in red, vestments especially for the Forty Martyrs of England and Scotland. An American couple are donating them and they don't mind what they spend; they wanted pure silk, handwoven and I was just writing to say we could not fill the order for a year or more, but now! Dame Benita has a design for red tongues of fire on gold.'

'It sounds ambitious.'

'I could do it with Sister Kazuko, Mother. She is, as I said, expert. As we work I could help her with her Latin and the chant. It would be another way to teach her.'

None of them had thought of Dame Colette as a teacher. She had cowed many young nuns sent to her for embroidery or weaving; it was only Dame Anselma's Irish warmth and humour, Dame Sophie's imperturbability that saved them. 'Dame Colette is wonderful but she is fierce,' said the young nuns – 'And Sister Kazuko seems so timid,' said Dame Clare.

'Yet . . .' The Abbess was thoughtful. 'Dame Philippa, what do you think?'

The Abbess had sent for her novice mistress and zelatrix to consult; Philippa as the most junior had stayed in the background. 'I don't know Sister Kazuko,' said Philippa. 'That is the point; none of us know her, not even Sister Yoko. It would seem Dame Colette has found a key. If Sister Kazuko is doing something she is able to do well – and to please Dame Colette she must do it extremely well – she might be freed from this blockage that is inhibiting her. Then she may learn the rest easily.'

'You would let her try?'

'I should let her try.'

Abbess Catherine tapped thoughtfully with her pencil. She was seeing Stefan Duranski's face as he worked on his stone, absorbed, making, creating; there was no room for pettiness in that large act, for jealousies or shame. Weaving was an art, a craft, but, 'Dame Colette will be accepting an exacting order with these vestments,' she said.

'Yes. If Sister Kazuko fails, the church work will be in a difficult position,' Dame Clare saw that.

'Sister Kazuko won't fail,' said Philippa. 'She has been trained in discipline and steadiness.'

'All the same, it's a risk,' said Dame Clare.

'One I think we shall take,' said Abbess Catherine.

It was the beginning of a friendship that budded fresh and strong yet as unobtrusively as the plum blossom of Kazuko's native province Fukuoka, in Kyushu.

It was Dame Colette who was able to tell, quite naturally, where Kazuko came from and who she was.

'An Eta,' said Yoko to whom it was confided. 'So!' That was drawn out like a whistle. 'Eta!' said Yoko. 'That explains it.'

The Eta, she told them, were an especial people. 'A tribe they could be called, folk that once, long long ago, were looked down on,' said Yoko, 'outcasts.'

'Like the untouchables in India,' said Philippa.

'Yes, but not now. It is going...' said Yoko firmly – but could it ever be gone from the Eta themselves, wondered Philippa.

Kazuko's father had been accepted at a mission school – the only one, in those days, possible for him – and had made friends with the son of a local Catholic. 'Rich good man,' said Kazuko. 'Benefactor.' He had had pity on the boy and took him as an apprentice, 'for silk,' said Kazuko. 'My father, he very skilful, made money to send me to good school. I like to weave but he say, "No. Go away, go to city." In city nobody know, none find out, but here,' said Kazuko, 'we all very close. I think they guess. Mariko guess.'

'It *doesn't matter*.' Yoko was insistent but, 'Look at your hands,' said Kazuko, 'fine, quick.'

'Yours are too, Sister Kazuko. Far cleverer than mine.'

'When I weave! Look at Mariko's.'

'Sister Mariko can't weave,' said Philippa quickly, but, 'Little hands,' said Kazuko longingly. 'Pale, soft; nails – how you say ... like pink shell. Mine like horn. That Eta,' said Kazuko.

'Which is nonsense,' Yoko spoke with firmness. 'Their hands are like anybody else's.'

352

Philippa's guess had been right. Kazuko learned Latin and the chant while Dame Colette learned some Japanese and then, at Abbess Catherine's suggestion, joined the lessons that Yoko was giving to several of the nuns – 'in case there is ever a foundation' – Dame Bridget: Dame Monica: Dame Sophie: Sister Scholastica and Sister Xaviera, but Dame Colette, Yoko reported, surpassed them all.

'Well, to learn Japanese is a matter for the intelligence, not?' said Dame Colette.

'It's extraordinarily difficult,' sighed Dame Bridget, and Yoko reiterated, 'Even for Japanese it is difficult to read and write our language – even for Japanese.'

'One must apply oneself,' said Dame Colette severely.

Under her fierceness, the quick Frenchwoman was devoted and very kind. The nuns would hear her voice, uplifted with Kazuko's strengthening and encouraging. The lengths of red silk grew on the loom and woven with it were hours of growing knowledge and confidence. 'You see, Sister, this is where our Abbey earns some of its living, in our church work-room,' she told Kazuko, 'and if you can help to do that, it is your gift to us.'

'And I always thinking I have no gift,' said Kazuko, and she said with a return of her sullenness, 'Mariko bring much much money.'

'But not in her fingers, like yours.'

'No.' The gloom lightened and soon Kazuko, they noticed, no longer spoke of horn nails.

16

'Mother, may I ask you to do something without telling you the reason?' Cecily was kneeling by the Abbess's chair.

This 'serene beauty' of Bishop Mark's, Dame Maura's 'knowledgeable one', Abbess Catherine found a startling child. She had not forgotten that grave, 'Because you have made a mistake,' over Cecily's Clothing. No young person in the Abbey had said that to a superior before – and the girl had been right, thought the Abbess. There seemed no doubt of a vocation now.

Cecily was in her fifth year at Brede, almost at the end of the time of trial; in less than two months she would make her Solemn Profession. 'She is due the second week of May,' said Dame Domitilla. Everything seemed serene, well set, but now Sister Cecily had come with this new and, again, unusually couched request.

'Not tell me the reason?' Abbess Catherine looked down on the young face, as grave now as in that other time, upturned in its wimple to hers. 'That makes it difficult for me to judge whether I should or shouldn't, doesn't it?'

'Yes,' said Cecily.

'And you can't tell me?'

'No.'

'Could you tell Mother Mistress?'

'No.' That was sharper.

'What is it you want me to do?'

'Stop my music.'

Again the Abbess was taken aback. That had been Dame Agnes's long-ago recommendation. 'I don't mean for choir, of

354

course,' said Cecily, 'but the organ and the extra singing. Please, Mother.'

Abbess Catherine considered. Now, as when Sister Cecily had come to her before, she felt there was a strong, and right, reason behind this. Did Sister Cecily feel the music – in Dame Maura's enthusiasm – was encroaching too much on her spiritual life? Had the others been teasing her, perhaps a little jealous, about it? The Abbess could picture Sister Louise and she knew Cecily was sensitive. After a moment Abbess Catherine said, 'I will have a word with Dame Maura.'

Not the usual slow flush but a flood of crimson stained Cecily's face from neck to forehead, painful crimson. 'Couldn't you ... order it, Mother, without anyone?'

After Sext, in the few minutes' pause before dinner, Abbess Catherine beckoned Dame Clare apart and walked with her. 'Sister Cecily?' said Dame Clare. 'No. She seems going on well now. She's less exalted, very level. At one time I thought she went rather too much to Dame Maura, there's all the work on these gramophone records of course' – the All Saints recording had been such a success that Dame Maura was doing a second – 'but Dame Maura, I think, gently discouraged her. Now Sister Cecily only goes when it is necessary, I will say that for her.'

When Abbess Catherine walked away, her hands under her scapular, she was so deep in thought that as she turned the corner to her room she almost walked over Sister Ellen, down on her hands and knees, polishing the floor of the alcove. 'Sister, I'm so sorry. I must have hurt you.'

Sister Ellen could not deny it. Abbess Catherine must have weighed nearly eleven stone, and she had trodden on Sister Ellen's fingers, but the Sister managed to wrap the tingling hurt in her apron for a moment, squeeze her hands together and then go on with her work with the other hand. My Lady is worried, was all she thought.

That afternoon Sister Hilary appeared. 'How I like that child of yours,' Abbot Bernard had told Abbess Catherine. He had been at Brede the autumn before, giving the nuns a retreat.

'Which child?'

'The solid one, with freckles and big spectacles. It's refreshing to meet such sense. She's a soldier.'

Hilary was soldierly now, blunt, straightforward. 'Mother, will you look at Sister Cecily?'

Hilary was kneeling where Cecily had knelt that morning, but where Cecily seemed slender, upright as a wand, Hilary was solid, a solid block; Cecily was gilded with good looks from head to foot where Hilary had freckles as Abbot Bernard had said, grey-green eyes, ugly spectacles – 'Why do the young want them to have such heavy frames?' wondered Abbess Catherine. Sister Scholastica's: Sister Louise's: Dame Sophie's were the same – yet Hilary was more attractive than Cecily – except to those who fell in love. Hilary's background had given her sureness, confidence and, more importantly, wise love, while Cecily's was strained, uncomfortably aspiring, often false. No two girls could be more different, but they were dear friends and both equally one in purpose – Abbess Catherine was sure of that – and, 'Tell me what is wrong, Sister,' she said.

'I don't know,' said Hilary. 'But something real. I would have talked to her but I'm clumsy and though Mother Mistress is so patient and clever, for some reason Sister Cecily is like a clam with her. I would have gone to Dame Philippa but she has all the Japanese ... Cecily was so happy,' and Hilary asked almost indignantly, 'What stopped her being like that? Every day she was happy, not up and down like us, but up ... without being uplifted. I used to think she was putting it on, but not now; we tease her too much. Now she's wretched. She ... flinches. I don't know how else to put it. At night I hear her crying in her cell, it's next to mine.'

'And you have no idea why?'

The eyes seemed bright through the spectacles. 'No, but it happened after we picked the nettles.'

'Nettles?'

'For St Benedict's soup.'

The twenty-first of March was the feast of St Benedict; it was kept with pomp and honour in every Benedictine house, 'and at Brede with nettle soup,' the novitiate said feelingly. The soup was pleasant, rather like spinach, but it was the novitiate who gathered the nettles. 'Grasp them firmly and they won't sting,' said Dame Clare. The nettles certainly did not sting her. 'She must be firmer than we are,' Hilary had said ruefully.

They had gathered them as usual this year but later that day Abbess Catherine had given a sharp order that, in future, for gathering nettles, or any other rough work, novices and juniors were all to wear leather gloves.

'Mother Prioress, would you mind? I need to speak to Mother alone.'

Dame Beatrice rose at once – she had not seen Dame Maura look like this and, 'Mother,' Dame Maura turned to the Abbess, 'would you ask for a short while, not to be disturbed?'

'I will stay in the alcove,' said Dame Beatrice, 'and keep anybody who comes.'

'Sit down, Dame,' but the precentrix stayed where she was, a strange darkness on her face which was wooden with her struggle to contain herself, then, 'Let me kneel,' said Dame Maura. Dame Maura's movements were always swift but now she came forward slowly, knelt – and bowed down, thought Abbess Catherine – a dread gathering in her own heart. She was beginning to guess.

'Mother, I have come to ask you to help me.' Dame Maura had raised her head and now, kneeling, she was as tall as the seated Abbess. 'To help me because I cannot help myself ... any longer.' Again Dame Maura bowed as if in pain. 'Mother, help me.'

'Is it something to do with St Benedict's day and your coming to me about the nettle stings on Sister Cecily's hands?'

Dame Maura nodded dumbly. All the novitiate had been stung but for Cecily that day there was an organ rehearsal practice for the recording and she had told Hilary, 'I shall have to go.'

'You can't play with those hands.'

'I'll manage.' Cecily had not gathered the nettles before, 'Somehow, all these years, I have missed this for St Benedict's day,' and she had had no idea what damage had been done, but, 'Sister, you're *fumbling*,' Dame Maura had called and at last in perplexed astonishment had gone swiftly up to the organ loft from the choir where she had been listening. Cecily had tried to hide her blistered hands but, 'Play that again,' Dame Maura had ordered, then, 'stop.' Her eyes were acute. 'You can't stretch, can you?' and she lifted Cecily's hands from the keyboard. As she turned them over, her eyes had blazed. 'Stay in the ante-chapel,' Dame Maura had said and gone straight to the Abbess.

'You were quite right,' said Abbess Catherine now.

'Yes, but I came back,' said Dame Maura. 'Sister Cecily was standing just under the Duranski statue, waiting for me. I believe she thought I was angry with her. With *her*! I said, "Show me those hands," and, unwillingly, Mother, she held them out for me to see. I don't know what came over me ... it was the sight of those swollen blistered ... I never exaggerate, never,' said Dame Maura fiercely, 'but I went down on my knees and ... kissed her hands.' There was a pause. Then Dame Maura went on. 'If I had put my arms round her, hugged her or petted her as any of us might have done, it would have been all right but ... this was different – and she knew it was different.' Dame Maura lifted her head and spoke more loudly as if she wanted Abbess Catherine to hear through walls of disbelief. 'Mother, I have become too ... fond ... of Sister Cecily.

'I have known it,' said Dame Maura, 'for weeks, perhaps for months. When we began the rehearsals for the All Saints record I could not hear her singing.'

'Not hear her?' The Abbess was puzzled.

'No. It used to be her voice, only the voice that I was fostering, and training, honouring. Then it was the girl.'

'What did you do?'

'Kept it down.' The fierceness came back. 'Kept it down, I thought, very well. No one had an inkling, least of all she. Thousands of us have been through this and got over it; it passes, unless,' and now Dame Maura bowed her head again, 'we ... betray ourselves.'

Abbess Catherine was silent a moment, then asked, 'When you kissed her hands, what did Sister Cecily do?'

'She couldn't have been more startled if I had hit her. I'm sure she would have preferred it,' said Dame Maura bitterly. Cecily had uttered a stifled, 'No! Dame, no!' torn her hands away and whipped them behind her like a schoolgirl as she backed towards the door. She found the handle, opened the door and fled. It was the first time anyone had slammed a door so near the choir, and Dame Maura said, 'Mother, I shall hear that slam all my life. I may have damaged that girl.'

'I ... I have to ask you,' said Cecily. 'Is ... is Dame Maura's going away so suddenly, the recording stopped ... anything to do with me?'

There were all sorts of answers Abbess Catherine could have given. She could have sheltered Sister Cecily with a snub, 'A precentrix doesn't go away because of a junior nun,' but she paid Cecily a tribute as she said, 'You were among the reasons.'

'Isn't there somewhere I could go for a while?' Dame Maura had asked when, as calmly as the Abbess could make it, they had discussed the situation. 'Somewhere? Anywhere?'

'Only Charlestown.'

'Charlestown Priory? But that's in Canada. I remember we sent them tapes.'

'Yes, the tapes started it. They have written to Father President begging for help. It seems the foundation isn't doing well, there are too many nuns without experience, and Father thought if they could be brought back to the chant, sing the Office properly the rest would follow – as it does. It seems the need is urgent and I had thought of asking Dame Monica, but you would have far more effect.'

'Canada!'

'Five years, perhaps longer.'

Dame Maura's head had still been bowed, then, in one movement, she had risen. 'Mother, it's right. I must go. When you said "five years" my first thought was, "For five years I shan't see Cecily".'

'Dame Maura was not "sent",' Abbess Catherine said now. 'I have no power to "send" anyone anywhere. She went of her own choice, because someone very strong and gifted is needed at Charlestown Priory,' but Cecily's hands were clenched. 'I should have been the one to leave.'

'That wouldn't have been fair or practical. You haven't taken your final vows yet ... besides, I said "among the reasons".' Cecily was not deceived. 'Dame Maura is valuable. I'm not.'

'That's morbid,' said the Abbess briskly. 'Get up, child, and sit down,' and, when Cecily had obeyed, 'we have no idea who is valuable, as you call it, and who isn't. We mustn't take ourselves too seriously, Sister.'

Cecily could not help it. 'When this ... this love happens to me – and you said it probably would – what can I do, Mother?' It was almost a wail.

'See it coming and try to prevent it.'

'But how? *How?*'

'Be more aware of the other person,' said Abbess Catherine. 'Put yourself in her place. That's the answer, Sister, then you can nip it in the bud ... don't let things reach this stage.'

'How can I do that with ... with a senior?'

'Do as Sister Hilary does, be a little flippant.'

'Flippant!' Cecily looked at her as if she were slightly shocked.

'It helps,' said the Abbess. 'We have custody of the eyes, Sister, and not only to keep them from distractions and curiosity; if you let yours shine, light up with response, what do you expect?'

'But with Dame Maura I never dreamed ...'

'Exactly. You should have dreamed. You and Dame Maura are kindred spirits, and an attachment of spirit to spirit is far stronger than between bodies – and more precious; but out of balance it can become a kind of ecstasy. You were unconscious I know, but that means not sensitive to Dame Maura, in a way thick-skinned.'

Cecily shrank from the word, but the Abbess repeated, 'Yes, thick-skinned, with her and Larry Bannerman. I could almost wish, Sister, that you could suffer a little from someone else, know what it is to be bereft.'

'Bereft.' The word seemed like a cry in the room but, 'I'm going to keep away from everyone. Everyone!' said Cecily, and Abbess Catherine knew she had not reached her at all.

When the silk woven red vestments were finished they were put on show to the community and Kazuko, now in her black veil as a junior, bowed again and again in gratitude and delight as the nuns admired them and congratulated her.

'Is Dame Colette,' Kazuko insisted by smiling broadly. 'Is Dame Colette.'

'Is Sister Kazuko,' said Dame Colette in equal delight.

This spring had brought too, the battle of the cats. 'If I were never unpopular before,' said Abbess Catherine, 'I am unpopular now.'

'Mother!' Sister Xaviera had come rushing in. 'Wimple has had her kittens – that's the fifth batch – and, just think, in the printing room in a cupboard full of pages; six of them.'

'Six pages or six kittens?'

'Kittens of course. Dame Edith is furious. Mother, don't let her hurt them.'

Sister Xaviera's pages were stitched copies of Brede's latest publication waiting for their hand binding. 'At least thirty are ruined!' lamented Dame Edith, but it was not the spoiled books that brought Abbess Catherine's decision to a head; it was the nuns.

Wimple, belieing her name, had been steadily producing kittens. Grock, the one-eyed, had died of old age, but there were at least twenty cats in the monastery. 'Soon we'll have more cats than nuns,' said Abbess Catherine. The nuns were forever cosseting and cradling them. 'Sister Xaviera is positively maudlin,' said Dame Agnes, 'and so is Sister Mary.'

'Well, now Dame Simone has gone, Sister Mary has nothing helpless to love,' said the prioress – Dame Simone had died the year before – but the cats, once past kittens, were not helpless; in fact, 'Is Brede run for them?' asked Dame Agnes.

'It's not as bad as that,' said Abbess Catherine, 'but they are becoming a preoccupation.' It was a hard lesson but one that, for a nun, had to be learned. 'We must go without,' and the edict went forth. Wimple was to go to the vet for spaying. 'She has had enough kittens to satisfy any cat!' Of the present new litter, one kitten could be kept. Burnell must dispatch the others, quickly and painlessly: of the pet population, all but two must go.

'Go where?'

'We will ring up the RSPCA.'

There was almost a rebellion. 'I am sorry but it must be done.' Abbess Catherine faced the community in chapter. 'Not even cats, beloved cats, must come between us and our duty. We have let this get out of bounds,' she said. 'Sad as I am, the balance must be restored.'

It was Sister Renata who restored it. Sister Renata had taken the Abbess's words to heart; in fact, anticipated them. 'It's Bonnie,' she said, 'our little extern cat. Mother, I knew I was getting too attached, so I tried to put him in the enclosure,' but Bonnie would not be put; he had come straight back to Sister Renata. 'He is old now,' said the Abbess, 'and you extern sisters have only the one cat – besides, the fact that you know you were getting too attached, shows that you weren't . . .' 'unbalanced' was the word she would not use.

'But the others . . .' the little Sister was visibly distressed. 'Mother, I think I could . . . you see, I have many friends in the town and farms around. Don't send for the RSPCA just yet. Give me six months.' Sister Renata had a way with her – people instinctively liked her – and it took her six weeks, not six months. With her big basket containing something that mewed and clawed, she would get in the car and quietly deport another black and white, or ginger, or tabby. 'I'm afraid Wimple is promiscuous,' said Dame Beatrice.

'Over and over again,' said the Abbess.

'Yes,' the prioress sighed. 'Now it isn't only Wimple. It's her daughters as well.'

Soon the monastery was restored to its original cat family numbers, Bonnie as the extern cat; Wimple in the enclosure with her one remaining kitten, a handsome tabby called, by Sister Xaviera, 'Tom'.

'He can't be called that,' said the Abbess. 'It is belieing fact,' and his name was changed to Tim.

'Sister Xaviera will never forgive me,' said Abbess Catherine.

'Which is worse,' asked the prioress in the privacy of the Abbess's room, 'Dame Veronica exalted or humble?'

As if the spring sap that rose in her was heady, Dame Veronica was brimful of ideas. 'And such ideas!' said the Abbess.

'Mother, you won't let these books appear as "By a Benedictine of Brede Abbey"?' Dame Colette had asked that in Council. 'That would be a little too shaming, I think.'

'Flowerets!' groaned Dame Agnes. ' "Petals from the Little Flower".'

'It's either that or the haiku,' said Abbess Catherine.

Set off by the Japanese, Dame Veronica had been studying the form of these little poems – 'That has staved it off for a year,' said Abbess Catherine.

'And at least she knows she has to study them,' Dame Agnes said in fairness.

'Indeed yes. They are not easy to write, only seventeen syllables, but now she wants to write the Childhood of Christ in haiku, so that it will do equally well for western or Japanese children.'

'She will translate them of course,' Dame Anselma asked that with a straight face, 'translate from one to the other?' The Council had to laugh.

'I think you are quite safe,' said Dame Ursula, as usual far behind. 'Dame Veronica will never learn Japanese.'

She had insisted on trying but it was the hurdle at which many of the would-be pioneers fell. Sister Xaviera had picked up most of hers colloquially from Sumi who helped her now in the laundry. Dame Monica and Dame Bridget were making headway by dogged persistence, 'though we shall never be much good,' said Dame Monica. Dame Sophie, with her gift for languages, did better and Sister Scholastica was, as her name implied, a scholar; besides, she and Dame Sophie were young. 'I was young when I learned Japanese,' Philippa said to console Dame Veronica. 'I doubt if I could do it now,' but then Dame Colette, older than any of them, had 'sailed in,' as Dame Veronica said, and mastered it. Dame Veronica had immediately given it up. 'That will not stop her writing haiku,' said Dame Anselma.

'But we know scarcely anything about the Childhood of Christ,' Dame Ursula objected.

'Dame Veronica does,' said the prioress.

'But Mother,' said Dame Edith who had taken Dame Maura's place on the Council, 'You won't let her *publish* any of these books?'

'Think of the reputation of the house,' said Dame Ursula.

'I shall have to try to bring her down,' Abbess Catherine said when the councillors had gone and she and the prioress were alone. It was then that Dame Beatrice had asked, 'Which is worse, Dame Veronica exalted or humble?'

'Humble is more dangerous,' said the Abbess and sighed.

'You mean none of my ideas for Mortimer and Digby are acceptable?' Dame Veronica was in the Abbess's room.

'None of *those* ideas,' Abbess Catherine corrected her.

'Did the Councillors say that?'

'Yes, Dame.'

'Attack a poet's work and you find a savage.' Abbess Catherine had heard that said and the poet was rampant in Dame Veronica at present. She stood with her hands pressed together, her head high but her chin of course quivering. 'I am to tell Mr Digby that?'

'I will tell him. He may put forward an idea of his own, or you may think of something better.'

'You once said, Mother, that we at Brede are intellectual snobs. How right you were.'

'Thank heaven,' said Dame Beatrice unexpectedly and then spoke as prioress. 'Dame, don't take this attitude. This is for your good as well as ours.'

'How can it be for my good?'

'You have a talent,' Abbess Catherine said and gravely, 'have been given a talent.'

'Then let me use it.'

'Willingly, but not abuse it. Dame, don't you see . . .'

'I see,' said Dame Veronica shaken with passion, 'I see that as Dame Agnes cannot get published, I'm not to be published either.'

'Don't be absurd.' The Abbess was curt, but Dame Veronica was too angry to take warning.

'I am to be tied down to her.'

'Tied down!' and Abbess Catherine's own temper exploded. 'Dame Agnes is a scholar, an expert, brilliant . . . you can't claim . . .' she broke off trying to contain herself.

'While you write jingles,' said Dame Beatrice flatly.

'Thank you,' said Dame Veronica. By now she was thoroughly dramatic. 'You have always been against me,' she flung at Abbess Catherine. 'Always.'

The silence that followed her words – and Dame Beatrice's bowed head and unhappy face – made Dame Veronica pause and catch herself back for a moment. 'I know you have been good to me this winter . . .'

There had been an unexpected darkness for Dame Veronica that winter 'which, of course, is why she is so edgy,' Abbess Catherine said afterwards. Paul was in prison again. 'Even Abbot Bernard can't stop him,' Dame Veronica had said despairingly. All had been going well; Paul had worked for a few months, been so enthusiastic that he was promoted, given responsibility, 'which I'm afraid is fatal,' said Abbot Bernard. He had fiddled his firm's accounts and stolen money. 'It seems Shaws are incorrigible,' said Dame Veronica. And Fanshawes, the Abbess thought despairingly. 'At least this time your little mother won't have to bear it alone,' she said it aloud. She had tried to console Dame Veronica; she had asked Mrs Shaw to the guest house – Bishop Mark had paid the expenses – and let mother and daughter be together as much as she could, given much time to them herself.

'I am grateful,' Dame Veronica went on now. 'Of course I am, but Lady Abbess' – there was an emphasis on the 'Lady' – 'did it for charity.'

'Charity is love, Dame,' said the prioress beseechingly, but Dame Veronica shook her head.

'I meant charity as a duty – charity that is cold because the old grudge is there.'

'Can you still say that?' asked Abbess Catherine grieved.

'Yes, I can.'

'What grudge could there be?' Dame Beatrice asked. 'I don't understand.'

'Don't you? A grudge because Mother Hester, our own dear Mother, deposed Dame Catherine as cellarer for me.' It was out at last and, for the moment, Dame Veronica was triumphant. 'Isn't that true?' she challenged the Abbess.

'I suppose there was a grain of truth in it,' Abbess Catherine told Dame Beatrice afterwards.

'Less than one quarter of one per cent!' said Dame Beatrice, 'and understandably. You were grieving for the office – with reason,' but now, 'I don't know whether to laugh or cry,' said Abbess Catherine helplessly.

'Laugh!' blazed Dame Veronica. 'Yes, laugh. You can afford to. You have made me a laughing stock.'

'My dear child. I think you had better go.'

'Gladly,' Dame Veronica made her bow and swept to the door. She opened it sharply and almost collided with Dame Philippa who had her hand raised ready to knock. The sudden opening of the door, Dame Veronica's sweeping passage, eyes blazing, cheeks red and the two nuns beyond, the prioress standing, made it clear that Philippa had stepped into a tense situation. 'I'm sorry, Mother. I will come back another time.'

'No, come in, Dame.' Both Abbess and prioress felt it was a relief to see the level Dame Philippa.

'Unless ... should I go to Dame Veronica?' asked Dame Beatrice.

'I should let her cool,' said the Abbess.

'You know how sorry she will be.'

'Yes,' said Abbess Catherine. 'I know. It gets a little weary-ing,' and she turned to Philippa.

By coincidence, Philippa had also come to speak about writing. 'About Dame Agnes's book.' Abbess and prioress exchanged glances.

'The news about the rejections has ... filtered down,' said Philippa, 'and I wondered, Mother, if you would consider trying it in America.'

'I hadn't thought of America and I'm sure Dame Agnes had not. But do you think there would be interest?'

'I think there would. Professor Dunstan Cornell of Ballatot University is the foremost expert on Early English literature. Dame Agnes must know his work. Ballatot has its own press and is immensely rich. I – used to know Professor Cornell. If you give me permission I will write to him.'

'But, please,' said Philippa when it was arranged, 'please, Mother, this time don't let anybody know. I will ask Professor Cornell not to mention me. Let Dame Agnes think it was your idea.'

'Wouldn't that be masquerading under false pretences?'

'Isn't an Abbess entitled to use what her community can bring her?' Then Philippa dropped her lighter tone. 'If Dame Agnes thought I had anything to do with it, it would ruin it for her.' But as Philippa came out she thought she saw the end of a black skirt and veil whisk around the corner of the corridor.

'If it is possible as late as this, Mother Mistress,' said Cecily, 'I should like to go to another house under stricter rule.' Perhaps it was Dame Maura's going that had put the idea into Cecily's head. 'I think I want to be a Cistercian.'

'At this last minute?'

'Yes, Mother.'

Dame Clare considered seriously but considered, Cecily felt, not the question but Cecily herself; then, 'Is Brede not strict enough?' asked Dame Clare.

'Not for me. I don't mean that conceitedly,' said Cecily, 'but

I feel . . . Mother, wouldn't I do better under a tougher rule? Life is so easy here.'

'Is it?' Dame Clare was looking into Cecily's face. 'I don't think any of us find it so. You know it is not easy, Sister, if it is lived to the full – and it gives much freedom and happiness.'

That 'to the full' was meant to reach Cecily, but Cecily was already going on: 'I have been reading about the Cistercians at Wimborne in Dorset. Mother, they keep the Rule of St Benedict too but far more strictly. They have silence always, don't have recreation, give themselves more wholly . . .'

'Do they?' Cecily wished Dame Clare would not ask these – tripping-up questions that upset the sweep of her new purpose. 'Of course I feel I am letting Brede down . . .'

'It existed for a hundred and thirty years before you came, and I think will continue to exist if you go,' said Dame Clare.

'Oh, Mother, I didn't mean . . .'

'Of course you didn't. I was teasing but . . . such thoughts mustn't weigh. You must go where you can fulfil God's purpose for you best.'

'Then do you think I should try?'

'I could answer that better,' said Dame Clare, 'if I knew if this desire for more strictness, more silence, was because you want to turn more to God – or whether it is, rather, because you want to turn away from people.' Cecily was silent and Dame Clare said very kindly, 'Sister, I think this is simply because you are missing Dame Maura more than you know.'

'Missing her!' Cecily wanted to cry in recoil and, 'All I want is to get away from everyone for ever,' but one did not argue with Mother Mistress.

'There isn't much time,' said Dame Clare, 'but still, I should give it a little more time, even if it means postponing your Profession. If you are still of the same mind in, say, a fortnight, shall we talk of it again?'

How could I be missing Dame Maura? Yet Dame Clare had a way of being right. Certainly all the joy had gone out of playing the organ and from choir practice; Cecily could not bring herself to like working with Dame Monica, who was temporarily precentrix, but then joy had gone out of everything. 'Know what it is to be bereft,' Lady Abbess had said. 'Reft' means to be torn, split, as if there were a great hole. Is that what is the matter with me? asked Cecily. But to have a hole or void in one was dangerous and she thought of the parable of the seven devils that had come in where one had been dispossessed – because its place was left empty. Empty, thought Cecily.

She tried to go into the choir to pray quietly in that place of prayer, or in her cell; to make herself walk in the accustomed ways, truly accustomed now, to give herself willingly to help Dame Monica – and Cecily knew that she could help – but she felt suddenly 'satiated,' thought Cecily. Brede, loved, longed for, fought for, had turned into an arid desert; even the Divine Office which had been her perpetual spring and inspiration seemed now merely sounds and words – nothing. As the slow days passed Cecily thought that the only one who could help her was Dame Philippa, but when Cecily went up to the attic floor where Philippa as zelatrix had her little office, Cecily held on to the banisters to stop herself from going in. 'Keep away from everyone,' she told herself. Everyone! Then one afternoon Philippa herself asked her if she would like to come to the parlour and see Penny Stevens's new baby.

The first one, Don, was almost two years old now; this was a girl to be called Philippa, 'Pippa to us,' said Penny, and 'Donald is mad about her. I only hope she will look like him and not like me,' said Penny.

At the moment Pippa did not look like anything as much as a pink poppy bud, crinkled and wrinkled in its sheath, not of green calyx but of white shawl. 'I wanted you to see her at once,' said Penny. 'For some reason she and Donald seem to think they owe their babies to us,' Philippa told Cecily, 'which they don't at all.' 'We do,' said Penny, 'you jerked us back into thinking.'

'Come and see her,' Philippa coaxed Cecily. 'I find unde-served gratitude a bit overwhelming.' The truth was that Philippa shrank as always – 'still' she would have said – from seeing a small boy. 'And you are Penny's age. You can talk to her better than I.'

'I wish you could hold her,' said Penny, 'but she won't go through the bars.' No, one cannot hold a baby through a grille, thought Cecily with a pang. To be jealous was such an unknown sensation for Cecily that she did not recognize the pang for what it was and incautiously put her hand through the grille to touch the baby's with her finger: Pippa's hand was unexpectedly warm and suddenly the minute fingers closed round Cecily's finger and held it in a surprisingly strong grip.

It was not long but Cecily felt that baby grip all that day and night, and through the days and nights that followed. 'Penny is just your age.' When Cecily had drawn back her finger and sat with her hand tingling under her scapular, she could have killed Penny for the casual way in which she shifted the baby to her other arm, held her against a shoulder, idly patting the tiny back as she talked, while the little boy Don, from whom, had Cecily known it, Philippa averted her eyes, pressed against his mother, rubbing his round head against her. Why do little boys have such outsize heads? thought Cecily with another pang. 'My son . . . my boy . . . my little son.' Cecily could not shut Penny's voice out of her ears.

Philippa had shown Cecily the way up to the tower long ago and there was one place on the roof where, standing at the parapet, one could look down from its height on to a glimpse of the town. Cecily more and more found herself stealing up there to look. She could see a glimpse of gardens, roofs, walls, windows; a vignette of a lawn with flower beds of wallflowers and daffodils; and homely objects; a shed, wheelbarrow, a hose, tools, sometimes a perambulator. What would it be like, thought Cecily, to have planted your own bulbs for spring? Your own, not bulbs for Dame Margaret who had succeeded Dame Mildred, bulbs chosen for your own garden? What would it be like to pick up your own warm sleeping baby? Cecily would cradle her arms in their black sleeves on the cold stone, but there was nothing in them and never would be.

In May, as Dame Domitilla said, she, Sister Cecily, would make her Solemn Profession; on the evening before it she would go to the chapter house where there would be two tables; on one the ring, cowl and mitra – the little silver crown

of a virgin – would be laid out; on the other the clothes she
had come in, her last worldly clothes, the blue dress and coat,
lined with pink, the blue hat bought – to make me fit for
Larry; they would look old-fashioned now. 'Yes, what frumps
we should look if we did walk out,' said Hilary. She said it
because, at this, the Tacit Profession, they would have to
choose for the last time. In front of all the nuns, Cecily would
have to go up and lay her hand on one table or the other.

It was only a formula; it was a foregone conclusion that she
would put her hand on the cowl – or I shouldn't have reached
that far – but what if I didn't, thought Cecily. Even at this, not
eleventh hour but eleventh and fifty-nine minutes? A trembling seemed to come up from her knees as she stood.

A dress and coat for Larry. Long long ago, when Cecily was
only sixteen, they had gone out shooting, Cecily walking with
the guns. To Mrs Scallon's immense gratification, Cecily had
been invited to the Bannerman shoot. Larry had lifted her
down from a stile; the beaters were out of sight, the keeper
gone after a young dog – Haig, the clumber spaniel who would
never come back, thought Cecily. Larry had lifted her down
but not at once; he had held her, letting her slide down against
him so that she had felt him, a man. For a moment on the
tower, her serge was his rough coat, and she seemed to feel his
quick breath as he had kissed her, kissed her eyes as he set her
down; then with one hand he had tilted her face up and kissed
her lips. It was only once, thought Cecily, but I remember it –
as she remembered the baby's hand.

'What should I have done?' she asked Dame Clare afterwards.

Dame Clare's answer was simple. 'If you wanted to stay,
stop going up to the tower.'

One moment I want to be a Cistercian, most solitary of
Orders, thought Cecily, the next I pine and long to have a
baby. What is the matter with me? and, as in this alternately
rain-filled or oddly warm spring weather, the evening mists
steamed off the ground, 'vapours,' Cecily told herself, 'that's
what is the matter, nothing but vapours' but she still went up
the tower.

371

The nun carrying round the post, pausing on her silent round, slid a letter under the door of Dame Agnes's cell and noticed that the large oblong envelope was American, edged in red, white and blue, it's left-hand corner printed: University of Ballatot, Illinois.

Almost any nun would have burst out of her cell and hurried with the sheet of paper to the Abbess's room, but the first toll for None was due to go in a few minutes and Dame Agnes, stickler to the Rule of never being late for Office, stayed where she was at her desk, 'Only every minute I picked the letter up and read it again.' When the bell sounded, she folded the letter carefully, slipped it into her breviary and, going downstairs, fetched her cowl and went quietly to her stall, but there was a look about her, a radiance, that made one or two glance at her. As soon as the Office was over, she hurried to the Abbess's room, but the dispenser was carrying in the small tea tray and Dame Agnes waited in the alcove to give time for Abbess Catherine to drink her tea in peace. At last she knocked.

'Deo gratias.'

Dame Agnes went in and as she laid the letter on the desk, her cheeks did colour, her hand shook and her voice was as shy and eager as a novice's. 'Mother, it's a letter from Professor Dunstan Cornell. *The* Dunstan Cornell. Does it say – what I think it does?'

'It confirmed,' said the Abbess next day at recreation, 'what Professor Cornell had written to me. You all know how long Dame Agnes has worked on her book, with what scrupulous care and patience, and with her permission I should like to read you what this notably erudite man has said.' Abbess Catherine read while the nuns made soft exclamations of congratulation and admiration. 'It must be a wonderful book,' said Dame Sophie.

'It is,' said Dame Paula who had been allowed to help in some of the work for it.

'I shouldn't understand a word of it, I expect,' said Dame Perpetua which, to her, was sure measure of the book's worth.

All that week, Dame Agnes went about the Abbey as if she, so prosaic and exact, were walking on air. 'The letter would have been enough,' she said, 'but their Press will publish it.'

'And with a wide distribution,' said the Abbess. 'It will be available in Britain.'

The Professor had written, 'It will become the classic reference on its subject.'

'I haven't deserved this,' Dame Agnes said when, too full of gratitude to find words, she went into the choir and knelt in the familiar quiet of her stall. 'From the bottom of my heart,' prayed Dame Agnes, 'I will try to be better, soften my tongue, not insist on my judgements, only give thanks and praise. Praise.'

Afterwards, as she walked down the long cloister she met Dame Veronica; Dame Agnes would have given her a small bow and passed on, but Dame Veronica stopped, beckoned Dame Agnes to step just outside the arches where there was a small embrasure. 'I didn't think I should congratulate you just with the others' – Dame Veronica's tone seemed to say 'we authors are a race apart' – 'You must be very happy.'

'I am,' said Dame Agnes simply. She would have moved on – this did not seem to her to be necessary talk – but Dame Veronica stopped her again.

'Yes ... happy. I was, even with my poor little despised effort.'

'Why despised? You had a wonderful success.'

'Wonderful seems the right word for some of the community,' Dame Veronica gave a little mirthless laugh. 'But at least I have the satisfaction that I did it all myself.'

'I'm afraid I don't follow you.'

'When my name-day poems were finished,' said Dame Veronica, 'I sent them to Mr Digby who took them at once on what he thought was their merit.'

'Dame Veronica, what are you trying to say? Please be plain.'

'I thought you knew.' Dame Veronica opened her eyes with innocent astonishment.

'Knew what?'

'Don't you know that Dame Philippa intervened? After your many disappointments, Mother let her write to Ballatot.'

'How do you know this?' Dame Agnes was sharp.

'I ... happen to know. American Universities often have a great deal of superfluous money. They even publish students' theses, and Dame Philippa is a great friend of Professor Dunstan Cornell.'

If Dame Veronica had expected a reaction from Dame Agnes, a recoil of anger or distress, she did not get it. The older nun looked at her for a moment and with disdain, then again she gave the inclination of her head. 'Thank you for telling me,' she said and stepped back into the long cloister.

'What are you going to do?'

Dame Agnes had found Abbess Catherine with the prioress. As soon as Abbess Catherine heard her step – she was growing adept at distinguishing the nuns' almost silent steps – she knew that the grateful unalloyed joy had gone. Something had happened to damage it, and, 'Mother, Mother Prioress...' Even in her distress Dame Agnes did not forget her manners though she could hardly bring herself to speak. 'Is it true that it was Dame Philippa who wrote to Professor Cornell about me?'

'She wrote the preliminary letter,' said Abbess Catherine. 'I sent the manuscript at his request.'

'Then – I owe this to her?'

'She had the thought but you owe it to your book.'

Dame Agnes did not answer. The struggle in her was visible. Dame Beatrice's soft eyes were full of pity as she watched, the Abbess's thoughtful, steady; Dame Agnes's lips twitched as if she were fighting for words; her little eyes, so unattractive with their reddened lids and sandy lashes, but so fearless and honest, looked far over their heads. 'Coals of fire,' said Dame Agnes, 'and they hurt.'

'I am sure they do.'

She lifted her chin. 'They must hurt,' and turned to go.

'What are you going to do?'

'If you will give me permission to break silence, Mother, to thank Dame Philippa with all my heart.'

Abbess Catherine rose and putting her arm round Dame

Agnes pressed her shoulders. Then she struck her bell. 'Let's have Dame Philippa here,' she said. 'There is something I want to ask her.'

'I – opened negotiations,' said Philippa. 'You see, Professor Cornell, though I honour him as a savant and a kind man, is a fierce and narrow-minded agnostic. The word "nun" would have conjured up for him a French or Irish peasant – or a timid sort of rabbit. He would not even have opened the manuscript; but I have lectured for him at Ballatot. I thought he might take my word, but it wasn't I who won him. You did that, Dame Agnes. Ballatot is not a philanthropic institution and he wouldn't waste one moment on any book if it were not of value to him or the university; a measure of its value is that nothing would induce him to set foot in a monastery, if it were not to see you.'

'And he says he is coming,' said Dame Beatrice, 'when he is next in England. Down to Brede to see you.'

Dame Agnes was flushed again with a near return of the joy – perhaps even deeper joy, thought the Abbess, because she had brought herself to thank Dame Philippa – but now Abbess Catherine had to ask, 'Dame Philippa, how did you come to let this out to Dame Veronica?'

'I didn't,' and they saw Philippa blush, saw a shocked realization in her eyes and Dame Beatrice, still sweetest and gentlest of them all in spite of her toughening as prioress, leant forward and said, 'Mother, I must remind you that Dame Veronica had been with us just before, in that – not pleasant – scene about her book. She went out as Dame Philippa came in. Yes,' said the prioress, 'Dame Veronica must have listened outside the door – eavesdropped!'

'I ought to have guessed,' Philippa remembered that veil disappearing round the corner and, too, a small encounter she had had later with Dame Veronica that had left her uneasy. Dame Veronica had come up to Philippa at recreation. 'I must say I admire you, my dear, for doing this for Dame Agnes.'

'Doing what?'

'Hush!' Dame Veronica had laid a finger to her lips. 'I

know it's a secret. Well, it's safe with me.'

'Doing what?' Philippa spoke with quiet persistence.

'Writing to Professor Dunstan Cornell. It was so kind because I know Dame Agnes has not always been exactly kind to you.'

'Hasn't she?' Philippa was fencing.

'It was she, wasn't it, who said of you, "*She* will never go all the way."' Again Dame Veronica's eyes were innocent but little drops of poison, thought Philippa, little grains of spite. Why?

'May I ask who told you about the Professor?'

'A little bird,' Dame Veronica had said airily and turned away, but, 'listened at the door!' said Dame Beatrice and Philippa remembered the whisk of that black skirt and veil. She was still silent but, 'I believe you are right,' said the Abbess now.

There was no need to tax Dame Veronica with 'this growing spite,' as the prioress called it; as always with Dame Veronica the remorse had been as quick as the damage and, guessing that Dame Agnes would be with the Abbess, she had gone to Mother Prioress's room hoping to find her; instead she found the subprioress Dame Perpetua. By this time Dame Veronica was in tears, longing to tell, but she met no sympathy or forbearance from Dame Perpetua who was so furious that Dame Veronica got the full roughness of her tongue, 'All the old Billingsgate,' as Dame Perpetua confessed to the Abbess afterwards and, 'an old Cockney like me should never have been appointed subprioress.'

'Why, what did you say?' asked Abbess Catherine.

'If I told you, I hope you wouldn't know the meaning, Mother, but among others I called her "a mean jealous little spoilsport".'

'Of all the dirty tricks,' Dame Perpetua had said, 'to listen at Mother's door. You're not fit to be a woman, let alone a nun.'

'Yes, yes I know, but when I lose my temper I do dreadful things. But now what am I to do? What am I to do?'

'Do? You've done it. Better see Father Gervase and get this

376

off your conscience. God will have to forgive you. I can't. When Dame Agnes was so happy! I'm disgusted – disgusted – disgusted.' Dame Veronica's tears were streaming down but they did not move Dame Perpetua. 'Go and do what you're told. Go!'

Abbess Catherine came down the short passage from her rooms to the infirmary to find Dame Joan. 'Do you think Dame Emily is well enough to talk?'

'She always loves to see you, Mother, and she has just had her "cocktail". You could try.'

Dame Emily's long ordeal was still going on. After she came back to Brede, for a few years she was better, then a fresh tumour showed. 'We blasted that with X-rays,' Doctor Avery told Abbess Catherine. X-rays had been tried again: 'It's difficult to gauge when to stop fighting,' Doctor Avery had said. Often Dame Emily was in bad pain yet it was seldom, even now, that she would take what she called the 'sleepy medicine', but Doctor Avery gave her his 'Brompton cocktail', 'a mixture of heroin and cocaine to kill the pain,' said Doctor Avery – 'gin as a lift and honey to hide the bitter taste. She does not know what is in it,' and, 'She's always better after that,' said Dame Joan.

Abbess Catherine saw Dame Emily every day, often twice a day; sometimes she went in to her in the night, but it was only now and again, 'in extremis' as she said, that she took a problem to her. She did not want to disturb the evening or ending of the days which, in spite of the pain and sickness, the near-starvation – 'one peeled grape for breakfast,' reported Dame Joan – was calm. Dame Emily's cell in the infirmary was a place of peace to which the nuns loved to come, her especial friends taking their turn one by one, so as not to tire her. She liked to see the Japanese, especially Yoko – and she loved Sister Cecily. 'I received her and shall never forget the beauty of her Clothing.' Dame Emily had her books near her; though, some days, she was too weak to hold them, the nuns read aloud to her, and her rosary was often twined in her fingers. On good days her bed was wheeled to the sick tribune to hear Mass, 'and she follows every word of the Office,' said Dame Joan. Now Dame Emily's face smiled from the pillow as the Abbess came in.

'Benedicite, Mother,' her voice was a whisper.

It was always about one of the older nuns that, on these rare occasions, Abbess Catherine consulted her. Now, 'Mother,' said Abbess Catherine, 'Mother, what am I to do with Dame Veronica?' and she told the sorry tale.

The thin fine hands with their wedding ring – too loose now – holding the beads, were still as Dame Emily thought; Dame Veronica had been one of her novices and she knew her through and through. 'She's a trying legacy for you,' said Dame Emily and sighed. 'She will always be Dame Veronica. It's too late to change her now – if it ever had been possible.'

'What shall I do with her?'

'Give her something difficult,' said Dame Emily.

There had been the usual interview of contrition, tears and promises from Dame Veronica: 'How *could* I have said it? How could I?' Now the Abbess sent for her again and, before Dame Veronica had a chance 'to embark' as Dame Beatrice said, Abbess Catherine picked up a letter from her desk, that capacious desk from which so many problems had been solved, providentially, miraculously, somehow – it often seemed to Abbess Catherine she had, not to decide, but follow pointers, keep herself aware, and the answer would come – 'Dame, I have this letter from the Prior of Whitforth. Please read it.'

Dame Veronica read, 'He wants a translation of Rufinus.'

'As you see, he says he needs it, really needs it and has no brother with time to do it, they are so busy preaching and giving retreats. I want you to do it.'

'*I*? But ... Rufinus is a stylist. It would be appallingly difficult to do him justice.'

'That's why he asks Brede to do it – and why I ask you.'

'It's work for Dame Agnes,' said Dame Veronica.

'You are a good Latinist too, but I'm sure she would help you.' Dame Veronica flinched. 'Will you try?'

'If you ask me, Mother,' – then I must, was unspoken.

378

'I do ask.'

'And my work for children? That is to go by the board?' Dame Veronica's chin was threatening its quiver, but Abbess Catherine was expecting that.

'Indeed no, you could do the two together and about the book for children I should like you to talk to Dame Emily.'

'Dame Emily?' There was a gleam of hope in the eyes that had been growing moist.

'Lying there, she has thought of an idea that I believe you would like, a valuable idea that would be acceptable to everyone, including Mr Digby: a record of what children have done – and written – for the faith all down the centuries. Think of the Children's Crusade, of the Japanese Thomas Tamaki and the smaller Thomas who was burned alive; of St Agnes and Maria Goretti. It would be a true record and an astonishing one. Go and ask Dame Emily.'

Dame Veronica seized Abbess Catherine's hand, kissed it, then sped like a bird.

17

'A Mrs Bannerman asking to see Sister Cecily.' Dame Domitilla had come to the prioress's cell. 'Sister Cecily – only she said "Miss Scallon".'

'Miss Scallon. Then it will be a friend of her mother's. Is the poor child never to have any peace?' and Dame Beatrice said, 'I must ask Lady Abbess.' She went to the Abbess whom she had undertaken to guard for an hour or two from all usual requests; this, Dame Beatrice judged, was not usual. 'Mother, would you rather I saw her? It will only unsettle Sister Cecily.'

'She is unsettled now,' said the Abbess. 'Dame Clare was very worried in her last report.'

'How odd it is,' said Dame Beatrice. 'So often it is the firmest, the most fervent, who get an attack of doubt at the eleventh hour,' and Abbess Catherine said what Cecily had thought herself, 'It's more than the eleventh; one could say eleven and more than three quarters. We are in April.' She rose. 'I think I must see Mrs Bannerman myself.'

On her way to the parlour she made a detour to pause for a moment at the Duranski statue. 'She is truly our Lady of Peace,' she had written to him. 'Some of the nuns did not like her at first, they were attached to what you called the "abomination". Now I often find them saying a prayer here – we pass her as we go in and out, and she seems very much our Lady with her hand protecting the world,' and how I wish she would spread it over us, thought Abbess Catherine.

Spring in the Abbey, just as spring in the outside world, was

380

always a difficult time. It was as if the sight of the chains of celandines along the bog garden – always the first of the flowers – the spreading of anemones and violets along the avenue, the first primrose and, always, the sound of bleating carried far on the wind from the new lambs on the marshes, the busy birds, the cloudy wind-torn sky shook the Abbey for a while out of its calm. Novice mistresses often found their novitiate as quarrelsome and restless as a nestful of young jays. This, Hilary's and Cecily's fifth in the novitiate, was especially difficult.

'Sister! Sister! Sister! I feel as if I'm being wiped out,' that was the new American, Sister Agatha.

Sister Louise said smugly that that was the idea.

'Mother Mistress, can I have your permission to *murder* Sister Louise?'

'I don't know what's the matter with me,' said Sister Polycarp, 'but I think I might feel better if I could play a good hard game of hockey.'

'I know,' said Hilary. 'My legs want to kick and run. Why do we have to wear skirts? If I could get a pair of jodhpurs and have a good gallop . . .' All this was natural, but this spring the worrying over Sister Cecily increased every day and Abbess Catherine, looking up as she came out on the garth from the choir, watched the weathercock on the tower spinning round and round – Like my mind, thought Abbess Catherine – and she said aloud, 'I do not know what to do about this girl. I do not know.'

'Where is the old one?'

'The old one?'

'The old Abbess. Carlotta Scallon, the only time we talked of this, said you were very old.'

The abruptness, almost rudeness, came, Abbess Catherine saw, from acute nerves. Mrs Bannerman's thin hands were trembling; she's skin and bone, thought Abbess Catherine, as ashen pale as Dame Emily, and the Abbess noticed the telltale nodules in the glands of her neck; advanced leukaemia, thought the Abbess. Poor soul! She looked, too, at the cut of

Mrs Bannerman's tweeds, the doeskin gloves, the diamond brooch that fastened a small cockade of feathers in the felt hat, and then at the eyes ringed by shadow, the fierce nose that seemed stabbing at everything – and everyone. Rich, ill and filled with misery to the point of anguish, diagnosed the Abbess. Aloud she said, 'I expect Mrs Scallon was speaking of Lady Abbess Hester Cunningham Proctor. She was eighty-five and died the day after Sister Cecily entered.'

'Sister Cecily?'

'Elspeth Scallon, as she was then.' There was a quick movement of negation. 'I am Abbess Catherine Ismay. Can I help you?'

'You won't.'

'I will if I can.'

'Larry – my son – would kill me if he knew I had come but, Lady Abbess, or whatever I call you, that girl is killing my son.'

'Sister Cecily has . . .'

'Elspeth,' Mrs Bannerman interrupted. 'I know her as Elspeth. She *is* Elspeth.'

'She has told me a little . . .'

'It isn't a little. Since he first saw her . . . she must have been six, he a little older . . . Larry is like his father, a silly dogged loyalty.' There were angry tears in the dark eyes that were proud too. 'Why they fall in love like this no one knows. I was fifteen when his father fell in love with me; he never looked at anyone else. God knows why. We're yeoman stock,' said Mrs Bannerman, 'plain people but Bannermans have been at Lamberton for five hundred years and there's only Larry. He should have children, sons, but because it's Elspeth . . . What is it here?' Mrs Bannerman asked it in anguish. 'What is it they find? What do you do?'

'We do nothing. We just are. If a girl has a vocation . . .'

'Give her back,' Mrs Bannerman interrupted again. 'Lady Abbess, I am going to die very soon. Doctors are fools but they are right about that. I can't leave my son like this.'

'I think,' said Abbess Catherine, 'you had better see Sister Cecily.'

'Larry saw her – through these bars.' The voice trembled. 'He said she was like marble.'

'A young girl can be very hard – if she has set her heart on something or if—' but Abbess Catherine did not say it – if she is afraid.

After Dame Clare's last report the Abbess had seen Cecily and tried to penetrate those mists. 'Mother Mistress tells me you are attracted towards the Cistercians.'

'Yes,' said Cecily, then, 'No.' The vapours had risen until Cecily felt she was wrapped in swirling mists in which she could not find her way, or even stand still; she felt she was drowning, going down in them.

'Would you like to go home?'

The reaction to that had been prompt. 'Never! Never! Not my home!' That at least was positive. 'In less than six weeks,' Abbess Catherine had said, 'you should be received for Solemn Profession, *Solemn*, dear child. That can't be like this. You must think, seriously and positively what you want to do.'

For a moment the old strong serenity had come back. 'I'm waiting for God to tell me.'

'I find myself in the same position,' Abbess Catherine had told the prioress afterwards. Then was this the answer? Here, in the parlour with Mrs Bannerman? 'Elspeth is older now,' said Abbess Catherine. 'She is still in Simple Vows.'

'You mean you...'

'It's not for me to decide, Mrs Bannerman, nor for you. It is for Elspeth – Sister Cecily. I can't give her back. She isn't mine to give. That would be turning her out and, as we have no fault to find with her, she has earned the right to stay at Brede until her death; but she can still elect to go. We have a door,' said Abbess Catherine, 'as well as bars. I will send her to you.'

When Cecily came in, Mrs Bannerman stood up; she hardly recognized the tall girl in the black habit who shut the door so quietly murmuring, to Mrs Bannerman, unknown Latin words; the soft curves had gone, the rounded cheeks, but the eyes were the same, their depths enhanced by the white bands that enhanced too the symmetry of the face. As Cecily came to the grille, Mrs Bannerman began to shake. The bag and gloves she had held so tightly dropped on the sill and she stretched her hands through the bars while tears ran down her ravaged face. 'Elspeth,' she said, 'Elspeth, come home.'

Home. It seemed to Cecily that every nerve in her ran to meet that; not home to the Scallon household, home to Lamberton, her home. 'Yes,' breathed Cecily silently. 'Yes.' She put out her hands too but, perhaps because she was dazed, they closed, not on Mrs Bannerman's, but on the grille bars. The parlour seemed to tilt and lift round Cecily. Am I going to faint? She held to the iron until its cold dispelled the mists and levelled her again.

'Elspeth, I beg of you . . .'

'I shall have to ask,' said Cecily.

'Your Lady Abbess said you could elect to go.'

'Not ask Lady Abbess,' the words seemed jerked out of Cecily. 'Ask myself.'

Cecily went to the choir, not to her usual place but away in a corner of the chapel of the Crown of Thorns where she would be hidden.

It was the answer to her prayers. Yes, prayers are answered, thought Cecily. In Mrs Bannerman's eyes she had seen Larry's steadfast ones. 'So long,' those had been Larry's last words in the parlour and it had been a long, long time, more than four years, thought Cecily. If she shut her eyes she could see Lamberton: the old house in its lawns and trees, its every beam and brick steeped in the sun and rain, wind and snow of centuries: its rose-brick chimneys and strong thatched roof – 'the most expensive kind of roof you can have nowadays,' Larry said ruefully, 'and it has to be fire-proofed too,' but Larry would not change it, nor do away with the white pigeons that were so ornamental but spoiled the gutters. The rooms were panelled, but not dark, thought Cecily, remembering the small green parlour as it was still called, with its lily-green panelling that caught deep reflections from the lawns outside. The stairs were wide and comfortable and there were deep window-sills where, as Cecily knew, a child could curl up with a book. We

384

used to play hide and seek in the attics – she seemed to hear running feet; a houseful of children, she thought, hers and Larry's. Hers.

Cecily opened her eyes. Suddenly in the bare little chapel she smelled the scent of box leaves. There could not be box here, but it was the scent of box. The chapel was cool, not chill but cool, yet the scent was of box, warm, aromatic in sun and Cecily was transported back to the Lamberton fête, when the Bannermans had lent the garden and a field to the village; all at once she had walked away from the people and the chatter, the marquee on the lawn for tea; away from the band and the stalls – the white elephant stall where I should have been helping Mummy – away from the lucky dip, the ponies, sixpence for a ride, and the coconut shy run by Larry. Cecily had walked away by herself across the lawn to the sunk garden.

She knew several pairs of eyes had followed her and that the same thought was in many minds: Is she thinking of the time when this will all be hers? Young mistress of Lamberton? 'I only want to see you married,' Mrs Bannerman had said, 'then I shall retire in peace,' but all Cecily had been thinking, as she wandered along the paths between low hedges kept clipped, dense and green, was, I hope my convent, wherever it is, will have box hedges like these – she had not known of Brede then, nor that nuns had monasteries – I hope it has a garden enclosed with box. She had broken off a sprig of it, crushed it in her hand and smelled it – as she smelled it now, kneeling in the chapel of the Crown of Thorns, 'And I came back to my senses,' she told Abbess Catherine.

She had been lost in the mists but now she had found her feet. 'I thought I was sinking but I was standing on a rock. Of course I can't go back.' If she went with Mrs Bannerman to Larry, dear, dear Larry, it would be an unforgivable wrong. I went apart by myself that day because I must always be apart. If I went back for Larry's sake, and for Lamberton's, it wouldn't be any good, thought Cecily, because I should be haunted, haunted so that – 'I could never be any use to you,' she felt she cried to Larry. 'I shouldn't even be satisfactory and you deserve far more than that. It is never right to take away what belongs to one and give it to another, and I belong to You.'

What was it her mother had said, that long-ago day when she, Cecily, was to be clothed. 'You are marrying an idea.'

Cecily's own voice came back to her. 'People often do marry ideas.'

'But a day comes,' Mrs Scallon had said, 'when you find the idea is a person. That's when the marriage holds or breaks.'

In that cocksure, ignorant voice Cecily had said, 'Mine won't break.' 'But it nearly did,' whispered Cecily. 'How nearly!' and she shivered.

She left her corner and went into the choir and knelt again, facing the high altar. In six weeks she should be there in the sanctuary kneeling before Bishop Mark, standing to sing her responses, prostrating, going in procession through the outer garden and the forecourt for the last time.

She knew now, quite certainly, that she would be there – because I shall have put my hand on the table with the cowl and the ring and the narrow crown of a virgin, consecrated to Him alone, thought Cecily: 'I know now in whom I have believed.' The words filled her and, 'No one else,' whispered Cecily. 'No human husband, no Larry, no children.' She would have to live without them for ever.

'I want you to know the price,' Lady Abbess had said, and 'I wish you could feel what it is to be bereft.' 'Don't delude yourself; you will never cease to feel the pang,' that had been Dame Clare. 'I was encouraging myself,' Cecily could admit that now. Yet kneeling here before the altar she was glad of these last few desperate and unhappy weeks, because, 'I did not know the price,' said Cecily, know what it meant to give, as Dame Philippa had said, the whole orchard. But blossom and fruit? No children! and then into Cecily's mind came other words said centuries ago to Anna in the temple: 'Why do you weep? Am I not more to thee than many sons?' For a further moment Cecily knelt, then, 'Amen, so be it.' She got up from her knees, dusted her habit and straightened her veil.

Elspeth – and Sister Cecily of even a week, an hour, ago – thought Cecily, would have gone to Lady Abbess and asked her to tell Mrs Bannerman, or even gone out into the park and hidden until she was sure Mrs Bannerman must have gone. This Sister Cecily went back to the parlour to talk gently, pityingly, but quite inexorably to Mrs Bannerman.

18

For the first time at Brede – 'and this may be the only time,'
warned Abbess Catherine – television was set up in the large
parlour so that the nuns could watch the opening of Vatican
Council II in Rome.

'In the long history of Christendom,' Abbess Catherine said
in the conference she gave on the Council, 'there have only
been twenty councils, and the last, the Vatican Council of
1869–70, was hurried and unfinished.' Pope John knew he had
not many years to live, he knew that the Curia, the group of
cardinals who were his helpers in governing the Church,
moved slowly – 'as slowly as what they are,' said Dame Agnes,
'the mills of God,' but, 'Our soul was illumined with a great
idea,' said Pope John, 'which we received with indescribable
trust.' It was indescribable trust: 'It will be impossible to open
the Council in 1963,' the prelates had said. 'Then we shall
open it in 1962,' said Pope John.

To many of the nuns, Rome was a fabled city. Sister Ellen,
for instance, saw it as one of those heavenly groups of buildings, castles and turrets lit by gold rays, that are seen in the
visions of sacred pictures, or offered on a tray to the Virgin
Mary as in the Crivelli Annunciation. 'Rome has the great
dome of St Peter's, I know that,' said Sister Ellen.

'And the Bernini colonnades; the Pope's balcony and the
Square where a multitude of people can gather,' said Sister
Priscilla, but now, suddenly, it had become real, almost as real
as it was for Philippa and Dame Gertrude and the rest of the
nuns who had been there. As Philippa watched, she could
smell the streets of Rome, hot dust and gutters, coffee – those

frothing capuccinos – and see the elegance of the women and cars, the flower sellers under their giant umbrellas below the Spanish steps among the tourists and students and fountains, and hear the shouts of the children playing in the Pincio gardens; Italian little girls have voices like klaxons too, she thought.

The nuns watched the concourse of clergy assembling, imagining the scarlet and purple, black, white and gold and the canary yellow and blue of the papal guard. They saw the crowd gathered outside between the colonnades. 'How large is the Square?' asked Sister Priscilla and when Dame Gertrude told her it would hold Brede Abbey, gardens and park, she looked dazed, as they all were dazed by the size of the Council. 'Two thousand, six hundred cardinals, patriarchs, archbishops and bishops,' said Dame Clare, 'and with them as observers, Anglicans, Methodists, Quakers, Congregationalists, Lutherans, Presbyterians and priests of the Abyssinian and Greek Orthodox churches.'

'And Uncle Tom Cobbleigh and all!' Hilary could not resist saying.

'Never before,' Dame Clare's eyes shone, but, 'Once they start, they won't know where to stop,' Dame Agnes predicted.

Most of the younger nuns were ready to adore Pope John but there were others, whose minds, perhaps steadier, went back to Pope Pius, 'who started so many of what you call the "new things",' said Dame Perpetua. 'They too were things for the people. He remitted the long fast before communion, he gave us evening Mass, he helped the people without giving away our riches.' It had been a gentle, steady liberalizing. 'But now. . . ?' said the nuns.

News came of Pope John's worsening health; then, on the last day of May, internal bleeding and an attack of peritonitis. At Brede prayers were intensified, faces were serious, voices hushed as the community waited; the town below was waiting too, as Sister Renata reported, 'This hasn't happened with any other pope. There isn't a television set down there that isn't switched on.' Pope John died on June the third as Cardinal Traglia offered Mass in the open in St Peter's Square, where tens of thousands had gathered, keeping watch, 'and millions beyond them,' as Abbess Catherine told the community when they were brought together by the tolling of the bell. Once more the yellow and white flag flew at half mast from the tower. The Pope had drawn his last breath – it might have been a sigh of satisfaction – as the words came from the Square, 'Ite, Missa est. Go, the Mass is ended.'

A reign of five short years – 'an interim pope' – yet a world of upheaval. Under Pope Paul the Council went on.

The wheel of the year seemed, for Philippa, to have turned faster since her Solemn Profession. 'Well, I have been so busy.' 'You have been at Brede eight years,' Dame Domitilla had told her when the Council first assembled. 'Eight years and ten months. How time flies,' but eight years, or nine, then ten into eleven, to Philippa it seemed a lifetime. 'Perhaps all of my life that matters.' She felt fixed, firmly attached to Brede ways; then how firmly attached must be nuns of forty, fifty, sixty or more years' standing? Changes had been on the way even in the last years of Abbess Hester, but she had stood against them, distrusted them. It had fallen to Abbess Catherine to be plunged into their midst. 'This is where we learn what obedience is,' she said.

The Abbesses of every house in the English Benedictine Congregation were called together to discuss changes in the future of claustral sisters. 'About time too,' Sister Louise, another leader of the hotheads had said. 'We should be done away with.'

'Why? Aren't we valuable?' asked Hilary.

'You know I didn't mean that; I mean the name; the distinction.'

'There is a distinction.'

'Yes. We should all be equal,' contended Sister Louise.

'But we're not.'

'Those times are past. We are all educated now.'

'Huh!' Hilary had said it almost rudely. 'Most of us *could* pass an ordinary examination if we were pushed and coached, but a choir nun has to have exceptional qualifications before she can even begin. I don't know about you,' said Hilary to Sister Louise, 'but I can't equal Sister Cecily's music, let alone Dame Perpetua's, Dame Monica's or Dame Maura's, or have Dame Scholastica's brain or Sister Polycarp's, or even understand most of the arguments in chapter. If we were allowed a seat there, we should probably leap to conclusions, because we haven't enough balance – or ballast if you like – to keep us steady, enough knowledge of the world, of history, theology, philosophy. We can't make wise decisions. To say otherwise is pretence,' said Hilary. 'It's using politeness instead of truth.' They had all listened with amazement to this long speech from Hilary, but for all Hilary's sense and Dame Agnes's endorsement, 'Yes, we want quality, not quantity,' the old order was being shaken out of its ways. 'Never before.' Those two words were becoming familiar at Brede. Never before in the Abbey have we done this: had that: seen this: been that. 'It's since Pope John,' said the nuns, or 'since Lady Abbess Catherine took the reins.'

'Since she was elected,' said Dame Paula, 'Brede Abbey's scope seems to have become twice as large.' As first of the leaders of the progressive nuns she was gratified. 'Twice as large!'

'Which makes it twice as hard to keep it monastic.' To Dame Agnes it was more necessary than ever to be on the alert. 'Be watchful and vigilant, for thine enemy the devil goeth about seeking whom he may devour,' she could have said. 'It's changes, changes, nothing but changes,' she mourned. 'It's the climate of the world,' Dame Paula assured her. Pope John had announced, 'We are going to shake off the dust that has collected on the throne of St Peter since the time of Constantine, let in fresh air,' and the chill of fresh air, blowing in a closed atmosphere, is always painful; new ideas, new thoughts, new changes were blowing through the monastery, not a fresh breeze as perhaps Pope John had intended, but in gusts, damaging storms.

'Nothing will ever be the same,' said Dame Ursula.

'It's not meant to be,' said Dame Paula.

'It will all settle down,' Abbess Catherine remained calm

and, 'at least the apathy, the contented torpor, has gone; Mark says you see it in the churches.'

'That's the vernacular,' cried Paula with enthusiasm.

'Vernacular.' The word, to Dame Agnes, was flaming red as hell fire. 'I'm glad they call it "vernacular". It's not even English,' and, 'Where is our universal Church?' she demanded. 'Once upon a time, from the north pole to the south, in either hemisphere, you would have found the Mass the same, and could join in and worship in it; now we are split into divisions,' said Dame Agnes. 'If you,' she told those – to her – insular ignoramuses, Sister Polycarp and Sister Michael, 'went to Mass in Venice, Delhi, Istanbul, you wouldn't understand a word.'

'But ... we want to pray in our own language.'

'Pray in it then, but privately. Keep it for private prayer, but the Mass and the Opus Dei are *liturgy*.'

'And even I,' said Dame Perpetua, 'can understand that Latin.'

'People can still be educated surely?' Dame Veronica, as the new scholarly translator of Rufinus, was on the side of Dame Agnes.

'And the English won't *fit*!' Cecily, now Dame Cecily, was one of the few among the younger nuns who wanted the old ways, but then she understood and was devoted to the chant with its cadences and melodies bound so closely with the words; now under Dame Monica – who was holding office as precentrix until Dame Maura came back – Cecily had to do what went sorely against the grain – 'and against all sense,' she and Dame Monica said despairingly – arrange English words to music meant for Latin. They were translating a version for Sister Polycarp's Solemn Profession. 'Solemn Profession in *English*!' Some of the nuns rejoiced, but at least half recoiled.

'Veni,' said harassed Cecily. 'The Bishop has to sing that three times and melodies have *notes*. "Veni" is sung on four; how can "come" be spun out to that – "Come ... c-om-mm-me", it sounds ridiculous. It's laughable.'

'Try "come on, come on", like a view hulloa,' suggested Hilary.

'When Dame Maura hears this she will weep,' said Cecily.

Almost everyone in the house though endorsed Abbess Catherine's desire for simplicity – 'If it's not taken too far,' cautioned Dame Agnes. 'We must think of the meaning of some of our ways.' The deep bows when they met the Abbess, bows now questioned by followers of Pope John's bonhomie, were not 'just for Lady Abbess, but for our Lord whom we see in her. Which is why we kneel to speak to her.' But they were all glad when Abbess Catherine did away with the kisses, 'and often those who want to kiss my hand are not the most obedient'. As Julian long ago had wanted, many of the nuns wanted the simplicity to be humble; 'Why not a wooden paten, and earthenware chalice?' they asked, and, 'Tiens!' said Dame Colette, 'the gold and silver is for the Seigneur, not for us,' and, 'Muddled thinking, muddled thinking,' said Dame Agnes, as one cherished tradition after another was felled by popular vote. Soon many of the nuns were asking in anguish, 'Does any good ever come out of a Council?'

'So much,' said some, 'is slipping away – being lost.' 'So much,' said others, 'is coming in.' 'I wish I could share with you,' wrote Dom Gervase, now a schoolteacher again, 'share the joy I felt in celebrating Mass with sixty-four of our boys when we were in camp in Switzerland at St Maurice in the Valais. There was not room in the tiny village chapel so, as it was fine, we had a table outside and now I understand once for all what the cardinals were about. As I faced them, the boys, still as mice, gathered united round a table at a banquet and a sacrifice. I rejoiced at the new simplicity, all those kisses and crossings and bowings done away with, and I loved the consecration which all could see and hear, and the prayers which all could join in and understand.'

'Humph!' said Dame Agnes and, 'are children nowadays so much less intelligent than their parents?' But she could not fault the truth and spirit of the letter.

'Everything must be challenged,' cried the enthusiasts.

'Challenged doesn't mean abolished.'

Most of the older nuns tried to act as a balance; they knew more of philosophy, of history, of the value of the Rule, but to the younger go-aheads they seemed to drag. 'You are thinking B.C.' was the cry, not meaning 'before Christ', but 'before the Council'. 'It's almost mob thinking,' said Dame Beatrice.

'It isn't thinking at all,' said Dame Agnes.

Some of the monks at Udimore were trying to persuade Abbot Bernard to have a factory in the monastery, 'though why a factory is more in keeping with the times than a farm, I do not know,' he said wearily to Abbess Catherine. 'It isn't as if we were quaintly antiquated, we use up-to-date machinery.'

Abbess Catherine laughed. 'We have a new electric printing machine, typewriters not quill pens, tape-recorders, a washing machine, and it's not enough,' but Abbot Bernard did not smile. 'They want to shorten the Office, run the Hours together, to leave more time for practical work.'

'So do some of mine,' said Abbess Catherine.

'Contemplatives want to do the work of active Orders, the active Orders of lay people,' said Abbot Bernard.

'Perhaps the lay people will turn to contemplation,' said Abbess Catherine.

'Then they will need the very grilles your progressives are seeking to take down; renew the solitude and silence, the prayer we are letting decay with all this busy-ness. They should read the Rule – and the Council documents that tell us to go back to our sources – but it seems they cannot read any more, not with their minds.'

'Yes. They have forgotten the meaning of things,' said Dame Agnes.

Brede, according to the new recommendations, had modified its habit; skirts were clear of the ground now, some of the fullness taken out, there were more sensible underclothes, 'praise be,' said the nuns; no petticoats, only one plain black underskirt; a few of the younger nuns extolled the new dress of some of the visiting nuns; suits, plain dresses, cardigans – 'Ugh!' said Philippa, 'no grown woman should wear a cardigan.'

'We want to look like anybody else,' said Dame Paula.

'Why?' asked Philippa, 'when you are a nun.'

394

'Why shouldn't nuns be in the fashion?'

'You think you would be in the fashion? It changes more quickly than you would know. Shorten your skirts and next year you will need to make them long again, and where is our poverty? Our habits that last us fifteen years?'

'Do away with the wimple.' 'Perhaps the most becoming wear ever invented for women,' as elegant Dame Colette used to say. 'Grow and show our hair.' 'Which you cannot dress properly,' said Dame Agnes. 'How do these new nuns look? Dowdy and blowsy, like Edwardian nurses.'

'We could learn hairdressing.'

'You haven't time to say your Office, yet you have time to wave and set your hair. Queer kind of nuns!' And, 'Poor lambs!' said Lady Seaton, seeing a pair of visiting sisters come out of the Abbey front door in a high wind, trying with one hand to clutch their veils over untidy hair and keep their skirts down with the other, while Sister Renata in her wimple and long skirt stood unruffled on the doorstep talking to them.

'But it is deeper than looks or even convenience.' Dame Agnes was deeply troubled. 'The habit, the veil, our cut hair under the cap, are meant for self-effacement – we need to be free of the preoccupations that plague other women, preoccupations with self – which was precisely why we did away with these time-consuming frills!'

Abbesses of some houses firmly kept the changes out; they had examined the ways of their house, they said, and found them good. Others cast away tradition, 'right and left,' as Dame Agnes said.

'I have fought,' she said bitterly to Abbess Catherine, 'to keep danger from this house. Sister Julian and her ideas, Dame Philippa and hers. Am I to be defeated now by these Paulas and Louises, Michaels and Polycarps?'

'Not by them,' Abbess Catherine could have said, 'by time.' Instead of which, she put her arms round Dame Agnes and hugged her close. 'It's very hard for you,' she said.

Abbess Catherine tried to steer a middle course; 'Let it bubble up, come out, rather than ferment; something will

395

emerge,' she said, though the perpetual 'Why?' 'Why?' of both sides buzzed in her ears. There was hardly a nun who did not give her opinion, 'required or not required,' the Abbess could have said wryly.

'Why didn't God make us all Catholics? Then there wouldn't be all this upsetting talk about unity,' said Sister Priscilla who liked things plain and settled.

'We were all Catholics once,' and Sister Louise, who had 'done' the Tudors at school, explained about Henry VIII and the Reformation.

'Ah, if there's a judy in the case, a man can make himself believe anything,' said Sister Priscilla.

'The Church has got blood poisoning,' said Dame Perpetua, 'and I think because it has lost the disinfectant of the Creed.' The Creed, touchstone and measure of the Faith, was only said now at Mass on Sundays and on important feast days. 'We used to say it every day – and we need it. If we had it, had to keep to it, there couldn't be all the defections, and the small things wouldn't matter.'

The old content and peace was gone but, 'There has to be upset,' said Abbess Catherine and, trying to hearten the troubled nuns, reminded them of the pool of Bethsaida. 'The angel came down and troubled the waters and the people were healed.' But would they be? She did not know and sometimes at the end of a long day, listening, considering, reconsidering, making or not making changes – 'I don't know how Mother *can*,' or, 'I don't know why Mother *can't*' – Abbess Catherine would find herself riven – tattered, she thought, would be a better word – and then she would go, under cover of the dark, to where she had found Philippa that long-ago night, to the pleached alley where she could see the Abbey with its lights. From here it looked peaceful and, as always, like Dame Clare's great ship riding the night, its tower high above the church and Abbess Catherine thought of its dedication those centuries ago. That very morning she had been able to tell the nuns of a new dedication. 'Here, in the seaside town that has grown up round Brede,' she had said as she gave the news to the community. 'People say the Church is shaken, but this new growth is going steadily on. In our diocese alone there have been eleven new churches built in the last twenty years. This one, of St Peter the Fisherman, at Brede Bay, so near to us, was dedicated last Friday, and since so few of you have witnessed a dedication, I thought you might like Dame Agnes to tell us about it.'

'The dedication of a church is the most important of all our rites,' said Dame Agnes. 'A ceremony so full of beauty and meaning that I pray *it* won't be robbed' – she could not forbear saying that, but, 'Go on please, Dame,' said Abbess Catherine.

'The consecration puts the whole building, the roof, walls and the spaces between them into a state of holiness. People often say they can feel the atmosphere in a church; so they should; it is, as the lesson from the dedication Mass tells us, "God's tent pitched here on earth".

'Before its consecration the church is locked, empty; it stays locked while the bishop circles it three times, three for the Blessed Trinity; only then is the door opened and he, representative of our Lord, signs it with his cross. "Veni Creator" is sung, the invocation of the Holy Spirit who unfolds all mysteries to us; Greek and Latin letters are traced in ashes on the floor by the bishop's staff, ashes for the humility needed to accept the teaching to be given here. The altar, the symbol of Christ, is signed in five places for his five wounds with the Gregorian water which holds ashes for death, salt for resurrection, wine for Christ; then the whole church is sprinkled. Relics are brought, representing the members of Christ, and are enshrined and sealed with chrism in a hollow in the altar and altar stone, then the whole altar is covered with the oils, signifying the anointing: the fire of the Holy Spirit, charity, is lit on it, four piles of incense burnt at the corners.

'Twelve crosses with candles are anointed too and put on the walls; twelve for the twelve apostles; those crosses are the sign of a consecrated church. It is now the expression of all the mysteries which make the essence of the Church militant, God's vast temple on earth and, too, the vision of the Church triumphant, which is eternal,' said Dame Agnes.

'Eternal,' and, walking in the dark, Abbess Catherine thought of that: eternal, militant but imperturbable: 'Upon this rock I shall build my church and the gates of hell shall not prevail against it.'

19

'Julia Yoko Sama.'
  'Grace Mariko Sama.'
  'Susanna Sumi.'
  'Colette Kazuko Sama.'
  'Sama', it had been decided, was the Japanese equivalent of Dame.

There had not been such an unusual Solemn Profession at Brede, 'nor in any other Benedictine house,' as Abbess Catherine said, addressing the community in Chapter. The Bishop of the province of Nagano had flown from Tokyo to act as master of ceremonies for the Cardinal, with Brede's own bishop assisting. Abbot Bernard was there with Thomas Miko, now a fully professed monk and on the way to being ordained priest. 'Then, one day, perhaps, he shall become our Chaplain,' said Mr Konishi. The matrons of honour had flown too from Japan; Yoko had her sister and brother-in-law and, at Mr Konishi's expense, the Tanakas, parents of Sumi, were there – 'I myself will bring them,' Mr Konishi had said. As for Mariko, she had cousins – 'Some may join, I think' – uncles, aunts, two godmothers. Kazuko did not want anyone: 'My mother now is Dame Colette,' said Kazuko, but there seemed a swarm of people and the town, as well as the Abbey, was electrified at the sudden invasion of Japanese gentlemen in morning coats, grey waistcoats, striped trousers and Japanese ladies in full ceremonial dress. Newspapers reported, photographs were taken – but not of the new nuns except Yoko. 'As she is the most accustomed she can pose,' suggested Mr Konishi. The others saw only their relations and spent the day in recollected quietness until the Cardinal, walking with the Abbess across the garth, came to visit them, when each bent herself double to kiss his ring and, sitting Japanese fashion on their heels round him on the floor, heads bent, hands folded, listened to him as he talked.

They were going now from Dame Clare's jurisdiction to their places in the community, where for another few years they would live and pray and work as fully professed nuns – 'disappear among us,' said Abbess Catherine – 'and then we shall see what develops.' Mr Konishi had already bought a site on which to build a possible house. 'The garden – so important – is already growing,' he said. 'The water lilies were exquisite this year. It only awaits . . .' Mr Konishi was still exhilarated from the great day. 'Why not let us start the house at once?'

'Don't be impatient,' Abbess Catherine pleaded. 'This is only the beginning. More postulants must come. I'm sure they will – in time. Don't be impatient.'

'I cannot help but be.'

'You are letting your garden mature. Let ours.'

'Madam Abbess, you know just how to catch me,' said Mr Konishi.

'There are no ambitions for me now,' Cecily wrote to Dame Maura, 'only to go on here.'

Cecily had started writing to Dame Maura two years ago. 'Her own idea,' wrote Abbess Catherine, 'not my suggestion,' but it had been the Abbess's suggestion over writing to Larry that had sparked these letters off. Dame Maura had written back and slowly, as the exchange grew more familiar, the old and rich relationship came back. 'I am helping Dame Monica in the choir until you come,' wrote Cecily. 'How we are looking forward to that.'

Larry Bannerman had married Cecily's cousin Jean. Mrs Scallon had come to Brede especially to break the news to Cecily. 'I knew it would happen. I told Elspeth so. I thought at least she would feel a pang.'

'And didn't she?' asked Abbess Catherine.

'No,' said Mrs Scallon crossly, 'she looked . . . irradiated.

It beats me!' said Mrs Scallon, and Abbess Catherine felt that perhaps at last it had.

'But how could I look sad?' asked Cecily when the Abbess told her. 'I was glad – glad! Jean has loved Larry for years and I feel as if a piece of lead had gone out of my heart. Now I can give it all.'

For her now there was nothing exciting and dramatic. 'Dame Cecily is one of the quietest of the nuns – except in choir,' wrote the Abbess to Dame Maura, 'where her voice seems to grow stronger and purer.' Her day was the same as that of all the nuns and, 'There isn't much leisure,' wrote Cecily. 'What there is must go in organ practice – I am working at Paul de Maleingreau's "Élévations Liturgiques" – but there isn't any boredom and, thank God, nowadays no ecstasy.' Cecily could laugh now at that starry-eyed young visionary and, *What* price ecstasy, she thought, as Hilary might have said, when you can have love.

Dame Maura came home in the late afternoon of the first Sunday of Advent when the nuns were in choir. Dame Domitilla was waiting at the enclosure door to greet her and let her in. 'You are just in time for Benediction,' she whispered after a welcoming kiss. Dame Maura put down her cloak and bag and the two nuns walked the length of the long cloister where dusk was lying across the garth and the lit church windows shone out red and blue and gold. 'Home,' whispered Dame Maura and squeezed Dame Domitilla's hand, 'Home at last!' They knelt in the ante-chapel as the choir began the Rorate Coeli. A solo voice rose and Dame Maura stiffened; it was Cecily's. '*Drop down dew, ye heavens, from above ... and let the clouds rain the Just One.*' The haunting plaintiveness filled the church, beautifully controlled as the choir took up the melody. Dame Maura lifted her face, an older face now, marked by loneliness and suffering – it had not been easy in Canada so far away; but Canada, its pains and turmoils, was forgotten now. The voice singing the verse was pleading, in the words of Isaiah, pleading with God; it was the voice of ancient Israel awaiting the coming Messiah, of a young mother waiting for the Child who was to be the saviour of the world, the voice of the whole Church crying aloud for the coming of the Lord in glory at the end of time. Then the refrain came again, *'Drop down dew, ye heavens, from above . . .'*

Dame Maura was listening, herself forgotten too. In the last verse Cecily's voice rose in the full sweep of an octave – a crescendo of trust and assurance – and with what power, thought Dame Maura, thrilling. *'I will save thee, fear not, for I am the Lord thy God, the Holy One of Israel, thy redeemer.'*

It was Cecily's voice unmistakably, but not the voice of the girl, Sister Cecily; she was Dame Cecily now, thirty-four years old, and there was no trace of that undertone of anxiety, the subtle asking for affection, pathos that had wrung Dame Maura's heart; no wanting human approval, no conscious art. It was selfless, pure, and Dame Maura could listen to it coolly, yet filled with an immense joy. She closed her eyes and the song seemed to well up from her own soul in thankfulness. *'I will save thee, fear not . . .'* and, *'Drop down dew, ye heavens, from above . . .'*

20

On the eve of Corpus Christi, a warm June night, Philippa was leaning on the sill of the window in the passage outside the infirmary, waiting for Dame Emily Lovell to die.

The water lilies in Mr Konishi's garden had to bloom three more times before Abbess Catherine had judged that the 'samas', as the Japanese choir nuns were called, and little Sister Sumi, were in no more need of Dame Philippa's especial guidance in the community, her unremitting care. 'I don't know what office I haven't helped to hold, in these last years,' she wrote to McTurk. 'Did you ever think I could be a washerwoman? Helping Sister Sumi in her work in the laundry as aid to Sister Xaviera, I have become quite a good one. They are teaching me to iron, too. Maggie would be proud of me. From these I go to show Kazuko her work in the sacristy and then to interpret musical terms for Mariko. Perhaps one day she will be precentrix at Suwa.'

Now another two years had passed and 'perhaps' had become a certainty; the Japanese foundation was no longer a hope, a vision, but a fact. The house at Suwa was ready, in its park and gardens above the lake, and in sight of the peak Kirigamine. 'You can truly lift up your eyes unto the hills,' said Mr Konishi.

Father Vincent's letters endorsed this. 'Your nuns will be pleased,' he wrote to the Abbess. 'Mr Konishi is truly an artist. The house, really a pavilion or series of pavilions, is of wood and paper, Japanese style, roofed with old dark tiles and set among gardens that are an extension of the house because the walls slide back so that the rooms are open. The gardens, in their turn, have vistas to the enclosure park which opens into another park for the public, that is a sanctuary of birds, flowers and silence.

'Don't worry about too much luxury; the rooms have a simplicity that is truly monastic. There are rows of small cells, each with matting on the floor and each with its small niche or shrine, arranged with flowers below a crucifix. I wish I could convey to you the loving care he has given. For your nuns, there will be beds; the Japanese will have their quilts and pillows which are folded up in the daytime; and for each, there is a little writing desk without legs that stands on the floor; no prie-dieu because they will use a cushion for kneeling. Instead of bells, there are gongs, made of bronze with different deep tones; they seem to fit the house. They are the gift of Julia Yoko Sama's sister.'

The little contingent was due to leave Brede at the end of this very month, on the twenty-seventh of June. 'The lilies will be in flower,' said Mr Konishi joyfully.

As it was only five years – 'Instead of the ten or fifteen we had visualized,' said Abbess Catherine – since the Japanese nuns' Solemn Profession, Dame Colette Aubadon had accepted the appointment of prioress – it would be several years before the foundation could qualify as an Abbey. Julia Yoko Sama was subprioress; 'Until she is really ready to lead,' said Abbess Catherine. 'Which may not be for ten, or even twenty years,' said Dame Colette. Every day she had to blink back tears at the thought of leaving Brede, and not only Brede, leaving her church work-room to Dame Anselma. 'In twenty years I shall be old,' said Dame Colette. 'You will not only be prioress,' Abbess Catherine reminded her. 'You will help Kazuko as mistress of church work and Kazuko is very much your daughter.' Mariko would be precentrix – 'though samisen is not right training for the choir'– but she would have Dame Monica to help and guide her. Dame Bridget was to be cellarer, with Sumi as her second, and Sumi would also run the kitchen with Sister Xaviera. Dame Scholastica was appointed sacristan and the novice mistress would be Dame Sophie, Yoko sharing the duties; two more postulants had come to Brede, were now juniors and would go with the others; more postulants were waiting at Suwa. Tickets had been booked on a Japanese air line, and Mr Konishi and Thomas Miko would act as escorts, while boxes of books, vestments, altar and chapter house furnishings had gone ahead by sea. Everything was ready for the twenty-seventh, feast of our Lady of Perpetual Succour, which was to be the title of the new house, though Mr Konishi called it 'Megumi-no-Sono, Garden of Grace'. Pope Paul had sent his blessing.

It all seemed scarcely to concern Philippa; just as, before the Japanese had come, she had been shut away in the choir, so now she was fast in the world of the infirmary. 'I! Imagine me!' she had written to McTurk.

When Abbess Catherine had officially released her from her Japanese charges, Philippa had climbed the tower stairs and stood there at the parapet, taking a new breath. I can go back to my own life, she had thought, with gratitude and content. 'I can abrogate responsibility,' she said as she had said before. Perhaps, too, she had thought unconsciously that there should be some sort of easement or reward. It had been the shock of shocks, when the Distribution of Offices came round, to find herself named infirmarian.

'*Infirmarian!* I! I!' She could not believe it. 'Besides, how can anyone imagine the infirmary without Dame Joan?'

'Exactly,' said the Abbess. 'It's time somebody did. Dame Joan has done a long hard term. She deserves a change.'

'Mother, I ... I know nothing about ill people.' Philippa had been incoherent with dismay. 'I have only one instinct with anyone ill and that is to run in the opposite direction,' but Abbess Catherine had not shown a jot of sympathy. 'Then this will be a new experience for you,' she said, and, 'no work can give you more closeness with and experience of the community; with your long time with the Japanese you have been specialized too long.'

'But *Mother*! Think of the poor patients,' Philippa pleaded but Abbess Catherine had ignored that. 'Go to Mother Prioress, she will tell you what you have to do,' and Philippa was dismissed.

Dame Beatrice had been more comforting. 'You have a good second in Dame Nichola, and Sister Mary is a tower of strength. You will do very well – you will see,' and Philippa had had to suppress a grimace.

She was used to it now, after two years, and the Abbess had been right; no work could have brought her closer to the community; nuns whom she had scarcely spoken to had become almost intimate. 'You really know someone when you have helped her through a spell of frightening asthma, attacks of vomiting, inflicted pain on her by hot-poulticing a virulent abscess. One thing I have learned,' Philippa told the Abbess, 'and that is how fastidious I was, how I guarded myself as if *I* were precious.' She had flinched from much of it, often felt impatient, but never with Dame Emily Lovell; to tend her was a privilege. No one had expected Dame Emily to live so long. Dame Frances Anne had died the autumn before and, a more personal grief for the Abbess, Sister Ellen, at the age of ninety-seven; 'I can never see a polished floor without thinking of her.' Abbess Catherine had been tempted to take Sister Hilary in her place – it would have been good to have Hilary so near her – but again, 'No favouritism,' the Abbess told herself and Sister Dorothy had been appointed to look after the Abbess's rooms. 'I must never show what I feel for anyone to anyone,' Abbess Catherine still told herself that.

Those old ones were gone, but Dame Emily lingered, though she was dying by inches and, when Philippa and Sister Mary, who specialized in looking after the old and very ill, lifted the emaciated body to ease her position, wash her, or change the sheets, Philippa could not put enough of tenderness and strength into it. 'If only I had a touch like yours,' she told Sister Mary. 'I so hate to hurt her but am afraid I do.' The last week had been one of great suffering, but there had not been a murmur of self-pity or complaint. Now Dame Emily was mercifully not conscious but in a world of her own; her hands moved over the counterpane, doing some remembered work or her lips made soundless words and she smiled, lingering over some movement, some work or prayer made long ago; this was the third night, but for all the hours of vigil, waiting, wiping away the sweat, cleansing and changing, Philippa would not have hurried her. 'We will let her take her time,' said Doctor Avery, putting away his needle. There was no need of morphia now, and Philippa was thankful. 'Something very wonderful is happening here,' she had said.

Dame Emily's pulse and breathing had not changed for the last hour and Philippa had come out of her cell for a moment's cool and air by the window.

She remembered the night of vigil for Penny. Philippa had taken part in many night vigils since then and was used now to lying down and going to sleep almost at any time, to getting up lightly, wide awake. She was wide awake now.

The window looked out on to the garth. Though the cloisters were built all round it, the garth did not seem shut in, but looked spacious with its lawn and rose beds making a circle round the pool where Abbess Hester's fountain, as the nuns called it, restored now, was gently splashing as it fell over the edge of the fountain basin to the pool below.

The moon was so bright that the roses showed in the ghostly soft colours in its light. Philippa could hear when Dame Emily's shallow breathing changed to stertorous; there was no other sound but that and the water falling, but the world seemed to be filled with expectancy of something ... tremendous, thought Philippa, something just out of sight waiting for Dame Emily. Philippa felt the promise, 'Eye hath not seen, nor ear heard, neither hath it entered into the heart of man, what things God hath prepared for them that love Him' was, in a few minutes? Hours? A day? to be fulfilled. All around was waiting, expectancy – and longing. If only I could go with her, thought Philippa this moonlit night, but as clearly as if a voice had told her, Philippa knew the expectancy was for Dame Emily – 'and not for me.'

Like Philippa, Dame Emily had been a convert. 'When I was eighteen, a high-headed proud young girl,' she had told Philippa, 'we were on holiday in Folkestone and on a rainy day when I was bored, having nothing particular to do, I wandered into a church to listen to the music. For me it might have been any church – I knew nothing of the denominations then – but it was Catholic. The time was the octave of Corpus Christi and I heard the priest preach on the Real Presence: 'This is My body,' and I thought, 'If this is true . . . the rest followed,' said Dame Emily.

It was Corpus Christi now, the Quarant Ore, forty hours of Exposition of the Blessed Sacrament that, at Brede, always marked the feast. How fitting, thought Philippa, if Dame Emily died today. It would soon be daybreak; the first cocks were crowing as Sister Mary came to relieve Dame Philippa who went straight to the choir for her hour of 'watch'. She took the thought of Dame Emily, of that expectancy, with her and, as she came into the choir, felt too the intensity, life lived at its very core, which always seemed to mark the Quarant Ore. As four o'clock struck she took her place on one of the two prie-dieux; Dame Veronica was on the other.

Bowls of flowers surrounded the high altar; the candles made points of flame above them and, in the centre, the disc of the white Host was enthroned in the glittering monstrance. Was it fancy because she was so tired, thought Philippa, a mere illusion, or was the Host penetrated by a light of its own? A kind of window through which, had she the eyes, she could have looked straight into heaven; but it's only the dying, or the very holy, who have the eyes like that, she thought.

At twenty minutes past four, with a rustling, then a chirp, one or two notes, a bird-scale, the dawn chorus in the garden began, the birds singing their own Lauds outside and suddenly, through the open window, hurling themselves in an ecstasy of joy at the dawn of another day, came two martlets, sweeping, gliding, soaring, twittering. Dame Veronica and Philippa both half rose, thinking the skimming and circling might knock over a candle, but the loops were perfectly timed in a mastery of soaring and gliding. For a brief moment the two nuns looked at one another and, for once, thought Philippa, she was able to equal Dame Veronica's smile of rapture; it seemed exactly right to both of them that, at this early hour, the court of the Lord should be tongues of flame, the lustre of pink poppies, two blue-black birds gashed with colour, and two nuns kneeling in silent adoration. Then the martlets were gone through the window into the day.

The soul of St Scholastica, St Benedict's sister, was said to have left her body as a white dove. Could Dame Emily's be a martlet? thought Philippa – she was getting fanciful, probably from lack of sleep – but a martlet suited Dame Emily, fearless, so swift once she had come to believe – from the time of hearing that sermon to her entry at Brede had been only two years, the minimum time needed. 'Life in Christ is no trick of the imagination,' she had often said, 'but solid theological fact.' She had been so sure in the glidings and loops she had made round the difficulties with Abbess Hester and, as the martlets had made their way among the candles without scorching a feather, so she had kept her soul unscathed through the long illness, operations and pain. Yes, Dame Emily was like a martlet, thought Philippa – but why two?

The last antiphon had just been given out by Abbess Catherine when Dame Domitilla appeared in the choir, waited until the words were finished and beckoned the Abbess out. The nuns took no particular notice – the portress was a stickler for taking every trifle to the Abbess herself – and the Office went smoothly on through the psalms, verse answering verse. A few moments later the passing bell began to ring – then, they thought, it is Dame Emily after all. The high note seemed more than ever like an agitation; then the deep note of the death bell rang, a minute between each knell.

Philippa had risen and slipped out of her stall, but at the entrance she met Abbess Catherine, come back and standing just inside the door. She put out a hand and stopped Philippa. The hand was cold and held Philippa's tightly.

Abbess Catherine looked tired, white – and shocked. One by one, quick glances divined that. Shocked? Why should she be shocked? All that week they had expected Dame Emily to die at any moment but Abbess Catherine was clearly thrown off balance and a stir went through the community as they sang: something has happened ... something, not Dame Emily.

The Office went steadily on but everyone was conscious of the Abbess's still figure in the doorway.

At the end of Prime she turned and, as the nuns came out, led them into the cloister. There, in the sunny early morning beauty of this June feast day, she spoke – was hardly able to speak, thought the community. 'Sisters ... I have news for you, sad news, that will shock you as much as it has shocked me.' Her voice broke for a moment then she went on: 'While we were in choir our sister, Dear Dame Colette, died in the infirmary, died in a matter of minutes ... our dear Dame Colette.'

It had happened so quickly and quietly that even Dame Nichola and Sister Mary who had been in the room with her, had not seen. 'I couldn't believe it,' said Dame Nichola. 'I cannot believe it now.'

'Nor I,' said Abbess Catherine. 'Dame Colette had been with me the evening before, talking over details for Suwa. She seemed perfectly well,' but when the caller knocked at the cell door that morning, Dame Colette had told her she felt ill. 'Her voice sounded odd. She asked me to fetch someone from the infirmary.' It was Dame Nichola who went. 'Sister Mary had just come on duty and I left her with Dame Emily. I asked what was the matter,' said Dame Nichola. 'Dame Colette said she had a pain; she thought it was bad indigestion as she had such heartburn. "It must have been those tomatoes we had for supper. They were a little hard." Indigestion and heartburn did not seem to me serious.' Dame Nichola was in tears. 'So I asked her to come to the infirmary where I would mix her a dose. If only I had looked at her,' said Dame Nichola. 'I should have seen how grey and drawn she was. Sister Mary and I both saw when she came in to the infirmary – she must have dragged herself there because it was a little time, but I thought she was dressing. We helped her to a chair and I turned to get the dose while Sister Mary got a bed ready. Then ...' and Dame Nichola's tears really came now, 'there was a sound like a sigh, sort of ... giving-out of breath and Dame Colette slid to the floor.' It must, said Doctor Avery, have been a coronary thrombosis. Dame Colette was dead.

Dame Emily – the first martlet, thought Philippa, died at noon without giving time to call the Abbess, slipping away so quietly that Philippa, who was watching, could not tell when she drew her last breath.

'I do not understand,' said Mr Konishi. 'I ... do ... not ... understand,' and he struck his fist into his palm in despair.

He was staying in the town and had come at once when the news was broken to him by Sister Renata.

'It is hard for you to understand,' said Abbess Catherine, 'but try. Be patient, and trust us.'

'Madam Abbess, there is not time to trust. You know the position. Dame Bridget is good, very good, but she is not a leader. Nor is Dame Monica. Dame Sophie is young. Julia Yoko Matsudaira is making wonderful headway but has short experience.' It was the first time Abbess Catherine had seen Mr Konishi neither cheerful nor imperturbable; even his paintbrush moustache seemed stiff with dismay and he made that gesture of angry frustration, striking his fist into his palm. It was not from the shock of Dame Colette's death – 'In religion one must subtract oneself and not give way to grief,' he had said. The frustration and perplexity were caused by Abbess Catherine's, to him, extraordinary attitude.

'But you are Abbess. You can command.'

'Not this,' said Abbess Catherine. 'Even an Abbess has no power to order this. Every nun here, Mr Konishi, has the right to live and end her days in her own house, as your professed nuns will have at Suwa.'

'But what shall we *do*?' Mr Konishi said it in agony. 'Time is so close. What will *you* do?'

'The need is known.' Abbess Catherine was calm. 'There will be results.'

'Are you sure?'

'I am sure,' said Abbess Catherine.

With Sister Mary and Dame Agnes, Philippa had been too busy that morning for any moments of thought; even when they came to lay out Dame Colette, the implications of her death

411

had not dawned, though Philippa noticed Dame Agnes looking at her, Philippa, shrewdly once or twice; but when, after a hasty late dinner, she came out into the garth though recreation was nearly over, she found the Japanese nuns waiting for her. They made such a frightened, small huddle of pathos that Philippa instinctively opened her arms and they ran to her like children; Kazuko, she could see, was almost beside herself and, holding her close, letting Sumi cling to her other arm, Philippa talked to them calmly, reassuringly, tenderly as had become Dame Philippa's way, and in their own language. Slowly, under her familiar voice, the tension relaxed until, looking up over Kazuko's head, Philippa saw the Abbess.

Abbess Catherine had come out from the cloister and was watching with such open approval that, suddenly, Philippa was warned. She felt a chill as if a cloud had come across the sun; she took her arm from around Kazuko, loosed Sumi's hold and, 'It isn't possible,' she breathed. It was the barest whisper but it seemed to split the Abbey apart, from garth to tower. Philippa felt her knees giving way; the grass seemed to rise and hit her between the eyes and she was dizzy. Then she felt two hands take her shoulders and turn her, while holding her up. 'Dame Philippa is very tired.' It was Abbess Catherine's voice. 'She has had Dame Emily's death as well as dear Dame Colette's. We must let her sit down,' and Philippa was steered into the quiet of the long cloister to a sun-warmed stone seat of one of the embrasures. Then Abbess Catherine mercifully took the Japanese nuns away.

The cloister was in sun, the afternoon almost stiflingly hot, yet Philippa shivered. Still dizzy, she shut her eyes and, curiously on this glorious still day, she seemed to hear seagulls in gusts of wind around the tower, mourning her, seeking her, wailing – a foreboding, thought Philippa; she remembered how she had heard them that long-ago day when she was left in the choir to wait for news of her Simple Profession. Odd, I never seriously visualized leaving Brede, she had thought then. 'How much less now. How much less now.' She whispered that aloud; the words seemed to hit the old stone walls and come back to her.

She did not need to be told what would await her as Superior at Suwa – she knew, without dissembling, it would have to be as Superior. She had seen enough of Abbess Catherine's lot at Brede, yet Brede was long established, with a pattern for everything, and a legion of strong, well-schooled nuns to help. Suwa would be different, as every Benedictine house was different, having to make its own way, find its particular flavour, but in strange surroundings: though I do know a little of Japan, thought Philippa, I am still a foreigner. There would be a thousand difficulties, big or petty, to encounter and counter – things that neither Mr Konishi, nor Father Vincent, could help her with, or even know. Can I be patient and wise enough, she asked? At that her gorge rose – or almost rose. Everything she had counted on at Brede would be gone, the peace, the anonymity, the shield of Abbess Catherine, the friendships – and the fun, thought Philippa. It had been bad enough for Dame Colette to have to go – 'but she had had decades of Brede, while I, so pitifully little,' whispered Philippa.

Self-pity would not help, but she could have a moment's private rebellion. The gulls around the tower. She saw herself standing at the parapet, gazing out to the silver line of sea. 'I shall never see the sea again.' Fool! thought Philippa now. Fool to say 'never'. She saw the almond trees in flower, those treacherous almond trees. They had made her give herself away – and at once the inevitable answer came back. Isn't that what you came for? To give yourself away? She remembered her Solemn Profession, her vows and the moment when she had lain before the altar – a holocaust. A little thing, thought Philippa, but the greatest anyone can give: yourself.

A bell sounded over her head, little St Luke, marking the end of recreation. Silence, work, had re-begun. She could take refuge in that; she had medicines to give, a dressing to be done, trays to get ready for tea. Work, she thought, would shut this out, but it would not be shut out.

In the cloister she met Cecily. Cecily did not stop at the token bow, the small inclination of the head, with which the nuns passed one another. Cecily, so undemonstrative now, stopped and put her arms round Philippa in a hug; her eyes were big with tears as she tightened it. Behind Cecily was Polycarp – Dame Polly. She took Philippa's hands and wrung them before she went on her way. Neither of them broke silence but more eloquently than if they had used torrents of words, it was a foretaste of 'goodbye'.

'Dame Philippa can only go of her own will,' Abbess Catherine had explained that to Mr Konishi a dozen times.

'Let me talk to her. I shall will her.'

'That wouldn't be fair,' and Abbess Catherine protected Philippa when next morning Mr Konishi met the community in the large parlour. Before Dame Colette died, it had been arranged that he should give a talk, describing the house at Suwa, and tell the nuns what the journey would be like and the reception prepared for the new community when they landed at Tokyo. Though everyone was acutely conscious of the two pall-covered biers in the choir, candles set round them, four nuns kneeling to keep vigil, Abbess Catherine decided to have the talk as planned. Mr Konishi, she knew, would show impeccable taste and it should help to solve the present dilemma – if it were a dilemma.

'Out of nearly a hundred nuns, why should I be the only one?' That was Philippa's silent cry of anguish.

'Because you are the only one.' The answer did not need to be said. It filled the whole monastery.

'I am too old,' Dame Agnes had said in Council when, for Philippa's sake, they tried to think of alternatives. 'Too old.'

'And I,' said Dame Ursula, 'am too old-fashioned.'

'Dame Maura is strong,' said Abbess Catherine, 'but she has been away six years and I feel I cannot let her go again, even if she volunteered; besides if she went it would mean Dame Monica must stay here; they won't need two musicians – and Dame Monica speaks Japanese.'

'I would offer,' said Dame Anselma, 'but Mother, you know I am no administrator, and I don't speak Japanese.'

'Nor I,' said Dame Thecla. 'Besides, they need somebody English.'

'Dame Veronica has offered. She has a smattering of Japanese,' said the Abbess.

'You are not serious, Mother.'

'No, this is far too serious for that.'

Time was so short. In a few days the Japanese nuns' friends and relatives would be gathering in Tokyo. Father Vincent would soon be on his way there, the bishop too, while the four new postulants had already come down-country.

'Is it all to be cancelled?' Mr Konishi asked mournfully.

'We shall hope not,' said Abbess Catherine. 'But you must give us time to think.'

At that, he lost his tact. 'What need to think when it is ob-vi-ous.'

Once again, Philippa was St Sebastian shot with arrows, but this time the arrows were of sympathy, compassion, sadness, more frightening than criticism; Philippa could not toughen herself against these, hunch herself in, only suffer. No one spoke to her that day, except of necessary things and she kept herself busy, working like a fury as she had in the months after Keith's death. That evening she was suddenly sick down the infirmary sluice: that night she could not sleep.

Morning brought the double funeral. Once more the day was hot and thundery and the long Requiem was exhausting; when the nuns went in to dinner, few wanted to eat, but they had hardly sat down when there was a thunderstorm, sudden and so loud that it drowned the reader's words. After it was over, coolness crept into the room, touching the nuns' faces, bringing freshness, a fresh light, and the sun shone out.

Philippa's place at table was directly opposite one of the tall windows and, as the sun came out, its first shaft fell on her – it was as if it picked her out in the dark refectory. For a moment she was dazzled, then she was warm for the first time for two days, warm and relaxed? thought Philippa.

Abbess Catherine gave the knock and announced that after Grace, everyone was to spend recreation in the garden. 'It may be wet but I feel we need air.'

Philippa could not go straight out; she had patients to settle to rest, doses to be given, trays to clear and put away and it was half an hour before she was free to walk down the cloister to the park. There she met Dame Agnes who, as cellarer, had tasks that kept her too; with Dame Agnes's usual rustle of linen and skirts she walked beside Philippa.

Some of the nuns were pacing near the flower beds, in the pleached alley, or on the brick path – those who revelled in sun – or in the avenue, those who liked shade. Philippa, long in the East, distrusted sun for head and eyes – we haven't dark glasses – and made for the shade of the avenue with Dame Agnes who, for a while was silent; then she stopped and looked through the trees across the park to the walls with their espaliered fruit trees, and along the pleached alley, over the bog garden and pond; the paths were dotted with figures in black and white sunning themselves, sitting or walking; the wind ruffled the trees and brought a scent of flowers; soft talk and laughter came on it. 'Very pleasant,' said Dame Agnes. 'Yes,' said Philippa and, like the Abbess, 'we need it.' Forty minutes' life-giving relaxation in a day of fourteen hours' work, seven days a week, year in, year out. 'You were right and I was wrong,' she said to Dame Agnes. 'Thank God, that idea of planning permission didn't have to go through. I must have been mad.'

'Not mad,' said Dame Agnes, 'another person, very dear sister.' She put her hand, quietly and kindly on Philippa's arm. Philippa gave the hand a grateful squeeze.

Dame Agnes had made up her mind but she was too intelligent not to be wary; she did not use her third red eye, but she guessed that Philippa was prickly, taut in every nerve and sick at heart. It would be better not to be too direct, a slant would be more tactful – a sort of parable – and she drew Philippa towards a seat under a great beech tree. 'Let's sit down.' Dame Agnes seated herself and, her eyes carefully kept away from the other's face, began to speak.

'You know, of course, it was Elinor Hartshorn, the last surviving member of the Hartshorn family, who gave Brede to us?'

'Yes, it's a wonderful story,' said Philippa, still standing.

'Did you know that when she offered it, she made one condition?'

'I didn't know.'

'Yes,' Dame Agnes went on, almost dreamily; her eyes followed the moving black and white figures as, slowly, in her deliberate way, she recounted the Hartshorn history. 'Elinor was the last left – her niece had become our Dame Gertrude but, when she offered us Brede, there was one small bit Elinor wanted to keep for herself.' Dame Agnes carefully kept her head turned away. 'It was the land around the dingle which she particularly loved. Yes, she wanted to build herself a modest house there,' said Dame Agnes. 'The gift was most handsome even without that ... just one little enclave that she wanted to keep for herself but, though we needed Brede so badly – we were badly cramped – a house just here would have spoilt the enclosure, so we had to refuse.' Dame Agnes paused invitingly, her eyes still on the figures. Philippa should have said, 'And?' – but nothing was forthcoming and Dame Agnes had to go on. 'Of course, she surrendered that enclave. She withdrew her condition and gave the whole gift. It was inevitable. Nothing less than the whole is good enough for God.'

Silence.

Dame Agnes still did not look but waited. The silence went on. Was Dame Philippa offended? Had she withdrawn into herself, as in the old days, she often and icily withdrew? Dame Agnes could not believe it, not of this Philippa. Then, as the silence continued, Dame Agnes turned to look.

No wonder there was silence; no wonder Dame Philippa had not asked the needed 'and?' The place Dame Agnes had indicated beside her on the seat was empty. Dame Agnes had a shrewd idea it had been empty all the time.

Philippa was with the Abbess.

As Dame Agnes had begun her parable, Philippa had known, suddenly and clearly, that she must make her offer now, 'This moment,' she could have said, 'or I can never nerve myself to it again.' Across the park she had seen a tall unmistakable figure going into the house and, forsaking Dame Agnes, Philippa followed. Dame Agnes had been too intent to hear the murmured apology, nor did she see Philippa as she crossed

417

the park to the garth – Philippa was always elusive. 'I must do this as quickly and decisively as a surgeon's cut,' she had told herself and almost ran up the stairs to the Abbess's room and knocked.

Never did a Deo Gratias have more meaning than Abbess Catherine's as she told Philippa to come in – she had recognized the swift step. She turned in her chair and held out both hands. Philippa knelt and put her own between them.

ENVOI

Penny, Donald and Joyce Bowman stood at the rail of the viewers' terrace with the other nuns' relatives waiting for the plane to take off. 'It isn't worth it,' Donald had said. 'All you will see is a glimpse through the glass as they come down the ramp to get into the bus, perhaps dots of figures as they go up the gangway to the plane. You have said goodbye. It isn't worth it,' but Penny obstinately stayed.

Philippa would have liked to have gone up to London by train, the way she had come, changing from the little train at Ashford, but it had to be what Yoko proudly called 'a motorcade'. McTurk met it at London Airport.

'I'm going with them,' he said on the telephone to Abbess Catherine. 'After fourteen years' enclosure, Philippa will be dazed, even our Philippa, and she may need me as well as Mr Konishi.' When the Abbess had tried to thank him, 'I am truly, truly grateful,' McTurk said, 'I have always wanted to see Japan – Buddhist Japan,' he had added as a parting shot.

'Who would have dreamed of this?' said Penny now. 'Dame Philippa thought she would be at Brede for the rest of her life. Poor Philippa.'

'Poor? Surely she welcomed this opportunity, wanted to go?' said Donald, but Penny knew better than that. 'I can guess it was like that verse when Christ said to Peter something about "Now you gird yourself and take yourself where you want to go . . . but one day another will gird you and take you where you do not want to go." I can guess it is just like that,' said Penny.

'We honour you,' Dame Maura, who was not given to compliments, had told Philippa, 'every one of us.'

'Well, Dame Agnes said I wouldn't go all the way,' Philippa had said shakily. 'I wanted the distinction of being the first nun to prove her wrong – though Dame Polly is coming up,' she added.

Though she had tried to make light of it, there was not one in the community who had not known what it meant for Philippa, when they went in procession with the travellers to the enclosure door.

In their black cloaks, holding their travelling bags – light grips lettered Japan Air Lines – the thirteen had looked a small group 'to conquer a new world,' as Dame Veronica dramatically said. For the Japanese, as far as they could tell, it was a final goodbye, but the Brede nuns would come back – 'One day,' said Abbess Catherine hopefully.

In ten, fifteen years, Philippa had thought, maybe twenty, maybe never. I am fifty-seven now. With Abbess Catherine it might very well be never; in twenty years the Abbess would be over eighty. Dame Agnes, Dame Maura ... so many, many nuns Philippa knew she would never see again, but she was a leader once more, in control, and amid the embraces and kisses and sobbings and tears, she had had to keep her face, as Abbess Catherine kept hers. 'Little Sophie, I know you will be brave.'

'Monica!' 'Dearest Sister Xaviera.' 'Scholastica.'

'Bridget, cheer up. There will be birds in Japan.'

'Mother, it's not the birds . . .'

'I know it's not, dearest child.'

Philippa had been grateful for the Abbess's formal blessing; neither she nor Abbess Catherine could have trusted their own words.

Now, on the airport terrace, 'Penny,' said Donald in a whisper, 'isn't that Sir Richard Taft?'

It was Sir Richard, standing as they were at the railing to see ... 'For Mercy's sake, don't look,' whispered Joyce Bowman.

At last the nuns came, among a file of other passengers

420

walking down the slanted ramp to the bus. As Donald had predicted, Penny caught only a glimpse of the tall black figure – even cloaked, she looks elegant, thought Penny – much taller than McTurk beside her, or any of the other twelve black-veiled and cloaked figures she was shepherding into the bus after the small plump bulk of Mr Konishi.

When they were all in, Philippa turned, as each nun had turned, on the step of the bus to wave. Philippa's face was framed in the white wimple and straight blackness of her veil. Her eyes sought out Joyce Bowman, Donald and Penny; she saw them and waved, but Penny had stiffened. Looking sideways, she had seen her chief take off his hat and wave too. Would Philippa see? Would she stop and pause? For a moment Philippa's eyes went over the crowd then, with another wave, she was gone, followed by McTurk. 'She didn't even notice him,' whispered Penny.

Sir Richard, still bare-headed, still stood at the railing. '*He* thought it worth while,' said Penny to Donald.

The plane took off, jets of white following its trail. A few minutes later it was over the sea.

PUBLISHER'S NOTE

Benedictine, Cistercian, Carmelite, Brigittines and Visitandine nuns all live in monasteries, not convents. The name convent was applied first to communities in simple vows which were not *permanent*. Usually these communities were for women (though the mendicant friars lived in convents) and the word became the common usage for any community of women whether nuns (in solemn vows living in monasteries) or Sisters (in simple vows living in convents).

THE BENEDICTINE LIFE

The Rule and Constitutions

St Benedict laid down the final form of his Rule in AD 540. Though each Benedictine house has its own constitution that can be adapted and changed, the founder's own monastery of Monte Cassino still provides the pattern for each, as it provided the pattern for the author's imaginary Abbey of Brede: the ideal of the unceasing round of prayer, praise and work continuing 'without sloth or haste' through the hours, days, years and centuries.

The Opus Dei

Liturgical prayer is the Benedictine's characteristic form of service; in Brede Abbey the Divine Office is shown as sung with full solemnity, i.e. sung in plainchant by the full choir divided into two 'sides', dexter and sinister, each led by a chantress – on feast days two chantresses. In every choir the most coveted office is that of the hebdomadarian, the nun appointed each week to lead, intoning or singing, the Canonical Hours, with their antiphons, passages of scripture and collects. On great feasts the hebdomadarian is always the Abbess; and each nun, on her own feast or name day, holds this office.

Different houses have different timetables but that of Brede is typical, ie, the times of the Hours, as they are called, do not change throughout the year; the nuns get up at five, half past four on feast days, for the exquisite daybreak Office of Lauds; pure praise. Prime, coming directly after, is the morning prayer, asking blessing on the day; Terce is at nine, the 'third hour', of the ancient world, when the Holy Spirit had come down on the apostles at Pentecost; fittingly Terce comes before the Conventual Mass. Sext is at midday, the 'sixth hour': None at three o'clock, the 'ninth hour' at which Christ died. Vespers, longer, more formal and of great beauty, is the evening prayer, a re-creation of the evening sacrifice in the Temple at Jerusalem. Compline at eight, intimate and quiet, closes the Canonical Hours and the community gathers its strength to sing Matins, the great Office of the night. The Great Silence, that must not be broken except in grave emergency, begins after Compline and stills the house until after Prime next day.

Lectio Divina

It was St Benedict who named it 'lectio divina', 'reading of divine things'. All nuns are bound to spend some part of the day in reading – the younger the nun the more time she is given for it. They are not restricted to theological books and at Brede there were books on philosophy, comparative religion, music, art, poetry, even novels. There were no newspapers: the Abbess marked anything she thought important in the news, to be read out by the Reader in the refectory during meals. All reading is tuned to the same end – spiritual understanding.

Postulants, Novices, Simple Profession, Solemn Profession

At every monastery, as at Brede, postulants come to try the life, and be tried by it, for six months during which they can leave at any time – or be asked to leave. Then, if the desire still holds, the postulant is clothed in the religious habit but with the white veil of a novice. Novices too can leave without notice. At the end of a year, after a thorough examination, written and oral, before the Council, and when the Abbess has asked the opinion of every member of the monastery, even the fellow novices, the novice takes temporary vows for three years and ranks as a junior differentiated from the community by a shorter black veil. For the whole four and a half years she keeps up intensive study and rigorous training under novice-mistress and zelatrix and certain 'teacher' nuns. At the end comes final acceptance. The time of probation, may be extended; it can never be lessened. The nun then renounces all her property, takes vows for life, enclosure at Brede and, if she is a choir nun, is given the ring and cowl, a stall in choir, a seat in the chapter; if claustral she simply has the ring, takes what part she can in choir and does not concern herself with affairs in chapter.

A recent Instruction from the Vatican calls for the postulant or probationary period to be extended up to two years before Clothing, followed by a novitiate of a further two years – this last is already enforced in many Benedictine houses. Then it is suggested that instead of taking Simple Vows the junior should make promises lasting from three to five years to the community. This change is important because a vow, even a temporary one, is made to God and is therefore so sacred that dispensation can only be granted for grave reasons. A promise is an agreement between the novice and the Order or house and can be dispensed with by mutual agreement. The Vatican makes it clear that temporary promises must be understood as a step towards Perpetual Vows which are unaffected by this recommendation; they are the basis of religious life. The Instruction also wants the age at entry to be higher – at least nineteen.

Vows

Benedictine vows are slightly different from those of other orders. The first vow is of Stability to the chosen house –

house not Order: the second is of Conversion of Manners which includes chastity, poverty and renunciation of all possessions: the third is of Obedience.

Dowries

A dowry for a choir nun is supposed to be a minimum of six hundred pounds – 'supposed' because in many cases it is waived and a suitable 'vocation' is accepted without any money at all. Dowries are kept on deposit until Solemn Profession and every nun has the right to dispose of her property in any way she chooses during the last two months before taking her final vows. Claustral sisters bring twenty pounds when they enter, but this also is often waived.

The Deposition and Distribution of Offices

At many houses as at Brede, this is held once a year. The whole community is called to the chapter house where the Abbess deposes them from their offices, one by one, beginning with the least. Any nun who holds keys rises as she is named and puts them symbolically on the table in front of the Abbess.

For three or four days the monastery is, as it were, in a state of suspension – only the most necessary work, such as that of sacristan, bellringer, infirmarian, portress being carried out until the community is summoned again for the Distribution when, beginning with the highest office, i.e. the prioress, the Abbess makes her appointments or reappointments.

The Chapter of Faults

The Chapter of Faults is held once a week in the chapter house, the Abbess calling out six nuns, one by one, to make a full confession of any external faults, or open transgressions against the Rule. Then the Abbess asks for 'acknowledgements', so that anyone who has transgressed, even slightly, has the opportunity to acknowledge it, not only for humility's sake, but because she feels marred or disfigured by the fault.

The nuns also go to confession in the usual way, either to their own chaplain or to a visiting priest, but this is their own, and private, affair.

The Turn

The Turn is not a door; every cloistered nunnery has both its main enclosure door, which is only opened on formal occasions, and its outer gate, through which traffic, lorries, vans, etc., can go in and out, but for the everyday perpetual flow of letters, messages, parcels, boxes, baskets, the turn is used – a sort of revolving table with shelves which can be loaded on the inner or outer side and spun to the other. There is a turn between the enclosure and the outer hall used by the extern sisters, another between the two sacristies. Anything and everything of manageable size goes through the turn.

'Down the Community'

The term is used when a nun goes to each of her sisters in turn, from the Abbess down to the newest professed; for instance, to be given the Pax, to say goodbye, on a special mission, etc.

Oblates

St Benedict is described as 'the leader and master of a countless multitude of souls'. This multitude is made up, not only of monks and nuns, but also of people living in the world and sharing in the spiritual life of the monasteries by an act of 'self-oblation' prompted by the desire for spiritual perfection and union with God. For Oblates a symbolic scapular – simply two small tabs, white on black joined by a black ribbon – represents the religious habit and they wear it secretly as a constant reminder of what they have undertaken.

The Habit

The habit of a religious is not only a dress or uniform; it is invested with a far deeper meaning and symbolism which explains why many people feel that those Orders which have substituted what is almost a 'lay dress' have suffered a loss they do not realize. It is understandable that nuns cannot drive cars, go in aeroplanes, walk busy streets, in such headdresses as the ancient and beautiful 'cornettes' once worn by the Sisters

426

of Charity, but habits can be modified without losing their meaning and grace.

One has only to read the prayers said at a Benedictine Clothing to understand what the habit represents: the leather girdle is 'to gird thee with justice and purity'; the scapular, a straight piece of material hanging back and front from the shoulders where it is joined – originally an apron for work – symbolizes 'the yoke of Christ': the veil is the token of chastity and obedience and the 'hidden' life: the ring, just as a wedding ring, is a symbol of dedication, a binding of the nun's life to Christ: the cowl is the official choir dress of the Benedictine Monk or nun, a loose, flowing garment worn over the habit; according to custom it is of ample width and almost reaching to the ground, with sleeves long enough when let down – they are worn turned back – to touch the ground, and wide enough to reach the knees when the hands are folded on the breast.

Skirts are long, not only for dignity but for self-effacement; heels are low because the nun's life is one of work.

Hair is cut short, the wimple worn simply to free the nun from 'women's fuss', preoccupation with self; a monastery or convent has, or used to have, no looking-glasses.

The Miserere

is the 50th psalm, 51st in non-catholic liturgy, one of the seven great penitential psalms: verse after verse is the plea of an over-burdened humiliated heart: the verse

'Sprinkle me with hyssop and I shall be cleansed;
wash me and I shall be made whiter than snow.'

is used in all Catholic churches before the chief Mass on Sunday when the celebrant comes down the nave, sprinkling the people with holy water. Hyssop twigs were used in the Jewish rites for ceremonies of purification.

Greetings

The nuns' answer of 'Deo Gratias' to a knock at the door comes from the Rule of St Benedict: 'If a knock comes to the

427

door the monk is to answer Deo Gratias,' (Rule, Chapter 66). 'Benedicite' is equivalent to 'give a blessing', and an invitation to bless God or the person speaking. Chapter 63 of the Rule says: 'Whenever the brethren meet one another, let the junior ask the senior for his blessing.'

The author of ONE PAIR OF HANDS

MONICA DICKENS

THE LANDLORD'S DAUGHTER 35p

Every page of this absorbing novel, which ranges from the Depression days of the thirties to the pop stars and 'dropouts' of today, is richly and compulsively readable . . . one of today's top-selling authors, at the very top of her form!

'Clever and highly complex murder story' – DAILY MAIL.

THE ROOM UPSTAIRS 25p

'Here is a grim, relentless story, with touches of the macabre, about a proud woman hanging grimly on to what is left of her well-remembered past; a mad woman ready to kill to preserve her peace of mind' – MANCHESTER EVENING NEWS.

A SELECTION OF POPULAR READING IN PAN

CRIME

Agatha Christie

THEY DO IT WITH MIRRORS 25p

Victor Canning

QUEEN'S PAWN 30p

THE SCORPIO LETTERS 30p

Dick Francis

FLYING FINISH 25p

BLOOD SPORT 25p

James Eastwood

COME DIE WITH ME 25p

Ed McBain

SHOTGUN 25p

GENERAL FICTION

Mario Puzo

THE GODFATHER 45p

Rumer Godden

IN THIS HOUSE OF BREDE 35p

Katheryn Hulme

THE NUN'S STORY 30p

George MacDonald Fraser

ROYAL FLASH 30p

Rona Jaffe

THE FAME GAME 40p

Leslie Thomas

COME TO THE WAR 30p

C. S. Forester

THE MAN ON THE YELLOW RAFT 30p

Andrea Newman

A BOUQUET OF BARBED WIRE 35p

Arthur Hailey

HOTEL 35p

IN HIGH PLACES 35p

Nevil Shute

REQUIEM FOR A WREN 30p

Kyle Onstott
DRUM 40p
MANDINGO 30p
Kyle Onstott & Lance Horner
FALCONHURST FANCY 35p
THE TATTOOED ROOD 35p
Lance Horner
HEIR TO FALCONHURST 40p

ROMANTIC FICTION
Juliette Benzoni
MARIANNE Book 1:
The Bride of Selton Hall 30p
MARIANNE Book 2:
The Eagle And The Nightingale 30p
Georgette Heyer
COUSIN KATE 30p
FREDERICA 30p
BATH TANGLE 30p
Sergeanne Golon
THE COUNTESS ANGELIQUE: Book One
In The Land Of The Redskin 30p
THE COUNTESS ANGELIQUE: Book Two
Prisoner Of The Mountains 30p

HISTORICAL FICTION
Frederick E. Smith
WATERLOO 25p
Jean Plaidy
MADAME SERPENT 30p
GAY LORD ROBERT 30p
MURDER MOST ROYAL 35p
Colin Forbes
TRAMP IN ARMOUR 30p

NON-FICTION

Dr. Laurence J. Peter & Raymond Hull
THE PETER PRINCIPLE · 30p

Peter F. Drucker
THE AGE OF DISCONTINUITY · 60p

Jack Olsen
SILENCE ON MONTE SOLE · 35p

Jim Dante & Leo Diegel
THE NINE BAD SHOTS OF GOLF (illus.) · 35p

Adrian Hill
HOW TO DRAW (Illus.) · 30p

Maurice Woodruff
THE SECRET OF FORETELLING YOUR OWN
FUTURE · 25p

William Sargant
THE UNQUIET MIND · 45p

Graham Hill
LIFE AT THE LIMIT (illus.) · 35p

Ken Welsh
HITCH-HIKER'S GUIDE TO EUROPE (illus.) · 35p

Miss Read
MISS READ'S COUNTRY COOKING · 30p

Gavin Maxwell
RAVEN SEEK THY BROTHER (illus.) · 30p

Obtainable from all booksellers and newsagents. If you have any difficulty, please send purchase price plus 5p postage to P.O. Box 11, Falmouth, Cornwall.

While every effort is made to keep prices low, it is sometimes necessary to increase prices at short notice. PAN Books reserve the right to show new retail prices on covers which may differ from the text or elsewhere.

I enclose a cheque/postal order for selected titles ticked above plus 5p a book to cover postage and packing.

NAME ....

ADDRESS ....

....

I 'nheulu i gyd a'r merched

Un

"Tynnwch, y ffycars! Be sy'n bod 'no chi? Be chi'n feddwl yw'r lle 'ma – AGM y WI?

"Ie, ie, Nerys fach, ishde di ar y rhaff, a gad i Heledd gario dy bwyse di. Pan wyt ti lawr fyn'na, ma Hels yn cario dy ben-ôl mowr di *a'i* phen-ôl 'i hunan 'fyd.

"Nawr dalwch e. DALWCH E wedes i, a gadewch e lawr. Aaaaaaraaaaaf, aaaaaaraaaaaaf. A wow nawr de, stop.

"Dalwch hi fan'na.

"Nawr te, co ni off, lan i'r top de plis, a llai o fflipin wenwn. Fi moyn gweld y rhaff 'na'n torri. Dau ddewis sy 'da chi ar ôl cymryd y stra'n – ennill ne' gwmpo'n ffycin farw. Deall? Nawr dalwch e am ddeg.

"Deg… Naw… Wyth… Saith…

"Symudodd y rhaff? Ddechreuwn ni 'to de.

"Deg… Wyth… Saith… Whech… Pump… Pump… Pump… Pump… Pump… Pedwartridaun. 'Na fe – lawr â fe, slo bach.

"Da iawn, hoe am bum munud."

Trodd y rhaff o fod yn dynn fel tant telyn i fod yn llysywen yn sleifio i'r borfa. Fel wede Les, "troi o goc tarw i gwt buwch". Roedd e ar 'i ore heddiw, yn cerdded o gwmpas y lle fel ceiliog a'r merched i gyd wedi blino'n blet ac Awen yr angor yn rhwbio'i chefn. Roedd Siân ar y llawr yn sugno cymysgedd o sgwash a halen o botel blastig fel oen swci ar sbîd, a Non yn aildrefnu'i chrys dan ei cheseiliau gan ddyfyrio'r pothellau ar ei bysedd.

Dou fis i fynd tan y 'big one', a dim blydi siâp arnon ni – er bod y fan lle ro'n ni'n tynnu'r gasgen lan y goeden wedi'i droelio'n foel. Roedden ni 'di bod yn dod i'r cae 'ma beder gwaith yr wythnos ers pum mis bellach, ac ro'dd newydd-deb y peth yn dechre troelo mor dene â'r borfa.

"Cym on de, ladies, 'na ddigon o'r iapan 'ma – ar eich tra'd!"

Ro'dd Les wedi dihuno 'to.

"Chi'n gwbod pam fi'n gweiddi arnoch chi fel hyn, on'd 'ych chi?" gofynnodd. "Ni'n amddiffyn y teitl – chi'n gwbod 'ny, on'd 'ych chi? Nid tîm tafarn leol y'n ni nawr. Nid namby-pamby-pink-nail-filing-lager-and-lime-drinking-skirt-wearing-giggle-when-he-fiddles-with-your-tits team y'n ni nawr.

"Ry'n ni'n adeiladu 'bach o'r stamina 'ma. Pan fyddwn ni'n y gystadleuaeth 'na, a chi 'di blino, a chi'n ffycd, a ma liffts y tîm arall yn tynnu'ch breichie chi o'ch corff, a chi ise hwydu, 'na pryd ma'r gwaith 'ma'n talu. 'Na pryd ni'n galler mynd at y banc manijer 'na a withdrawo chydig o'r stamina 'na chi 'di'i dalu mewn heno. 'Helô, Mr Banc Manijer, ga i gasho siec plis?' 'Wrth gwrs 'ny, dim problem,' fydd e'n gweud, achos ry'ch chi wedi talu digon i mewn, yndofe? Dy'n ni ddim yn y coch, odyn ni? Bydd y time erill yn trial gwneud run peth ac yn mynd at y banc manijer hefyd, yn byddan nhw? A beth fyddan nhw'n ga'l? E? Digon i dalu am Rolls Royce? Nage, glei – fflipin Robin Reliant ga'n nhw, ondife?

"Nawr te, run peth 'to, dim ffycian ambwti a tynnwch fel 'se whant 'no chi, wir Dduw. 'Bach o natur, os gwelwch chi fod yn dda. Dou fis sydd i fynd cyn i ni orffod wynebu'r gelyn, a chithe fan hyn fel blydi lloi. Sefwch wrth y rhaff."

Wyth merch, rhai cyhyrog erbyn hyn, yn sefyll fel petaen nhw'n cymryd cymun wrth y rhaff, yn troi i'r ochr ac yn estyn eu dwylo i fesur y pellter rhyngddynt. Wyth pâr o lygaid yn edrych ar Les.

"Pick up the rope." Wyth troed yn bachu'r rhaff a'i jacio i fyny dan wyth cesail.

"Take the strain." Wyth sawdwl chwith yn hacio i mewn i'r stecs fel teirw.

"Edrychwch arna i... Edrychwch arna i... a... TYNNWCH!"

Weiren y rhaff yn tynnu'n dynn, y crac yn lledu trwy gyhyrau ac esgyrn – a chasgen o gerrig yn ymbellhau oddi wrth y llawr.

"And pull and pull a 'nôl a 'nôl, and pull and pull a 'nôl a 'nôl. Tynnwch fel tîm!"

Roedd y rhaff wedi codi pothellau wrth fôn fy mysedd, a'r rheini wedi troi'n galed gan ei gwneud hi'n anoddach i gydio'n dynn.

"Nerys, ffor ffyc sêcs, tynna achan!"

Roedd y rhaff yn cripio mla'n gan fynd â chroen fy nwylo 'da hi.

"DEFEND! Chi'n gwbod beth i neud pan ma hyn yn digwydd – so newch e! Anghofiwch y blino 'ma. Os 'ych chi ofan 'bach o waith, cerwch gatre i weu. Beth am barti bach Tupperware, neu aerobics nos Iau 'da'r merched bach pert 'na yn y gym? Chi 'ma i neud job. Nawr DO the ffycin job! Plough 'em into the ground. Nawr te, gadewch hi lawr 'm bach. Dalwch chi fan'na am ryw bum munud."

Ebychiadau a rhegfeydd yn rhedeg i lawr y rhaff fel weiren deliffon.

"Beth yw'r holl wenwn 'ma? Wedi blino, ife? Wel fe newn ni fe'n chwe munud de!" Edrychodd i fyw llygaid

Kel, oedd ar flaen y rhaff. "O, 'na drueni, fi'n mynd i lefen. Os na ddalwch chi fe'n llonydd fe ga i'r blydi donci 'na draw 'ma i ddelio 'da'r cwbwl lot 'no chi."

Rodd Ner o mla'n i'n crynu, a holl bwysau'r cerrig yn gwneud i'w chorff hi galedu fel gwialen bysgota ryfedd. Teimlais Non y tu ôl i mi'n gorwedd yn is ar y rhaff, a'i rhegfeydd yn cynhesu 'ngwar.

"Tair munud ar ôl. Mwynhewch e."

Pengliniau Les yn pasio heibio.

"Hanner munud!"

Roedd fy nwylo'n troi'n wyn wrth i'r gwaed redeg i rannau arall o 'nghorff. O dan fy seicling siorts du roedd cyhyr yn fy mhen-glin dde yn chwyddo a'r boen ynddo'n llosgi.

"Cym on, ladies, chi'n edrych yn dda."

Pwysais fy mhen yn ôl dros y rhaff.

"'Na fe, cadwch eich penne 'nôl. Ma pob un o'ch penne chi'n pwyso pedwar pwys – wel, heblaw am un Ner. Tase chi gyd yn 'u pwyso nhw 'nôl, 'na bron i ddwy stôn arall o bwyse'n referso.

"Dalwch hi fan'na. Dalwch hi. Nawr y'n ni'n gweld pwy sy 'di bod yn gneud 'bach o waith, on'd 'yn ni, e? Gweld pwy sy 'di bod yn meddwl, 'www i'r diawl â hi, sa i'n treino heno 'ma, ma 'na ffilm bach mla'n a ma'r sboner yn dod draw, a fi ise mynd i'r gwely'n gynnar… NO BLYDI GOOD, YW E? Pa iws yw'r ffilm 'na i chi nawr? Bydde chi'n well tase chi wedi gneud awr fach ar y weights, yn bydde chi? YN BYDDE CHI? BE TI'N WEUD, NER?"

"NO GOOD, LES" gwaeddodd Ner, gan ei ddilyn dan ei hanadl 'da "Heil Hitler!"

Dyma fi'n dechre chwerthin, a'r boen yn neidio trwy 'mreichiau.

"Be sy mor ddoniol?" gofynnodd Les gan droi ar ei sawdl. Wyth ceg ar gau. "Wel, os y'n ni'n mwynhau gymaint â 'na, a bod digon o egni 'da ni i chwerthin, neith munud fach arall ar y rhaff ddim dolur wedyn, neith e?"

"Hwp hi, y bwch â ti…" cychwynnodd Ner.

"Ca' dy ben nawr de, heblaw bo ti'n moyn bod 'ma hyd bore fory," gwaeddodd Awen o'r cefen.

Dwy funud yn mynd heibio fel oriau, a'r cryndod yn tynnu o'r dwylo i'r ysgwyddau, i lawr y cefen a thrwy'r coese.

"A lawr yn ara bach."

Wrth i'r geiriau lacio'r cyhyrau, dyma un deg chwech esgid yn cripian ymlaen a'r gasgen yn rhoi ei phen-ôl ar y pridd.

"Nawr eisteddwch."

Plygais ymlaen i sythu 'nghefn. Ma'n siŵr taw fel hyn o'dd unrhyw un ga'th y rac yn teimlo. Llacies i 'ngharre ac eistedd i lawr. Roedd y seicling siorts yn glynu wrth fy nhin, a'r chwys yn rhedeg rhwng fy mronne. Tynnais siwmper drwchus dros 'y mhen rhag ofn i mi oeri.

"Nawr te, ladies, chat bach. Pwy nosweth yw hi heno?"

Pawb yn edrych yn fud ar ei gilydd. Roedd hyn yn anarferol. Doedd e byth yn gofyn dim inni fel arfer.

"Pwy nosweth yw hi heno?"

Edrychodd Ner arno fe'n dwp.

"Odych chi'n ffycin fyddar, de? Be sy ise arnoch chi? Pâr o nicyrs ar gyfer pob dydd, ac enwe'r diwrnode arnyn nhw?"

Closiodd Les at Ner nes bod ei drwyn ddim ond modfedd oddi wrth ei thrwyn hi.

"Nawr te, Nerys fach, pa ddiwrnod sy wedi'i sgwennu ar dy nicyrs di heddi?"

"O, ffycin dydd Sadwrn," medde Ner.

"Da iawn," atebodd Les, "fe ei di'n bell. A beth y'n ni'n neud nos Sadwrn?"

Pawb yn dawel.

"Mynd mas, ondefe? Blow fifty quid ar Snakebite and Black, meddwi hyd y stŷd a shelffo rhyw foi tu ôl i'r clwb rygbi, ondefe? Rhyw undeserving little scroat fydd yn gweud tho'i fêts pwy seis o'dd 'ych tits chi, a faint o bositions o'ch chi'n fodlon wneud. Deffro yn y bore – sic ar 'ych sgidie a phwrs gwag. Training nesa, a ffycin wasto'i hanner e'n chwysu'r crap 'na mas o'ch pores chi. Cymysgedd o gin a chicken korma. Allen i'ch lluo chi fory a mynd yn pissed fy hunan. Nawr te, ladies, less of it please. Newch ffafr â fi, a ffafr â Mr Banc Manijer a'r STD clinic. Eniwe, ma'ch hips chi fel rhai Neil Jenkins nawr, so ddyle neb fod yn galler jwmpo'ch bones chi. Reit te, 'na ddigon am heddi. Ffyc off."

A 'na'r ymarfer drosto am heno 'to, a phawb yn troi am y giât tra bod yr hen ddonci druan yn edrych yn ddigon nerfus yng nghornel y cae. Pawb yn dawel, a rhyw frân ddu yn pasio uwch ein pennau gan feddwl beth uffach o'dd wyth merch yn neud yn ymlwybro'n ôl i'r pentre ar bnawn Sadwrn a golwg mor ofnadw arnyn nhw. Edrychais 'nôl wrth roi'r tsiaen dros bostyn y giât rhag ofn i'r donci ein dilyn ni mas. Roedd Les yn penlinio wrth y rhaff, yn smygu ffàg.

Dou

Ar ôl i ni gyrradd y pentre, ma'r cleber yn dechre chwyddo 'to. Ma'r myfyrdod yn cracio, a'r tsiaen o ferched yn gwasgaru bob yn linc i wahanol gyfeiriadau gan dincial 'wela i di wedyn' a 'be ti'n wisgo heno?' i bob man.

Rhyw gymysgedd go ryfedd o'n ni 'fyd. Cerys y stiwdent (oedd hefyd yn cael ei galw'n Kelloggs (Kel) a Tacs-dodjer), pum troedfedd wyth modfedd o gyhyrau brown a llyged fel llo bach. Llinos, ces a hanner a oedd wastad yng nghanol y bwrlwm. Nerys, fy ffrind gore, yn goese tene ac yn wallt melyngoch i gyd, a Non, oedd yn gweithio mewn siop yn y dre. Treuliodd hi flynydde'n cael ei chlatsho 'da rhyw foi. Dihunodd hi o'r diwedd, a nawr ma hi'n cydio yn y rhaff fel se hi'n dychmygu taw 'i wddwg e sy yn ei llaw hi bob tro. Roedd gweddill y tîm yn cynnwys Heini, merch fferm o'r pentre – uffarn o ben busnes 'da hi, ond fowr o sens fel arall; Awen yr angor oedd â thamed mwy o wind resistance na'r gweddill ohonon ni; a Siân, llygoden o ferch ond fel tarw ar y rhaff – a finne.

Cerddai Ner a fi adre 'da'n gilydd, ar hyd y lôn gefn i'r un cyfeiriad. Roedd hi'n byw yn y fferm drws nesa i ni, hi ym Mhantglas a finne yn Nhyddyn Gwyn. Ac roedd ein hanes ni'n mynd 'nôl ymhell – ro'n ni'n arfer neidio fel ceffylau dros y rhesi gwair yn ryw beder neu bump oed, a chwarae yn yr ydlan, ac eistedd ar ben cydau 20:10:10 i lithro i lawr Cae Mawr yn yr eira, gan wlychu ein nicyrs yn sopen. Ro'n ni'n dwy wedi bod yn yr ysgol 'da'n gilydd, wedi cusanu'r un bechgyn ar ôl meddwi ar seidr, wedi bod bant yn y coleg, un yng Nghymru, a'r llall yn Lloegr, ac wedi dod 'nôl i'r pentre mewn penbleth. Heno, roedd Ner yn dawel, y mwd wedi sychu'n ole ar hyd ei choesau, a'i siwmper yn gachu i gyd dan ei chesail dde lle bu'n cydio yn y rhaff.

"Be sy'n bod? Picture-no-sound heno 'to," meddwn.

"O sai'n 'bo." Ciciodd garreg ag un o'r sgidie lleder oedd yn llawer rhy fawr iddi – roedden nhw'n edrych yn gomic gan fod ei choesau hi mor denau.

"Ma Mam yn wa'th heddi 'to, a damo Dad… "

O'n i'n gwbod o brofiad pryd i gau 'mhen pan ddechreue hi siarad fel hyn.

"Sdim cliw 'da fe, ma fe fel se fe'n grac arni am 'i bod hi'n sâl. Ffindies i hi bore 'ma ar y clos – o'dd hi 'di trial mynd mas i fwydo'r Westies ac wedi cwmpo a ffaelu codi."

Cododd y teimlad 'na yn fy ngwddf, y teimlad ry'ch chi'n ga'l pan does dim i weud, a rhyw fflach o angau'r blydi byd yn mynd trwyddo chi. Yr un teimlad chi'n ga'l pan welwch chi hen fenyw fach yn ymbalfalu am ei phwrs wrth drio talu am rywbeth a ffaelu'n deg â chael gafael ynddo fe.

"O'dd hi ddim wedi gweiddi – do'dd dim pwynt, medde hi; fydde neb wedi'i chlywed hi dros sŵn y parlwr godro ta beth. Ti'n dod mas heno? Ma ise sesh arna i."

"Sai'n gwbod, cofia; ti'n gwbod be wedodd Les."

"O twll 'i din e! Dere, plis, ddaliwn ni'r bws wyth. Bydd raid i fi neud swper i'r bois gynta, ond deith Dat i nôl ni fel fflipin arfer."

Erbyn hyn, ro'n ni wedi cyrraedd pen lôn cartre Ner.

"Iawn," medde fi, "gerdda i i gwrdd â ti tua hanner 'di saith."

Trodd Ner i lawr ei lôn hi gan gamu ychydig bach yn ysgafnach. Edrychais arni'n mynd am sbelen, a gwrando ar fwcwl y weightbelt yn clincian gyda'i charne. Faint o weithiau o'n ni'n dwy wedi ffarwelio fan hyn gan wneud cynlluniau i gwrdd nes mla'n? Miloedd, siŵr o fod.

Cariais mla'n am ryw ganllath a throi i mewn i'n lôn ni. Ro'n i wedi cerdded y lôn 'ma gannoedd o weithiau, a doedd hi byth yn edrych yr un peth. Heno roedd y borfa'n dechre troi'n rhyw las tebyg i inc tywyll, a'r awel yn chwythu'r borfa hir yn y caeau cyfagos gan droi ei liw fel rhwbio melfed yn groes i'r graen. Roedd yr hewl yn hir ac yn ymestyn at droad pen draw dau gae cyn mynd lawr at y clos. Yr adeg hyn o'r flwyddyn, roedd y cloddiau'n wyrdd ac yn wyllt, gyda'r drysni'n gwneud ei orau i gwrdd yn y canol. Ar ganol y ffordd byddai rhibyn o borfa werdd benderfynol yn gwthio'i ffordd trwy'r cerrig a'r mwd. Ers i mi ddod 'nôl o'r coleg yn Llundain, roedd y wac yma'n baradwys. Roedd y da'n pori'n swnllyd gan daro llygaid heibio i mi, a thros y ffens drydan lle roedd 'nhad wedi eu cau nhw mas o'r caeau silwair. Sôn am y borfa'n wyrddach yr ochr arall, roedd yr olwg yn eu llygaid yn gweud ei fod yn fwy blasus ta beth.

Meddyliais am Ner yn cyrradd gartre. Beth fydde'n 'i disgwyl hi heno, tybed? Roedd Emyr, 'i thad, yn un od. Roedd ganddo fe obsesiwn 'da modelau o awyrennau ac roedd e'n casáu drychau o unrhyw fath. Roedd e'n uffernol o galed ar Ner, ise iddi fod adre erbyn rhyw amser pendant neu'n mynnu 'i phigo hi lan o bobman. Boi go ryfedd o'dd e, ma'n rhaid cyfadde, er 'i fod e mor dawel. Ond, fel wede 'nhad yn aml, ci tawel sy'n cnoi.

Wrth gyrraedd y clos, edrychais i mewn trwy ffenest y gegin tra o'n i'n llacio 'ngharre a defnyddio slaben y drws cefn i dynnu'r sgidie oddi ar fy nhra'd. Roedd y pum leier o sane'n wlyb gan chwys. Heno, roedd yr haul yn machlud yn ara gan daflu cysgod lliw aur dros y clos, a'r parlwr godro'n dawel. Es i mewn i'r tŷ, gan adael ôl fy nhroed yn ddu ar y llechen las.

Tri

"Un, dau, tri a lawr â fe, bois!"

Lluo'r halen, llyncu'r tequila a sugno'r lemwn. Pedwar gwydryn yn clecio'n ôl ar y bwrdd gan wneud i'r gronynnau halen oedd arno ddawnsio.

YYhhhacchhhhhh, ych-a-fi Iesu," medde Awen gan grychu'i thrwyn o achos chwerder y lemwn. "Fi 'di dechre'i dal hi nawr, bois."

"Hei, chi'n gwbod shwt ma neud 'na'n iawn, on'dych chi?" holodd Ner.

"Shwt de?"

"Ffindio bachan bach pert, rhoi'r lemwn yn 'i geg e, lluo dy fys i wlychu'i nipyl a wedyn rhwbio'r halen arno fe. Lluo hwnnw o'i jest, downo'r tequila a hôl y lemwn o'i geg."

"Beth os o's hen jest blewog 'da fe?" gofynnodd Llinos yn hollol o ddifri.

"Ych, ie," medde Awen. "Gaet ti lond ceg o hen flew wedyn."

"Weles i rioed flew ar nipyls dyn," medde Ner.

"Weles i ryw ben-ôl blewog ar y diawl unwaith," ychwanegodd Awen.

"Wel, ti ddim yn mynd i roi halen ar din rhywun, wyt ti?" wedodd Ner 'bach yn fwy uchel nag oedd eisie.

"M'bod, mwy diddorol na lot o bethe fi 'di'i weld yn y gwely, siŵr o fod. Yn lle spice up your love life, season your love life, ondefe."

Awen yn rhochio chwerthin cyn datgan ei bod hi'n

teimlo'n sic. Beth oedd pwrpas blew ar din dyn oedd testun y drafodaeth nesaf.

"O, 'co ni off," medde Llinos. "Os y'n ni'n dechre trafod pethe fel hyn, ma angen bob o beint arnon ni, glei. Nawr te, kitty carrier at y bar plis!"

Dyma fi'n mynd at y bar gan edrych o 'nghwmpas i weld a o'dd Sion wedi dod allan. Digon tebyg 'i fod e'n fisi heno'n trwsio teclynnau ar gyfer y seilej. Ymlwybrais trwy'r gymysgedd o fechgyn oedd yn llawer rhy ifanc i fod mewn tafarn yn y lle cyntaf, merched oedd yn arfer bod yn yr ysgol 'da fi, a chydig o bobol y Clwb Ffermwyr Ifanc.

"Iawn, Hels?" gofynnodd llais o'r tu ôl i'r bar.

Chwe troedfedd o gorff, a hwnnw 'di ca'l tan hyfryd, gwallt du, llygaid glas a gwefusau o'n i'n methu tynnu'n llygaid oddi arnyn nhw.

"Blydi hel, Deian! Shwd wyt ti ers... wel ers dyddie ysgol?" medde finne, gan deimlo'n ymwybodol yn sydyn o'r ffordd ro'n i'n edrych.

"Ti'n edrych yn grêt," atebodd gan bwyso'n groes y bar i roi cusan ar fy moch. "Be ti lan i nawr de?" gofynnodd gan wenu ac anwybyddu'r boi wrth fy ochr oedd isie pedwar peint o lager top a phecyn o grisps.

"O, hyn a'r llall, t'mod. Trio cadw allan o drwbwl," medde fi'n ysgafn, gan feddwl – shit, wy'n fflyrto!

"Adre am ychydig dw i – ma 'da fi waith yn Llunden cyn bo hir, ac ma'n neis i ga'l tipyn o amser 'da'r oldies, t'mod. Eniwe, be ti ise?"

Finne'n rhoi'r ordyr diodydd iddo fe gan geisio peidio ag edrych ar ei din. Uffarn, o'dd y boi 'ma wedi newid er pan weles i fe ddwetha! Dyma fi'n dyfeisio mantra cyflym: 'paid edrych ar 'i din e, paid edrych ar 'i din e, paid edrych ar 'i din… '

"Wyth bunt pymtheg ceiniog, plis."

"E?"

"Y drincs… wyth bunt pymtheg."

"O ie, sori," medde fi wrth ymbalfalu am y cwdyn kitty.

"Ma dy ddiod di am ddim, wrth gwrs."

"O, diolch."

"Wela i di 'to, gobeitho?" wedodd e gan wincio'n secsi ddiawledig.

"Ie, bet your life."

A dyma fi'n troi am 'nôl i weld y merched i gyd yn edrych arna i'n dod tuag atyn nhw ac yn gwneud siapse ar ei gilydd. 'Bet your life?' Be uffarn o'n i'n weud? Pwy o'n i'n meddwl o'n i, de – rhywun ar *Friends*? A dyma fi'n meddwl wrth gerdded 'nôl, 'gobeithio bod e'n edrych ar 'y nhin i… gobeithio bod e'n edrych ar 'y nhin i… gobeithio bod e'n edrych ar 'y nhin i'. O'dd yr hen dintws yn edrych yn weddol ar ôl yr holl ymarfer. Clywais y gigyls yn dod i gwrdd â fi o gyfeiriad y ford.

"Heledd wedi tynnu, Heledd wedi tynnu," gwaeddodd Kelloggs ar dop ei llais.

"Ca' dy ben!" sibrydais yn dawel gan gochi hyd at fôn fy ngwallt.

"Pam ti'n mynd yn goch, de?" gofynnodd Llinos.

"Tin bach go lew 'da fe 'fyd," ychwanegodd Kelloggs. "Ond bydd rhaid inni ddweud wrth Sion dy fod ti'n tynnu dynion pert pan dyw e ddim mas!"

"O hisht," medde finne gyda'r teimlad cynnes 'na'n dal yn fy mhen ac mewn rhanne eraill o'r corff na ddyle fe fod, o feddwl bod gen i gariad.

"Chi'n meddwl bod chance 'da ni de?" gofynnodd Awen gan fy achub o'r diwedd.

"Gan 'i fod e'n edrych fel'na, ma bownd o fod rhyw ddol o fenyw 'da fe, 'da gwallt melyn a bronne o fan hyn i gopa'r Wyddfa," wedodd Llinos gan geisio tynnu'i llygaid oddi ar ei din.

"Dim 'da fe, y wali – 'da'r gystadleuaeth," chwarddodd Awen.

"'M'bod," medde Ner. "Ni'n well leni na llynedd, glei. Ni 'di bod yn treino'n galetach a fi 'di codi o 'ngwely cyn bo fi'n gall i fynd mas i redeg lot gormod."

"Un peth sy'n dda," ychwanegodd Kel, "yw'n bod ni'n ca'l ein pwyso ar yr un glorian â'r bois – we-hei! Gweld y talent yn eu pants cyn dechre. Neith e safio lot o swmpo'r nosweth 'ny!"

Roedd Kelloggs yn enwog am dri pheth: faint o fodca o'dd hi'n medru'i yfed, faint o ddynion o'dd hi'n mynd efo nhw (serial shagger) a hefyd am wneud i bawb yn y cartre hen bobl lle o'dd hi'n gweithio i ddwlu arni ac i chwerthin nes bod y Matron yn dweud 'u bod nhw'n mynd trwy fwy o bedpans nag unrhyw un o'r cartrefi cyfagos.

"Reit te," medde Ner gan godi'n sigledig ar ei thraed mewn pâr o sodle uchel. "I'm in the mood for dancing, bois… Up here for thinking, down here for dancing… Dewch mla'n, fi 'di cadw lle inni ar y llawr danso heno, bois."

"O's rhaid inni?" cwynodd Awen, o'dd wastad yn casáu dawnsio. "Chi'n gwbod faint fi'n hêto danso; ma' co-ordination jeli-ffish meddw 'da fi."

"Paid bod yn sili," medde finne. "Jeli-ffish falle, ond dim un meddw!"

"O blydi hel, Hels!"

"Dim ond jocan o'n i, achan!" medde finne gan gydio'n 'i braich.

"Sym dy din," medde Ner. "Meddylia amdano fe fel training, tynnu fel y diawl!"

A gyda'r geiriau hyn dyma Ner yn troi ar ei sawdl ac yn cwmpo'n bendramwnwgl ar hyd y bwrdd nesa, a hwnnw'n llawn gwydrau a dynion. Fe gododd y sgert fach wen dros ei thin a dyma lathenni o goesau'n chwifio dan drwynau'r bois. O'dd hi'n debyg i granc wedi'i droi ar ei gefn. Dyma Awen yn dechre chwerthin, a Llinos yn pisho'i hun, a neb â digon o nerth i fynd i'w helpu. Rhegfeydd yn dechre codi o'r coese ar y bwrdd, a breichiau'r bechgyn yn ei chodi ar ei thraed. Ner yn ceisio cadw'i chŵl a thorri'r embaras.

"Sori, bois – chi mor gorgeous, 'nes i gwmpo amdanoch chi'n strêt."

"O, ffor ffyc sêcs!" medde finne. "Dere, ti moyn dawnsio? O leia fydd 'na fwy o le, a llawr gwastad yn y Square."

Sgwâr concrid o le oedd y clwb nos lleol 'da décor oedd yn rhyw hanner cyfoes, a phapur wal bloc wedi'i beintio 'da phaent neon gan obeithio na sylwai neb. Roedd y staff hefyd yn edrych yn rhyfedd tu ôl i'r bar modern: Brian, boi tua hanner cant oed a oedd wastad yn ceisio bachu'r merched mwyaf meddw, a merched wedi'u dewis am bod eu bronne nhw'n cyfarfod â chi pan o'ch chi'n ordro drincs. Roedden ni'n gallu dychmygu Brian ar y casting couch yn rhoi interviews i'r pŵr-dabs. Eistedd wrth rhyw fwrdd oedd yn edrych fel 'se rhywun o *Homefront* wedi gwneud botched job arno fe, a Ner yn dod â threied arall o tequila draw. Pawb yn clecio.

"Ych-ych-ych," gwaeddodd Ner dros y miwsig, "ma 'ngwallt i'n sownd yn fy lipgloss i!"

"Duw, ar ddiwedd y noson fel arfer ma blew yn fy lipgloss i… " medde Kel.

"O'r fflipin hwch â ti!" rhochiodd Awen. "Ti'n rêl tarten!"

Llinos bron ar y llawr yn chwerthin.

"Nawr te, pwy sydd am bŵgi bach, de?" medde finne gan gydio ym mraich Awen cyn iddi sleifio i'r toiledau.

"Cym on de, ladies, dewch i ddangos be sy 'da ni, de." Ner yn arwain y ffordd fel arfer, a llygaid y dynion yn ei dilyn a'u tafodau'n creu carped coch inni gerdded drosto. Un peth oedd mynd allan 'da criw o ferched; peth arall oedd mynd allan 'en masse' 'da criw o ferched ffit yr olwg oedd yn edrych fel cymysgedd rhyfedd o aelodau'r maffia a'r Playboy bunnies. Roedd Awen yn dilyn, yn edrych 'bach yn sigledig ac yn gwneud ei gore i dynnu'i thop dros ei thin.

Roedd pethe'n dechre mynd 'bach yn niwlog. Diodydd, clebran â rhyw ddynion, cymharu fy mronne 'da rhai rhyw ferched yn y toiledau, hen ffrind ysgol yn dweud ei fod wedi fy ngharu i erioed cyn dweud 'tho Awen ei fod wedi ei charu hithau erioed hefyd, Llinos yn chwydu yn y toiledau, Kel yn snogio bownser a Brian yn winco arna i drwy'r nos ac yn colli'i eyeballs yn fy wonderbra bob tro ro'n i'n prynu diod. Roedd y diodydd yn dechre amrywio 'fyd, a bydde hynna wastad yn arwydd gwael. Poteli o ryw stwff lliw anti-ffrîs, caniau, peint o seidr, a shorts. Roedd Awen wedi ca'l gafel ar fodca jeli ac roedd hi'n brysur yn dawnsio gan ddal y peth wrth ei thin ac yn ceisio gweld pa un oedd yn crynu fwyaf. Ner yn edrych fel tase hi'n trio mogi un o'r bois landiodd hi arno yn y dafarn â'i bronnau. Sa i'n cofio dim byd wedyn 'mond yr arferol – pizza, a cholli hanner y merched i ryw gorneli tywyll. Emyr yn disgwyl am Ner a finne, a 'mhen i dal yn llawn o ryw foi tal a gwallt tywyll.

Pedwar

Dihuno'n chwys i gyd. Pedwar y bore, a'r lleuad llawn yn mynnu gwthio'i fysedd i mewn rhwng y llenni tenau. Damo Nerys, gorfod mynd i'w nôl hi yn orie mân y bore er bod ei mam yn sâl. Estyn llaw draw i ochr arall y gwely cyn cofio bod Gaynor yn y stafell sbâr. Ar ôl mynd â Heledd adre, a rhoi dŵr i Nerys i sobri dipyn arni hi, rhoi 'mhen i mewn drwy'r drws i weld sut oedd hi. Edrychai fel plentyn yn y gwely sengl, a'r papur wal Tomos y Tanc yn dal ar y welydd ar ôl y crwt. Gwrando am yr anadlu ysgafn cyn mynd yn ôl i'r gwely a thrial cysgu.

Does dim aer yn y nos. Rwy'n methu anadlu – mae'n sgyfaint i wedi mynd yn fach, fach ac mae 'na rywun wedi gosod clustog anweledig dros fy wyneb i. Rwy'n methu anadlu – blydi hel! Mae'r stafell yn troi rownd a rownd ac rwy'n cwympo'n ôl i gysgu unwaith eto. Cwympo dros ddibyn, cwympo fel 'chi'n gneud weithiau wrth fynd i gysgu, ond yn lle'r sioc o ddihuno ar fatras, dal i gwympo dros ryw glogwyn diwaelod. Gweld drych ar wal, a'r llosgi a'r panig yn chwyddo yn fy mrest i nes iddo fygwth ffrwydro allan trwy'r asennau a rhwygo'r esgyrn drwy'r cnawd. Rwy'n methu teimlo 'nwylo, maen nhw'n binne bach i gyd. Oerni'n teithio o un darn o 'nghorff i'r llall, yn debyg i anaesthetig cyn llawdriniaeth. Sŵn y gwynt yn anadlu tu allan gan fwrw dail yn erbyn y ffenest. Methu anadlu, methu teimlo, ond rwy'n gweld y drych mawr a'm wyneb i fy hun yn edrych yn ôl arna i. A beth wela i? Y rhychau, y llinellau coch tenau fel hewlydd ar fap lle mae'r gwynt wedi ffindio'i ffordd dros fy mochau. Tyllau fan hyn a fan draw lle mae'r gwynt wedi naddu pyllau yn y croen, a'r baw wedi aros ynddynt. Mae fy wyneb i'n hongian ar y wal.

Drwyn yn drwyn â mi fy hun, rwy'n medru gweld y bywyd arall tu ôl i'r wal, tu ôl i'r adlewyrchiad. Tu ôl i'r wyneb yn y drych mae 'na fywyd arall, a dyna'r lle rwy i i fod. Rwy'n symud fy ngheg, ond mae'r un ar y wal yn llonydd. Cragen fy wyneb a'r cig a'r gwaed tu ôl iddo wedi pydru a'i grafu o 'na. Cragen ar draeth arian y drych. Rwy'n mogi, yn methu teimlo rhagor; mae 'na ryw dynfa boenus yn fy mrest yn anfon afonydd o drydan i 'mhen gan wneud i'r meddyliau stumio allan o bob rheolaeth. Yr holl bethau rwy wedi meddwl amdanyn nhw erioed. Ffenestr eglwys o feddyliau, a'r plwm wedi toddi. Fy llygaid fy hun yn edrych arnaf. Wyneb sy'n arswydus o gyfarwydd. Ceisiaf gydio yn yr wyneb, gan ymbalfalu i dynnu'r mwgwd oddi am fy mhen, a gwthio fy mysedd i'r wyneb tu ôl i'r cnawd, ond rwy'n methu teimlo 'mysedd – teimlad meddw.

Dihuno eto a chodi i daro golwg ar Gaynor. Mynd ar draws y landin a golau'r lleuad yn dod trwy ffenest y stafell wely ac yna drwy'r banistr gan wneud patrwm barrau ar y llawr pren, a ffenest y landin yn bedwar sgwâr perffaith o olau. Clywed sŵn sibrwd tawel – Nerys yn siarad yn ei chwsg eto. Mynd i mewn i stafell Gaynor.

Pan briodon ni gyntaf, ro'n i wastad yn rhyfeddu sut roedd hi'n cysgu. Wrth godi yn y bore, roedd hi'n amhosib dweud ei bod hi wedi bod yn y gwely o gwbl. Roedd hi'n hynod o lonydd a thawel, ac yn llithro allan o'r gwely yn y bore fel llythyr o amlen. Yna daeth y baglu a'r lletchwithdod. Methu teimlo bysedd ei thraed yn y bàth ryw nosweth. Sŵn dail yn y gwynt gyda phob anadl. Byddwn weithiau'n eistedd yn y caeau yn gwrando ar y sŵn yna. Yn y gwanwyn byddai'r ffawydden yn anwylo'r awyr â dail oedd â rhyw wrid ysgafn o flew arian arnynt. Yn yr haf, dail iachus gwyrdd tywyll, ac yn yr hydref y sisial olaf cyn iddynt ddisgyn. Roedd y disgyn yn anochel, ond roedd y canu a'r sibrwd yn mynd ymlaen hyd y diwedd. Meddwl ar ôl i bopeth ddigwyddd y byddwn wastad yn teimlo hiraeth wrth glywed sŵn y dail; y byddent yn fy ngyrru'n wallgof wrth i mi weithio yn y caeau.

Penliniais wrth y gwely gan wrando ar y siffrwd yn ei hanadlu, a'r croen glân fel eira oer yng ngolau'r lleuad. Edau ei gwallt golau yn codi a disgyn o gwmpas ei cheg. Mae ei gwefusau'n sych, a rhyw wrid gwyn arnyn nhw fel y caeau ar fore o Hydref. Rwy'n rhoi bys yn fy ngheg i'w wlychu ac yn rhwbio'r sychder i ffwrdd. Mae'r siffrwd yn troi'n sibrwd yn ei chwsg, a cheisiaf ei ddehongli. Siffrwd dail yn blaguro enw… "Huw"… "Huw". Codi ar fy nhraed a mynd yn ôl i'm stafell. Sefyll wrth y ffenestr ac agor y llenni. Mae'n fore braf, a'r golau cyntaf yn ceisio cripio drwy'r cloddiau gan greu effaith brodwaith yn erbyn yr awyr. Y nen yn rhyw liw llechen, a'r cymylau fel sialc wedi'i rwbio i ffwrdd. Rhaid meddwl am dorri fory os dalith y tywydd. Mae cnwd da 'leni, yn llawn meillion, a gobeithio, fel llynedd, y bydd 'na beth dros ben i'w werthu ar ddiwedd y tymor. Rhaid cofio mynd at y cyfrifydd ddydd Llun. Sŵn drws yn agor groes y landin. Nerys. Traed ansicr yn mynd i'r tŷ bach. Sŵn chwydu. Tawelwch. Siffrwd cefn mewn gŵn-nos tenau yn llithro i lawr wal y stafell ac yna'n eistedd ar y llawr. Llefen. Dagrau tawel. Gallaf ei gweld hi nawr – merch un ar hugain oed mewn gŵn-nos tedi bêrs, y mascara'n rhedeg i lawr ei gruddiau gyda'r dagrau tawel. Doedd dim pwynt mynd ati – byddai'n eistedd a'i choesau wedi'u croesi fel y byddai hi'n wneud pan oedd yn blentyn bach, a'i phen fel lili wen fach yn pendwmpian. Sŵn y dail drws nesaf. O leiaf doedd Gaynor ddim wedi dihuno.

Cysgu unwaith eto a gweld y drych ar y wal. Cael fy llyncu gan gwsg a breuddwydion tywyll. Mwgwd. Yr un peth yn union.

Pump

Bore dydd Sul – ceg fel cesail camel a dim sgwash wrth ymyl y gwely. Rhoi un droed ar lawr ac arbrofi gydag eistedd lan. Edrych ar fy nhraed – un droed â hosan amdani, y llall heb; un glust â chlustdlws ynddi, y llall heb. Roedd bra neithiwr yn cydio'n rhy dynn o lawer yn fy nghroen a 'nhafod i fel twll tin sbaniel. Edrych i gyfeiriad y drws, a'm golwg yn cyrraedd ddeg eiliad ar ôl fy mhen.

Codi ar fy nhraed a'm stumog yn sur. Cael trafferth sefyll. Mynd i'r tŷ bach – dillad neithiwr ar y llawr dan y sinc, a'r êring-cypord yn arllwys dillad lle fues i'n twrio am wn-nos neithiwr. Yfed peint o ddŵr a 'nôl â fi i'r gwely. O na – mae 'na ymarfer mewn dwy awr! Gorwedd 'nôl a meddwl am neithiwr. Brith atgofion yn dod 'nôl ata i – Awen a'r fodca jeli a Ner 'da'r boi 'na ac Emyr yn ein dyfyrio ni'n dwy am fod mor hwyr wrth iddo fy ngollwng wrth giât y clos. Fy stumog fel tonnau'r môr. Sŵn Mam yn siarad 'da rhywun lawr sta'r a'r stof yn troi'r gwres ymlaen gan anfon siffrwd trwy'r peipiau dŵr. Sŵn traed ar y sta'r ac wedyn yn groes y landin. Cyrhaeddodd y cwestiwn y stafell cyn y person.

"A ble o't ti neithwr, 'de?" Roedd Sion mewn hwyl wael uffernol.

"A bore da i tithe 'fyd, cariad," atebais. "Ble ti'n feddwl o'n i neithwr? Mas 'da'r merched, on'defe? Ffones i ti cyn mynd – sdim bai arna i bod neb yn rhoi negeseuon i ti, nago's e?" A setlais 'nôl ar y gobennydd.

"Handi iawn! Bob tro ti isie mynd mas 'da'r criw tynnu rhaff 'na, dyw'r neges ddim yn 'y nghyrra'dd i. Od, ondife?" Roedd e'n cerdded 'nôl a mla'n ar hyd y llawr fel ffŵl. "A beth yw'r pwynt ca'l mobile os nad wyt ti'n ei adel e 'mlaen? Y? Galle unrhyw un feddwl bo' ti ddim isie i fi wbod lle o't ti. Unwaith wyt ti mas 'da'r merched 'na, rwyt ti'n newid yn llwyr. Be sy'n bod arna ti?"

"Beth uffarn ti'n feddwl?" holais, a 'nhymer yn dechre codi.

"O, dim byd… "

"Beth uffarn sy'n bod 'no ti, gwed? Be ti'n ddisgwl i fi neud? Hongian ambwti fan hyn fel ryw hen wraig fach nes bo' ti 'di bennu gwaith, ife?"

"Wel, ma' *rhai* o' ni'n gorfod gweithio, yn do's e?"

"Be ma 'na fod meddwl?"

"Wel, dyw pawb ddim yn galler fforddio ca'l rhyw jobyn bach cwshdi, ran-amser, ar ôl bod off yn y coleg, tra bo' ni'n whilo rhywbeth gwell, y'n ni? Ma' Dadi 'da ti yn dy gadw di'n net."

"O, diolch yn fowr i ti, Sion. 'Na beth ti'n meddwl ohono i, ife? 'Na beth ti'n meddwl fi'n neud, ife? Sbynjo off Mam a Dad?"

Roedd 'na gant a mil o bethe'n hedfan drwy fy meddwl. Edrychodd Sion ar y llawr a thawelu.

"Sori, Hels, o'n i ddim yn 'i feddwl e, t'mod… "

"Na? Swnio fel 'ny 'fyd!" gwylltiais, gan gicio'r garthen oddi arna i. Roedd hi'n anodd cwympo mas 'da rhywun a chithe ar eich cefen! "Fues i ddim yn y coleg am yr holl flynydde 'na am byger-ol, t'mod. Sa i moyn taflu'r cyfan bant a dechre gweithio mewn ryw siop rownd ffor hyn… "

"Dyw hynny ddim digon da i ti rhagor, yw e? Ise mynd off wyt ti, ondife, ca'l rhyw joben ffansi yn y ddinas a

drinks 'da'r bechgyn mewn siwts ar ôl gwaith. Callia,
Heledd – ti'n byw mewn ryw blydi soap opera, achan."

"Cer i grafu… "

"Ise ca'l gyment o bae â'r ffrindie ffansi 'na o'dd 'da ti
yn y coleg wyt ti, ondife? Yn syden reit, ma 'na bethe erill
yn bwysig yn do's e, Hels?"

"Wel, fi 'di colli ti nawr, no," brathais yn ôl. "O ble
ma hyn i gyd wedi dod? O't ti'n iawn amser cino ddo' pan
siarades i â ti ar y ffôn. O, gad fi feddwl nawr – ma Mother
wedi bod yn ca'l gair 'da ti yw hi?"

"Be ti'n feddwl?"

"O, cym off it, Sion; ti fel blydi llyfyr, achan. Madam
wedi bod yn gwenwyno 'to, odi ddi?"

"Nadi ddim, a paid â siarad amdani hi felna."

"Be ti'n ddisgwl 'te, Sion? Fydd dy fam ddim yn hapus
nes ein bod ni'n diwedd lan ar ffarm fach neis – bord
dderw yn y gegin, blode wedi sychu ar y chest-o-drôrs, a
hanner dwsin o blant. Ma hi 'di bod yn galw fi'n snoben
to, odi ddi?"

"Rwyt ti ise pethe na allith y lle 'ma, na finne chwaith,
'u roi iti achan."

"Wel, fe ddwgest ti'r geire mas o'i phen hi yndofe?
Llais dy fam o'dd hwnna os glywes i fe erioed. Sion, wir
Dduw, ma 'na fywyd ochor draw y ffycin stand laeth 'na,
ti'n gwbod."

Ro'n i'n crynu i gyd.

"Fi'n gwbod 'ny," gwaeddodd yn ôl, "er mod i ddim
wedi bod off mewn rhyw ffycin coleg ffansi fel ti… "

"O, 'co ni off 'to… "

"Ond alla i addo i ti nad yw e cystel â be sy 'da ti fan
hyn, Hels; alla i ffycin addo iti."

"A beth fi fod neud, Sion? Be ti ise fi neud? Ca'l ryw

joben fach cosy rownd ffordd hyn 'da'r cyngor neu rywbeth, ca'l plant a'u hela nhw i ryw ysgol fach leol – 'na beth fydde'n iawn i fi neud, ife? 'Na be fydde ore i *fi*, ife? Cym on, gwed. Ma'n debyg bod gan bob diawl awgrym am sut ddylwn i fyw fy mywyd, glei. Wyt ti'n mynd i roi pregeth i fi am fynd mas i yfed 'to? Falle ddylwn i gymryd cross-stitch lan a phrynu *House and Home…* "

"Ti'n siarad nonsens nawr," wedodd e. "Ti'n cofio pan est ti off i ddechre? 'Na i gyd o't ti'n siarad am o'dd ca'l gorffen yn y coleg a dod 'nôl ata i fan hyn, ondife? Ti'n cofio dod 'nôl am wylie a dod mas i fwydo'r defed 'da fi ac edrych mla'n tan gallet ti neud 'na o hyd? Llefen pan o't ti'n gorfod mynd yn ôl?"

"Ie?"

"Wel, alla i ddim symud y tir, Heledd; taswn i'n galler fe fydden i'n neud e i ti ga'l beth ti moyn, ond 'na fe, fi'n ffaelu. Fi 'di gweud o'r dechre, fi 'di byw ar ffarm trwy'n oes. 'Na i gyd fi'n gwbod, a mwy na 'ny, sa i moyn neud dim byd arall."

"A ma rhaid i fi blygu i 'na, o's e? Gwed wrtha i, Sion, odw i wedi gofyn i ti symud y tir er 'y mwyn i?"

Edrychodd arna i a'i lygaid yn ddolurus.

"Nag wyt," atebodd a dagrau yn ei lais, "dyna'r broblem." A cherddodd at y drws.

"Ble ti'n mynd?"

"Ma raid i fi fynd â'r invoices contracto o gwmpas."

"O ie, a galw am un bach yn y pyb ar y ffordd, ife?"

"Da iawn, Hels, good guess."

Caeodd y drws yn glep ar ei ôl.

"Ffor ffyc sêcs," mwmiais dan fy anadl wrth syrthio 'nôl ar y gwely. Doedd dim ffycin ennill i ga'l; pum mlynedd o berthynas a dyna fe'n cerdded allan i'r pyb. Man a man i ni fod wedi bod yn briod am ugain mlynedd! Tynnais y garthen yn dynnach o'm hamgylch; roedd 'y mhen i'n corco. Clywn sŵn car Sion yn mynd lan y lôn. Beth uffarn o'dd yn bod arno fe? Pan o'n i yn y coleg roedd e'n browd ohona i ac yn edrych mla'n at 'y ngweld i'n gneud rhywbeth ohona i fy hun. Ond nawr, ar ôl i mi orffen yno, roedd rhyw batrwm bach wedi'i gerfio allan i fi, a phawb – Ner, Awen, Non, Mam, Dad a'r mam-gus – i gyd yn disgwyl i fi hwylio i fewn i'r patrwm heb droi'n ôl. O'dd Sion yn iawn, 'na i gyd o'n i'n moyn pan o'n i yn y coleg o'dd ca'l dod adre er mwyn ca'l bod yn agos ato fe a'r ffarm. A beth o'dd yn od o'dd bod hynny ddim wedi newid o gwbl – jest 'mod i eisie lot o bethe erill o'dd ddim i ga'l 'ma 'fyd.

Bip Bip! wrth fy ochr. Ymbalfalu ar y ford wrth y gwely – neges testun ar y ffôn oddi wrth Ner: METHU SYMUD, V BRON MARW. TRAINING UGH

Ateb 'nôl: DITTO. NWDD GWMPO MAS DA S

Dwy funud yn mynd heibio.

PAID BECS - PMT DA FE. CU STAND LATH

Ateb 'nôl: FAINT O GLCH B T NA?

Munud arall yn mynd heibio.

AWR. MAM CAL BORE UFFERNOL

Es i ga'l cawod, a thynnu'r hen ddillad ymarfer mas o'r fasged olchi a'u gwisgo. Roedd drewdod hen chwys yn codi wrth iddyn nhw gynhesu am fy nghorff. Hanner darn o dost sych, cwpwl o gnau a charton cyfan o sudd oren. Wel, roedd hynna'n well na chyfuniad Awen o Milky Way a Dr Pepper.

* * * *

Cerddais yn araf am y cae i gyfarfod Ner. Roedd hi'n dawel iawn eto heddiw, a'i llygaid yn dangos ôl llefen. Roedd ganddon ni ddealltwriaeth – do'n i byth yn gofyn cwestiynau pan o'dd hi fel hyn.

"Gantri heddi, ferched. Kit up – bach o waith caled heddi nawr 'de.

"Beth yw'r gwenwn 'ma? Os 'ych chi 'di bod mas neithwr, fi'n mynd i wbod, dydw i? Cym on, ni'n mynd i ga'l newid bach rownd ffordd hyn. Shit work ar fore dydd Sul o nawr mla'n. Os 'ych chi 'di bod mas, fe fydda i'n galler gweud, a bydd y donci'n ca'l bach o action. Nawr get on with it, you gorgeous beasts."

Iesu, o'n ni'n ryff – Llinos yn dawel reit, Ner wedi bennu Abergafenni ac Awen yn treial cwato uffarn o lovebite dan ei chlust.

"Reit, pawb wrth y rhaff plis," cyfarthodd Les. "Ma 'da fi announcement bach i neud gynta. Ry'n ni'n chwilo am angor newydd."

Edrychodd pawb yn syn – beth uffach o'dd yn mynd mla'n? Edrychais 'nôl ar Awen, ac roedd honno'n edrych mor siocd â phawb arall.

"Ma'n debyg bod ein angor ni ddim lan i'r job rhagor, achos ma hi'n rhy ysgafn, ma hi 'di colli gormod o bwyse."

O'n ni i gyd yn hollol ar goll nawr.

"It seems, my darlings, bod rhywun wedi cymryd uffarn o hansh mas ohoni hi neithiwr. Ma'n debyg bod 'i chlust hi ym mola rhyw sgroat bach o ochre Aberystwyth bore 'ma."

Dechreuodd Ner giglan. Edrychai Llinos yn confused.

"Nawr te, sefwch wrth y rhaff," meddai Les gan gilwenu. "Ry'n ni'n mynd i ga'l chat fach gynta heddi ladies – so ffycin gwrandwch, y wasters!"

Daeth ebychiad o'r tu ôl i mi.

"Beth ry'n ni'n neud 'ma heddi?" gofynnodd Les.

Pawb yn dawel.

"O's rhywun yn mynd i ateb? Ner – tafla berl i mi, cariad."

Rhythodd Ner arno a'i llygaid wedi chwyddo i gyd.

"Tynnu rhaff."

"Da iawn, Ner, ti on the ball fel arfer; the wheel's still spinning and the hamster's not quite dead. Y peth yw, fy nghariadon annwyl, ein bod ni fel Cymry yn colli tamed fynna mewn cyfieithad, chi'n gweld."

Trodd Les ar ei sawdl a cherdded 'nôl ar hyd y llinell. Arafodd ar bwys Awen. Closiodd at ei chlust. "TUG-O'-WAR!" gwaeddodd nerth ei ben.

Neidiodd Awen droedfedd o'r llawr. "Iesu Grist, ddyn, beth uffarn sy'n bod 'no chi?" gwaeddodd hithau 'nôl.

"Sori, cariad, o's pen tost 'da ti?" gwenodd Les. "Tasen i'n gwbod 'nny, fyddwn i byth wedi gweiddi shwt gymint." Yna, ar ôl ychydig eiliadau o dawelwch, dechreuodd fyfyrio. "Tug-o'-war," meddai, "dyna i chi eirie, ondife. Rhyfel. Rhyfel… chi'n gweld. Dyna beth ni'n neud fan hyn heddiw yw dysgu sut mae rhyfela. Mewn cystadleuaeth ma'n rhaid ichi ddysgu atgasedd. You've got to hate their fucking guts – those stupid tarts who were arrogant enough to think they could come up against you and walk away." Dechreuodd ei lais godi eto. "RHYFEL, chi'n deall? Meddyliwch am y Gododdin. 'Co ni ar y cae a'r cigfrain yn hedfan dros ein penne. Ma'r adar 'na yn mynd i ga'l ffîd a chi'n mynd i neud yn dam siŵr nad eich eyeballs chi fyddan nhw'n fyta i frecwast. COMPRENDE? Nhw yn erbyn ni. Anghofiwch y ffycin 'y peth pwysig yw cymryd rhan', 'parchwch eich cyd-chwaraewyr' shite 'ma chi 'di ddysgu 'wrth ryw groten o ysgol Gwmrâg rywle wrth chware pêl-rwyd. 'Na i gyd ma nhw'n wbod yw sut ma neud sioe ffycin gerdd. RHYFEL yw hyn. Wyneb yn wyneb, pwy sy gryfa? O'dd y Vikings yn tynnu'i gilydd dros goelcerthi, felly cowntwch 'ych hunen yn lwcus. Ni mas i goncro ac i ladd, a ma hynna'n digwydd pan ma nhw ar 'u ffycin tine ar 'yn hochor ni o'r llinell." Closiodd at Non. "Deall?"

"Odw, Les."

"Odw, Les," ailadroddodd e gan ddynwared llais bach merchetaidd. "Gwed e felse ti'n 'i feddwl e, de!"

"ODW, LES!" gwaeddodd Non.

"Da iawn." A cherddodd ar hyd y lein eto. "Byddwn ni'n tynnu time o bobman, a ni'n mynd i'w casáu nhw – bob shagging jac wan ohonyn nhw. Prynwch ddrinc iddyn nhw ar ôl 'nny ar bob cyfri, ond ar y cae ry'n ni'n udo am waed. Beth wy'n moyn yw'r bitchiness 'stare the cow in the face – look at her as if you've scraped her off your shoe,' as only women can do. Ry'ch chi'n neud e ar nos Sadwrn pan ma rhyw ferch yn edrych yn right state mewn ryw dress, on'd ych chi? Ma fe'n dod yn naturiol i chi, y bygers, so nawr put it to some use. NATUR.

"Pick up the rope," a dyma ni'n codi'r rhaff.

"Take the strain!" Sŵn fel palu gardd.

"Edrychwch arna i... Edrychwch arna i... a TYNNWCH!"

Breichiau Les yn cwympo a'r 'HY' yn canu 'nôl ar hyd y llinell.

Uffarn, roedd lot o bwyse yn y gasgen heddi, ac roedd pizza neithiwr yn mynnu codi 'nôl i 'ngheg i. Roedd Ner druan yn syffro 'fyd, a'r rhaff yn cripian yn ôl yn arafach nag arfer.

"AND pull and pull and pull," deuai llais Les wrth fy ochr.

"Cod dy fflipin din," gwaeddodd Llinos ar Ner. "Be sy'n bod arnot ti?"

A Ner dan straen yn brathu, "Piss off, Llinos!"

Chwifiai'r gasgen 'nôl a mla'n ar y sgaffold.

"Ewch 'nôl â hi, de, ferched; chi'n stablan ambwti 'ma felse'r holl amser yn y blydi byd 'da chi."

Dyma rhif un yn rhoi plwc ac yn codi rhythm, a ninnau'n ei dilyn hi fel ryw chain gang chwyslyd am 'nôl.

"'Na fe, 'na fe, ma 'bach o siâp 'ma nawr, a dalwch hi ar y top fynna am ryw ddwy funud inni ga'l cynhesu lan 'm bach."

Roedd fy nwylo i'n llosgi a'r blas afiach 'na yn codi 'nôl i'm ceg. Iesu, ro'n i'n wan!

"Munud ar ôl," meddai llais Les wrth fy ochr. "O, Hels, fi'n joio clywed ti'n moanan."

"Piss off!"

"'Na fe, ladies," meddai Les gan gerdded mla'n wrth y rhaff. "Ma Hels fan hyn wedi ennill munud fach arall ichi."

Roedd e'n chware 'da ni 'to, ac ro'n i'n casáu 'na. Roedd y cyhyrau yn fy mreichiau'n crynu a finne'n gorfod jacio'r rhaff ar fy weightbelt. Roedd Llinos ar y warpath.

"Heledd, paid jacio, myn uffarn i. Rwyt ti'n rhoi uffarn o ginc yn y rhaff, achan."

"Sori," ymddiheurais.

"Beth uffarn yw iws sori? Jest blydi stopa."

"Sori," meddwn inne 'to.

Daeth Les draw. "Nawr te, ladies, pwy sy 'di bod ar y pop 'ma? Nawr ry'n ni'n gweld, ondife? O'dd y fodca'n ffein, Llinos?"

"Yfes i ddim fodca, diolch," cyfarthodd Llinos.

"O, sori! You're a lager girl, ife Llinos?"

Roedd Ner yn dechre gwenwyno a thynnodd hi un llaw oddi ar y rhaff i gael gwa'd yn ôl iddi.

Aeth Les yn boncyrs. "Be ffyc weles i fan'na?" gwaeddodd yn ei chlust. "Joiest ti'r hoe fach 'na?"

"Ffyc off, Les."

"Os wela i unrhyw beth felna 'to, fydd hi off 'ma – 'na'n gwmws beth ma nhw'n aros amdano, yn edrych amdano. Cofiwch, bydd dyn 'da nhw yn 'ych gwylio chi ac yn aros i chi neud rhywbeth mor ffycin stiwpid."

Roedd Ner yn dechre'i cholli hi a mwy a mwy o bwyse'n ca'l ei drosglwyddo i 'mreichiau i a 'nôl ar hyd y rhaff.

"CYM ON, PEIDWCH RHOI LAN!" Roedd ei wyneb yn prysur gochi a ninne'n meddwl ei fod yn mynd i ga'l harten. Gwaeddodd unwaith eto ar Ner. "WHAT DOES NOT KILL ME MAKES ME STRONGER! Deg, naw, wyth, saith, whech, pedwar, tri, dau a lawr â hi. Swig a hoe a 'nôl ar y rhaff."

Roedd clytie mawr ar fy sgidie, a'r platie metel yn slic fel rhew. Eisteddodd pawb mewn cylch am eiliad, a Les yn mynd i roi rhagor o gerrig yn y gasgen. Roedd pawb yn dawel am sbel, a Ner yn edrych fel petai ar fin llefen. Newidiodd Heini y sgwrs: "Beth uffarn o'dd y boi 'na'n trio neud iti, 'de, Awen?"

"O, ca dy ben," atebodd, "dim ond lovebite yw e."

"Iesu, weden i bo fe 'di ca'l three course meal wrth 'i golwg hi," chwarddodd Llinos. "Cer â chwpwl o dog chews mas 'da ti tro nesa, for Pete's sake!"

"Reit 'te, ferched, cadwch e hyd ar ôl training, plis. 'Nôl ar y rhaff – ry'n ni'n mynd i ymarfer liffts nawr."

Pawb yn mynd 'nôl ar y rhaff, a'r wyth ohonon ni'n nacyrd ac yn fwd o'r top i'r gwaelod yn barod.

"Pick up the rope, take the strain… and pull!"

Dechreuodd y rhaff gripio 'nôl ac roedd y pwysau ychwanegol yn gwneud gwahaniaeth. Pawb yn rhoi plwc 'da'i gilydd a'r rhythm yn codi unwaith eto.

"And pull and pull and pull… Cadwch hi ar y top am sbelen fach plis ferched, 'na fe."

Tawelwch wrth inni ddal y pwysau, tawelwch oedd yn cael ei dorri weithiau gan sawdl yn cael ei hailgladdu yn y stecs. Tawelwch hir a phoenus.

Sŵn car.

Sawdl arall yn hacio.

Sŵn drws yn cau.

Ner o'm bla'n yn gorwedd yn iselach.

Sŵn traed ar goncrid.

Rhaff yn crynu.

Sŵn llais o'r gât. "Nerys!"

Naw pen yn troi i edrych.

Emyr fel delw a'i wyneb gwelw fel y galchen yn dweud y cyfan.

Ner yn edrych i fyw llygaid Emyr.

Gadawodd hi'r rhaff i fynd, a dyma wyth merch yn cwympo mla'n, gan lithro yn y stecs hyd at waelod y ffens. O'n ni'n ffaelu dal gafel, ac wrth inni gael ein tynnu mla'n dyma fi'n bwrw Ner allan o'r ffordd nes ei bod hi ar ei phengliniau yn y mwd. Bwrodd y gasgen y llawr gan wasgaru'r cerrig i bob cyfeiriad. Roedd pobman yn dawel heblaw am sŵn y dail. Roedd dwylo pawb yn gwaedu.

Whech

"Ti'n mynd draw heddi 'ma 'to, Heledd?" Daeth llais Mam o waelod y sta'r.

"Nadw, dim heno, falle a' i nos fory. Fi'n mynd am jog 'da Les nes mla'n."

Allwn i ddim stumogi mynd draw eto heddi. Neithwr, roedd Ner yn edrych yn uffernol, fel tase hi wedi heneiddio deng mlynedd dros nos. Ydi pobl yn edrych yn wahanol pan mae pethau fel hyn yn digwydd, neu ni sy'n edrych yn wahanol arnyn nhw? Roedd Sion wedi galw heibio ac fe aethon ni, heb siarad, â bara brith i Emyr. Roedd llond y lle o gacs i ga'l 'na, a chwaer Emyr, Eirwen, wedi dod lawr i edrych ar ôl pethe a hclpu 'da'r trefniade. Roedd Emyr yn eistedd ar y sgiw yn cydio yn tsiaen gwddwg Gaynor. Roedd e wedi rhoi ei modrwyau hi ar y tsiaen, a dyna lle roedd e'n eu troi nhw'n ddi-stop fel rosari o gwmpas ei law. Troi a throi o gwmpas ei fysedd nes gwneud imi deimlo awydd rhedeg allan drwy'r drws.

"Ddrwg iawn 'da fi," medde Sion. Chwarae teg, roedd e'n eitha da mewn sefyllfaoedd fel hyn.

"Diolch iti. Fe wneith Eirwen de ichi nawr."

"Na, na, peidiwch â phoeni, newydd ga'l swper ry'n ni," medde finne.

"Well i chi ga'l rhywbeth, siŵr o fod."

"Na wir, diolch."

Do'n ni ddim yn gwbod be i neud wedyn. Rhyw fath o ddeud jôcs bach a phawb yn siarad yn bwrpasol ysgafn.

Roedd Rhys, brawd bach Ner, yn eistedd ar y llawr yn chware 'da ryw dractors, er ei fod e bron yn bymtheg oed. Roedd e wastad yn dawel, ond heddi do'dd dim bwm i' ga'l 'da fe. Edrychodd Sion arna i gan godi'i eiliau. Doedd dim smic o sŵn yn unman, heblaw olwynion y tractors yn crafu dros y leino ar y llawr ac Emyr yn troelli'r tsiaen.

"Ble ma Ner?" holais i dorri ar y tawelwch.

Tra bod Sion ac Emyr yn trafod y cynhaeaf, es inne lan sta'r at Ner, gan deimlo'n uffernol o falch o gael dianc. Roedd Ner yn eistedd yn ei stafell.

Tŷ rhyfedd oedd Pantglas, gyda ryw sta'r llydan yn mynd lan yng nghanol y tŷ a chilfachau bach od fan hyn a fan draw. Roedd rhai o'r rheini wedi cael eu gorchuddio yn y chwedegau, pan o'dd cwato popeth 'da bwrdd plastar a'i bapuro 'da papur graen-pren mewn ffasiwn. Roedd modelau o awyrennau ym mhobman, a darnau ohonyn nhw fel lego plentyn bach ar y llawr. Do'dd 'na ddim drychau o gwbl yn y tŷ – ro'n i wedi sylwi hynny ryw dro pan ddes i yma i aros a methu dod o hyd i ddrych pan o'n i'n stryffaglu i roi fy nghontacts i fewn.

Stafell Ner oedd un o'r rhai mwyaf yn y tŷ a'r lle tân mawr ynddi wedi'i gau â bwrdd pren a rhyw flodau sidan wedi'u gosod o'i flaen. Er hyn, roedd y gwynt yn canu yn y wal ar ddiwrnodau gaeafol. Stafell oeraidd oedd hi, gyda hen ddrws lliw hufen a chlicied yn ei gau, ac atig yn rhedeg ochr yn ochr iddi. Hen garped brown wedi'i orchuddio â blodau mawr ar y llawr, a phapur wal yn pilo fel hen groen o gwmpas y ffenestri cul. Posteri o geffylau ar y welydd, a'r sgarffiau sidan roedd Ner yn arfer eu gwisgo yn ei gwallt yn hongian ar gornel y gwely. Stafell merch fach oedd hi, gyda rhai cliwiau – fel y casgliad o fatiau cwrw ar y wal a'r lluniau o grwpiau o fyfyrwyr –

yn dangos bod y ferch fach bellach wedi tyfu lan. Blodau sidan oedd yr unig beth addurniadol yno. Eisteddai Ner ar y gwely, a'i choese wedi'u croesi oddi tani. Yr unig awgrym o ddigwyddiadau'r diwrnod oedd y siwt ddu a hongiai ar waelod y gwely a'r pentwr o bapurach wrth ochr Ner. Cododd ei llygaid i edrych arna i. Roedd y gath wrth ei thraed yn cysgu'n anymwybodol braf ar ei chefn, a'i chynffon wedi'i chwrlo o gwmpas ei thraed.

"Ti'n edrych yn bygyrd." Fedrwn i ddim meddwl am ddim byd call i weud.

"Charming as ever, Miss Davies," medde hithau gan wneud ei gorau i wenu.

"O, dere 'ma," dwedais wrth eistedd ar ei phwys a chydio ynddi. Bu'r ddwy ohonom yn eistedd glust yn nghlust yn dawel am sbelen. "Be ni'n mynd i neud â ti 'de, groten? Mm?" medde fi wedyn.

"M'bod," sibrydodd Ner i mewn i'm gwallt.

"Shwt ma pethe mewn fynna 'de?" holais, gan wasgu llaw ar ei mynwes.

"Neud dolur," atebodd Ner. "Licen i taswn i'n galler cymryd rhwbeth, rhyw dabled neu rwbeth, i ga'l gwared o'r teimlad – jest i ga'l llonydd am sbelen fach. Wedyn fi'n teimlo'n euog achos mod i ddim isie teimlo…"

"Ti'n galler ca'l tabledi 'wrth y doc, rhywbeth i helpu 'bach arnat ti am sbelen, dim yn hir, dim ond nes iti droi'r gornel… "

"Na, ma gormod o fflipin dabledi wedi bod yn y tŷ 'ma ers sbel. Ma Dat arnyn nhw'n barod, a rhyngddo fe a Mam wy'n credu taw dim ond fi a Rhys sy 'di bod yn gall 'ma ers misodd." Yna bu tawelwch am eiliad. "O'n i mas pan ddigwyddodd e, Heledd."

"O't ti ddim i wbod… "

"O'n i'n gwbod 'i bod hi'n sâl uffernol."

"Ond o'dd hi 'di bod yn sâl am mor hir, achan – shwt o't ti i fod i wbod? O'dd e'n eitha sydyn yn y diwedd, ma rhaid iti gyfadde."

"Ddylen i ddim fod mas, a ddylen i ddim fod wedi dod i'r ymarfer 'na chwaith. Dylen i fod wedi aros gartre gyda hi. Pan dda'th hi mas o'r ysbyty yn y diwedd felna, ddylen i fod wedi gwbod bod e'n dod yn agosach; o'n nhw'n ffaelu neud dim byd, o'n nhw?" Roedd ei llygaid hi'n goch i gyd a'r lliw glas fel tase fe'n gwaedu dros ei bochau.

"Ti'n meddwl fydde hi ise i ti roi'r cwbwl lan? O'dd hi'n gwbod bod angen iti gadw rhyw fath o fywyd dy hun, yn do'dd hi? Wedodd hi 'na ar y dechre."

"Do, ond... "

"Nest ti beth o'dd hi isie i ti neud; alli di ddim beio dy hunan am 'na."

"M'bod."

Fe driais i droi'r sgwrs. "A'th popeth yn iawn heddi, yn dofe? Pam does neb 'ma heno?"

"Do'dd Dat ddim isie ffys heno eto; wedodd e bod heddi wedi bod yn ddigon o stra'n."

"O." Eisteddodd y ddwy ohonom yn dawel am sbel. "O'dd lot o barch 'da pobol at dy fam, no; weles ti faint o flode o'dd 'na?"

"Do, ac i beth? Dyw hi ddim yn galler 'u gweld nhw; gwywo 'nan nhw, dim ond rhywbeth i hela pethe i edrych yn well."

"Paid â gweud pethe felna... "

"Gwneud hi'n hawdd i bobol deimlo'n well – dyna yw pwrpas blodau, ondife, 'run peth â fflipin casgliad at elusen."

Roedd y gath yn dechre diflasu ar gael ei gwasgu, a neidiodd yn ysgafn oddi ar y gwely gan daro golwg hiraethus 'nôl at y garthen.

"Beth fydd hi fel 'ma nawr, sdim syniad 'da fi. Ma Dat yn mynd i reoli'n holl fywyd i nawr – o leia ro'n i'n ca'l 'bach o lonydd pan o'dd Mam ambwti'r lle."

"Weithith pethe mas to," meddwn inne gan dynnu slifren o wallt o'i llygaid a'i wasgu tu ôl i'w chlust.

"Ti'n gwbod bod Dat a fi fel ci a hwch trwy'r amser, a finne'n methu madde rhai o'r pethe wedodd e 'tho Mam."

"Ti'n mynd o fla'n gofid nawr, achan. Falle fydd pethe'n well – ro'dd y stra'n o weld dy fam felna'n bownd o effeithio arno fe."

"O't ti'n gwbod bod Mam wedi gadel llythyr i Rhys a fi?"

"Nagon i."

"Do, i weud wrtho ni bod hi'n 'yn caru ni... "

Roedd y dagre'n llifo o'i llygaid ac fe orffwysodd ei phen ar fy mrest fel plentyn bach.

"Cymer dy amser... "

"Sgwennodd hi i weud bod hi'n meddwl y byd ohonon ni'n dou, ac yn gobeithio bydde ni'n ei chofio hi – fel tase ni'n galler anghofio! Wedodd hi hefyd 'i bod hi'n moyn i'w gweddillion ga'l 'u gwasgaru ar y Ffridd."

"Ar y Ffridd?" holais yn syfrdan.

"Ie'n gwmws – ges i mo'r llythyr nes ginne fach gan Anti Eirwen."

"Ti 'di siarad â dy dad?"

"Sa i'n galler edrych arno fe, heb sôn am siarad ag e."

"Falle do'dd e ddim yn gwbod taw dyna'i dymuniad hi."

"Wrth gwrs 'i fod e. Ti'n meddwl y gallet ti fod yn sâl

mor hir â 'na heb siarad am y pethe 'ma?"

"Wel, fydde fe ddim yn rhwydd, na fydde fe?"

"Na fydde, ond fydde ti'n trio'i neud e beth bynnag. Ma'n rhy hwyr nawr, on'dyw hi?"

"Sa i'n gwbod beth i weud."

"Nei di aros 'ma heno 'da fi?" gofynnodd Ner, a'i llygaid yn llenwi.

"Wrth gwrs naf i, y bwp!" atebais, gan ddangos y gŵn-nos a'r brwsh dannedd oedd gen i'n barod mewn cwdyn Spar.

Gwenodd hithau.

"Ond iti beido rhechen, ac i ti addo gwisgo fest i gadw'r bola na'n gynnes!"

Gorweddodd Ner 'nôl ar y gwely a chau ei llygaid.

Es i lawr y sta'r i drefnu bod Sion yn dod i 'nghasglu i yn y bore, yna es i mewn i'r gwely at Ner a'r ddwy ohonom yn gorwedd fel llwyau dan y garthen. Cysgodd Ner yn drwm drwy'r nos, ond weithiau byddai'n crynu'n ddireolaeth. Codais rywbryd i wneud potel ddŵr poeth i'w gwasgu rhyngom, a chlywn ochneidio'n dod o stafell Emyr. Cyn llenwi'r botel roedd yn rhaid i mi symud y teclyn oedd yn arfer codi Gaynor i mewn i'r bàth.

Roedd hi'n noson lonydd a'r lleuad yn lliwio popeth ar y clos yn wêr arian. Sefais wrth y ffenest am funud gan edrych allan i'r clos. Roedd 'na stlumod yn chwarae yn yr aer fel pysgod yn dartio o un gornel i'r llall, gan newid cyfeiriad ar onglau heb iddynt weld dim.

Yn y bore, dihunodd Ner a minnau drwyn wrth drwyn, a syllu ar ein gilydd heb eiriau am amser hir cyn codi.

Saith

Roedd Les ar y sgwâr pan gyrhaeddais, yn gwisgo tracsiwt lwyd a thair streipen lliw leim ar hyd y coese. Roedd e wrthi'n twymo lan yn erbyn polyn 'lectric."Looking radiant today, darling," wedodd e, heb hyd yn oed troi 'i ben i edrych arna i.

"Ta, Les; not looking so bad yourself – ond trueni am yr hairy chest, ondife," atebais.

"Cariad, tase ti'n teimlo'r static sy'n dod o'r blew 'ma, fydde ti'n tyfu peth dy hunan."

"Rywbryd arall falle," atebais cyn ymuno gydag e yn y twymo lan. "Lle ni'n mynd heddi,'de?"

"Pentre nesa, lan i Rhiwfelen, rownd y Mownt a gartre," medde fe gan dynnu'i goes am 'nôl ar ongl annaturiol.

"O's rhywun arall yn dod?"

"Just you and me baby, ac os bydd Awen ar dop ei lôn hi ma hi am ymuno â ni ar yr home straight. Ma tamed mwy o wind resistance 'da hi na ni."

"Bitch!"

"So sue me," medde fe gan ddechre trotian i gyfeiriad Rhiwfelen.

Cychwyn am y pentre nesa, a'r ddau ohonom yn cwympo mewn i gam yn weddol hawdd. Am unwaith, ro'n i'n hoffi rhedeg yng nghwmni rhywun arall. Roedd rhedeg ar eich pen eich hun yn medru bod yn boen yn y pen, yn enwedig os oeddech chi'n tueddu i hel meddyliau wrth fynd. Roedd meddyliau a sŵn eich traed yn codi rhythm yn eich pen o'dd yn medru eich gyrru chi'n wallgo weithiau, ond roedd rhedeg 'da rhywun arall yn ddigon tebyg i gael rhyw – wrth gyfathrebu drwy'r corff, ry'ch chi'n cwympo i fewn i rythm person arall ac yn ymateb i'w hanghenion nhw. Ry'ch chi'n gwrando ar yr anadlu ac yn ymateb i'r patrymau hynny, yn arafu weithiau ac yn cyflymu dro arall. Ac yn union fel rhyw, roedd rhedeg yn medru llacio'ch ceg chi 'fyd.

Gwrandewais ar fyfyrio Les.

"Ma angen i ti a Kel weithio ar aerobics, wedyn yn agosach at y gystadleuaeth allwch chi neud mwy ar y gwaith pwyse. Ma ise inni weitho fel mashîn, ti'n gweld, fel bod y cwbwl yn dod yn naturiol. 'Excellence is an art won by habituation.' 'Na pam ma gyment o slapyrs a pissheads ambwti'r lle, tweld, a digon o fastards yn malu cachu. PRACTIS. Ma fe'n dod mor naturiol nes bod hanner knobsters a nirks y byd 'ma ddim yn sylweddoli 'u bod nhw, t'weld. Ma angen trimo lawr 'yn bach ar Awen – rhoi planad fach iddi, a wedyn lot o waith pwyse yn yr wythnose nesa 'ma. Allith y lleill nofio mwy – ac ma angen lot o waith pwyse ar goese Ner. Ma nhw fel dwy lasen ar Slimfast."

"Cym on Les, alli di ddim disgwl iddi hi neud llawer am sbel."

"Pam lai?" holodd a syndod yn ei lais.

"Ma hi newydd gladdu'i mam, for Pete's sake," medde finne'n ddiamynedd.

"Do's 'na ddim byd allith hi neud ambwti fe. Ma'n rhaid iddi ddod 'nôl i rwtîn cyn gynted ag ma hi'n galler – deith dim lles o wandran ambwti'r lle fel cysgod. Y peth gore alle hi neud nawr yw ailddechre'n syth gyda phopeth ro'dd hi arfer neud, gan gynnwys training. Sa i'n bod yn entirely selfish fan hyn, ond ma 'bach o waith caled ar y corff yn galler neud wonders."

"Mmm," meddais gan feddwl tybed pa mor barod fydden i i neud circuits taswn i yn yr un sefyllfa.

Rhedeg heibio'r cloddie, ambell gar yn mynd heibio, a finne'n cwympo 'nôl tu ôl i Les ac wedyn yn codi cyflymder i redeg wrth ei ochr unwaith eto. Mynd heibio ffermydd, a Les yn rhedeg ar yr ochr fewnol rhag ofn i ryw gi defed ddod ar ein holau. Roedd e'n gwybod faint o'n i'n casáu hynna. O'dd pobl yn meddwl oherwydd eu bod yn byw yn nghanol y wlad bod hawl 'da nhw i gadw cŵn fydde'n gwneud i'r Hound of the Baskervilles edrych fel yr Andrex puppy.

"Les?"

"Ie?"

"Sut gwrddes ti â Gwyneth?"

"'Bach yn feddylgar i ti, Hels, yr amser hyn o'r bore."

"Sori, o'n i jest yn meddwl... "

"Na, na, iawn bach; basically weles i ddi mas ryw nosweth yn Aberteifi pan o'n i lawr 'na 'da ryw fenyw arall. Weles i ddi – a 'na fe, been in love ever since. Pen-ôl bach siapus – ro'dd hyn cyn iddi ddechre byta fel Bwda, cofia – gwên bert a gwyneb fel angel. Dragies i hi i'r stafell gefn a wnaethon ni runner trwy'r toiledau a mas y bac. Lucky girl!"

"Beth am y fenyw arall, 'de?"

"She married your father, darling!"

"Na! Na, o'dd Mam... "

"Ah, the sweet ironies of life! Galle hwn fod yn father-daughter jog nawr."

"O mei god – fi'n teimlo'n sic."

"Ha, ha! Ti gollodd mas, cofia – achos fe fydde ti'n lot mwy gwd-lwcing tase gen i rywbeth i neud â'r peth."

Cariodd y ddau ohonom ymlaen i redeg am ychydig.

"Be sy'n bod?" holodd Les.

"Dim byd."

"Cariad, sa i 'di studio, rhedeg wrtho, ca'l fy nala efo, traino na ffycin shaggo menwod ar hyd 'yn o's heb wbod bod 'dim byd' yn meddwl rhywbeth."

Yn sydyn reit o'n i'n teimlo'n gas tuag ato fe.

"Nawr 'te," medde fe cyn anfon pelen o boer crwn at ryw flodyn bach diniwed yn y clawdd. "Ma merched fel arfer yn becso am bethe na ddylen nhw fecso amdanyn nhw, ac esgeuluso'r pethe ddylen nhw fod yn becso amdanyn nhw. Nawr 'te, be sy'n dy fecso di? Seis dy din di?" cynigiodd.

"Nage."

"Dy fam a dy dad?"

"Nage."

"STD?"

"Piss off!"

"Oh dear, Elizabeth, have we been jilted admirably?"

"Naddo, Mr fflipin Bennett."

"Rhywun yn tynnu'r penwas bach yn rhy dynn, falle?" Gwrandawais ar sŵn fy nhreiners yn bwrw'r tarmac.

"Ha, ha – bingo!"

"Ca dy lap, Les."

"Ah, the independent woman! What a marvellous thing, a phenomenon of our time. Blynydde 'nôl ro'dd pethe mor hawdd. Ro'dd dyn yn mynd lawr i'r local, yfed peintiau o mild, prynu Babycham a brandy i ryw fenyw, mynd â hi adre yn y Cortina – a Bob's your uncle and Fanny's your aunt!"

Car arall yn mynd heibio a finne'n falch o gael cwympo tu ôl i Les.

"Ti'n meddwl byddwn i'n tynnu rhaff a gneud yr holl blydi training 'ma tasen i'n iste gartre yn gwneud fy ngwinedd a disgwl galwad ffôn 'wrth Mr Mild?"

"Na fyddech chi, ddim un ohonoch chi, a 'na pam fi'n lyfo chi i gyd, hynny a'r ffaith mod i'n galler edrych ar eich tine chi pan chi'n traino."

"Cer i grafu!"

Troi'r cornel a gweld ffigwr yn y pellter.

"'Co Awen!" medde fi.

"Da iawn, Hels; do's dim byd fel newid 'bach ar y testun, o's e?"

"Dim ond gweud o'n i… "

"Observant iawn, Ms Attenborough, specimen plump neis o Birdicus Ceredigionus wrth dop y lôn – well spotted."

Dyma Awen yn dechre trotian tuag atom.

"Byddi di'n iawn," sibrydodd Les, "ma pethe fel hyn yn gweitho mas yn sweet yn y diwedd. A beth yw'r peth gwaetha alle ddigwydd? Allet ti dorri i ffwrdd a difaru dy blydi ened, neu aros a difaru dy ened – it's your choice, baby, and the price is right!"

"Difaru be?" holodd Awen wrth iddi ddala lan 'da ni.

"Difaru na fase ti wedi dod yr holl ffordd rownd 'da ni o'n i, wrth weld dy dits di yn y sports bra 'na."

"Ca' dy lap, Les," medde Awen gan gydgamu â ni.

"O, how sharper than a serpent's tooth it is to have a thankless tug-o'-war team."

Ro'n i'n dechre oeri, ac o'n i 'di blino'n rhacs. Roedd Awen yn ffres ac yn pwsho'r pês a Les heb flino dim. Roedd fy nghoese i'n 'yn lladd i gan nad oedden nhw wedi cael hoe ers dyddie.

"Cym on, Hels," gwaeddodd Les. "Ti fel hwyaden gloff heddi."

Ar ôl tipyn dyma'r pentre'n dod i'r golwg a'r ddau arall yn arafu wrth y capel er mwyn inni gael rhedeg i mewn i'r pentre gyda'n gilydd. Wrth inni gyrraedd dyma John Torrwr Bedde'n dod allan o'i dŷ.

Arhosodd Les i siarad 'da fe.

"Shwmai, Les? Shwmai, ferched? Shwt ma'r traino'n mynd?" holodd gan wincio'n ddwl ar Les.

Roedd gwyneb Awen fel bitrwt a f'un inne fel tomato wrth i ni ateb, "Iawn diolch, John."

"Ble chi off heddi, de, John?" holodd Les.

"Torri heddi lawr yn Pentreisa, ac wrth olwg y ddwy 'ma falle dylen i fynd draw i'r fynwent fan hyn i baratoi cwpwl o lefydd!"

"Wwww, ych!" medde Awen, a Les a John yn chwerthin.

"Pwy sda ti heddi, de?" gofynnodd Les.

"Wel, ar ôl pwy ddwrnod a Gaynor Pantglas, ma heddi'n bleser. Hen fenyw fach o ochre Tregaron yw hon, yn dod 'nôl i Pentreisa i ga'l 'i chladdu. Ma hi dros ei phedwar ugen, wedi ca'l innings da − ac yn well na dim, ma hi mor ysgafn â dryw."

"O blydi hel, esgusodwch fi," medde Awen gan drotian i ffwrdd i gyfeiriad y patshyn glas o fla'n y tai cownsil.

"Finne 'fyd, hwyl," medde finne a'i dilyn.

"Wela i chi cyn bo hir, ferched," gwaeddodd John ar ein holau.

"Ddim am sbel, gobeitho!" oedd ymateb y ddwy ohonom wrth ddiflannu i'r pellter.

Twymo lawr ar y patshyn glas cyn gorwedd ar ein cefne ar y borfa. Dyma'r rhan ore o'r rhedeg. Gorwedd ar dy gefn a gwres dy gorff di'n cyfnewid lle 'da'r oerfel braf yn y borfa. Chwys yn dy wallt a rhwng dy fronne, a'r awydd rhyfedda am ddiet coke.

"O, ma'r teimlad 'ma'n well 'na'r teimlad ar ôl ca'l jwmp, o beth fi'n gofio," medde Awen gan dorri ar y myfyrdod.

"Ma jog yn para'n hirach," medde finne gan glywed sŵn trainers Les yn dod yn nes.

"Da iawn, ferched, good effort; cofiwch neud bricen a wela i chi'n y training nesa. Heledd, ti sy â'r job o ga'l Ner i ddod 'da ti."

"O, diolch Les."

"Ie, wel, 'na fe, felna ma hi, life's a bitch and then you join a tug-o'-war team."

Les yn trotian i ffwrdd gan fethu peidio â gweiddi dros ei ysgwydd, "a cheer up, Hels, ne fyddi di'n blydi baglu dros dy swch di cyn bo hir."

Edrychodd Awen ar din Les yn diflannu rownd y gornel.

"Ti yn edrych 'bach yn ddiflas," medde hi. "Odi'r busnes 'ma 'da Ner yn dy boeni di?"

"Hynny a lot o bethe erill." Eisteddais i fyny a dechre chwarae â thafod fy nhreiner. "Ma pethe 'bach yn chwithig 'da Sion, 'na i gyd."

"Be sy'n bod? O'ch chi'n iawn yn angladd Gaynor, popeth i weld yn iawn."

"Wel, ma pawb yn clymu at ei gilydd mewn angladde, so ti 'di sylwi?"

"Ma Sion yn gweitho lot, on'd yw e?"

"Gweitho, odi, trwy'r fflipin amser. Awen, ga i ofyn rhywbeth i ti?"

"Ffeiar awê," medde hi gan godi ar ei heistedd.

"Wyt ti'n gweld dy hunan yn dal 'ma mewn ugen mlynedd? T'mod, setlo lawr a ddim mentro i unrhyw le arall?"

Edrychodd Awen yn galed ar ei thrainers hithe. "Odw i, cofia. Sai'n credu byddwn i'n hapus yn unrhyw le arall. Os wy'n hapus heddi, 'na i gyd fi'n poeni am; falle fydda i ddim 'ma i joio fory, ond un peth fi'n gwbod, sa i'n moyn byw yn rhywle lle does neb yn gwbod fy enw i nac yn becso mo'r dam amdana i. Uffarn, o'dd rhai ffrindie 'da fi yn coleg o'dd ddim yn gwbod pwy o'dd yn byw drws nesa iddyn nhw. Rownd ffor hyn ti'n gwbod pa liw pants ma nhw'n gwisgo a pryd yw'r amser gore i alw heibo am dc achos ti'n gwbod pryd ma nhw'n cwca cacen!" Edrychodd arna i am eiliad cyn ychwanegu, "Pam ti'n gofyn?"

"O, fi sy'n bod yn sili," atebais. "Dere, gwell inni gychwyn am adre."

Finne'n sefyll ar ei threiners, cydio yn ei dwy law a'i thynnu ar ei thraed, a'r ddwy ohonon ni'n dechrau cyd-gerdded.

"Hei, sôn am fod yn sili," wedodd hi, "weles ti pwy o'dd yn yr angladd?"

"Pwy?" atebais, gan esgus nad o'n i'n gwybod beth o'dd hi'n mynd i ddweud.

"Deian; o'dd e'n edrych ar dy din di drwy'r adeg! O'n i'n meddwl 'i fod e'n mynd i faglu dros ei dafod unwaith neu ddwy!"

"Awen! Mewn angladd?!"

"Wel," medde hi gan wincio, "ma bywyd yn mynd yn 'i fla'n ta beth ti'n ddweud – natur, ondife?"

Atseiniai sŵn ein chwerthin trwy'r pentre tawel.

Wyth

"Heledd! Fydde'n dda 'da fi tase ti ddim yn gadel dy hen ddillad brwnt ar hyd y lle 'ma – ti'n trin y lle 'ma fel Chinese Laundry," gwaeddodd Mam o'r gegin. "Ddysgon nhw ddim i ti shwt i olchi dillad yn y coleg, de? Ma'r cwbwl yn gagle ac yn glêd i gyd."

Roedd Mam â chroen ei thin ar ei thalcen, a Dat ddim llawer gwell.

"Sori, Mam."

"O's syniad 'da ti faint o amser fi'n dreulio'r diwrnode hyn yn golchi hen git sy'n bwdlacs i gyd?"

"Sori, Mam."

"A pheth arall, weden i 'i bod hi'n hen bryd iti chwilo am joben 'bach mwy sefydlog. Alli di ddim gweithio yn yr hen Ganolfan Groeso 'na am byth, ti'n gwbod."

"Reit, Mam."

"Wyt ti 'di bod mas o'r coleg ers sbelen fach nawr. Dyle fod syniad 'da ti erbyn hyn beth ti am neud."

"Iawn, Mam. Mam?"

"Ie?"

"Faint yw 'n oedran i?"

"Wel, weden i bod ti'n dal yn dair ar ddeg yn ôl y ffordd ti'n bihafio. Gyda llaw, odi Sion yn dod draw heno?"

"Sai m'bod."

"Wel os nad wyt ti'n gwbod, pwy sy? Y'ch chi 'di cwmpo mas 'to? Beth sy'n bod 'no chi? Ers iti adel y coleg ry'ch chi 'di bod fel ci a hwch. Weles i ei fam e heddi yn

52

Spar – do'n i ddim yn gwbod beth i ddweud wrthi."

"Peidwch gweud dim de."

"Alla i ddim anwybyddu'r fenyw ne fydd hi'n meddwl bo fi'n od."

"Wel siaradwch 'da hi de."

"Ambwti beth?"

"Ambwti'r Kama Sutra, falle? Sai m'bod, Mam, beth bynnag liciwch chi."

"Sdim ise bod felna, o's e? Nawr, o's rhywbeth arall 'da ti i olchi? Ma whant arna i i wneud dy holl ddillad gwyn di'n llwyd heddi, ac os o's jîns 'da ti i shrinco, dere â nhw 'ma."

"Typical," wedes i o dan fy ngwynt. Roedd Mam on-form heddi.

"Ma iwnifform lân i ga'l yn yr êring-cypord os wyt ti'n moyn hi; ddyle hi fod yn gras erbyn hyn. Ma 'na fra glân yn dy gwpwrth di, ond ma'r weiers wedi dod mas ohono fe, mae arna i ofan – aethon nhw'n sownd ym mherfedd y peiriant. Neith e ddim drwg iti – ti'n ddigon ifanc. Pan fyddi di'r un oedran â fi, alli di'u tycio nhw i fewn i dy sgert."

"Diolch, Mam."

Ro'n i'n gweithio am un ar ddeg, ac roedd Sion am roi lifft imi i'r dre. Roedd e wedi ffonio neithiwr i ddweud ei fod yn sori am be wedodd e a gofyn a alle fe siarad â fi heddi. O'n i'n eitha swta wrtho fe, a gweud y gwir; yn un peth ro'n i wedi ca'l llond bol o gwmpo mas, a hefyd ro'n i bron trigo oherwydd y rhedeg ddoe. Doedd hyd yn oed bàth Rêdocs ddim wedi gwneud unrhyw wahaniaeth. Dechreuais wisgo. Roedd iwnifform y Ganolfan Groeso yn ddigon erchyll i wneud i unrhyw un chwydu o gan llath i ffwrdd, a chymaint o blastig ynddi hi nes ei bod yn fy

nghadw'n sych yn y glaw. Roedd hi'n edrych fel petai Dad
wedi pasio heibio gyda'r peiriant gwasgaru dom, a hwnnw'n
llawn o baent. Roedd gen i hanner chwant ei chynnig hi i'r
fyddin, a gweud y gwir, achos fe fyddai hi'n fwy effeithiol
na stun-gun unrhyw bryd. Clywais landrofer Sion yn
cyrraedd y clos a Mam yn gweiddi unwaith eto.

"Heledd! Sym' dy din, siapa stwmps – ma Sion 'ma."

Roedd Mam yn hoff iawn o Sion, a gallwn ei
dychmygu hi nawr yn ei gôcso i gael te a chacen o flaen y
stof, ac yntau, wedi hen arfer â'r seremoni, yn gwrthod yn
boléit i ddechre cyn rhoi i fewn gan ganmol ei chacen i'r
cymyle.

Roedd 'na inspection i fod yn y gwaith, felly fe dries i
wneud i'r llathenni o neilon edrych yn hanner teidi cyn
rhedeg i lawr y sta'r.

Safai Sion wrth y stof a'r bara brith yn ei law.
Edrychodd arna i gan wenu a dweud, "Wel, Heledd, ga i
fynd â ti allan am swper heno?"

"Iawn," medde finne.

"Ar un amod."

"Beth yw honno?"

"Dy fod ti ddim yn newid allan o dy iwnifform."

"Piss off!"

"Angharad?" Llais Dad o ddrws y gegin. Roedd e'n
hongian i mewn i'r stafell wrth un fraich, yn methu dod
ymhellach oherwydd ei fod yn gwisgo welingtons brwnt.

"Wyt ti'n dwyno stepen fy nrws i?" gofynnodd Mam.

"Dim o gwbwl," atebodd gan wincio'n ddwl arna i.

"Be ti moyn?"

"Alli di 'mestyn y papur newydd 'na i fi? Ma rhyw
ddafad wedi bwrw mamog yn y lle mwya twp welsoch chi
erio'd."

"Chi ise help?"

"Na, ma'n iawn diolch, Sion; tase hi'n fuwch, cofia, fe fydde hi'n stori wahanol. O'n i'n meddwl bo ti Heledd yn gweitho heddi?"

"Wy'n mynd nawr."

"Well ti fynd i newid gloi, 'de, ne fyddi di'n hwyr," meddai gan daflu winc fach ddwl arall i gyfeiriad Mam.

"O, ha ha! Cer i stwffo dy famog ne rywbeth, nei di?"

Roedd Dad hefyd yn hoff o Sion, ond mewn ffordd dawelach. Roedd e'n llawer mwy gofalus gyda fe oherwydd ei fod yn gwybod mai ffarmwr oedd Sion, a tasen ni'n diweddu lan gyda'n gilydd, Sion fyddai'n cymryd y lle 'ma drosodd yn y diwedd gan mai fi oedd yr unig blentyn. Wedodd e ddim byd erioed, ond ro'n i'n ei adnabod e'n ddigon da. Roedd Mam wedi methu ca'l rhagor o blant, a bu'n rhaid iddi gael yr op whap ar ôl fy ngeni i. Merch oedd hi wastad wedi bod eisiau, beth bynnag, gan iddi golli ei chwaer ei hun yn ifanc. Doedd hi'n ddim byd ond gwyneb mewn lluniau i mi, er fy mod i'n teimlo rhyw agosatrwydd ati weithiau oherwydd Mam, a'r ffaith fy mod wedi cael ei henw, Iona, yn ail enw i mi. Yn y lluniau ohoni o gwmpas y tŷ, gwelwn ferch ifanc tua phymtheg oed, mewn ffrog gwta lliw oren a chlustdlysau mawr crwn. Roedd hi'n debyg iawn i Mam, yr un llygaid a rhyw wên fach ddwl. Roedd Mam yn siarad amdani weithiau, ond do'n i byth yn gwasgu am fanylion am y ddamwain achos ro'n i'n galler gweld y boen yn ei llygaid pan oedd hi'n siarad amdani.

Casglais weddill fy mhethe. I ffwrdd â Sion a fi i'r dre mewn Land Rover llawn caniau Teremeisin, poteli gwyn o benisilin, nod dafad a phaceidi o polo mints. Roedd Sion yn frawl i gyd, a'i wallt gole'n oleuach fyth oherwydd ei fod yn treulio cymaint o'i amser tu fas y diwrnode hyn; roedd ei war yn frown fel cneuen. Heddiw, gwisgai hen grys ffelt yn sgwariau i gyd – crys hambon fel bydde Awen yn 'i alw fe – a waterprwffs gwyrdd dros y cyfan. Roedd e'n ceisio dal fy llygaid drwy'r amser ac yn gwneud ei orau i wneud imi chwerthin drwy chwibanu caneuon pop yn hollol allan o diwn.

"Y'n ni'n ffrindiau nawr?" gofynnodd o'r diwedd.

"Be ti'n feddwl?"

"Wel, o leia alla i ga'l jwmp?"

"Ca dy ben," medde finne gan ymladd yn erbyn yr awydd i wenu.

"Drycha, fi'n gwbod alli di ddim bod yn grac 'da fi am hir achos fi'n rhy gorgeous, so paid â teimlo'n wael os oes awydd arno ti i dynnu'n nhrowser i a dangos gwd teim i fi fan hyn. Fi'n cyfadde bod yr iwnifform yn troi fi mla'n – 'bach yn cinci, rili, fel ca'l jwmp 'da aelod o'r capel."

Gwenais, ond daliais i edrych mas drwy'r ffenest.

Troiodd y landrofer i mewn i dop lôn fferm.

"Be ti'n neud?" gofynnais gan wneud fy ngore i beidio edrych arno.

"Cym on, dere â snog – ti'n gwbod bod ti'n moyn."

"Nadw ddim, fi'n mynd i fod yn hwyr i'r gwaith. Nawr dere!"

Cydiodd yn f'ysgwyddau a throi fy mhen i edrych arno. Fe aeth yn ddifrifol yn sydyn. "Sori, Hels, am be wedes i. Fi'n gweld dy ise di, 'na i gyd, yn enwedig pan wyt ti off o hyd 'da'r merched. O'n i'n gweld mwy ohono ti pan o't ti yn y coleg."

"Bachan, rwyt ti'n gweitho 'fyd – bob awr o'r dydd. Shwt ti'n meddwl fi'n teimlo am 'nna?"

"Fi'n gwbod – sori, ond ma pethe wedi bod yn fisi'n ddiweddar ac ma'r hen foi yn mynd off 'i ben am bethe. Ma'n hen bryd iddo fe roi'r gore iddi a mynd i fyw ar iot yn y Caribî, glei – wel, fydde Bytlins yn agosach at beth alle ni fforddio – ond ma fe'n pallu gadel fynd, ti'n gweld. Isie neud pethe mewn ryw ffordd arbennig achos 'na felna ma fe wastad wedi'u gneud nhw. Ma rhai jobsys yn hela fflipin deirgwaith mor hir. Fi'n gwbod 'i bod hi'n anodd iti ddeall. Ga i neud e lan iti a mynd â ti am Chinese heno 'ma?"

Nodiais fy mhen.

"Ac os wyt ti'n ferch dda, fe gei di'r prawn crackers 'na sy'n sugno dy dafod ti pan ti'n trio'u byta nhw!"

Chwarddais ac fe blannodd gusan ar fy ngwefusau a chydio'n dynn yno i. Rhedodd ei ddwylo dros fy nghefn cyn tynnu'r flowsen allan o'm sgert a rhedeg ei ddwylo dros fy mronnau. Roedd ei ddwylo'n galed ac wedi cracio mewn mannau ond roedd e'n deimlad braf, yn well na rhyw ddwylo meddal fel merch. Cydiodd yn fy mra a'i dynnu i lawr dros f'ysgwyddau. Cusanodd fy ngwddw ac aeth ei fysedd ati i agor botymau'r flowsen afiach. Plygodd ei ben i gusanu 'mronne gan sugno'r nipyls fel tase nhw'n blasu mor dda â chwrw. Aeth car heibio.

Chwarddodd Sion cyn llithro'i ddwylo rownd fy mhen-ôl a'm codi i eistedd yn ei gôl a'm cefn yn gwasgu i fewn i'r olwyn lywio. Dechreuodd anadlu'n ddyfnach a throdd ei wyneb yn ddifrifol i gyd wrth iddo ganolbwyntio. Teimlais ei fysedd yn ymgripio i fyny 'nghlunie, a'm cnawd yn mynd yn binne bach i gyd dan ei fysedd. Cusanais ochr ei wddf wrth iddo wthio fy nicers i'r ochr a dechrau cyffwrdd yn ofalus rhwng fy nghoesau.

Roedd e'n uffernol o dda efo'i fysedd; pan gwrddon ni am
y tro cyntaf roedden ni'n treulio penwythnosau cyfan yn y
gwely, a nosweithiau gwallgo pan ddown i 'nôl o'r coleg
i'w weld, a ninnau wedi bod ar wahân cyn hired. Cododd
rythm ar fy nghlitoris nes i'r teimlad tyn 'na ddwysáu a
minnau'n wlyb sopen ac yn methu peidio â gwasgu 'nôl yn
erbyn ei law.

"Odi 'nna'n neis?" gofynnodd â gwen fach ddrwg.

"Ti'n gwbod yn iawn bod e," atebais a'm hanadl yn
brin.

Aeth car arall heibio – cododd Sion ei law rydd arno a
gweiddi "Bore da, Mr Evans," allan drwy'r ffenest.

Chwarddais inne, ac wrth imi wneud dyma'r tensiwn yn
mynd yn ormod a'r pinne bach yn ymledu trwy 'nghorff.

"O, Miss Davies," meddai Sion. "Chi'n groten fach
ddrwg," cyn fflicio'i dafod yn bryfoclyd dros fy ngwefusau.
Sythais innau rhag ofn i rywun ein gweld ac fe gododd
yntau ei ben-ôl i aildrefnu'i drowser.

"Uffach," meddai, "ma rhaid gneud lle i'r Eiffel Tower!
Os wyt ti'n lwcus, gei di day trip i'r top heno iti ga'l gweld
yr olygfa!"

Chwarddais wrth inni ailgychwyn am y dre. Ro'n i'n
eistedd yn agosach ato ac yntau ag un fraich frown yn
hongian allan o'r ffenest a'r llall yn gorwedd rhwng fy
nghoesau.

Naw

Bip Bip!

CYSTAD LLAI NA 8NOS. PENTRE 12 SEMIS – THIS IS ROUND 1 LADIES. LES

Bip Bip!

TI DI CAL NEG LES? 6 TIM – DIM MAS NOS WEN. AWEN

Anfon 'nôl.

OES TRAINING HENO?

Munud yn mynd heibio.

OES. 7.30 DERE A NER. AWEN

Bip Bip!

SHIT CYST SAD – RYN NI FEL BWPS. MA NHW FEL DYNION. LLINOS

Anfon 'nôl.

PAID BECS – GWISGO WONDERBRAS I DISTRACTO NHW DE

Munud yn mynd heibio.

HA HA C U TOC – LLINOS

Bip Bip!

YN GWAITH. CAL ROW – ANGHOFIO RHOI BEDPAN YN Y COMOD. PW AR Y LLAWR. KEL

Bydde Kelloggs yn gwneud pethau fel hyn drwy'r amser, ac yn llwyddo i ga'l get-awê bob tro. Unwaith fe roddodd hi mêc-ofyr i rai o'r hen fenywod a'u ca'l nhw i fodelu shower caps. Pan dda'th y sister 'nôl, roedd y fenyw hena o'dd 'na – o'dd bron yn gant oed – yn walzo lawr y ward yn modelu, a stand y drip o'dd yn 'i braich hi'n ei dilyn hi fel ci bach. Dro arall fe benderfynodd Kel bod angen ailwampio'r llyfrgell yn y day room, ac fe ddaeth â llyfrau o'r gyfres Black Lace gyda hi o gartre a llenwi'r silffoedd 'da nhw. Roedd un dyn bach wedi mynd mor ecseited, roedd e 'di trio mynd i mewn i ward y menywod yn y nos.

Bip Bip!

SISTER WEDI GADEL FI OFF OND FI AR SLUICE DUTY AM FIS - SHIT! KEL

Ateb 'nôl.

NA PISSING OFF - GET IT! CU X

Bip Bip!

HELS GET OFF FAT ARSE A RHEDA. LES

Anfon 'nôl.

BORE DA I TI HEFYD LES - ON THE WE

Bip Bip!

CLWDDGAST! TASE FE'N BOLLOKING COMP ITD B NO CNTEST - LES

Anfon neges at Ner.

FFNSI TRINING? BYDDEN NEIS GWELD TI. PS KEL YN DISASTER ETO X

Munud bach yn mynd heibio.

GN NI WELD - DI BLINO. NER

Ateb 'nôl.

7.30. LES ISE TI DDOD. C U WEDYN FALLE X

Bip Bip!

IAWN X

Deg

"Rhys, cer i fwydo'r Westies 'na nei di? A bo ti'n hela gyment o amser 'da nhw, ddylet ti fod yn cofio pryd ma angen 'u bwydo nhw."

Pam na alle fe neud rhywbeth 'i hunan am unwaith, yn lle mod i'n gorfod gweiddi arno fe bob munud? Dyma sŵn traed yn dod lawr y sta'r. Nerys.

"Ble uffarn ti meddwl ti'n mynd?"

"Ble ti'n meddwl, wedi gwisgo fel hyn? I'r Sydney Opera House?"

"Ti'n mynd i training, wyt ti?"

"Odw, pam 'nny?"

Os oedd un ohonyn nhw'n pallu neud dim 'da neb, dim ond aros gartre, roedd hon wedyn fel tase hi wedi anghofio'r cwbwl ambwti beth o'dd wedi digwydd. Gwasgais y llinyn i grombil y mwg yn fy nhymer. "Cer di, Ner fach, paid becso dim."

"Beth ma 'na fod meddwl? Os o's 'da ti rywbeth i weud, jest blydi gwed e."

"O's ma fe. Ers i dy fam farw rwyt ti'n fi fi fi; cofia, do't ti ddim lot gwell pan o'dd hi'n fyw, o't ti?" Roedd 'y nwylo i'n crynu wrth imi sychu'r mwg.

"Fi'n hunanol, ife?"

"Mynd ambwti'r lle yn neud yn gwmws fel ti moyn. Ti ddim wedi bod gartre un nosweth, a phan wyt ti, ma rhywun 'da ti o hyd."

"Heledd yw hyn 'to, ondife? Beth uffarn yw dy broblem di 'da hi?"

"O, ma'r haul yn sheino mas o din Heledd 'da ti, on'dyw e?"

"A beth uffarn wna'th hi i ti erio'd? Ma hi 'di bod yn fwy o gefen i fi yn y miso'dd dwetha 'ma nag unrhyw un. Os yw hi'n broblem ca'l fy ffrindie i draw, jest gwed – af i i'w tai nhw."

"Yn gwmws; o's rhywbeth yn bod ar fod gartre?"

"O's, pan wyt ti'n siarad â fi fel hyn o hyd."

"'Na'r unig siawns s'da fi i siarad â ti; nid dim ond ti sy'n mynd trwy hyn, t'mod." Ro'n i'n gwbod mai'r ffordd i'w dolurio hi fydde dod â Rhys i fewn i'r peth. "Ti 'di siarad â Rhys, wyt ti? Ti 'di sylwi ei fod e ddim yn gweud bwm 'tho neb? Chwarae â'r blydi tois 'na felse fe'n saith oed 'to?"

"Odw, diolch yn fowr; ddeith e drosto fe – fel'na ma fe'n ymdopi â phethe."

"O, a 'na fe, ife? Ti ddim yn meddwl falle ddylet ti siarad â fe? Ma fe'n ifancach na ti a ti'n gwbod fel ma fe, mor dawel â dryw ond mor feddal ag ma nhw'n dod, achan." Roedd 'na ryw angen ynof i anfon euogrwydd fel gwlyborwch trwyddi. "Ac rwyt ti'n cario mla'n fel arfer, mynd off i training felse dim byd yn bod." Roedd y cyhuddiadau'n llifo a dim rheolaeth gen i drostyn nhw.

"Be fi fod neud, Dad? Aros fan hyn yn edrych ar y blydi stair lift 'na ife? A siarad am fod yn selfish, pwy o'dd yn grac 'da Mam drw'r amser achos bod hi'n sâl?"

Neidiodd rhyw gynnwrf ynof i gan wneud i'm nerfau dynhau fel rhaff.

"Mynd yn grac pan o'dd hi'n cwmpo pethe, a gweiddi am gost pethe o'dd hi'n 'u torri?" Roedd hi'n crynu erbyn hyn.

"Jest ca dy ben, ti ddim yn gwbod be ti'n siarad ambwti, wyt ti? O'n ni'n deall ein gilydd yn iawn, a paid â meddwl bod ti'n galler gneud fel fynno ti, a gweud fel mynno ti nawr bod hi ddim 'ma chwaith."

"Deall eich gilydd, o'ch chi? Pam o'dd hi wastad yn llefen 'de? Pam o'dd hi'n neidio bob tro roeddet ti'n dod mewn i'r stafell? Deall eich gilydd, ife?"

Gwegiais wrth i ffrwd o ddelweddau o Gaynor lifo'n ôl i'm meddwl a boddi popeth yn fy mhen. Roedd popeth yn drwch o Gaynor a'r dagrau'n dechrau cronni. Roedd gwyneb Ner yn goch a'r cryndod wedi symud i'w llais. Rhythodd arna i.

"Dere mla'n de, man a man siarad am bopeth tra bod ni wrthi."

"O'n i'n meddwl bod ti'n mynd i'r training." Ro'n i ise mynd mas, mas i neud rhywbeth.

"Stwffo'r training," medde Ner wrth daflu'i phethe ar hyd y llawr. "Shwt ma hi'n mynd i fod 'ma o hyn mla'n, e? Fi sy'n cymryd lle Mam, ife? Be sy'n mynd i ddigwydd? Ti'n mynd i ddod i moyn fi o bob man fel arfer? Wyt ti'n mynd i adel i fi ffycin ddysgu dreifo? O's rhaid i fi ofyn caniatâd cyn ca'l ffrind draw?"

"Dwyt ti ddim yn deall y cwbwl, Ner," medde fi'n dawel, "er bod ti'n meddwl dy fod ti."

"Wel tria fi, Dad; wy'n un ar hugen, ti'n gwbod, a fi'n gwbod be fi 'di'i weld dros y blynydde 'fyd – fi ddim yn dwp. A pheth arall, yn y llythyr 'na ges i 'da Anti Eirwen ar ôl yr angladd fe wedodd Mam bod hi am i'w llwch gael ei chwalu ar Ffridd-y-mynydd. Pam ga'dd hi 'i chladdu, Dad? Ma fe'n hollol glir o'r llythyr 'na beth o'dd hi moyn – na'th hi dy drystio di, yn do fe? Ac mae'n amlwg na nest ti ddim gneud beth roet ti wedi'i addo."

"Beth arall odd yn y llythyron 'na?" gofynnais gan ddangos llawer mwy o ddiddordeb nag ro'n i wedi'i fwriadu.

"Dim."

"Wedes i wrthi am beidio sgwennu'r fath nonsens."

Cochodd Ner. "NONSENS? Dyna be ti'n galw'i geirie ola hi, ife?" A dechreuodd Ner feichio llefen.

"Wedes i wrthi bydde nhw'n ypseto chi." Ceisiais gydio ynddi a'i chysuro.

"Paid twtsh â fi!"

Triais i esbonio wrthi. "Ma geirie heb berson tu ôl iddyn nhw'n ein harwain ni i lefydd sy ddim yn bod, Ner: celwydd, ry'n ni'n gweld pethe sy ddim 'na, ysbrydion... Do'dd hi ddim yn gwbod beth o'dd hi moyn erbyn y diwedd. 'Na beth ma edrych ar dy farwoleth dy hunan cyn hired yn neud i ti, ac a gweud y gwir, y ffordd fi'n teimlo nawr, 'na'r lle gore i fi fydde wrth 'i hochor hi."

Clywais sŵn traed yn rhedeg i fyny'r sta'r; ro'dd Rhys wedi gorffen bwydo'r cŵn, a Duw a ŵyr faint roedd e wedi'i glywed.

"O shit," medde Ner gan symud tuag at y sta'r.

"Gad e," dwedais yn dawel, "af i lan ato fe wedyn ar ôl iddo fe ga'l munud ar 'i ben 'i hun." Edrychais arni. "Do'n i ddim yn meddwl y pethe wedes i wrth dy fam at y diwedd, a wedodd hi lawer o bethe hurt 'fyd; ro'dd hi 'di colli arni'i hunan. Do'dd hi ddim yn gwbod beth odd hi ise ac ro'dd rhaid inni wneud rhai penderfyniade drosti. Ma'n well inni'i chofio hi fel o'dd hi, a pheido meddwl gormod am bethe."

Roedd hi'n edrych ar y llawr. "Cer nawr 'de," medde fi wrth fynd allan o'r stafell i chwilio am Rhys.

Un ar ddeg

Dydd Sadwrn a 'mola i'n troi. Neges testun peth cynta'n y bore.

ARSES IN GEAR – GOING TO WAR – BUS 11 PENTRE – DIM BRECWAST – LES

Bydden ni'n gorfod starfo tan ar ôl pwyso heddi gan ein bod ni mor agos i'r uchafswm pwyse yn y training diwetha.

Bip Bip!

BWTI STARFO – FE DRIGA I CYN PWYSO GLEI – AWEN

Anfon 'nôl.

BACN BUTIES, FREI UPS, WY TOST SOS BROWN

Aros am funud.

BUWCH! GWLD TI WEDN – AWEN

Anfon neges at Ner gan 'i bod hi heb droi lan i training tan ddiwedd yr wythnos ddwetha. O'dd hi di bod am wac, medde hi. Bollocing 'da Les yn ddiweddarach ac ro'n i 'di addo gneud yn siŵr y bydde hi 'na ar amser heddi.

BAROD? HELS

Munud yn mynd heibio.

AYE – PAID BECS C U STAND LATH 11.30 – NER

Roedd peil o waith paco 'da fi i neud hefyd. Tynnais allan hen fag Adidas oedd yn perthyn i Sion a'i lenwi 'da dillad – siorts du, sane di-ben-draw, sports bra, crys-T gwyn a thop tynnu wedi'i smwddo. Gosod y sgidie mewn cwdyn plastig a'u plannu yng nghanol y bag. Roedd angen dillad ar gyfer y parti nos hefyd. Roedd y gystadleuaeth ar gae pêl-droed ar gyrion Abertawe a pharti ar ôl 'nny mewn ryw glwb rygbi ar bwys Caerfyrddin. Ar ôl yr holl ymarfer roedd 'y nghoese i wedi mynd braidd yn gyhyrog i sgert, felly stwffiais bâr o hipsters du i'r cwdyn a'u dilyn gan wonderbra coch, a thop bach i ddangos y belly stud. Cofiais bacio plastar i roi dros hwnnw rhag ofn iddo gydio'n y rhaff. Tywel a nicers glân, a dyna fi'n barod – ac yn starfo.

Roedd Ner yn aros amdana i wrth y stand la'th ac fe gydgerddon ni'n ara tuag at y pentre.

"Nerfus 'de?" holais.

"M'bod. Ydw, 'bach – sa i 'di ca'l llawer o chance yn ddiweddar i feddwl ambwti fe, a gweud y gwir. Garantîd fydda nhw fel heffrod. Jest gobeitho bod 'na ddynion go smart 'na i neud lan am y lwndad ry'n ni'n mynd i ga'l."

"Mm, fi'n credu bod Kel yn edrych mla'n at dynnu yn y ddwy ffordd heddi. Ma siŵr o fod gwd chance 'da ni ar ôl yr holl waith 'da Les."

"Co ni off," medde hi wrth inni droi'r cornel. "Speak of the devil... "

"... and the devil appears," gorffennes inne, "in trainers."

Roedd Les yn sefyll ar y sgwâr yn sgwennu ar ryw fwrdd nodiade. Gwisgai ei dracsiwt ore, sane gwyn, a thrainers a'u tafode'n rhy fowr.

Gwaeddodd draw. "Cym on ferched, tynnwch eich ffycin bysedd mas, dewch inni ga'l 'ych pwyso chi."

Roedd pawb arall yn eistedd yn y bws yn barod, a golwg fel aelodau trip Ysgol Sul ar steroids arnyn nhw. Cael ein pwyso tu allan i'r bws, ac wedyn llwytho'r cyfan. Cododd Les ar ei benglinie ar y sedd flaen i areithio.

"Nawr te ferched, ry'n ni'n uffernol o agos i bwyse, felly os dala i un ohono chi'n byta, chi'n dead – a sa i'n jocan." Taflodd ei lygaid droston ni gan adael iddyn nhw aros braidd yn hir ar Awen.

"Paid edrych arna i, y sod salw," medde hithe'n bwdlyd.

Dechreuodd Llinos chwerthin.

"Shut up, Llinos," medde Les. "'Sda ti ddim lot i weud. Dim ots 'da fi be chi'n neud, ond dim bwyd, dim dŵr, dim byd. Rhechwch, cewch i'r toilet faint gallwch chi. Nawr 'te, checklist cyn dachre: trainers, sgidie, beltie codi pwyse, dŵr, bwyd ar ôl pwyso, condoms erbyn heno... " Gigyls yn codi o bob cyfeiriad. "Nawr 'te, un peth sy ar ôl fel blydi arfer." Finne'n edrych rownd – doedd Kel ddim yna. "Kel as bloody usual; man a man inni fynd draw i bigo hi lan, ynta – ma hi fel rhech."

Neidiodd Les i sedd y gyrrwr ac off â ni. Codi Kel yn ei chartre, a hithe'n rhedeg at y bws yn ei hiwnifform – cwdyn mowr dan ei chesail a marmalêd rownd ei cheg. Pawb yn codi bloedd wrth iddi neidio i sedd sbâr gan chwistrellu ymddiheuriadau dros y lle am night shift a dim digon o staff.

"Pnawn da, Kel, be wedes i am ffycin brecwast?" gofynnodd Les a'i aeliau wedi codi i dop ei ben.

"Shit, swper o'n i'n meddwl o'n ni ddim fod byta. Ro'n i bwyti starfo neithwr yn y gwaith, jest â craco pan o'n ni'n rhoi swper mas."

Roedd Les yn ei gwylio hi yn nrych y bws. "Paid â becso," medde fe, "os ti ddim 'di ca'l swper fe ddyle ni fod yn iawn. Be ti 'di ga'l? Dim ond tost?"

"Ie," atebodd Kel gan gochi, "ar ôl bacwn ac wy a miwsli – o'n i'n meddwl bod angen 'bach o nerth heddi.

'Daw bola'n gefen,' and all that." Ochneidiodd pawb.
"Sori bois, o'n i'n starfo ar ôl neithwr."

Roedd gwyneb Les yn welw. "Wel, sdim byd i neud
ond trio hela ti fynd i'r toiled a gneud i ti fynd am jog fach
mewn deunaw siwmper cyn y pwyso. Os wyt ti dros
bwyse wedyn, wel elli di gadw'r iwnifform 'na mla'n achos
ti'n mynd i orfod cadw cwmni i fi heno fel fforffit."

"Shit," medde Kel, "gadewch fi lawr – fi'n mynd i
redeg lawr i Abertawe."

"Ti'n ploncer, Kel," medde Les. "Pawb 'da'i gilydd,
ladies... "

"TI'N PLONCER, KEL," ailadroddodd pawb 'da'i
gilydd nes bod Kel druan yn cochi at ei chlustiau.

"Nawr 'te bawb – ymlaciwch a shut up am sbelen."

Roedd Awen yn eistedd godderbyn â fi, yn gwasgu'i
thrwyn ar y ffenest; Llinos yn ca'l fforti wincs; Non yn
darllen cylchgrawn; Ner yn gwrando ar fiwsig; Siân yn
chwarae I-spy 'da Kel, a Heini yn trio cwato'i nerfau drwy
ganu 'Oes gafr eto' gan anghofio pwy liw o'dd yn dod nesa
bob tro.

****

Cyrraedd, dadbacio a thrio pheidio edrych ar ferched y
time erill, oherwydd eu bod nhw wastad yn edrych yn
anferth ac mor galed â pit bull terriers 'da pwynt i brofi a
peils yn y fargen. Anfon Kel am jog, ac ar ôl iddi fynd
dyma Les yn cyfadde bod ein pwyse ni'n iawn, ond fe
wnâi e les i glustie Kel tase hi'n gorfod mynd am run.

Pwyso mewn ryw neuadd ar bwys y cae a'r cyfanswm yn
576 kilo. Mynd 'nôl i'r bws ac anelu'n syth am y brechdane.
Awen am y cynta 'da'r mini Mars bars, a phawb yn sugno
poteli fel tase dim fory i ga'l.

Rodd pum tîm arall yn y gystadleuaeth, a ninne'n gorfod aros i gystadlaethau'r dynion orffen yn gyntaf. Eistedd yn y bws gan geisio peidio gwrando ar y gweiddi a'r tuchan yn dod o'r cae. Gwrando ar ryw foi mewn carafán a megaffon yn mynd trwy enwau'r time i gyd, a'r gystadleuaeth yn dod yn agosach.

"Reit 'te, kit up." Neidiodd Les o'r sedd flaen a phawb yn mynd ati i wisgo'n dawel. Llinos yn tynnu'i sane i fyny, Non yn edrych fel tase hi'n mynd i gyfarfod â firing squad, Ner yn tynnu'i belt o gwmpas ei chanol, a Kel yn chwifio'i breichiau fel melin wynt i baratoi.

Yna daeth llais o gyfeiriad y cae. "Cystadlaethau Merched, Ladies' Competition. Coaches to caravan, please – alla i ga'l yr hyfforddwyr draw fan hyn os gwelwch chi fod yn dda? Nawr 'te, Rhosgarn yn erbyn Llandinas, a Merched Dowlais yn erbyn Merched Tafarn y Rhos."

Wrth i'r geirie godi dros ein penne, ffurfiodd pawb gylch cyn cyfri i ddeg gan godi'n lleisie wrth rifo i fyny. Ffwrdd â ni tuag at y cylch o bobl lle roedd y pitsh wedi'i farcio. Dwy raff ar y llawr yn edrych yn ddiniwed iawn – dim byd tebyg i arfau rhyfel. Roedd y merched eraill mewn rhesi ar bwys y garafán yn gweiddi ar ei gilydd ac yn ceisio gwylltio'u hunain i fewn i natur. Roedd Les wrth y garafán yn siglo llaw 'da hyfforddwr arall, a'r reff yn sefyll rhyngddon nhw yn taflu darn deg ceiniog i'r awyr i benderfynu pwy oedd yn tynnu i fyny ac i lawr y cae. Roedd 'na dipyn o oledd yn y cae ac fe fydde mantais fawr 'da'r tîm oedd yn tynnu am lawr yn gyntaf. Galwyd 'pen' a 'chwt' ond fe gollon ni a gollyngodd Les reg. Daeth draw atom a dweud celwydd gole.

"Dim problem – ry'n ni'n gwbod beth i neud – gadel iddyn nhw ennill y pull cynta, gadel iddyn nhw feddwl bod nhw'n agos at y diwedd."

Leinio i fyny godderbyn â'r lleill a chlywed un o ferched y tîm arall yn sibrwd 'ast' i gyfeiriad Awen.

"O Iesu," clywes Ner tu ôl imi, "'co ni off!"

Cerdded tuag at y rhaff, leinio i fyny a dechrau'r broses o drio gwasgu popeth arall o'm meddwl a chanolbwyntio ar beth oedd o'm bla'n.

Craffu ar y dyfarnwr.

"Pick up the rope."

Jacio'r rhaff o dan fy nghesail a chlywed Kel yn gweiddi, "Cym on, ferched." Wyth sawdl yn creithio'r cae.

"Take the strain." Breichiau'r dyfarnwr yn codi dros ei ben ac yn craffu ar y marc coch rhwng y ddau dîm. "And PULL!"

Crac yn mynd i lawr y rhaff; roedd y drop wedi mynd yn iawn. Gorweddai pawb yn y tîm 'nôl yn gyfforddus yn y siâp iawn; mae'n debyg taw tîm cyfrwys oedd rhain.

Les yn cerdded ar hyd y llinell. "Iawn ferched, iawn ferched, canolbwyntio, nawr 'te, gorwedd 'nôl 'yn bach, gorwedd 'nôl, teimlwch y tensiwn, teimlwch e, nawr 'te, power horse yn y bla'n plis... "

Roedd y tensiwn yn y rhaff yn codi a'r tîm arall yn paratoi i'n codi ni. Yn sydyn dyma'r rhaff yn slacio gan wneud i Non yn y blaen golli'i thraed dani hi.

Les yn codi'i lais: "Cym on ferched, ry'n ni'n gwbod beth i neud; os y'n nhw'n rhoi rhaff i chi, cymrwch e. Nawr 'te, 'co un arall yn dod."

Y rhaff yn slacio eto a finne'n ceisio cadw fy sodle wedi'u claddu cyn hired â phosib. Sibrydodd Les yn 'y nghlust i, "Heledd, for god's sake cwyd ar dy dra'd yn lle wilibowan lawr fan'na."

Jacio'n hunan i fyny ar 'y nhraed a chlywed y rhaff yn sythu yn fy ngafael; roedd Kel wedi codi rhythm a phawb yn cwympo i fewn iddo'n araf.

"And pull, and pull and pull... " Roedd Les yn mynd yn ddwl bared. "'Na fe, ferched, sdim hast – 'nôl â nhw'n slo bach, and pull and pull and pull... " Roedd pawb yn codi am 'nôl yn ara bach ac ro'n i'n ymwybodol o wyneb 'u frontman nhw'n crychu dan y straen. "And pull and pull and pull!"

A breichiau'r dyfarnwr yn taflu draw i'n ochr ni. Un ochr i ddim. Codi oddi ar y llawr lle roedden ni wedi cwympo, a Les yn gweiddi arnon ni'n syth.

"Reit 'te, ferched – dim segura nawr; yfwch sip fach o ddŵr a chadwch 'ych cefne at y dyfarnwr. Os yw e moyn i ni ailddechre geith e ofyn i ni." Techneg Les oedd hon i ga'l 'bach mwy o hoe rhwng pulls.

Roedd 'y mreiche i'n crynu i gyd – roedd hyn wastad yn digwydd ar ôl tynnu am y tro cynta mewn cystadleuaeth oherwydd bod y cyhyrau ddim yn gyfarwydd â'r straen. Dechreuodd y dyfarnwr neud stumie a ninnau'n mynd tuag at ochr arall y cae. Bydde'n haws tro hyn, gobeithio – roedd y merched erill yn edrych wedi blino wrth inni eu pasio. Roedd Les yn iawn, os o'dd tîm ffit 'da chi do'dd dim hast i dynnu'r tîm arall i ddechre – llabyddio nhw oedd eisie.

Ailddechrau'r broses eto: cloi pob meddwl allan o'r pen a chodi'r rhaff, craffu ar y beirniad, a lawr â ni eto fel rhyw neidr gantroed a thynnu o'r dechrau. Roedd y dechneg wedi gweithio, a'r merched erill yn disgwyl inni ddal eto am hir. Oherwydd eu bod nhw 'di blino do'dd 'na ddim tensiwn i gael 'nôl, ac roedden ni fel tase ni ar y gantri yn y cae ymarfer a Les ar ei benliniau yn taro'r llawr gan weiddi "And pull and pull and pull," gyda phob cam yn ôl. Came ceiliog oedden nhw, ond came am 'nôl yn sicr.

Dwylo'r dyfarnwr yn cwympo eto, a ninnau am yr ail dro wedi tynnu'r lleill ar eu tinau dros y llinell goch ar ganol y cae.

Leinio i fyny i ysgwyd llaw gyda'r lleill, ac wrth adael y cylch clywais lais Awen yn sibrwd wrth ryw ferch, "Gwell ast na gwahadden – bron i ti fynd o'r golwg, cariad."

Roedd Les wedi cerdded o'r cae fel sowldiwr, a'i frest mas. Clywed llais o'r garafán yn datgan y canlyniad: "Merched Tafarn y Rhos wedi ennill, tynfa hira: dwy funud tri deg pedwar eiliad."

"Nawr 'te ferched, performance go lew, ond fi 'di gweld gwell."

"Blydi enillon ni achan," medde Non gan geisio tynnu'i nicers gwlyb a mwdlyd o'i phen-ôl.

"Da iawn, Einstein," atebodd Les yn siarp reit, "ond fi 'di gweld chi'n ennill yn well na 'na."

"Be ti moyn ni neud?" gofynnodd Awen. "Rhoi arabesque mewn neu rywbeth, neu neud triple lutz?"

"Ca dy ffycin ben, Awen, a gwrandwch newch chi? Nawr ma ise edrych 'bach mwy hyderus os gwelwch chi fod yn dda, ddim cerdded ar y cae yn edrych fel tase'n well 'da chi fynd i neud bara brith yn rhywle. Dy'ch chi'n dda i ddim fel'na – edrychwch fel tase chi o ddifri. Nawr 'te, ry'n ni arno 'to."

Naw pull yn ddiweddarach roedden ni ymhell ar y blaen ond yn gorfod tynnu'r tîm anodda olaf a ninnau a'n breichiau bron â chyffwrdd y llawr a'n stumogau'n gwasgu i mewn i'r beltiau lledr rownd ein canolau. Yn ystod y pull diwetha roedd y rhaff wedi cydio rhwng fy nghrys a'm belt gan binsho'r croen oddi tano – ro'n i'n gwbod heb orfod edrych ei fod yn biws a choch. Roedd y tîm arall wedi gwneud yn dda hefyd ac roedden nhw'n edrych fel tase nhw'n cryfhau bob eiliad. Roedd hi'n glawio'n drwm a'r bandyn o amgylch fy mhen yn methu cadw'r holl law allan o'm llygaid. Ro'n i'n socian hyd y croen a'r dŵr yn rhedeg lawr fy ngefn. Roedd y glaw yn gwlychu'r mwd ar hyd fy nghoese a hwnnw'n llifo lawr am fy sgidiau. Fe gasglon ni o gwmpas Les am air bach cyn mynd i fewn i'r cylch am y tro olaf. Tynnodd e botel o smelling salts mas o'i boced a'i rhoi i Kel oedd wrth ei ochr. Cymerodd honno anadl ddofn cyn ei basio ymlaen rownd y cylch.

"Nawr 'te ferched, ry'n ni'n perfformio'r tro ola 'ma fel tase ni'n perfformio am y tro cynta. Dyma lle ma'r bastard training 'ma'n dod mewn. Ma nhw'n ffycin bygyrd a ninne jest yn dechre."

Roedd rhywbeth yn fy mhen i'n gweud ei fod yn trio'n calonogi ni yn hytrach na gweud y gwir.

"Byddwn ni trwyddo i'r gystadleuaeth drwy Bryden os enillwn ni hon, ferched; yn cynrychioli ein gwlad – ry'ch chi'n moyn 'na o'nd y'ch chi? O's syniad 'da chi faint o bobol fydde'n lladd i ga'l y cyfle 'na? Cyfle i dynnu'r crys coch dros eu penne gan wbod taw nhw yw'r gore 'sda'u gwlad nhw i' gynnig. Y'ch chi'n moyn 'na?"

Pawb yn nodio'u penne.

"Dewch i fi ga'l ffycin clywed chi 'de."

"ODYN LES!" gwaeddodd pawb gyda'i gilydd trwy'r glaw.

"Nawr dewch mla'n, a dangoswch i'r bastards beth chi'n galler neud."

Ac i ffwrdd â ni fel neidr wlyb tuag at y cylch.

Roedd y pull cynta'n galed, a 'mreichiau i wedi blino'n rhacs. Roedd y lleill yn ein tynnu ni'n galed, y llawr wedi gwlychu'n sopen a'r cae yn stecs i gyd. Teimlais fomentwm y tîm arall trwy'r rhaff ac ro'n i'n gwbod na allwn ddal hon; cyn pen deg eiliad roedd ein sodlau'n dechrau cael eu tynnu allan o'r nythod roedden ni wedi'u gneud iddyn nhw yn y pridd. Roedd Kel ar y llawr a'r dyfarnwr yn gneud arwydd iddi godi neu fe fydden ni'n ca'l rhybudd swyddogol.

Roedd Les yn gweiddi arni i godi. "Cym on, Kel, ar dy dra'd!"

Roedd ongl y rhaff yn golygu bod rhan y fwya o'r straen ar ei chefen hi ac roedd hi'n gwingo dan y boen.

"Cwyd Kel, plis; Kel get your ass off the ffycin floor!"

Y dyfarnwr yn cwympo'i ddwylo ac yn gweiddi, "Rhybudd i Ferched Tafarn y Rhos."

Kel yn hyrddio ac yn codi'i phen-ôl oddi ar y llawr, a ninne'n cael ein tynnu mla'n oherwydd inni golli'r rhythm. O gornel fy llygaid gweles y marcyn coch yn mynd heibio. Eistedd yn y pwdel yn wlyb o'm coryn i'm sodle – fy nghefen yn sgrechen a'm hochor yn gwingo – gan feddwl beth oedd yn bod ar chwarae tennis neu bêl-droed. Les yn dod â photel o ddŵr imi a minnau'n ei chymryd er nad o'n i'n gallu teimlo 'nwylo. Codi ar ein traed a ffurfio cylch unwaith eto

"Nawr 'te ferched, pwy sy fel donci 'ma e? Pwy sy'n mynd i gydio yn y rhaff y tro hyn a gweud, 'Cym on 'te, yr eist, triwch 'na eto; cym on, triwch e. Triwch chi gladdu fi yn y llawr ac fe gladda i chithe hyd y bôn, y diawled uffern'? Nawr ma gyts yn dod i mewn i chware, nawr ry'n ni'n gweld pwy sy'n galler tynnu rhaff."

Pawb yn dechre sgwario i fyny. Newid ochr a dechrau eto. Roedd y straen yr un mor uffernol, a'r ffaith eu bod nhw wedi ennill y pull olaf wedi rhoi hyder iddyn nhw, ac roedd eu cefnogwyr yn bloeddio wrth ochr y cylch. Yn sydyn dyma Kel yn rhoi sgrech ac yn claddu'i sawdl i fewn i'r mwd gan wneud i glotsen godi i'r aer a chwistrellu siorts Les â stecs. Teimlais y cryndod yn y rhaff yn siarad â chyhyrau pawb ac yn ein galluogi i wybod pryd oedd ychwanegu pwysau. Pwyso 'mhen am 'nôl gan gofio bod 'na beth pwysau yn hwnnw, er nad o'n ni'n medru gweld hynny nawr a ninnau'n sgrechian ar ganol cae ar ddydd Sadwrn yn lle bod yn y dre yn siopa a wedyn mynd allan am gwpwl o beints.

Roedd y dorf yn mynd yn ddwl bared, a Les ar ei bengliniau unwaith eto yn gweiddi nerth ei ben. Roedd 'na wres rhyfedd yn codi trwy fy nghyhyrau a'r bandyn o gwmpas fy mhen yn teimlo'n dynnach nag erioed. A dyna'r camgymeriad ar eu rhan nhw yn digwydd. Fe ollyngon nhw'r rhaff gan obeithio ein disodli. Ond roedden ni wedi bod yn aros am hyn, ac wrth iddyn nhw roi inni fe dynnon ni'n syth gan eu codi nhw ar eu man gwanna. Unwaith gododd y rhythm, roedd y linell derfyn mewn golwg hawdd. Roedden nhw wedi colli'u grip a ninnau'n eu tynnu tuag at y terfyn. Roedd y dorf yn bloeddio a Les yn cynhyrfu'n ddwl.

"Nawr 'te ferched, ar eich traed. Un dynfa sy rhyngddon ni a'r cryse coch nawr. Chi'n gwbod faint y'n ni ise fe – yr holl orie 'na o dreino a styfnigo a seiens a dim yfed. Nawr yw ein cyfle ni. Fi moyn i chi neud hyn mewn steil."

Edrychais ar y tîm arall. Roedden nhw'n eistedd ar y llawr neu'n plygu mla'n a'u dwylo ar eu pengliniau.

"Ma nhw wedi blino, so nawr ma galw ffafr mewn 'da Mr Stamina Banc Manijer, ondife? Felly cashwch y sieciau 'na, ferched – this is it!"

Mynd am yr ochr arall a doedden ni ddim yn ymwybodol o'r tîm arall o gwbl. Doedd ganddyn nhw ddim wynebau; roedden nhw wedi shrinco i fod yn ddim mwy na rhyw elyn pell, rhyw olau coch oedd angen ei ddiffodd. Dyma ddwylo'r dyfarnwr yn cwympo a ninnau'n mynd lawr i bosition. Tensiwn cyfartal ar bob ochr, a dyna lle buon ni'n arbrofi ar gryfder ein gilydd nes bod rhaid i rhywbeth newid. Les, am unwaith, yn cyfarwyddo'r tîm. Roedd yn sibrwd ac yn cerdded y lein gan ddweud rhywbeth 'tho pob merch yn ei thro.

"Reit Hels, this is for the Welsh shirt, baby... " meddai wrth basio.

Pawb yn rhoi plwc 'da'i gilydd a'r tîm arall yn rhoi plwc 'nôl ar yr un pryd fel ein bod yn siglo 'nôl a mla'n rhwng ein gilydd. Dyna godi'r momentwm wrth i'r rhaff wegian ar ein hochr ni – a dyna'r stêlmêt wedi'i dorri. Wyth sawdl yn hacio'r ddaear a'r mwd yn codi gyda phob cam. Rhaff yn llosgi'r dwylo ac yn ara bach yn dod am 'nôl. Roedd y llosgi'n treiddio trwy groen y dwylo ac i fyny i'm breichiau ac i'm gwar a Les yn colli arno'i hun yn llwyr.

"CYMMMM ONNNNNNNNNNN! ANNNNND PULL ANNNNND PULL ANNNNND PULL!"

Rhaffed o ferched yn mynd am 'nôl, a feddylies i rioed y bydde ugain llath mor blydi pell. O'r diwedd, ac ar ôl i bob nerf yn fy nghorff glustfeinio amdano, dyma chwiban y dyfarnwr yn canu a 'mhen-ôl yn cyfarfod â'r llawr ar ochr iawn y llinell. Roedd y cwbwl yn dawel er bod y dorf yn gweiddi nerth eu pennau. Ro'n i'n eistedd yn y pwll dŵr, yn hollol anymwybodol, nes i Ner landio ar 'y mhen i gan gusanu fy nhrwyn.

Roedd ei llygaid yn disgleirio unwaith eto. "Cym on, baby, ma cwpwl o beints i fod heno."

Roedd Les yn ceisio ein casglu i ryw fath o drefen a'i wyneb mor syth â phocer. "Nawr 'te ferched, professionalism plis – codwch ar 'ych tra'd, shiglwch eu dwylo a ffyc off i'r gawod. Cym on, dewch!"

Dadblico Ner oddi arna i, a ffwrdd â ni i'r bloc molchi. Roedd Les yn gweiddi arnom i'w gyfarfod yn y bar am de-briefing.

Erbyn i Ner a finne gyrraedd y cawodydd, roedd Awen yn rhoi perfformiad gwych o 'Mambo Number 5' gyda soap on a rope a Llinos yn gwneud rhyw gymysgedd o salsa a dawns werin i gyfeiliant Awen. Dadwisgodd Ner a fi gan fynd i ymuno â nhw. Roedd pawb yn fwd o'u pen i fysedd eu traed ac fe gawson ni hwyl yn chwilio pwy oedd â'r clais mwyaf diddorol gan addo prynu peint i'r perchennog. Siân oedd yr enillydd gyda chlais mawr glas oedd yn prysur felynu jest ar tu fewn ei chlun. Erbyn inni gyrraedd y bar roedd Les wedi bod yn y gawod hefyd, ac yn eistedd ar un o'r seddi melfed coch yn edrych fel rhywbeth allan o gatalog o'r saithdegau. Pawb yn codi peint ac yn edrych fel merched unwaith eto, yn eu sgertiau a'u wonderbras.

"SHHH," medde Les. "Gwrandwch nawr 'te. Reit, ry'n ni wedi ennill y fraint o dynnu dros ein gwlad, a sa i'n credu bo chi'n ddigon da."

Gwyneb pawb yn cwympo.

"Dwi'n ryw feddwl gofyn i'r ail dîm 'na a fydde nhw'n fodlon cymryd ein lle ni."

"Beth?" bytheiriodd Kel. "Enillon ni bron bob pull heddi! Ro'n ni'n dda, achan – beth yn y byd sy'n bod arno chi?"

"Ca dy ben, Kel; gweud ydw i nad y'ch chi wedi'i neud e â steil. Fi'n gwbod, er enghraifft, eich bod chi wedi bod ar y piss yn ddiweddar; fi'n gwbod bod rhai ohonoch chi â llai o ddiddordeb na'r lleill, bod rhai ohonoch chi ddim yn codi ddigon cynnar er mwyn mynd i redeg. Chi'n trin y peth fel ryw half bit, poncy woncy girly team – ac i ddweud y gwir do's dim amser 'da fi ichi. Ma digon o bethe 'da fi i neud heblaw rhedeg ar ôl chi'r diawled – ac os nad o's newid mawr yn yr agwedd 'ma fe fydda i'n gwneud yr alwad ffôn 'na i dîm merched y Parc. Ry'n ni'n mynd i wisgo'r crys coch 'na, a ddyle neb neud hynny â hanner calon. Cofiwch, dim rygbi y'n ni'n chware."

Pawb yn syllu i berfeddion eu gwydrau lagyr.

"Nawr 'te, meddyliwch chi am y peth a gadewch imi wbod be chi ise neud – fe ddisgwylia i alwad ffôn 'wrth bob aelod erbyn pnawn fory neu fe fydda i'n gwneud galwad ffôn nos fory a gartre fyddwn ni. Am heno, fi am i bawb feddwi'n barlat a does dim esgus dros ga'l gwydryn gwag. Chi'n haeddu fe heddi, ond meddyliwch be wedes i. Nawr 'te, lawr â fe – the next round's on the coach."

Douddeg

Un ar ddeg y nos a 'mhen i'n troi. Beth bynnag ddwedai Les, roedd yr holl ymarfer 'ma yn cael effaith ar y diawl arna i. Roedd y peints wedi mynd yn strêt i 'mhen a'r merched i gyd fel tase nhw heb weld cwrw ers chwe mlynedd a hanner.

Roedd y clwb yn llawn, a thîm pêl-droed y dre a nifer fawr o'r time tynnu erill yno. Roedd Kel wrthi'n dawnsio'n ddigon secsi 'da ryw foi i wneud i Rasputin gochi, ac Awen wrth fy ochr yn pregethu tra bod Ner wrth y bar yn codi rownd.

"Sai'n gwbod beth uffarn o'dd yn bod 'no fe, no, y diawl diflas!" medde Awen. "Myn uffarn i, allen ni ddim fod wedi gneud mwy na beth naethon ni. Beth o'dd e'n ddisgwl – ennill drwy dynnu ag un llaw? Bachan bachan, ma fe fel bat! Ti 'di ffono Sion 'de?"

"E?"

"Ti 'di ffono Sion?"

"I beth?"

"I weud be ddigwyddodd, achan; jiawl, wyt tithe fel slej 'fyd!"

"O, do, ginne fach."

"Be wedodd e?"

"Dim byd lot – o'dd e ar ei ffordd mas i rywle."

"Shw ma pethe erbyn hyn?"

"T'mod fel ma nhw," wedes inne. "Uffarn, ma ise drinc arall arna i glei."

Daeth Ner 'nôl o'r bar a'r dorf o ddynion yn ymrannu wrth iddyn nhw edrych arni a cheisio dal ei llygaid hi. Tri tequila ar hambwrdd, potyn cyfan o halen, a lemwn plastig cyfan o sudd Jif.

"Dowch mla'n," medde hithe, "ma'r barmed yn cadw llygad arnon ni – ma hi ise'r halen a phethe 'nôl."

"Uffarn, classy," medde Awen.

Tri gwydryn yn clecio ar fwrdd, ac i lawr y lôn goch â nhw. Sgwyrt o'r lemwn allan o'r Jif ac roedd y cyfan drosodd – nes i Awen gamgymryd lle roedd ei llygad a chwistrellu'r sudd reit i'w chanol.

"AHHHHHHHHHHHHHHH!" sgrechiodd ac fe droiodd pawb o gwmpas i edrych arnon ni.

"Shit, Ner – der 'da fi i'r toiled. Alla i ddim mynd fy hunan – weles i'r ferch 'na fuodd yn gas i fi pnawn 'ma yn mynd yno."

Ffwrdd â nhw i'r tŷ bach gan adael imi fynd am y bar i nôl diod arall gan geisio edrych fel petai fy ffrindie i wastad yn gweiddi blue murder pan o'n nhw'n yfed tequila. Roedd 'y mhen i'n troi wrth imi ymbalfalu am fy mhwrs a phrin y teimlais y llaw ar fy mraich wrth imi ofyn am fodca a soda.

"Haia," medde rhyw lais uwch 'y mhen i. Edrychais i fyny ac fe ddiflannodd pob gair a ddysgais erioed.

"Shwt wyt ti 'de? Fancy seeing a girl like you in a place like this," medde Deian a'i lygaid yn rhedeg yn ysgafn dros fy nghorff.

"Haia," medde finne wrth iddo bwyso dros y bar a thalu am fy nrinc. "O, sdim angen i ti neud 'na... "

"Na, ma'n iawn, fyddi di arno rhywbeth i fi wedyn, a fe fydd esgus 'da fi i roi guilt trip iti a pherswadio ti i ddod 'nôl 'da fi heno a neidio mewn i'r gwely," meddai'n ysgafn gan setlo'i lygaid yn ôl ar fy ngwefusau.

Roedd unrhyw eiriau o'n i wedi ceisio'u cofio wedi diflannu am byth nawr.

"Ti'n dod i eistedd?"medde fe. "Fi'n gweld bod dy ffrindie di'n otherwise engaged," ychwanegodd, gan edrych ar Kel.

Wrth inni edrych ar y ddau'n cusanu a dawnsio, cododd gwrid ar fy mochau."O'n i'n iste draw fan hyn, os ti am," medde finne.

"Iawn, lead the way."

Roedd e'n gwisgo ryw grys ysgafn a hwnnw wedi'i agor o gwmpas ei wddwg. 'Nes i ddim mentro edrych ymhellach, rhag ofn.

"Be ti'n neud 'ma?" medde fi wrtho.

"Wel, ma mrawd i'n tynnu i'r tîm heddlu lawr fan hyn, ti'n gweld. Ro'n i lawr am y penwythnos ac yn meddwl, wel, ma'n siŵr gwrdden ni â rhywun o'n i'n nabod 'ma heno... a weles i ti yn dy siorts pnawn 'ma a nawr dwi'n stalko."

Chwarddais gydag e cyn meddwl, unwaith eto, beth uffarn o'n i'n neud.

"Wnaethoch chi'n dda," mynte fe, ac wrth iddo ynganu'r geirie roedd gen i uffarn o awydd plannu anferth o gusan ar ei wefusau.

"O do, iawn," atebais, gan geisio serio gwyneb Sion yn fy meddwl.

"Ti'n iawn?" gofynnodd. "Ti'n dawel iawn; cofia, os o's well 'da ti fod yn rhywle arall, gwed wrtha i – dim problem."

"O na," medde fi'n syth gan ddifaru wedyn mod i'n swnio mor bendant, "wedi blino'n rhacs a gweud y gwir."

"Trueni," atebodd gan ychwanegu, "o'n i'n mynd i

ofyn iti am ddawns."

Roedd e wedi symud yn agosach. Gwelais Awen a Ner yn dychwelyd o'r tŷ bach a mascara Awen yn rhedeg hyd ei bochau. Gwelodd Deian nhw'n dod.

"Ym... wela i ti nes mla'n?" gofynnodd.

"Ie," atebais gan ddamio Awen a Ner dan fy anadl am ddod 'nôl yn syth at y ford.

Eisteddodd y ddwy i lawr wrth imi ddilyn pen-ôl Deian yn diflannu i mewn i'r dorf.

Roedd Awen yn esbonio sut roedd lemwn yn teimlo mewn llefydd nad oedd e i fod, a Ner yn esbonio iddi lle roedd cariadon Rasputin yn rhoi'u lemwn nhw. Wrth lwc, ddaethon ni allan o'r esboniad yna pan ddaeth un o dime'r dynion aton ni a hawlio'r seddau nesa atom.

"Shwmai ferched! Chi ffansi tynnu heno fel dynnoch chi heddi?"

Roedd Awen wrth ei bodd, a gwyneb Ner yn dangos llai o straen nag o'n i wedi'i weld ers misoedd. Daeth Non, Heini, Siân a Llinos draw gan adael i Kel wneud beth o'dd hi'n neud ore, sef cystadleuaeth yfed a oedd yn cynnwys codi ar ben eich stôl gan geisio cofio cant a mil o bethau. Os oeddech chi'n methu cofio popeth, y gosb oedd gorfod yfed hanner eich diod a rhoi cusan ar foch pwy bynnag oedd ar eich ochr chwith. Yn fuan iawn roedd y cyfan wedi mynd yn gymysgedd o fwynhau sylw'r bechgyn, yfed gormod, teimlo'n sâl a gweud jôcs brwnt. Aeth hydoedd heibio, a'r merched yn diflannu bob yn un gyda'r bechgyn. Ro'n innau'n chwilio am ben tywyll Deian bob tro ro'n in mynd i'r tŷ bach.

O'r diwedd, daeth Les heibio. "Cym on y diawled, off â ni; ma 'da ni dipyn o siwrne 'nôl i ga'l. Chop chop you lovelies, a rhowch y bois 'na lawr, newch chi! Smo chi'n gwbod lle ma nhw 'di bod na beth ma nhw 'di'i ddala tra bod nhw 'na."

Awen a finne'n cerdded tua'r bws wedi colli pawb arall ers hydoedd, a'r aer oer tu allan yn sioc i'r sgyfaint. Yna gwelais rywbeth wnaeth i'r aer neidio allan o 'mrest i unwaith eto.

Roedd Non newydd rhoi right hook i'r boi oedd 'da Kel ac roedd Kel a hithau'n beichio crio a'r boi ar ei hyd ar y llawr.

"Beth uffarn sy'n mynd... " dechreuodd Les.

"O'dd e'n dechre mynd yn ryff gyda Kel," esboniodd Non gan fagu'i dwrn. "Des i mas fan hyn ac ro'dd e'n cydio yn ei gwallt hi a'i thynnu tu ôl tuag at y wal. Beth arall allen i neud?"

Aeth Les lan at y corff ar y llawr. "Y cachwr uffarn," gwaeddodd, gan wneud ei ore i beidio rhoi cic iddo. "Dere 'ma, Kel," meddai gan gydio ynddi a chusanu top ei phen. Roedd hi'n crynu ac yn llefen.

Ar hyn dyma fi'n codi mhen i weld pen golau Ner a rhyw foi yn dod rownd y gornel law yn llaw wedi clywed yr halibalŵ. Ro'n i'n nabod y pen tywyll wrth ei hochor. Deian o'dd e.

Wrth i'n llygaid gyfarfod fe edrychodd ar ei draed. Cwympodd fy nghalon i'm sodle, ond bydde well 'da fi ga'l fy nharo'n farw na dangos dim byd. Es ar fy mhengliniau a theimlo am guriad calon y bachgen ar y llawr. Yn sydyn, roedd rhywun arall yn penlinio wrth fy ochr.

"Iwan... Iwan, dihuna achan! Deian sy 'ma, Iwan. Ti'n clywed fi? O, shit, be wedith Mam am hyn? Iwan, achan, dy frawd sy 'ma... "

Codais ar fy nhraed ac anelu am ddrws y bws, ond fe

chwydais cyn ei gyrraedd. Teimlais fraich Awen o amgylch fy nghanol – ond does gen i ddim llawer o gof o ddim ddigwyddodd wedyn, wrth inni fynd â Non i'r sbyty iddi gael plastar a'r wobr amwys o fod y ferch gyntaf erioed i gael ei chludo yno 'da boxer's fracture.

O'r diwedd, gollyngodd y bws ni wrth dop y lôn ac fe dda'th Kel gyda fi gan ei bod hi'n dal yn sigledig. Plannais hi yn fy ngwely gyda photel ddŵr poeth a thynnais fy nghontacts. Roedd Kel yn cysgu'n barod. Gwisgais sanau tewion am ei thraed a rhoi cusan iddi. Wrth orwedd wrth ei hochor dechreuodd hi lefen yn ei chwsg; cydiais yn ei llaw ac aeth y cyfan yn ddu.

Tri ar ddeg

Edrych ar y cloc unwaith eto. Dau o'r gloch, a'r nerfau'n tician. Mae hi'n oer ar ôl i'r gwres droi i ffwrdd. Codi a mynd at y ffôn. Codi'r derbynnydd i tsecio am dôn; cymryd llwnc arall o chwisgi; eistedd i lawr. Codi i edrych drwy'r llenni am ole yn dod lawr y lôn. Sŵn cŵn yn cyfarth yn y sièd. Mynd i'r stafell ore i ga'l golwg well o'r lôn. Dim byd i'w glywed ond sŵn y da'n pori yn y ca'. Mynd 'nôl i'r gegin, a theimlo 'bach o bendro wrth eistedd i lawr. Sŵn sodle'n agosáu at y drws. Dyma hi'n dod i mewn heb droi rownd; mae'n rhoi'r bag i lawr a throi'r gole mla'n.

"Ffycin hel, Dat! Be sy arno ti'n hela ofan arna i felna?"

"Ble uffarn ti 'di bod? O'n i'n gwbod ddylen ni wedi dod i dy nôl di. Iesu, ferch, dyw e ddim hyd yn o'd yn croesi dy feddwl di i ffono i weud bod ti'n iawn?"

"Jest gad hi, nei di? Fi'n feddw a fi isie mynd i'r gwely."

"Aros di fynna, lodes. Tra 'mod i mas yn y caeau 'na bob awr o'r dydd, a dy fod tithe'n byw fan hyn, fe fydde'n beth da iti gofio pwy sy'n rhoi bwyd ar y ford." Damo hi'n meddwl bod hi'n galler trin y lle 'ma fel fflipin gwesty. Roedd 'na fêc-yp ar ei gruddiau, a dilynais ei llygaid tuag at y botel wag o'dd ar y ford.

"O ie, 'na be sy'n bod ife?" medde hi. "Bender bach arall, ife? Wel, cer i dy wely a phaid â chodi nes bo ti'n gall 'to. Odi Rhys wedi gweld ti fel hyn?"

"Ma Rhys a fi'n deall ein gilydd yn iawn."

"Ble 'ma fe?"

"Ble uffarn ti'n meddwl ma fe yr amser hyn o'r bore?" Ceisiodd hi gydio yn y botel cyn imi ei chipio o'i gafael.

"Dere â hwnna i fi!"

Am eiliad roedd ei llaw hi'n gynnes am f'un i. Tynnodd hi i ffwrdd fel tase hi wedi cyffwrdd â rhywbeth poeth. Cerddodd at y stof. Cododd glawr y hotplet, rhoi'r tegyl i ferwi ac estyn siwmper oddi ar y stôl.

"Gwd – allet ti neud â gwisgo honna. Ti'n edrych fel reial tarten fach heno." Dihangodd y geiriau o'm gwefusau a oedd wedi'u llacio braidd gan y Grouse. "Ro'dd y bechgyn i gyd yn meddwl bod ti'n rywbeth bach tsiep, siŵr o fod. Ti'n codi cywilydd arna i wrth fynd mas felna. Bydde dy fam yn mynd off 'i phen."

"Bydde Mam yn gwbod 'mod i'n deall beth fi'n neud ac yn ddigon hen i wbod beth sy ore 'fyd."

"Gwbod beth ti'n neud, ife? Ti ddim wedi neud dim â beth ddysges ti'n y coleg 'na, wyt ti? Gweithio mewn swyddfa fach wyt ti, ondife, yn gneud beth ma pobol erill yn gweud tho ti neud. Da iawn, Ner. Ddarllenes i ddim un llyfyr erio'd, a nath e ddim drwg i fi."

"Naddo fe nawr."

"Blydi nonsens yw e i gyd; lle i blant fynd i wasto arian ac amser yn lle bod mas yn y byd go iawn. Pryd ti'n mynd i ddefnyddio dy gomon sens, Ner, a neud rhywbeth o werth? Fe fydd dy frawd yn mynd i'r Brifysgol; ma rhwbeth yn 'i ben e, yn wahanol i rai."

Roedd hi'n gwneud coffi.

"Gad hi nawr, Dad, jest cer i'r gwely."

"Ie 'na fe, 'na le wyt ti'n hela'r rhan fwya o dy amser, ondife; os nad wyt ti'n y gwely rwyt ti'n trainio."

Cerddodd tuag ata i a rhoi'r mwg o'm bla'n.

"Yfa hwnna a cer i'r gwely. Alla i ddim siarad â ti pan wyt ti fel hyn. Plis jest cer."

"Fydde dy fam di ddim yn siarad â fi felna; fydde wastad amser 'da hi i siarad â fi."

"Wel sori, Dad, ond ma'n hen bryd iti ddeall 'i bod hi wedi mynd. Dyw hi ddim yn mynd i gerdded drwy'r drws 'na byth 'to."

Gwylltiais yn uffern dân. "Paid byth â siarad â fi felna 'to; do's 'da ti ddim hawl, dim hawl o gwbwl. Pwy uffarn wyt ti'n meddwl wyt ti?" gwaeddais gan wthio bys i'w gwddf. Ro'n i'n teimlo fel tase rhywun arall wedi cymryd rheolaeth o 'nghorff. Bwrais y mwg yn glep 'nôl ar y ford. Ro'n i'n crynu.

"Dim hawl?" sgrechiodd hi'n ôl gan godi ar ei thraed. "Dim hawl i siarad am fy mam fy hun? Sa i'n gwbod beth uffarn welodd hi ynddo ti!"

Wrth i'r geiriau fy nghyrraedd trwy'r niwl, teimlais ryw glwyf ynof yn dechrau gwaedu. Cwympais yn ôl yn glep ar y stôl. Plethais fy nwylo o gwmpas y mwg coffi. Roedd 'na ddagrau poeth yn dod o rywle a rheini'n rhedeg dros y baw oedd mewn siâp gwêr cor ar fy mysedd.

"O'dd hi yn fy ngharu i! Alle hi ddim peidio 'ngharu i os o'dd hi'n 'i garu fe."

"Beth ti'n weud?"

"O'dd hi yn fy ngharu i trwy'r amser, ti'n gweld; ma Rhys yn caru fi."

"Beth wyt ti'n frowlan ambwti? Drycha, ti'n feddw; yfa hwnna a cer i'r gwely."

"At bwy?" gofynnais gan edrych i fyw ei llygaid. "Beth sy'n digwydd nawr, Nerys?"

"Dim byd, 'na beth; do's 'na ddim allwn ni neud."

Cododd ar ei thraed a throi am y sta'r. Oedodd am eiliad fel tasai hi'n disgwyl clywed rhywbeth arall. Roedd y niwl yn tewhau a'r blinder mwyaf ofnadwy yn llethu 'nghorff. Daeth cwsg ata i ac aeth y cyfan yn ddu.

"Beth o't ti'n feddwl, 'os o'dd hi'n 'i garu fe?' Dat... Dat... ?"

Pedwar ar ddeg

Bip Bip!

Clywais y sŵn wrth fy ochr, ac yn ara bach dyma fi'n dod ataf fy hun. Roedd Kel wrth fy ochor yn cysgu fel twrch, a 'mhen inne'n teimlo fel tase Mam wedi'i roi e yn y tymbl dreier. Ymbalfalais am y ffôn, ac wrth wneud hynny sylwais bod pob cyhyr yn fy nghorff yn stiff fel procer. O'n i'n methu symud yn dda iawn ac ro'n i'n galler teimlo pob clais yn gwingo ar hyd fy nghorff. Fel hyn roedd bocsiwr yn teimlo y diwrnod ar ôl ffeit, siwr o fod.

V FFYCD - KEL YN IAWN? AWEN

Anfon 'nôl.

CYSGU. V HORIBLEDIG FYD

Anfon 'nôl.

CAFFI 12 FFREI UP

* * * *

Wrth inni gerdded tuag at y caffi'n nes mla'n, a Kel yn edrych yn eitha llipa, ro'n i'n methu cael y llun o Deian a Ner allan o 'mhen. Roedd e'n beth twp mewn gwirionedd, achos doedd dim rheswm 'da fi i fod yn sili amdano'r peth – ac eniwe, sut oedd Ner fod i wybod 'mod i'n 'i ffansïo fe? Ar ôl rhoi'r ordyr i fewn eisteddon ni i lawr i ddisgwyl y lleill. Roedd mwg ffags y ddwy weitres yn cymylu draw tuag aton ni wrth iddyn nhw eistedd wrth y bwrdd fformeica yn cnoi'u gwinedd.

Cyrhaeddodd Llinos ac eistedd lawr. "Sa i byth am yfed 'to, no," mynte hi gan wneud gwyneb sur. "So fe werth e, achan; ma naill ai rhaid iti fod yn ffit ne ma rhaid iti fod yn piss-head; do's dim pwynt neud dim byd in-bitwîn achos ma fe'n rhy boenus."

"Ca dy lap, nei di? Wîcend nesa, fyddi di 'nôl ar y pop fel whippet," atebodd Kel gan geisio yfed cwpaned o goffi lla'th oedd yn rhy boeth iddi.

"Rhwng 'y mhen i, a'r ffaith bo fi mor stiff â phostyn ffenso, dyw hi ddim yn dda 'ma."

"Be ni'n mynd i neud 'de?" holais wrth edrych i fyny i weld Ner yn dod i mewn a Heini ar ei hôl. Roedd golwg llwyd iawn ar Ner, a'i gwallt yn ffluwch.

"Ffyc knows. Y'n ni'n mynd i ffono Les 'de?" gofynnodd Llinos.

"Jocan o'dd e, siŵr o fod," wedodd Heini.

"Sai'n siŵr, t'mod; ma fe'n ddigon o un, cofia."

"Wel man a man inni gario mla'n, glei, ar ôl yr holl blydi ffwdan 'ma; ni 'di dod mor bell â hyn."

"Ie, ond ry'n ni un yn brin 'ma nawr, cofiwch. Shwt ma Non? O's rhywun wedi clywed 'wrthi?" gofynnais.

"Beauty o dorrad, mewn pedwar lle, mae'n debyg; ges i neges bore 'ma," atebodd Ner.

"Beth am y boi 'na?" gofynnodd Llinos. "Dim bod lot o ots am y ba'dd."

Teimlais Kel yn mynd yn llai a llai wrth fy ochr a'i phen yn cwympo at ei brest.

"Sai'n credu bod dim byd pellach yn mynd i ddigwydd; ro'dd e'n gwbod bod e'n y rong a 'na ddiwedd arni fi'n credu."

Dyma Kel yn dechre llefen a phawb yn teimlo'n wael wedyn.

"Ddylen i ddim fod wedi'i lîdo fe mla'n fel'na; bai fi oedd e... " dechreuodd sniffian.

"Bai ti?" medde Awen, oedd wedi ymuno â ni yn dawel bach, "paid bod yn sili − fe o'dd y bastard. Ma 'na' yn golygu 'na' mewn unrhyw iaith ac mewn unrhyw ffordd, ac os gwela i fe, fe geith e gic yn ei bwrs i fatsho'i lygad."

Gwenodd Kel yn ddiolchgar. "Ddylen i ddim bod mor fforward 'da nhw, ddylen i; chi i gyd yn siŵr o fod yn meddwl bo fi'n real slapyr."

"Paid bod yn sili, y bat; ma unrhyw un sy'n nabod ti'n meddwl bod ti'n lyfli − a twll tin pawb arall eniwe."

"Chi'n meddwl 'ny?"

"Wrth gwrs bod ni, a ry'n ni angen ti, achos bydde'n shares ni yn Durex yn cwmpo trwy'r llawr se ti ddim ambwti'r lle."

Heini'n chwerthin a Siân yn rhoi cusan ar dop ei phen.

"Nawr 'te, ca dy seiens inni ga'l cymryd fôt," medde fi. "Cofiwch, fydd dim stynts nac yfed na dim nonsens os y'n ni'n mynd i neud hyn. Reit, pawb sy moyn cario mla'n, dwylo lan."

Saethodd llaw Awen yn syth i'r awyr. "Fi moyn colli rhagor o'r tin 'ma," wedodd hi.

"Iawn, rheswm da."

Dilynwyd llaw Awen gan f'un i, Kel, Heini a Siân. Ro'dd Ner yn dal yn ôl gan edrych o'i chwmpas. Aeth llaw Llinos lan, a dyna fe.

"Overall majority, bois. Ry'n ni'n cario mla'n ond ma angen rhoi'n thinking caps arno − ma angen aelod arall arnon ni." Daeth y weitres draw â sawl plataid o fwyd ac aeth pawb ati'n brysur i fyta. Llenwyd y caffi 'da rhyw gleber a chwerthin a sŵn cyllyll a ffyrcs.

"Be am Bethan Boulder?"

"Ddim digon ffit."

"Honna sy'n crafu tato 'da Dai Chips 'de?"

"Rhy dew."

"Beth am chwaer Sion?"

"Rhy llipa."

"Wel, ffycin hel, bois – sdim lot o ddewis 'da ni o's e?"

"Shwt y'n ni'n mynd i ga'l rhywun lan i sbîd yn yr amser?"

"Beth am chwaer y boi pert 'na, beth yw'i enw fe – Deian?"

"Weles i hi'n chware hoci a ma hi fel peth wyllt; falle fydde hi'n un dda," medde Llinos.

"Wel os yw hi'n debyg i'w brawd mowr, dy'n ni ddim moyn gwbod," ychwanegais gan roi fy llaw ar fraich Kel.

"Sda hi ddim byd i neud â'i brawd, a ma hi'n iawn. Sara yw 'i henw hi fi'n credu."

"Eniwe," dwedais gan drio newid y testun, "os o's rhywun yn galler meddwl am enw, ma training nos Fowrth – a cofiwch ffono Les heno 'ma."

Aeth pawb ati i lusgo'u darnau tost trwy'u melyn wyau a chwrso'r bêcd bîns ola o gwmpas eu platie.

Pymtheg

Wrth inni nesáu at y cae ymarfer, dyma sŵn chwerthin
dwl yn dod i'n cyfarfod, ynghyd â sŵn fel rheinoseros a
phen tost arno fe. Edrychodd Ner a finne ar ein gilydd a
rhedeg rownd y gornel. Roedd y merched i gyd yn sefyll o
gwmpas malwen fawr o fan wen, a honno'n gollwng digon
o fwg du allan i'r awyr i roi harten i unrhyw greeny.

Eisteddai Les wrth y llyw, yn wafo arnon ni'n dwy i
neidio i mewn. Roedd y merched i gyd yn mynd i fewn
fesul un gan edrych yn betrusgar ofnadwy – yn cynnwys
merch wallt tywyll, Sara. Roedd pawb yn pesychu, a dŵr
yn rhedeg o lygaid ambell un. Roedd Llinos yn holi am
seat belt.

"Don't be bloody stupid, woman," medde Les. "Be
chi'n feddwl yw hon – luxury liner? Nawr 'te, ma syrpreis
bach 'da fi i chi heddi – fel tase hon ddim yn ddigon o
syrpreis ynddi'i hunan. Shut the ffycin sardine can and let's
go!"

Dyma Awen yn cau'r drws trwm gan anfon cawod o
rwd dros Heini.

"This is the Tug-o'-War War Bus, bois," gwaeddodd
Les dros y twrw. "This is the all-mobile, all-dancing, all-
singing puller-carrier. Eisteddwch 'nôl and enjoy the ride."

Roedd Llinos mewn stitches, ac Awen yn chwerthin
oherwydd bod ei phen-ôl hi'n gwichian ar y seddi feinil
bob tro roedden ni'n mynd rownd cornel. Roedd 'na dwll
yn y llawr, a hwnnw'n ddigon mawr i roi eich troed

trwyddo, a rhyw dwll yn y to a oedd wedi'i batsho 'da darn o gwdyn sment Blue Circle.

"Dim byd fel trafaelu mewn steil, o's e?" wedodd Heini cyn i'r bws daro rhywbeth ar yr hewl a ninnau'n cael hyrddiad o un ochr y sedd i'r llall. Hedfanodd y mud-flaps heibio i'r ffenest.

Ugain munud yn ddiweddarach dyma ni'n troi am y môr a chario mla'n am lawr. Roedd y cynnwrf yn fy stumog yn dweud wrtha i 'mod i'n gwbod lle ro'n ni'n mynd. Ymlaen ac ymlaen tuag at y môr, nes i'r tyrau ddod i'r golwg. Troi lawr lôn fach, trwy rhyw fariers, a dyna ni. Diffoddodd Les yr injan a rhoddodd y bws naid nes i bob merch lanio yng nghôl y ferch drws nesa. Pawb yn neidio allan ar gae cwrs assault yr Armi.

"Ti'n ca'l ffycin laff, on'd wyt ti?" holodd Awen, yn methu credu ei llygaid.

Daeth tri dyn mewn iwnifforms gwyrdd tuag aton ni.

"You see, ladies," medde Les, "fi ddim jest yn rhoi'r training gore yn y byd i chi, ond fi'n rhoi tidy bit of ass i chi edrych arno fe 'fyd."

Cochodd Ner yn syth; roedd dau ohonyn nhw'n edrych yn gorjys, gyda gwallt tywyll a chyhyrau amlwg, a thine y gallech chi agor poteli Bud ynddyn nhw.

"My god," medde Heini, "ma mwy o dits 'da hwnna na fi!"

Cael ein rhannu'n ddau dîm a chael ordyrs i gyrraedd pen pella'r cwrs mewn llai na hanner awr, neu bydde'n rhaid inni fynd yn ôl a dechre o'r dechre eto. Roedd rhaid inni hefyd gael pob aelod o'r tîm yn groes y llinell orffen oherwydd ein bod ni'n dysgu gweithio fel tîm. Dyma Awen, Heini, Llinos a fi'n ca'l ein rhannu 'wrth y lleill, a finne'n falch 'mod i ddim yn yr un tîm â Ner a Sara am nawr.

Roedd y cae'n llawn dop o bethe oedd yn edrych fel tasen nhw'n mynd i wneud uffarn o ddolur. Roedd 'na ryw rwydi ar y llawr, pyllau dŵr, welydd mawr uchel a dim stepiau atyn nhw. Doedden ni ddim yn hapus.

"Ni'n mynd i farw," cwynodd Awen y tu ôl imi, a sŵn llefen yn ei llais.

"Paid bod yn soft, achan," atebais. "Duw duw, fyddwn ni'n iawn." Llyncais fy mhoer.

"Reit 'te ferched," medde un o'r dynion ffit, "bydd naill ai fi, Liwtenant Harris neu Liwtenant Davies yn dod rownd 'da chi, rhag ofn, a geith Les aros amdanon ni ar y llinell derfyn. Cofiwch y rheolau, a chofiwch ein bod ni'n gweithio fel tîm. Reit!"

Dyma fe'n chwythu'r chwiban a ninne'n rhedeg at y ddrychiolaeth gynta fel pac o gŵn hela.

"O ffyc," medde fi wrth gwmpo ar fy mhenglinie i fynd dan y rhwyd ar y llawr. Aeth Awen trwyddo fel shot oherwydd ei brechiau cryf. Ro'n inne ar ei hôl hi. Daeth Llinos allan fel gwahadden, a smotie o gachu defaid ar hyd ei chrys-T. Dyma ni'n disgwyl am Heini o grombil y rhwyd, a chlywed rhyw fwmial.

"Sdim sens yn y peth, myn uffarn i; nid fflipin caterpillar ydw i – ma 'da fi dits i ga'l."

Roedd Siân a'r tîm arall ar y rhwystr nesa yn barod. Twll sgwâr yn y ddaear o'dd hwnnw, yn llawn dop o ddŵr brwnt o'dd yn drewi i'r cymyle. Daliodd Heini i fyny â ni.

"Wel myn uffarn i – dip defed, glei!"

Roedd yn rhaid inni gerdded trwyddo gan fynd oddi tano weithie i osgoi weiren bigog oedd yn gorwedd ar draws wyneb y dŵr mewn mannau.

Neidiodd Llinos i mewn heb destio'r dyfnder. Aeth hi'n grwn o'r golwg.

"Llinos, achan, dere lan! Ble wyt ti?" gwaeddodd Heini.

"Wel dyw hi ddim yn mynd i glywed o dan fan'na, odi ddi," medde Awen.

Edrychais yn bryderus ar y dŵr tywyll a gweiddi, "Lle ma hi 'de? Dyle hi fod wedi dod lan erbyn nawr glei!"

Dyma Liwtenant Harris yn rhedeg tuag at y dŵr a ninnau'n dechre panicio. Yn sydyn, dyma fybls yn codi o ochr arall y pwll a phen Llinos yn ymddangos yn wên i gyd.

"Fifty yards underwater badge Ysgol Gynradd y Rhos – jôc fach i gadw'n iach, ladies."

Taflodd Heini glotsen fawr o fwd ati am ei dwli a chafodd ei churo slap yng nghanol ei thalcen.

Aeth Heini i mewn wedyn gan wenwyno am ei gwallt, a dilynodd Awen a fi, yn dal dwylo. Roedd y dŵr yn oer, oer, a'r cyhyrau yn fy nghoesau'n tynhau. Dyma oedd y nod, mae'n siŵr – eich oeri a'ch diflasu cyn dechrau. Dal anadl ac ymbalfalu o dan y weiren. Daeth Awen i'r golwg ar f'ôl i, a'i gwallt yn sownd yn y pige.

"Awwww, awww byger awww!" gwaeddodd cyn rhoi uffach o blwc i'w phen a dod yn rhydd. Tynnodd Heini a Llinos ni allan. Ochr draw y cae roedd y tîm arall yn dal i berswadio Sara i fynd i mewn i'r pwll, a hithe'n gweiddi rhywbeth am gontact lensys.

Dringo oedd nesa – dringo wal uchel, uchel heb raff na dim i helpu. Edrychodd y bedair ohonon ni lan arni.

"Reit 'te," medde Awen, "af i ar y gwaelod, a Heini ar ben fi; Llinos, cer di lan ar ben Heini, a Hels dringa di drosto ond gad dy goese lawr i Llinos ga'l dringo lan nhw."

Dyma stranco a styrnigo nes yn y diwedd roedden ni fel Tower of Pisa gwlyb, a finne'n hongian lawr fel rhaff. Dringodd Llinos drosta i gan blannu'i sawdl yn fy llygad; daeth Heini ar ei hôl a thynnwyd Awen lan gan y dair ohonon ni.

"So far so good," medde finne cyn gweld beth oedd o'n blaene – tiwb concrid a hwnnw hanner o dan ddŵr. Roedd e'n ymestyn am tua can llath ac roedd disgwyl i ni i gyd fynd drwodd.

"O ych a fi, fi'n casáu bod mewn llefydd confined fel'na," medde Heini.

"Shwt uffarn fi fod ffito trwyddo hwnna?" gofynnodd Awen, a'r cryndod cynnar yn dod yn ôl i'w llais.

"Bydd rhaid iti gripian yn isel," medde Llinos.

"A ffycin boddi tra bo fi wrthi, ife?" brathodd Awen yn ôl. Roedden ni'n deall ei phroblem – roedd y diwben yn uffernol o gul. Aeth Heini i mewn yn gyntaf fel petai eisiau profi bod modd ei wneud. Roedd y dŵr yn tasgu'n ôl i'w gwyneb, a sŵn tisian yn dod o berfeddion y diwben. Aeth Llinos i mewn nesa, a wedyn finne.

"Drycha, os ei di'n sownd, jest cydia yn fy nghoese i," medde fi wrth Awen cyn diflannu i mewn i'r tywyllwch.

Roedd siorts Llinos o 'mlaen i'n wlyb sopen a'i g-string gwyn hi'n goleuo'r ffordd trwy'r tywyllwch i ddechrau.

"Iesu, mai'n dynn 'ma," clywais Awen yn gwenwyno tu ôl imi. "Ddo i byth mas o fan hyn, bois – hon fydd 'yn arch i."

"Cadw'n iselach, 'de," gwaeddais 'nôl, a'r cyfyngdra'n dechrau codi panig ynof inne 'fyd. Duw a ŵyr sut oedd pobol yn medru mynd i lawr i ryw ogofâu bach.

"Wel, fe fydden i taset ti ddim yn tasgu'r dŵr 'ma 'nôl ata i bob whip stitch."

"Sori."

"Ca dy lap 'de."

Roedd fy mhenglinie i'n dost i gyd, a'r lleithder yn dripian o nenfwd y diwben. Rownd rhyw gornel â ni, ac roedd hi'n dywyll bitsh. Ro'n i'n medru clywed anadlu'r lleill, ond dyna i gyd. Roedd fy nghalon yn curo'n galetach a minne'n trio mynd yn gyflymach i gyrraedd y pen draw. Roedd 'na gornel arall, a chlywais lais Heini yn y pellter yn gweiddi "golau!"

Cripiais mla'n a mla'n wrth i'r düwch droi'n llwyd, a hwnnw wedyn yn rhyw hanner golau. Roedd 'na un tro cas iawn jest wrth y diwedd, a'r dŵr yn ddwfn ddwfn gan ddod lan ymhell heibio i 'mrest. Crafais trwyddo gan deimlo'r croen yn codi oddi ar fy sgwyddau. Roedd Llinos a Heini mas yn barod, ac yn edrych 'nôl i mewn i'r diwben i weld lle ro'n i.

Yn sydyn teimlais blwc ac aeth fy mhen yn glir o dan y dŵr; roedd fy ngheg ar agor a dechreuais dagu. Chwifiais fy mreichiau i drio safio fy hun, a bwrais fy mhen yn erbyn y concrid. Roedd popeth yn troi. O'r diwedd, dyma fi'n teimlo dwylo Llinos yn codi fy ngwyneb uwchben y dŵr.

"Beth uffach… " pesychais. "Be ddigwyddodd?" Roedd 'na ddŵr i fyny 'nhrwyn a twshialais e i wyneb Llinos.

"Blydi hel, paid achan!"

"Sori, be ffyc… "

"Hels, callia nawr; ti'n iawn, est ti tano am sbel, 'na i gyd."

Roedd y dŵr yn llosgi fy llygaid a swnd yn crensian bob tro y byddai 'nannedd i'n cyfarfod. Dyma lais yn codi o'r tu ôl imi.

"Hei bois... hei bois... fi'n styc, sai'n jocan nawr, fi'n styc solid."

"Wel, sdim ise ffycin boddi fi, o's e?" gwaeddais.

"Sori, ond wedes ti... "

"Jest cydia yn fy nghoes i a geith Llinos a Heini dynnu ni mas."

Roedd Liwtenant Harris yn ceisio peidio chwerthin a finne'n teimlo awydd rhoi wad iddo. Dyma Heini a Llinos yn cydio yn fy nwylo a theimlais Awen yn cadwyno'i bysedd o gwmpas fy mhigyrne. Dyma fi'n dechrau symud a'r straen yn codi i fyny f'asgwrn cefn.

"Cym on ferched, PULL," gwaeddodd Liwtenant Harris ac yna dechreuodd chwerthin a galw'i fêt draw i gael gweld.

"Pwy rododd ffiffti pens yn dy slot di, was?" medde Heini'n swta.

"O feri ffyni, nawr ffyc off," ychwanegodd Llinos.

Gyda'r geiriau olaf dyma fi'n saethu allan o'r diwben ac Awen ar fy ôl, fel bwled mas o ddryll. Dyma'r chwerthin yn cynyddu, a Heini a Llinos yn sefyll yn stond. Edrychais yn ôl i weld Awen ar y llawr a'm trowser yn ei dwylo. Er mor boeth oedd fy mochau, roedd bochau fy nhin yn wyn ac yn wincio'n bert ar bawb.

"O mei god," llefais gan edrych ar y ddau Liwtenant yn eu dwble'n chwerthin. Taflodd Llinos siwmper drosta i, ond dechreuodd Heini chwerthin 'fyd a dyna ni, dyna'i diwedd hi. Roedd pawb yn chwerthin nes eu bod nhw'n blet, a phawb yn rhy wan i wisgo amdanaf. Roedd y tîm arall ymhell ar y blaen, ond yn sydyn doedd dim ots. Ar ôl stablan ar ein traed a cheisio cwblhau'r cwrs heb golli rhagor o ddillad, roedd pawb yn ffrwydro chwerthin bob nawr ac yn y man gan wneud i'r holl dasgau bara am byth. Wrth inni groesi'r llinell, cododd bloedd anferthol a chyfle o'r diwedd imi gael paratoi ar gyfer y jôcs diddiwedd oedd yn sicr o fod o mla'n i.

Cafodd pawb gawod a barbiciw y tu allan wrth i'r haul fachlud. Cyflwynwyd pâr o drowser armi i mi a chusan, un ar bob boch, 'wrth y ddau liwtenant.

Un ar bymtheg

"Nawr te, ladies, croeso 'nôl, croeso 'nôl, falch gweld eich bod chi wedi penderfynu tynnu'ch ffycin bysedd mas a chario mla'n; ry'n ni wedi ca'l ein trip blynyddol nawr, so this is it. Croeso i Sara, new recruit – byddi di'n mynd trwy uffern i ddechre, ond tough shit – ti sy 'di penderfynu dod 'ma. Nawr te, steddwch lawr am sbel fach."

Dydd Sadwrn, a ninne 'nôl ar y cae a chleisiau dydd Sadwrn diwetha'n dechre pylu a slwtshio'n rhyw frown a melyn gole. Roedd pawb â thamed bach mwy o fflach ynddyn nhw wedi'r ymweliad â'r camp armi, a'r brwdfrydedd yn dechre berwi 'to.

"Fel wedes i ginne fach, neis gweld chi gyd 'to, especially ti Heledd; can't seem to see enough of you these days, sexy bum."

"Ffyc off!"

"Diolch; reit te, this is not ffycin linedancing, bois. Os bydd un o chi'n torri'r rheole, fydda i lawr arno chi fel post-knocker – deall? Sai'n jocan, fuck me about and I'll fuck you about. Dim booze, dim slaco, dim 'ww, ma period pains 'da fi'. FFYC THAT, DEALL? Os byddwch chi 'di tyfu pâr o geillie erbyn y gystadleuaeth 'ma, fe fydda i wedi neud y job yn iawn."

Aeth Les lan at Nerys, oedd yn eistedd a'i choese wedi'u croesi ar y llawr, a gwthio'i grotsh i fewn i'w gwyneb.

"Gweld rhein?" gofynnodd.

"Na, sdim magnifying glass 'da fi, sori."

"Wel, fe fydd pâr dy hunan 'da ti cyn bo hir i edrych arno."

"Dere inni obeithio bydda nhw'n fwy na rheina, de."

Gwenodd Les arni; roedd e'n falch 'i bod hi wedi ffeindio'i thafod unwaith eto.

"Reit, ma raid i mi eich pwyso chi nawr. 580k yw'r pwyse, a ma 'da fi ryw syniad falle fyddwn ni 'bach drosto."

Roedd tafol fawr yng nghornel y cae a cherddodd Les ati gan dynnu'r tarpowlin oddi arni.

"Reit, dillad off, gyment â gallwch chi, trainers off hefyd."

Aeth pawb ati i dynnu faint galle nhw i ffwrdd a'r eidion yn y cae nesa yn pipo dros y clawdd. Neidiodd pawb ar y dafol a Les yn edrych ar y deial a golwg bryderus arno.

"Sefwch yn llonydd... reit, off â chi a gwisgwch 'to.

"Nawrte, y bastards, ma raid colli 'bach o'r blydi pwyse 'ma. Ma'r fformiwla'n eitha syml – bytwch ffycin llai a rhedwch ffycin fwy. Na'th Duw ddim rhoi ni ar y ddaear 'ma i fynd i aerobics neu i ffartan ambwti yn y gym. Rhedeg i ffwrdd o'wrth llewod a mynd mas i hela y'n ni i fod neud, so get your fucking arse in gear. Welsoch chi rywun tew yn dod mas o Fietnam? Do fe? Rhywun tew yn dod mas o'r armi? Ble mae'r fat bastards i gyd wedi mynd? O'n nhw wedi starfo yn do'n nhw? O'n nhw'n ffit yn do'n nhw? Glywsoch chi un ohonyn nhw'n gweud, 'O, glands fi yw e', 'O, metabolism fi sy'n slo', 'O, pêr shêp yw'n teulu ni'. Na, dim ffycin wan jac, do fe; oedd pob un o' nhw fel rhaca on'd o'n nhw? Stwffiwch y diet sheets a'r nonsens a ffys a'r low-fat foods a shit felna. Peidiwch byta a ffycin rhedwch – it's a simple formula, so sticwch ati. Reit – dou fis sy 'da ni; off rownd y cae 'na nawr te i weld sut y'n ni'n mynd. Siapwch hi!"

Cododd pawb oddi ar y llawr a phatshyn gwlyb ar din pob un ohonon ni. Ffwrdd â ni o gwmpas y cae, a Les yn gwylio o'r canol fel ryw gi defaid. Roedd Sara'n hongian tua'r cefen gan edrych fel tase hi'n difaru dod i'r byd. Pryd tywyll oedd hi, run peth â'i dau frawd, ac yn eitha tenau – yn debyg i lyngeren hollt, fel wede mam-gu. Daeth Nerys ata i.

"Shwmai, ti'n iawn?" Doedden ni ddim wedi siarad llawer ers nos Sadwrn diwethaf.

"Aye, iawn," atebais gan drio meddwl beth yn gwmws oedd achos y lletchwithdra.

"Be ti neud heno?" gofynnodd, gan gamu rhwng yr ysgall oedd yn tyfu'n gryf o gwmpas y cae.

"Sion yn mynd â fi i'r Mill am swper."

"Uffach! Posh, glei. Beth yw'r achlysur?"

"Dim byd," medde fi, "wedi'i drefnu ers sbel."

"Ti ddim yn dod mas de?"

"Na, fydd hi'n rhy hwyr ar ôl 'ny, siŵr o fod. So chi'n yfed, odych chi?" gofynnais, gan feddwl y bydde Les yn 'u lladd nhw os ffindiai allan.

"Un ne ddou bach, dim sesiwn gachu bants."

"O."

"Watsha di, swper yn y Mill – bydd 'na focs bach yn dod mas o'i boced e cyn diwedd y nos siŵr o fod."

"O ca' dy lap!" Saethodd rhyw binne bach drwydda i a doedd dim cysylltiad rhyngddon nhw a'r danal poethion o gwmpas fy nghoese. Roedd Sion wedi trefnu heno ers oese, ac roedd e fel llo am drefnu pethe fel arfer. Doedden ni ddim wedi bod yn y Mill ers ein dêt cynta, a gweud y gwir; roedd e'n trio fy impresio i bryd hynny. Roedd fy meddylie'n dechre troi cyn i lais Les dorri ar fy nhraws.

"KIT UP, YOU BASTARDS!"

Roedd e 'di gwlychu'r swnd yn y gasgen heno fel ei bod hi mor drwm â phosib, ac ro'n i'n medru clywed Sara yn tuchan ac yn stryglio ar y rhaff. Roedd Les yn gweiddi'n ddi-stop arni.

"Sara, ti'n hopeless, achan! Galle dy fam-gu neud job well!"

"Sara fach, ti'n gadel pawb lawr 'ma."

"Ie, ie Sara, mwynhea di, y blydi pasinjer. Paid â dod ar gyfyl y cae 'ma 'to, 'na i gyd!"

Dyma'i dechneg e, i weld a fydde rhywun yn medru cymryd y cwbl wrtho fe. Os oeddech chi'n medru peidio rhoi i mewn iddo fe – neu, yn well fyth, yn trio dal wad iddo fe – roedd y rhagolygon yn go lew. Roedd Awen wedi'i rhybuddio hi, ond er hynny roedd hi'n edrych yn go druenus weithie.

Hanner ffordd trwy'r ymarfer dechreuodd rhai o fechgyn y pentre ymgynnull wrth giât y cae. Roedden nhw'n chwerthin ac yn jocian, a rhai ohonyn nhw wedi dod yn syth mas o'r dafarn. Aeth y cwbwl ohonyn nhw ar y dafol, a dyma Les yn chwerthin wrth eu pwyso nhw. Gwaeddodd Dai Siop arnon ni:

"Ma hanner tunnell o bwyse yn John Tomos fi, siŵr o fod!"

"Mwy nag sy yn dy ben di de," gwaeddodd Sara'n ôl. Roedd hi'n dechre ymlacio o gwmpas y merched erill ac yn edrych yn ferch neis, er mod i'n gweld ei brawd bob tro yr edrychwn arni.

Daeth Gerallt Garej draw gan neidio dros y giât ac ymuno â'r bechgyn erill ar y dafol.

"Uffarn," meddai Kel wrth f'ochor, "'na ti bishyn!"

"Gerallt yw e – ma fe'n gwitho yn y garej."

"Ww," wedodd hi, "geith e roi MOT i fi unrhyw bryd!"

"Rho hi i gadw, wir," wedodd Awen. Roedd hi'n gwisgo siaced ledr i amddiffyn ei hysgwyddau.

"Reit te ladies, ma'r bechgyn yn mynd i rhoi lwndad i chi nawr, er mwyn i chi ga'l gwbod beth yw gwaith. Ma nhw'n lot trymach na chi, so peidiwch â meddwl gallwch chi'u tynnu nhw – ond fe fydd hi'n sbort gweld chi'n treial!"

Roedd y dynion yn torchi'u llewyse ac yn ffurfio rhes gan chwerthin a jocian ymysg ei gilydd. Roedd John Torrwr Bedde ar y blaen.

"O's ise i fi ddod â chwpwl o focsys pren draw 'ma ar ôl hyn?"

"I bwy? I chi?" atebodd Heini, a chwarddodd y merched.

"Gobeitho bod lean-to's ar y bocsys 'na o weld seis dy fola di," ychwanegodd Llinos.

"Ca di dy lap, groten," atebodd yn bwdlyd gan rwbio'i fola. "Ma hwn yn all paid for – storage chamber ar gyfer y diesel i'n love machine i yw e."

"Reit, bois, pan fydda i'n codi mreiche uwch 'y mhen, codwch y rhaff – ond peidwch tynnu nes fydda i'n dod â 'nwylo i lawr at fy ochre."

Aeth Les tuag at ganol y rhaff.

"Codwch y rhaff, cymrwch y straen a PULL!"

Dyma'r rhaff yn dechre cratshian oherwydd ei bod hi'n sych, a'r dynion yn ein dal yn llonydd wrth inni brofi cryfder ein gilydd.

"Cym on, ferched," gwaeddodd Gerallt, "fi'n dala fe ag un bys fan hyn!"

Yn sydyn dyma nhw'n rhoi mwy o raff inni gan geisio ein disodli, ac aeth fy mhen-ôl i lawr at y llawr.

"Coda, coda, cwyd ar dy dra'd – bydden ni'n ca'l rhybudd am 'na mewn cystadleuaeth!"

Roedd y straen yn llosgi trwy'r corff.

"'Na fe bois, dalwch nhw, tynnwch nhw, llabyddiwch nhw; 'na beth sy ise arnyn nhw – 'bach o waith sy ise 'ma."

Ar ôl tua tair munud, roedd y straen yn ormod a 'mreichie i'n crynu i gyd. Dyma nhw'n rhoi plwc a ninne'n colli llathen.

"Cym on, dewch mla'n, ymladdwch e, peidwch rhoi mewn. Ma rhaid ichi ymladd – it's not over till the whistle goes. Cym on – dalwch, dalwch, dalwch..."

Gyda pob 'dalwch' roedden ni'n cripian mla'n gam a fedrwn i ddim gweld traed y ferch gynta'n croesi'r linell. O'r diwedd, canodd y chwiban.

"'Na fe, hoe fach nawr. Da iawn, ferched, rhoioch chi ddim mewn; 'na be sy ise, dogged determination. Os yw'ch braich chi'n cwmpo off, ffwc o ots, dalwch y rhaff 'da'r llall; os yw honno'n cwmpo off, cydiwch yn y rhaff 'da'ch dannedd and tighten on it ac edrychwch draw a meddyliwch 'cym o'n then, fat heifers, try it again'."

Roedd hi'n dechrau nosi, y goleuadau lliwgar o gwmpas y dafarn wedi'u troi mla'n a rhai ymwelwyr yn cerdded lawr o'r seits carafannau i'r dafarn i gael pryd o fwyd gan edrych yn hurt dros y ffens arnon ni. Roedd y gwybed yn cnoi'n ddiawledig a llygaid yr eidion yn y cae nesa'n goleuo wrth i'r haul felynu. Daeth diwedd iddi tua cwarter i chwech, yn hwyrach nag arfer achos 'sneb yn mynd mas eniwe, o's e?' fel wedodd Les. Gadawodd pawb y cae yn flinedig, gan adael Kel a Gerallt yn pwyso ar y giât yn siarad. Ymlwybrais 'nôl am adre 'da Nerys gan gerdded mewn cwmwl o wybed oedd yn cael eu denu gan arogl chwys. Y ddwy ohonon ni'n gwahanu wrth y stand la'th, a hithau'n mynd gatre i newid gan daflu 'Hwyl, Miss Married!' dros 'i hysgwydd.

Dou ar bymtheg

"Ie, ble ti'n mynd heno de?" gofynnodd Mam yn fusnes i gyd, gan godi ryw ddillad oddi ar y llawr er mwyn cael esgus i fod yn yr un stafell â fi.

"Mill."

"Www, posh glei; ti ddim yn mynd fel'na, wyt ti?"

"Fel shwt?"

"Wedi gwisgo fel'na – ma'r lle 'na'n posh, cofia."

"Beth fi fod gwisgo de? Ball gown?" gofynnais, gan edrych ar fy nhrowser du a'r fest fach wen oedd amdana i.

"Paid bod yn sili – beth am y top bach pinc 'na oedd 'da ti yn parti Dat llynedd?"

"Rhy fach."

"Pam?"

"Rhywun wedi shrinco fe."

"Wel beth am y top bach lês arall 'na de?"

"Gormod o gleise ar 'y mreiche i."

"Ych-a-fi," meddai Mam gan ysgwyd tywel gwlyb fel aligetor mewn pwll. "Bydde'n dda 'da fi tase ti'n bennu neud y nonsens 'na; 'na beth yw straino dy hunan heb ise. Sut bydd dy gefen di mewn blynydde, gwed? 'Na beth licen i wbod." Oedodd am funud gan blygu pâr o sane yn y ffordd dyw neb ond mamau'n neud. "Pam chi'n mynd i'r Mill heno, de?"

"M'bod," medde finne gan osgoi'r llygaid pelydr-X a cheisio rhwbio mousse i mewn i'r mwng afreolus ar fy mhen.

"O wel, rho rywbeth teidi amdanat ti, for Pete's sake; sdim ise cerdded ambwti fel sachabwndi, o's e?"

"Nago's, Mam."

"A rho dy wallt lan neu rywbeth – ti'n edrych fel coeden fale."

"Iawn, Mam."

"A paid ag ordro bolonês fel nest ti tro dwetha fuon ni mas; fues ti bron tynnu llygad dy dad mas."

"Ocê, Mam."

* * * *

Cyrhaeddodd Sion ar amser; roedd e'n gwisgo'r crys glas brynes i iddo fe ar ei ben-blwydd a'r lliw yn adleisio'i lygaid yn berffaith. Roedd y gwesty'n llawn, a llond y lle o bobl yn mwynhau ac yn chwerthin. Roedd Sion yn dawel wrth inni eistedd wrth y ford a'r weitar yn tynnu'r arwydd 'Bwrdd Cadw' oddi ar y lliain.

"Ti'n edrych yn sbeshal," meddai a gwên fawr ar ei wyneb. Roedd e'n swnio fel tase fe wedi bod yn rhedeg ras.

"Diolch," medde fi heb edrych lan. Un peth ro'n i'n gasáu'n fwy na dim byd oedd yn unrhyw un yn gneud ffys ohona i.

"Beth ni'n mynd i ga'l de?" gofynnais, gan geisio newid trywydd y sgwrs. "Ma 'da fi le i jiráff ar dost."

"Mmm, ga i stêc, run peth ag arfer," meddai Sion, ar ôl edrych ar y fwydlen.

Sylwais fod ei ddwylo'n crynu, a theimlais fy stumog yn rhoi naid; falle fod Ner yn iawn wedi'r cwbl.

Wedi i'r bwyd gyrraedd, sylwais bod Sion heb gyffwrdd â'i blât. Edrychais arno.

"Sion... "

"Ie?" atebodd gan geisio ffindio rhywbeth hynod ddiddorol mewn ryw bysen ar ei blât.

"Be sy'n bod?"

"Dim byd." Edrychodd arna i a rhoi ei fforc a'i gyllell 'nôl ar y plât. "Hels... "

"Ie?"

"Wyt ti'n cofio pryd ddaethon ni 'ma ddiwetha?"

"Wrth gwrs bo fi, achan." Roedd fy nghalon i'n gwneud ei ffordd lan fy ngwddf.

"Wel, fi 'di bod yn meddwl... "

"Ie?"

"Ry'n ni wedi bod 'da'n gilydd ers blynydde a... "

"A beth?"

"Wel, meddwl o'n i... "

"Meddwl beth?" Roedd fy ngheg i'n sych gorcyn.

"Meddwl falle ddylen ni hela 'bach o amser ar wahân... "

Aeth y bwyty'n dawel jest fel roedd e'n ynganu'r geiriau olaf. Cwympodd fy nghalon a theimlwn fel tasai rhywun wedi tynnu 'mherfedd i mas.

"Ti'n gweld, fi 'di bod yn meddwl am fynd bant am sbel... "

"I ble?"

"I Awstralia. A gweud y gwir, bues i'n y dre ddoe, a fi 'di bwco ar gyfer mynd i gneifo yno am flwyddyn."

Ro'n i'n galler gweld ei geg e'n symud, ond yn methu clywed y geire.

"Am flwyddyn?"

"Ie."

"I Awstralia?"

"Ie. Drycha, fi'n sori am hyn, ond ry'n ni 'di bod yn cwmpo mas lot yn ddiweddar, a meddwl o'n i falle naethe fe les inni ga'l bach o le... "

"Wel, gei di ddigon o hwnna yn Awstralia, ta beth. O't ti jest yn mynd i fynd heb weud dim wrtha i, jest trefnu fel'na?"

"Wel, o'n i'n ofan fydde ti'n trio newid 'yn meddwl i."

Estynnodd law dros y bwrdd gan geisio gafael yn fy llaw i. Codais ar fy nhraed a sylwi fod 'na ddagre'n rhedeg i lawr fy moche. Aeth gwyneb Sion ar goll yn y niwl. Cerddais am y drws heb wrando ar ei bledio imi ddod yn ôl a siarad am y peth.

Wrth i'r gwynt fy nharo i allan yn y stryd, dechreuais deimlo'n sâl. Rhedais tu ôl i'r siop fara a chwydu, gan sylwi ynghanol popeth nad oedd e wedi rhedeg ar fy ôl fel y bydde fe'n wneud bob tro y bydden ni'n cwmpo mas. Cerddais heibio i'w gar gan feddwl yn sydyn na fyddwn yn cael mynd 'da fe ynddo fe fyth eto. Dyna beth rhyfedd i sylwi arno fe! Cerddais tuag adre; roedd hi'n bum milltir o wac, ond doedd dim awydd arna i i ffonio Mam i ddod i 'nghasglu i, ac roedd y merched i gyd mas.

Wrth i mi ymbelláu oddi wrth y dre, a'r gwyll yn dechre tewhau, bwrodd y sioc fi eto. Roedd hi'n noson dawel, a'r sêr yn dechrau tyllu'u ffordd trwy'r cymylau. Roedd y lôn yn dywyll, a'r unig ffordd y gallwn i neud yn siŵr 'mod i yng nghanol y ffordd oedd edrych i fyny i weld lle roedd y gofod rhwng y coed uwchben. Goleuodd y gwyll wrth i olau car ddod i gwrdd â fi, a sefais wrth fôn y clawdd. Arafodd y car a stopio, a theimlais am y tro cynta falle nad oedd cerdded adre'n beth doeth iawn yr amser hyn o'r nos. Sefais a dal f'anadl. Diolch byth! Deian oedd yn gyrru'r car, a Sara wrth ei ochr.

"Heledd, ti'n iawn? Beth uffarn ti'n neud fan hyn, achan?"

Methais feddwl am unrhyw esgus call, a mwmiais rywbeth am fynd adre. Daeth Deian allan o'r car gan sefyll yn dal drosta i.

"Hei, ti'n oer; cymer hon."

Tynnodd ei siwmper dros ei ben a'i rhoi amdana i. Aroglais gwmwl o aftershêf wrth iddo ei thynnu dros fy mreichiau.

"Dere, gei di lifft nawr. Fi'n mynd â Sara lawr i'r dre i gwrdd â'r merched. A' i â ti adre wedyn. Dere!"

"Na, dim diolch, gerdda i."

"Ond ma fe'n rhy bell, a ti'n ypsét. Dere, ti ddim yn gwbod pwy sy ar hyd y lle yr amser hyn o'r nos."

Meddyliais am Nerys a Deian a Sion, a theimlais yn sâl unwaith eto. Gwthiais heibio iddo.

"Diolch am y siwmper, gei di 'ddi 'nôl yn strêt," medde fi gan gario mla'n ar hyd yr hewl ac anwybyddu'i ymbilio. Roedd y nos yn cau amdanaf a'r oerfel yn teimlo fel ryw ryddhad. Ar ôl sbel daeth 'na oleuadau eto o'r tu ôl imi. Neidiais i mewn i gae cyfagos a gwylio Deian yn mynd heibio unwaith eto gan feddwl fy nghodi i fyny ar y ffordd adre. Gwyliais e'n gyrru'n araf heibio i giât y cae, a'r da yn pori'n dawel y tu ôl imi.

Deunaw

Roedd Mam yn smwddio ar bwys y ford gan fwmial yn dawel am faint o waith golchi oedd 'da hi i neud, a faint o'r gloch oedd hi fod i fynd i lanhau'r eglwys, a finne'n iste wrth y ford yn treial gwthio darn o dost sych lawr y lôn goch.

"Dere mla'n nawr, byt rywbeth; fi ddim ise ti ambwti'r lle 'ma fel delw."

"Fi'n treial."

Cariodd mla'n 'da'i smwddio gan wthio pig yr harn i bob twll a chornel o'r crys ar y bwrdd smwddio.

"Sai'n gwbod, wir, na dw i; beth sy'n bod 'no fe de?"

Rhoddodd hi'r harn ar ei cistedd a chymryd llwnc o'r coffi lla'th o'r mwg ar y seidbord cyn dechrau eto.

"Synnen i fochyn tase rhywun arall 'da fe, cofia."

Gyda'r geirie yna, dyma fy stumog i'n rhoi naid. "O, ffycin diolch, Mam, jest beth o'n i ise clywed."

"Sori, cariad, dim ond meddwl mas yn uchel o'n i."

"Wel, stopwch hi!"

Daeth sŵn traed yn cerdded tuag at y drws, a thic-tician ewinedd pawennau Carlo'n gymysg. Gwthiodd Carlo ei drwyn blewog, gwlyb drwy'r drws cilagored. Gwelodd Mam e.

"Cer mas y ci, ma slops tu fas fynna i ti. Whisht!" A dyma hwnnw'n troi'n sydyn gan dwmblo'r welingtons roedd Dat newydd 'u tynnu oddi ar ei draed.

Daeth Dat i mewn heb ddweud gair; pwysodd ar y bwlyn a chôcsio gwaelod ei drowsus mas o'i sane gwlân. Roedd e'n 'i deall hi mewn sefyllfaoedd fel hyn – gweud dim oedd y peth gore alle fe neud. Eisteddodd wrth y bwrdd gan ddechre cymhennu ryw ronynne o siwgwr oedd wedi cwympo ar yr oilcloth.

"O's te 'ma de?"

"O's, yn y tebot; gwed 'cym bei' wrtho fe a falle ddeith e draw i arllwys ei hun iti."

Cododd ar ei draed eto a mynd yn herc at y stof. Edrychodd arna i wrth fynd heibio.

"Sdim gwaith 'da ti heddi de?"

"Nagos, ma wythnos o wylie 'da fi nawr."

"Braf ar rai! Sa i 'di ca'l gwylie ers i dy fam a finne fynd i Sir Benfro i'r garafán 'na flynydde'n ôl. Be ti'n fwriadu neud heddi de?"

"M'bod," dwedais gan geisio peidio edrych ar yr wy 'di'i ferwi roedd Dat wedi'i roi o mla'n wrth iddo basio'n ôl am ei gader gan gario'r tebot poeth yn y llaw arall. Gosododd gap gwlanog am y tebot a thwymodd ei ddwylo o'i gwmpas.

Roedd Dat a Mam yn meddwl taw stwffio oedd yr ateb i bopeth. Pan fyddai rhywun yn sâl yn y pentre, bydde toreth o gacs yn cyrraedd o bob cyfeiriad – er bod y person mwy na thebyg yn methu bwyta, a'r peth diwetha oedd 'i angen arno oedd cacen ffrwythe drom.

Neithiwr, ar ôl i fi gyrradd adre, roedd Mam 'di gwneud brecwast anferth imi, a finne newydd fod mas am swper – er 'mod i wedi'i adel ar bwys y siop 'na yn y dre. Roedd hi'n wallgo neithiwr, yn dyfyrio Sion a'i fam am mai 'un od yw hi 'di bod erio'd', a bod y 'crwt 'na'n mynd i golli mas oherwydd rhyw freuddwyd twp am fynd mas i Awstralia'. Gadewais i'r storm gasglu a thorri drosof – a ddwedais i run gair.

Es at y Rayburn ac estyn siwmper i mi fy hun, cyn sylwi bod siwmper Deian yn crasu uwchben y barrau. Teimlais fy stumog yn troi. Es at y drws.

"Lle ti'n mynd, Miss Pws? Ti heb dwtsh â dy frecwast."

"Am wac; fydda i 'nôl cyn bo hir."

Cerddais i fyny'r lôn a heibio'r cae lle fuodd Sion a fi'n caru tua mis yn ôl yn y borfa hir. Heibio i'r stand la'th a lawr am y pentre. Roedd y blode'n wyllt yr amser hyn o'r flwyddyn gan fritho'r clawdd gyda darnau lliwgar fel tu mewn i focs gwinio mam-gu. Chwythai'r gwynt yn ysgafn. Cerddais heb wybod ble ro'n i'n mynd.

Des i at y tŷ, agor y giât a cherdded heibio'r ddafad oedd wedi cael ei chlymu yn yr ardd. Roedd 'na goler goch o gwmpas ei gwddf a 'Flymo' wedi'i sgrifennu mewn llythrennau du arni. Cnociais ar y drws, a daeth sŵn cyfarth o'r tu fewn. Cnociais eto.

"Ffyc off heblaw bod rhywbeth pwysig 'da chi i weud," meddai llais Les o rywle.

Camais i mewn dros y llechen anwastad wrth y drws, ac er ei bod yn fore braf, fe gymerodd fy llygaid rai eiliade i gynefino â'r tywyllwch tu fewn. Yn sydyn, wrth fy nhraed roedd y ci lleia weles i erioed – rhyw groes rhwng toi pwdl a fferet.

"O, ti sy 'na; o'n i'n dy ddisgwl di a gweud y gwir." Edrychodd Les ar y ci oedd yn brysur yn marcho fy esgid chwith. "Ti 'di cwrdd â Romeo, fi'n gweld." Codais fy llygaid a'i weld yn eistedd wrth y ford.

"Les, ma fe'n trio mownto'n esgid i!"

"Ti'n lwcus – ma fe'n galler mynd am lefydd lot mwy embarrassing. Isde," medde fe gan gario mla'n i glymu'r pry pysgota yn ei ddwylo.

Edrychais o nghwmpas gan chwilio man clir i barcio 'nhin. Roedd llond y lle o bethe ym mhob twll a chornel: arfe hela, dryllau, ffonau, gwialenni pysgota, rhesi o getrys coch, a llyfre ymhobman, llyfre bach a mawr, rhai tew, rhai tenau. Llyfre barddonieth yn benna, llyfre hanes, llyfre am gefn gwlad, llyfre am grefydd. Llond bocsys fan hyn a fan draw wedyn o hen rifynnau o *Reader's Digest* a rheini'n melynu i gyd. Eisteddodd Les 'nôl gan alw Romeo ato. Edrychodd arna i wrth imi sodro fy hun rhwng copi o *Western Religion and the Sands of Time* a *Cerddi Dic Jones*.

"Ie."

"Be?"

"Ie, wedes i."

"Beth?"

"Glywes i am neithwr."

"Syrpreis syrpreis, shwt?"

"Un o'r merched – neges testun."

"O."

Pwysodd yn ôl unwaith eto. "Be ti moyn de?"

Yn sydyn, teimlwn yn gas tuag ato. "Dim byd rili; af i o'ma os ti moyn."

"Na, isde di fan'na."

Estynnodd dros y ford i ganol yr annibendod lle roedd potel o rywbeth lliw brown tywyll. Llenwodd y gwydryn wrth ei benelin a chydio mewn un arall oddi ar y sgiw. Rhwbiodd hwnnw gyda chlwtyn oedd yn barddu, ac arllwys mesur o'r ddiod mas.

"Cymer hwn."

"Sai fod, fi'n traino," mwmblais.

"Ffyc off nawr de," wedodd e gan wthio'r tymbler i'm dwylo. "Nawr te Hels, let's get this over with. This is the first one, the first big love down the tubes, wedi went. Tra faint o't ti'n lico fe, fe ddaw 'na bâr arall o bolycs heibio cyn bo hir."

"O, diolch Les. Ti 'di cysidro gyrfa mewn marriage counselling erio'd?"

"Benefit of my experience, ti'n gweld. Cofia, ar y llaw arall, falle nad hwn oedd y boi. Ma pob menyw yn gorfod colli un dyn ma nhw'n garu, ffact iti; rite of passage, ma arna i ofan."

Cymerais lwnc o'r stwff lliw aur, a llosgodd ei ffordd lawr i 'mola i.

"Ond paid poeni dy ben bach pert am bethe felna; fyddi di 'nôl yn meddwi hyd y stŷd cyn bo hir, yn joio mynd mas a shelffo rhyw foi a hwdu ar y ffordd gatre a chofio dim byd diwrnod wedyn, a bod yn real classy lady bob whip stitch."

"Sai'n teimlo fel 'nny nawr."

"Na, fyddi di ddim. 'Na'r peth am fod yn ifanc, ti'n gweld; ti'n straffaglio dy ffordd drwyddo fe yn wenwn i gyd, a ti ddim yn sylweddoli dy fod ar dy gryfa tra bod ti'n neud e. Yr unig beth sda ti i neud pan ti yn f'oedran i yw coacho tîm o ferched ifanc a trio sugno a lluo'r egni o'u croen nhw fel paraseit." Roedd hanner gwên ar ei wyneb.

"Diolch, Les."

"The pleasure's all mine, believe me," meddai gan arllwys bob o fesur arall o'r chwisgi.

"Uffach, dal mewn; fydd dim bagal dana i cyn mynd o 'ma."

Roedd Romeo wedi dod draw i eistedd wrth fy ochor ac yn edrych lan arna i a'i lygaid yn llawn cariad.

"Be sy'n bod ar y ci 'ma, Les?"

"Felna ma fe, rhywbeth i neud â'i bwrs e, fi'n credu. Fe drion ni 'i sbaddu fe, ond methodd y fet am ryw reswm a ma fe wedi bod felna ers 'nny."

"Dim llawer gwa'th na rhai o'r dynion yn y Sgwâr nos Sadwrn, I suppose," medde fi gan wenu.

"'Na ti, Hels, that's the way; bollocks to him!"

Ro'n i'n teimlo'n wan i gyd – cymysgedd o gerdded gatre neithwr, llefen drwy'r nos a theimlo fel tasai cerrig Pentre Ifan i gyd yn fy mola.

"Gewn ni lwncdestun de," cynigiodd Les. "I dynnu rhaff," meddai gan godi'i wydryn, "sy'n debyg i farddonieth a physgota, y pethe mwya anodd yn y byd i neud yn iawn, ac sy'n ymddangos yn hollol ddibwrpas i bobl y byd." Roedd ei dafod yn dew. "Ac i Heledd a'r pâr nesa o bolycs."

Ymunais ag e gan godi fy ngwydryn uwch fy mhen, a Romeo'n mynd yn ecseited bost. Meddyliais am ennyd am rywbeth i ddweud.

"Ie, i fi a'r pâr nesa o bolycs."

"Well done, Hels, oratorical fireworks as usual."

"Piss off! Uffach, beth yw'r stwff 'ma de Les? Ma fe'n tasto fel diesel coch, achan."

"Ie, paid smoco ffàg ar ôl yfed y baby hyn," meddai gan edrych yn gariadus ar yr hylif tew.

Topiodd ein gwydrau hyd yr ymyl unwaith eto. Roedd Romeo wedi mynd am dacteg wahanol, ac erbyn hyn yn gorwedd ar ei gefen yn gwenu arna i.

"Nawr te, Miss Davies, beth yn ni'n mynd i neud â chi a Nerys de?"

"Be ti feddwl?"

"My only working eye may be in my pants but, my dear,

alla i weld bod pethe ddim yn happy families rhyngoch chi rhagor."

"Pam ti'n gweud ny?"

"Cym off it, Hels. The essence of pulling like a team yw i ddod yn un corff."

"Ti'n swno fel manual, achan."

"Wel, dynnwch chi ddim ar eich gore os na weithwch chi gyda'ch gilydd. Neith tynnu ar draws neud byger all ichi'n gorfforol nac yn feddyliol, dim ond nacro chi mas ynghynt na alli di weud 'take the strain'. Ma unrhyw un yn galler chware 'da pêl, ti'n gweld – rho di bêl i gi ac fe chwaraeith e 'da hi drwy'r dydd heb feddwl dim byd, a'r dung beetles mowr 'na'n gwthio peli o gachu rownd y jyngl. Rhowch bêl i ddyn a 'na fe, ma fe wrth 'i fodd, yn 'i gwthio hi 'nôl a mla'n ar hyd y cae wrth chware pêl-droed, neu dros fwrdd yn chware snwcer, a ffag yn ei ben – ond dim pawb sy'n medru chware 'da rhaff. Do's dim chware 'da rhaff i ga'l, dim ond y dynfa ryfeddol 'na rhwng popeth. 'Na beth ni'n siarad am fan hyn, bois, dim ffwcin cwmpo mas."

"So ni 'di cwmpo mas."

"Fi'n gwbod, ond o'ch chi mor dynn â thwll tin hwyad pythowrnod, a fydden i'n meddwl bydde'r holl fusnes 'ma 'da Gaynor wedi dod â chi'n agosach."

"Ni'n iawn."

"Beth ti'n neud fan hyn de, Hels?"

"E?"

"Newydd orffen 'da dy gariad wyt ti – ddylet ti ddim fod yn llefen ar ei hysgwydd hi a wedyn mynd mas yn gwisgo sgert fach a ca'l un o'r chats 'stwffo fe, ti'n rhy dda 'ddo fe, ei golled e yw e' 'na 'da hi de?"

"Wel... "

"Ca hi, Hels; nawr te, sort it out ne sorta i fe mas i chi. Ry'n ni i gyd yn gorffod neud e – cnoi dy dafod a rhoi dy gefen 'nôl mewn iddi. That's the way of the world unless bo ti moyn fi ffacso Duw a neud ti'n special case."

Roedd fy mhen i'n nofio ac ro'n i'n ffaelu teimlo'n stumog a oedd yn wag heblaw am hanner litr o'r stwff diesel 'ma. Roedd Romeo wedi mynd i gysgu ar ei gefen, a'i gwt wedi cyrlio'n un cwrlyn main rhwng ei goese.

"Odi'r ffycin Emyr 'na 'di ca'l gair 'da Nerys 'to de?"

"Ambwti be?"

"Nadi felly."

"Gair am beth?"

"Anghofia fe." Cododd Les yn sigledig ar ei draed cyn eistedd i lawr eto.

"Beth ti'n siarad am Nerys, Les?"

"O, ffycin hel... "

"Beth?" Roedd y stwff aur wedi gwneud imi deimlo'n llawer mwy busneslyd nag arfer.

"Drycha, ma lot gormod o hen chitter-chatter yn y pentre 'ma'n barod heb i ni adio ato fe; hen sibrwd tu ôl i ddwylo, hen snigger fach pan ma rhywbeth drwg yn digwydd i rywun, hen droi lan mewn angladd gyda phlated o sangwejis jest i ga'l gweld pwy sy 'na, lot gormod o hen ddringo'r ysgol nes bod dim rheng arall i gydio ynddi, ac ma hi'n ffordd bell i lawr wedyn."

Roedd e 'di mynd yn goch i gyd ac roedd awydd cysgu yn dod drosta i.

"Be ti'n siarad am, Les?"

"Nerys ac Emyr, achan."

"E?"

"Heledd, Heledd achan, Heledd... HELEDD!"

Dihunais; roedd Les yn gweiddi yn fy nghlust.

"Dere, fe af i â ti adre nawr."

Cofio ca'l fy llusgo trwy ddrws, i mewn i ryw gar glas ac wedyn cerdded yn ara bach lawr y lôn. Cofio Dat yn gweiddi arna i, a chofio eistedd ar y clos yn canu, a Carlo dan fy nghesail mewn head-lock. Cofio gweud wrth Carlo bod 'da fi gariad iddo ac y bydde Romeo'n dod draw i'w weld. Dihuno yn y nos a methu symud, fy stumog ar dân, a rhyw atgof pell o Mam yn gweud na chawn i byth fynd i dynnu rhaff 'to.

Pedwar ar bymtheg

Codais cyn Mam a Dat gan wbod na fydde ddim croeso imi rownd y bwrdd brecwast beth bynnag. Wythnos i ffwrdd o'r gwaith, a finne wedi bod yn meddwl mynd am ryw dridie i rywle neis 'da Sion. Syndod sut ma pethe'n newid. Ro'n i wedi dechre hen arfer hefyd â checio'r ffôn bob dwy eiliad rhag ofn bod Sion wedi tecstio neu adael neges neu rywbeth. Dim gair.

Gwisgais fy hen jîns a'n sgidie a dechre cerdded lan y lôn cyn i Dat ddod allan o'r parlwr godro. Roedd y da yn yr iard yn edrych dros y giât arna i fel tase nhw'n fy nghyhuddo i'n dawel bach o actio fel ffŵl. Daeth Carlo 'da fi; dim ond fe oedd wedi mwynhau'r olygfa neithwr am ei fod wedi ca'l gyment o ffys. Cerddes lan hyd y lôn a'r tarth yn codi oddi ar y caeau. Roedd hi'n mynd i fod yn ddiwrnod poeth. Penderfynais alw heibio Ner a siarad â hi go iawn am beth oedd yn mynd ymlaen. Roedd y gwenoliaid yn mynd ar fy nerfe, yn clebran yn swnllyd fel tase nhw'n chwerthin ar fy mhen i.

Cyrhaeddais ben y lôn a daeth car heibio. Sion. Arafodd a thynnu draw ar fy mhwys cyn mynd heibio. Gwelais ei fam yn sedd y pasinjer yn stumio arno fe i fynd heibio. Edrychais ar y car yn mynd, a'r llwch yn codi ar ei ôl. Ma'n siŵr eu bod nhw'n mynd i'r dre i brynu pethe ar gyfer ei daith i Awstralia. Roedd 'na boen yn fy mrest, rhyw dynfa ar y diawl, a sylweddolais unwaith eto 'mod i'n llefen.

Trois i mewn i lôn Ner gan obeithio y byddai hi gatre. O'r diwedd dyma dri ci defaid yn dod i gwrdd â fi, cŵn Emyr, a gwelais y Westies yn chwarae o gwmpas drws y tŷ, oedd led y pen ar agor. Roedd gweiddi i'w glywed yn dod o'r gegin, ac arhosais yn y fan a'r lle.

"Well iti neud cino inni, neu fydd hi ddim yn dda 'ma; ti'n ffaelu ca'l dynion draw ar gynhaea a dim bwyd iddyn nhw. Nawr shapa hi." Llais Emyr oedd e, o gyfeiriad y gegin.

"Iawn." Llais Nerys. "Fe 'na i fe, ond bydd raid i ti ffono'r gwaith a gweud bo fi ddim yn dod mewn."

"Na wna i! Jobyn ceinog a dime sda ti eniwe; tase ti'n mynd ar goll am fis wele neb mo dy ise di."

Dyma fi'n troi ar fy sawdl a dod wyneb yn wyneb â Rhys, oedd ar ei ffordd mas o'r ydlan a llond ei gôl o wair.

"Haia," medde fi wrtho. Roedd ei lygaid fel tase nhw wedi mynd ar goll yn ei ben a'i groen yn welw uffernol. Roedd e 'di colli lot o bwyse. "Ti'n iawn?" gofynnais cyn ymresymu 'i fod e'n gwestiwn twp uffernol.

Nodiodd Rhys ei ben. "Ni 'di bod yn cliro stwff Mam mas heddi."

Doedd 'da fi ddim syniad beth i ddweud.

"Ma ryw ddyn yn dod pnawn 'ma i dynnu'r stair lifft 'na lawr; ma Dat ar y seilej a Ner yn y tŷ."

Gyda hyn dyma sŵn traed y tu ôl imi. Dyna lle roedd Emyr, a hwyl wael uffernol i weld arno. Aeth heibio heb weud gair, heblaw snapo ar Rhys, "Siapa hi 'da'r gwair 'na, wir dduw."

"Af i i'r tŷ 'te," medde fi, gan feddwl taw dyna'r peth ola yn y byd ro'n i'n moyn neud. Cerddodd Rhys i'r sièd isaf.

Roedd Ner ar ei phenglinie yn paro pare o sane at ei gilydd ar y leino a dagre'n twmblo lawr ei boche. Yn sydyn roedd cywilydd ar y diawl arna i. Cododd Ner ei phen i edrych arna i.

"Shwd wyt ti?" gofynnais gan benlinio lawr ar ei phwys hi, ac yn sydyn reit dyma ni'n dwy yn gweud 'Sori' ar yr un pryd yn union, a gwenu'n wan ar ein gilydd. Ymunes yn y paro sane.

"Beth o'dd yn bod 'no charmer bore 'ma de?"

"Ma'r bêler 'di torri lawr a ma fe'n methu ca'l part hyd ddiwedd yr wythos; ma can erw lawr 'da fe a fi'n gorffod mynd i'r gwaith heddi. Ma fe wedi galw bois mewn i bêlo a sdim bwyd 'ma iddyn nhw."

"Wel, fi gatre am wythnos," medde fi gan deimlo'n falch yn sydyn mod i'n medru bod o help i rywun. "Ffona di'r gwaith a gweud bo ti ddim yn dda. Wedyn allwn ni neud uffarn o ffîd i'r bois a fyddwn ni ddim wincad."

Edrychodd Ner yn ddiolchgar arna i.

Codais a chymryd pip rownd y gegin. "Wel, ma wye 'ma, a tomatos a 'bach o ham; duw duw ma digon o fwyd fan hyn am wythnos, a ma letysen yn yr ardd a shibwnsyn, dim problem."

"Mam blannodd rheina."

Suddodd fy nghalon unwaith eto. "O, gadwn ni rheina de," medde fi'n dawel.

"Na, ma'n iawn; fydde hi ddim yn lico gweld pethe'n mynd yn wastraff – ti'n gwbod fel oedd hi."

A dyna lle buon ni am weddill y bore yn coginio a berwi tato newydd a'u llwytho â menyn a shibwns a'u rhoi yn ffwrn waelod y stof i'w cadw'n gynnes. Roedd yn deimlad rhyfedd tynnu'r letys o'r ardd a'r shibwns oedd Gaynor wedi'u plannu, a rheini'n edrych mor iach a llewyrchus. Codon ni'r bitrwt hefyd er mwyn eu berwi ar gyfer swper. Erbyn inni orffen coginio a mynd lan â the deg i'r cae, roedd y bore wedi hedfan.

Roedd Ner yn siarad lot am Gaynor, yn sôn am sut y bydde hi wastad yn mynd o gwmpas yr ardd yn ei chader olwyn ar blanciau pren roedd Emyr wedi'u gosod iddi led y whîls 'wrth ei gilydd, a sut y bydde hi'n mynd yn benwan am y malwod oedd yn gneud eu gore i ddifetha unrhyw beth roedd hi'n ei blannu. Roedd hi hyd yn oed wedi bod yn ceisio'u meddwi trwy rhoi soseri o gwrw mas i'r "diawled" fel roedd hi'n eu galw nhw. Roedd un o'r cŵn wedi ca'l gafel yn y soseri ryw ddiwrnod ac yfed y cwrw i gyd. Treuliodd weddill y diwrnod yn cerdded ar dro, a rhochian cysgu ar ei gefen!

Daeth sŵn cerbyde i'r clos a lleisie prysur. Gydag Emyr roedd 'na ddau ddyn ro'n i'n eu hanner nabod o rywle. Daeth Emyr i'r tŷ mewn fest werdd, a'r blew cyrliog dros ei sgwyddau wedi cydio ym mhob llwchyn strae o'r aer, a'r croen yn goch sgald oddi tano. Gwelodd y bwyd ar y ford. Safodd yn stond.

"Beth uffarn yw hwnna?" Rhoddais y mygaid o de ro'n i'n ei yfed yn ôl ar y ford ac edrych ar Ner.

"Cino, be ti'n feddwl yw e?" atebodd hithau.

Gwelais wyneb Emyr yn cochi wrth iddo droi'n sydyn a mynd mas i'r ardd. Roedd y ddou foi arall wrthi'n tynnu'u welingtons ac yn esgus anwybyddu popeth. Rhuthrodd Emyr yn ôl heibio iddyn nhw.

"Chi 'di codi pethe Gaynor! Beth uffarn chi'n meddwl chi'n neud?" bytheiriodd. Cerddodd at y ford, codi'r bowlen salad a'i lluchio i'r llawr.

Cerddodd Emyr draw at Ner a chydio yn ei sgwyddau. "Fe ffycin ladda i di," meddai, "beth uffarn ti'n neud? Rhai Gaynor yw rheina, hi ddewisodd nhw, hi blannodd nhw, a be ti'n feddwl ni'n mynd i neud – iste fynna'n byta nhw fel tase dim byd yn bod?"

"Gad fi fynd," gwaeddodd Nerys, a'r ofn rhyfedda'n dod dros ei gwyneb.

Aeth y ddau foi arall mas a chau'r drws ar eu holau. Edrychodd Emyr arna i. "Cer o'ma," meddai'n dawel.

"Dyw Heledd yn mynd i unman," atebodd Ner drosto i.

Roedd dwylo Emyr yn crynu ac yn gwasgu patshys gwyn i mewn i groen sgwyddau Ner.

"Pam uffarn wyt ti'n neud rhywbeth fel hyn heddi? Meddwl ca'l gwared ohoni hi i gyd mewn un diwrnod, ife? Ffonio'r boi sta'r 'na a cha'l gwared o honno, ca'l gwared o'i dillad hi, a nawr ti'n palu'i gardd hi lan."

"Syniad fi oedd hôl y llysie... " mentrais.

"Ca dy ben."

"Beth yw'r ots?" atebodd Nerys gan wthio'i freichiau i ffwrdd. "Beth o't ti'n feddwl neud de? Gadel i'r cwbwl lot bydru fynna yn y ddaear fel hi?"

Roedd y dynfa rhyngddynt yn ormod, a meddyliais am eiliad ei fod yn mynd i'w bwrw hi.

"Bydde Mam wedi bod isie i ni godi popeth a'u mwynhau nhw; 'na pam o'dd hi'n plannu nhw, o'dd hi'n gwbod na fydde hi byth 'ma i fyta nhw." Roedd llais Ner yn uchel a'r dagrau'n llifo'n dawel i lawr ei bochau.

"Ti'n meddwl gallwn ni 'i hanghofio hi, on'd wyt ti? Ei chladdu hi a 'na ddiwedd arni. Anghofia i byth mohoni hi, byth bythoedd, ac fe wna i'n siŵr na nei di byth chwaith."

Daeth Rhys i lawr y sta'r lle roedd e 'di bod yn golchi'i ddwylo ar gyfer cinio.

"Stopwch hi, just ffwcin stopwch chi, newch chi?" gwaeddodd ac edrychodd y tri ohonon ni arno fel tase ni'n ei weld am y tro cynta. "Beth chi'n meddwl ddeith o hyn i gyd? Ma hi wedi mynd!" Roedd 'i lais yn crynu.

"Beth yw rheina sy 'da ti?" gofynnodd Emyr gan sylwi fel finne ar y papure yn nwylo Rhys.

Dechreuodd y crwt lefen a finne ddim yn gwybod beth i neud na lle i edrych.

"Beth y'n nhw?" gwaeddodd Emyr gan fynd amdanyn nhw. Camodd Rhys yn ei ôl.

"I Nerys ma rhein; ma'n bryd i bawb weud y gwir 'ma."

"Am beth ti'n siarad, Rhys?" Roedd Ner yn llefen yn waeth nawr wrth weld ei brawd yn llefen. Dyma'r tro cyntaf iddo fe golli deigryn dros ei fam.

"Ffindies i rhein yn y parlwr dan y leino sbel 'nôl."

"Dere â rheina 'ma," gwaeddodd Emyr gan gamu mla'n i'w cipio o ddwylo Rhys. Edrychodd ar y papure a'r chwys yn rhedeg lawr ei wddwg. "Y bitsh fach iddi, yn cadw rhein wedyn; y bitsh fach, yn cwato pethe a meddwl amdano *fe...* "

Aeth Nerys at Rhys a chipio'r bwndel cyn iddo ga'l cyfle i symud o'i ffordd. Edrychodd arnyn nhw fel tase hi'n blentyn bach yn darllen am y tro cyntaf. Sefais y tu ôl iddi gan ddarllen dros ei hysgwydd. Toriadau o hen bapurau newydd oedden nhw, yn adrodd hanes ryw ddamwain. Edrychais ar y lluniau cyn i'r enwau yn y penawdau wneud imi deimlo awydd chwydu.

... *Tragic suicide of Huw Williams after his lover Iona dies in motorbike crash...*

Roedd y lluniau yn yr ail bapur yn dangos dyn oedd yn edrych yn gwmws fel Emyr, a'r llall o ferch ifanc gyda gwên hardd, yr un ferch ag oedd yn y llun ar y pentan 'da Mam. Anti Iona. Roedd Emyr wedi dechrau llefen erbyn hyn, ac yn holi Rhys.

"Pryd ffindies ti rhein? Ble o'n nhw? Ers faint wyt ti'n gwbod?"

Roedd Nerys wedi suddo i'r llawr ac yn darllen y penawdau drosodd a throsodd. Roedd fy mhen i'n troi. Rhedodd Emyr mas gan adael y drws led y pen ar agor. Eisteddodd Rhys i lawr wrth y bwrdd.

Roedd y geirie'n pefrio ar y dudalen: *hanged himself on family farm... tragic circumstances... leaves his fiancée Gaynor Williams.*

Edrychais ar Rhys a oedd yn magu'i ben ac yn edrych ar Ner ar y llawr fel tase fe'n disgwyl ymateb ganddi.

"Roedd efaill 'da Dad, Ner; fe o'dd dy dad di. Roedd e wedi dyweddïo 'da Mam cyn i'r ddamwain 'ma ddigwydd gyda Iona, anti Heledd. Roedd gyment o gas 'da fe, fe bennodd e 'i hunan."

"O'dd Gaynor yn disgwl pan briododd hi ag Emyr?" gofynnais.

"O'dd."

Edrychais ar Ner a oedd mor wyn â'r galchen, gan ddisgwyl iddi weud rhywbeth.

"Does dim mam na thad 'da fi," medde hi gan edrych yn syn ar y papurau, "a dwyt ti ddim yn frawd i fi chwaith."

Dechreuodd Rhys wylo'n drymach fyth.

"Pam na fydde ti wedi gweud?" gofynnodd iddo. "Pam?" Roedd ei llais hi'n codi ac yn llawn dagrau.

"Do'n i ddim yn gwbod fy hun nes i Mam farw – dyna pryd ffeindies i nhw – ac ro'n i'n aros i Dad weud rhywbeth."

"Emyr, ti'n feddwl? Dyw e ddim yn dad i fi!" Cododd Ner ar ei thraed. "'Na pam felly o'dd hi moyn ca'l gwasgaru'i llwch ar y Ffridd; yn fan'no o'dd y ddamwain, ac ro'dd hi'n ei garu fe hyd y diwedd."

Eisteddais i lawr gan geisio gneud rhywfaint o synnwyr o'r holl beth. "Ond pam na fase rhywun wedi gweud

rhywbeth cyn hyn?" gofynnais, gan fethu deall pam na
fyddai Mam wedi sôn am y peth.

"Roedd 'na rywfaint o sôn am gyffuriau, fi'n credu... "

Clywais y dynion yn mynd yn ôl i'w cerbydau a gyrru
mas o'r clos. Roedd Ner ar ei phengliniau unwaith eto yn
casglu darnau'r fowlen salad oedd yn chwilfriw ar lawr.
Dechreuais roi help llaw iddi – fedrwn i ddim meddwl am
unrhyw beth arall i neud. Cydiais mewn darn o'r fowlen a
theimlo'r boen wrth i ddarn o'r crochenwaith gladdu ei
hun hyd y bôn yn fy mys. Roedd 'na waed yn pistyllio i
bobman. Ro'n i jest â marw isie mynd gatre a gofyn i
Mam pam 'i bod hi 'di cuddio amgylchiadau marwolaeth
Iona oddi wrtha i, ond ro'n i hefyd isie aros 'da Ner tra
bod y newyddion yn suddo i mewn gyda hi.

Ar ôl cliro rhoddais y bwyd i gyd 'nôl yn y ffrij tra
eisteddai Ner wrth y ford yn edrych ar ei dwylo. Estynnais
ddau wydryn a chwilio dan y sinc am botel o chwisgi –
roedd ei thad wastad yn cadw peth yno. Arllwysais beth i'r
gwydrau ac eistedd ar bwys Ner. Roedd hi'n edrych fel
tase hi'n gweld pethau ymhell i mewn yn nhywyllwch ei
meddyliau. Roedd ei llygaid yn symud yn ôl a mla'n, ond
doedd hi'n gweud dim.

Llyncodd y chwisgi cyn estyn am un arall a llyncodd
hwnnw wedyn. Estynnodd am y botel cyn i minne estyn
yr un pryd a rhoi fy llaw i dros ei llaw hi. Edrychodd arna
i.

"Dy anti di oedd wedi mynd â Huw 'wrth Mam."

"Beth?"

"O'dd e ar ei foto-beic 'da dy anti di er bod e 'di
dyweddïo 'da Mam."

Roedd y geiriau yn swnio'n estron, rywsut, ac roedd
'na galedwch rhyfedd yn ei llygaid.

"Dyw e ddim byd i neud â fi, achan – paid bod yn sili."

"Do's dim mam na thad 'da fi rhagor."

Ceisiais gydio yn ei llaw eto.

"Cer," dwedodd gan edrych yn rhyfedd arna i.

"Sai'n dy adel di fan hyn," dwedais i. "Chei di ddim bod ar ben dy hunan."

"Cer," meddai hi eto, yn hollol bendant. "Sa i moyn ti 'ma."

Roedd 'na olwg hanner gwyllt, hanner oer yn ei llygaid ac ro'n i'n gwbod bod dim dewis 'da fi. Codais a mynd at y drws.

"Ner, os ti moyn fi, ti'n gwbod lle ydw i."

"Cer," meddai hi eto wrth imi gau'r drws ar f'ôl.

Cerddais tuag adre a 'mhen i bron â ffrwydro; roedd popeth wedi newid. Roedd yr holl fyd wedi mynd yn ddieithr o fewn ychydig orie – Sion yn mynd i ben draw'r byd a Mam wedi bod yn celu'r gwir 'wrtha i ers blynydde. Doedd Emyr ddim yn dad i Ner bellach, ac roedd gan Gaynor fywyd hollol wahanol na wyddai neb amdano. Roedd Les yn amlwg yn gwbod, a'r pentre bach wedi llyncu'r gyfrinach yn gyfan gwbl gan adael dim ond un darn o ddafedd rhydd ar ôl i Rhys ei ffindio.

Wrth i mi gyrraedd pen y lôn, dyma gar arall yn tynnu i fyny. Deian. Rholiodd y ffenest lawr.

"Haia, shwt wyt ti?" gofynnodd â gwên fawr.

"Ie, iawn," medde fi gan feddwl sut y gallwn i ei wared er mwyn imi ga'l mynd adre a meddwl.

Daeth allan o'r car. "Drycha," medde fe, "isie esbonio am 'y mrawd i a beth ddigwyddodd 'da Nerys 'n i. Fi'n credu bod angen inni siarad, ond o'n i isie gweld a o't ti wedi cyrradd adre'n saff hefyd."

"Do, iawn, diolch."

"Beth o'dd yn bod de?"

"Ymm... " Ro'n i'n methu canolbwyntio o gwbwl.

"Heledd? Ti'n iawn? Ti 'di gneud dolur i dy law di?"

"Drycha, dyw hyn ddim yn amser da... "

"Wyt ti dal yn grac 'da fi? Ti'n gwbod cystel â fi bod rhywbeth rhyngddo ni. O'n i jest moyn i ti wbod taw clust i wrando i Nerys o'n i'r noson 'na a dim byd arall; ddigwyddodd dim byd, a fi'n credu bo ti'n gwbod 'na yn y bôn."

Symudodd yn agosach ata i gan dynnu cudyn o wallt allan o'm ceg a'i wthio dros fy moch.

"Glywes i bod ti a Sion wedi bennu."

"Ym, do."

"O'n i'n meddwl tybed fydde unrhyw siawns... "

Roedd ei law tu ôl i'm gwddf.

"Ym, drycha, dyw hyn ddim yn amser da; sori ond ma pethe'n gymhleth, sai m'bod beth sy'n digwydd, diolch am boeni amdana i, ond... "

"O, iawn, sori," meddai gan gamu'n ôl. "Os nad wyt ti'n teimlo run fath... "

"Na, na... ddim 'na beth... beth fi'n treial gweud yw odw, ond ma... "

"Beth?"

"O, ma rhaid i fi fynd i'r tŷ bach," medde fi gan redeg lawr ein lôn ni heb edrych yn ôl unwaith.

Igen

Erbyn i Mam esbonio popeth, roedd hi wedi dechre nosi.
Buodd hi'n llefen am dipyn a roedd e felse fe'n ryw fath o
ryddhad iddi gael siarad am bopeth oedd wedi digwydd.
Roedd hi wedi dod â sangwej banana imi yn y gwely, fel
oedd hi wastad yn neud pan o'n ni wedi cwmpo mas, ac
wedi dod mewn i'r gwely ata i i siarad. Roedd Dat yn
neud beth oedd e wastad yn neud pan oedd unrhyw beth
pwysig i siarad amdano, sef mynd mas i symud lectric ffens
y da. Roedd Rhys wedi ca'l gafel yn yr un darn o ddafedd
rhydd, a heno roedd Mam am dynnu'r we o gelwydd yn
ddarnau.

Wrth i Mam siarad roedd hi mewn rhyw fyd bach arall
– rhyw amser pell i ffwrdd, a hwnnw'n teimlo mor fyw â
ddoe iddi hi yn ei meddwl. Buodd hi'n siarad a siarad am
oriau heb aros a heb adael imi ofyn un cwestiwn. Roedd
hi'n arllwys ei meddyliau i bob man gan adael imi geisio
pysgota am synnwyr yn y llif geiriau.

Yn yr armi roedd Huw ac roedd e wedi rhoi e lan i
ddyweddïo â Gaynor. Roedd Emyr i ffwrdd yn was ffarm
yn y gogledd. Wedi danto â bod 'nôl yn y pentre, roedd
Huw yn cymryd cymysgedd o gyffuriau ac yn chware'r
rebel yn berffaith. Roedd e 'di cipio calon Gaynor o'r
funud gyntaf a bodlonodd hi ei briodi, ond nid hi oedd yr
unig ferch yn ei fywyd. Roedd sawl menyw briod 'da fe
oedd yn chwilio am 'bach o gynnwrf, a merched ifainc
oedd ddim yn gwbod dim gwell. Pan ddigwyddodd y

ddamwain, Iona, chwaer Mam, oedd ar gefn ei foto-beic, a
chafodd ei lladd yn syth. Y noson honno daeth Gaynor
draw a chyhuddo Mam o wybod bod Huw yn mynd 'da
Iona, a fuodd dim llawer o Gymraeg rhyngddon nhw wedi
'nny. Roedd y peth yn sgandal mawr, a phawb yn beio
Huw am farwolaeth Iona.

Roedd pob atgof yn tynnu deigryn arall o lygaid Mam,
a hithau'n dal i siarad a siarad. Ddaeth Huw ddim i'r
angladd, roedd gormod o gywilydd arno fe, ac aeth e byth
i weld Gaynor i esbonio pam oedd e 'da Iona y noson
honno. Ar ôl cyrraedd gatre o'r angladd, aeth ei deulu i
chwilio amdano a'i ffindio'n crogi yn y beudy. Roedd e
wedi marw ers y bore, mae'n debyg. Doedd dim nodyn,
dim byd, dim ond ei ddillad wedi'u plygu'n daclus yn y
cornel a chwdyn plastig am ei ben.

Roedd 'na donnau o emosiynau'n torri drosta i –
cymysgedd o anghredinedd bod y fath beth wedi'i guddio
cyhyd, a phiti tuag at Mam, a rhyw ddicter hefyd am iddi
golli'i chwaer mewn amgylchiadau mor uffernol. Claddwyd
yr hanes gyda Huw; daeth Emyr gatre o'r gogledd ar gyfer
yr angladd, a chyfarfod â Gaynor. Cwympodd mewn cariad
â hi, ac er 'i bod hi'n gwbod na allai ei garu gymaint ag
roedd hi'n caru ei frawd, fe briododd y ddau a chododd e
Nerys fel ei ferch ei hun. Wedodd neb ddim byd am eu
bod nhw'n meddwl taw Emyr a Gaynor ddylai ddeud wrth
Nerys cyn i neb arall neud. Doedd Mam ddim am ddeud
gair wrtha i am 'mod i'n gymaint o ffrindiau 'da Nerys.
Byddai'r cyfrifoldeb a'r celwydd yn annheg.

Roedd golau'r dydd yn melynu, a sŵn Dat i'w glywed
tu fas yn symud ryw bethe yn y sièd. Roedd ein te wedi
oeri heb ei yfed a sglein gwyn ar hyd ei wyneb. Buon ni'n
siarad wedyn am dipyn cyn i Mam syrthio i gysgu'n

sownd, fel tase hi wedi cael rhyddhad roedd hi wedi bod yn aros amdano ers blynyddoedd.

Gorweddais am sbel yn methu cysgu, nac yn methu deffro'n iawn chwaith, yn gwrando ar guriad hamddenol y cloc lawr sta'r ac anadlu tawel Mam wrth fy ochor. Clywais Dat yn dod i mewn ar ôl cau Carlo yn ei gwt, ac yn gneud paned o goffi lla'th iddo fe'i hun. Clywais ef wedyn yn golchi'i gwpan cyn cloi'r drws mas a dod lan y sta'r. Clywais gil fy nrws yn agor a dyma fi'n esgus cysgu. Daeth Dat i mewn i droi'r lamp i ffwrdd a thynnu carthen dros Mam a fi cyn mynd allan gan fwmblian,

"Nos da, ferched bach."

Un ar higen

Ma hi'n bwrw heno. Tri llond cae o seilej yn gwlychu fan hyn yn y glaw. Yn pydru'n dawel. Ma'r dŵr yn disgyn ar y rhesi gwair gan ryddhau arogl sur. Yng ngolau'r lleuad ma'r rhesi'n edrych fel gwallt y merched duon 'na welodd Gaynor a finne yn Antigua ar ein mis mêl. Rhesi o wallt tywyll wedi'i dynnu'n rychau dros y pen gan adael y gwyn rhyngddynt. Ma'r gwair yn sgleinio'n ddu yn y nos, a fan hyn a fan draw ma 'na ffrwydrad o bridd coch lle ma'r peiriant torri wedi gwaedu'r ddaear. O fan hyn rwy'n medru gweld y tŷ, a golau stafell wely Nerys yn diffodd. Does dim golau yn Nhyddyn Gwyn chwaith. Ma'n siŵr eu bod nhw i gyd yn cysgu. Ma'r cŵn wedi tawelu. Noson gynnes, a'r dafnau dŵr yn rhedeg o 'ngwallt lawr i wlychu'r fest amdanaf, gan olchi halen y chwys i mewn i'm llygaid. Teimlad fel nofio'n y môr. Ma'r awel yn goglais y dail yn ysgafn i sibrwd arna i, i chwerthin yn dawel.

Roedd Rhys yn gwybod, yn cario'r cwbwl yn ei ben am yr holl wythnose 'na. Gwybod bod ei dad erioed wedi bod yn ddigon i'w fam. Ma cleber y pentre yn nail y coed. Y pinne bach yn dechre eto a'r tyndra'n boen yn y frest. Methu'n lân â cha'l unrhyw aer allan o'r nos; teimlad fel anadlu dŵr. Weithie ma'r cwbwl yn tywyllu nes bod dim i'w weld ond y borfa'n pydru ar lawr.

Yn y pellter ma 'na ambell gar yn mynd dros y Mownt gan oleuo'r nos o'i amgylch. Pobol yn prysuro i fynd adre i

gael mynd i'r gwely mewn parau. Dynion wedi cael eu
hanfon ar neges munud-olaf i Spar, neu'n codi aelod o'r
teulu a mynd â nhw gatre. Goleuadau yn niwl y glaw, gan
ei gwneud yn bosib gweld y dafnau unigol am eiliad. Am
eiliad. Yr ochr arall ma'r môr i'w weld yn anadlu'n rhwydd.

Eistedd wrth y clawdd a gwrando ar dic-tician y glaw
yn y dail uwchben fel sŵn ewinedd Carlo ar lawr. Tractor
yr ochr arall i'r cae lle gadewais e amser cinio yn edrych fel
tegan yng ngolau'r lleuad. Rhoi'r rhaff i lawr wrth fy ochr.
sŵn y dail yn y coed uwchben, a'r lleuad wedi'i ddal yn y
brigau, wedi'i ddal yng nghrafangau'r pren. Ma fe'n edrych
yn brydferthach nag erioed, gyda'r sêr sy wedi'u mogi gan
gymylau duon. Does dim cystadleuaeth iddo wedyn.

Byddai Gaynor a finne'n dod 'ma weithiau gyda
basgedaid o fwyd; gadael i Nerys i chwarae gerllaw a Rhys
yn fabi yn ei chôl. Byddai Heledd yn dod i chwarae 'da
Nerys, a Gaynor a fi'n eu gwylio'n dawnsio drwy'r borfa
hir neu'n neidio dros y rhesi gwair. Wrth i'r nos nesáu,
byddai bysedd y machlud yn dal darnau o ddwst gwair, a'u
goglais yn yr aer cyn eu gadael i ddisgyn. Byddai Gaynor
yn pesychu bryd hynny, ond yn mynnu bod yr haul a'r
gwres yn gwneud lles iddi. Eisteddai hi a'i gwallt gole
wedi'i dwtio tu ôl i'w chlustiau a'r brychau haul yn
tywyllu dros ei thrwyn. Byddai ei gwallt yn dal yr haul gan
ddatgelu'r lliwiau ynddo, o felyn gole gole i goch tywyll.

Dafnau trymion o ddŵr ar fy nghefn – maen nhw'n
casglu yn y dail uwchben cyn cwympo. Ymgynnull ac oedi
cyn cwympo i'r llawr. Dail gwyrddion yn sianelu'r dŵr
yn barod am y gwymp. Ma'r glaw'n trymhau. Rwy'n
methu'n lân â cha'l ysgyfaint llawn o aer. Bob nos ers
blynyddoedd yr un hen beth, y teimlad bod rhywun yn
eistedd ar fy mhen yn gwasgu'r gwynt allan ohona i.

Rhwydi o nerfau'n neidio. Bysedd yn dwyn yr ocsigen allan o'r aer. Weithiau'n dihuno yn y nos, weithiau'n cael fy ngharcharu mewn breuddwydion o wynebau a drychau a rhaffau. Weithiau'n gwylio Gaynor gan deimlo bod ei symudiadau hi'n perthyn i mi. Dihuno ambell fore a'm nerfau'n neidio ac yn tician yn fywyd i gyd. Bysedd duon y nos yn gwthio i'm gwyneb. Bysedd y nos yn sleifio i mewn i'm llygaid, dros fy nghroen, i mewn i'm clustiau ac i bobman. Tagu a mogi. Bysedd y nos dros y gwyneb, y gwyneb a ddaeth yn arf i'r dail gael fy ngwawdio. Rwy'n methu gweld, a'r ofn dyfnaf erioed yn tyfu trwy fy nghorff.

Codi, a sŵn y dail yn anadlu yn fy mhen. Taflu'r rhaff dros y gangen isaf.

Dou ar higen

"Codwch y rhaff nawr de, dim ffwcio ambwti, codwch hi, dalwch y straen a PULL, a cym on, cym on, cym on, CYM ON!"

Les yn fy nghlust i, a'r merched i gyd yn straffaglio dan y pwyse aruthrol yn y gasgen.

"Hasssa Hasssa Hasssa!"

Roedd y rhan fwya o ddynion y pentre lan yn y cae heddi i weld ein ymarfer olaf cyn mynd am y ffeinal.

"Reit Heledd, off y rhaff plis; cer i redeg rownd y ca'."

"E?"

"Cer i redeg rownd y ca' – ti'n ffycin byddar ne be?"

Dyma fi'n gollwng y rhaff gan adael mwy o bwyse i'r merched i'w ddala a dechre rhedeg cyn gyflymed ag y gallwn i rownd y cae.

"CYM ON, PEIDWCH RHOI MEWN, CYM ON, THIS IS IT – 'BACH O BOEN YN NEUD DIM DRWG ICHI!"

Wrth imi gyrraedd man pella'r cae, ro'n i'n medru clywed y merched yn gweiddi arna i.

"Cym on Hels, ffwcin siapa hi!"

"Dere Hels, 'nôl ar y rhaff plis."

"Plis Hels, alla i ddim â... "

"Do's dim 'fi ffaelu' neu 'alla i ddim' yn perthyn i'r ffwcin tîm 'ma! Peidiwch byth â gadel i fi glywed chi'n siarad felna 'to."

Rhedeg nerth fy nghoesau rownd y cae ac ailgydio yn y

rhaff – roedd yn crynu dan afael y merched.

"Reit te, deg eiliad a lawr â hi."

Deg eiliad yn llusgo heibio, yn goglais traed y rhifau ar watsh Les cyn iddo ostwng ei ddwylo a gadael inni roi'r gasgen i lawr. Saith merch yn cwympo i'r ddaear.

"Da iawn, 'na'r pull ola chi'n mynd i neud nawr cyn cydio yn y rhaff 'na yn y ffeinal. Gobeitho bo chi wedi mwynhau e. Reit, af i i hôl sgwash ichi nawr."

Roedd pawb yn gorwedd ar y borfa wlyb yn ymladd i gael eu hanadl yn ôl. Awen oedd wrth fy ochor.

"O's rhywun wedi pwynto mas i'r ploncyr 'na bod ni un yn brin, de?" meddai gan godi'i braich i gymryd potel ddŵr 'wrth Kel heb symud un rhan arall o'i chorff.

"Ti'n cynnig gweud tho fe?" holais.

"Nadw i, ond ma pawb yn gwbod bod Ner druan â phethe mwy pwysig ar 'i meddwl hi nawr."

"Shwt ma ddi de?" gofynnodd Kel gan cistedd lan. Roedd y merched erill yn gwrando'n astud hefyd.

"Paid gofyn i fi," atebais, "dyw hi ddim isie gweld fi o gwbwl."

"Es i draw 'na bore ddo' a gweud y gwir," medde Awen.

"Shwt oedd hi de?" holodd Kel yn glustie i gyd.

"Wel, fel fyddet ti'n disgwl, wedi ca'l uffarn o sioc ac yn gynddeiriog at Emyr am y celwydd – ond mwy na 'nny am y claddu 'ma."

"Alla i ddeall 'nny."

"Shwt ma fe de?"

"Ro'dd e'n edrych yn bygyrd pan weles i fe; wedodd Ner fod e ddim 'di cysgu winc y nosweth cyn 'nny – ro'dd e 'di dod 'nôl i'r tŷ yn y bore yn wlyb sopen ac mor wyn â'r galchen. Duw a ŵyr lle o'dd e 'di bod."

"Sneb arall 'da fe, o's e? A bod e wedi aros mas trwy'r nos?" gofynnodd Siân yn fusnes i gyd.

"Na, sai'n credu 'ny; wedi bod mas yn cerdded neu rywbeth, siŵr o fod."

"Ma 'da fi drueni drosto fe, cofia; o'dd e'n dwlu ar Gaynor yn 'i ffordd fach 'i hunan. Uffarn o beth cymryd rhywun arno felna a gwbod bod hi'n disgwyl," ychwanegodd Heini.

Daeth Les yn ei ôl gyda llond basged o boteli ffres o sgwash. Roedd y dynion wedi mynd adre i gyd heblaw am Gerallt, oedd yn disgwyl am Kel.

"Be sy mla'n 'da chi'ch dou de?" holodd Awen gan edrych ar Kel.

"Fi'n credu bo fi in love."

"E?"

"Fi rili yn lico fe, t'mod, a dyw'r ffaith bo 'da fe blentyn ddim yn becso fi o gwbwl."

"Plentyn?" medde fi'n syn. Roedd hyn yn newyddion i fi.

"Beth sy'n bod ar 'nny?" gofynnodd hithe, yn amddiffynnol yn sydyn.

"Dim, whatever tickles your pickle, on'dife," atebodd Awen.

"Ma fe wedi gofyn i fi fynd am wylie 'da fe ar ôl y ffeinal. Fi mor ecseited!"

"Faint yw 'i oedran e de?"

"Tri deg."

"O."

"Be?"

"Dim."

"Yfwch rhein nawr de ferched, a gewn ni chat bach wedyn."

Gyda'r geiriau ola 'na, roedd pawb yn teimlo araith fach arall yn dod. Pawb yn yfed ac yn rhoi siwmperi am eu cefne.

"Reit te ferched, this is the lie of the land; in a nutshell, we're shagged."

Pawb yn edrych ar ei gilydd.

"Ry'n ni one member lawr, a gewn ni neb arall o'r pwyse iawn lan i sbîd erbyn y gystadleuaeth. Os na gewn ni Ner 'nôl i dynnu, allwn ni anghofio am y gystadleuaeth, a ma'r holl waith caled 'ma wedi bod yn wastraff."

Roedd pawb yn edrych ar y llawr wrth gymryd hyn i gyd i mewn.

"Reit, ma pawb yn gwbod beth sy 'di digwydd iddi hi; not nice, shit happens, ond ein nod ni nawr yw 'i cha'l hi 'nôl i bach o fywyd normal. Ry'n ni'n gyfrifol amdani nawr achos ma hi'n un ohonon ni. Beth fi'n trial weud yw bod military operation yn mynd i ddigwydd 'ma. Fi'n gwbod faint chi'n mcddwl o Ner, ond ma'n hen bryd i chi'r bastards dynnu'ch bysedd mas o'ch tine. We've seen the worst of this inbred bastard place – nawr dewch inni weld y gore plis. I'll leave it to you. Os chi'n moyn ymddwyn fel hanner y diawled rownd ffor hyn a gweud 'duw, da iawn, neis gweld teulu felna'n ca'l 'i dynnu lawr peg ne ddou,' carry on weda i. ''Na be ni'n lico on'dife? Gwên fach tu ôl i'r cydymdeimlo 'na i gyd', ma fe lan i chi. Sort it out. Peth arall yw'r gystadleuaeth 'ma. Fi'n gwbod bo chi'n disgwl pregeth, ond dim ond un peth sda fi i weud. Chi wedi ennill y fraint o wisgo'r crys coch 'na, crys Cymru. Pan fyddwch chi'n tynnu hwnna dros eich pen, chi'n gwbod beth chi'n gorffod neud. Fe anfona i negeseuon atoch chi am drefniade ddydd Sadwrn. Reit, ffyc off nawr de."

Cydgerdded o'r cae ymarfer am y tro ola, a sylwi bod pawb yn cerdded 'da'i gilydd erbyn hyn.

"Af i draw heno," cynigiodd Llinos.

"A finne nos fory," wedodd Heini.

"Ma 'da fi siwmper i roi 'nôl iddi o'r ymarfer diwetha fuodd hi ynddo fe. Alla i fynd â honno 'nôl fel esgus i alw draw," ychwanegodd Sara.

"Be amdanat ti?" holodd Awen i fi.

"'Na gwestiwn, dyw hi ddim isie gweld fi hyd yn o'd."

"Ry'n ni i gyd yn gwbod mai 'da ti ma'r afael ore drosti hi."

"Gewn ni weld, falle af i draw i'w gweld hi; gore oll os na fydd Emyr 'na."

Roedd pawb yn frawl i gyd am sut roedden nhw'n mynd i fod yn gymorth i Nerys; ro'n i'n falch achos doedd neb wedi sôn am Sion a fi, ac roedd hynny, o leia, yn gysur. Gwahanodd pawb yn y pentre a chytuno i anfon negeseuon at ein gilydd yn dweud sut oedd 'Operation Nerys' yn dod yn ei fla'n.

Heini a Siân yn cerdded am y pentre yn gleber gwyllt, Kel a Gerallt law yn llaw, Sara, Llinos ac Awen yn gwneud cynlluniau i fynd i'r sinema, a finne'n troi am y lôn gefn.

Tri ar higen

Bip Bip!

DIGON CARBS. DIM FAT. DIGON DWR. LES

Amser swper, a Les yno ar fy ysgwydd drwy'r amser. Drainio'r pasta drwy'r rhidell a'i arllwys yn mygu i gyd ar y plât. Mam yn llenwi ryw ffurflenni wrth y bwrdd a Dat yn eistedd yn ei gadair yn darllen taflen arall o'r Cynulliad yn dweud pryd a sut oedd e fod i symud ei anifeiliaid. Sylwais ei fod yn ei ddal a'i ben ucha isa.

Bip Bip!

NER YN WELL – WEDI BOD AM SWPER YN DRE. AWEN

Anfon 'nôl.

NATH HI WEUD RHWBETH AM FI?

Bip Bip!

NA – PAID BECS

"Beth yw'r sŵn tragwyddol 'na 'da ti, ferch?" Roedd Mam yn gwisgo sbectol oedd yn medru curo rheole gravity ac yn eistedd yn berffaith ar ben ei thrwyn. "Wyt ti'n bip bip fan hyn a bip bip fan draw – ti'n ddigon o farn, wir."

"Sori, Mam."

"A beth yw'r bwyd 'na ti'n fyta? Ych-a-fi, byt dato wir, neithe fe les iti."

"Ocê, Mam."

Roedd Mam yn un o'r rhain oedd yn meddwl mai'r unig bethau oedd eu hangen mewn bywyd oedd bwyd sybstansial, dyn sybstansial a nicyrs sybstansial.

"Ti 'di siarad 'da'r crwt 'na 'to te?"

"A pwy grwt yw hwnnw nawr te?"

"Ti'n gwbod yn iawn pwy, a paid â bod yn cheeky – ti ddim rhy hen i ga'l llwy bren, t'mod."

"Nadw, a sai moyn siarad amdano fe, diolch."

"O 'na fe 'te, g'na di beth ti moyn. Sdim pwynt i fi bregethu fan hyn -- ti'n gwmws run peth â dy dad."

"Beth?"

"Fel donci."

"Hei," medde Dat wrth edrych dros ben ei bapur, "os yw'r groten moyn llonydd, rho lonydd iddi hi, dim mynd fel terrier ar 'i hôl hi felna."

"Bydd ddistaw," medde hithe a Dat yn diflannu eto tu ôl i'r papur fel tase Mam wedi damsgen ar 'i bawen e.

"A pheth arall, sai'n deall pam wyt ti'n llabyddio dy hunan fel ti'n neud 'da'r hen raff 'na."

Aeth hi'n ôl at ei ffurflenni, a Dat yn mentro edrych dros ei bapur unwaith eto. Eisteddais wrth y bwrdd.

Bip Bip!

FI IN LUV. KEL

Anfon 'nôl.

TI SHWR?

Bip Bip!

MA FE'N BIWTIWIWTIFFWL. KEL

Meddyliais tybed lle roedd Sion heno. Yn pacio, siŵr o fod. Roedd hi'n ddiwedd y mis ar ôl y wîcend. Doedd dim pwynt cysylltu 'da fe, er i fi bron â bwrw bogail isie gneud weithie. Felna oedd e, unwaith roedd e wedi gneud ei benderfyniad doedd dim troi 'nôl. Roedd Mam wedi dechre clebran am rywbeth, rhywun yn gweud celwydd fel ci yn trotian neu rywbeth. Roedd Deian hefyd yn siŵr o fod yn meddwl erbyn hyn bo fi'n reial ploncyr. Doedd

dim ots; roedd popeth wedi mynd o chwith beth bynnag.
Sylwais bod ei siwmper yn dal i grasu uwchben y stof.
Roedd Mam yn disgwyl imi fynd â hi o 'na.

Bip Bip!

4 DIWNOD I FYND – EX8TING! LLINOS

Anfon 'nôl.

AYE – CRYSE COCH AMDANI DE

Roedd y gystadleuaeth yn cael ei chynnal ar gae rygbi
ger Hwlffordd, a'r parti ar ôl 'nny mewn neuadd rhyw
goleg cyfagos. Gan fod gymaint o bobol isie dod lawr i'n
gweld ni'n tynnu, roedd Les wedi trefnu bws mawr – a
bydde hwnnw'n dod â ni 'nôl hefyd fel bod neb yn gorfod
dreifio. Duw a ŵyr pwy fyddai arno fe.

Bip Bip!

DDOI DI AM WAC DA V FORY? NER

Neidiodd fy nghalon am ryw reswm.

Anfon 'nôl.

IAWN 12? STAND LATH

Bip Bip!

IWN

Roedd fy nghalon i beth yn ysgafnach gan wybod ei
bod hi am drafod pethe – er bod Mam yn gweud bod dim
llawer mwy i weud yn y bôn a bod dim bai ar neb heblaw
Huw a Iona. Gorffennais fy swper a mynd lan sta'r.
Glanhau 'nannedd a meddwl am eiliad beth o'n i'n mynd i
wisgo ar gyfer y parti mawr ar ôl y tynnu. Yn ddiweddar
roedd ffasiwn a phethe felna yn bell o 'meddwl i. Lle o'r
blaen bydden i'n genfigennus ar y diawl wrth weld ryw
ferch dene, ro'n i'n meddwl nawr sut bydde hi'n edrych ar
ddiwedd rhaff neu ar jog hir 'da Les 'da llond bac-pac o
bwyse ar 'i chefen. Roedd popeth wedi newid.

Bip Bip!

NOS DA X - AWEN
Anfon 'nôl.
NOS DA X

Pedwar ar higen

Roedd Ner yn mynnu mynd am y Ffridd, a gallen i ddeall pam, mewn ffordd. Roedd hi wedi ffono'i Anti Eirwen ac wedi darganfod yr union fan lle ddigwyddodd y ddamwain. Do'n i ddim yn siŵr a o'n i isie gweld, a gweud y gwir. Ar ôl cwrdd, fe gerddon ni y bedair milltir i fyny'r Mownt ac i'r Ffridd. Ardal o dir pori gwael agored yw'r Ffridd, fel tir comin, gyda hewl gul yn sleifio'n dwyllodrus drwyddo. Roedd 'na ambell dwffyn o wlân fan hyn a fan draw ar y ffensys, ond dim llawer o sôn am ddefaid. Cydgerddodd y ddwy ohonon ni'n dawel gan nad oedd llawer i ddeud. Roedd Ner yn edrych yn llwyd ac wedi colli pwyse'n ofnadw. Roedd hi'n gwisgo rhyw grys-T oedd mor hen ag Adda, a throwser marchogaeth ceffyle. O leia roedd y ffaith ein bod yn mynd i rywle'n rhoi esgus inni siarad.

"Ble ma fe de?"

"Lan tua canllath to, fi'n credu. Ma hen goeden 'na; ma hi'n nychlyd uffernol ond ma'n debyg bod y moto-beic wedi mynd i mewn iddi hi wrth droi'r cornel."

Wrth inni gerdded i fyny dyma'r goeden yn dod i'r golwg – hen goeden oedd wedi plygu yn 'i chwman gan y gwynt am fod y tir lan fan hyn mor agored. Hen goeden debyg i'r rhai roedd Ner a finne'n chware ynddyn nhw flynyddoedd yn ôl; coeden ddringo go iawn. Sefon ni'n dwy'n llonydd a distaw ac edrych arni. Roedd yr hewl yn codi tipyn tuag at y copa ac roedd 'na gornel siarp jest cyn hynny.

Wrth sefyll mewn tawelwch am sbel, cofiais am y disgrifiad roddodd Mam i fi yn y gwely y noson honno. Y ffono, y chwilio am Huw am ei fod wedi rhedeg i ffwrdd o'r ddamwain. Y cerddwr ddaeth ar draws y corff wrth ochor yr hewl. Y ffrog oren oedd am Iona, a'r gwaed yn gymysg â'i gwallt. Y moto-beic wedi'i falurio a'i lapio o amgylch y goeden, a'r harn mor feddal â chroen. Yn y fan hon y penderfynodd Huw na allai e fyw 'da'r cyfrifoldeb. O'r fan hon roedd y cerddwr wedi cario'r corff yn ôl lawr i'r pentre at y doctor, gan wybod drwy'r amser ei bod hi'n rhy hwyr.

"Ma hi'n dawel 'ma, on'dyw hi?" meddai Ner o'r diwedd.

"Odi."

Roedd 'na galedwch newydd yn llygaid Nerys oedd yn gwneud i'r dagre a gwympai o'i llygaid edrych fel rhai damweiniol.

"Fan hyn ffindiodd Les hi achos bod fy nhad i wedi rhedeg bant."

"Beth?"

"Les ffindiodd hi; o't ti ddim yn gwbod?"

"Na, wedodd Mam ddim."

"Sdim lot i weud, o's e?"

"Les gariodd hi 'nôl i'r pentre?"

"Ie – peder milltir; roedd e mas yn cerdded, ac yn gwbod yn ei galon taw corff oedd e'n gario."

Roedd y newyddion yn llosgi drwyddaf. Edrychais ar Ner; roedd y gwynt wedi codi lympie bach ar hyd ei breichie i gyd.

"Colles i 'nhad y nosweth 'ny, collodd Mam ei chariad, a chollest ti dy Anti. Digwyddodd y cwbwl fan hyn, a run ohonon ni'n gwbod dim amdano fe."

"Od, on'dyw e? Doeddet ti na fi ddim i ga'l, hyd yn o'd."

"Fan hyn oedd hi moyn bod, lan fan hyn 'da'i hatgof ohono fe."

"Oedd e bownd o fod yn anodd i dy da—... i Emyr, cofia," medde fi, a bron yn rhoi 'nhroed ynddi eto.

"Mmm."

Sefon ni'n dwy yn edrych ar y goeden am o leiaf deg munud cyn i gar dorri'r tawelwch. Dau dwrist yn edrych arnon ni'n syllu'n ddwys ar ryw goeden gyffredin ar ganol darn anghysbell o dir.

"Excuse me? Can you direct us to the nearest cashpoint, please?"

Llais Sais tu ôl imi, a'r ddwy ohonon ni'n troi i edrych arno ac yn methu deud gair o'n penne. Caeodd y Sais ffenest y car o'r diwedd gan ddeud yn ddigon uchel inni ga'l clywed:

"Bloody Welsh – they're so fucking ignorant!"

Edrychodd Nerys arna i a gwenu'n drist. Cydiais innau yn ei llaw a cherddon ni tuag adre 'da'n gilydd.

Pump ar higen

Bip Bip!

COCK A DOODLE DOO BASTARDS – GET UP!
D DAY – LES

Edrych ar y cloc, hanner awr wedi chwech. Roedd hyn
yn cadarnhau popeth ro'n i wedi dechre 'i feddwl am Les –
roedd y boi off 'i blydi ben! Roedd hi'n dal yn ganol nos.
Trois drosodd a cheisio mynd yn ôl i gysgu. Doedd y bws
ddim yn mynd tan naw, a finne wedi paco popeth neithiwr
– dillad tynnu, sane, crys coch wedi'i smwddo deirgwaith,
ac wrth gwrs dillad i wisgo yn y parti. Cwarter awr o
lonydd, yna:

Bip Bip!

GET UP OR I'LL COME OVER AND SHAG YOU
– LES

Wyth merch yn neidio mas o'r gwely. Ar ôl i mi gael
cawod, clywais Dat yn codi er mwyn mynd i hôl y da, a'r
beic pedair olwyn yn cychwyn lan y lôn. Wedyn, mewn
ryw ugen munud, curiad calon y peiriant godro'n cychwyn.
Roedd meddwl am ddigwyddiadau'r dydd o mla'n yn
anfon tonnau o nerfusrwydd drwydda i, felly ceisio
anwybyddu'r peth fyddai ore. Wedodd Les bod nerfe'n
bethe da achos bydde nhw'n ein cadw ni'n siarp ac ar
ddihun. Os taw fel hyn o'n i'n mynd i deimlo drwy'r bore,
byddwn i wedi bennu erbyn heno.

Roedd y pwyso'n digwydd rhwng hanner dydd ac un yn
y clwb rygbi, a'r stampiau pwyse'n ca'l eu rhoi ar ein coese

fel nod ar wartheg. Roedd pawb wedi colli pwyse, felly fe ddylen ni fod yn iawn o ran hynny. Roedd pedwar tîm arall yn y gystadleuaeth – Iwerddon, yr Alban, Jersi, ac wrth gwrs y pencampwyr, Lloegr. Doedden ni ddim i fod i gael brecwast, felly es lawr sta'r i adel Carlo mas o'i gwt a rhoi maldod iddo am sbel. Roedd hwnnw'n edrych yn nerfus hefyd. Es lan unwaith eto i neud yn siŵr 'mod i wedi cofio popeth.

Bip Bip!

9 BWS PENTRE SHARPISH. LES

Ro'n i wedi trefnu cyfarfod Nerys ar dop y lôn. Doedd hi ddim isie cyrredd ar 'i phen 'i hunan achos bydde lot o bobol y pentre ar y bws. Roedd awydd uffernol arna i i ffono Sion. Dyna un o'r pethe anodda – bob tro roedd rhywbeth yn fy mhoeni, neu rywbeth cyffrous yn digwydd, dyna'r person cyntaf ro'n i'n ei ffono fel arfer. Nawr, roedd arna i angen rhywun i siarad, a fedrwn i ddim meddwl am neb gwell na Sion. Rhois y ffôn yn fy mag ac addo i mi fy hunan y byddwn i'n ei ffono taswn i'n dal i deimlo'r un peth mewn awr. Awr yn pasio, a finne'n addo run peth eto mewn awr – cyn i mi gychwyn, heb ffono, am dop y lôn.

Roedd hanner y pentref wedi codi i ffarwelio â ni, ac roedd y teimlad yn gwmws fel tase ni'n mynd i ffwrdd i ryfel. Roedd rhai'n dod lawr mewn ceir hefyd oherwydd bod dim digon o le ar y bws. Roedd y merched i gyd yno, a hyd yn oed Kel wedi neud special early showing i ddangos ei bod hi'n keen. Roedd Gerallt yn sownd wrth ei hochor fel Prit Stick. Pawb yn cael eu pwyso cyn mynd ar y bws, a Les yn gneud syms yn ei ben. Roedd e'n edrych yn arbennig o smart heddiw, mewn tracsiwt goch a chap fflat gwyn. Edrychai fel tase fe'n mynd i rasys milgwn yn hytrach nag i gystadleuaeth tynnu rhaff. Roedd Les yn awyddus inni beidio â chymysgu 'da'r bobl erill ar y bws, ac i eistedd yn y cefen fel tîm.

"Don't go talking to these bastards," medde fe gan fwynhau'r diawlio roedd yn ei gael ganddyn nhw. "These are blydi plebs – so sportspeople in the back, please. Dyw rhai o'r rhein ddim wedi efolfo digon 'to, ma nhw'n dal i lusgo'u nycls ar y llawr."

Esgid yn cael 'i thaflu o flaen y bws ac yn bwrw Les yn ei ben. Hwnnw'n chwerthin. Ar ôl gneud yn siŵr fod popeth gyda ni, a checio am yr ail dro, dyma ni'n cychwyn. Roedd tipyn o bobl y pentre yna – John Torrwr Bedde a'i wraig, Gwyneth gwraig Les, a phwy neidiodd ar y bws yn hwyr ond Deian. Sylwes i ar Awen yn edrych yn bwrpasol i 'nghyfeiriad i pan ddaeth e i'r golwg. Diolch byth 'i fod e'n eistedd yn rhan flaen y bws!

"Reit te, y diawled, ymlaciwch nawr de a mwynhewch y diwrnod."

"O'n i'n treial ymlacio am hanner awr wedi chwech bore 'ma," medde Awen yn bwdlyd.

* * * *

Dwy awr yn ddiweddarach, dyma ni'n cyrraedd y cae. Roedd y time erill i gyd yn eu citiau'n barod am eu bod nhw wedi aros mewn gwestai cyfagos dros nos. Roedd 'na nifer o dime dynion yno hefyd, ac roedden nhw eisoes yn pwyso i mewn gan eu bod nhw'n tynnu'n gyntaf. Roedden nhw'n sefyll o gwmpas yn eu dillad isa, yn gyhyrau ac yn liw haul i gyd. Am unwaith daeth dim pip mas o Kel – roedd hi'n rhy brysur yn edrych yn gariadus ar Gerallt.

"Mei god, ma hi wedi cwmpo am hwn no," wedodd Llinos y tu ôl inni. "Fel arfer, erbyn hyn ma hi fel ci hela sy wedi gweld cadno a'i bronne fel dwy red setter."

Heini'n giglo ac Awen yn cytuno'n dawel. Gofynnodd Les i bobol y pentre fynd mas er mwyn inni gael eiliad fach ar ein pennau'n hunain i ganolbwyntio. Gwelais Deian yn mynd am y bar yn y clwb rygbi gyda Gerallt, ar ôl i Les hôl crowbar i dynnu Kel oddi wrtho.

"Reit te ladies." Roedd Les allan o wynt i gyd a'i wyneb yn goch. "Dyma ni, dyma beth ry'n ni wedi bod yn freuddwydio amdano, a galla i ddweud heb air o bolycs bo fi'n prowd ohono chi i gyd, yn arbennig Ner, am ddod 'ma heddi – not an easy thing, but let's cut the crap, let's do it. Gnewch y'ch gore, ladies; gnewch y'ch hunen a Chymru'n browd taw chi sy'n gwisgo'r cryse coch."

Gyda'r geirie ola 'na gan Les, dyma ryw don ryfedd yn mynd reit trwof i, fel ry'ch chi'n teimlo wrth sefyll yn Stadiwm y Mileniwm yn canu 'Hen Wlad fy Nhadau'.

"Let's go!"

Wrth i ni i gyd gamu oddi ar y bws, roedden ni'n cael ein llygadu gan y time merched erill, ac ambell un o dime'r dynion. Roedd pawb yn broffesiynol iawn ar y lefel yma o gystadleuaeth, a bydde'r awyrgylch yn rhoi sioc i unrhyw un oedd yn meddwl bod tynnu rhaff ddim yn gamp go iawn. Roedd nifer fawr o stiwardiaid ar hyd y lle hefyd mewn siacedi smart a bathodynnau defnydd wedi'u gwinio arnyn nhw, yn helpu pobl i ffindio'r gwahanol stafelloedd. Wedi dadbacio ac edrych ar ein gilydd am sbel, dyma ni'n mynd tuag at y dafol. Roedden ni isie bod yno gynta er mwyn cael dod 'nôl i'r stafell a chael rhywbeth i fwyta. Roedd Lloegr a'r Alban yno'n barod. Dyma ni'n stripio pob dilledyn posib heb adael ein hunain yn agored i gael ein harestio, a'r dynion yn methu cuddio'r ffaith eu bod nhw'n edrych arnon ni.

Camu ar y dafol bob yn un, a gwylio gwyneb y dyfarnwr yn ofalus. Siân oedd yr un ddiwetha i sefyll ar y dafol – a dyna fe, sefyll yn llonydd.

"Iawn, 576 kilo, stampiwch nhw."

Roedd y rhyddhad yn amlwg ar wyneb Les a phob un ohonon ni'r merched. Roedd y pwysau'n berffaith, ddim yn rhy ysgafn nac yn rhy drwm chwaith. Dyma ninnau'n cael ein stampio ac yn gwisgo eto cyn inni oeri.

"Reit, bwyd!" medde Awen a gwên fawr ar ei gwyneb. "Fi bron â starfo!"

'Nôl â ni i'r bws a byta a byta a byta. Roedd mynd heb fwyd yn ddigon gwael, ond roedd mynd heb ddiod yn waeth fyth. Wedi byta dyma ni'n tynnu ein tracsiwts ac yn dechre gwisgo'n 'dillad rhyfel'. Roedd 'na gynnwrf yn yr aer wrth i'r crysau coch fynd dros ein pennau, a phob un am unwaith heb lawer i weud. Roedd Awen yn edrych yn nerfus uffernol ac yn mynd trwy'r symudiadau yn ei phen. Roedd y dynion wrthi'n tynnu, a'r tuchan a'r gweiddi i'w glywed ar ein bws ni. Roedd y time merched erill hefyd yn barod i dynnu, ac yn edrych draw i'n cyfeiriad ni gan obeithio hela ofan arnon ni. Roedd Les wedi ein paratoi am hyn ac roedden ni wedi cael rhybudd i beidio edrych o gwbwl arnyn nhw. Eu trin fel tase nhw ddim yn bod – hen dric armi, mae'n debyg, negyddu bodolaeth y gelyn neu rywbeth. Clymais fandyn am ben Nerys a gwnaeth hithau run peth i mi. Roedd y tywydd yn go lew, o leia, a'r ddaear ddim yn rhy galed nac yn rhy sych. Roedd Nerys yn cerdded 'nôl a mla'n a Kel yn chwilio am ben Gerallt yn y dorf.

Clywed tîm bechgyn Cymru'n cael eu galw. Llais o'r cae yn gweud taw yr Alban oedd yn eu herbyn i ddechrau. Roedd sawl baner Draig Goch yn chwifio wrth i'r crysau coch gerdded tuag at y cae. Aeth Les draw i ganol y cae er mwyn taflu'r geiniog i sefydlu pwy oedd yn tynnu gyntaf. Gan taw cystadleuaeth Round Robin oedd hi, byddai'n rhaid tynnu pawb yn ei dro. Ond fe fyddai'n fanteisiol i ni dynnu'r time cryfa yn ola; roedden ni'n dibynnu ar y ffaith ein bod ni'n fwy ffit na'r lleill, felly byddai 'mwy ar ôl yn y banc' gyda ni, fel wedai Les.

Yn y cyfamser, aeth pawb ati i gynhesu'r cyhyrau. Chwifio breichiau, tynnu coesau'n ôl a chysuro'n gilydd. Daeth Les yn ei ôl – Iwerddon yn gynta, wedyn yr Alban, wedyn Jersi ac wedyn Lloegr yn ola, yn dibynnu sut roedd pethe'n mynd. Ni oedd yn tynnu'n gyntaf. Roedd cystadlaethau'r bechgyn yn dal i fynd mla'n a ninnau ar ail raff ar eu pwys. O leia bydde hynny'n dipyn o gysur.

"Reit te ferched, mewn cylch os gwelwch chi fod yn dda." Pawb yn ymgynnull. "Reit, chi'n gwbod faint o waith chi wedi neud, a nawr chi 'ma yn gwisgo'r cryse coch. Sdim rhaid i fi weud 'tho chi am neud eich gore. Fi'n gwbod newch chi, achos chi'n diamond girls. Un peth, peidwch colli'ch penne nawr, easy does it, ry'n ni 'ma for the long run. Un peth fi isie chi neud, a hynny yw dod off y cae 'na heddi yn gwbod bo chi wedi rhoi popeth gallech chi. Os gwnewch chi 'nny, bydd dim byd 'da neb i weud. Ni i gyd wedi gweld time Cymru'n mynd mewn i gystadlaethe'n dân i gyd, a beth sy'n digwydd? Ma nhw'n colli, naill ai colli'u penne ne'n colli achos bo nhw'n crap. Wel, alla i addo ichi, dy'ch chi ddim yn crap, so peidwch colli'ch penne a gwnewch eich gwlad yn browd ohonoch chi. This is it: RHYFEL!" gwaeddodd gan gynhyrfu pob un ohonon ni'n wallgo.

Cerdded tuag at y cae heb edrych ar y rhes o ferched mewn cryse gwyrdd. Cerdded tuag at y rhaff oedd yn mesur y pellter, a chraffu ar y beirniad. Penlinio wrth y rhaff wrth i un o'r stiwardiaid edrych ar ein sgidiau i neud yn siŵr eu bod nhw'n gyfreithlon. Roedd Les wrth ein hochor, yn dawel reit. Y pull cynta oedd waetha, ond 'na fe, roedd rhaid ei gwneud hi.

"Are you ready, Wales?" Albanwr oedd y beirniad ta beth. Les yn nodio'i ben.

"Ireland, are you ready?"

Boi bach mewn het ddu yn nodio'i ben.

"Right, pick up the rope, take the strain and PULL!"

Pawb yn cwympo a'r rhaff yn crensian. Roedd y rhain am drio tynnu o'r dechre ac roedden nhw'n gweiddi nerth eu pennau.

"Hasssa Hasssa Hasssa!"

Yna roedden nhw'n gorwedd yn ôl yn galetach ar y rhaff.

"Na fe ferched, gadewch iddyn nhw neud y gwaith; 'na fe, gadewch iddyn nhw labyddio'u hunen – ma nhw'n neud y job droston ni. Sdim pwynt tynnu nawr, blinwch nhw 'bach."

Roedd y rhaff yn neidio lan a lawr wrth i'r tîm arall drio mynd yn ôl â hi. Roedd hi'n edrych fel petai trydan yn rhedeg ar ei hyd.

"Warning, Ireland, jacking. First warning."

Roedd un o ferched Iwerddon yn jacio'r rhaff dan ei braich yn anghyfreithlon. Dau rybudd arall a bydde nhw mas o'r gystadleuaeth. Roedd Ner o mla'n i'n crynu dipyn, ond 'na fe – doedd hi ddim wedi bod yn yr ymarferion yn ddiweddar.

"Reit te ferched, cewch â nhw, ma nhw wedi bennu os y'n nhw'n jacio, cewch â nhw ar ôl tri, UN DAU TRI, ANNNND PULL ANNNND PULL ANNNND PULL!"

Dyma'r rhaff yn dechre symud a merch flaen y tîm arall yn dechre llithro. Unwaith cododd y rhythm, daeth y rhaff am yn ôl heb drafferth hyd at chwiban y dyfarnwr.

"First end to Wales, two minutes three seconds; change ends please."

Doedd gen i ddim teimlad yn fy mreichie, a'r wefr oedd yn fy nghorff yn dechre setlo.

"Da iawn, ferched. Reit, bennu rhein sy isie, peidio gadel iddyn nhw ga'l gafel ynddi y tro hyn. Lladdwch nhw cyn iddyn nhw sylweddoli beth sy wedi digwydd."

Newid ochor a Les unwaith eto wrth ein hochor. Roedd hi'n anodd ei golli yn y tracsiwt 'na.

"Wales, are you ready?"

Les yn nodio.

"Ireland, are you ready?"

Y dyn bach yn nodio unwaith eto.

"Pick up the rope, take the strain and PULL!"

Roedd dwylo'r dyfarnwr wedi disgyn yn gloi y tro 'ma, a ninne dipyn bach ar ei hôl hi. Dyma Kel yn rhoi hyrddiad, a phawb arall yn dilyn ei hesiampl. Roedd y lleill wedi mynd am dacteg wahanol y tro hwn, ac yn awr yn gorwedd 'nôl a dala. Ar ôl ryw ddeg eiliad, dyma'r symudiad yn codi, ac er mawr ryddhad i Les, daeth y rhaff am 'nôl. Cwmpais ar fy nhin wrth i'r mwd dan fy nhraed fynd yn llithrig, ac wrth i mi drio codi dyma chwiban y dyfarnwr yn mynd â'r marc ar ein hochor ni o'r llinell. A dyna ni wedi curo Iwerddon.

"Iawn, ladies, ar eich tra'd; cymrwch rywbeth i yfed a siglwch law, wedyn 'nôl at y bws."

Doedd dim teimlad ar ôl yn fy nwylo wrth i mi gynnig llaw lipa i'r Gwyddelod, a rheini'n ein llongyfarch ar hyd y llinell.

'Nôl wrth y bws roedd Les wedi cynhyrfu'n bost. Roedd

e'n wyn fel gwêr, a'r cap am ei ben wedi'i wthio'n ôl.

"Reit te, ddim yn ddrwg, ond ma peil o waith ar ôl 'da ni. Roe'ch chi'n edrych yn go lew, ond fi 'di gweld gwell. Watshiwch y drop 'na; yn yr ail dynfa 'na gaethoch chi'ch dala mas, y diawled. Keep your eye on the ball, dim colli penne nawr a tynnu'n ddwl. Control, 'na be sy isie 'ma."

"Next Ladies' match, Scotland v Wales. Ladies to the rope, please."

Roedd John Torrwr Bedde wedi'i fabwysiadu fel water boy, er taw dyna'r peth lleia tebyg i water boy welsoch chi rioed. Roedd Kel wedi gweud bod y rhaff yn rhy sych, ac roedd John wedi cael ei anfon i'r bws i moyn tac. Rhododd ddarn bach o bren yn y pot jam ac wedyn llusgo hwnnw ar draws cledr llaw pob merch. Pawb yn clapio i wneud y cymysgedd rhyfedd oedd fel glud ar eu dwylo, ac arogl petrol yn codi ohono. Mynd am y cae, a chryse glas tywyll yr ochr arall i'r rhaff y tro hwn. Les yn cerdded y llinell gan sibrwd:

"Put your thoughts away, this is it, concentrate, just another job to be done, kill the enemy!"

"Scotland ready?"

"Wales ready?"

"Pick up the rope, take the strain and PULL!"

Roedd ei ddwylo wedi cyrraedd ei ochr cyn inni sylweddoli beth oedd wedi digwydd, a ninne ar ei hôl hi unwaith eto. Damo, roedden nhw wedi cael y drop, a ninne'n dal arno wedi plygu i gyd. Roedd fy nhraed i ymhell o flaen fy nghorff, a 'nghefen yn grwm. Damo ffycin damo! Clywed hyfforddwr yr Alban yn eu hannog nhw i dynnu.

"Come on, girls, give 'em some stick!"

A llais Les yn y glust arall yn gweiddi nerth ei ben:

"PEIDWCH PANICO, PEIDWCH PANICO, FE FLINAN NHW NAWR!"

Dal a dal a dal am funudau di-ben-draw. Ner o mla'n i yn hyrddio a finne'n dilyn, ac Awen yn y cefn yn ffindio'i hun 'nôl yn y position iawn.

"REIT TE FERCHED, CO NHW NAWR – MA'U GWENDID NHW'N DOD – CO NHW'N DACHRE HWTHU!"

Dyma finne'n rhoi un cam bach ymlaen er mwyn i mi fedru sythu 'nghefn. Camgymeriad mawr.

"PAID Â FFWCIN STABLAN AR Y RHAFF, PEIDWCH SYMUD Y DIAWLED!"

Munudau hirion yn mynd heibio a thamed o raff yn dod ffordd ni.

"REIT FERCHED, CYMRWCH E OS Y'N NHW'N RHOI E ICHI, SDIM AMSER DA CHI I WILIBOWAN."

Gorwedd 'nôl a theinilo'r rhaff yn dod am 'nôl yn ara bach ond yn sicr. Roedd y merched erill yn gorfod neidio mla'n mewn camau bach er mwyn ceisio amddiffyn, ond roedd eu nerth nhw wedi mynd.

"First end to Wales, longest pull of the competition – three minutes and twenty seconds."

Gorweddai Awen ar y llawr yn gwenwyno bod ei chefen hi wedi bennu.

"Ca dy blydi seiens nawr, wir; gewn ni wenwyno wedyn yn y bar," oedd ymateb swta Les.

"Change ends please, ladies."

"Run dechneg â'r tro dwetha," medde Les, "ond watshiwch y blydi drops 'ma. Chi labyddiodd y'ch hunen fan'na drwy fod fel lloi ar y drops. Fydde 'na ddim wedi digwydd tase chi 'bach yn siarpach."

Daeth yr ail pull i'w ddiwedd yn go gyflym. Roedden ni'n dechre gweld pa mor bwysig oedd bod yn ffit, ac yn gweld pwrpas yr holl foreau 'na roedden ni 'di'u treulio'n codi'n gynnar a mynd allan i redeg. Roedd y merched yn y cryse glas tywyll wedi bennu.

'Nôl wrth y bws, roedd 'na rywbeth newydd i'w weld yng ngwyneb Les, rhyw olwg penderfynol nad oedden ni wedi'i weld o'r blaen. Roedd Awen yn gwingo am fod ei chefen hi mor dost, a Ner yn edrych fel tase hi'n diodde hefyd. Roedd Kel yn edrych yn wyllt reit, fel tase tân ar fin dod mas o'i ffroene.

"Reit, tîm Jersi nesa. Ma nhw'n gry, ond ry'ch chi'n gryfach. Let's do the job unwaith eto, ma 'da chi ddwy funud fach i ga'l tra bod rheina'n tynnu'i gilydd."

Roedd merched Jersi mewn cryse oren, ac am unwaith doedd ganddon ni ddim cliw beth oedden nhw'n weud wrth ei gilydd am eu bod nhw'n siarad fersiwn o Ffrangeg. Wrth i ddwylo'r dyfarnwr gwympo, dyma ninnau'n cwympo hefyd, ac am y tro cynta yn teimlo bod 'na rywun yr ochr arall i'r rhaff. Roedd rhain yn gry, yn uffernol o gry.

"CYM ON FERCHED, RHOWCH O'CH GORE NAWR, HAAASA HAAASA HASSA AND PUUUUUUUULL AND PUUUUUUUULL AND PUUUUUUUULL!"

Doedd y rhaff ddim yn symud ac roedd gen i deimlad na fydde fe'n symud chwaith. Dechreuodd eu hyfforddwr nhw weiddi yn Ffrangeg, a'r tîm yn dechre codi rhythm. Mewn chwinciad, roedden ni wedi ca'l ein llusgo i'r llinell.

"First end to Jersey, change ends please."

Roedd y dorf yn mynd yn boncyrs, a phawb fel tase nhw ar ein hochor ni.

"CYM ON FERCHED, SO CHI'N MYND I ADEL

RHEIN NEUD 'NA ICHI, ODYCH CHI, A CHERDDED OFF YN FYW? BE SY'N BOD 'NO CHI? DIHUNWCH!"

Unwaith eto dyma ni'n cwympo 'nôl i'n lle a'r tro hwn gawson ni afael yn y rhaff yn gyntaf. Ychwanegu pwyse'n ara o hyd nes bod fy nwylo'n troi'n wyn o ddiffyg gwaed, a chyhyrau fy nghoese'n llosgi fel tân. Doedd dim yn symud rhein. Wedyn, ar ôl hanner munud, dyma raff yn dod allan o ddim un man, a ninnau ddim yn barod. Pob un ohonon ni wedi'n disodli a minnau heb ddewis ond mynd i bosition amddiffyn. Hwn oedd y position mwya anodd i'w ddal am amser hir oherwydd y straen ar y cefn. Aros a dal a dal tra bod y rhaff yn tasgu 'nôl a mla'n. Roedd Les yn dechre colli'i cŵl.

"CYM ON FERCHED, PEIDWCH RHOI MEWN I'R DIAWLED, CYM ON, DEWCH NAWR MYN UFFARN!"

Roedd y dala'n gwneud i mi deimlo'n sâl, a phob darn o nghorff wedi mynd yn galed reit. Aros a chyfri i ddeg er mwyn rhoi'r boen allan o'r meddwl. Aros eto a chyfri i ddeg, aros ac aros iddyn nhw flino, ond yn sydyn dyma nhw'n hyrddio a ninnau'n cael ein tynnu mla'n a mla'n. Ceisio amddiffyn yr holl ffordd, a pheidio rhoi i mewn o gwbl ond, yn anochel, dyma'r chwiban yn chwythu.

Damo shit!

"This round to Jersey. Thank you, ladies."

Doedd bloeddiadau'r dyrfa ddim yn bod bellach a'r byd unwaith eto wedi mynd yn dawel reit. Ro'n i'n methu teimlo dim o 'nghorff, ac roedden ni wedi cael ein curo 'fair and square', fel wede Les.

"Reit, codwch ar eich tra'd a siglo llaw; dyw hi ddim drosodd eto."

Roedd pawb yn ddistaw wrth y bws a phob un ohonon ni'n gwbod ein bod wedi cael ein curo gan dîm gwell na ni, a hynny ar ôl inni roi popeth i mewn i'r ymarfer. Peth diflas yw cael eich curo beth bynnag, ond roedd cael eich curo pan roeddech chi wedi rhoi popeth allech chi i mewn i'r gamp yn waeth. Doedd dim gwella i ga'l wedyn, oedd e?

"Y ffycers, beth uffarn yw'r penne lawr 'ma? Beth uffarn sy mla'n 'ma?" Cerddodd Les o gwmpas gan roi slap ar wyneb pob merch wrth iddo fynd heibio. Roedd pawb mewn sioc. "Rhoi fyny nawr, ife? 'Na beth ni'n mynd i neud? Rhoi fyny a meddwl 'o, wel, 'na fe; ni 'di colli, so wa'th inni fynd at y bar' ife? 'Na beth sy'n mynd trw'ch penne chi? Os 'na beth sy'n mynd mla'n yn y coconuts 'na, wel ry'n ni 'di gwastraffu misoedd ar fisoedd yn y cae 'na'n chwysu. Achos chi'n gwbod beth ddylsech chi fod yn meddwl? E? Chi'n gwbod, e?" Cydiodd ym mhen Kel ac edrych i mewn i'w llygaid. "Dyma be ddylech chi ddeud, 'COME ON AND TRY THAT AGAIN, YOU SILLY TWAT! SO YOU DID IT ONCE, BUT OVER MY DEAD BODY WILL YOU BE DOING IT AGAIN.' Think teabags!"

Edrychodd pawb ar ei gilydd mewn penbleth. "It's only when you're in hot water that you find out how strong you are! Nawr Lloegr sy nesa; chi'n gwbod fel ma nhw, ma nhw'n mynd i feddwl bo chi'n easy pickings nawr, so let's do it you buggers, get back in there and do it in style!"

Pawb yn codi'u penne ac yn cymryd arogl hir mas o'r botel smelling salts roedd Les yn ei phasio o gwmpas.

"England v. Wales, please, ladies."

"Cym on de, ferched, dewch i gladdu'r diawled," gwaeddodd Awen, a oedd yn edrych yn barod i dynnu'r rhaff ar 'i phen 'i hunan tase rhaid iddi.

"England, are you ready?"

"Wales, are you ready?" Les yn nodio.

"Pick up the rope, take the strain and PULL!"

Lawr â ni fel tase dim fory i gael a rhoi'n holl bwyse i mewn i'r rhaff. Unwaith eto roedd hi'n ddigon amlwg bod rhywun ar ochr arall y rhaff. Roedd rhein yn dda hefyd.

"CYM ON FERCHED, CHI'N GWBOD BETH SY RAID ICHI NEUD!"

Eu hyfforddwr nhw'n gweud wrthyn nhw am ein codi, a'r tîm yn rhoi rhaff gan ddisgwyl ein disodli. Ninnau'n cymryd y rhaff ac eistedd arno. Munud arall yn mynd heibio, a'r blinder yn gweithio'i ffordd drwy 'nghorff; ro'n i bron â llwgu hefyd erbyn hyn. Roedd hi'n syndod sut oedd y corff yn treulio bwyd o dan y fath amgylchiadau. Cyhyrau yn fy mol yn crynu i gyd. Teimlad od.

"Pwyswch 'nôl nawr de ferched," meddai Les wrth gerdded y llinell unwaith eto.

Roedd y dyrfa'n mynd yn boncyrs, a finne'n sylweddoli bod y gystadleuaeth hon rhyngon ni a Lloegr bron mor bwysig ag ennill y gystadleuaeth. O gornel fy llygad, sylwais ar Deian yn sefyll ar bwys Gerallt. Roedd y ddau'n bloeddio nerth eu penne.

Yn sydyn dyma Nerys yn rhoi uffarn o floedd ac yn codi'i choes dde i'r aer a'i chladdu yn y mwd nes ei bod hi hyd y bôn o'r golwg. Dyma finne'n ei dilyn a Kel yn gneud run peth. Clywais lais Awen o'r cefen, "Do's dim blydi ffordd yn y byd 'ma fi'n mynd am mla'n!"

Roedd y rhaff yn gwichian a Les yn pasio heibio unwaith eto.

"Reit ferched, cymrwch nhw."

Hyrddio am 'nôl gyda'n gilydd, ac yn sydyn teimlo'n bod yn eu disodli. Roedd eu merch flaen nhw'n edrych dan straen, a Kel yn rhythu arni fel petai'n ei herio hi i dynnu'n galetach. Dyma Kel a Ner a finne'n cydgerdded yn ôl, a'r rhaff yn dod yn raddol gan wichian yr holl ffordd tuag at y llinell.

"First end to Wales. Swap ends, please."

Les yn anwybyddu'r beirniad am eiliad inni gael ein gwynt atom.

"Run peth 'to ferched, fi moyn ichi drin y pull 'ma fel yr un gyntaf, proffesiynol y'n ni, so do the job a cewch o 'ma gyda'ch penne'n uchel. Ma pawb fan hyn isie i chi ennill hon ac yn y'ch calonne chi i gyd yn gwbod fydde hi'n beauty -- so come on, newch e i fi. Do the job!"

Roedd Kel yn rhythu unwaith eto ar y ferch ar flaen eu rhaff nhw. Doedd hi ddim wedi cau ei llygaid unwaith. Roedd hi'n edrych fel tase hi'n barod i ladd unrhyw un a fentrai gydio yn ochr arall y rhaff. Canolbwyntiais ar beth oedd i'w wneud. Rhoi pob meddwl arall mas o'r pen a gweld y gole coch lawr y rhaff.

"Pick up the rope, take the strain... " a gyda hyn dyma ein merched ni'n hacio i mewn i'r ddaear fel teirw gan ollwng 'HY' fawr i'r awyr.

"... and PULL!"

Lawr â ni a'i dal hi unwaith eto. Roedden nhw wedi gwylltio ac yn tynnu fel yr uffarn, a ninne'n dal ac yn eistedd 'nôl gan aros iddyn nhw flino.

"DALWCH HI, DALWCH HI, DALWCH HI!"

Nerys yn bloeddio mewn poen, a Heini y tu ôl imi'n gweiddi, "Iesu Grist, myn uffarn i, dewch mla'n, tynnwch y diawled! Bois bach, sdim sens achan, bachan bachan... "

Ac Awen yn gweiddi o'r cefen, "Watshiwch hi, ma nhw'n mynd i roi, co fe'n dod, co fe'n dod... "

Dyma ninnau 'nôl ar ein penolau wrth iddyn nhw rhoi rhaff a ninnau jest yn gadel iddyn nhw'n codi ni 'nôl lan.

"Warning Wales, sitting. First warning."

"Oce de ferched, ar eich tra'd; llaw lawr a codwch, ond cadwch y pressure arno, peidiwch â gadel iddyn nhw ga'l hon nawr."

Roedd y ffaith ein bod wedi cael rhybudd wedi rhoi ail wynt iddyn nhw a ninnau'n ara bach yn cael ein tynnu mla'n. Damo! Roedd Ner yn troi'n goch o mla'n i, a Llinos yn gweiddi nerth ei phen. Roedd y marcyn yn dod yn agosach ac yn agosach, a Kel ar flaen y rhaff ddim isie mynd heibio iddo.

"REIT TE, DEWCH MLA'N, UN IDDYN NHW Y DIAWLED UFFARN!" Llais Ner o mla'n i a phawb yn methu deall beth oedd wedi digwydd iddi. "CYM ON FERCHED, SO NI'N MYND GATRE HEB GURO RHEIN!" A gyda'r geiriau hyn dyma hi'n claddu ei sawdl unwaith eto gan godi clytsen i'r aer; aeth honno'n syth am y dyfarnwr ac ar hyd ei drowser gwyn i gyd. Roedd Kel tua 15 cm o'r llinell. Bloeddiodd Awen, ac yn sydyn roedd gafael 'da ni ar y rhaff.

Cododd Kel ar ei thraed a dechre gweiddi, "Dde CHWITH Dde CHWITH Dde CHWITH!"

Roedd y cryse gwynion wedi cael gymaint o sioc nes iddyn nhw edrych lan a ninnau'n cymryd mantais o bob gwendid. Cynyddodd bloeddiadau'r dorf a neb yn medru credu'r peth wrth inni gerdded yn araf yn ôl â'r rhaff, ac mewn hanner munud yn eu llusgo nhw ar eu tinau yn groes y llinell. Roedd y rhyddhad yn anodd i'w ddisgrifio, a dyma Les yn dod draw ata i a rhoi uffarn o gusan ar fy moch. Roedd y merched mewn cylch yn neidio lan a lawr, a finne'n sefyll yna yn edrych ar fy nwylo er bod 'na ddim teimlad ynddyn nhw.

"Cym on, siglwch law, ac off â ni i'r bws."

Wrth inni gyrraedd y bws roedd pobol y pentre 'na'n barod. Rhuthrodd Kel i freichie Gerallt. Deian oedd y person cynta i mi 'i weld. Cydiodd ynof i a rhoi gwasgad i fi.

"Da iawn, Hels – sterling performance!"

Roedd fy mhen i'n ysgafn yn barod, ond roedd e'n ysgafnach fyth erbyn hyn. Aeth Deian ymlaen i gydio yn Sara. Doedd y time erill heb orffen tynnu eto, a Lloegr a'r Alban yn tynnu am y drydedd safle. Galwodd Les am dawelwch, ac roedd golwg ddifrifol ofnadwy arno fe.

"Shhhhh ferched, shhhh nawr de, gwrandwch arna i nawr. Alla i weud un peth, a fi'n meddwl e o waelod 'y nghalon ac yn hollol ddiffuant. FFYCIN BEAUTY!"

Bloeddiodd pawb, a'r merched i gyd yn prysuro am y cawodydd. Roedd Awen druan yn dal i boeni am ei chefen, a finnau'n meddwl am Sion.

Whech ar higen

"Dewch mla'n, ferched, ma dathlu ar y diawl i fod heno," meddai Awen yn uchel ei chloch. "Llinos, rhwbia 'nghefen i, nei di?" meddai hi wedyn wrth roi tywel i Llinos noethlymun, a honno'n sychu cefen Awen gan ganu fersiwn o 'Bing bong' nad oedd yn ffit i gael ei ailadrodd.

Roedd pob un ohonon ni mewn ffrogiau heno, gan fod y cinio'n un go swanc. Ffrog ddu oedd 'da fi; helpodd Mam fi i'w dewis hi ha' dwetha erbyn fy seremoni raddio. Roedd Sion yn honno hefyd, yn ei siwt smart.

Ar ôl gwneud fy ngwallt, dyma Ner yn zipio cefn fy ffrog a finnau'n botymu ei ffrog hithe. Ffrog lliw pinc tywyll oedd 'da hi. Roedd rhaid gweud, wedi inni orffen a gweld Kel yn ymladd 'da pâr o syspenders 'yn sbeshal i lyfer boi', ro'n ni i gyd yn edrych yn ddigon smart, a hyd yn oed Awen, oedd yn casáu ffrogiau, yn edmygu ei hun yn y drych.

Dringo ar y bws unwaith eto i gael mynd i'r cinio, ac wrth imi gamu arno dyma fi'n dod wyneb yn wyneb â Deian. Edrychodd arna i heb weud gair, a minnau'n mynd yn goch ac yn meddwl bod pawb wedi sylwi. Roedd e wedi newid hefyd i siwt ddu, a honno'n gweddu'n berffaith i'w lygaid glas. Blydi hel, roedd y boi 'ma'n secsi. Gwthiais heibio iddo a llusgodd yntau ei law ar draws fy nghefen gan ddihuno pilipalas yn fy stumog.

Roedd Les wedi prynu bocsaid mawr o win a chwpanau plastig ar gyfer y siwrne a phawb yn pitsho i mewn. Roedd pobol y pentre i gyd mewn hwyliau uffernol o dda gan fod eu hanner nhw wedi bod yn y tent cwrw drwy'r pnawn cyn mynd i newid ar gyfer y nos. Roedd 'na benillion yn mynd 'nôl a mla'n, a nifer ohonyn nhw'n gneud i yrrwr y bws fynd yn goch fel twrci. Wrth inni agosáu at y neuadd, dyma'r gyrrwr yn galw am dawelwch drwy'r meicroffon a ninnau'n disgwyl pregeth am yr iaith oedd 'da ni. Ond na, dyma Gerallt, yn llwyd ac yn chwyslyd, yn cydio yn y meic. Edrychodd pawb ar ei gilydd.

"Ym... alla i weud, cyn bo ni'n cyrradd," a chliriodd ei wddf, "alla i weud 'llongyfarchiadau' i'r merched ar eu llwyddiant heddi." Daeth bloeddiadau o bob cyfeiriad, a'r merched i gyd yn gweiddi. "A hefyd ma rhywbeth 'da fi i holi i rywun ar y bws 'ma."

Dyma ninnau'n edrych ar ein gilydd wrth sylweddoli'n sydyn beth oedd ar fin digwydd. Roedd Kel yn eistedd yn lyged i gyd. "Fi wedi bod yn gweld Kel nawr am rai wythnose ac wedi penderfynu na alla i fyth fyw hebddi hi, felly dim ond un peth sy i neud." Dyma fe'n estyn i mewn i'w boced a thynnu bocs bach allan. "Kel, nei di fod yn wraig i fi?"

Roedd y bws i gyd yn dawel, a dim gair yn dod wrth neb; roedd y gyrrwr wedi tynnu mewn i ochr yr hewl heb i neb sylwi, a phob llygad ar y bws wedi'i sodro ar Kel. Dyma hi'n codi ac yn rhedeg at Gerallt ffwl sbîd, cyn i'w ffrog ddal yn un o'r seddi a hithau'n cael ei thynnu'n ôl a'i thaflu ar ei thin.

"O shit," medde Awen gan ei chodi ar ei thraed unwaith eto.

"Wrth gwrs 'naf i!" oedd ateb Kel.

Dyma pawb ar y bws yn edrych ar ei gilydd ac yn dechre llongyfarch y pâr ar unwaith. Roedd y merched i gyd mewn sioc a phopeth wedi digwydd mor gyflym. Yn sydyn, roedd un ohonon ni ar fin priodi, a hynny'n deimlad uffernol o od ond neis ar yr un pryd. Ailgychwyn y bws a mynd i'r neuadd; pawb mor ecseited, a rhywbeth ychwanegol i'w ddathlu'n awr.

Wrth inni gamu oddi ar y bws, dyma Les yn ein cadw ar ôl mewn grŵp. Roedd e wedi tynnu'r stops mas heno ac yn gwisgo siwt biws gole oedd wedi'i smwddo mor dda nes bod modd i chi hogi cyllyll ar y sîms.

"Nawr 'te ferched, dewch i fi ga'l y'ch gweld chi nawr." Edrychodd arnon ni i gyd bob yn un. "Feri neis, 'na i gyd alla i weud. Fi'n browd ohonoch chi a bydd yn bleser mowr i'ch esgorto chi i gyd i'r ddawns 'ma. Reit, pawb i gydio llaw a let's make our entrance."

Roedd y neuadd wedi'i haddurno fwy ar gyfer gwledd briodas na chinio ar ôl cystadleuaeth tynnu rhaff, ond falle dan yr amgylchiadau bod hynny'n addas. Roedd ein bwrdd ni ar bwys tîm y dynion o Iwerddon, a rheini mewn hwyliau uchel iawn wrth i bawb gyflwyno'i gilydd a rhannu gwin. Roedd Kel a Gerallt godderbyn â fi, ac Awen wrth fy ochr. Ro'n i'n medru gweld Deian ar waelod y bwrdd yn siarad yn dawel gyda Ner, ac aeth ryw saeth o genfigen twp trwyddof.

"Os gwela i wydryn gwag, fydd hi ddim yn dda 'ma!" Daeth llais Les o waelod y ford a ninnau'n dilyn ei gyfarwyddiadau fel arfer ac yn gwagio sawl potel cyn i'r cinio ddod i ben. Ar ôl symud y celfi dyma ryw hen foi a wig am ei ben, a honno'n matshio'r blew ar ei jest, yn dod i chwarae ryw CDs o'r unfed ganrif ar bymtheg. Doedd dim ots, roedd pawb yn cael hwyl beth bynnag. Roedd Llinos a Siân a Heini wrthi'n tynnu rhai o'r Gwyddelod, a ninnau wedi bod yn clebran gyda ryw ferched o Jersi.

Roedd Les ar ben stôl yn canu 'Calon Lân', a Gwyneth wrth ei ochor yn edrych fel tasai hi'n difaru dod i'r byd. R oedd John Torrwr Bedde'n siarad yn dawel gyda grŵp o'r pentre am brisie eirch, fel bydde fe bob tro ar ôl cael un neu ddau yn ormod, a Kel a Gerallt yn sownd yn ei gilydd ar y dance floor.

"Aros fan'na – fi'n mynd i'r bog; dal fy mag i nei di?"

Gwyliais Awen yn cerdded am y toiledau, a rhyw foi tal yn dod tuag ataf. Edrychais lan. Deian oedd yna, yn edrych lawr arna i heb ddeud run gair. Edrychais arno.

"Beth?"

"Dim."

"Ar be ti'n edrych?"

"Be ti'n feddwl?" Oedodd fel tase fe'n asesu'r sefyllfa. "Dere mas am eiliad."

"Be, nawr?"

"Na, wythnos i fory."

"O."

"Ti'n dod de?"

"Ocê, 'na i adel bag Awen 'da Ner nawr."

Gadel y bag ar y ffordd mas, a meddwl beth oedd e isie. Roedd 'na gynnwrf fel ryw groten fach yn corddi yn fy mola. Y tu allan i'r neuadd, cydiodd yn fy llaw heb weud gair a cherdded am y bws. Roedd hi bron â nosi ac roedd goleuadau'r parti ar goll yng nghymylau'r niwl ar y ffenestr. Cerddodd Deian fi tuag at y bws a'm gosod i rhyngddo ef a'r drws. Edrychais arno. Cydiodd yn fy ngwyneb yn dawel, a rhedeg ei fysedd dros fy ngwefusau. Doedd dim cliw 'da fi beth oedd e'n neud, ond roedd tensiwn y sefyllfa'n gweithio i fi. Tynnodd gudyn o 'ngwallt allan o'm llygaid ac roedd 'na rannau ohono i'n gweiddi arno i gyffwrdd â fi.

Daeth ei ben yn agosach a dechreuodd gusanu fy llygaid ac wedyn fy mochau cyn mentro'n ara bach tuag at fy ngwefusau. Roedd ei gusanau'n mynd yn ddyfnach a'i anadlu'n gyflymach. Gwasgodd fi'n ôl a'm cefen ar y metel oer y tu ôl imi. Cydiais ynddo. Roedd ei gorff yn galed, ac wrth redeg fy nwylo dros ei gorff roedd 'na arogl aftershêf sbeislyd yn codi o'i groen. Teimlais ei ddwylo yng ngwaelod fy nghefen ac wedyn dros fy ngwddf. Roedd angen y boi 'ma arna i yn fwy na dim byd yn y byd. Llithrodd ei fysedd lawr rhwng defnydd y ffrog a'm bronne, ac roedd yr effaith fel troi switsh golau mla'n. Cydiais yn ei grys a'i agor gan redeg fy nwylo dros ei gorff. Wrth iddo fy ngwasgu yn erbyn y metel roedd hi'n hollol amlwg ei fod e isie finne hefyd.

Datodais ei felt wrth iddo estyn i lawr i godi hem fy ffrog. Teimlais ei ddwylo'n rhedeg lan heibio i'm pengliniau ac i fyny fy nghluniau. Roedd e'n anwesu'r croen ac roedd y teimlad mor sensitif nes ei fod bron â bod yn boenus. Ro'n i'n gwbod mod i'n wlyb sopen. Cydiodd yn fy mhen-ôl gan fy nghodi damed o'r llawr; roedd ei wyneb ar goll yn fy ngwallt.

"Ti'n siŵr?" sibrydodd.

"Wyt ti?" holais a bron dim llais ar ôl.

"Fi wedi bod isie neud hyn ers i fi weld ti'r tro cynta 'na yn y gwaith."

"Odw, fi'n siŵr; o's 'da ti ym... "

"O oes."

"Cheeky, well prepared!"

"Dib Dib Dob Dob and all that!"

Chwarddais; roedd y metel wrth fy ngefen yn cyferbynnu â'r gwres rhyngom.

Cusanodd fy ngwddf gan lusgo'i dafod dros y croen yn ara bach. Wrth wneud hyn dyma fe'n cyffwrdd rhwng fy nghoese a bron i fi neidio allan o'm croen.

"Ti'n iawn?"

"Odw."

Datododd gefn fy ffrog a'm gwasgu'n ôl unwaith eto ar y drws. Tynnodd strapiau fy mra dros fy sgwyddau. Sefodd yn ôl.

"Be sy'n bod?"

"Dim, jest isie edrych arno ti, 'na i gyd."

Rhoiodd fys yn fy ngheg, a'i daenu wedyn lawr fy ngwddwg a thros fy mronne.

"Ti'n uffernol o bert, Hels."

"Paid... "

"Fi'n gweud y gwir."

Roedd yr edrych yma'n gwneud imi deimlo'n anghyfforddus. Cydiais ynddo a'i dynnu'n gryf tuag ataf. Suddais ar fy mhengliniau a'i gymryd yn fy ngheg. Roedd e'n blasu o sebon. Roedd ei anadlu'n trymhau ac yn cyflymu. Estynnais i mewn i'w boced gan chwilio'r condom, ei agor yn araf a'i roi amdano wrth ei wthio i lawr ei fin gyda'm ceg. Cydiodd yndda i fel tase fe'n ca'l trafferth dal yn ôl. Pwysodd drosof gan roi ei ddwylo rhwng fy nghoesau; gwthiodd un bys ynof a mwytho'm clitoris gyda'r llall. Roedd yn deimlad uffernol o dda. Ar ôl ennyd dyma fe'n fy nghodi i unwaith eto a gwthio'i hun i mewn imi. Dyma finne'n rhoi ebychiad bach. Roedd e'n symud yn araf ynof, a'i lygaid ar gau fel tase fe'n canolbwyntio ar bethe. Roedd effaith y gwin, a theimlad ei groen ar fy mronne, yn gneud i'r byd deimlo'n bell i ffwrdd. Roedd e'n symud yn gyflymach ac yn fwy caled gan wthio fy mhen-ôl yn erbyn y metel oer. Roedd y dynfa gyfarwydd yna'n codi ynof, ac wrth iddo ddod dyma fe'n mwytho rhwng fy nghoese gan wneud yn siŵr 'mod inne'n dod hefyd.

Sefyll am sbel heb air rhyngom cyn ail-wisgo rhag ofn i rywun ddod mas o'r neuadd. Cydiodd amdana i wedyn am amser hir, a'i freichiau'n amgylchynu 'nghorff. Dyma fe'n cusanu 'nhrwyn a sychu tamaid o golur a oedd wedi symud o'm llygaid yn y chwys.

"Dere, weden i bod angen drinc 'ma," medde fe gan fy arwain i 'nôl. Ro'n i'n teimlo'n benysgafn ac yn hanner meddwl hefyd ble fyddai pawb yn meddwl o'n ni wedi bod. Doedd dim angen poeni am hir.

"Wahey, finally shagged then have we?" gwaeddodd Les ar dop ei lais, a finne isie i'r ddaear agor a'm llyncu i. "That's my girl, Hels, classy bird as ffycin usual, beauty; wel, weden ni bod 'na'n haeddu toten fach arall o wisgi."

"Da iawn, Hels; o'n ni'n dechre meddwl naethech chi byth mo fe – about time, really." Llinos yn chwerthin 'da Siân.

"O wel," medde Deian gan chwerthin, "fodca a tonic?"

Aeth gweddill y noson heibio mewn cymysgedd o fodca a dawnsio. Roedd Sion am unwaith yng nghornel dywyllaf fy meddwl a finne'n medru meddwl am ddim ond am lygaid Deian. Roedd Kel a Gerallt yn edrych yn hapus dros ben a ninnau i gyd yn cymryd ein tro i edmygu'r fodrwy ar ei bys. Roedd Les yn dawnsio gyda Gwyneth ac yn damsgen ar ei thraed bob dwy funud nes bod ei gweiddi hi'n dod mor gyson â churiadau'r drymiau. Pawb yn stablan 'nôl i'r bws, a John Torrwr Bedde'n canu emynau gyda Gerallt. Roedd pawb yn dechrau tawelu a'r unig sŵn oedd y poteli cwrw gwag yn rholio o un ochr y bws i'r llall wrth fynd rownd y corneli.

Bip Bip!

Pawb yn cydio yn eu ffonau. Nerys yn ymbalfalu yn ei bag.

"O shit!"

"Be?"

"Ma Rhys wedi mynd ar goll."

Saith ar higen

Arhosodd Deian ar y bws ar ôl i fi addo y bydden i'n ei ffono i drefnu cinio y diwrnod wedyn. Ddes i o'r bws 'da Nerys a hithe'n banics gwyllt. Doedd cerdded y lôn ddim yn broblem fel arfer ond heno, yn ein ffrogiau a'n sodle, roedd pethe 'bach yn wahanol. Trwy'r tywyllwch gwelson ni bod Emyr wedi gadel y beic pedair olwyn inni ar dop y lôn, ac am unwaith roedden ni'n falch ohono, Nerys yn gyrru a finne'n cydio am ei chanol. Doedd dim ots 'da'r ddwy ohonon ni am am ein ffrogiau rhagor – roedd f'un i'n frwnt beth bynnag a Ner yn poeni gormod am Rhys. Roedd Ner wedi ffono Emyr yn syth i gael yr hanes. Roedd Rhys wedi mynd mas am bump ac wedi addo bod 'nôl tua saith, ond doedd neb wedi'i weld ers 'nny ac roedd 'i ffôn e wedi'i droi i ffwrdd. Parcio'r beic yn y garej a ninne'n mynd am y tŷ. Roedd hi'n oer, tua tri o'r gloch y bore, a Ner a finne wedi sobri'n weddol.

Roedd Emyr yn eistedd wrth y ford a'r ffôn symudol wrth ei ochr. Edrychodd arnon ni'n cerdded i mewn.

"Unrhyw newydd?" gofynnodd Ner.

"Na, dim byd."

Roedd y ddwy ohonon ni'n gwbod taw'r peth gorau oedd newid i ddillad erill achos bydde'n gweld ni yn ein dillad ffansi'n gwylltio Emyr. Aethon ni lan sta'r a newid yn gloi. Benthycais hen bâr o drowser a siwmper gan Ner. Aethon lawr y sta'r eto heb gyfnewid gair.

"Ti wedi trial ffono... ?"

"Fi wedi ffono pawb; sai'n ffycin dwp, fi 'di trial bob ffrind fi'n gwbod amdanyn nhw, a phob perthynas a phawb yn y pentre bron – pawb heblaw am y pissheads 'na oedd ar y bws 'da chi, a bydde neb gatre 'da rheini beth bynnag."

"Wedodd e lle oedd e'n mynd de?"

"Be ti'n feddwl?"

"Olreit, dim ond gofyn… "

"Wel paid 'te."

Cerddais at y stof a dechrau llenwi'r tegyl ar bwys y sinc. Roedd Emyr yn siarad â'i hunan.

"Fi 'di bod lawr ar bwys yr afon rhag ofan a fi 'di checo'r pit slyrri, ond do's dim sôn amdano fe."

Dechreuais neud brechdanau bron heb feddwl be o'n i'n neud. Sylweddolais 'mod i'n troi mewn i Mam.

"Sneb arall allwn ni dreial de?"

"Heblaw bo ti'n gwbod am ryw ffrindie erill fi ddim yn gwbod amdanyn nhw, nagos."

"Beth am yr heddlu?"

"Ma nhw'n ffaelu neud dim achos ei oedran nes ei fod wedi bod ar goll am beder awr ar higen."

"O."

"Dyw e ddim fel e i neud hyn heblaw bod rhywbeth yn bod, yw e?" wedodd Ner gan edrych ar y llawr a meddwl am eiliad am y gwaethaf.

"Ma fe wedi ca'l amser digon caled yn ddiweddar, on'dyw e?" wedais i, heb sylwi beth o'n i'n ddeud.

Craffodd Emyr arna i.

"Do, falle."

Doedd dim i neud ond aros a gweld be ddigwydde. Roedd y tensiwn bron yn ormod, a phob un ohonon ni'n edrych ar y cloc nawr ac yn y man. Roedd Emyr yn mynd mas i edrych ar y clos weithiau a ddim yn cau'r drws yn iawn ar ei ffordd 'nôl. Ffoniais Mam a Dad jest i ddweud fy mod i'n saff, rhag ofn iddyn nhw feddwl 'mod inne ar goll hefyd. Roedd y ddau'n iawn, a'r unig beth ges i oedd clust dost gan Dat am 'i ddihuno fe. Typical!

Roedd y cloc yn cripian tuag at bedwar o'r gloch, a'r straen yn cynyddu. Roedd hanner whant arna i i ofyn a oedden nhw wedi bod yn edrych ar y Ffridd; fanna oedd un o'r llefydd mwya amlwg os taw teimlo'n isel oedd e. Cefais fy achub gan Ner.

"Ti wedi bod lan ar y Ffridd de?"

Tywyllodd gwyneb Emyr.

"Do, dim byd."

"O."

Dychmygais ef yn mynd yn ôl yno. Yn chwilio am Rhys rhwng y borfa hir. Am unwaith teimlais biti drosto am iddo garu Gaynor gymaint a methu byw yn ei groen ei hun.

Yn sydyn dyma sŵn cerdded ar y clos; Emyr yn edrych ar Nerys a'r ddau'n codi ar yr un pryd a rhedeg at y drws. Yn ymlwybro'n ara bach, fel sowldiwr o ryfel, daeth Rhys allan o'r tywyllwch yn wên i gyd.

"Sssshhhhhhhhhwmai Dad! Hey sis, hey lwcing shecshy heno babe."

Roedd y gymysgedd o ryddhad ac anghredinedd ar wyneb Emyr yn bictiwr.

"Dere 'ma, y diawl!"

"Hey, gimme five big man," medde Rhys gan geisio gwneud high five 'da Emyr cyn i hwnnw'i golero a'i lusgo i mewn i'r gegin a'i eistedd ar y sgiw.

"Lle uffarn ti 'di bod?" holodd a'i lygaid yn fflachio.

"Hey, chill man, take a chiiiiiiiiiiiiiiiill pill, ti'n stressed out father dear."

Roedd yr holl sefyllfa'n codi whant chwerthin arna i, ac roedd yn rhaid i mi gnoi 'nhafod yn galed.

"Fiiiiiiii di bod 'da mêt newydd fi a gaethon ni un neu ddou drinky bach. Sa i'n hwyr, ydw i?"

Gyda hyn, dyma Nerys yn ffrwydro chwerthin a finne'n gneud yr un peth. Edrychodd Emyr ar y ddwy ohonon ni, ac yn mwyaf annisgwyl yn ymuno â ni yn y chwerthin. 'Na'r tro cynta erioed i fi 'i weld e'n chwerthin yn braf o'i fola.

"Be? Be sy'n bod?" gofynnodd Rhys yn ffwndrus i gyd.

"Dim byd o gwbwl," medde Emyr a mynd i nôl dŵr iddo fe. "Yfa hwn a cer i'r ca' nos, a sai moyn dy weld ti hyd bore fory."

Tra bod Rhys yn yfed a ninnau dwy'n dal i chwerthin, aeth Emyr mas i'r parlwr godro i nôl bwced i'w roi ar bwys gwely Rhys. Pan ddaeth yn ôl, roedd Rhys wedi ca'l gafael ar un o'r Westies oedd Emyr wedi'i adael allan i gyfarth os dôi Rhys yn ôl.

"Shwdi twtsen, ti'n lyfli ti yn, a fi'n caru chwa'r fi – ma hi'n neis. A fi'n caru Heledd, na fi ddim yn caru Heledd, fi'n lico Heledd ond fi ddim yn caru hi, a fi'n mynd i ga'l job yn y dre 'ma cyn bo hir a phrynu moto-beic a mynd neeeeeeeooooowwwwww rownd y lle 'ma. Be ti'n weud, father?"

Cydiodd Emyr ynddo a'i fachu wrth ei fraich.

"Dere nawr de, y gob mowr; gewn ni weld faint o sŵn fydd 'da ti'n y bore."

Cafodd Ner a finne baned arall, ac mewn sbel daeth Emyr lawr i gwrdd â ni a llai o lawer o straen ar ei wyneb na welais i ers sbel.

"A'th e i gysgu."

"Do, a fan'na fydd e am sbel 'fyd, wrth 'i olwg e."

Eisteddodd Emyr gyda ni. "Wel, 'na'r ddrama 'na drosto 'to te; fe flinga i'r diawl yn y bore."

"O leia ma fe'n dechre ymddwyn fel ma fe i fod, ac ystyried bod e yn 'i arddegau."

"Wel, ie, ma'n hen bryd iddo fe ddechre dod mas o'i gragen."

Yn sydyn roedd Emyr a Ner yn siarad fel na wnaethon nhw ers misoedd, yn cloncan am les Rhys a sut oedd angen iddo ddatblygu heb gysgod drosto fe. Yn yr eiliad honno gwelais rywbeth yn llygaid y ddou a wnaeth imi deimlo falle bydde popeth yn iawn rhyngddyn nhw wedi'r cwbwl. Meddyliais taw nawr oedd yr amser i fi fynd i'r gwely.

Wyth ar higen

Codais cyn Nerys a chychwyn am adre. Gadewais nodyn yn gofyn iddi gwrdd â fi amser cinio wrth y stand la'th i fi gael clywed beth ddigwyddodd. Ymlwybrais i fyny'r lôn, wedi ailwisgo fy ffrog a gadael dillad Ner wrth ei gwely. Cwrddais â Dat ar y lôn a hwnnw'n chwerthin yn braf yn fy ngweld i'n dod yn fy ffrog. Cerddais y tu ôl i'r da gyda fe wrth i fi sôn am helyntion y noson cynt. Cyrhaeddais adre a chael bàth cyn checio fy ffôn. Roedd 'na dair neges gan Deian a'r un ddiwetha'n deud ei fod yn mynd i bigo fi lan am ginio tua un. Meddyliais am neithiwr a theimlad ei groen llyfn. Dihunodd y pilipalas unwaith eto.

Cwrddais â Ner wrth y stand la'th. Roedd hi yno o mlaen i ac yn edrych yn llawer gwell nag oedd hi wedi edrych ers sbel, er iddi gael diwrnod a noson mor galed. Eisteddais ar ei phwys. Roedd hi ac Emyr wedi siarad hyd oriau mân y bore.

"Be sy'n mynd i ddigwydd nawr de?" holais.

"M'bod, fi'n meddwl falle mynd off am sbel."

"I ble?"

"Sai'n gwbod, rhywle newydd, jest am sbel fach i fi ga'l start, t'mod?"

Edrychodd arna i a'i llygaid yn sgleinio am unwaith.

"Be ti'n mynd i neud de?"

"Am beth?"

"Lyfer boi, job?"

"M'bod. Ma fe'n dod i hôl fi wedyn i fynd â fi am ginio."

"W, cîn glei."

"Odi, ond ma fe'n mynd off cyn bo hir 'to."

"O, odi, o'n ni wedi anghofio am 'na."

"Mmmm... "

"Reit, well i fi fynd i neud cino i'r bois," medde Ner gan neidio i'r llawr. "Hala i neges atat ti wedyn."

"Ocê."

Gwyliais hi'n mynd lawr y lôn a'i gwallt yn bownsio ar ei chefen gyda phob cam. Trois inne lawr ein lôn ni hefyd gan feddwl i ble bydde Deian yn mynd â fi am ginio. Roedd hi'n fore braf er bod diwedd yr haf yn nesáu, 'ha bach Mihangel' fel bydde Mam yn ei alw.

Ar ôl newid fy nillad a thrio rhoi mêc-yp i guddio'r cylchoedd tywyll dan fy llygaid, dyma fi'n edrych ar y cloc. Roedd hi bron yn un o'r gloch, ac roedd 'na sŵn car ar y clos. Arhosais am eiliad i ddisgwyl y gnoc ar y drws. Aeth cynnwrf drwydda i wrth feddwl am weld Deian eto, ac anadlais yn ddwfn cyn mynd lawr sta'r. Agorais y drws i weld gwyneb Sion. Roedd e'n ddagrau i gyd. Ro'n i'n teimlo'n sâl. Roedd 'na fagiau wrth ei draed.

"Hels, allen i byth... o'n i'n ffaelu mynd ar yr awyren... allen i byth, dim hebddo ti... "

Nofel dditectif wefreiddiol...

Dyma gyfrol finiog llawn dychan sy'n sicr o'ch cadw ar bigau'r drain.
- *Islwyn Ffowc Elis*

£6.95
0 86243 661 3

Nofelau diweddar gan Y Lolfa

Pelé, Gerson a'r Angel - Daniel Davies (£5.95)

Os Dianc Rhai - Martin Davis (£9.95)

Dim Heddwch - Lyn Ebenezer (£5.95)

Amdani! - Bethan Gwanas (£5.95)

Diolch i 'Nhrwyn - Rocet Arwel Jones (£6.95)

O'r Canol i Lawr - Emyr Huws Jones (£6.95)

Dyddiadur Alci Hypocondriac - Gruffydd Meredith (£5.95)

Dan Gadarn Goncrit - Mihangel Morgan (£7.95)

Y Ddynes Ddirgel - Mihangel Morgan (£5.95)

Dial yr Hanner Brawd - Arwel Vittle (£6.95)

Talu'r Pris - Arwel Vittle (£7.95)

Y cyfan i'w gael mewn siopau llyfrau Cymraeg lleol

Am restr gyflawn o holl gyhoeddiadau'r Lolfa,
mynnwch gopi o'n Catalog newydd lliw-llawn — neu
hwyliwch i mewn i **www.ylolfa.com**

TAL-Y-BONT CEREDIGION CYMRU SY24 5AP
e-bost ylolfa@ylolfa.com
y We www.ylolfa.com
ffôn 01970 832304
ffacs 832782
isdn 832813